AGATHA CHRISTIE OMNIBUS

1920s

VOLUME ONE

D1330184

BY THE SAME AUTHOR

AGATHA CHRISTIE

OMNIBUS

1920S

VOLUME ONE

The Mysterious Affair at Styles
The Secret Adversary
Murder on the Links

Background Notes by Jacques Baudou

HarperCollins*Publishers*

HarperCollins*Publishers*
77-85 Fulham Palace Road
Hammersmith, London w6 8jb

This paperback edition 1995
3 5 7 9 8 6 4 2

ISBN 0 00 649630 X

Set in Linotron Baskerville by
Rowland Phototypesetting Ltd
Bury St Edmunds, Suffolk

Printed and bound in Great Britain by
Caledonian International Book Manufacturing Ltd, Glasgow

Contents

THE MYSTERIOUS
AFFAIR AT STYLES

CHAPTER I

I Go to Styles

The intense interest aroused in the public by what was known at the time as 'The Styles Case' has now somewhat subsided. Nevertheless, in view of the world-wide notoriety which attended it, I have been asked, both by my friend Poirot and the family themselves, to write an account of the whole story. This, we trust, will effectually silence the sensational rumours which still persist.

I will therefore briefly set down the circumstances which led to my being connected with the affair.

I had been invalided home from the Front; and, after spending some months in a rather depressing Convalescent Home, was given a month's sick leave. Having no near relations or friends, I was trying to make up my mind what to do, when I ran across John Cavendish. I had seen very little of him for some years. Indeed, I had never known him particularly well. He was a good fifteen years my senior, for one thing, though he hardly looked his forty-five years. As a boy, though, I had often stayed at Styles, his mother's place in Essex.

We had a good yarn about old times, and it ended in his inviting me down to Styles to spend my leave there.

'The mater will be delighted to see you again – after all those years,' he added.

'Your mother keeps well?' I asked.

'Oh, yes. I suppose you know that she has married again?'

I am afraid I showed my surprise rather plainly. Mrs Cavendish, who had married John's father when he was a widower with two sons, had been a handsome woman of middle-age as I remembered her. She certainly could not be a day less than seventy now. I recalled her as an energetic, autocratic personality, somewhat inclined to charitable and social notoriety, with a fondness for opening bazaars and playing the Lady Bountiful. She was a most generous woman, and possessed a considerable fortune of her own.

Their country-place, Styles Court, had been purchased by Mr Cavendish early in their married life. He had been completely under his wife's ascendancy, so much so that, on dying, he left the place to her for her lifetime, as well as the larger part of his income; an arrangement that was distinctly unfair to his two sons. Their stepmother, however, had always been most generous to them; indeed, they were so young at the time of their father's remarriage that they always thought of her as their own mother.

Lawrence, the younger, had been a delicate youth. He had qualified as a doctor but early relinquished the profession of medicine, and lived at home while pursuing literary ambitions; though his verses never had any marked success.

John practised for some time as a barrister, but had finally settled down to the more congenial life of a country squire. He had married two years ago, and had taken his wife to live at Styles, though I entertained a shrewd suspicion that he would have preferred his mother to increase his allowance, which would have enabled him to have a home of his own. Mrs Cavendish, however, was a lady who liked to make her own plans, and expected other people to fall in with them, and in this case she certainly had the whip hand, namely: the purse strings.

John noticed my surprise at the news of his mother's remarriage and smiled rather ruefully.

'Rotten little bounder too!' he said savagely. 'I can tell you, Hastings, it's making life jolly difficult for us. As for Evie – you remember Evie?'

'No.'

'Oh, I suppose she was after your time. She's the mater's factotum, companion, Jack of all trades! A great sport – old Evie! Not precisely young and beautiful, but as game as they make them.'

'You were going to say –'

'Oh, this fellow! He turned up from nowhere, on the pretext of being a second cousin or something of Evie's, though she didn't seem particularly keen to acknowledge the relationship. The fellow is an absolute outsider, anyone can see that. He's got a great black beard, and wears patent leather boots in all weathers! But the mater cottoned to him at once, took him on as secretary – you know how she's always running a hundred societies?'

I nodded.

'Well, of course, the war has turned the hundreds into thousands. No doubt the fellow was very useful to her. But you could have knocked us all down with a feather when, three months ago, she suddenly announced that she and Alfred were engaged! The fellow must be at least twenty years younger than she is! It's simply bare-faced fortune hunting; but there you are – she is her own mistress, and she's married him.'

'It must be a difficult situation for you all.'

'Difficult! It's damnable!'

Thus it came about that, three days later, I descended from the train at Styles St Mary, an absurd little station, with no apparent reason for existence, perched up in the midst of green fields and country lanes. John Cavendish was waiting on the platform, and piloted me out to the car.

'Got a drop or two of petrol still, you see,' he remarked. 'Mainly owing to the mater's activities.'

The village of Styles St Mary was situated about two miles from the little station, and Styles Court lay a mile the other side of it. It was a still, warm day in early July. As one looked out over the flat Essex country, lying so green and peaceful under the afternoon sun, it seemed almost impossible to believe that, not so very far away, a great war was running its appointed course. I felt I had suddenly strayed into another world. As we turned in at the lodge gates, John said:

'I'm afraid you'll find it very quiet down here, Hastings.'

'My dear fellow, that's just what I want.'

'Oh, it's pleasant enough if you want to lead the idle life. I drill with the volunteers twice a week, and lend a hand at the farms. My wife works regularly "on the land". She is up at five every morning to milk, and keeps at it steadily until lunch-time. It's a jolly good life taking it all round – if it weren't for that fellow Alfred Inglethorp!' He checked the car suddenly, and glanced at his watch. 'I wonder if we've time to pick up Cynthia. No, she'll have started from the hospital by now.'

'Cynthia! That's not your wife?'

'No, Cynthia is a protégée of my mother's, the daughter of an old schoolfellow of hers, who married a rascally solicitor. He came a cropper, and the girl was left an orphan and penni-less. My mother came to the rescue, and Cynthia has been with us nearly two years now. She works in the Red Cross Hospital at Tadminster, seven miles away.'

As he spoke the last words, we drew up in front of the fine old house. A lady in a stout tweed skirt, who was bending over a flower bed, straightened herself at our approach.

'Hullo, Evie, here's our wounded hero! Mr Hastings – Miss Howard.'

Miss Howard shook hands with a hearty, almost painful, grip. I had an impression of very blue eyes in a sunburnt face. She was a pleasant-looking woman of about forty, with a deep voice, almost manly in its stentorian tones, and had a large sensible square body, with feet to match – these last encased in good thick boots. Her conversation, I soon found, was couched in the telegraphic style.

'Weeds grow like house afire. Can't keep even with 'em. Shall press you in. Better be careful!'

'I'm sure I shall be only too delighted to make myself useful,' I responded.

'Don't say it. Never does. Wish you hadn't later.'

'You're a cynic, Evie,' said John, laughing. 'Where's tea today – inside or out?'

'Out. Too fine a day to be cooped up in the house.'

'Come on then, you've done enough gardening for today. "The labourer is worthy of his hire," you know. Come and be refreshed.'

'Well,' said Miss Howard, drawing off her gardening gloves, 'I'm inclined to agree with you.'

She led the way round the house to where tea was spread under the shade of a large sycamore.

A figure rose from one of the basket chairs, and came a few steps to meet us.

'My wife, Hastings,' said John.

I shall never forget my first sight of Mary Cavendish. Her tall, slender form, outlined against the bright light; the vivid sense of slumbering fire that seemed to find expression only in those wonderful tawny eyes of hers, remarkable eyes, different from any other woman's that I have ever known; the intense power of stillness she possessed, which nevertheless conveyed the impression of a wild untamed spirit in an exquisitely civilized body – all these things are burnt into my memory. I shall never forget them.

She greeted me with a few words of pleasant welcome in a low clear voice, and I sank into a basket chair feeling distinctly glad that I had accepted John's invitation. Mrs Cavendish gave me some tea, and her few quiet remarks heightened my first impression of her as a thoroughly fascinating woman. An appreciative listener is always stimulating, and I described, in a humorous manner, certain incidents of my Convalescent Home, in a way which, I flatter myself, greatly amused my hostess. John, of course, good fellow though he is, could hardly be called a brilliant conversationalist.

At that moment a well-remembered voice floated through the open french window near at hand:

'Then you'll write to the Princess after tea, Alfred? I'll write to Lady Tadminster for the second day, myself. Or shall we wait until we hear from the Princess? In case of a refusal, Lady Tadminster might open it the first day, and Mrs Crosbie the second. Then there's the Duchess – about the school fête.'

There was the murmur of a man's voice, and then Mrs Inglethorp's rose in reply:

'Yes, certainly. After tea will do quite well. You are so thoughtful, Alfred dear.'

The french window swung open a little wider, and a handsome white-haired old lady, with a somewhat masterful cast of features, stepped out of it on to the lawn. A man followed her, a suggestion of deference in his manner.

Mrs Inglethorp greeted me with effusion.

'Why, if it isn't too delightful to see you again, Mr Hastings, after all these years. Alfred, darling, Mr Hastings – my husband.'

I looked with some curiosity at 'Alfred darling'. He certainly struck a rather alien note. I did not wonder at John objecting to his beard. It was one of the longest and blackest I have ever seen. He wore gold-rimmed pince-nez, and had a curious impassivity of feature. It struck me that he might look natural on a stage, but was strangely out of place in real life. His voice was rather deep and unctuous. He placed a wooden hand in mine and said:

'This is a pleasure, Mr Hastings.' Then, turning to his wife: 'Emily dearest, I think that cushion is a little damp.'

She beamed fondly on him, as he substituted another with every demonstration of the tenderest care. Strange infatuation of an otherwise sensible woman!

With the presence of Mr Inglethorp, a sense of constraint and veiled hostility seemed to settle down upon the company. Miss Howard, in particular, took no pains to conceal her feelings. Mrs Inglethorp, however, seemed to notice nothing unusual. Her volubility, which I remembered of old, had lost nothing in the intervening years, and she poured out a steady flood of conversation, mainly on the subject of the forthcoming bazaar which she was organizing and which was to take place shortly. Occasionally she referred to her husband over a question of days or dates. His watchful and attentive manner never varied. From the very first I took a firm and rooted dislike to him, and I flatter myself that my first judgements are usually fairly shrewd.

Presently Mrs Inglethorp turned to give some instructions about letters to Evelyn Howard, and her husband addressed me in his painstaking voice:

'Is soldiering your regular profession, Mr Hastings?'

'No, before the war I was in Lloyd's.'

'And you will return there after it is over?'

'Perhaps. Either that or a fresh start altogether.'

Mary Cavendish leant forward.

'What would you really choose as a profession, if you could just consult your inclination?'

'Well, that depends.'

'No secret hobby?' she asked. 'Tell me – you're drawn to something? Every one is – usually something absurd.'

'You'll laugh at me.'

She smiled.

'Perhaps.'

'Well, I've always had a secret hankering to be a detective!'

'The real thing – Scotland Yard? Or Sherlock Holmes?'

'Oh, Sherlock Holmes by all means. But really, seriously, I am awfully drawn to it. I came across a man in Belgium once, a very famous detective, and he quite inflamed me. He was a marvellous little fellow. He used to say that all good detective work was a mere matter of method. My system is based on his – though of course I have progressed rather further. He was a funny little man, a great dandy, but wonderfully clever.'

'Like a good detective story myself,' remarked Miss Howard. 'Lots of nonsense written, though. Criminal discovered in last chapter. Everyone dumbfounded. Real crime – you'd know at once.'

'There have been a great number of undiscovered crimes,' I argued.

'Don't mean the police, but the people that are right in it. The family. You couldn't really hoodwink them. They'd know.'

'Then,' I said, much amused, 'you think that if you were mixed up in a crime, say a murder, you'd be able to spot the murderer right off?'

'Of course I should. Mightn't be able to prove it to a pack of lawyers. But I'm certain I'd know. I'd feel it in my finger-tips if he came near me.'

'It might be a "she",' I suggested.

'Might. But murder's a violent crime. Associate it more with a man.'

'Not in a case of poisoning.' Mrs Cavendish's clear voice startled me. 'Dr Bauerstein was saying yesterday that, owing to the general ignorance of the more uncommon poisons among the medical profession, there were probably countless cases of poisoning quite unsuspected.'

'Why, Mary, what a gruesome conversation!' cried Mrs Inglethorp. 'It makes me feel as if a goose were walking over my grave. Oh, there's Cynthia!'

A young girl in VAD uniform ran lightly across the lawn.

'Why, Cynthia, you are late today. This is Mr Hastings – Miss Murdoch.'

Cynthia Murdoch was a fresh-looking young creature, full of life and vigour. She tossed off her little VAD cap, and I admired the great loose waves of her auburn hair, and the smallness and whiteness of the hand she held out to claim her tea. With dark eyes and eyelashes she would have been a beauty.

She flung herself down on the ground beside John, and as I handed her a plate of sandwiches she smiled up at me.

'Sit down here on the grass, do. It's ever so much nicer.'

I dropped down obediently.

'You work at Tadminster, don't you, Miss Murdoch?'

She nodded.

'For my sins.'

'Do they bully you, then?' I asked, smiling.

'I should like to see them!' cried Cynthia with dignity.

'I have got a cousin who is nursing,' I remarked. 'And she is terrified of "Sisters".'

'I don't wonder. Sisters *are*, you know, Mr Hastings. They simp-ly *are*! You've no idea! But I'm not a nurse, thank heaven, I work in the dispensary.'

'How many people do you poison?' I asked, smiling.

Cynthia smiled too.

'Oh, hundreds!' she said.

'Cynthia,' called Mrs Inglethorp, 'do you think you could write a few notes for me?'

'Certainly, Aunt Emily.'

She jumped up promptly, and something in her manner reminded me that her position was a dependent one, and that Mrs Inglethorp, kind as she might be in the main, did not allow her to forget it.

My hostess turned to me.

'John will show you your room. Supper is at half-past seven. We have given up late dinner for some time now. Lady Tadminster, our Member's wife – she was the late Lord Abbotsbury's daughter – does the same. She agrees with me that one must set an example of economy. We are quite a war household; nothing is wasted here – every scrap of waste paper, even, is saved and sent away in sacks.'

I expressed my appreciation, and John took me into the house and up the broad staircase, which forked right and left half-way to different wings of the building. My room was in the left wing, and looked out over the park.

John left me, and a few minutes later I saw him from my window walking slowly across the grass arm in arm with Cynthia Murdoch. I heard Mrs Inglethorp call 'Cynthia' impatiently, and the girl started and ran back to the house. At the same moment, a man stepped out from the shadow of a tree and walked slowly in the same direction. He looked about forty, very dark with a melancholy clean-shaven face. Some violent emotion seemed to be mastering him. He looked up at my window as he passed, and I recognized him, though he had changed much in the fifteen years that had elapsed since we last met. It was John's younger brother, Lawrence Cavendish. I wondered what it was that had brought that singular expression to his face.

Then I dismissed him from my mind, and returned to the contemplation of my own affairs.

The evening passed pleasantly enough; and I dreamed that
night of that enigmatical woman, Mary Cavendish.

The next morning dawned bright and sunny, and I was full
of the anticipation of a delightful visit.

I did not see Mrs Cavendish until lunch-time, when she
volunteered to take me for a walk, and we spent a charming
afternoon roaming in the woods, returning to the house about
five.

As we entered the large hall, John beckoned us both into
the smoking-room. I saw at once by his face that something
disturbing had occurred. We followed him in, and he shut the
door after us.

'Look here, Mary, there's the deuce of a mess. Evie's had
a row with Alfred Inglethorp, and she's off.'

'Evie? Off?'

John nodded gloomily.

'Yes; you see she went to the mater, and – oh, here's Evie
herself.'

Miss Howard entered. Her lips were set grimly together,
and she carried a small suitcase. She looked excited and determined, and slightly on the defensive.

'At any rate,' she burst out, 'I've spoken my mind!'

'My dear Evelyn,' cried Mrs Cavendish, 'this can't be true!'

Miss Howard nodded grimly.

'True enough! Afraid I said some things to Emily she won't
forget or forgive in a hurry. Don't mind if they've only sunk
in a bit. Probably water off a duck's back, though. I said right
out: "You're an old woman, Emily, and there's no fool like
an old fool. The man's twenty years younger than you, and
don't you fool yourself as to what he married you for. Money!
Well, don't let him have too much of it. Farmer Raikes has
got a very pretty young wife. Just ask your Alfred how much
time he spends over there." She was very angry. Natural! I
went on: "I'm going to warn you, whether you like it or not.
That man would as soon murder you in your bed as look at
you. He's a bad lot. You can say what you like to me, but
remember what I've told you. He's a bad lot!"'

'What did she say?'

Miss Howard made an extremely expressive grimace.

'"Darling Alfred" – "dearest Alfred" – "wicked calumnies" – "wicked lies" – "wicked woman" – to accuse her "dear husband"! The sooner I left her house the better. So I'm off.'

'But not now?'

'This minute!'

For a moment we sat and stared at her. Finally John Cavendish, finding his persuasions of no avail, went off to look up the trains. His wife followed him, murmuring something about persuading Mrs Inglethorp to think better of it.

As she left the room, Miss Howard's face changed. She leant towards me eagerly.

'Mr Hastings, you're honest. I can trust you?'

I was a little startled. She laid her hand on my arm, and sank her voice to a whisper.

'Look after her, Mr Hastings. My poor Emily. They're a lot of sharks – all of them. Oh, I know what I'm talking about. There isn't one of them that's not hard up and trying to get money out of her. I've protected her as much as I could. Now I'm out of the way, they'll impose upon her.'

'Of course, Miss Howard,' I said, 'I'll do everything I can, but I'm sure you're excited and overwrought.'

She interrupted me by slowly shaking her forefinger.

'Young man, trust me. I've lived in the world rather longer than you have. All I ask you is to keep your eyes open. You'll see what I mean.'

The throb of the motor came through the open window, and Miss Howard rose and moved to the door. John's voice sounded outside. With her hand on the handle, she turned her head over her shoulder, and beckoned to me.

'Above all, Mr Hastings, watch that devil – her husband!'

There was no time for more. Miss Howard was swallowed up in an eager chorus of protests and goodbyes. The Inglethorps did not appear.

As the motor drove away, Mrs Cavendish suddenly detached herself from the group, and moved across the drive to the lawn to meet a tall bearded man who had been evidently making for the house. The colour rose in her cheeks as she held out her hand to him.

'Who is that?' I asked sharply, for instinctively I distrusted the man.

'That's Dr Bauerstein,' said John shortly.

'And who is Dr Bauerstein?'

'He's staying in the village doing a rest cure, after a bad nervous breakdown. He's a London specialist; a very clever man – one of the greatest living experts on poisons, I believe.'

'And he's a great friend of Mary's,' put in Cynthia, the irrepressible.

John Cavendish frowned and changed the subject.

'Come for a stroll, Hastings. This has been a most rotten business. She always had a rough tongue, but there is no stauncher friend in England than Evelyn Howard.'

He took the path through the plantation, and we walked down to the village through the woods which bordered one side of the estate.

As we passed through one of the gates on our way home again, a pretty young woman of gipsy type coming in the opposite direction bowed and smiled.

'That's a pretty girl,' I remarked appreciatively.

John's face hardened.

'That is Mrs Raikes.'

'The one that Miss Howard –'

'Exactly,' said John, with rather unnecessary abruptness.

I thought of the white-haired old lady in the big house, and that vivid wicked little face that had just smiled into ours, and a vague chill of foreboding crept over me. I brushed it aside.

'Styles is really a glorious old place,' I said to John.

He nodded rather gloomily.

'Yes, it's a fine property. It'll be mine some day – should be mine now by rights, if my father had only made a decent will. And then I shouldn't be so damned hard up as I am now.'

'Hard up, are you?'

'My dear Hastings, I don't mind telling you that I'm at my wits' end for money.'

'Couldn't your brother help you?'

'Lawrence? He's gone through every penny he ever had, publishing rotten verses in fancy bindings. No, we're an impecunious lot. My mother's always been awfully good to us, I must say. That is, up to now. Since her marriage, of course –' He broke off, frowning.

For the first time I felt that, with Evelyn Howard, something indefinable had gone from the atmosphere. Her presence had spelt security. Now that security was removed – and the air seemed rife with suspicion. The sinister face of Dr Bauerstein recurred to me unpleasantly. A vague suspicion of everyone and everything filled my mind. Just for a moment I had a premonition of approaching evil.

CHAPTER II

The 16th and 17th of July

I had arrived at Styles on the 5th of July. I come now to the events of the 16th and 17th of that month. For the convenience of the reader I will recapitulate the incidents of those days in as exact a manner as possible. They were elicited subsequently at the trial by a process of long and tedious cross-examinations.

I received a letter from Evelyn Howard a couple of days after her departure, telling me she was working as a nurse at the big hospital in Middlingham, a manufacturing town some fifteen miles away, and begging me to let her know if Mrs Inglethorp should show any wish to be reconciled.

The only fly in the ointment of my peaceful days was Mrs Cavendish's extraordinary and, for my part, unaccountable preference for the society of Dr Bauerstein. What she saw in the man I cannot imagine, but she was always asking him up to the house, and often went off for long expeditions with him. I must confess that I was quite unable to see his attraction.

The 16th of July fell on a Monday. It was a day of turmoil. The famous bazaar had taken place on Saturday, and an entertainment, in connection with the same charity, at which Mrs Inglethorp was to recite a War poem, was to be held that night. We were all busy during the morning arranging and decorating the Hall in the village where it was to take place. We had a late luncheon and spent the afternoon resting in the garden. I noticed that John's manner was somewhat unusual. He seemed very excited and restless.

After tea, Mrs Inglethorp went to lie down to rest before her efforts in the evening and I challenged Mary Cavendish to a single at tennis.

About a quarter to seven, Mrs Inglethorp called to us that we should be late as supper was early that night. We had rather a scramble to get ready in time; and before the meal was over the motor was waiting at the door.

The entertainment was a great success, Mrs Inglethorp's recitation receiving tremendous applause. There were also some tableaux in which Cynthia took part. She did not return with us, having been asked to a supper party, and to remain the night with some friends who had been acting with her in the tableaux.

The following morning, Mrs Inglethorp stayed in bed to breakfast, as she was rather over-tired; but she appeared in her briskest mood about 12.30, and swept Lawrence and myself off to a luncheon party.

'Such a charming invitation from Mrs Rolleston. Lady Tadminster's sister, you know. The Rollestons came over with the Conqueror – one of our oldest families.'

Mary had excused herself on the plea of an engagement with Dr Bauerstein.

We had a pleasant luncheon, and as we drove away Lawrence suggested that we should return by Tadminster, which was barely a mile out of our way, and pay a visit to Cynthia in her dispensary. Mrs Inglethorp replied that this was an excellent idea, but as she had several letters to write she would drop us there, and we could come back with Cynthia in the pony-trap.

We were detained under suspicion by the hospital porter, until Cynthia appeared to vouch for us, looking very cool and sweet in her long white overall. She took us up to her sanctum, and introduced us to her fellow dispenser, a rather awe-inspiring individual, whom Cynthia cheerily addressed as 'Nibs'.

'What a lot of bottles!' I exclaimed, as my eye travelled round the small room. 'Do you really know what's in them all?'

'Say something original,' groaned Cynthia. 'Every single person who comes up here says that. We are really thinking of bestowing a prize on the first individual who does *not* say: "What a lot of bottles!" And I know the next thing you're going to say is: "How many people have you poisoned?"'

I pleaded guilty with a laugh.

'If you people only knew how fatally easy it is to poison someone by mistake, you wouldn't joke about it. Come on, let's have tea. We've got all sorts of secret stores in that cupboard. No, Lawrence – that's the poison cupboard. The big cupboard – that's right.'

We had a very cheery tea, and assisted Cynthia to wash up afterwards. We had just put away the last teaspoon when a knock came at the door. The countenances of Cynthia and Nibs were suddenly petrified into a stern and forbidding expression.

'Come in,' said Cynthia, in a sharp professional tone.

A young and rather scared-looking nurse appeared with a bottle which she proffered to Nibs, who waved her towards Cynthia with the somewhat enigmatical remark:

'*I*'m not really here today.'

Cynthia took the bottle and examined it with the severity of a judge.

'This should have been sent up this morning.'

'Sister is very sorry. She forgot.'

'Sister should read the rules outside the door.'

I gathered from the little nurse's expression that there was not the least likelihood of her having the hardihood to retail this message to the dreaded 'Sister'.

'So now it can't be done until tomorrow,' finished Cynthia.

'Don't you think you could possibly let us have it to-night?'

'Well,' said Cynthia graciously, 'we are very busy, but if we have time it shall be done.'

The little nurse withdrew, and Cynthia promptly took a jar from the shelf, refilled the bottle and placed it on the table outside the door.

I laughed.

'Discipline must be maintained?'

'Exactly. Come out on our little balcony. You can see all the outside wards there.'

I followed Cynthia and her friend and they pointed out the different wards to me. Lawrence remained behind, but after a few moments Cynthia called to him over her shoulder to come and join us. Then she looked at her watch.

'Nothing more to do, Nibs?'

'No.'

'All right. Then we can lock up and go.'

I had seen Lawrence in quite a different light that afternoon. Compared to John, he was an astoundingly difficult person to get to know. He was the opposite of his brother in almost every respect, being unusually shy and reserved. Yet he had a certain charm of manner, and I fancied that, if one really knew him well, one could have a deep affection for him. I had always fancied that his manner to Cynthia was rather constrained, and that she on her side was inclined to be shy of him. But they were both gay enough this afternoon, and chatted together like a couple of children.

As we drove through the village, I remembered that I wanted some stamps, so accordingly we pulled up at the post office.

As I came out again, I cannoned into a little man who was just entering. I drew aside and apologized, when suddenly, with a loud exclamation, he clasped me in his arms and kissed me warmly.

'*Mon ami* Hastings!' he cried. 'It is indeed *mon ami* Hastings!'

'Poirot!' I exclaimed.

I turned to the pony-trap.

'This is a very pleasant meeting for me, Miss Cynthia. This is my old friend, Monsieur Poirot, whom I have not seen for years.'

'Oh, we know Monsieur Poirot,' said Cynthia gaily. 'But I had no idea he was a friend of yours.'

'Yes, indeed,' said Poirot seriously, 'I know Mademoiselle Cynthia. It is by the charity of that good Mrs Inglethorp that I am here.' Then, as I looked at him inquiringly: 'Yes, my friend, she has kindly extended hospitality to seven of my country-people who, alas, are refugees from their native land. We Belgians will always remember her with gratitude.'

Poirot was an extraordinary-looking little man. He was hardly more than five feet four inches, but carried himself with great dignity. His head was exactly the shape of an egg, and he always perched it a little on one side. His moustache was very stiff and military. The neatness of his attire was almost incredible; I believe a speck of dust would have caused him more pain than a bullet wound. Yet this quaint dandified little man who, I was sorry to see, now limped badly, had been in his time one of the most celebrated members of the Belgian police. As a detective, his flair had been extraordinary, and he had achieved triumphs by unravelling some of the most baffling cases of the day.

He pointed out to me the little house inhabited by him and his fellow Belgians, and I promised to go and see him at an early date. Then he raised his hat with a flourish to Cynthia, and we drove away.

'He's a dear little man,' said Cynthia. 'I'd no idea you knew him.'

'You've been entertaining a celebrity unawares,' I replied.

And, for the rest of the way home, I recited to them the various exploits and triumphs of Hercule Poirot.

We arrived back in a very cheerful mood. As we entered the hall, Mrs Inglethorp came out of her boudoir. She looked flushed and upset.

'Oh, it's you,' she said.

'Is there anything the matter, Aunt Emily?' asked Cynthia.

'Certainly not,' said Mrs Inglethorp sharply. 'What should there be?' Then catching sight of Dorcas, the parlourmaid, going into the dining-room, she called to her to bring some stamps into the boudoir.

'Yes, m'm.' The old servant hesitated, then added diffidently: 'Don't you think, m'm, you'd better get to bed? You're looking very tired.'

'Perhaps you're right, Dorcas – yes – no – not now. I've

some letters I must finish by post-time. Have you lighted the fire in my room as I told you?'

'Yes, m'm.'

'Then I'll go to bed directly after supper.'

She went into her boudoir again, and Cynthia stared after her.

'Goodness gracious! I wonder what's up?' she said to Lawrence.

He did not seem to have heard her, for without a word he turned on his heel and went out of the house.

I suggested a quick game of tennis before supper and, Cynthia agreeing, I ran upstairs to fetch my racquet.

Mrs Cavendish was coming down the stairs. It may have been my fancy, but she, too, was looking odd and disturbed.

'Had a good walk with Dr Bauerstein?' I asked, trying to appear as indifferent as I could.

'I didn't go,' she replied abruptly. 'Where is Mrs Inglethorp?'

'In the boudoir.'

Her hand clenched itself on the banisters, then she seemed to nerve herself for some encounter, and went rapidly past me down the stairs across the hall to the boudoir, the door of which she shut behind her.

As I ran out to the tennis court a few moments later, I had to pass the open boudoir window, and was unable to help overhearing the following scrap of dialogue. Mary Cavendish was saying in the voice of a woman desperately controlling herself: 'Then you won't show it to me?'

To which Mrs Inglethorp replied:

'My dear Mary, it has nothing to do with that matter.'

'Then show it to me.'

'I tell you it is not what you imagine. It does not concern you in the least.'

To which Mary Cavendish replied, with a rising bitterness: 'Of course, I might have known you would shield him.'

Cynthia was waiting for me, and greeted me eagerly with:

'I say! There's been the most awful row! I've got it all out of Dorcas.'

'What kind of a row?'

'Between Aunt Emily and *him*. I do hope she's found him out at last!'

'Was Dorcas there, then?'

'Of course not. She "happened to be near the door". It was a real old bust-up. I do wish I knew what it was all about.'

I thought of Mrs Raikes's gipsy face, and Evelyn Howard's warnings, but wisely decided to hold my peace, whilst Cynthia exhausted every possible hypothesis, and cheerfully hoped, 'Aunt Emily will send him away, and will never speak to him again.'

I was anxious to get hold of John, but he was nowhere to be seen. Evidently something very momentous had occurred that afternoon. I tried to forget the few words I had overheard; but, do what I would, I could not dismiss them altogether from my mind. What was Mary Cavendish's concern in this matter?

Mr Inglethorp was in the drawing-room when I came down to supper. His face was impassive as ever, and the strange unreality of the man struck me afresh.

Mrs Inglethorp came down last. She still looked agitated, and during the meal there was a somewhat constrained silence. Inglethorp was unusually quiet. As a rule, he surrounded his wife with little attentions, placing a cushion at her back, and altogether playing the part of the devoted husband. Immediately after supper, Mrs Inglethorp retired to her boudoir again.

'Send my coffee in here, Mary,' she called. 'I've just five minutes to catch the post.'

Cynthia and I went and sat by the open window in the drawing-room. Mary Cavendish brought our coffee to us. She seemed excited.

'Do you young people want lights, or do you enjoy the twilight?' she asked. 'Will you take Mrs Inglethorp her coffee, Cynthia? I will pour it out.'

'Do not trouble, Mary,' said Inglethorp. 'I will take it to Emily.' He poured it out, and went out of the room carrying it carefully.

Lawrence followed him, and Mrs Cavendish sat down by us.

We three sat for some time in silence. It was a glorious night, hot and still. Mrs Cavendish fanned herself gently with a palm leaf.

'It's almost too hot,' she murmured. 'We shall have a thunderstorm.'

Alas, that these harmonious moments can never endure! My paradise was rudely shattered by the sound of a well-known, and heartily disliked, voice in the hall.

'Dr Bauerstein!' exclaimed Cynthia. 'What a funny time to come.'

I glanced jealously at Mary Cavendish, but she seemed quite undisturbed, the delicate pallor of her cheeks did not vary.

In a few moments, Alfred Inglethorp had ushered the doctor in, the latter laughing, and protesting that he was in no fit state for a drawing-room. In truth, he presented a sorry spectacle, being literally plastered with mud.

'What have you been doing, doctor?' cried Mrs Cavendish.

'I must make my apologies,' said the doctor. 'I did not really mean to come in, but Mr Inglethorp insisted.'

'Well, Bauerstein, you are in a plight,' said John, strolling in from the hall. 'Have some coffee, and tell us what you have been up to.'

'Thank you, I will.' He laughed rather ruefully, as he described how he had discovered a very rare species of fern in an inaccessible place, and in his efforts to obtain it had lost his footing, and slipped ignominiously into a neighbouring pond.

'The sun soon dried me off,' he added, 'but I'm afraid my appearance is very disreputable.'

At this juncture, Mrs Inglethorp called to Cynthia from the hall, and the girl ran out.

'Just carry up my despatch-case, will you, dear? I'm going to bed.'

The door into the hall was a wide one. I had risen when Cynthia did, John was close by me. There were, therefore, three witnesses who could swear that Mrs Inglethorp was carrying her coffee, as yet untasted, in her hand. My evening was utterly and entirely spoilt by the presence of Dr Bauerstein. It seemed to me the man would never go. He rose at last, however, and I breathed a sigh of relief.

'I'll walk down to the village with you,' said Mr Inglethorp. 'I must see our agent over those estate accounts.' He turned to John. 'No one need sit up. I will take the latch-key.'

CHAPTER III

The Night of the Tragedy

To make this part of my story clear, I append the following plan of the first floor of Styles. The servants' rooms are reached through the door B. They have no communication with the right wing, where the Inglethorps' rooms were situated.

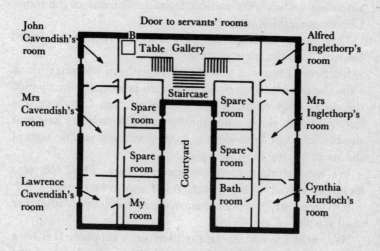

It seemed to be the middle of the night when I was awakened by Lawrence Cavendish. He had a candle in his hand, and the agitation of his face told me at once that something was seriously wrong.

'What's the matter?' I asked, sitting up in bed, and trying to collect my scattered thoughts.

'We are afraid my mother is very ill. She seems to be having some kind of fit. Unfortunately she has locked herself in.'

'I'll come at once.'

I sprang out of bed, and, pulling on a dressing-gown, followed Lawrence along the passage and the gallery to the right wing of the house.

John Cavendish joined us, and one or two of the servants were standing round in a state of awe-stricken excitement. Lawrence turned to his brother.

'What do you think we had better do?'

Never, I thought, had his indecision of character been more apparent.

John rattled the handle of Mrs Inglethorp's door violently, but with no effect. It was obviously locked or bolted on the inside. The whole household was aroused by now. The most alarming sounds were audible from the interior of the room. Clearly something must be done.

'Try going through Mr Inglethorp's room, sir,' cried Dorcas. 'Oh, the poor mistress!'

Suddenly I realized that Alfred Inglethorp was not with us – that he alone had given no sign of his presence. John opened the door of his room. It was pitch dark, but Lawrence was following with the candle, and by its feeble light we saw that the bed had not been slept in, and that there was no sign of the room having been occupied.

We went straight to the connecting door. That, too, was locked or bolted on the inside. What was to be done?

'Oh, dear, sir,' cried Dorcas, wringing her hands, 'whatever shall we do?'

'We must try and break the door in, I suppose. It'll be a tough job, though. Here, let one of the maids go down and wake Baily and tell him to go for Dr Wilkins at once. Now then, we'll have a try at the door. Half a moment, though, isn't there a door into Miss Cynthia's room?'

'Yes, sir, but that's always bolted. It's never been undone.'

'Well, we might just see.'

He ran rapidly down the corridor to Cynthia's room. Mary Cavendish was there, shaking the girl – who must have been an unusually sound sleeper – and trying to wake her.

In a moment or two he was back.

'No good. That's bolted too. We must break in the door. I think this one is a shade less solid than the one in the passage.'

We strained and heaved together. The framework of the door was solid, and for a long time it resisted our efforts, but at last we felt it give beneath our weight, and finally, with a resounding crash, it was burst open.

We stumbled in together, Lawrence still holding his candle. Mrs Inglethorp was lying on the bed, her whole form agitated by violent convulsions, in one of which she must have overturned the table beside her. As we entered, however, her limbs relaxed, and she fell back upon the pillows.

John strode across the room and lit the gas. Turning to Annie, one of the housemaids, he sent her downstairs to the dining-room for brandy. Then he went across to his mother whilst I unbolted the door that gave on the corridor.

I turned to Lawrence, to suggest that I had better leave them now that there was no further need of my services, but the words were frozen on my lips. Never have I seen such a ghastly look on any man's face. He was white as chalk, the candle he held in his shaking hand was sputtering on to the carpet, and his eyes, petrified with terror or some such kindred emotion, stared fixedly over my head at a point on the further wall. It was as though he had seen something that turned him to stone. I instinctively followed the direction of his eyes, but I could see nothing unusual. The still feebly flickering ashes in the grate, and the row of prim ornaments on the mantelpiece, were surely harmless enough.

The violence of Mrs Inglethorp's attack seemed to be passing. She was able to speak in short gasps.

'Better now – very sudden – stupid of me – to lock myself in.'

A shadow fell on the bed and, looking up, I saw Mary Cavendish standing near the door with her arm around Cynthia. She seemed to be supporting the girl, who looked utterly dazed and unlike herself. Her face was heavily flushed, and she yawned repeatedly.

'Poor Cynthia is quite frightened,' said Mrs Cavendish in a low clear voice. She herself, I noticed, was dressed in her white land smock. Then it must be later than I thought. I saw that a faint streak of daylight was showing through the curtains of the windows, and that the clock on the mantelpiece pointed to close upon five o'clock.

A strangled cry from the bed startled me. A fresh access of pain seized the unfortunate old lady. The convulsions were of a violence terrible to behold. Everything was confusion. We thronged round her, powerless to help or alleviate. A final convulsion lifted her from the bed, until she appeared to rest upon her head and her heels, with her body arched in an extraordinary manner. In vain Mary and John tried to administer more brandy. The moments flew. Again the body arched itself in that peculiar fashion.

At that moment, Dr Bauerstein pushed his way authoritatively into the room. For one instant he stopped dead, staring at the figure on the bed, and, at the same instant, Mrs Inglethorp cried out in a strangled voice, her eyes fixed on the doctor:

'Alfred – Alfred –' Then she fell back motionless on the pillows.

With a stride, the doctor reached the bed, and seizing her arms worked them energetically, applying what I knew to be artificial respiration. He issued a few short sharp orders to the servants. An imperious wave of his hand drove us all to the door. We watched him, fascinated, though I think we all knew in our hearts that it was too late, and that nothing could be done now. I could see by the expression on his face that he himself had little hope.

Finally he abandoned his task, shaking his head gravely. At that moment, we heard footsteps outside, and Dr Wilkins, Mrs Inglethorp's own doctor, a portly, fussy little man, came bustling in.

In a few words Dr Bauerstein explained how he had happened to be passing the lodge gates as the car came out, and had run up to the house as fast as he could, whilst the car went on to fetch Dr Wilkins. With a faint gesture of the hand, he indicated the figure on the bed.

'Ve – ry sad. Ve – ry sad,' murmured Dr Wilkins. 'Poor dear lady. Always did far too much – far too much – against my advice. I warned her, "Take it easy". But no – her zeal for good works was too great. Nature rebelled. Na – ture – re – belled.'

Dr Bauerstein, I noticed, was watching the local doctor narrowly. He still kept his eyes fixed on him as he spoke.

'The convulsions were of a peculiar violence, Dr Wilkins. I am sorry you were not here in time to witness them. They were quite – tetanic in character.'

'Ah!' said Dr Wilkins wisely.

'I should like to speak to you in private,' said Dr Bauerstein. He turned to John. 'You do not object?'

'Certainly not.'

We all trooped out into the corridor, leaving the two doctors alone, and I heard the key turned in the lock behind us.

We went slowly down the stairs. I was violently excited. I have a certain talent for deduction, and Dr Bauerstein's manner had started a flock of wild surmises in my mind. Mary Cavendish laid her hand upon my arm.

'What is it? Why did Dr Bauerstein seem so – peculiar?'

I looked at her.

'Do you know what I think?'

'What?'

'Listen!' I looked round, the others were out of earshot. I lowered my voice to a whisper. 'I believe she has been poisoned! I'm certain Dr Bauerstein suspects it.'

'*What?*' She shrank against the wall, the pupils of her eyes dilating wildly. Then, with a sudden cry that startled me, she cried out: 'No, no – not that – not that!' And breaking from me, fled up the stairs. I followed her, afraid that she was going to faint. I found her leaning against the banisters, deadly pale. She waved me away impatiently.

'No, no – leave me. I'd rather be alone. Let me just be quiet for a minute or two. Go down to the others.'

I obeyed her reluctantly. John and Lawrence were in the dining-room. I joined them. We were all silent, but I suppose I voiced the thoughts of us all when I at last broke it by saying:

'Where is Mr Inglethorp?'

John shook his head.

'He's not in the house.'

Our eyes met. Where *was* Alfred Inglethorp? His absence was strange and inexplicable. I remembered Mrs Inglethorp's dying words. What lay beneath them? What more could she have told us, if she had had time?

At last we heard the doctors descending the stairs. Dr Wilkins was looking important and excited, and trying to conceal an inward exultation under a manner of decorous calm. Dr Bauerstein remained in the background, his grave bearded face unchanged. Dr Wilkins was the spokesman for the two. He addressed himself to John:

'Mr Cavendish, I should like your consent to a post-mortem.'

'Is that necessary?' asked John gravely. A spasm of pain crossed his face.

'Absolutely,' said Dr Bauerstein.

'You mean by that –?'

'That neither Dr Wilkins nor myself could give a death certificate under the circumstances.'

John bent his head.

'In that case, I have no alternative but to agree.'

'Thank you,' said Dr Wilkins briskly. 'We propose that it should take place tomorrow night – or rather tonight.' And he glanced at the daylight. 'Under the circumstances, I am afraid an inquest can hardly be avoided – these formalities are necessary, but I beg that you won't distress yourselves.'

There was a pause, and then Dr Bauerstein drew two keys from his pocket, and handed them to John.

'These are the keys of the two rooms. I have locked them and, in my opinion, they would be better kept locked for the present.'

The doctors then departed.

I had been turning over an idea in my head, and I felt that the moment had now come to broach it. Yet I was a little chary of doing so. John, I knew, had a horror of any kind of publicity, and was an easy-going optimist, who preferred never to meet trouble half-way. It might be difficult to convince him of the soundness of my plan. Lawrence, on the other hand, being less conventional, and having more imagination, I felt I might count upon as an ally. There was no doubt that the moment had come for me to take the lead.

'John,' I said, 'I am going to ask you something.'

'Well?'

'You remember my speaking of my friend Poirot? The Belgian who is here? He has been a most famous detective.'

'Yes.'

'I want you to let me call him in – to investigate this matter.'

'What – now? Before the post-mortem?'

'Yes, time is an advantage if – if – there has been foul play.'

'Rubbish!' cried Lawrence angrily. 'In my opinion the whole thing is a mare's nest of Bauerstein's! Wilkins hadn't an idea of such a thing, until Bauerstein put it into his head. But, like all specialists, Bauerstein's got a bee in his bonnet. Poisons are his hobby, so, of course, he sees them everywhere.'

I confess that I was surprised by Lawrence's attitude. He was so seldom vehement about anything.

John hesitated.

'I can't feel as you do, Lawrence,' he said at last, 'I'm inclined to give Hastings a free hand, though I should prefer to wait a bit. We don't want any unnecessary scandal.'

'No, no,' I cried eagerly, 'you need have no fear of that. Poirot is discretion itself.'

'Very well then, have it your own way. I leave it in your hands. Though, if it is as we suspect, it seems a clear enough case. God forgive me if I am wronging him!'

I looked at my watch. It was six o'clock. I determined to lose no time.

Five minutes' delay, however, I allowed myself. I spent it in ransacking the library until I discovered a medical book which gave a description of strychnine poisoning.

CHAPTER IV

Poirot Investigates

The house which the Belgians occupied in the village was quite close to the park gates. One could save time by taking a narrow path through the long grass, which cut off the detours of the winding drive. So I, accordingly, went that way. I had nearly reached the lodge, when my attention was arrested by the running figure of a man approaching me. It was Mr Inglethorp. Where had he been? How did he intend to explain his absence?

He accosted me eagerly.

'My God! This is terrible! My poor wife! I have only just heard.'

'Where have you been?' I asked.

'Denby kept me late last night. It was one o'clock before we'd finished. Then I found that I'd forgotten the latch-key after all. I didn't want to arouse the household, so Denby gave me a bed.'

'How did you hear the news?' I asked.

'Wilkins knocked Denby up to tell him. My poor Emily! She was so self-sacrificing – such a noble character. She over-taxed her strength.'

A wave of revulsion swept over me. What a consummate hypocrite the man was!

'I must hurry on,' I said, thankful that he did not ask me whither I was bound.

In a few minutes I was knocking at the door of Leastways Cottage.

Getting no answer, I repeated my summons impatiently. A window above me was cautiously opened, and Poirot himself looked out.

He gave an exclamation of surprise at seeing me. In a few brief words, I explained the tragedy that had occurred, and that I wanted his help.

'Wait, my friend, I will let you in, and you shall recount to me the affairs whilst I dress.'

In a few moments he had unbarred the door, and I followed him up to his room. There he installed me in a chair, and I related the whole story, keeping back nothing, and omitting no circumstance, however insignificant, whilst he himself made a careful and deliberate toilet.

I told him of my awakening, of Mrs Inglethorp's dying words, of her husband's absence, of the quarrel the day before, of the scrap of conversation between Mary and her mother-in-law that I had overheard, of the former quarrel between Mrs Inglethorp and Evelyn Howard, and of the latter's innuendoes.

I was hardly as clear as I could wish. I repeated myself several times, and occasionally had to go back to some detail that I had forgotten. Poirot smiled kindly on me.

'The mind is confused? Is it not so? Take time, *mon ami*. You are agitated; you are excited – it is but natural. Presently, when we are calmer, we will arrange the facts, neatly, each in his proper place. We will examine – and reject. Those of importance we will put on one side; those of no importance, pouf!' – he screwed up his cherub-like face, and puffed comically enough – 'blow them away!'

'That's all very well,' I objected, 'but how are you going to decide what is important, and what isn't? That always seems the difficulty to me.'

Poirot shook his head energetically. He was now arranging his moustache with exquisite care.

'Not so. *Voyons!* One fact leads to another – so we continue. Does the next fit in with that? *A merveille!* Good! We can proceed. The next little fact – no! Ah, that is curious! There is something missing – a link in the chain that is not there. We examine. We search. And that little curious fact, that possibly paltry little detail that will not tally, we put it here!' He made an extravagant gesture with his hand. 'It is significant! It is tremendous!'

'Y – es –'

'Ah!' Poirot shook his forefinger so fiercely at me that I quailed before it. 'Beware! Peril to the detective who says: "It is so small – it does not matter. It will not agree. I will forget it." That way lies confusion! Everything matters.'

'I know. You always told me that. That's why I have gone into all the details of this thing whether they seemed to me relevant or not.'

'And I am pleased with you. You have a good memory, and you have given me the facts faithfully. Of the order in which you present them, I say nothing – truly, it is deplorable! But I make allowances – you are upset. To that I attribute the circumstance that you have omitted one fact of paramount importance.'

'What is that?' I asked.

'You have not told me if Mrs Inglethorp ate well last night.'

I stared at him. Surely the war had affected the little man's brain. He was carefully engaged in brushing his coat before putting it on, and seemed wholly engrossed in the task.

'I don't remember,' I said. 'And, anyway, I don't see –'

'You do not see? But it is of the first importance.'

'I can't see why,' I said, rather nettled. 'As far as I can remember, she didn't eat much. She was obviously upset, and it had taken her appetite away. That was only natural.'

'Yes,' said Poirot thoughtfully, 'it was only natural.'

He opened a drawer, and took out a small despatch-case, then turned to me.

'Now I am ready. We will proceed to the château, and study matters on the spot. Excuse me, *mon ami*, you dressed in haste, and your tie is on one side. Permit me.' With a deft gesture, he rearranged it.

'*Ça y est!* Now, shall we start?'

We hurried up the village, and turned in at the lodge gates. Poirot stopped for a moment, and gazed sorrowfully over the beautiful expanse of park, still glittering with morning dew.

'So beautiful, so beautiful, and yet, the poor family, plunged in sorrow, prostrated with grief.'

He looked at me keenly as he spoke, and I was aware that I reddened under his prolonged gaze.

Was the family prostrated by grief? Was the sorrow at Mrs Inglethorp's death so great? I realized that there was an emotional lack in the atmosphere. The dead woman had not the gift of commanding love. Her death was a shock and a distress, but she would not be passionately regretted.

Poirot seemed to follow my thoughts. He nodded his head gravely.

'No, you are right,' he said, 'it is not as though there was a blood tie. She has been kind and generous to these Cavendishes, but she was not their own mother. Blood tells – always remember that – blood tells.'

'Poirot,' I said, 'I wish you would tell me why you wanted to know if Mrs Inglethorp ate well last night? I have been turning it over in my mind, but I can't see how it has anything to do with the matter.'

He was silent for a minute or two as we walked along, but finally he said:

'I do not mind telling you – though, as you know, it is not my habit to explain until the end is reached. The present contention is that Mrs Inglethorp died of strychnine poisoning, presumably administered in her coffee.'

'Yes?'

'Well, what time was the coffee served?'

'About eight o'clock.'

'Therefore she drank it between then and half-past eight – certainly not much later. Well, strychnine is a fairly rapid poison. Its effects would be felt very soon, probably in about an hour. Yet, in Mrs Inglethorp's case, the symptoms do not manifest themselves until five o'clock the next morning: nine hours! But a heavy meal, taken at about the same time as the poison, might retard its effects, though hardly to that extent. Still, it is a possibility to be taken into account. But, according to you, she ate very little for supper, and yet the symptoms do not develop until early the next morning! Now that is a curious circumstance, my friend. Something may arise at the autopsy to explain it. In the meantime, remember it.'

As we neared the house, John came out and met us. His face looked weary and haggard.

'This is a very dreadful business, Monsieur Poirot,' he said. 'Hastings has explained to you that we are anxious for no publicity?'

'I comprehend perfectly.'

'You see, it is only suspicion so far. We have nothing to go upon.'

'Precisely. It is a matter of precaution only.'

John turned to me, taking out his cigarette-case, and lighting a cigarette as he did so.

'You know that fellow Inglethorp is back?'

'Yes. I met him.'

John flung the match into an adjacent flower bed, a proceeding which was too much for Poirot's feelings. He retrieved it, and buried it neatly.

'It's jolly difficult to know how to treat him.'

'That difficulty will not exist long,' pronounced Poirot quietly.

John looked puzzled, not quite understanding the portent of this cryptic saying. He handed the two keys which Dr Bauerstein had given him to me.

'Show Monsieur Poirot everything he wants to see.'

'The rooms are locked?' asked Poirot.

'Dr Bauerstein considered it advisable.'

Poirot nodded thoughtfully.

'Then he is very sure. Well, that simplifies matters for us.'

We went up together to the room of the tragedy. For convenience I append a plan of the room and the principal articles of furniture in it.

Poirot locked the door on the inside, and proceeded to a minute inspection of the room. He darted from one object to the other with the agility of a grasshopper. I remained by the

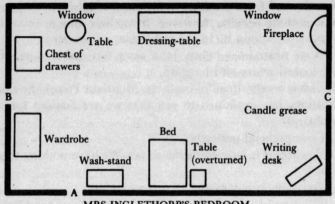

MRS INGLETHORP'S BEDROOM

A – Door into passage
B – Door into Mr Inglethorp's room
C – Door into Cynthia's room

door, fearing to obliterate any clues. Poirot, however, did not seem grateful to me for my forbearance.

'What have you, my friend?' he cried, 'that you remain there like – how do you say it? – ah, yes, the stuck pig?'

I explained that I was afraid of obliterating any footmarks.

'Footmarks? But what an idea! There has already been practically an army in the room! What footmarks are we likely to find? No, come here and aid me in my search. I will put down my little case until I need it.'

He did so, on the round table by the window, but it was an ill-advised proceeding; for, the top of it being loose, it tilted up, and precipitated the despatch-case on to the floor.

'*En voilà une table!*' cried Poirot. 'Ah, my friend, one may live in a big house and yet have no comfort.'

After which piece of moralizing, he resumed his search.

A small purple despatch-case, with a key in the lock, on the writing-table, engaged his attention for some time. He took out the key from the lock, and passed it to me to inspect. I saw nothing peculiar, however. It was an ordinary key of the Yale type, with a bit of twisted wire through the handle.

Next, he examined the framework of the door we had broken in, assuring himself that the bolt had really been shot. Then he went to the door opposite leading into Cynthia's room. That door was also bolted, as I had stated. However, he went to the length of unbolting it, and opening and shutting it several times; this he did with the utmost precaution against making any noise. Suddenly something in the bolt itself seemed to rivet his attention. He examined it carefully, and then, nimbly whipping out a pair of small forceps from his case, he drew out some minute particle which he carefully sealed up in a tiny envelope.

On the chest of drawers there was a tray with a spirit lamp and a small saucepan on it. A small quantity of a dark fluid remained in the saucepan, and an empty cup and saucer that had been drunk out of stood near it.

I wondered how I could have been so unobservant as to overlook this. Here was a clue worth having. Poirot delicately dipped his finger into the liquid, and tasted it gingerly. He made a grimace.

'Cocoa – with – I think – rum in it.'

He passed on to the debris on the floor, where the table by the bed had been overturned. A reading-lamp, some books, matches, a bunch of keys, and the crushed fragments of a coffee-cup lay scattered about.

'Ah, this is curious,' said Poirot.

'I must confess that I see nothing particularly curious about it.'

'You do not? Observe the lamp – the chimney is broken in two places; they lie there as they fell. But see, the coffee-cup is absolutely smashed to powder.'

'Well,' I said wearily, 'I suppose someone must have stepped on it.'

'Exactly,' said Poirot, in an odd voice. 'Someone stepped on it.'

He rose from his knees, and walked slowly across to the mantelpiece, where he stood abstractedly fingering the ornaments, and straightening them – a trick of his when he was agitated.

'*Mon ami*,' he said, turning to me, 'somebody stepped on that cup, grinding it to powder, and the reason they did so was either because it contained strychnine or – which is far more serious – because it did not contain strychnine!'

I made no reply. I was bewildered, but I knew that it was no good asking him to explain. In a moment or two he roused himself, and went on with his investigations. He picked up the bunch of keys from the floor, and twirling them round in his fingers finally selected one, very bright and shining, which he tried in the lock of the purple despatch-case. It fitted, and he opened the box, but after a moment's hesitation, closed and relocked it, and slipped the bunch of keys, as well as the key that had originally stood in the lock, into his own pocket.

'I have no authority to go through these papers. But it should be done – at once!'

He then made a very careful examination of the drawers of the wash-stand. Crossing the room to the left-hand window, a round stain, hardly visible on the dark brown carpet, seemed to interest him particularly. He went down on his knees, examining it minutely – even going so far as to smell it.

Finally, he poured a few drops of the cocoa into a test tube, sealing it up carefully. His next proceeding was to take out a little notebook.

'We have found in this room,' he said, writing busily, 'six points of interest. Shall I enumerate them, or will you?'

'Oh, you,' I replied hastily.

'Very well, then. One, a coffee-cup that has been ground into powder; two, a despatch-case with a key in the lock; three, a stain on the floor.'

'That may have been done some time ago,' I interrupted.

'No, for it is still perceptibly damp and smells of coffee. Four, a fragment of some dark green fabric – only a thread or two, but recognizable.'

'Ah!' I cried. 'That was what you sealed up in the envelope.'

'Yes. It may turn out to be a piece of one of Mrs Inglethorp's own dresses, and quite unimportant. We shall see. Five, *this!*' With a dramatic gesture, he pointed to a large splash of candle grease on the floor by the writing-table. 'It must have been done since yesterday, otherwise a good housemaid would have at once removed it with blotting-paper and a hot iron. One of my best hats once – but that is not to the point.'

'It was very likely done last night. We were very agitated. Or perhaps Mrs Inglethorp herself dropped her candle.'

'You brought only one candle into the room?'

'Yes. Lawrence Cavendish was carrying it. But he was very upset. He seemed to see something over here' – I indicated the mantelpiece – 'that absolutely paralysed him.'

'That is interesting,' said Poirot quickly. 'Yes, it is suggestive' – his eye sweeping the whole length of the wall – 'but it was not his candle that made this great patch, for you perceive that this is white grease; whereas Monsieur Lawrence's candle, which is still on the dressing-table, is pink. On the other hand, Mrs Inglethorp had no candlestick in the room, only a reading-lamp.'

'Then,' I said, 'what do you deduce?'

To which my friend only made a rather irritating reply, urging me to use my own natural faculties.

'And the sixth point?' I asked. 'I suppose it is the sample of cocoa.'

'No,' said Poirot thoughtfully. 'I might have included that in the six, but I did not. No, the sixth point I will keep to myself for the present.'

He looked quickly round the room. 'There is nothing more to be done here, I think, unless' – he stared earnestly and long at the dead ashes in the grate. 'The fire burns – and it destroys. But by chance – there might be – let us see!'

Deftly, on hands and knees, he began to sort the ashes from the grate into the fender, handling them with the greatest caution. Suddenly, he gave a faint exclamation.

'The forceps, Hastings!'

I quickly handed them to him, and with skill he extracted a small piece of half-charred paper.

'There, *mon ami*!' he cried. 'What do you think of that?'

I scrutinized the fragment. This is an exact reproduction of it:

I was puzzled. It was unusually thick, quite unlike ordinary notepaper. Suddenly an idea struck me.

'Poirot!' I cried. 'This is a fragment of a will!'

'Exactly.'

I looked up at him sharply.

'You are not surprised?'

'No,' he said gravely, 'I expected it.'

I relinquished the piece of paper, and watched him put it away in his case, with the same methodical care that he bestowed on everything. My brain was in a whirl. What was this complication of a will? Who had destroyed it? The person who had left the candle grease on the floor? Obviously. But how had anyone gained admission? All the doors had been bolted on the inside.

'Now, my friend,' said Poirot briskly, 'we will go. I should like to ask a few questions of the parlourmaid – Dorcas, her name is, is it not?'

We passed through Alfred Inglethorp's room, and Poirot delayed long enough to make a brief but fairly comprehensive examination of it. We went out through that door, locking both it and that of Mrs Inglethorp's room as before.

I took him down to the boudoir which he had expressed a wish to see, and went myself in search of Dorcas.

When I returned with her, however, the boudoir was empty.

'Poirot,' I cried, 'where are you?'

'I am here, my friend.'

He had stepped outside the french window, and was standing, apparently lost in admiration, before the various-shaped flower beds.

'Admirable!' he murmured. 'Admirable! What symmetry! Observe that crescent; and those diamonds – their neatness rejoices the eye. The spacing of the plants, also, is perfect. It has been recently done; is it not so?'

'Yes, I believe they were at it yesterday afternoon. But come in – Dorcas is here.'

'*Eh bien, eh bien!* Do not grudge me a moment's satisfaction of the eye.'

'Yes, but this affair is more important.'

'And how do you know that these fine begonias are not of equal importance?'

I shrugged my shoulders. There was really no arguing with him if he chose to take that line.

'You do not agree? But such things have been. Well, we will come in and interview the brave Dorcas.'

Dorcas was standing in the boudoir, her hands folded in front of her, and her grey hair rose in stiff waves under her white cap. She was the very model and picture of a good old-fashioned servant.

In her attitude towards Poirot, she was inclined to be suspicious, but he soon broke down her defences. He drew forward a chair.

'Pray be seated, mademoiselle.'

'Thank you, sir.'

'You have been with your mistress many years, is it not so?'

'Ten years, sir.'

'That is a long time, and very faithful service. You were much attached to her, were you not?'

'She was a very good mistress to me, sir.'

'Then you will not object to answering a few questions. I put them to you with Mr Cavendish's full approval.'

'Oh, certainly, sir.'

'Then I will begin by asking you about the events of yesterday afternoon. Your mistress had a quarrel?'

'Yes, sir. But I don't know that I ought –' Dorcas hesitated. Poirot looked at her keenly.

'My good Dorcas, it is necessary that I should know every detail of that quarrel as fully as possible. Do not think you are betraying your mistress's secrets. Your mistress lies dead, and it is necessary that we should know all – if we are to avenge her. Nothing can bring her back to life, but we do hope, if there has been foul play, to bring the murderer to justice.'

'Amen to that,' said Dorcas fiercely. 'And, naming no names, there's *one* in this house that none of us could ever abide! And an ill day it was when first *he* darkened the threshold.'

Poirot waited for her indignation to subside, and then, resuming his business-like tone, he asked:

'Now, as to this quarrel? What is the first you heard of it?'

'Well, sir, I happened to be going along the hall outside yesterday –'

'What time was that?'

'I couldn't say exactly, sir, but it wasn't teatime by a long way. Perhaps four o'clock – or it may have been a bit later. Well, sir, as I said, I happened to be passing along, when I heard voices very loud and angry in here. I didn't exactly mean to listen, but – well, there it is. I stopped. The door was shut, but the mistress was speaking very sharp and clear, and I heard what she said quite plainly. "You have lied to me, and deceived me," she said. I didn't hear what Mr Inglethorp replied. He spoke a good bit lower than she did – but she answered: "How dare you? I have kept you and clothed you and fed you! You owe everything to me! And this is how you repay me! By bringing disgrace upon our name!" Again I didn't hear what he said, but she went on: "Nothing that you can say will make any difference. I see my duty clearly. My mind is made up. You need not think that any fear of publicity, or scandal between husband and wife will deter me." Then I thought I heard them coming out, so I went off quickly.'

'You are sure it was Mr Inglethorp's voice you heard?'

'Oh, yes, sir, whose else's could it be?'

'Well, what happened next?'

'Later, I came back to the hall; but it was all quiet. At five o'clock, Mrs Inglethorp rang the bell and told me to bring her a cup of tea – nothing to eat – to the boudoir. She was looking dreadful – so white and upset. "Dorcas," she says, "I've had a great shock." "I'm sorry for that, m'm," I says. "You'll feel better after a nice hot cup of tea, m'm." She had something in her hand. I don't know if it was a letter, or just a piece of paper, but it had writing on it, and she kept staring at it, almost as if she couldn't believe what was written there. She whispered to herself, as though she had forgotten I was there: "These few words – and everything's changed." And then she says to me: "Never trust a man, Dorcas, they're not worth it!" I hurried off, and got her a good strong cup of tea, and she thanked me, and said she'd feel better when she'd drunk it. "I don't know what to do," she says. "Scandal between husband and wife is a dreadful thing, Dorcas. I'd rather hush it up if I could." Mrs Cavendish came in just then, so she didn't say any more.'

'She still had the letter, or whatever it was, in her hand?'

'Yes, sir.'

'What would she be likely to do with it afterwards?'

'Well, I don't know, sir, I expect she would lock it up in that purple case of hers.'

'Is that where she usually kept important papers?'

'Yes, sir. She brought it down with her every morning, and took it up every night.'

'When did she lose the key of it?'

'She missed it yesterday at lunch-time, sir, and told me to look carefully for it. She was very much put out about it.'

'But she had a duplicate key?'

'Oh, yes, sir.'

Dorcas was looking very curiously at him and, to tell the

truth, so was I. What was all this about a lost key? Poirot smiled.

'Never mind, Dorcas, it is my business to know things. Is this the key that was lost?' He drew from his pocket the key that he had found in the lock of the despatch-case upstairs.

Dorcas's eyes looked as though they would pop out of her head.

'That's it, sir, right enough. But where did you find it? I looked everywhere for it.'

'Ah, but you see it was not in the same place yesterday as it was today. Now, to pass to another subject, had your mistress a dark green dress in her wardrobe?'

Dorcas was rather startled by the unexpected question.

'No, sir.'

'Are you quite sure?'

'Oh, yes, sir.'

'Has anyone else in the house got a green dress?'

Dorcas reflected.

'Miss Cynthia has a green evening dress.'

'Light or dark green?'

'A light green, sir; a sort of chiffon, they call it.'

'Ah, that is not what I want. And nobody else has anything green?'

'No, sir – not that I know of.'

Poirot's face did not betray a trace of whether he was disappointed or otherwise. He merely remarked:

'Good, we will leave that and pass on. Have you any reason to believe that your mistress was likely to take a sleeping powder last night?'

'Not *last* night, sir, I know she didn't.'

'Why do you know so positively?'

'Because the box was empty. She took the last one two days ago, and she didn't have any more made up.'

'You are quite sure of that?'

'Positive, sir.'

'Then that is cleared up! By the way, your mistress didn't ask you to sign any paper yesterday?'

'To sign a paper? No, sir.'

'When Mr Hastings and Mr Lawrence came in yesterday evening, they found your mistress busy writing letters. I suppose you can give me no idea to whom these letters were addressed?'

'I'm afraid I couldn't, sir. I was out in the evening. Perhaps Annie could tell you, though she's a careless girl. Never cleared the coffee-cups away last night. That's what happens when I'm not here to look after things.'

Poirot lifted his hand.

'Since they have been left, Dorcas, leave them a little longer, I pray you. I should like to examine them.'

'Very well, sir.'

'What time did you go out last evening?'

'About six o'clock, sir.'

'Thank you, Dorcas, that is all I have to ask you.' He rose and strolled to the window. 'I have been admiring these flower beds. How many gardeners are employed here, by the way?'

'Only three now, sir. Five, we had, before the war, when it was kept as a gentleman's place should be. I wish you could have seen it then, sir. A fair sight it was. But now there's only old Manning, and young William, and a new-fashioned woman gardener in breeches and such-like. Ah, these are dreadful times!'

'The good times will come again, Dorcas. At least, we hope so. Now, will you send Annie to me here?'

'Yes, sir. Thank you, sir.'

'How did you know that Mrs Inglethorp took sleeping powders?' I asked, in lively curiosity, as Dorcas left the room. 'And about the lost key and the duplicate?'

'One thing at a time. As to the sleeping powders, I knew by this.' He suddenly produced a small cardboard box, such as chemists use for powders.

'Where did you find it?'

'In the wash-stand drawer in Mrs Inglethorp's bedroom. It was Number Six of my catalogue.'

'But I suppose, as the last powder was taken two days ago, it is not of much importance?'

'Probably not, but do you notice anything that strikes you as peculiar about this box?'

I examined it closely.

'No, I can't say that I do.'

'Look at the label.'

I read the label carefully: One powder to be taken at bedtime, if required. Mrs Inglethorp. 'No, I see nothing unusual.'

'Not the fact that there is no chemist's name?'

'Ah!' I exclaimed. 'To be sure, that is odd!'

'Have you ever known a chemist to send out a box like that, without his printed name?'

'No, I can't say that I have.'

I was becoming quite excited, but Poirot damped my ardour by remarking:

'Yet the explanation is quite simple. So do not intrigue yourself, my friend.'

An audible creaking proclaimed the approach of Annie, so I had no time to reply.

Annie was a fine, strapping girl, and was evidently labouring under intense excitement, mingled with a certain ghoulish enjoyment of the tragedy.

Poirot came to the point at once, with a business-like briskness.

'I sent for you, Annie, because I thought you might be able to tell me something about the letters Mrs Inglethorp wrote last night. How many were there? And can you tell me any of the names and addresses?'

Annie considered.

'There were four letters, sir. One was to Miss Howard, and one was to Mr Wells, the lawyer, and the other two I don't think I remember, sir – oh, yes, one was to Ross's, the caterers in Tadminster. The other one, I don't remember.'

'Think,' urged Poirot.

Annie racked her brains in vain.

'I'm sorry, sir, but it's clean gone. I don't think I can have noticed it.'

'It does not matter,' said Poirot, not betraying any sign of disappointment. 'Now I want to ask you about something else. There is a saucepan in Mrs Inglethorp's room with some cocoa in it. Did she have that every night?'

'Yes, sir, it was put in her room every evening, and she warmed it up in the night – whenever she fancied it.'

'What was it? Plain cocoa?'

'Yes, sir, made with milk, with a teaspoonful of sugar, and two teaspoonfuls of rum in it.'

'Who took it to her room?'

'I did, sir.'

'Always?'

'Yes, sir.'

'At what time?'

'When I went to draw the curtains, as a rule, sir.'

'Did you bring it straight up from the kitchen then?'

'No, sir, you see there's not much room on the gas stove, so Cook used to make it early, before putting the vegetables on for supper. Then I used to bring it up, and put it on the table by the swing door, and take it into her room later.'

'The swing door is in the left wing, is it not?'

'Yes, sir.'

'And the table, is it on this side of the door, or on the farther – servants' side?'

'It's this side, sir.'

'What time did you bring it up last night?'

'About quarter-past seven, I should say, sir.'

'And when did you take it into Mrs Inglethorp's room?'

'When I went to shut up, sir. About eight o'clock. Mrs Inglethorp came up to bed before I'd finished.'

'Then, between 7.15 and 8 o'clock, the cocoa was standing on the table in the left wing?'

'Yes, sir.' Annie had been growing redder and redder in the face, and now she blurted out unexpectedly:

'And if there *was* salt in it, sir, it wasn't me. I never took the salt near it.'

'What makes you think there was salt in it?' asked Poirot.

'Seeing it on the tray, sir.'

'You saw some salt on the tray?'

'Yes. Coarse kitchen salt, it looked. I never noticed it when I took the tray up, but when I came to take it into the mistress's room I saw it at once, and I suppose I ought to have taken it down again, and asked Cook to make some fresh. But I was in a hurry, because Dorcas was out, and I thought maybe the cocoa itself was all right, and the salt had only gone on the tray. So I dusted it off with my apron, and took it in.'

I had the utmost difficulty in controlling my excitement. Unknown to herself, Annie had provided us with an important piece of evidence. How she would have gaped if she had realized that her 'coarse kitchen salt' was strychnine, one of the most deadly poisons known to mankind. I marvelled at Poirot's calm. His self-control was astonishing. I awaited his next question with impatience, but it disappointed me.

'When you went into Mrs Inglethorp's room, was the door leading into Miss Cynthia's room bolted?'

'Oh! Yes, sir; it always was. It had never been opened.'

'And the door into Mr Inglethorp's room? Did you notice if that was bolted too?'

Annie hesitated.

'I couldn't rightly say, sir; it was shut but I couldn't say whether it was bolted or not.'

'When you finally left the room, did Mrs Inglethorp bolt the door after you?'

'No, sir, not then, but I expect she did later. She usually did lock it at night. The door into the passage, that is.'

'Did you notice any candle grease on the floor when you did the room yesterday?'

'Candle grease? Oh, no, sir. Mrs Inglethorp didn't have a candle, only a reading-lamp.'

'Then, if there had been a large patch of candle grease on

the floor, you think you would have been sure to have seen it?'

'Yes, sir, and I would have taken it out with a piece of blotting-paper and a hot iron.'

Then Poirot repeated the question he had put to Dorcas:

'Did your mistress ever have a green dress?'

'No, sir.'

'Nor a mantle, nor a cape, nor a – how do you call it? – a sports coat?'

'Not green, sir.'

'Nor anyone else in the house?'

Annie reflected.

'No, sir.'

'You are sure of that?'

'Quite sure.'

'*Bien!* That is all I want to know. Thank you very much.'

With a nervous giggle, Annie took herself creakingly out of the room. My pent-up excitement burst forth.

'Poirot,' I cried, 'I congratulate you! This is a great discovery.'

'What is a great discovery?'

'Why, that it was the cocoa and not the coffee that was poisoned. That explains everything! Of course, it did not take effect until the early morning, since the cocoa was only drunk in the middle of the night.'

'So you think that the cocoa – mark well what I say, Hastings, the *cocoa* – contained strychnine?'

'Of course! That salt on the tray, what else could it have been?'

'It might have been salt,' replied Poirot placidly.

I shrugged my shoulders. If he was going to take the matter that way, it was no good arguing with him. The idea crossed my mind, not for the first time, that poor old Poirot was growing old. Privately I thought it lucky that he had associated with him someone of a more receptive type of mind.

Poirot was surveying me with quietly twinkling eyes.

'You are not pleased with me, *mon ami*?'

'My dear Poirot,' I said coldly, 'it is not for me to dictate

to you. You have a right to your own opinion, just as I have
to mine.'

'A most admirable sentiment,' remarked Poirot, rising
briskly to his feet. 'Now I have finished with this room. By
the way, whose is the smaller desk in the corner?'

'Mr Inglethorp's.'

'Ah!' He tried the roll top tentatively. 'Locked. But perhaps
one of Mrs Inglethorp's keys would open it.' He tried several,
twisting and turning them with a practised hand, and finally
uttering an ejaculation of satisfaction. '*Voilà!* It is not the key,
but it will open it at a pinch.' He slid back the roll top, and
ran a rapid eye over the neatly filed papers. To my surprise,
he did not examine them, merely remarking approvingly as
he relocked the desk: 'Decidedly, he is a man of method, this
Mr Inglethorp!'

A 'man of method' was, in Poirot's estimation, the highest
praise that could be bestowed on any individual.

I felt that my friend was not what he had been as he rambled
on disconnectedly:

'There were no stamps in his desk, but there might have
been, eh, *mon ami*? There might have been? Yes' – his eyes
wandered round the room – 'this boudoir has nothing more
to tell us. It did not yield much. Only this.'

He pulled a crumpled envelope out of his pocket, and
tossed it over to me. It was rather a curious document.
A plain, dirty-looking envelope with a few words scrawled
across it, apparently at random. The following is a facsimile
of it:

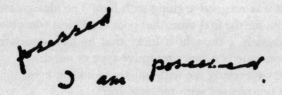

He is possessed

I am possessed

possessed

CHAPTER V

'It Isn't Strychnine, Is It?"

'Where did you find this?' I asked Poirot, in lively curiosity.

'In the waste-paper basket. You recognize the handwriting?'

'Yes, it is Mrs Inglethorp's. But what does it mean?'

Poirot shrugged his shoulders.

'I cannot say – but it is suggestive.'

A wild idea flashed across me. Was it possible that Mrs Inglethorp's mind was deranged? Had she some fantastic idea of demoniacal possession? And, if that were so, was it not also possible that she might have taken her own life?

I was about to expound these theories to Poirot, when his own words distracted me.

'Come,' he said, 'now to examine the coffee-cups!'

'My dear Poirot! What on earth is the good of that, now that we know about the cocoa?'

'Oh, *là là*! That miserable cocoa!' cried Poirot flippantly.

He laughed with apparent enjoyment, raising his arms to heaven in mock despair, in what I could not but consider the worst possible taste.

'And, anyway,' I said, with increasing coldness, 'as Mrs Inglethorp took her coffee upstairs with her, I do not see what you expect to find, unless you consider it likely that we shall discover a packet of strychnine on the coffee tray!'

Poirot was sobered at once.

'Come, come, my friend,' he said, slipping his arm through mine. *'Ne vous fâchez pas!* Allow me to interest myself in my coffee-cups, and I will respect your cocoa. There! Is it a bargain?'

He was so quaintly humorous that I was forced to laugh; and we went together to the drawing-room, where the coffee-cups and tray remained undisturbed as we had left them.

Poirot made me recapitulate the scene of the night before, listening very carefully, and verifying the position of the various cups.

'So Mrs Cavendish stood by the tray – and poured out. Yes. Then she came across to the window where you sat with Mademoiselle Cynthia. Yes. Here are the three cups. And the cup on the mantelpiece, half drunk, that would be Mr Lawrence Cavendish's. And the one on the tray?'

'John Cavendish's. I saw him put it down there.'

'Good. One, two, three, four, five – but where, then, is the cup of Mr Inglethorp?'

'He does not take coffee.'

'Then all are accounted for. One moment, my friend.'

With infinite care, he took a drop or two from the grounds in each cup, sealing them up in separate test tubes, tasting each in turn as he did so. His physiognomy underwent a curious change. An expression gathered there that I can only describe as half puzzled, and half relieved.

'*Bien!*' he said at last. 'It is evident! I had an idea – but clearly I was mistaken. Yes, altogether I was mistaken. Yet it is strange. But no matter!'

And, with a characteristic shrug, he dismissed whatever it was that was worrying him from his mind. I could have told him from the beginning that this obsession of his over the coffee was bound to end in a blind alley, but I restrained my tongue. After all, though he was old, Poirot had been a great man in his day.

'Breakfast is ready,' said John Cavendish, coming in from the hall. 'You will breakfast with us, Monsieur Poirot?'

Poirot acquiesced. I observed John. Already he was almost restored to his normal self. The shock of the events of the last night had upset him temporarily, but his equable poise soon swung back to the normal. He was a man of very little imagination, in sharp contrast with his brother, who had, perhaps, too much.

Ever since the early hours of the morning, John had been

hard at work, sending telegrams – one of the first had gone to Evelyn Howard – writing notices for the papers, and generally occupying himself with the melancholy duties that a death entails.

'May I ask how things are proceeding?' he said. 'Do your investigations point to my mother having died a natural death – or – or must we prepare ourselves for the worst?'

'I think, Mr Cavendish,' said Poirot gravely, 'that you would do well not to buoy yourself up with any false hopes. Can you tell me the views of the other members of the family?'

'My brother Lawrence is convinced that we are making a fuss over nothing. He says that everything points to its being a simple case of heart failure.'

'He does, does he? That is very interesting – very interesting,' murmured Poirot softly. 'And Mrs Cavendish?'

A faint cloud passed over John's face.

'I have not the least idea what my wife's views on the subject are.'

The answer brought a momentary stiffness in its train. John broke the rather awkward silence by saying with a slight effort:

'I told you, didn't I, that Mr Inglethorp has returned?'

Poirot bent his head.

'It's an awkward position for all of us. Of course, one has to treat him as usual – but, hang it all, one's gorge does rise at sitting down to eat with a possible murderer!'

Poirot nodded sympathetically.

'I quite understand. It is a very difficult situation for you, Mr Cavendish. I would like to ask you one question. Mr Inglethorp's reason for not returning last night was, I believe, that he had forgotten the latch-key. Is not that so?'

'Yes.'

'I suppose you are quite sure that the latch-key *was* forgotten – that he did not take it after all?'

'I have no idea. I never thought of looking. We always keep it in the hall drawer. I'll go and see if it's there now.'

Poirot held up his hand with a faint smile.

'No, no, Mr Cavendish, it is too late now. I am certain that you will find it. If Mr Inglethorp did take it, he has had ample time to replace it by now.'

'But do you think –'

'I think nothing. If anyone had chanced to look this morning before his return, and seen it there, it would have been a valuable point in his favour. That is all.'

John looked perplexed.

'Do not worry,' said Poirot smoothly. 'I assure you that you need not let it trouble you. Since you are so kind, let us go and have some breakfast.'

Everyone was assembled in the dining-room. Under the circumstances, we were naturally not a cheerful party. The reaction after a shock is always trying, and I think we were all suffering from it. Decorum and good breeding naturally enjoined that our demeanour should be much as usual, yet I could not help wondering if this self-control were really a matter of great difficulty. There were no red eyes, no signs of secretly indulged grief. I felt that I was right in my opinion that Dorcas was the person most affected by the personal side of the tragedy.

I pass over Alfred Inglethorp, who acted the bereaved widower in a manner that I felt to be disgusting in its hypocrisy. Did he know that we suspected him, I wondered. Surely he could not be unaware of the fact, conceal it as we would. Did he feel some secret stirring of fear, or was he confident that his crime would go unpunished? Surely the suspicion in the atmosphere must warn him that he was already a marked man.

But did everyone suspect him? What about Mrs Cavendish? I watched her as she sat at the head of the table, graceful, composed, enigmatic. In her soft grey frock, with white ruffles at the wrists falling over her slender hands, she looked very beautiful. When she chose, however, her face could be sphinx-like in its inscrutability. She was very silent, hardly opening her lips, and yet in some queer way I felt that the great strength of her personality was dominating us all.

And little Cynthia? Did she suspect? She looked very tired

and ill, I thought. The heaviness and languor of her manner were very marked. I asked her if she were feeling ill, and she answered frankly:

'Yes, I've got the most beastly headache.'

'Have another cup of coffee, mademoiselle?' said Poirot solicitously. 'It will revive you. It is unparalleled for the *mal de tête.*' He jumped up and took her cup.

'No sugar,' said Cynthia, watching him, as he picked up the sugar-tongs.

'No sugar? You abandon it in the war-time, eh?'

'No, I never take it in coffee.'

'*Sacré!*' murmured Poirot to himself, as he brought back the replenished cup.

Only I heard him, and glancing up curiously at the little man I saw that his face was working with suppressed excitement, and his eyes were as green as a cat's. He had heard or seen something that had affected him strongly – but what was it? I do not usually label myself as dense, but I must confess that nothing out of the ordinary had attracted *my* attention.

In another moment, the door opened and Dorcas appeared. 'Mr Wells to see you, sir,' she said to John.

I remembered the name as being that of the lawyer to whom Mrs Inglethorp had written the night before.

John rose immediately.

'Show him into my study.' Then he turned to us. 'My mother's lawyer,' he explained. And in a lower voice: 'He is also Coroner – you understand. Perhaps you would like to come with me?'

We acquiesced and followed him out of the room. John strode on ahead and I took the opportunity of whispering to Poirot:

'There will be an inquest then?'

Poirot nodded absently. He seemed absorbed in thought; so much so that my curiosity was aroused.

'What is it? You are not attending to what I say.'

'It is true, my friend. I am much worried.'

'Why?'

'Because Mademoiselle Cynthia does not take sugar in her coffee.'

'What? You cannot be serious?'

'But I am most serious. Ah, there is something there that I do not understand. My instinct was right.'

'What instinct?'

'The instinct that led me to insist on examining those coffee-cups. *Chut!* no more now!'

We followed John into his study, and he closed the door behind us.

Mr Wells was a pleasant man of middle-age, with keen eyes, and the typical lawyer's mouth. John introduced us both, and explained the reason of our presence.

'You will understand, Wells,' he added, 'that this is all strictly private. We are still hoping that there will turn out to be no need for investigation of any kind.'

'Quite so, quite so,' said Mr Wells soothingly. 'I wish we could have spared you the pain and publicity of an inquest, but, of course, it's quite unavoidable in the absence of a doctor's certificate.'

'Yes, I suppose so.'

'Clever man, Bauerstein. Great authority on toxicology, I believe.'

'Indeed,' said John with a certain stiffness in his manner. Then he added rather hesitatingly: 'Shall we have to appear as witnesses – all of us, I mean?'

'You, of course – and ah – er – Mr – er – Inglethorp.'

A slight pause ensued before the lawyer went on in his soothing manner:

'Any other evidence will be simply confirmatory, a mere matter of form.'

'I see.'

A faint expression of relief swept over John's face. It puzzled me, for I saw no occasion for it.

'If you know of nothing to the contrary,' pursued Mr Wells, 'I had thought of Friday. That will give us plenty of time for the doctor's report. The post-mortem is to take place tonight, I believe?'

'Yes.'

'Then that arrangement will suit you?'

'Perfectly.'

'I need not tell you, my dear Cavendish, how distressed I am at this most tragic affair.'

'Can you give us no help in solving it, monsieur?' interposed Poirot, speaking for the first time since we had entered the room.

'I?'

'Yes, we heard that Mrs Inglethorp wrote to you last night. You should have received the letter this morning.'

'I did, but it contains no information. It is merely a note asking me to call upon her this morning, as she wanted my advice on a matter of great importance.'

'She gave you no hint as to what that matter might be?'

'Unfortunately, no.'

'That is a pity,' said John.

'A great pity,' agreed Poirot gravely.

There was silence. Poirot remained lost in thought for a few minutes. Finally he turned to the lawyer again.

'Mr Wells, there is one thing I should like to ask you – that is, if it is not against professional etiquette. In the event of Mrs Inglethorp's death, who would inherit her money?'

The lawyer hesitated a moment, and then replied:

'The knowledge will be public property very soon, so if Mr Cavendish does not object – '

'Not at all,' interpolated John.

'I do not see any reason why I should not answer your question. By her last will, dated August of last year, after various unimportant legacies to servants, etc., she gave her entire fortune to her stepson, Mr John Cavendish.'

'Was not that – pardon the question, Mr Cavendish – rather unfair to her other stepson, Mr Lawrence Cavendish?'

'No, I do not think so. You see, under the terms of their father's will, while John inherited the property, Lawrence, at his stepmother's death, would come into a considerable sum of money. Mrs Inglethorp left her money to her elder stepson, knowing that he would have to keep up Styles. It was, to my mind, a very fair and equitable distribution.'

Poirot nodded thoughtfully.

'I see. But I am right in saying, am I not, that by your English law that will was automatically revoked when Mrs Inglethorp remarried?'

Mr Wells bowed his head.

'As I was about to proceed, Monsieur Poirot, that document is now null and void.'

'*Hein!*' said Poirot. He reflected for a moment, and then asked: 'Was Mrs Inglethorp herself aware of that fact?'

'I do not know. She may have been.'

'She was,' said John unexpectedly. 'We were discussing the matter of wills being revoked by marriage only yesterday.'

'Ah! One more question, Mr Wells. You say "her last will". Had Mrs Inglethorp, then, made several former wills?'

'On an average, she made a new will at least once a year,' said Mr Wells imperturbably. 'She was given to changing her mind as to her testamentary dispositions, now benefiting one, now another member of her family.'

'Suppose,' suggested Poirot, 'that, unknown to you, she had made a new will in favour of someone who was not, in any sense of the word, a member of the family – we will say Miss Howard, for instance – would you be surprised?'

'Not in the least.'

'Ah!' Poirot seemed to have exhausted his questions.

I drew close to him, while John and the lawyer were debating the question of going through Mrs Inglethorp's papers.

'Do you think Mrs Inglethorp made a will leaving all her money to Miss Howard?' I asked in a low voice, with some curiosity.

Poirot smiled.

'No.'

'Then why did you ask?'

'Hush!'

John Cavendish had turned to Poirot.

'Will you come with us, Monsieur Poirot? We are going through my mother's papers. Mr Inglethorp is quite willing to leave it entirely to Mr Wells and myself.'

'Which simplifies matters very much,' murmured the lawyer. 'As technically, of course, he was entitled –' He did not finish the sentence.

'We will look through the desk in the boudoir first,' explained John, 'and go up to her bedroom afterwards. She kept her most important papers in a purple despatch-case, which we must look through carefully.'

'Yes,' said the lawyer, 'it is quite possible that there may be a later will than the one in my possession.'

'There *is* a later will.' It was Poirot who spoke.

'What?' John and the lawyer looked at him startled.

'Or rather,' pursued my friend imperturbably, 'there *was* one.'

'What do you mean – there was one? Where is it now?'

'Burnt!'

'Burnt?'

'Yes. See here.' He took out the charred fragment we had found in the grate in Mrs Inglethorp's room, and handed it to the lawyer with a brief explanation of when and where he had found it.

'But possibly this is an old will?'

'I do not think so. In fact I am almost certain that it was made no earlier than yesterday afternoon.'

'What?' 'Impossible!' broke simultaneously from both men.

Poirot turned to John.

'If you will allow me to send for your gardener, I will prove it to you.'

'Oh, of course – but I don't see –'

Poirot raised his hand.

'Do as I ask you. Afterwards you shall question as much as you please.'

'Very well.' He rang the bell.

Dorcas answered it in due course.

'Dorcas, will you tell Manning to come round and speak to me here.'

'Yes, sir.'

Dorcas withdrew.

We waited in a tense silence. Poirot alone seemed perfectly at his ease, and dusted a forgotten corner of the bookcase.

The clumping of hobnailed boots on the gravel outside proclaimed the approach of Manning. John looked questioningly at Poirot. The latter nodded.

'Come inside, Manning,' said John, 'I want to speak to you.'

Manning came slowly and hesitatingly through the french window, and stood as near it as he could. He held his cap in his hands, twisting it very carefully round and round. His back was much bent, though he was probably not as old as he looked, but his eyes were sharp and intelligent, and belied his slow and rather cautious speech.

'Manning,' said John, 'this gentleman will put some questions to you which I want you to answer.'

'Yessir,' mumbled Manning.

Poirot stepped forward briskly. Manning's eye swept over him with a faint contempt.

'You were planting a bed of begonias round by the south side of the house yesterday afternoon, were you not, Manning?'

'Yes, sir, me and Willum.'

'And Mrs Inglethorp came to the window and called you, did she not?'

'Yes, sir, she did.'

'Tell me in your own words exactly what happened after that.'

'Well, sir, nothing much. She just told Willum to go on his bicycle down to the village, and bring back a form of will, or such-like – I don't know what exactly – she wrote it down for him.'

'Well?'

'Well, he did, sir.'

'And what happened next?'

'We went on with the begonias, sir.'

'Did not Mrs Inglethorp call you again?'

'Yes, sir, both me and Willum, she called.'

'And then?'

'She made us come right in, and sign our names at the bottom of a long paper – under where she'd signed.'

'Did you see anything of what was written above her signature?' asked Poirot sharply.

'No, sir, there was a bit of blotting-paper over that part.'

'And you signed where she told you?'

'Yes, sir, first me and then Willum.'

'What did she do with it afterwards?'

'Well, sir, she slipped it into a long envelope, and put it inside a sort of purple box that was standing on the desk.'

'What time was it when she called you?'

'About four, I should say, sir.'

'Not earlier? Couldn't it have been about half-past three?'

'No, I shouldn't say so, sir. It would be more likely to be a bit after four – not before it.'

'Thank you, Manning, that will do,' said Poirot pleasantly.

The gardener glanced at his master, who nodded, whereupon Manning lifted a finger to his forehead with a low mumble, and backed cautiously out of the window.

We all looked at each other.

'Good heavens!' murmured John. 'What an extraordinary coincidence.'

'How – a coincidence?'

'That my mother should have made a will on the very day of her death!'

Mr Wells cleared his throat and remarked dryly:

'Are you so sure it is a coincidence, Cavendish?'

'What do you mean?'

'Your mother, you tell me, had a violent quarrel with – someone yesterday afternoon –'

'What do you mean?' cried John again. There was a tremor in his voice, and he had gone very pale.

'In consequence of that quarrel, your mother very suddenly

and hurriedly makes a new will. The contents of that will we shall never know. She told no one of its provisions. This morning, no doubt, she would have consulted me on the subject – but she had no chance. The will disappears, and she takes its secret with her to her grave. Cavendish, I much fear there is no coincidence there. Monsieur Poirot, I am sure you agree with me that the facts are very suggestive.'

'Suggestive or not,' interrupted John, 'we are most grateful to Monsieur Poirot for elucidating the matter. But for him, we should never have known of this will. I suppose I may not ask you, monsieur, what first led you to suspect the fact?'

Poirot smiled and answered:

'A scribbled-over old envelope, and a freshly planted bed of begonias.'

John, I think, would have pressed his questions further, but at that moment the loud purr of a motor was audible, and we all turned to the window as it swept past.

'Evie!' cried John. 'Excuse me, Wells.' He went hurriedly out into the hall.

Poirot looked inquiringly at me.

'Miss Howard,' I explained.

'Ah, I am glad she has come. There is a woman with a head and a heart too, Hastings. Though the good God gave her no beauty!'

I followed John's example, and went out into the hall, where Miss Howard was endeavouring to extricate herself from the voluminous mass of veils that enveloped her head. As her eyes fell on me, a sudden pang of guilt shot through me. This was the woman who had warned me so earnestly, and to whose warning I had, alas, paid no heed! How soon, and how contemptuously, I had dismissed it from my mind. Now that she had been proved justified in so tragic a manner, I felt ashamed. She had known Alfred Inglethorp only too well. I wondered whether, if she had remained at Styles, the tragedy would have taken place, or would the man have feared her watchful eyes?

I was relieved when she shook me by the hand, with her

well-remembered painful grip. The eyes that met mine were sad, but not reproachful; that she had been crying, bitterly, I could tell by the redness of her eyelids, but her manner was unchanged from its old blunt gruffness.

'Started the moment I got the wire. Just come off night duty. Hired car. Quickest way to get here.'

'Have you had anything to eat this morning, Evie?' asked John.

'No.'

'I thought not. Come along, breakfast's not cleared away yet, and they'll make you some fresh tea.' He turned to me. 'Look after her, Hastings, will you? Wells is waiting for me. Oh, here's Monsieur Poirot. He's helping us, you know, Evie.'

Miss Howard shook hands with Poirot, but glanced suspiciously over her shoulder at John.

'What do you mean – helping us?'

'Helping us to investigate.'

'Nothing to investigate. Have they taken him to prison yet?'

'Taken who to prison?'

'Who? Alfred Inglethorp, of course!'

'My dear Evie, do be careful. Lawrence is of the opinion that my mother died from heart seizure.'

'More fool, Lawrence!' retorted Miss Howard. 'Of course Alfred Inglethorp murdered poor Emily – as I always told you he would.'

'My dear Evie, don't shout so. Whatever we may think or suspect, it is better to say as little as possible for the present. The inquest isn't until Friday.'

'Not until fiddlesticks!' The snort Miss Howard gave was truly magnificent. 'You're all off your heads. The man will be out of the country by then. If he's any sense, he won't stay here tamely and wait to be hanged.'

John Cavendish looked at her helplessly.

'I know what it is,' she accused him, 'you've been listening to the doctors. Never should. What do they know? Nothing at all – or just enough to make them dangerous. I ought to know – my own father was a doctor. That little Wilkins is about the greatest fool that even I have ever seen. Heart seizure! Sort of thing he would say. Anyone with any sense could see at once that her husband had poisoned her. I always said he'd murder her in her bed, poor soul. Now he's done it. And all you can do is to murmur silly things about "heart seizure" and "inquest on Friday". You ought to be ashamed of yourself, John Cavendish.'

'What do you want me to do?' asked John, unable to help a faint smile. 'Dash it all, Evie, I can't haul him down to the local police station by the scruff of his neck.'

'Well, you might do something. Find out how he did it. He's a crafty beggar. Dare say he soaked fly papers. Ask Cook if she's missed any.'

It occurred to me very forcibly at that moment that to harbour Miss Howard and Alfred Inglethorp under the same roof, and keep the peace between them, was likely to prove a Herculean task, and I did not envy John. I could see by the expression of his face that he fully appreciated the difficulty of the position. For the moment, he sought refuge in retreat, and left the room precipitately.

Dorcas brought in fresh tea. As she left the room, Poirot came over from the window where he had been standing, and sat down facing Miss Howard.

'Mademoiselle,' he said gravely, 'I want to ask you something.'

'Ask away,' said the lady, eyeing him with some disfavour.

'I want to be able to count upon your help.'

'I'll help you to hang Alfred with pleasure,' she replied gruffly. 'Hanging's too good for him. Ought to be drawn and quartered, like in good old times.'

'We are at one then,' said Poirot, 'for I, too, want to hang the criminal.'

'Alfred Inglethorp?'

'Him, or another.'

'No question of another. Poor Emily was never murdered until *he* came along. I don't say she wasn't surrounded by sharks – she was. But it was only her purse they were after. Her life was safe enough. But along comes Mr Alfred Inglethorp – and within two months – hey presto!'

'Believe me, Miss Howard,' said Poirot very earnestly, 'if Mr Inglethorp is the man, he shall not escape me. On my honour, I will hang him as high as Haman!'

'That's better,' said Miss Howard more enthusiastically.

'But I must ask you to trust me. Now your help may be very valuable to me. I will tell you why. Because, in all this house of mourning, yours are the only eyes that have wept.'

Miss Howard blinked, and a new note crept into the gruffness of her voice.

'If you mean that I was fond of her – yes, I was. You know, Emily was a selfish old woman in her way. She was very generous, but she always wanted a return. She never let people forget what she had done for them – and, that way, she missed love. Don't think she ever realized it, though, or felt the lack of it. Hope not, anyway. I was on a different footing. I took my stand from the first. "So many pounds a year I'm worth to you. Well and good. But not a penny piece besides – not a pair of gloves, nor a theatre ticket." She didn't understand – was very offended sometimes. Said I was foolishly proud. It wasn't that – but I couldn't explain. Anyway, I kept my self-respect. And so, out of the whole bunch, I was the only one who could allow myself to be fond of her. I watched over her. I guarded her from the lot of them. And then a glib-tongued scoundrel comes along, and pooh! all my years of devotion go for nothing.'

Poirot nodded sympathetically.

'I understand, mademoiselle, I understand all you feel. It is most natural. You think that we are lukewarm – that we lack fire and energy – but trust me, it is not so.'

John stuck his head in at this juncture, and invited us both to come up to Mrs Inglethorp's room, as he and Mr Wells had finished looking through the desk in the boudoir.

As we went up the stairs, John looked back to the dining-room, and lowered his voice confidentially:

'Look here, what's going to happen when these two meet?'

I shook my head helplessly.

'I've told Mary to keep them apart if she can.'

'Will she be able to do so?'

'The Lord only knows. There's one thing, Inglethorp himself won't be too keen on meeting her.'

'You've got the keys still, haven't you, Poirot?' I asked, as we reached the door of the locked room.

Taking the keys from Poirot, John unlocked it, and we all passed in. The lawyer went straight to the desk, and John followed him.

'My mother kept most of her important papers in this despatch-case, I believe,' he said.

Poirot drew out the small bunch of keys.

'Permit me. I locked it, out of precaution, this morning.'

'But it's not locked now.'

'Impossible!'

'See.' And John lifted the lid as he spoke.

'*Mille tonnerres!*' cried Poirot, dumbfounded. 'And I – who have both the keys in my pocket!' He flung himself upon the case. Suddenly he stiffened. '*En voilà une affaire!* This lock has been forced!'

'What?'

Poirot laid down the case again.

'But who forced it? Why should they? When? But the door was locked!' These exclamations burst from us disjointedly.

Poirot answered them categorically – almost mechanically.

'Who? That is the question. Why? Ah, if I only knew. When? Since I was here an hour ago. As to the door being locked, it is a very ordinary lock. Probably any other of the door-keys in this passage would fit it.'

We stared at one another blankly. Poirot had walked over to the mantelpiece. He was outwardly calm, but I noticed his hands, which from long force of habit were mechanically straightening the spill vases on the mantelpiece, were shaking violently.

'See here, it was like this,' he said at last. 'There was something in that case – some piece of evidence, slight in itself perhaps, but still enough of a clue to connect the murderer with the crime. It was vital to him that it should be destroyed before it was discovered and its significance appreciated. Therefore, he took the risk, the great risk, of coming in here. Finding the case locked, he was obliged to force it, thus betraying his presence. For him to take that risk, it must have been something of great importance.'

'But what was it?'

'Ah!' cried Poirot, with a gesture of anger. 'That, I do not know! A document of some kind, without doubt, possibly the scrap of paper Dorcas saw in her hand yesterday afternoon. And I' – his anger burst forth freely – 'miserable animal that I am! I guessed nothing! I have behaved like an imbecile! I should never have left that case here. I should have carried it away with me. Ah, triple pig! And now it is gone. It is destroyed – but is it destroyed? Is there not yet a chance – we must leave no stone unturned –'

He rushed like a madman from the room, and I followed him as soon as I had sufficiently recovered my wits. But, by the time I had reached the top of the stairs, he was out of sight.

Mary Cavendish was standing where the staircase branched, staring down into the hall in the direction in which he had disappeared.

'What has happened to your extraordinary little friend, Mr Hastings? He has just rushed past me like a mad bull.'

'He's rather upset about something,' I remarked feebly. I really did not know how much Poirot would wish me to disclose. As I saw a faint smile gather on Mrs Cavendish's expressive mouth, I endeavoured to try and turn the conversation by saying: 'They haven't met yet, have they?'

'Who?'

'Mr Inglethorp and Miss Howard.'

She looked at me in rather a disconcerting manner.

'Do you think it would be such a disaster if they did meet?'

'Well, don't you?' I said, rather taken aback.

'No.' She was smiling in her quiet way. 'I should like to see a good flare-up. It would clear the air. At present we are all thinking so much, and saying so little.'

'John doesn't think so,' I remarked. 'He's anxious to keep them apart.'

'Oh, John!'

Something in her tone fired me, and I blurted out:

'Old John's an awfully good sort.'

She studied me curiously for a minute or two, and then said, to my great surprise:

'You are loyal to your friend. I like you for that.'

'Aren't you my friend, too?'

'I am a very bad friend.'

'Why do you say that?'

'Because it is true. I am charming to my friends one day, and forget all about them the next.'

I don't know what impelled me, but I was nettled, and I said foolishly and not in the best of taste:

'Yet you seem to be invariably charming to Dr Bauerstein!'

Instantly I regretted my words. Her face stiffened. I had the impression of a steel curtain coming down and blotting out the real woman. Without a word, she turned and went swiftly up the stairs, whilst I stood like an idiot gaping after her.

I was recalled to other matters by a frightful row going on below. I could hear Poirot shouting and expounding. I was vexed to think that my diplomacy had been in vain. The little man appeared to be taking the whole house into his confidence, a proceeding of which I, for one, doubted the wisdom. Once again I could not help regretting that my friend was so prone to lose his head in moments of excitement. I stepped briskly down the stairs. The sight of me calmed Poirot almost immediately. I drew him aside.

'My dear fellow,' I said, 'is this wise? Surely you don't want the whole house to know of this occurrence? You are actually playing into the criminal's hands.'

'You think so, Hastings?'

'I am sure of it.'

'Well, well, my friend, I will be guided by you.'

'Good. Although, unfortunately, it is a little too late now.'

'True.'

He looked so crestfallen and abashed that I felt quite sorry, though I still thought my rebuke a just and wise one.

'Well,' he said at last, 'let us go, *mon ami.*'

'You have finished here?'

'For the moment, yes. You will walk back with me to the village?'

'Willingly.'

He picked up his little suitcase, and we went out through the open window in the drawing-room. Cynthia Murdoch was just coming in, and Poirot stood aside to let her pass.

'Excuse me, mademoiselle, one minute.'

'Yes?' She turned inquiringly.

'Did you ever make up Mrs Inglethorp's medicines?'

A slight flush rose in her face, as she answered rather constrainedly:

'No.'

'Only her powders?'

The flush deepened as Cynthia replied:

'Oh, yes, I did make up some sleeping powders for her once.'

'These?'

Poirot produced the empty box which had contained powders.

She nodded.

'Can you tell me what they were? Sulphonal? Veronal?'

'No, they were bromide powders.'

'Ah! Thank you, mademoiselle; good morning.'

As we walked briskly away from the house, I glanced at him more than once. I had often before noticed that, if anything excited him, his eyes turned green like a cat's. They were shining like emeralds now.

'My friend,' he broke out at last, 'I have a little idea, a very strange, and probably utterly impossible idea. And yet – it fits in.'

I shrugged my shoulders. I privately thought that Poirot was rather too much given to these fantastic ideas. In this case, surely, the truth was only too plain and apparent.

'So that is the explanation of the blank label on the box,' I remarked. 'Very simple, as you said. I really wonder that I did not think of it myself.'

Poirot did not appear to be listening to me.

'They have made one more discovery, *là-bas*,' he observed, jerking his thumb over his shoulder in the direction of Styles. 'Mr Wells told me as we were going upstairs.'

'What was it?'

'Locked up in the desk in the boudoir, they found a will of Mrs Inglethorp's, dated before her marriage, leaving her fortune to Alfred Inglethorp. It must have been made just at the time they were engaged. It came quite as a surprise to Wells – and to John Cavendish also. It was written on one of those printed will forms, and witnessed by two of the servants – not Dorcas.'

'Did Mr Inglethorp know of it?'

'He says not.'

'One might take that with a grain of salt,' I remarked sceptically. 'All these wills are very confusing. Tell me, how did those scribbled words on the envelope help you to discover that a will was made yesterday afternoon?'

Poirot smiled.

'*Mon ami*, have you ever, when writing a letter, been arrested by the fact that you did not know how to spell a certain word?'

'Yes, often. I suppose everyone has.'

'Exactly. And have you not, in such a case, tried the word once or twice on the edge of the blotting-paper, or a spare scrap of paper, to see if it looked right? Well, that is what Mrs Inglethorp did. You will notice that the word "possessed" is spelt first with one "s" and subsequently with two – correctly. To make sure, she had further tried it in a sentence, thus: "I am possessed." Now, what did that tell me? It told me that Mrs Inglethorp had been writing the word "possessed" that afternoon, and, having the fragment of paper found in the grate fresh in my mind, the possibility of a will – a document almost certain to contain that word – occurred to me at once. This possibility was confirmed by a further circumstance. In the general confusion, the boudoir had not been swept that morning, and near the desk were several traces of brown mould and earth. The weather had been perfectly fine for some days, and no ordinary boots would have left such a heavy deposit.

'I strolled to the window, and saw at once that the begonia beds had been newly planted. The mould in the beds was exactly similar to that on the floor of the boudoir, and also I learnt from you that they *had* been planted yesterday after-noon. I was now sure that one, or possibly both of the gar-deners – for there were two sets of footprints in the bed – had entered the boudoir, for if Mrs Inglethorp had merely wished to speak to them she would in all probability have stood at the window, and they would not have come into the room at all. I was now quite convinced that she had made a fresh will, and had called the two gardeners in to witness her signature. Events proved that I was right in my supposition.'

'That was very ingenious,' I could not help admitting. 'I must confess that the conclusions I drew from those few scribbled words were quite erroneous.'

He smiled.

'You gave too much rein to your imagination. Imagination is a good servant, and a bad master. The simplest explanation is always the most likely.'

'Another point – how did you know that the key of the despatch-case had been lost?'

'I did not know it. It was a guess that turned out to be correct. You observed that it had a piece of twisted wire through the handle. That suggested to me at once that it had possibly been wrenched off a flimsy key-ring. Now, if it had been lost and recovered, Mrs Inglethorp would at once have replaced it on her bunch; but on her bunch I found what was obviously the duplicate key, very new and bright, which led me to the hypothesis that somebody else had inserted the original key in the lock of the despatch-case.'

'Yes,' I said, 'Alfred Inglethorp, without doubt.'

Poirot looked at me curiously.

'You are very sure of his guilt?'

'Well, naturally. Every fresh circumstance seems to establish it more clearly.'

'On the contrary,' said Poirot quietly, 'there are several points in his favour.'

'Oh, come now!'

'Yes.'

'I see only one.'

'And that?'

'That he was not in the house last night.'

' "Bad shot!" as you English say! You have chosen the one point that to my mind tells against him.'

'How is that?'

'Because if Mr Inglethorp knew that his wife would be poisoned last night, he would certainly have arranged to be away from the house. His excuse was an obviously trumped-up one. That leaves us two possibilities: either he knew what was going to happen or he had a reason of his own for his absence.'

'And that reason?' I asked sceptically.

Poirot shrugged his shoulders.

'How should I know? Discreditable, without doubt. This Mr Inglethorp, I should say, is somewhat of a scoundrel – but that does not of necessity make him a murderer.'

I shook my head, unconvinced.

'We do not agree, eh?' said Poirot. 'Well, let us leave it. Time will show which of us is right. Now let us turn to other aspects of the case. What do you make of the fact that all the doors of the bedroom were bolted on the inside?'

'Well –' I considered. 'One must look at it logically.'

'True.'

'I should put it this way. The doors *were* bolted – our own eyes have told us that – yet the presence of the candle grease on the floor, and the destruction of the will, prove that during the night someone entered the room. You agree so far?'

'Perfectly. Put with admirable clearness. Proceed.'

'Well,' I said, encouraged, 'as the person who entered did not do so by the window, nor by miraculous means, it follows that the door must have been opened from inside by Mrs Inglethorp herself. That strengthens the conviction that the person in question was her husband. She would naturally open the door to her own husband.'

Poirot shook his head.

'Why should she? She had bolted the door leading into his room – a most unusual proceeding on her part – she had had a most violent quarrel with him that very afternoon. No, he was the last person she would admit.'

'But you agree with me that the door must have been opened by Mrs Inglethorp herself?'

'There is another possibility. She may have forgotten to bolt the door into the passage when she went to bed, and have got up later, towards morning, and bolted it then.'

'Poirot, is that seriously your opinion?'

'No, I do not say it is so, but it might be. Now, to turn to another feature, what do you make of the scrap of conversation you overheard between Mrs Cavendish and her mother-in-law?'

'I had forgotten that,' I said thoughtfully. 'That is as enigmatical as ever. It seems incredible that a woman like Mrs Cavendish, proud and reticent to the last degree, should interfere so violently in what was certainly not her affair.'

'Precisely. It was an astonishing thing for a woman of her breeding to do.'

'It is certainly curious,' I agreed. 'Still, it is unimportant, and need not be taken into account.'

A groan burst from Poirot.

'What have I always told you? Everything must be taken into account. If the fact will not fit the theory – let the theory go.'

'Well, we shall see,' I said, nettled.

'Yes, we shall see.'

We had reached Leastways Cottage, and Poirot ushered me upstairs to his own room. He offered me one of the tiny Russian cigarettes he himself occasionally smoked. I was amused to notice that he stowed away the used matches most carefully in a little china pot. My momentary annoyance vanished.

Poirot had placed our two chairs in front of the open window which commanded a view of the village street. The fresh air blew in warm and pleasant. It was going to be a hot day.

Suddenly my attention was arrested by a weedy-looking young man rushing down the street at a great pace. It was the expression on his face that was extraordinary – a curious mingling of terror and agitation.

'Look, Poirot!' I said.

He leant forward. '*Tiens!*' he said. 'It is Mr Mace, from the chemist's shop. He is coming here.'

The young man came to a halt before Leastways Cottage, and, after hesitating a moment, pounded vigorously at the door.

'A little minute,' cried Poirot from the window. 'I come.'

Motioning to me to follow him, he ran swiftly down the stairs and opened the door. Mr Mace began at once.

'Oh, Mr Poirot, I'm sorry for the inconvenience, but I heard that you'd just come back from the Hall?'

'Yes, we have.'

The young man moistened his dry lips. His face was working curiously.

'It's all over the village about old Mrs Inglethorp dying so suddenly. They do say –' he lowered his voice cautiously – 'that it's poison?'

Poirot's face remained quite impassive.

'Only the doctors can tell us that, Mr Mace.'

'Yes, exactly – of course –' The young man hesitated, and then his agitation was too much for him. He clutched Poirot by the arm, and sank his voice to a whisper: 'Just tell me this, Mr Poirot, it isn't – it isn't strychnine, is it?'

I hardly heard what Poirot replied. Something evidently of

a non-committal nature. The young man departed, and as he closed the door Poirot's eyes met mine.

'Yes,' he said, nodding gravely. 'He will have evidence to give at the inquest.'

We went slowly upstairs again. I was opening my lips, when Poirot stopped me with a gesture of his hand.

'Not now, not now, *mon ami*. I have need of reflection. My mind is in some disorder – which is not well.'

For about ten minutes he sat in dead silence, perfectly still, except for several expressive motions of his eyebrows, and all the time his eyes grew steadily greener. At last he heaved a deep sigh.

'It is well. The bad moment has passed. Now all is arranged and classified. One must never permit confusion. The case is not clear yet – no. For it is of the most complicated! It puzzles *me*. *Me*, Hercule Poirot! There are two facts of significance.'

'And what are they?'

'The first is the state of the weather yesterday. That is very important.'

'But it was a glorious day!' I interrupted. 'Poirot, you're pulling my leg!'

'Not at all. The thermometer registered 80° in the shade. Do not forget that, my friend. It is the key to the whole riddle!'

'And the second point?' I asked.

'The important fact that Monsieur Inglethorp wears very peculiar clothes, has a black beard, and uses glasses.'

'Poirot, I cannot believe you are serious.'

'I am absolutely serious, my friend.'

'But this is childish!'

'No, it is very momentous.'

'And supposing the Coroner's jury returns a verdict of Wilful Murder against Alfred Inglethorp. What becomes of your theories, then?'

'They would not be shaken because twelve stupid men had happened to make a mistake! But that will not occur. For one thing, a country jury is not anxious to take responsibility upon itself, and Mr Inglethorp stands practically in the position of local squire. Also,' he added placidly, '*I* should not allow it!'

'*You* would not allow it?'

'No.'

I looked at the extraordinary little man, divided between annoyance and amusement. He was so tremendously sure of himself. As though he read my thoughts, he nodded gently.

'Oh, yes, *mon ami*, I would do what I say.' He got up and laid his hand on my shoulder. His physiognomy underwent a complete change. Tears came into his eyes. 'In all this, you see, I think of that poor Mrs Inglethorp who is dead. She was not extravagantly loved – no. But she was very good to us Belgians – I owe her a debt.'

I endeavoured to interrupt, but Poirot swept on.

'Let me tell you this, Hastings. She would never forgive me if I let Alfred Inglethorp, her husband, be arrested *now* – when a word from me could save him!'

CHAPTER VI

The Inquest

In the interval before the inquest, Poirot was unfailing in his activity. Twice he was closeted with Mr Wells. He also took long walks into the country. I rather resented his not taking me into his confidence, the more so as I could not in the least guess what he was driving at.

It occurred to me that he might have been making inquiries at Raikes's farm; so, finding him out when I called at Leastways Cottage on Wednesday evening, I walked over there by the fields, hoping to meet him. But there was no sign of him, and I hesitated to go right up to the farm itself. As I walked away, I met an aged rustic, who leered at me cunningly.

'You'm from the Hall, bain't you?' he asked.

'Yes. I'm looking for a friend of mine who I thought might have walked this way.'

'A little chap? As waves his hands when he talks? One of them Belgies from the village?'

'Yes,' I said eagerly. 'He has been here, then?'

'Oh, ay, he's been here, right enough. More'n once too. Friend of yours, is he? Ah, you gentlemen from the Hall – you'm a pretty lot!' And he leered more jocosely than ever.

'Why, do the gentlemen from the Hall come here often?' I asked, as carelessly as I could.

He winked at me knowingly.

'*One* does, mister. Naming no names, mind. And a very liberal gentleman too! Oh, thank you, sir, I'm sure.'

I walked on sharply. Evelyn Howard had been right then, and I experienced a sharp twinge of disgust, as I thought of Alfred Inglethorp's liberality with another woman's money. Had that piquant gipsy face been at the bottom of the crime, or was it the baser mainspring of money? Probably a judicious mixture of both.

On one point, Poirot seemed to have a curious obsession. He once or twice observed to me that he thought Dorcas must have made an error in fixing the time of the quarrel. He suggested to her repeatedly that it was 4.30, and not 4 o'clock when she heard the voices.

But Dorcas was unshaken. Quite an hour, or even more, had elapsed between the time when she had heard the voices and 5 o'clock, when she had taken tea to her mistress.

The inquest was held on Friday at the Stylites Arms in the village. Poirot and I sat together, not being required to give evidence.

The preliminaries were gone through. The jury viewed the body, and John Cavendish gave evidence of identification.

Further questioned, he described his awakening in the early hours of the morning, and the circumstances of his mother's death.

The medical evidence was next taken. There was a breathless hush, and every eye was fixed on the famous London specialist, who was known to be one of the greatest authorities of the day on the subject of toxicology.

In a few brief words, he summed up the result of the postmortem. Shorn of its medical phraseology and technicalities, it amounted to the fact that Mrs Inglethorp had met her death as a result of strychnine poisoning. Judging from the quantity recovered, she must have taken not less than three-quarters of a grain of strychnine, but probably one grain or slightly over.

'Is it possible that she could have swallowed the poison by accident?' asked the Coroner.

'I should consider it very unlikely. Strychnine is not used for domestic purposes, as some poisons are, and there are restrictions placed on its sale.'

'Does anything in your examination lead you to determine how the poison was administered?'

'No.'

'You arrived at Styles before Dr Wilkins, I believe?'

'That is so. The motor met me just outside the lodge gates, and I hurried there as fast as I could.'

'Will you relate to us exactly what happened next?'

'I entered Mrs Inglethorp's room. She was at that moment in a typical tetanic convulsion. She turned towards me, and gasped out: "Alfred – Alfred –"'

'Could the strychnine have been administered in Mrs Inglethorp's after-dinner coffee which was taken to her by her husband?'

'Possibly, but strychnine is a fairly rapid drug in its action. The symptoms appear from one to two hours after it has been swallowed. It is retarded under certain conditions, none of which, however, appear to have been present in this case. I presume Mrs Inglethorp took the coffee after dinner about eight o'clock, whereas the symptoms did not manifest themselves until the early hours of the morning, which, on the face of it, points to the drug having been taken much later in the evening.'

'Mrs Inglethorp was in the habit of drinking a cup of cocoa in the middle of the night. Could the strychnine have been administered in that?'

'No, I myself took a sample of the cocoa remaining in the saucepan and had it analysed. There was no strychnine present.'

I heard Poirot chuckle softly beside me.

'How did you know?' I whispered.

'Listen.'

'I should say' – the doctor was continuing – 'that I would have been considerably surprised at any other result.'

'Why?'

'Simply because strychnine has an unusually bitter taste. It can be detected in a solution of 1 in 70,000, and can only be disguised by some strongly flavoured substance. Cocoa would be quite powerless to mask it.'

One of the jury wanted to know if the same objection applied to coffee.

'No. Coffee has a bitter taste of its own which would probably cover the taste of the strychnine.'

'Then you consider it more likely that the drug was administered in the coffee, but that for some unknown reason its action was delayed?'

'Yes, but, the cup being completely smashed, there is no possibility of analysing its contents.'

This concluded Dr Bauerstein's evidence. Dr Wilkins corroborated it on all points. Sounded as to the possibility of suicide, he repudiated it utterly. The deceased, he said, suffered from a weak heart, but otherwise enjoyed perfect health, and was of a cheerful and well-balanced disposition. She would be one of the last people to take her own life.

Lawrence Cavendish was next called. His evidence was quite unimportant, being a mere repetition of that of his brother. Just as he was about to step down, he paused, and said rather hesitatingly:

'I should like to make a suggestion if I may?'

He glanced deprecatingly at the Coroner, who replied briskly:

'Certainly, Mr Cavendish, we are here to arrive at the truth of this matter, and welcome anything that may lead to further elucidation.'

'It is just an idea of mine,' explained Lawrence. 'Of course I may be quite wrong, but it still seems to me that my mother's death might be accounted for by natural means.'

'How do you make that out, Mr Cavendish?'

'My mother, at the time of her death, and for some time before it, was taking a tonic containing strychnine.'

'Ah!' said the Coroner.

The jury looked up, interested.

'I believe,' continued Lawrence, 'that there have been cases where the cumulative effect of a drug, administered for some time, has ended by causing death. Also, is it not possible that she may have taken an overdose of her medicine by accident?'

'This is the first we have heard of the deceased taking

strychnine at the time of her death. We are much obliged to you, Mr Cavendish.'

Dr Wilkins was recalled and ridiculed the idea.

'What Mr Cavendish suggests is quite impossible. Any doctor would tell you the same. Strychnine is, in a certain sense, a cumulative poison, but it would be quite impossible for it to result in sudden death in this way. There would have to be a long period of chronic symptoms which would at once have attracted my attention. The whole thing is absurd.'

'And the second suggestion? That Mrs Inglethorp may have inadvertently taken an overdose?'

'Three, or even four, doses would not have resulted in death. Mrs Inglethorp always had an extra large amount of medicine made up at a time, as she dealt with Coot's, the Cash Chemists in Tadminster. She would have had to take very nearly the whole bottle to account for the amount of strychnine found at the post-mortem.'

'Then you consider that we may dismiss the tonic as not being in any way instrumental in causing her death?'

'Certainly. The supposition is ridiculous.'

The same juryman who had interrupted before here suggested that the chemist who made up the medicine might have committed an error.

'That, of course, is always possible,' replied the doctor.

But Dorcas, who was the next witness called, dispelled even that possibility. The medicine had not been newly made up. On the contrary, Mrs Inglethorp had taken the last dose on the day of her death.

So the question of the tonic was finally abandoned, and the Coroner proceeded with his task. Having elicited from Dorcas how she had been awakened by the violent ringing of her mistress's bell, and had subsequently roused the household, he passed to the subject of the quarrel on the preceding afternoon.

Dorcas's evidence on this point was substantially what Poirot and I had already heard, so I will not repeat it here.

The next witness was Mary Cavendish. She stood very upright, and spoke in a low, clear, and perfectly composed voice. In answer to the Coroner's question, she told how, her alarm clock having aroused her at 4.30 as usual, she was dressing, when she was startled by the sound of something heavy falling.

'That would have been the table by the bed?' commented the Coroner.

'I opened my door,' continued Mary, 'and listened. In a few minutes a bell rang violently, Dorcas came running down and woke my husband, and we all went to my mother-in-law's room, but it was locked –'

The Coroner interrupted her.

'I really do not think we need trouble you further on that point. We know all that can be known of the subsequent happenings. But I should be obliged if you would tell us all you overheard of the quarrel the day before.'

'I?'

There was a faint insolence in her voice. She raised her hand and adjusted the ruffle of lace at her neck, turning her head a little as she did so. And quite spontaneously the thought flashed across my mind: 'She is gaining time!'

'Yes. I understand,' continued the Coroner deliberately, 'that you were sitting reading on the bench just outside the long window of the boudoir. That is so, is it not?'

This was news to me and glancing sideways at Poirot, I fancied that it was news to him as well.

There was the faintest pause, the mere hesitation of a moment, before she answered:

'Yes, that is so.'

'And the boudoir window was open, was it not?'

Surely her face grew a little paler as she answered:

'Yes.'

'Then you cannot have failed to hear the voices inside, especially as they were raised in anger. In fact, they would be more audible where you were than in the hall.'

'Possibly.'

'Will you repeat to us what you overheard of the quarrel?'

'I really do not remember hearing anything.'

'Do you mean to say you did not hear voices?'

'Oh, yes, I heard the voices, but I did not hear what they said.' A faint spot of colour came into her cheek. 'I am not in the habit of listening to private conversations.'

The Coroner persisted.

'And you remember nothing at all? *Nothing*, Mrs Cavendish? Not one stray word or phrase to make you realize that it *was* a private conversation?'

She paused, and seemed to reflect, still outwardly as calm as ever.

'Yes; I remember, Mrs Inglethorp said something – I do not remember exactly what – about causing scandal between husband and wife.'

'Ah!' The Coroner leant back satisfied. 'That corresponds with what Dorcas heard. But excuse me, Mrs Cavendish, although you realized it was a private conversation, you did not move away? You remained where you were?'

I caught the momentary gleam of her tawny eyes as she raised them. I felt certain that at that moment she would willingly have torn the little lawyer, with his insinuations, into pieces, but she replied quietly enough:

'No. I was very comfortable where I was. I fixed my mind on my book.'

'And that is all you can tell us?'

'That is all.'

The examination was over, though I doubted if the Coroner was entirely satisfied with it. I think he suspected that Mary Cavendish could tell more if she chose.

Amy Hill, shop assistant, was next called, and deposed to having sold a will form on the afternoon of the 17th to William Earl, under-gardener at Styles.

William Earl and Manning succeeded her, and testified to witnessing a document. Manning fixed the time at about 4.30, William was of the opinion that it was rather earlier.

Cynthia Murdoch came next. She had, however, little to tell. She had known nothing of the tragedy, until awakened by Mrs Cavendish.

'You did not hear the table fall?'

'No. I was fast asleep.'

The Coroner smiled.

'A good conscience makes a sound sleeper,' he observed. 'Thank you, Miss Murdoch, that is all.'

'Miss Howard.'

Miss Howard produced the letter written to her by Mrs Inglethorp on the evening of the 17th. Poirot and I had, of course, already seen it. It added nothing to our knowledge of the tragedy. The following is a facsimile:

July 17th   Styles Court
                             Essex

My dear Evelyn

    Can we not bury
the hatchet? I have
found it hard to forgive
the things you said
against my dear husband
but I am an old woman
    very fond of you
        Yours affectionately
            Emily Inglethorp

It was handed to the jury who scrutinized it attentively.

'I fear it does not help us much,' said the Coroner, with a sigh. 'There is no mention of any of the events of that afternoon.'

'Plain as a pikestaff to me,' said Miss Howard shortly. 'It shows clearly enough that my poor old friend had just found out she'd been made a fool of!'

'It says nothing of the kind in the letter,' the Coroner pointed out.

'No, because Emily never could bear to put herself in the wrong. But *I* know her. She wanted me back. But she wasn't going to own that I'd been right. She went round about. Most people do. Don't believe in it myself.'

Mr Wells smiled faintly. So, I noticed, did several of the jury. Miss Howard was obviously quite a public character.

'Anyway, all this tomfoolery is a great waste of time,' continued the lady, glancing up and down the jury disparagingly. 'Talk – talk – talk! When all the time we know perfectly well –'

The Coroner interrupted her in an agony of apprehension:

'Thank you, Miss Howard, that is all.'

I fancy he breathed a sigh of relief when she complied.

Then came the sensation of the day. The Coroner called Albert Mace, chemist's assistant.

It was our agitated young man of the pale face. In answer to the Coroner's questions, he explained that he was a qualified pharmacist, but had only recently come to this particular shop, as the assistant formerly there had just been called up for the army.

These preliminaries completed, the Coroner proceeded to business.

'Mr Mace, have you lately sold strychnine to any unauthorized person?'

'Yes, sir.'

'When was this?'

'Last Monday night.'

'Monday? Not Tuesday?'

'No, sir, Monday, the 16th.'

'Will you tell us to whom you sold it?'

You could have heard a pin drop.

'Yes, sir. It was Mr Inglethorp.'

Every eye turned simultaneously to where Alfred Inglethorp was sitting, impassive and wooden. He started slightly, as the damning words fell from the young man's lips. I half thought he was going to rise from his chair, but he remained seated, although a remarkably well-acted expression of astonishment rose on his face.

'You are sure of what you say?' asked the Coroner sternly.

'Quite sure, sir.'

'Are you in the habit of selling strychnine indiscriminately over the counter?'

The wretched young man wilted visibly under the Coroner's frown.

'Oh, no, sir – of course not. But, seeing it was Mr Inglethorp of the Hall, I thought there was no harm in it. He said it was to poison a dog.'

Inwardly I sympathized. It was only human nature to endeavour to please 'The Hall' – especially when it might result in custom being transferred from Coot's to the local establishment.

'Is it not customary for anyone purchasing poison to sign a book?'

'Yes, sir, Mr Inglethorp did so.'

'Have you got the book here?'

'Yes, sir.'

It was produced; and, with a few words of stern censure, the Coroner dismissed the wretched Mr Mace.

Then, amidst a breathless silence, Alfred Inglethorp was called. Did he realize, I wondered, how closely the halter was being drawn around his neck?

The Coroner went straight to the point.

'On Monday evening last, did you purchase strychnine for the purpose of poisoning a dog?'

Inglethorp replied with perfect calmness:

'No, I did not. There is no dog at Styles, except an outdoor sheepdog, which is in perfect health.'

'You deny absolutely having purchased strychnine from Albert Mace on Monday last?'

'I do.'

'Do you also deny *this*?'

The Coroner handed him the register in which his signature was inscribed.

'Certainly I do. The handwriting is quite different from mine. I will show you.'

He took an old envelope out of his pocket, and wrote his name on it, handing it to the jury. It was certainly utterly dissimilar.

'Then what is your explanation of Mr Mace's statement?'

Alfred Inglethorp replied imperturbably:

'Mr Mace must have been mistaken.'

The Coroner hesitated for a moment, and then said:

'Mr Inglethorp, as a mere matter of form, would you mind telling us where you were on the evening of Monday, July 16th?'

'Really – I cannot remember.'

'That is absurd, Mr Inglethorp,' said the Coroner sharply. 'Think again.'

Inglethorp shook his head.

'I cannot tell you. I have an idea that I was out walking.'

'In what direction?'

'I really can't remember.'

The Coroner's face grew graver.

'Were you in company with anyone?'

'No.'

'Did you meet anyone on your walk?'

'No.'

'That is a pity,' said the Coroner dryly. 'I am to take it then that you decline to say where you were at the time that Mr Mace positively recognized you as entering the shop to purchase strychnine?'

'If you like to take it that way, yes.'

'Be careful, Mr Inglethorp.'

Poirot was fidgeting nervously.

'*Sacré!*' he murmured. 'Does this imbecile of a man *want* to be arrested?'

Inglethorp was indeed creating a bad impression. His futile denials would not have convinced a child. The Coroner, however, passed briskly to the next point, and Poirot drew a deep breath of relief.

'You had a discussion with your wife on Tuesday afternoon?'

'Pardon me,' interrupted Alfred Inglethorp, 'you have been misinformed. I had no quarrel with my dear wife. The whole story is absolutely untrue. I was absent from the house the entire afternoon.'

'Have you anyone who can testify to that?'

'You have my word,' said Inglethorp haughtily.

The Coroner did not trouble to reply.

'There are two witnesses who will swear to having heard your disagreement with Mrs Inglethorp.'

'Those witnesses were mistaken.'

I was puzzled. The man spoke with such quiet assurance that I was staggered. I looked at Poirot. There was an expression of exultation on his face which I could not understand. Was he at last convinced of Alfred Inglethorp's guilt?

'Mr Inglethorp,' said the Coroner, 'you have heard your wife's dying words repeated here. Can you explain them in any way?'

'Certainly I can.'

'You can?'

'It seems to me very simple. The room was dimly lighted. Dr Bauerstein is much of my height and build, and, like me, wears a beard. In the dim light, and suffering as she was, my poor wife mistook him for me.'

'Ah!' murmured Poirot to himself. 'But it is an idea, that!'

'You think it is true?' I whispered.

'I do not say that. But it is truly an ingenious supposition.'

'You read my wife's last words as an accusation' – Ingle-thorp was continuing – 'they were, on the contrary, an appeal to me.'

The Coroner reflected a moment, then he said:

'I believe, Mr Inglethorp, that you yourself poured out the coffee, and took it to your wife that evening?'

'I poured it out, yes. But I did not take it to her. I meant to do so, but I was told that a friend was at the hall door, so I laid down the coffee on the hall table. When I came through the hall again a few minutes later, it was gone.'

This statement might, or might not, be true, but it did not seem to me to improve matters much for Inglethorp. In any case, he had had ample time to introduce the poison.

At that point, Poirot nudged me gently, indicating two men who were sitting together near the door. One was a little, sharp, dark, ferret-faced man, the other was tall and fair.

I questioned Poirot mutely. He put his lips to my ear.

'Do you know who that little man is?'

I shook my head.

'That is Detective-Inspector James Japp of Scotland Yard – Jimmy Japp. The other man is from Scotland Yard, too. Things are moving quickly, my friend.'

I stared at the two men intently. There was certainly nothing of the policeman about them. I should never have sus-pected them of being official personages.

I was still staring, when I was startled and recalled by the verdict being given:

'Wilful Murder against some person or persons unknown.'

CHAPTER VII

Poirot Pays His Debts

As we came out of the Stylites Arms, Poirot drew me aside by a gentle pressure of the arm. I understood his object. He was waiting for the Scotland Yard men.

In a few moments, they emerged, and Poirot at once stepped forward, and accosted the shorter of the two.

'I fear you do not remember me, Inspector Japp.'

'Why, if it isn't Mr Poirot!' cried the Inspector. He turned to the other man. 'You've heard me speak of Mr Poirot? It was in 1904 he and I worked together – the Abercrombie forgery case – you remember, he was run down in Brussels. Ah, those were great days, moosier. Then, do you remember "Baron" Altara? There was a pretty rogue for you! He eluded the clutches of half the police in Europe. But we nailed him in Antwerp – thanks to Mr Poirot here.'

As these friendly reminiscences were being indulged in, I drew nearer, and was introduced to Detective-Inspector Japp, who in his turn introduced us both to his companion, Superintendent Summerhaye.

'I need hardly ask what you are doing here, gentlemen,' remarked Poirot.

Japp closed one eye knowingly.

'No, indeed. Pretty clear case I should say.'

But Poirot answered gravely:

'There I differ from you.'

'Oh, come!' said Summerhaye, opening his lips for the first time. 'Surely the whole thing is clear as daylight. The man's caught red-handed. How he could be such a fool beats me!'

But Japp was looking attentively at Poirot.

'Hold your fire, Summerhaye,' he remarked jocularly.

'Me and Moosier here have met before – and there's no man's judgement I'd sooner take than his. If I'm not greatly mistaken, he's got something up his sleeve. Isn't that so, moosier?'

Poirot smiled.

'I have drawn certain conclusions – yes.'

Summerhaye was still looking rather sceptical, but Japp continued his scrutiny of Poirot.

'It's this way,' he said, 'so far, we've only seen the case from the outside. That's where the Yard's at a disadvantage in a case of this kind, where the murder's only out, so to speak, after the inquest. A lot depends on being on the spot first thing, and that's where Mr Poirot's had the start of us. We shouldn't have been here as soon as this even, if it hadn't been for the fact that there was a smart doctor on the spot, who gave us the tip through the Coroner. But you've been on the spot from the first, and you may have picked up some little hints. From the evidence at the inquest, Mr Inglethorp murdered his wife as sure as I stand here, and if anyone but you hinted the contrary I'd laugh in his face. I must say I was surprised the jury didn't bring in Wilful Murder against him right off. I think they would have, if it hadn't been for the Coroner – he seemed to be holding them back.'

'Perhaps, though, you have a warrant for his arrest in your pocket now,' suggested Poirot.

A kind of wooden shutter of officialdom came down over Japp's expressive countenance.

'Perhaps I have, and perhaps I haven't,' he remarked dryly.

Poirot looked at him thoughtfully.

'I am very anxious, Messieurs, that he should not be arrested.'

'I dare say,' observed Summerhaye sarcastically.

Japp was regarding Poirot with comical perplexity.

'Can't you go a little further, Mr Poirot? A wink's as good as a nod – from you. You've been on the spot – and the Yard doesn't want to make any mistakes, you know.'

Poirot nodded gravely.

'That is exactly what I thought. Well, I will tell you this.

Use your warrant: Arrest Mr Inglethorp. But it will bring you no kudos – the case against him will be dismissed at once! *Comme ça!*' And he snapped his fingers expressively.

Japp's face grew grave, though Summerhaye gave an incredulous snort.

As for me, I was literally dumb with astonishment. I could only conclude that Poirot was mad.

Japp had taken out a handkerchief, and was gently dabbing his brow.

'I daren't do it, Mr Poirot. I'd take your word, but there's others over me who'll be asking what the devil I mean by it. Can't you give me a little more to go on?'

Poirot reflected a moment.

'It can be done,' he said at last. 'I admit I do not wish it. It forces my hand. I would have preferred to work in the dark just for the present, but what you say is very just – the word of a Belgian policeman, whose day is past, is not enough! And Alfred Inglethorp must not be arrested. That I have sworn, as my friend Hastings here knows. See, then, my good Japp, you go at once to Styles?'

'Well, in about half an hour. We're seeing the Coroner and the doctor first.'

'Good. Call for me in passing – the last house in the village. I will go with you. At Styles, Mr Inglethorp will give you, or if he refuses – as is probable – I will give you such proofs that shall satisfy you that the case against him could not possibly be sustained. Is that a bargain?'

'That's a bargain,' said Japp heartily. 'And, on behalf of the Yard, I'm much obliged to you, though I'm bound to confess I can't at present see the faintest possible loophole in the evidence, but you always were a marvel! So long, then, moosier.'

The two detectives strode away, Summerhaye with an incredulous grin on his face.

'Well, my friend,' cried Poirot, before I could get in a word, 'what do you think? *Mon dieu!* I had some warm moments in that court; I did not figure to myself that the man would be so pig-headed as to refuse to say anything at all. Decidedly, it was the policy of an imbecile.'

'H'm! There are other explanations besides that of imbecility,' I remarked. 'For, if the case against him is true, how could he defend himself except by silence?'

'Why, in a thousand ingenious ways,' cried Poirot. 'See; say that it is I who have committed this murder, I can think of seven most plausible stories! Far more convincing than Mr Inglethorp's stony denials!'

I could not help laughing.

'My dear Poirot, I am sure you are capable of thinking of seventy! But, seriously, in spite of what I heard you say to the detectives, you surely cannot still believe in the possibility of Alfred Inglethorp's innocence?'

'Why not now as much as before? Nothing has changed.'

'But the evidence is so conclusive.'

'Yes, too conclusive.'

We turned in at the gate of Leastways Cottage, and proceeded up the now familiar stairs.

'Yes, yes, too conclusive,' continued Poirot, almost to himself. 'Real evidence is usually vague and unsatisfactory. It has to be examined – sifted. But here the whole thing is cut and dried. No, my friend, this evidence has been very cleverly manufactured – so cleverly that it has defeated its own ends.'

'How do you make that out?'

'Because, so long as the evidence against him was vague and intangible, it was very hard to disprove. But, in his anxiety, the criminal has drawn the net so closely that one cut will set Inglethorp free.'

I was silent. And in a minute or two, Poirot continued:

'Let us look at the matter like this. Here is a man, let us say, who sets out to poison his wife. He has lived by his wits as the saying goes. Presumably, therefore, he has some wits. He is not altogether a fool. Well, how does he set about it? He goes boldly to the village chemist's and purchases strychnine under his own name, with a trumped-up story about a dog which is bound to be proved absurd. He does not employ the poison that night. No, he waits until he has had a violent quarrel with her, of which the whole household is cognizant, and which naturally directs their suspicions upon him. He prepares no defence – no shadow of an alibi, yet he knows the chemist's assistant must necessarily come forward with the facts. Bah! do not ask me to believe that any man could be so idiotic! Only a lunatic, who wished to commit suicide by causing himself to be hanged, would act so!'

'Still – I do not see –' I began.

'Neither do I see. I tell you, *mon ami*, it puzzles me. *Me* – Hercule Poirot!'

'But if you believe him innocent, how do you explain his buying the strychnine?'

'Very simply. He did *not* buy it.'

'But Mace recognized him!'

'I beg your pardon, he saw a man with a black beard like Mr Inglethorp's, and wearing glasses like Mr Inglethorp, and dressed in Mr Inglethorp's rather noticeable clothes. He could not recognize a man whom he had probably only seen in the distance, since, you remember, he himself had only been in the village a fortnight, and Mrs Inglethorp dealt principally with Coot's in Tadminster.'

'Then you think –'

'*Mon ami*, do you remember the two points I laid stress upon? Leave the first one for the moment, what was the second?'

'The important fact that Alfred Inglethorp wears peculiar clothes, has a black beard, and uses glasses,' I quoted.

'Exactly. Now suppose anyone wished to pass himself off as John or Lawrence Cavendish. Would it be easy?'

'No,' I said thoughtfully. 'Of course an actor –'

But Poirot cut me short ruthlessly.

'And why would it not be easy? I will tell you, my friend: Because they are both clean-shaven men. To make up successfully as one of these two in broad daylight, it would need an actor of genius, and a certain initial facial resemblance. But in the case of Alfred Inglethorp, all that is changed. His

clothes, his beard, the glasses which hide his eyes – those are
the salient points about his personal appearance. Now, what
is the first instinct of the criminal? To divert suspicion from
himself, is it not so? And how can he best do that? By throwing
it on someone else. In this instance, there was a man ready
to his hand. Everybody was predisposed to believe in Mr
Inglethorp's guilt. It was a foregone conclusion that he would
be suspected; but, to make it a sure thing, there must be
tangible proof – such as the actual buying of the poison, and
that, with a man of the peculiar appearance of Mr Inglethorp,
was not difficult. Remember, this young Mace had never actually spoken to Mr Inglethorp. How should he doubt that the
man in his clothes, with his beard and his glasses, was not
Alfred Inglethorp?'

'It may be so,' I said, fascinated by Poirot's eloquence. 'But,
if that was the case, why does he not say where he was at six
o'clock on Monday evening?'

'Ah, why indeed?' said Poirot, calming down. 'If he were
arrested, he probably would speak, but I do not want it to
come to that. I must make him see the gravity of his position.
There is, of course, something discreditable behind his silence.
If he did not murder his wife, he is, nevertheless, a scoundrel,
and has something of his own to conceal, quite apart from the
murder.'

'What can it be?' I mused, won over to Poirot's views for
the moment, although still retaining a faint conviction that
the obvious deduction was the correct one.

'Can you not guess?' asked Poirot, smiling.

'No, can you?'

'Oh, yes, I had a little idea some time ago – and it has
turned out to be correct.'

'You never told me,' I said reproachfully.

Poirot spread out his hands apologetically.

'Pardon me, *mon ami*, you were not precisely *sympathique*.'
He turned to me earnestly. 'Tell me – you see now that he
must not be arrested?'

'Perhaps,' I said doubtfully, for I was really quite indifferent to the fate of Alfred Inglethorp, and thought that a good fright would do him no harm.

Poirot, who was watching me intently, gave a sigh.

'Come, my friend,' he said, changing the subject, 'apart from Mr Inglethorp, how did the evidence at the inquest strike you?'

'Oh, pretty much what I expected.'

'Did nothing strike you as peculiar about it?'

My thoughts flew to Mary Cavendish, and I hedged:

'In what way?'

'Well, Mr Lawrence Cavendish's evidence for instance?'

I was relieved.

'Oh, Lawrence! No, I don't think so. He's always a nervous chap.'

'His suggestion that his mother might have been poisoned accidentally by means of the tonic she was taking, that did not strike you as strange – *hein*?'

'No, I can't say it did. The doctors ridiculed it of course. But it was quite a natural suggestion for a layman to make.'

'But Monsieur Lawrence is not a layman. You told me yourself that he had started by studying medicine, and that he had taken his degree.'

'Yes, that's true. I never thought of that.' I was rather startled. 'It *is* odd.'

Poirot nodded.

'From the first, his behaviour has been peculiar. Of all the household, he alone would be likely to recognize the symptoms of strychnine poisoning, and yet we find him the only member of the family to uphold strenuously the theory of death from natural causes. If it had been Monsieur John, I could have understood it. He has no technical knowledge, and is by nature unimaginative. But Monsieur Lawrence – no! And now, today, he puts forward a suggestion that he himself must have known was ridiculous. There is food for thought in this, *mon ami*!'

'It's very confusing,' I agreed.

'Then there is Mrs Cavendish,' continued Poirot. 'That's another who is not telling all she knows! What do you make of her attitude?'

'I don't know what to make of it. It seems inconceivable that she should be shielding Alfred Inglethorp. Yet that is what it looks like.'

Poirot nodded reflectively.

'Yes, it is queer. One thing is certain, she overheard a good deal more of that "private conversation" than she was willing to admit.'

'And yet she is the last person one would accuse of stooping to eavesdrop!'

'Exactly. One thing her evidence *has* shown me. I made a mistake. Dorcas was quite right. The quarrel did take place earlier in the afternoon, about four o'clock, as she said.'

I looked at him curiously. I had never understood his insistence on that point.

'Yes, a good deal that was peculiar came out today,' continued Poirot. 'Dr Bauerstein, now, what was *he* doing up and dressed at that hour in the morning? It is astonishing to me that no one commented on the fact.'

'He has insomnia, I believe,' I said doubtfully.

'Which is a very good, or a very bad explanation,' remarked Poirot. 'It covers everything, and explains nothing. I shall keep my eye on our clever Dr Bauerstein.'

'Any more faults to find with the evidence?' I inquired satirically.

'*Mon ami*,' replied Poirot gravely, 'when you find that people are not telling you the truth – look out! Now, unless I am much mistaken, at this inquest today only one – at most, two persons were speaking the truth without reservation or subterfuge.'

'Oh, come now, Poirot! I won't cite Lawrence, or Mrs Cavendish. But there's John – and Miss Howard, surely they were speaking the truth?'

'Both of them, my friend? One, I grant you, but both –!'

His words gave me an unpleasant shock. Miss Howard's evidence, unimportant as it was, had been given in such a downright straightforward manner that it had never occurred to me to doubt her sincerity. Still, I had a great respect for

Poirot's sagacity – except on the occasions when he was what I described to myself as 'foolishly pig-headed'.

'Do you really think so?' I asked. 'Miss Howard has always seemed to me so essentially honest – almost uncomfortably so.'

Poirot gave me a curious look, which I could not quite fathom. He seemed about to speak, and then checked himself.

'Miss Murdoch too,' I continued, 'there's nothing untruthful about *her*.'

'No. But it was strange that she never heard a sound, sleeping next door; whereas Mrs Cavendish, in the other wing of the building, distinctly heard the table fall.'

'Well, she's young. And she sleeps soundly.'

'Ah, yes, indeed! She must be a famous sleeper, that one!'

I did not quite like the tone of his voice, but at that moment a smart knock reached our ears, and looking out of the window we perceived the two detectives waiting for us below.

Poirot seized his hat, gave a ferocious twist to his moustache, and, carefully brushing an imaginary speck of dust from his sleeve, motioned me to precede him down the stairs; there we joined the detectives and set out for Styles.

I think the appearance of the two Scotland Yard men was rather a shock – especially to John, though, of course, after the verdict, he had realized that it was only a matter of time. Still, the presence of the detectives brought the truth home to him more than anything else could have done.

Poirot had conferred with Japp in a low tone on the way up, and it was the latter functionary who requested that the household, with the exception of the servants, should be assembled together in the drawing-room. I realized the significance of this. It was up to Poirot to make his boast good.

Personally, I was not sanguine. Poirot might have excellent reasons for his belief in Inglethorp's innocence, but a man of the type of Summerhaye would require tangible proofs, and these I doubted if Poirot could supply.

Before very long we had all trooped into the drawing-room, the door of which Japp closed. Poirot politely set chairs for everyone. The Scotland Yard men were the cynosure of all eyes. I think that for the first time we realized that the thing was not a bad dream, but a tangible reality. We had read of such things – now we ourselves were actors in the drama. Tomorrow the daily papers, all over England, would blazon out the news in staring headlines:

'MYSTERIOUS TRAGEDY IN ESSEX'
'WEALTHY LADY POISONED'

There would be pictures of Styles, snapshots of 'The family leaving the Inquest' – the village photographer had not been idle! All the things that one had read a hundred times – things that happen to other people, not to oneself. And now, in this house, a murder had been committed. In front of us were 'the detectives in charge of the case'. The well-known glib phraseology passed rapidly through my mind in the interval before Poirot opened the proceedings.

I think everyone was a little surprised that it should be he and not one of the official detectives who took the initiative.

'*Mesdames* and *messieurs*,' said Poirot, bowing as though he were a celebrity about to deliver a lecture, 'I have asked you to come here all together, for a certain object. That object, it concerns Mr Alfred Inglethorp.'

Inglethorp was sitting a little by himself – I think, unconsciously, everyone had drawn his chair slightly away from him – and he gave a faint start as Poirot pronounced his name.

'Mr Inglethorp,' said Poirot, addressing him directly, 'a very dark shadow is resting on this house – the shadow of murder.'

Inglethorp shook his head sadly.

'My poor wife,' he murmured. 'Poor Emily! It is terrible.'

'I do not think, monsieur,' said Poirot pointedly, 'that you quite realize how terrible it may be – for you.' And as Inglethorp did not appear to understand, he added: 'Mr Inglethorp, you are standing in very grave danger.'

The two detectives fidgeted. I saw the official caution, 'Anything you say will be used in evidence against you,' actually hovering on Summerhaye's lips. Poirot went on:

'Do you understand now, monsieur?'

'No. What do you mean?'

'I mean,' said Poirot deliberately, 'that you are suspected of poisoning your wife.'

A little gasp ran round the circle at this plain speaking.

'Good heavens!' cried Inglethorp, starting up. 'What a monstrous idea! *I* – poison my dearest Emily!'

'I do not think' – Poirot watched him narrowly – 'that you quite realize the unfavourable nature of your evidence at the inquest. Mr Inglethorp, knowing what I have now told you, do you still refuse to say where you were at six o'clock on Monday afternoon?'

With a groan, Alfred Inglethorp sank down again and buried his face in his hands. Poirot approached and stood over him.

'Speak!' he cried menacingly.

With an effort, Inglethorp raised his face from his hands. Then, slowly and deliberately, he shook his head.

'You will not speak?'

'No. I do not believe that anyone could be so monstrous as to accuse me of what you say.'

Poirot nodded thoughtfully, like a man whose mind is made up. '*Soit!*' he said. 'Then I must speak for you.'

Alfred Inglethorp sprang up again.

'You? How can you speak? You do not know –' He broke off abruptly.

Poirot turned to face us. '*Mesdames* and *messieurs*! I speak! Listen! I, Hercule Poirot, affirm that the man who entered the chemist's shop, and purchased strychnine at six o'clock on Monday last, was not Mr Inglethorp, for at six o'clock on that day Mr Inglethorp was escorting Mrs Raikes back to her home from a neighbouring farm. I can produce no less than five witnesses to swear to having seen them together, either at six or just after and, as you may know, the Abbey Farm, Mrs Raikes's home, is at least two and a half miles distant from the village. There is absolutely no question as to the alibi!'

CHAPTER VIII

Fresh Suspicions

There was a moment's stupefied silence. Japp, who was the least surprised of any of us, was the first to speak.

'My word,' he cried, 'you're the goods! And no mistake, Mr Poirot! These witnesses of yours are all right, I suppose?'

'*Voilà!* I have prepared a list of them – names and addresses. You must see them, of course. But you will find it all right.'

'I'm sure of that.' Japp lowered his voice. 'I'm much obliged to you. A pretty mare's nest arresting him would have been.' He turned to Inglethorp. 'But, if you'll excuse me, sir, why couldn't you say all this at the inquest?'

'I will tell you why,' interrupted Poirot. 'There was a certain rumour –'

'A most malicious and utterly untrue one,' interrupted Alfred Inglethorp in an agitated voice.

'And Mr Inglethorp was anxious to have no scandal revived just at present. Am I right?'

'Quite right.' Inglethorp nodded. 'With my poor Emily not yet buried, can you wonder I was anxious that no more lying rumours should be started?'

'Between you and me, sir,' remarked Japp, 'I'd sooner have any amount of rumours than be arrested for murder. And I venture to think your poor lady would have felt the same. And, if it hadn't been for Mr Poirot here, arrested you would have been, as sure as eggs is eggs!'

'I was foolish, no doubt,' murmured Inglethorp. 'But you do not know, Inspector, how I have been persecuted and maligned.' And he shot a baleful glance at Evelyn Howard.

'Now, sir,' said Japp, turning briskly to John, 'I should like to see the lady's bedroom, please, and after that I'll have a little chat with the servants. Don't you bother about anything. Mr Poirot, here, will show me the way.'

As they all went out of the room, Poirot turned and made me a sign to follow him upstairs. There he caught me by the arm, and drew me aside.

'Quick, go to the other wing. Stand there – just this side of the baize door. Do not move till I come.' Then, turning rapidly, he rejoined the two detectives.

I followed his instructions, taking up my position by the baize door, and wondering what on earth lay behind the request. Why was I to stand in this particular spot on guard? I looked thoughtfully down the corridor in front of me. An idea struck me. With the exception of Cynthia Murdoch's, every room was in this left wing. Had that anything to do with it? Was I to report who came or went? I stood faithfully at my post. The minutes passed. Nobody came. Nothing happened.

It must have been quite twenty minutes before Poirot rejoined me.

'You have not stirred?'

'No, I've stuck here like a rock. Nothing's happened.'

'Ah!' Was he pleased, or disappointed? 'You've seen nothing at all?'

'No.'

'But you have probably heard something? A big bump – eh, *mon ami*?'

'No.'

'Is it possible? Ah, but I am vexed with myself! I am not usually clumsy. I made but a slight gesture' – I know Poirot's gestures – 'with the left hand, and over went the table by the bed!'

He looked so childishly vexed and crestfallen that I hastened to console him.

'Never mind, old chap. What does it matter? Your triumph downstairs excited you. I can tell you, that was a surprise to us all. There must be more in this affair of Inglethorp's with Mrs Raikes than we thought, to make him hold his tongue so persistently. What are you going to do now? Where are the Scotland Yard fellows?'

'Gone down to interview the servants. I showed them all our exhibits. I am disappointed in Japp. He has no method!'

'Hullo!' I said, looking out of the window. 'Here's Dr Bauerstein. I believe you're right about that man, Poirot. I don't like him.'

'He is clever,' observed Poirot meditatively.

'Oh, clever as the devil! I must say I was overjoyed to see him in the plight he was in on Tuesday. You never saw such a spectacle!' And I described the doctor's adventure. 'He looked a regular scarecrow! Plastered with mud from head to foot.'

'You saw him, then?'

'Yes. Of course, he didn't want to come in – it was just after dinner – but Mr Inglethorp insisted.'

'What?' Poirot caught me violently by the shoulders. 'Was Dr Bauerstein here on Tuesday evening? Here? And you never told me? Why did you not tell me? Why? Why?'

He appeared to be in an absolute frenzy.

'My dear Poirot,' I expostulated, 'I never thought it would interest you. I didn't know it was of any importance.'

'Importance? It is of the first importance! So Dr Bauerstein was here on Tuesday night – the night of the murder. Hastings, do you not see? That alters everything – everything!'

I had never seen him so upset. Loosening his hold of me, he mechanically straightened a pair of candlesticks, still murmuring to himself: 'Yes, that alters everything – everything.'

Suddenly he seemed to come to a decision.

'*Allons!*' he said. 'We must act at once. Where is Mr Cavendish?'

John was in the smoking-room. Poirot went straight to him.

'Mr Cavendish, I have some important business in Tadminster. A new clue. May I take your motor?'

'Why, of course. Do you mean at once?'

'If you please.'

John rang the bell, and ordered round the car. In another

ten minutes, we were racing down the park and along the high road to Tadminster.

'Now, Poirot,' I remarked resignedly, 'perhaps you will tell me what all this is about?'

'Well, *mon ami*, a good deal you can guess for yourself. Of course, you realize that, now Mr Inglethorp is out of it, the whole position is greatly changed. We are face to face with an entirely new problem. We know now that there is one person who did not buy the poison. We have cleared away the manufactured clues. Now for the real ones. I have ascertained that anyone in the household, with the exception of Mrs Cavendish, who was playing tennis with you, could have personated Mr Inglethorp on Monday evening. In the same way, we have his statement that he put the coffee down in the hall. No one took much notice of that at the inquest – but now it has a very different significance. We must find out who did take that coffee to Mrs Inglethorp eventually, or who passed through the hall whilst it was standing there. From your account, there are only two people whom we can positively say did not go near the coffee – Mrs Cavendish, and Mademoiselle Cynthia.'

'Yes, that is so.' I felt an inexpressible lightening of the heart. Mary Cavendish could certainly not rest under suspicion.

'In clearing Alfred Inglethorp,' continued Poirot, 'I have been obliged to show my hand sooner than I intended. As long as I might be thought to be pursuing him, the criminal would be off his guard. Now, he will be doubly careful. Yes – doubly careful.' He turned to me abruptly. 'Tell me, Hastings, you yourself – have you no suspicions of anybody?'

I hesitated. To tell the truth, an idea, wild and extravagant in itself, had once or twice that morning flashed through my brain. I had rejected it as absurd, nevertheless it persisted.

'You couldn't call it a suspicion,' I murmured. 'It's so utterly foolish.'

'Come now,' urged Poirot encouragingly. 'Do not fear.

Speak your mind. You should always pay attention to your instincts.'

'Well then,' I blurted out, 'it's absurd – but I suspect Miss Howard of not telling all she knows!'

'Miss Howard?'

'Yes – you'll laugh at me –'

'Not at all. Why should I?'

'I can't help feeling,' I continued blunderingly, 'that we've rather left her out of the possible suspects, simply on the strength of her having been away from the place. But, after all, she was only fifteen miles away. A car would do it in half an hour. Can we say positively that she was away from Styles on the night of the murder?'

'Yes, my friend,' said Poirot unexpectedly, 'we can. One of my first actions was to ring up the hospital where she was working.'

'Well?'

'Well, I learnt that Miss Howard had been on afternoon duty on Tuesday, and that – a convoy coming in unexpectedly – she had kindly offered to remain on night duty, which offer was gratefully accepted. That disposes of that.'

'Oh!' I said, rather nonplussed. 'Really,' I continued, 'it's her extraordinary vehemence against Inglethorp that started me off suspecting her. I can't help feeling she'd do anything against him. And I had an idea she might know something about the destroying of the will. She might have burnt the new one, mistaking it for the earlier one in his favour. She is so terribly bitter against him.'

'You consider her vehemence unnatural?'

'Y – es. She is so very violent. I wonder really whether she is quite sane on that point.'

Poirot shook his head energetically.

'No, no, you are on a wrong track there. There is nothing weak-minded or degenerate about Miss Howard. She is an excellent specimen of well-balanced English beef and brawn. She is sanity itself.'

'Yet her hatred of Inglethorp seems almost a mania. My

idea was – a very ridiculous one, no doubt – that she had intended to poison him – and that, in some way, Mrs Inglethorp got hold of it by mistake. But I don't at all see how it could have been done. The whole thing is absurd and ridiculous to the last degree.'

'Still you are right in one thing. It is always wise to suspect everybody until you can prove logically, and to your own satisfaction, that they are innocent. Now, what reasons are there against Miss Howard's having deliberately poisoned Mrs Inglethorp?'

'Why, she was devoted to her!' I exclaimed.

'Tcha! Tcha!' cried Poirot irritably. 'You argue like a child. If Miss Howard were capable of poisoning the old lady, she would be quite equally capable of simulating devotion. No, we must look elsewhere. You are perfectly correct in your assumption that her vehemence against Alfred Inglethorp is too violent to be natural; but you are quite wrong in the deduction you draw from it. I have drawn my own deductions, which I believe to be correct, but I will not speak of them at present.' He paused a minute, then went on. 'Now, to my way of thinking, there is one insuperable objection to Miss Howard's being the murderess.'

'And that is?'

'That in no possible way could Mrs Inglethorp's death benefit Miss Howard. Now there is no murder without a motive.'

I reflected.

'Could not Mrs Inglethorp have made a will in her favour?' Poirot shook his head.

'But you yourself suggested that possibility to Mr Wells?' Poirot smiled.

'That was for a reason. I did not want to mention the name of the person who was actually in my mind. Miss Howard occupied very much the same position, so I used her name instead.'

'Still, Mrs Inglethorp might have done so. Why, that will made on the afternoon of her death may –'

But Poirot's shake of the head was so energetic that I stopped.

'No, my friend. I have certain little ideas of my own about that will. But I can tell you this much – it was not in Miss Howard's favour.'

I accepted his assurance, though I did not really see how he could be so positive about the matter.

'Well,' I said, with a sigh, 'we will acquit Miss Howard, then. It is partly your fault that I ever came to suspect her. It was what you said about her evidence at the inquest that set me off.'

Poirot looked puzzled.

'What did I say about her evidence at the inquest?'

'Don't you remember? When I cited her and John Cavendish as being above suspicion?'

'Oh – ah – yes.' He seemed a little confused, but recovered himself. 'By the way, Hastings, there is something I want you to do for me.'

'Certainly. What is it?'

'Next time you happen to be alone with Lawrence Cavendish, I want you to say this to him. "I have a message for you from Poirot. He says: 'Find the extra coffee-cup, and you can rest in peace!'" Nothing more. Nothing less!'

'"Find the extra coffee-cup, and you can rest in peace!" Is that right?' I asked, much mystified.

'Excellent.'

'But what does it mean?'

'Ah, that I will leave you to find out. You have access to the facts. Just say that to him, and see what he says.'

'Very well – but it's all extremely mysterious.'

We were running into Tadminster now, and Poirot directed the car to the 'Analytical Chemist'.

Poirot hopped down briskly, and went inside. In a few minutes he was back again.

'There,' he said. 'That is all my business.'

'What were you doing there?' I asked in lively curiosity.

'I left something to be analysed.'

'Yes, but what?'

'The sample of cocoa I took from the saucepan in the bedroom.'

'But that has already been tested!' I cried, stupefied. 'Dr Bauerstein had it tested, and you yourself laughed at the possibility of there being strychnine in it.'

'I know Dr Bauerstein had it tested,' replied Poirot quietly.

'Well, then?'

'Well, I have a fancy for having it analysed again, that is all.'

And not another word on the subject could I drag out of him.

This proceeding of Poirot's, in respect of the cocoa, puzzled me intensely. I could see neither rhyme nor reason in it. However, my confidence in him, which at one time had rather waned, was fully restored since his belief in Alfred Inglethorp's innocence had been so triumphantly vindicated.

The funeral of Mrs Inglethorp took place the following day, and on Monday, as I came down to a late breakfast, John drew me aside, and informed me that Mr Inglethorp was leaving that morning, to take up his quarters at the Stylites Arms until he should have completed his plans.

'And really it's a great relief to think he's going, Hastings,' continued my honest friend. 'It was bad enough before, when we thought he'd done it, but I'm hanged if it isn't worse now, when we all feel guilty for having been so down on the fellow. The fact is, we've treated him abominably. Of course, things did look black against him. I don't see how anyone could blame us for jumping to the conclusions we did. Still, there it is, we were in the wrong, and now there's a beastly feeling that one ought to make amends; which is difficult, when one doesn't like the fellow a bit better than one did before. The whole thing's damned awkward! And I'm thankful he's had the tact to take himself off. It's a good thing Styles wasn't the mater's to leave to him. Couldn't bear to think of the fellow lording it here. He's welcome to her money.'

'You'll be able to keep up the place all right?' I asked.

'Oh, yes. There are the death duties, of course, but half my

father's money goes with the place, and Lawrence will stay
with us for the present, so there is his share as well. We shall
be pinched at first, of course, because, as I once told you, I
am in a bit of a hole financially myself. Still, the Johnnies will
wait now.'

In the general relief at Inglethorp's approaching departure,
we had the most genial breakfast we had experienced since the
tragedy. Cynthia, whose young spirits were naturally buoyant,
was looking quite her pretty self again, and we all, with the
exception of Lawrence, who seemed unalterably gloomy and
nervous, were quietly cheerful, at the opening of a new and
hopeful future.

The papers, of course, had been full of the tragedy. Glaring
headlines, sandwiched biographies of every member of the
household, subtle innuendoes, the usual familiar tag about the
police having a clue. Nothing was spared us. It was a slack
time. The war was momentarily inactive, and the newspapers
seized with avidity on this crime in fashionable life: 'The
Mysterious Affair at Styles' was the topic of the moment.

Naturally it was very annoying for the Cavendishes. The
house was constantly besieged by reporters, who were consist-
ently denied admission, but who continued to haunt the village
and the grounds, where they lay in wait with cameras, for any
unwary members of the household. We all lived in a blast of
publicity. The Scotland Yard men came and went, examining,
questioning, lynx-eyed and reserved of tongue. Towards what
end they were working, we did not know. Had they any clue, or
would the whole thing remain in the category of undiscovered
crimes?

After breakfast, Dorcas came up to me rather mysteriously,
and asked if she might have a few words with me.

'Certainly. What is it, Dorcas?'

'Well, it's just this, sir. You'll be seeing the Belgian gentleman today perhaps?' I nodded. 'Well, sir, you know how he
asked me so particular if the mistress, or anyone else, had a
green dress?'

'Yes, yes. You have found one?' My interest was aroused.

'No, not that, sir. But since then I've remembered what the young gentlemen' – John and Lawrence were still the 'young gentlemen' to Dorcas – 'call the "dressing-up box". It's up in the front attic, sir. A great chest, full of old clothes and fancy dresses, and what not. And it came to me sudden like that there might be a green dress amongst them. So, if you'd tell the Belgian gentleman –'

'I will tell him, Dorcas,' I promised.

'Thank you very much, sir. A very nice gentleman he is, sir. And quite a different class from them two detectives from London, what goes prying about, and asking questions. I don't hold with foreigners as a rule, but from what the newspapers says I make out as how these brave Belgies isn't the ordinary run of foreigners and certainly he's a most polite-spoken gentleman.'

Dear old Dorcas! As she stood there, with her honest face upturned to mine, I thought what a fine specimen she was of the old-fashioned servant that is so fast dying out.

I thought I might as well go down to the village at once, and look up Poirot; but I met him half-way, coming up to the house, and at once gave him Dorcas's message.

'Ah, the brave Dorcas! We will look at the chest, although – but no matter – we will examine it all the same.'

We entered the house by one of the windows. There was no one in the hall, and we went straight up to the attic.

Sure enough, there was the chest, a fine old piece, all studded with brass nails, and full to overflowing with every imaginable type of garment.

Poirot bundled everything out on the floor with scant ceremony. There were one or two green fabrics of varying shades; but Poirot shook his head over them all. He seemed somewhat apathetic in the search, as though he expected no great results from it. Suddenly he gave an exclamation.

'What is it?'

'Look!'

The chest was nearly empty, and there, reposing right at the bottom, was a magnificent black beard.

'*Ohó!*' said Poirot. '*Ohó!*' He turned it over in his hands, examining it closely. 'New,' he remarked. 'Yes, quite new.'

After a moment's hesitation, he replaced it in the chest, heaped all the other things on top of it as before, and made his way briskly downstairs. He went straight to the pantry, where we found Dorcas busily polishing her silver.

Poirot wished her good morning with Gallic politeness, and went on:

'We have been looking through that chest, Dorcas. I'm much obliged to you for mentioning it. There is, indeed, a fine collection there. Are they often used, may I ask?'

'Well, sir, not very often nowadays, though from time to time we do have what the young gentlemen call "a dress-up night". And very funny it is sometimes, sir. Mr Lawrence, he's wonderful. Most comic! I shall never forget the night he came down as the Char of Persia, I think he called it – a sort of Eastern King it was. He had the big paper knife in his hand, and "Mind, Dorcas," he says, "you'll have to be very respectful. This is my specially sharpened scimitar, and it's off with your head if I'm at all displeased with you!" Miss Cynthia, she was what they call an Apache, or some such name – a Frenchified sort of cut-throat, I take it to be. A real sight she looked. You'd never have believed a pretty young lady like that could have made herself into such a ruffian. Nobody would have known her.'

'These evenings must have been great fun,' said Poirot genially. 'I suppose Mr Lawrence wore that fine black beard in the chest upstairs, when he was Shah of Persia?'

'He did have a beard, sir,' replied Dorcas, smiling. 'And well I know it, for he borrowed two skeins of my black wool to make it with! And I'm sure it looked wonderfully natural at a distance. I didn't know as there was a beard up there at all. It must have been got quite lately, I think. There was a red wig, I know, but nothing else in the way of hair. Burnt corks they use mostly – though 'tis messy getting it off again. Miss Cynthia was a Negress once, and, oh, the trouble she had.'

'So Dorcas knows nothing about that black beard,' said Poirot thoughtfully, as we walked out into the hall again.

'Do you think it is *the* one?' I whispered eagerly.

Poirot nodded.

'I do. You noticed it had been trimmed?'

'No.'

'Yes. It was cut exactly the shape of Mr Inglethorp's, and I found one or two snipped hairs. Hastings, this affair is very deep.'

'Who put it in the chest, I wonder?'

'Someone with a good deal of intelligence,' remarked Poirot dryly. 'You realize that he chose the one place in the house to hide it where its presence would not be remarked? Yes, he is intelligent. But we must be more intelligent. We must be so intelligent that he does not suspect us of being intelligent at all.'

I acquiesced.

'There, *mon ami*, you will be of great assistance to me.'

I was pleased with the compliment. There had been times when I hardly thought that Poirot appreciated me at my true worth.

'Yes,' he continued, staring at me thoughtfully, 'you will be invaluable.'

This was naturally gratifying, but Poirot's next words were not so welcome.

'I must have an ally in the house,' he observed reflectively.

'You have me,' I protested.

'True, but you are not sufficient.'

I was hurt, and showed it. Poirot hurried to explain himself.

'You do not quite take my meaning. You are known to be working with me. I want somebody who is not associated with us in any way.'

'Oh, I see. How about John?'

'No, I think not.'

'The dear fellow isn't perhaps very bright,' I said thoughtfully.

'Here comes Miss Howard,' said Poirot suddenly. 'She is

the very person. But I am in her black books, since I cleared Mr Inglethorp. Still, we can but try.'

With a nod that was barely civil, Miss Howard assented to Poirot's request for a few minutes' conversation.

We went into the little morning-room, and Poirot closed the door.

'Well, Monsieur Poirot,' said Miss Howard impatiently, 'what is it? Out with it. I'm busy.'

'Do you remember, mademoiselle, that I once asked you to help me?'

'Yes, I do.' The lady nodded. 'And I told you I'd help you with pleasure – to hang Alfred Inglethorp.'

'Ah!' Poirot studied her seriously. 'Miss Howard, I will ask you one question. I beg of you to reply to it truthfully.'

'Never tell lies,' replied Miss Howard.

'It is this. Do you still believe that Mrs Inglethorp was poisoned by her husband?'

'What do you mean?' she asked sharply. 'You needn't think your pretty explanations influence me in the slightest. I'll admit that it wasn't he who bought strychnine at the chemist's shop. What of that? I dare say he soaked fly paper, as I told you at the beginning.'

'That is arsenic – not strychnine,' said Poirot mildly.

'What does that matter? Arsenic would put poor Emily out of the way just as well as strychnine. If I'm convinced he did it, it doesn't matter a jot to me *how* he did it.'

'Exactly. *If* you are convinced he did it,' said Poirot quietly. 'I will put my question in another form. Did you ever in your heart of hearts believe that Mrs Inglethorp was poisoned by her husband?'

'Good heavens!' cried Miss Howard. 'Haven't I always told you the man is a villain? Haven't I always told you he would murder her in her bed? Haven't I always hated him like poison?'

'Exactly,' said Poirot. 'That bears out my little idea entirely.'

'What little idea?'

'Miss Howard, do you remember a conversation that took place on the day of my friend's arrival here? He repeated it to me, and there is a sentence of yours that has impressed me very much. Do you remember affirming that if a crime had been committed, and anyone you loved had been murdered, you felt certain that you would know by instinct who the criminal was, even if you were quite unable to prove it?'

'Yes, I remember saying that. I believe it, too. I suppose you think it nonsense?'

'Not at all.'

'And yet you will pay no attention to my instinct against Alfred Inglethorp?'

'No,' said Poirot curtly. 'Because your instinct is not against Mr Inglethorp.'

'What?'

'No. You wish to believe he committed the crime. You believe him capable of committing it. But your instinct tells you he did not commit it. It tells you more – shall I go on?'

She was staring at him, fascinated, and made a slight affirmative movement of the hand.

'Shall I tell you why you have been so vehement against Mr Inglethorp? It is because you have been trying to believe what you wish to believe. It is because you are trying to drown and stifle your instinct, which tells you another name –'

'No, no, no!' cried Miss Howard, wildly, flinging up her hands. 'Don't say it! Oh, don't say it! It isn't true! It can't be true. I don't know what put such a wild – such a dreadful – idea into my head!'

'I am right, am I not?' asked Poirot.

'Yes, yes; you must be a wizard to have guessed. But it can't be so – it's too monstrous, too impossible. It *must* be Alfred Inglethorp.'

Poirot shook his head gravely.

'Don't ask me about it,' continued Miss Howard, 'because I shan't tell you. I won't admit it, even to myself. I must be mad to think of such a thing.'

Poirot nodded, as if satisfied.

'I will ask you nothing. It is enough for me that it is as I thought. And I – I, too, have an instinct. We are working together towards a common end.'

'Don't ask me to help you, because I won't. I wouldn't lift a finger to – to –' She faltered.

'You will help me in spite of yourself. I ask you nothing – but you will be my ally. You will not be able to help yourself. You will do the only thing that I want of you.'

'And that is?'

'You will watch!'

Evelyn Howard bowed her head.

'Yes, I can't help doing that. I am always watching – always hoping I shall be proved wrong.'

'If we are wrong, well and good,' said Poirot. 'No one will be more pleased than I shall. But, if we are right? If we are right, Miss Howard, on whose side are you then?'

'I don't know, I don't know –'

'Come now.'

'It could be hushed up.'

'There must be no hushing up.'

'But Emily herself –' She broke off.

'Miss Howard,' said Poirot gravely, 'this is unworthy of you.'

Suddenly she took her face from her hands.

'Yes,' she said quietly, 'that was not Evelyn Howard who spoke!' She flung her head up proudly. '*This* is Evelyn Howard! And she is on the side of Justice! Let the cost be what it may.' And with these words, she walked firmly out of the room.

'There,' said Poirot, looking after her, 'goes a very valuable ally. That woman, Hastings, has got brains as well as a heart.'

I did not reply.

'Instinct is a marvellous thing,' mused Poirot. 'It can neither be explained nor ignored.'

'You and Miss Howard seem to know what you are talking about,' I observed coldly. 'Perhaps you don't realize that *I* am still in the dark.'

'Really? Is that so, *mon ami*?'

'Yes. Enlighten me, will you?'

Poirot studied me attentively for a moment or two. Then, to my intense surprise, he shook his head decidedly.

'No, my friend.'

'Oh, look here, why not?'

'Two is enough for a secret.'

'Well, I think it is very unfair to keep back facts from me.'

'I am not keeping back facts. Every fact that I know is in your possession. You can draw your own deductions from them. This time it is a question of ideas.'

'Still, it would be interesting to know.'

Poirot looked at me very earnestly, and again shook his head.

'You see,' he said sadly, '*you* have no instincts.'

'It was intelligence you were requiring just now,' I pointed out.

'The two often go together,' said Poirot enigmatically.

The remark seemed so utterly irrelevant that I did not even take the trouble to answer it. But I decided that if I made any interesting and important discoveries – as no doubt I should – I would keep them to myself, and surprise Poirot with the ultimate result.

There are times when it is one's duty to assert oneself.

CHAPTER IX

Dr Bauerstein

I had no opportunity as yet of passing on Poirot's message to Lawrence. But now, as I strolled out on the lawn, still nursing a grudge against my friend's high-handedness, I saw Lawrence on the croquet lawn, aimlessly knocking a couple of very ancient balls about, with a still more ancient mallet.

It struck me that it would be a good opportunity to deliver my message. Otherwise, Poirot himself might relieve me of it. It was true that I did not quite gather its purport, but I flattered myself that by Lawrence's reply, and perhaps a little skilful cross-examination on my part, I should soon perceive its significance. Accordingly I accosted him.

'I've been looking for you,' I remarked untruthfully.

'Have you?'

'Yes. The truth is, I've got a message for you – from Poirot.'

'Yes?'

'He told me to wait until I was alone with you,' I said, dropping my voice significantly, and watching him intently out of the corner of my eye. I have always been rather good at what is called, I believe, creating an atmosphere.

'Well?'

There was no change of expression in the dark melancholic face. Had he any idea of what I was about to say?

'This is the message.' I dropped my voice still lower. ' "Find the extra coffee-cup, and you can rest in peace." '

'What on earth does he mean?' Lawrence stared at me in quite unaffected astonishment.

'Don't you know?'

'Not in the least. Do you?'

I was compelled to shake my head.

'What extra coffee-cup?'

'I don't know.'

'He'd better ask Dorcas, or one of the maids, if he wants to know about coffee-cups. It's their business, not mine. I don't know anything about the coffee-cups, except that we've got some that are never used, which are a perfect dream! Old Worcester. You're not a connoisseur, are you, Hastings?'

I shook my head.

'You miss a lot. A really perfect bit of old china – it's pure delight to handle it, or even to look at it.'

'Well, what am I to tell Poirot?'

'Tell him I don't know what he's talking about. It's double Dutch to me.'

'All right.'

I was moving off towards the house again when he suddenly called me back.

'I say, what was the end of that message? Say it over again, will you?'

'"Find the extra coffee-cup, and you can rest in peace." Are you sure you don't know what it means?' I asked him earnestly.

He shook his head.

'No,' he said musingly, 'I don't. I – I wish I did.'

The boom of the gong sounded from the house, and we went in together. Poirot had been asked by John to remain to lunch, and was already seated at the table.

By tacit consent, all mention of the tragedy was barred. We conversed on the war, and other outside topics. But after the cheese and biscuits had been handed round, and Dorcas had left the room, Poirot suddenly leant forward to Mrs Cavendish.

'Pardon me, madame, for recalling unpleasant memories, but I have a little idea' – Poirot's 'little ideas' were becoming a perfect byword – 'and would like to ask one or two questions.'

'Of me? Certainly.'

'You are too *aimable*, madame. What I want to ask is this: the door leading into Mrs Inglethorp's room from that of Mademoiselle Cynthia, it was bolted, you say?'

'Certainly it was bolted,' replied Mary Cavendish, rather surprised. 'I said so at the inquest.'

'Bolted?'

'Yes.' She looked perplexed.

'I mean,' explained Poirot, 'you are sure it was bolted, and not merely locked?'

'Oh, I see what you mean. No, I don't know. I said bolted, meaning that it was fastened, and I could not open it, but I believe all the doors were found bolted on the inside.'

'Still, as far as you are concerned, the door might equally well have been locked?'

'Oh, yes.'

'You yourself did not happen to notice, madame, when you entered Mrs Inglethorp's room, whether that door was bolted or not?'

'I – I believe it was.'

'But you did not see it?'

'No. I – never looked.'

'But *I* did,' interrupted Lawrence suddenly. 'I happened to notice that it *was* bolted.'

'Ah, that settles it.' And Poirot looked crestfallen.

I could not help rejoicing that, for once, one of his 'little ideas' had come to naught.

After lunch Poirot begged me to accompany him home. I consented rather stiffly.

'You are annoyed, is it not so?' he asked anxiously, as we walked through the park.

'Not at all,' I said coldly.

'That is well. That lifts a great load from my mind.'

This was not quite what I had intended. I had hoped that he would have observed the stiffness of my manner. Still, the fervour of his words went towards the appeasing of my just displeasure. I thawed.

'I gave Lawrence your message,' I said.

'And what did he say? He was entirely puzzled?'

'Yes. I am quite sure he had no idea of what you meant.'

I had expected Poirot to be disappointed; but, to my

surprise, he replied that that was as he had thought, and that he was very glad. My pride forbade me to ask any questions.

Poirot switched off on another tack.

'Mademoiselle Cynthia was not at lunch today? How was that?'

'She is at the hospital again. She resumed work today.'

'Ah, she is an industrious little demoiselle. And pretty too. She is like pictures I have seen in Italy. I would rather like to see that dispensary of hers. Do you think she would show it to me?'

'I am sure she would be delighted. It's an interesting little place.'

'Does she go there every day?'

'She has all Wednesdays off, and comes back to lunch on Saturdays. Those are her only times off.'

'I will remember. Women are doing great work nowadays, and Mademoiselle Cynthia is clever – oh, yes, she has brains, that little one.'

'Yes. I believe she has passed quite a stiff exam.'

'Without doubt. After all, it is very responsible work. I suppose they have very strong poisons there?'

'Yes, she showed them to us. They are kept locked up in a little cupboard. I believe they have to be very careful. They always take out the key before leaving the room.'

'Indeed. It is near the window, this cupboard?'

'No, right the other side of the room. Why?'

Poirot shrugged his shoulders.

'I wondered. That is all. Will you come in?'

We had reached the cottage.

'No. I think I'll be getting back. I shall go round the long way through the woods.'

The woods round Styles were very beautiful. After the walk across the open park, it was pleasant to saunter lazily through the cool glades. There was hardly a breath of wind, the very chirp of the birds was faint and subdued. I strolled on a little way, and finally flung myself down at the foot of a grand old

beech-tree. My thoughts of mankind were kindly and charitable. I even forgave Poirot for his absurd secrecy. In fact, I
was at peace with the world. Then I yawned.

I thought about the crime, and it struck me as being very
unreal and far off.

I yawned again.

Probably, I thought, it really never happened. Of course, it
was all a bad dream. The truth of the matter was that it was
Lawrence who had murdered Alfred Inglethorp with a croquet
mallet. But it was absurd of John to make such a fuss about
it, and to go shouting out: 'I tell you I won't have it!'

I woke up with a start.

At once I realized that I was in a very awkward predica-
ment. For, about twelve feet away from me, John and Mary
Cavendish were standing facing each other, and they were
evidently quarrelling. And, quite as evidently, they were
unaware of my vicinity, for before I could move or speak John
repeated the words which had aroused me from my dream.

'I tell you, Mary, I won't have it.'

Mary's voice came, cool and liquid:

'Have *you* any right to criticize my actions?'

'It will be the talk of the village! My mother was only buried
on Saturday, and here you are gadding about with the fellow.'

'Oh,' she shrugged her shoulders, 'if it is only village gossip
that you mind!'

'But it isn't. I've had enough of the fellow hanging about.
He's a Polish Jew, anyway.'

'A tinge of Jewish blood is not a bad thing. It leavens the'
– she looked at him – 'stolid stupidity of the ordinary Englishman.'

Fire in her eyes, ice in her voice. I did not wonder that the
blood rose to John's face in a crimson tide.

'Mary!'

'Well?' Her tone did not change.

The pleading died out of his voice.

'Am I to understand that you will continue to see Bauerstein
against my express wishes?'

'If I choose.'

'You defy me?'

'No, but I deny your right to criticize my actions. Have *you* no friends of whom I should disapprove?'

John fell back a pace. The colour ebbed slowly from his face.

'What do you mean?' he said, in an unsteady voice.

'You see!' said Mary quietly. 'You *do* see, don't you, that *you* have no right to dictate to *me* as to the choice of my friends?'

John glanced at her pleadingly, a stricken look in his face.

'No right? Have I *no* right, Mary?' he said unsteadily. He stretched out his hands. 'Mary –'

For a moment, I thought she wavered. A softer expression came over her face, then suddenly she turned almost fiercely away.

'None!'

She was walking away when John sprang after her, and caught her by the arm.

'Mary' – his voice was very quiet now – 'are you in love with this fellow Bauerstein?'

She hesitated, and suddenly there swept across her face a strange expression, old as the hills, yet with something eternally young about it. So might some Egyptian sphinx have smiled.

She freed herself quietly from his arm, and spoke over her shoulder.

'Perhaps,' she said; and then swiftly passed out of the little glade, leaving John standing there as though he had been turned to stone.

Rather ostentatiously, I stepped forward, crackling some dead branches with my feet as I did so. John turned. Luckily, he took it for granted that I had only just come upon the scene.

'Hullo, Hastings. Have you seen the little fellow safely back to his cottage? Quaint little chap! Is he any good, though, really?'

'He was considered one of the finest detectives of his day.'

'Oh, well, I suppose there must be something in it, then. What a rotten world it is, though!'

'You find it so?' I asked.

'Good Lord, yes! There's this terrible business to start with. Scotland Yard men in and out of the house like a jack-in-the-box! Never know where they won't turn up next. Screaming headlines in every paper in the country – damn all journalists, I say! Do you know there was a whole crowd staring in at the lodge gates this morning. Sort of Madame Tussaud's chamber of horrors business that can be seen for nothing. Pretty thick, isn't it?'

'Cheer up, John!' I said soothingly. 'It can't last for ever.'

'Can't it, though? It can last long enough for us never to be able to hold up our heads again.'

'No, no, you're getting morbid on the subject.'

'Enough to make a man morbid, to be stalked by beastly journalists and stared at by gaping moon-faced idiots, wherever he goes! But there's worse than that.'

'What?'

John lowered his voice:

'Have you ever thought, Hastings – it's a nightmare to me – who did it? I can't help feeling sometimes it must have been an accident. Because – because – who could have done it? Now Inglethorp's out of the way, there's no one else; no one, I mean, except – one of us.'

Yes, indeed, that was nightmare enough for any man! One of us? Yes, surely it must be so, unless –

A new idea suggested itself to my mind. Rapidly, I considered it. The light increased. Poirot's mysterious doings, his hints – they all fitted in. Fool that I was not to have thought of this possibility before, and what a relief for us all.

'No, John,' I said, 'it isn't one of us. How could it be?'

'I know, but, still, who else is there?'

'Can't you guess?'

'No.'

I looked cautiously round, and lowered my voice.

'Dr Bauerstein!' I whispered.

'Impossible!'

'Not at all.'

'But what earthly interest could he have in my mother's death?'

'That I don't see,' I confessed, 'but I'll tell you this: Poirot thinks so.'

'Poirot? Does he? How do you know?'

I told him of Poirot's intense excitement on hearing that Dr Bauerstein had been at Styles on the fatal night, and added:

'He said twice: "That alters everything." And I've been thinking. You know Inglethorp said he had put down the coffee in the hall? Well, it was just then that Bauerstein arrived. Isn't it possible that, as Inglethorp brought him through the hall, the doctor dropped something into the coffee in passing?'

'H'm,' said John. 'It would have been very risky.'

'Yes, but it was possible.'

'And then, how could he know it was her coffee? No, old fellow, I don't think that will wash.'

But I had remembered something else.

'You're quite right. That wasn't how it was done. Listen.' And then I told him of the cocoa sample which Poirot had taken to be analysed.

John interrupted just as I had done.

'But, look here, Bauerstein had had it analysed already?'

'Yes, yes, that's the point. I didn't see it either until now. Don't you understand? Bauerstein had it analysed – that's just it! If Bauerstein's the murderer, nothing could be simpler than for him to substitute some ordinary cocoa for his sample, and send that to be tested. And of course they would find no strychnine! But no one would dream of suspecting Bauerstein, or think of taking another sample – except Poirot,' I added, with belated recognition.

'Yes, but what about the bitter taste that cocoa won't disguise?'

'Well, we've only his word for that. And there are other

possibilities. He's admittedly one of the world's greatest toxicologists –'

'One of the world's greatest what? Say it again.'

'He knows more about poisons than almost anybody,' I explained. 'Well, my idea is, that perhaps he's found some way of making strychnine tasteless. Or it may not have been strychnine at all, but some obscure drug no one has ever heard of, which produces much the same symptoms.'

'H'm, yes, that might be,' said John. 'But look here, how could he have got at the cocoa? That wasn't downstairs?'

'No, it wasn't,' I admitted reluctantly.

And then, suddenly, a dreadful possibility flashed through my mind. I hoped and prayed it would not occur to John also. I glanced sideways at him. He was frowning perplexedly, and I drew a deep breath of relief, for the terrible thought that had flashed across my mind was this: that Dr Bauerstein might have had an accomplice.

Yet surely it could not be! Surely no woman as beautiful as Mary Cavendish could be a murderess. Yet beautiful women had been known to poison.

And suddenly I remembered that first conversation at tea on the day of my arrival, and the gleam in her eyes as she had said that poison was a woman's weapon. How agitated she had been on that fatal Tuesday evening! Had Mrs Inglethorp discovered something between her and Bauerstein, and threatened to tell her husband? Was it to stop that denunciation that the crime had been committed?

Then I remembered that enigmatical conversation between Poirot and Evelyn Howard. Was this what they had meant? Was this the monstrous possibility that Evelyn had tried not to believe?

Yes, it all fitted in.

No wonder Miss Howard had suggested 'hushing it up'. Now I understood that unfinished sentence of hers: 'Emily herself –' And in my heart I agreed with her. Would not Mrs Inglethorp have preferred to go unavenged rather than have such terrible dishonour fall upon the name of Cavendish?

'There's another thing,' said John suddenly, and the unexpected sound of his voice made me start guiltily. 'Something which makes me doubt if what you say can be true.'

'What's that?' I asked, thankful that he had gone away from the subject of how the poison could have been introduced into the cocoa.

'Why, the fact that Bauerstein demanded a post-mortem. He needn't have done so. Little Wilkins would have been quite content to let it go at heart disease.'

'Yes,' I said doubtfully. 'But we don't know. Perhaps he thought it safer in the long run. Someone might have talked afterwards. Then the Home Office might have ordered exhumation. The whole thing would have come out, then, and he would have been in an awkward position, for no one would have believed that a man of his reputation could have been deceived into calling it heart disease.'

'Yes, that's possible,' admitted John. 'Still,' he added, 'I'm blest if I can see what his motive could have been.'

I trembled.

'Look here,' I said, 'I may be altogether wrong. And, remember, all this is in confidence.'

'Oh, of course – that goes without saying.'

We had walked, as we talked, and now we passed through the little gate into the garden. Voices rose near at hand, for tea was spread out under the sycamore-tree, as it had been on the day of my arrival.

Cynthia was back from the hospital, and I placed my chair beside her, and told her of Poirot's wish to visit the dispensary.

'Of course! I'd love him to see it. He'd better come to tea there one day. I must fix it up with him. He's such a dear little man! But he *is* funny. He made me take the brooch out of my tie the other day, and put it in again, because he said it wasn't straight.'

I laughed.

'It's quite a mania with him.'

'Yes, isn't it?'

We were silent for a minute or two, and then, glancing in

the direction of Mary Cavendish, and dropping her voice, Cynthia said:

'Mr Hastings.'

'Yes?'

'After tea, I want to talk to you.'

Her glance at Mary had set me thinking. I fancied that between these two there existed very little sympathy. For the first time, it occurred to me to wonder about the girl's future. Mrs Inglethorp had made no provision of any kind for her, but I imagined that John and Mary would probably insist on her making her home with them – at any rate until the end of the war. John, I knew, was very fond of her, and would be sorry to let her go.

John, who had gone into the house, now reappeared. His good-natured face wore an unaccustomed frown of anger.

'Confound those detectives! I can't think what they're after! They've been in every room in the house – turning things inside out, and upside down. It really is too bad! I suppose they took advantage of our all being out. I shall go for that fellow Japp, when I next see him!'

'Lot of Paul Prys,' grunted Miss Howard.

Lawrence opined that they had to make a show of doing something.

Mary Cavendish said nothing.

After tea, I invited Cynthia to come for a walk, and we sauntered off into the woods together.

'Well?' I inquired, as soon as we were protected from prying eyes by the leafy screen.

With a sigh, Cynthia flung herself down, and tossed off her hat. The sunlight, piercing through the branches, turned the auburn of her hair to quivering gold.

'Mr Hastings – you are always so kind, and you know such a lot.'

It struck me at this moment that Cynthia was really a very charming girl! Much more charming than Mary, who never said things of that kind.

'Well?' I asked benignantly, as she hesitated.

'I want to ask your advice. What shall I do?'

'Do?'

'Yes. You see, Aunt Emily always told me I should be provided for. I suppose she forgot, or didn't think she was likely to die – anyway, I am *not* provided for! And I don't know what to do. Do you think I ought to go away from here at once?'

'Good heavens, no! They don't want to part with you, I'm sure.'

Cynthia hesitated a moment, plucking up the grass with her tiny hands. Then she said: 'Mrs Cavendish does. She hates me.'

'Hates you?' I cried, astonished.

Cynthia nodded.

'Yes. I don't know why, but she can't bear me and *he* can't either.'

'There I know you're wrong,' I said warmly. 'On the contrary, John is very fond of you.'

'Oh, yes – *John*. I meant Lawrence. Not, of course, that I care whether Lawrence hates me or not. Still, it's rather horrid when no one loves you, isn't it?'

'But they do, Cynthia dear,' I said earnestly. 'I'm sure you are mistaken. Look, there is John – and Miss Howard –'

Cynthia nodded rather gloomily. 'Yes, John likes me, I think, and of course Evie, for all her gruff ways, wouldn't be unkind to a fly. But Lawrence never speaks to me if he can help it, and Mary can hardly bring herself to be civil to me. She wants Evie to stay on, is begging her to, but she doesn't want me, and – and – I don't know what to do.' Suddenly the poor child burst out crying.

I don't know what possessed me. Her beauty, perhaps, as she sat there, with the sunlight glinting down on her head; perhaps the sense of relief at encountering someone who so obviously could have no connection with the tragedy; perhaps honest pity for her youth and loneliness. Anyway, I leant forward, and taking her little hand, I said awkwardly:

'Marry me, Cynthia.'

Unwittingly, I had hit upon a sovereign remedy for her tears. She sat up at once, drew her hand away, and said, with some asperity:

'Don't be silly!'

I was a little annoyed.

'I'm not being silly. I am asking you to do me the honour of becoming my wife.'

To my intense surprise, Cynthia burst out laughing, and called me a 'funny dear'.

'It's perfectly sweet of you,' she said, 'but you know you don't want to!'

'Yes, I do. I've got –'

'Never mind what you've got. You don't really want to – and I don't either.'

'Well, of course, that settles it,' I said stiffly. 'But I don't see anything to laugh at. There's nothing funny about a proposal.'

'No, indeed,' said Cynthia. 'Somebody might accept you next time. Goodbye, you've cheered me up *very* much.'

And, with a final uncontrollable burst of merriment, she vanished through the trees.

Thinking over the interview, it struck me as being profoundly unsatisfactory.

It occurred to me suddenly that I would go down to the village, and look up Bauerstein. Somebody ought to be keeping an eye on the fellow. At the same time, it would be wise to allay any suspicions he might have as to his being suspected. I remembered how Poirot had relied on my diplomacy. Accordingly, I went to the little house with the 'Apartments' card inserted in the window, where I knew he lodged, and tapped on the door.

An old woman came and opened it.

'Good afternoon,' I said pleasantly. 'Is Dr Bauerstein in?'

She stared at me.

'Haven't you heard?'

'Heard what?'

'About him.'

'What about him?'

'He's took.'

'Took? Dead?'

'No, took by the perlice.'

'By the police!' I gasped. 'Do you mean they've arrested him?'

'Yes, that's it, and –'

I waited to hear no more, but tore up the village to find Poirot.

CHAPTER X

The Arrest

To my extreme annoyance, Poirot was not in, and the old Belgian who answered my knock informed me that he believed he had gone to London.

I was dumbfounded. What on earth could Poirot be doing in London? Was it a sudden decision on his part, or had he already made up his mind when he parted from me a few hours earlier?

I retraced my steps to Styles in some annoyance. With Poirot away, I was uncertain how to act. Had he foreseen this arrest? Had he not, in all probability, been the cause of it? Those questions I could not resolve. But in the meantime what was I to do? Should I announce the arrest openly at Styles, or not? Though I did not acknowledge it to myself, the thought of Mary Cavendish was weighing on me. Would it not be a terrible shock to her? For the moment, I set aside utterly any suspicions of her. She could not be implicated – otherwise I should have heard some hint of it.

Of course, there was no possibility of being able permanently to conceal Dr Bauerstein's arrest from her. It would be announced in every newspaper on the morrow. Still, I shrank from blurting it out. If only Poirot had been accessible, I could have asked his advice. What possessed him to go posting off to London in this unaccountable way?

In spite of myself, my opinion of his sagacity was immeasurably heightened. I would never have dreamt of suspecting the doctor, had not Poirot put it into my head. Yes, decidedly, the little man was clever.

After some reflecting, I decided to take John into my confidence, and leave him to make the matter public or not, as he thought fit.

He gave vent to a prodigious whistle, as I imparted the news.

'Great Scot! You *were* right, then. I couldn't believe it at the time.'

'No, it is astonishing until you get used to the idea, and see how it makes everything fit in. Now, what are we to do? Of course, it will be generally known tomorrow.'

John reflected.

'Never mind,' he said at last, 'we won't say anything at present. There is no need. As you say, it will be known soon enough.'

But to my intense surprise, on getting down early the next morning, and eagerly opening the newspapers, there was not a word about the arrest! There was a column of mere padding about 'The Styles Poisoning Case', but nothing further. It was rather inexplicable, but I supposed that, for some reason or other, Japp wished to keep it out of the papers. It worried me just a little, for it suggested the possibility that there might be further arrests to come.

After breakfast, I decided to go down to the village, and see if Poirot had returned yet; but, before I could start, a well-known face blocked one of the windows, and the well-known voice said:

'*Bonjour, mon ami!*'

'Poirot,' I exclaimed, with relief, and seizing him by both hands I dragged him into the room. 'I was never so glad to see anyone. Listen, I have said nothing to anybody but John. Is that right?'

'My friend,' replied Poirot, 'I do not know what you are talking about.'

'Dr Bauerstein's arrest, of course,' I answered impatiently.

'Is Bauerstein arrested, then?'

'Did you not know it?'

'Not the least in the world.' But, pausing a moment, he added: 'Still, it does not surprise me. After all, we are only four miles from the coast.'

'The coast?' I asked, puzzled. 'What has that got to do with it?'

Poirot shrugged his shoulders.

'Surely, it is obvious!'

'Not to me. No doubt I am very dense, but I cannot see what the proximity of the coast has got to do with the murder of Mrs Inglethorp.'

'Nothing at all, of course,' replied Poirot, smiling. 'But we were speaking of the arrest of Dr Bauerstein.'

'Well, he is arrested for the murder of Mrs Inglethorp –'

'What?' cried Poirot, in apparently lively astonishment. 'Dr Bauerstein arrested for the murder of Mrs Inglethorp?'

'Yes.'

'Impossible! That would be too good a farce! Who told you that, my friend?'

'Well, no one exactly told me,' I confessed. 'But he is arrested.'

'Oh, yes, very likely. But for espionage, *mon ami*.'

'Espionage?' I gasped.

'Precisely.'

'Not for poisoning Mrs Inglethorp?'

'Not unless our friend Japp has taken leave of his senses,' replied Poirot placidly.

'But – but I thought you thought so too?'

Poirot gave me one look, which conveyed a wondering pity, and his full sense of the utter absurdity of such an idea.

'Do you mean to say,' I asked, slowly adapting myself to the new idea, 'that Dr Bauerstein is a spy?'

Poirot nodded.

'Have you never suspected it?'

'It never entered my head.'

'It did not strike you as peculiar that a famous London doctor should bury himself in a little village like this, and should be in the habit of walking about at all hours of the night, fully dressed?'

'No,' I confessed, 'I never thought of such a thing.'

'He is, of course, a German by birth,' said Poirot thoughtfully, 'though he has practised so long in this country that nobody thinks of him as anything but an Englishman. He was naturalized about fifteen years ago. A very clever man – a Jew, of course.'

'The blackguard!' I cried indignantly.

'Not at all. He is, on the contrary, a patriot. Think what he stands to lose. I admire the man myself.'

But I could not look at it in Poirot's philosophical way.

'And this is the man with whom Mrs Cavendish has been wandering about all over the country!' I cried indignantly.

'Yes. I should fancy he had found her very useful,' remarked Poirot. 'So long as gossip busied itself in coupling their names together, any other vagaries of the doctor's passed unobserved.'

'Then you think he never really cared for her?' I asked eagerly – rather too eagerly, perhaps, under the circumstances.

'That, of course, I cannot say, but – shall I tell you my own private opinion, Hastings?'

'Yes.'

'Well, it is this: that Mrs Cavendish does not care, and never has cared one little jot about Dr Bauerstein!'

'Do you really think so?' I could not disguise my pleasure.

'I am quite sure of it. And I will tell you why.'

'Yes?'

'Because she cares for someone else, *mon ami*.'

'Oh!' What did he mean? In spite of myself, an agreeable warmth spread over me. I am not a vain man where women are concerned, but I remembered certain evidences, too lightly thought of at the time, perhaps, but which certainly seemed to indicate –

My pleasing thoughts were interrupted by the sudden entrance of Miss Howard. She glanced round hastily to make sure there was no one else in the room, and quickly produced an old sheet of brown paper. This she handed to Poirot, murmuring as she did so the cryptic words:

'On top of the wardrobe.' Then she hurriedly left the room.

Poirot unfolded the sheet of paper eagerly, and uttered an

exclamation of satisfaction. He spread it out on the table.

'Come here, Hastings. Now tell me, what is that initial – J. or L.?'

It was a medium-sized sheet of paper, rather dusty, as though it had lain by for some time. But it was the label that was attracting Poirot's attention. At the top, it bore the printed stamp of Messrs Parkson's, the well-known theatrical costumiers, and it was addressed to '– (the debatable initial) Cavendish, Esq., Styles Court, Styles St Mary, Essex.'

'It might be T. Or it might be L.,' I said, after studying the thing for a minute or two. 'It certainly isn't a J.'

'Good,' replied Poirot, folding up the paper again. 'I, also, am of your way of thinking. It is an L., depend upon it!'

'Where did it come from?' I asked curiously. 'Is it important?'

'Moderately so. It confirms a surmise of mine. Having deduced its existence, I set Miss Howard to search for it, and, as you see, she has been successful.'

'What did she mean by "On top of the wardrobe"?'

'She meant,' replied Poirot promptly, 'that she found it on top of a wardrobe.'

'A funny place for a piece of brown paper,' I mused.

'Not at all. The top of a wardrobe is an excellent place for brown paper and cardboard boxes. I have kept them there myself. Neatly arranged, there is nothing to offend the eye.'

'Poirot,' I asked earnestly, 'have you made up your mind about this crime?'

'Yes – that is to say, I believe I know how it was committed.'

'Ah!'

'Unfortunately, I have no proof beyond my surmise, unless –' With sudden energy, he caught me by the arm, and whirled me down the hall, calling out in French in his excitement: 'Mademoiselle Dorcas, Mademoiselle Dorcas, *un moment, s'il vous plaît!*'

Dorcas, quite flurried by the noise, came hurrying out of the pantry.

'My good Dorcas, I have an idea – a little idea – if it should prove justified, what magnificent chance! Tell me, on Monday, not Tuesday, Dorcas, but Monday, the day before the tragedy, did anything go wrong with Mrs Inglethorp's bell?'

Dorcas looked very surprised.

'Yes, sir, now you mention it, it did; though I don't know how you came to hear of it. A mouse, or some such, must have nibbled the wire through. The man came and put it right on Tuesday morning.'

With a long-drawn exclamation of ecstasy, Poirot led the way back to the morning-room.

'See you, one should not ask for outside proof – no, reason should be enough. But the flesh is weak, it is consolation to find that one is on the right track. Ah, my friend, I am like a giant refreshed. I run! I leap!'

And, in very truth, run and leap he did, gambolling wildly down the stretch of lawn outside the long window.

'What is your remarkable little friend doing?' asked a voice behind me, and I turned to find Mary Cavendish at my elbow.

She smiled, and so did I. 'What is it all about?'

'Really, I can't tell you. He asked Dorcas some question about a bell, and appeared so delighted with her answer that he is capering about as you see!'

Mary laughed.

'How ridiculous! He's going out of the gate. Isn't he coming back today?'

'I don't know. I've given up trying to guess what he'll do next.'

'Is he quite mad, Mr Hastings?'

'I honestly don't know. Sometimes, I feel sure he is as mad as a hatter; and then, just as he is at his maddest, I find there is method in his madness.'

'I see.'

In spite of her laugh, Mary was looking thoughtful this morning. She seemed grave, almost sad.

It occurred to me that it would be a good opportunity to tackle her on the subject of Cynthia. I began rather tactfully,

I thought, but I had not gone far before she stopped me authoritatively.

'You are an excellent advocate, I have no doubt, Mr Hastings, but in this case your talents are quite thrown away. Cynthia will run no risk of encountering any unkindness from me.'

I began to stammer feebly that I hoped she hadn't thought – But again she stopped me, and her words were so unexpected that they quite drove Cynthia, and her troubles, out of my mind.

'Mr Hastings,' she said, 'do you think I and my husband are happy together?'

I was considerably taken aback, and murmured something about it not being my business to think anything of the sort.

'Well,' she said quietly, 'whether it is your business or not, I will tell you that we are *not* happy.'

I said nothing, for I saw that she had not finished.

She began slowly, walking up and down the room, her head a little bent, and that slim, supple figure of hers swaying gently as she walked. She stopped suddenly, and looked up at me.

'You don't know anything about me, do you?' she asked. 'Where I come from, who I was before I married John – anything, in fact? Well, I will tell you. I will make a father confessor of you. You are kind, I think – yes, I am sure you are kind.'

Somehow, I was not quite as elated as I might have been. I remembered that Cynthia had begun her confidences in much the same way. Besides, a father confessor should be elderly, it is not at all the role for a young man.

'My father was English,' said Mrs Cavendish, 'but my mother was a Russian.'

'Ah,' I said, 'now I understand –'

'Understand what?'

'A hint of something foreign – different – that there has always been about you.'

'My mother was very beautiful, I believe. I don't know, because I never saw her. She died when I was quite a little child. I believe there was some tragedy connected with her death – she took an overdose of some sleeping draught by mistake. However that may be, my father was broken-hearted. Shortly afterwards, he went into the Consular Service. Everywhere he went, I went with him. When I was twenty-three, I had been nearly all over the world. It was a splendid life – I loved it.'

There was a smile on her face, and her head was thrown back. She seemed living in the memory of those old glad days.

'Then my father died. He left me very badly off. I had to go and live with some old aunts in Yorkshire.' She shuddered. 'You will understand me when I say that it was a deadly life for a girl brought up as I had been. The narrowness, the deadly monotony of it, almost drove me mad.' She paused a minute, and added in a different tone: 'And then I met John Cavendish.'

'Yes?'

'You can imagine that, from my aunts' point of view, it was a very good match for me. But I can honestly say it was not this fact which weighed with me. No, he was simply a way of escape from the insufferable monotony of my life.'

I said nothing, and after a moment, she went on:

'Don't misunderstand me. I was quite honest with him. I told him, what was true, that I liked him very much, that I hoped to come to like him more, but that I was not in any way what the world calls "in love" with him. He declared that that satisfied him, and so – we were married.'

She waited a long time, a little frown had gathered on her forehead. She seemed to be looking back earnestly into those past days.

'I think – I am sure – he cared for me at first. But I suppose we were not well matched. Almost at once, we drifted apart. He – it is not a pleasant thing for my pride, but it is the truth – tired of me very soon.' I must have made some murmur of dissent, for she went on quickly: 'Oh, yes, he did! Not that it matters now – now that we've come to the parting of the ways.'

'What do you mean?'

She answered quietly:

'I mean that I am not going to remain at Styles.'

'You and John are not going to live here?'

'John may live here, but I shall not.'

'You are going to leave him?'

'Yes.'

'But why?'

She paused a long time, and said at last:

'Perhaps – because I want to be – free!'

And, as she spoke, I had a sudden vision of broad spaces, virgin tracts of forests, untrodden lands – and a realization of what freedom would mean to such a nature as Mary Cavendish. I seemed to see her for a moment as she was, a proud wild creature, as untamed by civilization as some shy bird of the hills. A little cry broke from her lips:

'You don't know, you don't know, how this hateful place has been prison to me!'

'I understand,' I said, 'but – but don't do anything rash.'

'Oh, rash!' Her voice mocked at my prudence.

Then suddenly I said a thing I could have bitten out my tongue for:

'You know that Dr Bauerstein has been arrested?'

An instant coldness passed like a mask over her face, blotting out all expression.

'John was so kind as to break that to me this morning.'

'Well, what do you think?' I asked feebly.

'Of what?'

'Of the arrest?'

'What should I think? Apparently he is a German spy; so the gardener had told John.'

Her face and voice were absolutely cold and expressionless. Did she care, or did she not?

She moved away a step or two, and fingered one of the flower vases. 'These are quite dead. I must do them again. Would you mind moving – thank you, Mr Hastings.' And she walked quietly past me out of the window, with a cool little nod of dismissal.

No, surely she could not care for Bauerstein. No woman could act her part with that icy unconcern.

Poirot did not make his appearance the following morning, and there was no sign of the Scotland Yard men.

But, at lunch-time, there arrived a new piece of evidence – or rather lack of evidence. We had vainly tried to trace the fourth letter which Mrs Inglethorp had written on the evening preceding her death. Our efforts having been in vain, we had abandoned the matter, hoping that it might turn up of itself one day. And this is just what did happen, in the shape of a communication, which arrived by the second post from a firm of French music publishers, acknowledging Mrs Inglethorp's cheque, and regretting they had been unable to trace a certain series of Russian folk-songs. So the last hope of solving the mystery, by means of Mrs Inglethorp's correspondence on the fatal evening, had to be abandoned.

Just before tea, I strolled down to tell Poirot of the new disappointment, but found, to my annoyance, that he was once more out.

'Gone to London again?'

'Oh, no, monsieur, he has but taken the train to Tadminster. "To see a young lady's dispensary," he said.'

'Silly ass!' I ejaculated. 'I told him Wednesday was the one day she wasn't there! Well, tell him to look us up tomorrow morning, will you?'

'Certainly, monsieur.'

But, on the following day, no sign of Poirot. I was getting angry. He was really treating us in the most cavalier fashion.

After lunch, Lawrence drew me aside, and asked if I was going down to see him.

'No, I don't think I shall. He can come up here if he wants to see us.'

'Oh!' Lawrence looked indeterminate. Something unusually nervous and excited in his manner roused my curiosity.

'What is it?' I asked. 'I could go if there's anything special.'

'It's nothing much, but – well, if you are going, will you

tell him' – he dropped his voice to a whisper – 'I think I've found the extra coffee-cup!'

I had almost forgotten that enigmatical message of Poirot's, but now my curiosity was aroused afresh.

Lawrence would say no more, so I decided that I would descend from my high horse, and once more seek out Poirot at Leastways Cottage.

This time I was received with a smile. Monsieur Poirot was within. Would I mount? I mounted accordingly.

Poirot was sitting by the table, his head buried in his hands. He sprang up at my entrance.

'What is it?' I asked solicitously. 'You are not ill, I trust?'

'No, no, not ill. But I decide an affair of great moment.'

'Whether to catch the criminal or not?' I asked facetiously.

But, to my great surprise, Poirot nodded gravely.

' "To speak or not to speak," as your so great Shakespeare says, "that is the question." '

I did not trouble to correct the quotation.

'You are not serious, Poirot?'

'I am of the most serious. For the most serious of all things hangs in the balance.'

'And that is?'

'A woman's happiness, *mon ami*,' he said gravely.

I did not quite know what to say.

'The moment has come,' said Poirot thoughtfully, 'and I do not know what to do. For, see you, it is a big stake for which I play. No one but I, Hercule Poirot, would attempt it!' And he tapped himself proudly on the breast.

After pausing a few minutes respectfully, so as not to spoil his effect, I gave him Lawrence's message.

'Aha!' he cried. 'So he has found the extra coffee-cup. That is good. He has more intelligence than would appear, this long-faced Monsieur Lawrence of yours!'

I did not myself think very highly of Lawrence's intelligence; but I forbore to contradict Poirot, and gently took him to task for forgetting my instructions as to which were Cynthia's days off.

'It is true. I have the head of a sieve. However, the other young lady was most kind. She was sorry for my disappointment, and showed me everything in the kindest way.'

'Oh, well, that's all right, then, and you must go to tea with Cynthia another day.'

I told him about the letter.

'I am sorry for that,' he said. 'I always had hopes of that letter. But, no, it was not to be. This affair must all be unravelled from within.' He tapped his forehead. 'These little grey cells. It is "up to them" – as you say over here.' Then, suddenly, he asked: 'Are you a judge of finger-marks, my friend?'

'No,' I said, rather surprised, 'I know that there are no two finger-marks alike, but that's as far as my science goes.'

'Exactly.'

He unlocked a little drawer, and took out some photographs which he laid on the table.

'I have numbered them, 1, 2, 3. Will you describe them to me?'

I studied the proofs attentively.

'All greatly magnified, I see. No. 1, I should say, are a man's finger-prints; thumb and first finger. No. 2 are a lady's; they are much smaller, and quite different in every way. No. 3' – I paused for some time – 'there seems to be a lot of confused finger-marks, but here, very distinctly, are No. 1's.'

'Overlapping the others?'

'Yes.'

'You recognize them beyond fail?'

'Oh, yes; they are identical.'

Poirot nodded, and gently taking the photographs from me locked them up again.

'I suppose,' I said, 'that as usual, you are not going to explain?'

'On the contrary. No. 1 were the finger-prints of Monsieur Lawrence. No. 2 were those of Mademoiselle Cynthia. They are not important. I merely obtained them for comparison. No. 3 is a little more complicated.'

'Yes?'

'It is, as you see, highly magnified. You may have noticed a sort of blur extending all across the picture. I will not describe to you the special apparatus, dusting powder, etc., which I used. It is a well-known process to the police, and by means of it you can obtain a photograph of the finger-prints on any object in a very short space of time. Well, my friend, you have seen the finger-marks – it remains to tell you the particular object on which they had been left.'

'Go on – I am really excited.'

'*Eh bien!* Photo No. 3 represents the highly magnified surface of a tiny bottle in the top poison cupboard of the dispensary in the Red Cross Hospital at Tadminster – which sounds like the house that Jack built!'

'Good heavens!' I exclaimed. 'But what were Lawrence Cavendish's finger-marks doing on it? He never went near the poison cupboard the day we were there.'

'Oh, yes, he did!'

'Impossible! We were all together the whole time.'

Poirot shook his head.

'No, my friend, there was a moment when you were not all together. There was a moment when you could not have been all together, or it would not have been necessary to call to Monsieur Lawrence to come and join you on the balcony.'

'I'd forgotten that,' I admitted. 'But it was only for a moment.'

'Long enough.'

'Long enough for what?'

Poirot's smile became rather enigmatical.

'Long enough for a gentleman who had once studied medicine to gratify a very natural interest and curiosity.'

Our eyes met. Poirot's were pleasantly vague. He got up and hummed a little tune. I watched him suspiciously.

'Poirot,' I said, 'what was in this particular little bottle?'

Poirot looked out of the window.

'Hydro-chloride of strychnine,' he said, over his shoulder, continuing to hum.

'Good heavens!' I said it quite quietly. I was not surprised. I had expected that answer.

'They use the pure hydro-chloride of strychnine very little – only occasionally for pills. It is the official solution, Liq. Strychnine Hydro-chlor. that is used in most medicines. That is why the finger-marks have remained undisturbed since then.'

'How did you manage to take this photograph?'

'I dropped my hat from the balcony,' explained Poirot simply. 'Visitors were not permitted below at that hour, so, in spite of my many apologies, Mademoiselle Cynthia's colleague had to go down and fetch it for me.'

'Then you knew what you were going to find?'

'No, not at all. I merely realized that it was possible, from your story, for Monsieur Lawrence to go to the poison cupboard. The possibility had to be confirmed, or eliminated.'

'Poirot,' I said, 'your gaiety does not deceive me. This is a very important discovery.'

'I do not know,' said Poirot. 'But one thing does strike me. No doubt it has struck you too.'

'What is that?'

'Why, that there is altogether too much strychnine about this case. This is the third time we run up against it. There was strychnine in Mrs Inglethorp's tonic. There is the strychnine sold across the counter at Styles St Mary by Mace. Now we have more strychnine, handled by one of the household. It is confusing; and, as you know, I do not like confusion.'

Before I could reply, one of the other Belgians opened the door and stuck his head in.

'There is a lady below, asking for Mr Hastings.'

'A lady?'

I jumped up. Poirot followed me down the narrow stairs. Mary Cavendish was standing in the doorway.

'I have been visiting an old woman in the village,' she explained, 'and as Lawrence told me you were with Monsieur Poirot I thought I would call for you.'

'Alas, madame,' said Poirot, 'I thought you had come to honour me with a visit!'

'I will some day, if you ask me,' she promised him, smiling.

'That is well. If you should need a father confessor, madame' – she started ever so slightly – 'remember, Papa Poirot is always at your service.'

She stared at him for a few minutes, as though seeking to read some deeper meaning into his words. Then she turned abruptly away.

'Come, will you not walk back with us too, Monsieur Poirot?'

'Enchanted, madame.'

All the way to Styles, Mary talked fast and feverishly. It struck me that in some way she was nervous of Poirot's eyes.

The weather had broken, and the sharp wind was almost autumnal in its shrewishness. Mary shivered a little, and buttoned her black sports coat closer. The wind through the trees made a mournful noise, like some giant sighing.

We walked up to the great door of Styles, and at once the knowledge came to us that something was wrong.

Dorcas came running out to meet us. She was crying and wringing her hands. I was aware of other servants huddled together in the background, all eyes and ears.

'Oh, m'am! Oh, m'am! I don't know how to tell you –'

'What is it, Dorcas?' I asked impatiently. 'Tell us at once.'

'It's those wicked detectives. They've arrested him – they've arrested Mr Cavendish!'

'Arrested Lawrence?' I gasped.

I saw a strange look come into Dorcas's eyes.

'No, sir. Not Mr Lawrence – Mr John.'

Behind me, with a wild cry, Mary Cavendish fell heavily against me, and as I turned to catch her I met the quiet triumph in Poirot's eyes.

CHAPTER XI

The Case for the Prosecution

The trial of John Cavendish for the murder of his stepmother took place two months later.

Of the intervening weeks I will say little, but my admiration and sympathy went out unfeignedly to Mary Cavendish. She ranged herself passionately on her husband's side, scorning the mere idea of his guilt, and fought for him tooth and nail.

I expressed my admiration to Poirot, and he nodded thoughtfully. 'Yes, she is of those women who show at their best in adversity. It brings out all that is sweetest and truest in them. Her pride and her jealousy have –'

'Jealousy?' I queried.

'Yes. Have you not realized that she is an unusually jealous woman? As I was saying, her pride and jealousy have been laid aside. She thinks of nothing but her husband, and the terrible fate that is hanging over him.'

He spoke very feelingly, and I looked at him earnestly, remembering that last afternoon, when he had been deliberating whether or no to speak. With his tenderness for 'a woman's happiness', I felt glad that the decision had been taken out of his hands.

'Even now,' I said, 'I can hardly believe it. You see, up to the very last minute, I thought it was Lawrence!'

Poirot grinned.

'I know you did.'

'But John! My old friend John!'

'Every murderer is probably somebody's old friend,' observed Poirot philosophically. 'You cannot mix up senti-ment and reason.'

'I must say I think you might have given me a hint.'

'Perhaps, *mon ami*, I did not do so, just because he *was* your old friend.'

I was rather disconcerted by this, remembering how I had busily passed on to John what I believed to be Poirot's views concerning Bauerstein. He, by the way, had been acquitted of the charge brought against him. Nevertheless, although he had been too clever for them this time, and the charge of espionage could not be brought home to him, his wings were pretty well clipped for the future.

I asked Poirot whether he thought John would be condemned. To my intense surprise, he replied that, on the contrary, he was extremely likely to be acquitted.

'But Poirot –' I protested.

'Oh, my friend, have I not said to you all along that I have no proofs. It is one thing to know that a man is guilty, it is quite another matter to prove him so. And, in this case, there is terribly little evidence. That is the whole trouble. I, Hercule Poirot, know, but I lack the last link in my chain. And unless I can find that missing link –' He shook his head gravely.

'When did you first suspect John Cavendish?' I asked, after a minute or two.

'Did you not suspect him at all?'

'No, indeed.'

'Not after that fragment of conversation you overheard between Mrs Cavendish and her mother-in-law, and her subsequent lack of frankness at the inquest?'

'No.'

'Did you not put two and two together, and reflect that if it was not Alfred Inglethorp who was quarrelling with his wife – and you remember, he strenuously denied it at the inquest – it must be either Lawrence or John? Now, if it was Lawrence, Mary Cavendish's conduct was just as inexplicable. But if, on the other hand, it was John, the whole thing was explained quite naturally.'

'So,' I cried, a light breaking in upon me, 'it was John who quarrelled with his mother that afternoon?'

'Exactly.'

'And you have known this all along?'

'Certainly. Mrs Cavendish's behaviour could only be explained that way.'

'And yet you say he may be acquitted?'

Poirot shrugged his shoulders.

'Certainly I do. At the police court proceedings, we shall hear the case for the prosecution, but in all probability his solicitors will advise him to reserve his defence. That will be sprung upon us at the trial. And – ah, by the way, I have a word of caution to give you, my friend. I must not appear in the case.'

'What?'

'No. Officially, I have nothing to do with it. Until I have found that last link in my chain, I must remain behind the scenes. Mrs Cavendish must think I am working for her husband, not against him.'

'I say, that's playing it a bit low down,' I protested.

'Not at all. We have to deal with a most clever and unscrupulous man, and we must use any means in our power – otherwise he will slip through our fingers. That is why I have been careful to remain in the background. All the discoveries have been made by Japp, and Japp will take all the credit. If I am called upon to give evidence at all' – he smiled broadly – 'it will probably be as a witness for the defence.'

I could hardly believe my ears.

'It is quite *en règle*,' continued Poirot. 'Strangely enough, I can give evidence that will demolish one contention of the prosecution.'

'Which one?'

'The one that relates to the destruction of the will. John Cavendish did not destroy that will.'

Poirot was a true prophet. I will not go into the details of the police court proceedings, as it involves many tiresome repetitions. I will merely state baldly that John Cavendish reserved his defence, and was duly committed for trial.

September found us all in London. Mary took a house in Kensington, Poirot being included in the family party.

I myself had been given a job at the War Office, so was able to see them continually.

As the weeks went by, the state of Poirot's nerves grew worse and worse. That 'last link' he talked about was still lacking. Privately, I hoped it might remain so, for what happiness could there be for Mary, if John were not acquitted?

On September 15th John Cavendish appeared in the dock at the Old Bailey, charged with 'The Wilful Murder of Emily Agnes Inglethorp', and pleaded 'Not Guilty'.

Sir Ernest Heavywether, the famous KC, had been engaged to defend him.

Mr Philips, KC, opened the case for the Crown.

The murder, he said, was a most premeditated and cold-blooded one. It was neither more nor less than the deliberate poisoning of a fond and trusting woman by the stepson to whom she had been more than a mother. Ever since his boyhood, she had supported him. He and his wife had lived at Styles Court in every luxury, surrounded by her care and attention. She had been their kind and generous benefactress.

He proposed to call witnesses to show how the prisoner, a profligate and spendthrift, had been at the end of his financial tether, and had also been carrying on an intrigue with a certain Mrs Raikes, a neighbouring farmer's wife. This having come to his stepmother's ears, she taxed him with it on the afternoon before her death, and a quarrel ensued, part of which was overheard. On the previous day, the prisoner had purchased strychnine at the village chemist's shop, wearing a disguise by means of which he hoped to throw the onus of the crime upon another man – to wit, Mrs Inglethorp's husband, of whom he had been bitterly jealous. Luckily for Mr Inglethorp, he had been able to produce an unimpeachable alibi.

On the afternoon of July 17th, continued Counsel, immediately after the quarrel with her son, Mrs Inglethorp made a new will. This will was found destroyed in the grate of her bedroom the following morning, but evidence had come to light which showed that it had been drawn up in favour of her husband. Deceased had already made a will in his favour

before her marriage, but – and Mr Philips wagged an expressive forefinger – the prisoner was not aware of that. What had
induced the deceased to make a fresh will, with the old one
still extant, he could not say. She was an old lady, and might
possibly have forgotten the former one; or – this seemed to
him more likely – she may have had an idea that it was revoked
by her marriage, as there had been some conversation on
the subject. Ladies were not always very well versed in legal
knowledge. She had, about a year before, executed a will in
favour of the prisoner. He would call evidence to show that it
was the prisoner who ultimately handed his stepmother her
coffee on the fatal night. Later in the evening, he had sought
admission to her room, on which occasion, no doubt, he found
an opportunity of destroying the will which, as far as he knew,
would render the one in his favour valid.

The prisoner had been arrested in consequence of the discovery, in his room, by Detective-Inspector Japp – a most
brilliant officer – of the identical phial of strychnine which
had been sold at the village chemist's to the supposed Mr
Inglethorp on the day before the murder. It would be for the
jury to decide whether or no these damning facts constituted
an overwhelming proof of the prisoner's guilt.

And, subtly implying that a jury which did not so decide
was quite unthinkable, Mr Philips sat down and wiped his
forehead.

The first witnesses for the prosecution were mostly those
who had been called at the inquest, the medical evidence being
again taken first.

Sir Ernest Heavywether, who was famous all over England
for the unscrupulous manner in which he bullied witnesses,
only asked two questions.

'I take it, Dr Bauerstein, that strychnine, as a drug, acts
quickly?'

'Yes.'

'And that you are unable to account for the delay in this
case?'

'Yes.'

'Thank you.'

Mr Mace identified the phial handed him by Counsel as that sold by him to 'Mr Inglethorp'. Pressed, he admitted that he only knew Mr Inglethorp by sight. He had never spoken to him. The witness was not cross-examined.

Alfred Inglethorp was called, and denied having purchased the poison. He also denied having quarrelled with his wife. Various witnesses testified to the accuracy of these statements.

The gardeners' evidence as to the witnessing of the will was taken, and then Dorcas was called.

Dorcas, faithful to her 'young gentlemen', denied strenuously that it could have been John's voice she heard, and resolutely declared, in the teeth of everything, that it was Mr Inglethorp who had been in the boudoir with her mistress. A rather wistful smile passed across the face of the prisoner in the dock. He knew only too well how useless her gallant defiance was, since it was not the object of the defence to deny this point. Mrs Cavendish, of course, could not be called upon to give evidence against her husband.

After various questions on other matters, Mr Philips asked:

'In the month of June last, do you remember a parcel arriving for Mr Lawrence Cavendish from Parkson's?'

Dorcas shook her head.

'I don't remember, sir. It may have done, but Mr Lawrence was away from home part of June.'

'In the event of a parcel arriving for him whilst he was away, what would be done with it?'

'It would either be put in his room or sent on after him.'

'By you?'

'No, sir, I should leave it on the hall table. It would be Miss Howard who would attend to anything like that.'

Evelyn Howard was called and, after being examined on other points, was questioned as to the parcel.

'Don't remember. Lots of parcels come. Can't remember one special one.'

'You do not know if it was sent after Mr Lawrence Cavendish to Wales, or whether it was put in his room?'

'Don't think it was sent after him. Should have remembered if it was.'

'Supposing a parcel arrived addressed to Mr Lawrence Cavendish, and afterwards it disappeared, should you remark its absence?'

'No, don't think so. I should think someone had taken charge of it.'

'I believe, Miss Howard, that it was you who found this sheet of brown paper?' He held up the same dusty piece which Poirot and I had examined in the morning-room at Styles.

'Yes, I did.'

'How did you come to look for it?'

'The Belgian detective who was employed on the case asked me to search for it.'

'Where did you eventually discover it?'

'On top of – of – a wardrobe.'

'On top of the prisoner's wardrobe?'

'I – I believe so.'

'Did you not find it yourself?'

'Yes.'

'Then you must know where you found it?'

'Yes, it was on the prisoner's wardrobe.'

'That is better.'

An assistant from Parkson's, Theatrical Costumiers, testified that on June 29th they had supplied a black beard to Mr L. Cavendish, as requested. It was ordered by letter, and a postal order was enclosed. No, they had not kept the letter. All transactions were entered in their books. They had sent the beard, as directed, to 'L. Cavendish, Esq., Styles Court.'

Sir Ernest Heavywether rose ponderously.

'Where was the letter written from?'

'From Styles Court.'

'The same address to which you sent the parcel?'

'Yes.'

Like a beast of prey, Heavywether fell upon him:

'How do you know?'

'I – I don't understand.'

'How do you know that letter came from Styles? Did you notice the postmark?'

'No – but –'

'Ah, you did *not* notice the postmark! And yet you affirm so confidently that it came from Styles. It might, in fact, have been any postmark?'

'Y – es.'

'In fact, the letter, though written on stamped notepaper, might have been posted from anywhere? From Wales, for instance?'

The witness admitted that such might be the case, and Sir Ernest signified that he was satisfied.

Elizabeth Wells, second housemaid at Styles, stated that after she had gone to bed she remembered that she had bolted the front door, instead of leaving it on the latch as Mr Inglethorp had requested. She had accordingly gone downstairs again to rectify her error. Hearing a slight noise in the West wing, she had peeped along the passage, and had seen Mr John Cavendish knocking at Mrs Inglethorp's door.

Sir Ernest Heavywether made short work of her, and under his unmerciful bullying she contradicted herself hopelessly, and Sir Ernest sat down again with a satisfied smile on his face.

With the evidence of Annie, as to the candle grease on the floor, and as to seeing the prisoner take the coffee into the boudoir, the proceedings were adjourned until the following day.

As we went home, Mary Cavendish spoke bitterly against the prosecuting counsel.

'That hateful man! What a net he has drawn around my poor John! How he twisted every little fact until he made it seem what it wasn't!'

'Well,' I said consolingly, 'it will be the other way about tomorrow.'

'Yes,' she said meditatively; then suddenly dropped her voice. 'Mr Hastings, you do not think – surely it could not have been Lawrence – oh, no, that could not be!'

But I myself was puzzled, and as soon as I was alone with Poirot I asked him what he thought Sir Ernest was driving at.

'Ah!' said Poirot appreciatively. 'He is a clever man, that Sir Ernest.'

'Do you think he believes Lawrence guilty?'

'I do not think he believes or cares anything! No, what he is trying for is to create such confusion in the minds of the jury that they are divided in their opinion as to which brother did it. He is endeavouring to make out that there is quite as much evidence against Lawrence as against John – and I am not at all sure that he will not succeed.'

Detective-Inspector Japp was the first witness called when the trial was reopened, and gave his evidence succinctly and briefly. After relating the earlier events, he proceeded:

'Acting on information received, Superintendent Summer-haye and myself searched the prisoner's room, during his temporary absence from the house. In his chest of drawers, hidden beneath some underclothing, we found: first, a pair of gold-rimmed pince-nez similar to those worn by Mr Inglethorp' – these were exhibited – 'secondly, this phial.'

The phial was that already recognized by the chemist's assistant, a tiny bottle of blue glass, containing a few grains of a white crystalline powder, and labelled: 'Strychnine Hydrochloride. POISON.'

A fresh piece of evidence discovered by the detectives since the police court proceedings was a long, almost new piece of blotting-paper. It had been found in Mrs Inglethorp's cheque book, and on being reversed at a mirror, showed clearly the words: '. . . everything of which I die possessed I leave to my beloved husband Alfred Ing . . .' This placed beyond question the fact that the destroyed will had been in favour of the deceased lady's husband. Japp then produced the charred fragment of paper recovered from the grate, and this, with the discovery of the beard in the attic, completed his evidence.

But Sir Ernest's cross-examination was yet to come.

'What day was it when you searched the prisoner's room?'

'Tuesday, the 24th of July.'

'Exactly a week after the tragedy?'

'Yes.'

'You found these two objects, you say, in the chest of drawers. Was the drawer unlocked?'

'Yes.'

'Does it not strike you as unlikely that a man who had committed a crime should keep the evidence of it in an unlocked drawer for anyone to find?'

'He might have stowed them there in a hurry.'

'But you have just said it was a whole week since the crime. He would have had ample time to remove them and destroy them.'

'Perhaps.'

'There is no perhaps about it. Would he, or would he not, have had plenty of time to remove and destroy them?'

'Yes.'

'Was the pile of underclothes under which the things were hidden heavy or light?'

'Heavyish.'

'In other words, it was winter underclothing. Obviously, the prisoner would not be likely to go to that drawer?'

'Perhaps not.'

'Kindly answer my question. Would the prisoner, in the hottest week of a hot summer, be likely to go to a drawer containing winter underclothing? Yes, or no?'

'No.'

'In that case, is it not possible that the articles in question might have been put there by a third person, and that the prisoner was quite unaware of their presence?'

'I should not think it likely.'

'But it is possible?'

'Yes.'

'That is all.'

More evidence followed. Evidence as to the financial difficulties in which the prisoner had found himself at the end of July. Evidence as to his intrigue with Mrs Raikes – poor Mary, that must have been bitter hearing for a woman of her pride. Evelyn Howard had been right in her facts, though her animosity against Alfred Inglethorp had caused her to jump to the conclusion that he was the person concerned.

Lawrence Cavendish was then put into the box. In a low voice, in answer to Mr Philips's questions, he denied having ordered anything from Parkson's in June. In fact, on June 29th, he had been staying away, in Wales.

Instantly, Sir Ernest's chin was shooting pugnaciously forward.

'You deny having ordered a black beard from Parkson's on June 29th?'

'I do.'

'Ah! In the event of anything happening to your brother, who will inherit Styles Court?'

The brutality of the question called a flush to Lawrence's pale face. The Judge gave vent to a faint murmur of disapprobation, and the prisoner in the dock leant forward angrily.

Heavywether cared nothing for his client's anger.

'Answer my question, if you please.'

'I suppose,' said Lawrence quietly, 'that I should.'

'What do you mean by you "suppose"? Your brother has no children. You *would* inherit it, wouldn't you?'

'Yes.'

'Ah, that's better,' said Heavywether, with ferocious geniality. 'And you'd inherit a good slice of money too, wouldn't you?'

'Really, Sir Ernest,' protested the Judge, 'these questions are not relevant.'

Sir Ernest bowed, and having shot his arrow proceeded.

'On Tuesday, the 17th July, you went, I believe, with another guest, to visit the dispensary at the Red Cross Hospital in Tadminster?'

'Yes.'

'Did you – while you happened to be alone for a few seconds – unlock the poison cupboard, and examine some of the bottles?'

'I – I – may have done so.'

'I put it to you that you did do so.'

'Yes.'

Sir Ernest fairly shot the next question at him.

'Did you examine one bottle in particular?'

'No, I do not think so.'

'Be careful, Mr Cavendish, I am referring to a little bottle of Hydro-chloride of Strychnine.'

Lawrence was turning a sickly greenish colour.

'N – o – I am sure I didn't.'

'Then how do you account for the fact that you left the unmistakable impress of your finger-prints on it?'

The bullying manner was highly efficacious with a nervous disposition.

'I – I suppose I must have taken up the bottle.'

'I suppose so too! Did you abstract any of the contents of the bottle?'

'Certainly not.'

'Then why did you take it up?'

'I once studied to be a doctor. Such things naturally interest me.'

'Ah! So poisons "naturally interest" you, do they? Still, you waited to be alone before gratifying that "interest" of yours?'

'That was pure chance. If the others had been there, I should have done just the same.'

'Still, as it happens, the others were not there?'

'No, but –'

'In fact, during the whole afternoon, you were only alone for a couple of minutes, and it happened – I say, it happened – to be during those two minutes that you displayed your "natural interest" in Hydro-chloride of Strychnine?'

Lawrence stammered pitiably.

'I – I –'

With a satisfied and expressive countenance, Sir Ernest observed:

'I have nothing more to ask you, Mr Cavendish.'

This bit of cross-examination had caused great excitement

in court. The heads of the many fashionably attired women present were busily laid together, and their whispers became so loud that the Judge angrily threatened to have the court cleared if there was not immediate silence.

There was little more evidence. The handwriting experts were called upon for their opinion of the signature of 'Alfred Inglethorp' in the chemist's poison register. They all declared unanimously that it was certainly not his handwriting, and gave it as their view that it might be that of the prisoner disguised. Cross-examined, they admitted that it might be the prisoner's handwriting cleverly counterfeited.

Sir Ernest Heavywether's speech in opening the case for the defence was not a long one, but it was backed by the full force of his emphatic manner. Never, he said, in the course of his long experience, had he known a charge of murder rest on slighter evidence. Not only was it entirely circumstantial, but the greater part of it was practically unproved. Let them take the testimony they had heard and sift it impartially. The strychnine had been found in a drawer in the prisoner's room. That drawer was an unlocked one, as he had pointed out, and he submitted that there was no evidence to prove that it was the prisoner who had concealed the poison there. It was, in fact, a wicked and malicious attempt on the part of some third person to fix the crime on the prisoner. The prosecution had been unable to produce a shred of evidence in support of their contention that it was the prisoner who ordered the black beard from Parkson's. The quarrel which had taken place between the prisoner and his stepmother was freely admitted, but both it and his financial embarrassments had been grossly exaggerated.

His learned friend – Sir Ernest nodded carelessly at Mr Philips – had stated that if the prisoner were an innocent man, he would have come forward at the inquest to explain that it was he, and not Mr Inglethorp, who had been the participator in the quarrel. He thought the facts had been misrepresented. What had actually occurred was this. The prisoner, returning to the house on Tuesday evening, had been authoritatively told that there had been a violent quarrel between Mr and Mrs Inglethorp. No suspicion had entered the prisoner's head that anyone could possibly have mistaken his voice for that of Mr Inglethorp. He naturally concluded that his stepmother had had two quarrels.

The prosecution averred that on Monday, July 16th, the prisoner had entered the chemist's shop in the village, disguised as Mr Inglethorp. The prisoner, on the contrary, was at that time at a lonely spot called Marston's Spinney, where he had been summoned by an anonymous note, couched in blackmailing terms, and threatening to reveal certain matters to his wife unless he complied with its demands. The prisoner had, accordingly, gone to the appointed spot, and after waiting there vainly for half an hour had returned home. Unfortunately, he had met with no one on the way there or back who could vouch for the truth of his story, but luckily he had kept the note, and it would be produced as evidence.

As for the statement relating to the destruction of the will, the prisoner had formerly practised at the Bar, and was perfectly well aware that the will made in his favour a year before was automatically revoked by his stepmother's re-marriage. He would call evidence to show who did destroy the will, and it was possible that that might open up quite a new view of the case.

Finally, he would point out to the jury that there was evidence against other people besides John Cavendish. He would direct their attention to the fact that the evidence against Mr Lawrence Cavendish was quite as strong, if not stronger than that against his brother.

He would now call the prisoner.

John acquitted himself well in the witness-box. Under Sir Ernest's skilful handling, he told his tale credibly and well. The anonymous note received by him was produced, and handed to the jury to examine. The readiness with which he admitted his financial difficulties, and the disagreement with his stepmother, lent value to his denials.

At the close of his examination, he paused, and said:

'I should like to make one thing clear. I utterly reject and disapprove of Sir Ernest Heavywether's insinuations against my brother. My brother, I am convinced, had no more to do with the crime than I have.'

Sir Ernest merely smiled, and noted with a sharp eye that John's protest had produced a very favourable impression on the jury.

Then the cross-examination began.

'I understand you to say that it never entered your head that the witnesses at the inquest could possibly have mistaken your voice for that of Mr Inglethorp. Is not that very surprising?'

'No, I don't think so. I was told there had been a quarrel between my mother and Mr Inglethorp, and it never occurred to me that such was not really the case.'

'Not when the servant Dorcas repeated certain fragments of the conversation – fragments which you must have recognized?'

'I did not recognize them.'

'Your memory must be unusually short!'

'No, but we were both angry, and, I think, said more than we meant. I paid very little attention to my mother's actual words.'

Mr Philips's incredulous sniff was a triumph of forensic skill. He passed on to the subject of the note.

'You have produced this note very opportunely. Tell me, is there nothing familiar about the handwriting of it?'

'Not that I know of.'

'Do you not think that it bears a marked resemblance to your own handwriting – carelessly disguised?'

'No, I do not think so.'

'I put it to you that it is your own handwriting!'

'No.'

'I put it to you that, anxious to prove an alibi, you conceived the idea of a fictitious and rather incredible appointment, and wrote this note yourself in order to bear out your statement!'

'No.'

'Is it not a fact that, at the time you claim to have been waiting about at a solitary and unfrequented spot, you were really in the chemist's shop in Styles St Mary, where you purchased strychnine in the name of Alfred Inglethorp?'

'No, that is a lie.'

'I put it to you that, wearing a suit of Mr Inglethorp's clothes, with a black beard trimmed to resemble his, you were there – and signed the register in his name!'

'That is absolutely untrue.'

'Then I will leave the remarkable similarity of handwriting between the note, the register, and your own, to the consideration of the jury,' said Mr Philips, and sat down with the air of a man who had done his duty, but who was nevertheless horrified by such deliberate perjury.

After this, as it was growing late, the case was adjourned till Monday.

Poirot, I noticed, was looking profoundly discouraged. He had that little frown between the eyes that I knew so well.

'What is it, Poirot?' I inquired.

'Ah, *mon ami*, things are going badly, badly.'

In spite of myself, my heart gave a leap of relief. Evidently there was a likelihood of John Cavendish being acquitted.

When we reached the house, my little friend waved aside Mary's offer of tea.

'No, I thank you, madame. I will mount to my room.'

I followed him. Still frowning, he went across to the desk and took out a small pack of patience cards. Then he drew up a chair to the table, and to my utter amazement, began solemnly to build card houses!

My jaw dropped involuntarily, and he said at once:

'No, *mon ami*, I am not in my second childhood! I steady my nerves, that is all. This employment requires precision of the fingers. With precision of the fingers goes precision of the brain. And never have I needed that more than now!'

'What is the trouble?' I asked.

With a great thump on the table, Poirot demolished his carefully built-up edifice.

'It is this, *mon ami*! That I can build card houses seven storeys high, but I cannot' – thump – 'find' – thump – 'that last link of which I spoke to you.'

I could not quite tell what to say, so I held my peace, and he began slowly building up the cards again, speaking in jerks as he did so.

'It is done – so! By placing – one card – on another – with mathematical – precision!'

I watched the card house rising under his hands, storey by storey. He never hesitated or faltered. It was really almost like a conjuring trick.

'What a steady hand you've got,' I remarked. 'I believe I've only seen your hand shake once.'

'On an occasion when I was enraged, without doubt,' observed Poirot, with great placidity.

'Yes, indeed! You were in a towering rage. Do you remember? It was when you discovered that the lock of the despatch-case in Mrs Inglethorp's bedroom had been forced. You stood by the mantelpiece, twiddling the things on it in your usual fashion, and your hand shook like a leaf! I must say –'

But I stopped suddenly. For Poirot, uttering a hoarse and inarticulate cry, again annihilated his masterpiece of cards, and putting his hands over his eyes swayed backwards and forwards, apparently suffering the keenest agony.

'Good heavens, Poirot!' I cried. 'What is the matter? Are you taken ill?'

'No, no,' he gasped. 'It is – it is – that I have an idea!'

'Oh!' I exclaimed, much relieved. 'One of your "little ideas"?'

'Ah, *ma foi*, no!' replied Poirot frankly. 'This time it is an idea gigantic! Stupendous! And you – *you*, my friend, have given it to me!'

Suddenly clasping me in his arms, he kissed me warmly on both cheeks, and before I had recovered from my surprise ran headlong from the room.

Mary Cavendish entered at that moment.

'What *is* the matter with Monsieur Poirot? He rushed past

me crying out: "A garage! For the love of Heaven, direct me to a garage, madame!" And, before I could answer, he had dashed out into the street.'

I hurried to the window. True enough, there he was, tearing down the street, hatless, and gesticulating as he went. I turned to Mary with a gesture of despair.

'He'll be stopped by a policeman in another minute. There he goes, round the corner!'

Our eyes met, and we stared helplessly at one another.

'What can be the matter?'

I shook my head.

'I don't know. He was building card houses, when suddenly he said he had an idea, and rushed off as you saw.'

'Well,' said Mary, 'I expect he will be back before dinner.'

But night fell, and Poirot had not returned.

CHAPTER XII

The Last Link

Poirot's abrupt departure had intrigued us all greatly. Sunday morning wore away, and still he did not reappear. But about three o'clock a ferocious and prolonged hooting outside drove us to the window, to see Poirot alighting from a car, accompanied by Japp and Summerhaye. The little man was transformed. He radiated an absurd complacency. He bowed with exaggerated respect to Mary Cavendish.

'Madame, I have your permission to hold a little *réunion* in the *salon*? It is necessary for everyone to attend.'

Mary smiled sadly.

'You know, Monsieur Poirot, that you have *carte blanche* in every way.'

'You are too amiable, madame.'

Still beaming, Poirot marshalled us all into the dining-room, bringing forward chairs as he did so.

'Miss Howard – here. Mademoiselle Cynthia. Monsieur Lawrence. The good Dorcas. And Annie. *Bien!* We must delay our proceedings a few minutes more until Mr Inglethorp arrives. I have sent him a note.'

Miss Howard rose immediately from her seat.

'If that man comes into the house, I leave it!'

'No, no!' Poirot went up to her and pleaded in a low voice.

Finally Miss Howard consented to return to her chair. A few minutes later Alfred Inglethorp entered the room.

The company once assembled, Poirot rose from his seat with the air of a popular lecturer, and bowed politely to his audience.

'*Messieurs, mesdames*, as you all know, I was called in by Monsieur John Cavendish to investigate this case. I at once examined the bedroom of the deceased which, by the advice of the doctors, had been kept locked, and was consequently exactly as it had been when the tragedy occurred. I found: first, a fragment of green material; secondly, a stain on the carpet near the window, still damp; thirdly, an empty box of bromide powders.

'To take the fragment of green material first, I found it caught in the bolt of the communicating door between that room and the adjoining one occupied by Mademoiselle Cynthia. I handed the fragment over to the police who did not consider it of much importance. Nor did they recognize it for what it was – a piece torn from a green land armlet.'

There was a little stir of excitement.

'Now there was only one person at Styles who worked on the land – Mrs Cavendish. Therefore it must have been Mrs Cavendish who entered the deceased's room through the door communicating with Mademoiselle Cynthia's room.'

'But that door was bolted on the inside!' I cried.

'When I examined the room, yes. But in the first place we have only her word for it, since it was she who tried that particular door and reported it fastened. In the ensuing confusion she would have had ample opportunity to shoot the bolt across. I took an early opportunity of verifying my conjectures. To begin with, the fragment corresponds exactly with a tear in Mrs Cavendish's armlet. Also, at the inquest, Mrs Cavendish declared that she had heard, from her own room, the fall of the table by the bed. I took an early opportunity of testing that statement by stationing my friend Monsieur Hastings, in the left wing of the building, just outside Mrs Cavendish's door. I myself, in company with the police, went to the deceased's room, and whilst there I, apparently accidentally, knocked over the table in question, but found that, as I had expected, Monsieur Hastings had heard no sound at all. This confirmed my belief that Mrs Cavendish was not speaking the truth when she declared that she had been dressing in her room at the time of the tragedy. In fact, I was convinced that, far from having been in her own room, Mrs Cavendish was actually in the deceased's room when the alarm was given.'

I shot a quick glance at Mary. She was very pale, but smiling.

'I proceeded to reason on that assumption. Mrs Cavendish is in her mother-in-law's room. We will say that she is seeking for something and has not yet found it. Suddenly Mrs Inglethorp awakens and is seized with an alarming paroxysm. She flings out her arm, overturning the bed table, and then pulls desperately at the bell. Mrs Cavendish, startled, drops her candle, scattering the grease on the carpet. She picks it up, and retreats quickly to Mademoiselle Cynthia's room, closing the door behind her. She hurries out into the passage, for the servants must not find her where she is. But it is too late! Already footsteps are echoing along the gallery which connects the two wings. What can she do? Quick as thought, she hurries back to the young girl's room, and starts shaking her awake. The hastily aroused household come trooping down the passage. They are all busily battering at Mrs Inglethorp's door. It occurs to nobody that Mrs Cavendish has not arrived with the rest, but – and this is significant – I can find no one who saw her come from the other wing.' He looked at Mary Cavendish. 'Am I right, madame?'

She bowed her head.

'Quite right, monsieur. You understand that, if I had thought I would do my husband any good by revealing these facts, I would have done so. But it did not seem to me to bear upon the question of his guilt or innocence.'

'In a sense, that is correct, madame. But it cleared my mind of many misconceptions, and left me free to see other facts in their true significance.'

'The will!' cried Lawrence. 'Then it was you, Mary, who destroyed the will?'

She shook her head, and Poirot shook his also.

'No,' he said quietly. 'There is only one person who could possibly have destroyed that will – Mrs Inglethorp herself!'

'Impossible!' I exclaimed. 'She had only made it out that very afternoon!'

'Nevertheless, *mon ami*, it was Mrs Inglethorp. Because, in no other way can you account for the fact that, on one of the hottest days of the year, Mrs Inglethorp ordered a fire to be lighted in her room.'

I gave a gasp. What idiots we had been never to think of that fire as being incongruous! Poirot was continuing:

'The temperature on that day, messieurs, was 80° in the shade. Yet Mrs Inglethorp ordered a fire! Why? Because she wished to destroy something, and could think of no other way. You will remember that, in consequence of the War economies practised at Styles, no waste paper was thrown away. There was, therefore, no means of destroying a thick document such as a will. The moment I heard of a fire being lighted in Mrs Inglethorp's room, I leaped to the conclusion that it was to destroy some important document – possibly a will. So the discovery of the charred fragment in the grate was no surprise to me. I did not, of course, know at the time that the will in question had only been made that afternoon, and I will admit that, when I learnt that fact, I fell into a grievous error. I came to the conclusion that Mrs Inglethorp's determination to destroy her will arose as a direct consequence of the quarrel she had that afternoon, and that therefore the quarrel took place after, and not before, the making of the will.

'Here, as we know, I was wrong, and I was forced to abandon that idea. I faced the problem from a new standpoint. Now, at 4 o'clock, Dorcas overheard her mistress saying angrily: "You need not think that any fear of publicity, or scandal between husband and wife will deter me." I conjectured, and conjectured rightly, that these words were addressed, not to her husband, but to Mr John Cavendish. At 5 o'clock, an hour later, she uses almost the same words, but the standpoint is different. She admits to Dorcas, "I don't know what to do; scandal between husband and wife is a dreadful thing." At 4 o'clock she has been angry, but completely mistress of herself. At 5 o'clock she is in violent distress, and speaks of having had a "great shock".

'Looking at the matter psychologically, I drew one deduction which I was convinced was correct. The second "scandal" she spoke of was not the same as the first – and it concerned herself!

'Let us reconstruct. At 4 o'clock, Mrs Inglethorp quarrels with her son, and threatens to denounce him to his wife – who, by the way, overheard the greater part of the conversation. At 4.30, Mrs Inglethorp, in consequence of a conversation on the validity of wills, makes a will in favour of her husband, which the two gardeners witness. At 5 o'clock, Dorcas finds her mistress in a state of considerable agitation, with a slip of paper – "a letter", Dorcas thinks – in her hand, and it is then that she orders the fire in her room to be lighted. Presumably, then, between 4.30 and 5 o'clock, something has occurred to occasion a complete revolution of feeling, since she is now as anxious to destroy the will as she was before to make it. What was that something?

'As far as we know, she was quite alone during that half-hour. Nobody entered or left that boudoir. What then occasioned this sudden change of sentiment?

'One can only guess, but I believe my guess to be correct. Mrs Inglethorp had no stamps in her desk. We know this, because later she asked Dorcas to bring her some. Now in the opposite corner of the room stood her husband's desk – locked. She was anxious to find some stamps, and, according to my theory, she tried her own keys in the desk. That one of them fitted I know. She therefore opened the desk, and in searching for the stamps she came across something else – that slip of paper which Dorcas saw in her hand, and which assuredly was never meant for Mrs Inglethorp's eyes. On the other hand, Mrs Cavendish believed that the slip of paper to which her mother-in-law clung so tenaciously was a written proof of her own husband's infidelity. She demanded it from Mrs Inglethorp who assured her, quite truly, that it had nothing to do with that matter. Mrs Cavendish did not believe her. She thought that Mrs Inglethorp was shielding her stepson. Now Mrs Cavendish is a very resolute woman, and, behind her mask of reserve, she was madly jealous of her husband. She determined to get hold of that paper at all costs, and in this resolution chance came to her aid. She happened to pick up the key of Mrs Inglethorp's despatch-case, which had been lost that morning. She knew that her mother-in-law invariably kept all important papers in this particular case.

'Mrs Cavendish, therefore, made her plans as only a woman driven desperate through jealousy could have done. Some time in the evening she unbolted the door leading into Mademoiselle Cynthia's room. Possibly she applied oil to the hinges, for I found that it opened quite noiselessly when I tried it. She put off her project until the early hours of the morning as being safer, since the servants were accustomed to hearing her move about her room at that time. She dressed completely in her land kit, and made her way quietly through Mademoiselle Cynthia's room into that of Mrs Inglethorp.'

He paused a moment, and Cynthia interrupted:

'But I should have woken up if anyone had come through my room?'

'Not if you were drugged, mademoiselle.'

'Drugged?'

'*Mais, oui!*

'You remember' – he addressed us collectively again – 'that through all the tumult and noise next door Mademoiselle Cynthia slept. That admitted of two possibilities. Either her sleep was feigned – which I did not believe – or her unconsciousness was induced by artificial means.

'With this latter idea in my mind, I examined all the coffee-cups most carefully, remembering that it was Mrs Cavendish who had brought Mademoiselle Cynthia her coffee the night before. I took a sample from each cup, and had them analysed – with no result. I had counted the cups carefully, in the event of one having been removed. Six persons had taken coffee, and six cups were duly found. I had to confess myself mistaken.

'Then I discovered that I had been guilty of a very grave oversight. Coffee had been brought in for seven persons, not six, for Dr Bauerstein had been there that evening. This changed the face of the whole affair, for there was now one cup missing. The servants noticed nothing, since Annie, the housemaid, who took in the coffee, brought in seven cups, not knowing that Mr Inglethorp never drank it, whereas Dorcas, who cleared them away the following morning, found six as usual – or strictly speaking she found five, the sixth being the one found broken in Mrs Inglethorp's room.

'I was confident that the missing cup was that of Mademoiselle Cynthia. I had an additional reason for that belief in the fact that all the cups found contained sugar, which Mademoiselle Cynthia never took in her coffee. My attention was attracted by the story of Annie about some "salt" on the tray of cocoa which she took every night to Mrs Inglethorp's room. I accordingly secured a sample of that cocoa, and sent it to be analysed.'

'But that had already been done by Dr Bauerstein,' said Lawrence quickly.

'Not exactly. The analyst was asked by him to report whether strychnine was, or was not, present. He did not have it tested, as I did, for a narcotic.'

'For a narcotic?'

'Yes. Here is the analyst's report. Mrs Cavendish administered a safe, but effectual, narcotic to both Mrs Inglethorp and Mademoiselle Cynthia. And it is possible that she had a *mauvais quart d'heure* in consequence! Imagine her feelings when her mother-in-law is suddenly taken ill and dies, and immediately after she hears the word "Poison"! She has believed that the sleeping draught she administered was perfectly harmless, but there is no doubt that for one terrible moment she must have feared that Mrs Inglethorp's death lay at her door. She is seized with panic, and under its influence she hurries downstairs, and quickly drops the coffee-cup and saucer used by Mademoiselle Cynthia into a large brass vase, where it is discovered later by Monsieur Lawrence. The remains of the cocoa she dare not touch. Too many eyes are upon her. Guess at her relief when strychnine is mentioned, and she discovers that after all the tragedy is not her doing.

'We are now able to account for the symptoms of strychnine

poisoning being so long in making their appearance. A narcotic taken with strychnine will delay the action of the poison for some hours.'

Poirot paused. Mary looked up at him, the colour slowly rising in her face.

'All you have said is quite true, Monsieur Poirot. It was the most awful hour of my life. I shall never forget it. But you are wonderful. I understand now –'

'What I meant when I told you that you could safely confess to Papa Poirot, eh? But you would not trust me.'

'I see everything now,' said Lawrence. 'The drugged cocoa, taken on top of the poisoned coffee, amply accounts for the delay.'

'Exactly. But was the coffee poisoned, or was it not? We come to a little difficulty here, since Mrs Inglethorp never drank it.'

'What?' The cry of surprise was universal.

'No. You will remember my speaking of a stain on the carpet in Mrs Inglethorp's room? There were some peculiar points about that stain. It was still damp, it exhaled a strong odour of coffee, and imbedded in the nap of the carpet I found some little splinters of china. What had happened was plain to me, for not two minutes before I had placed my little case on the table near the window, and the table, tilting up, had deposited it upon the floor on precisely the identical spot. In exactly the same way, Mrs Inglethorp had laid down her cup of coffee on reaching her room the night before, and the treacherous table had played her the same trick.

'What happened next is mere guesswork on my part, but I should say that Mrs Inglethorp picked up the broken cup and placed it on the table by the bed. Feeling in need of a stimulant of some kind, she heated up her cocoa, and drank it off then and there. Now we are faced with a new problem. We know the cocoa contained no strychnine. The coffee was never drunk. Yet the strychnine must have been administered between seven and nine o'clock that evening. What third medium was there – a medium so suitable for disguising the taste of strychnine that it is extraordinary no one has thought of it?' Poirot looked around the room, and then answered himself impressively. 'Her medicine!'

'Do you mean that the murderer introduced the strychnine into her tonic?' I cried.

'There was no need to introduce it. It was already there – in the mixture. The strychnine that killed Mrs Inglethorp was the identical strychnine prescribed by Dr Wilkins. To make that clear to you, I will read you an extract from a book on dispensing which I found in the dispensary of the Red Cross Hospital at Tadminster:

'The following prescription has become famous in textbooks:

Strychninae Sulph	gr. 1
Potass Bromide	ʒvi
Aqua ad	ʒviii
Fiat Mistura	

This solution deposits in a few hours the greater part of the strychnine salt as an insoluble bromide in transparent crystals. A lady in England lost her life by taking a similar mixture: the precipitated strychnine collected at the bottom, and in taking the last dose she swallowed nearly all of it!

'Now there was, of course, no bromide in Dr Wilkins's prescription, but you will remember that I mentioned an empty box of bromide powders. One or two of those powders introduced into the full bottle of medicine would effectually precipitate the strychnine, as the book describes, and cause it to be taken in the last dose. You will learn later that the person who usually poured out Mrs Inglethorp's medicine was always extremely careful not to shake the bottle, but to leave the sediment at the bottom of it undisturbed.

'Throughout the case, there have been evidences that the tragedy was intended to take place on Monday evening. On that day, Mrs Inglethorp's bell wire was neatly cut, and on Monday evening Mademoiselle Cynthia was spending the night with friends, so that Mrs Inglethorp would have been quite alone in the right wing, completely shut off from help of any kind, and would have died, in all probability, before medical aid could have been summoned. But in her hurry to be in time for the village entertainment Mrs Inglethorp forgot to take her medicine, and the next day she lunched away from home, so that the last – and fatal – dose was actually taken twenty-four hours later than had been anticipated by the murderer; and it is owing to that delay that the final proof – the last link of the chain – is now in my hands.'

Amid breathless excitement, he held out three thin strips of paper.

'A letter in the murderer's own handwriting, *mes amis*! Had it been a little clearer in its terms, it is possible that Mrs Inglethorp, warned in time, would have escaped. As it was, she realized her danger, but not the manner of it.'

In the deathly silence, Poirot pieced together the slips of paper and, clearing his throat, read:

'Dearest Evelyn,

   You will be anxious at hearing nothing. It is all right – only it will be tonight instead of last night. You understand. There's a good time coming once the old woman is dead and out of the way. No one can possibly bring home the crime to me. That idea of yours about the bromides was a stroke of genius! But we must be very circumspect. A false step –

'Here, my friends, the letter breaks off. Doubtless the writer was interrupted; but there can be no question as to his identity. We all know his handwriting and –'

A howl that was almost a scream broke the silence.

'You devil! How did you get it?'

A chair was overturned. Poirot skipped nimbly aside. A quick movement on his part, and his assailant fell with a crash.

'*Messieurs, mesdames*,' said Poirot, with a flourish, 'let me introduce you to the murderer, Mr Alfred Inglethorp!'

CHAPTER XIII

Poirot Explains

'Poirot, you old villain,' I said, 'I've half a mind to strangle you! What do you mean by deceiving me as you have done?'

We were sitting in the library. Several hectic days lay behind us. In the room below, John and Mary were together once more, while Alfred Inglethorp and Miss Howard were in custody. Now at last, I had Poirot to myself, and could relieve my still burning curiosity.

Poirot did not answer me for a moment, but at last he said:

'I did not deceive you, *mon ami*. At most, I permitted you to deceive yourself.'

'Yes, but why?'

'Well, it is difficult to explain. You see, my friend, you have a nature so honest, and a countenance so transparent, that – *enfin*, to conceal your feelings is impossible! If I had told you my ideas, the very first time you saw Mr Alfred Inglethorp that astute gentleman would have – in your so expressive idiom – "smelt a rat"! And then, *bonjour* to our chances of catching him!'

'I think that I have more diplomacy than you give me credit for.'

'My friend,' besought Poirot, 'I implore you, do not enrage yourself! Your help has been of the most invaluable. It is but the extremely beautiful nature that you have which made me pause.'

'Well,' I grumbled, a little mollified, 'I still think you might have given me a hint.'

'But I did, my friend. Several hints. You would not take them. Think now, did I ever say to you that I believed John

Cavendish guilty? Did I not, on the contrary, tell you that he would almost certainly be acquitted?'

'Yes, but –'

'And did I not immediately afterwards speak of the difficulty of bringing the murderer to justice? Was it not plain to you that I was speaking of two entirely different persons?'

'No,' I said, 'it was not plain to me!'

'Then again,' continued Poirot, 'at the beginning, did I not repeat to you several times that I didn't want Mr Inglethorp arrested *now*? That should have conveyed something to you.'

'Do you mean to say you suspected him as long ago as that?'

'Yes. To begin with, whoever else might benefit by Mrs Inglethorp's death, her husband would benefit the most. There was no getting away from that. When I went up to Styles with you that first day, I had no idea as to how the crime had been committed, but from what I knew of Mr Inglethorp I fancied that it would be very hard to find anything to connect him with it. When I arrived at the château, I realized at once that it was Mrs Inglethorp who had burnt the will; and there, by the way, you cannot complain, my friend, for I tried my best to force on you the significance of that bedroom fire in mid-summer.'

'Yes, yes,' I said impatiently. 'Go on.'

'Well, my friend, as I say, my views as to Mr Inglethorp's guilt were very much shaken. There was, in fact, so much evidence against him that I was inclined to believe that he had not done it.'

'When did you change your mind?'

'When I found that the more efforts I made to clear him, the more efforts he made to get himself arrested. Then, when I discovered that Inglethorp had nothing to do with Mrs Raikes, and that in fact it was John Cavendish who was interested in that quarter, I was quite sure.'

'But why?'

'Simply this. If it had been Inglethorp who was carrying on an intrigue with Mrs Raikes, his silence was perfectly comprehensible. But, when I discovered that it was known all over the village that it was John who was attracted by the farmer's pretty wife, his silence bore quite a different interpretation. It was nonsense to pretend that he was afraid of the scandal, as no possible scandal could attach to him. This attitude of his gave me furiously to think, and I was slowly forced to the conclusion that Alfred Inglethorp wanted to be arrested. *Eh bien!* from that moment, I was equally determined that he should not be arrested.'

'Wait a moment. I don't see why he wished to be arrested?'

'Because, *mon ami*, it is the law of your country that a man once acquitted can never be tried again for the same offence. Aha! but it was clever – his idea! Assuredly, he is a man of method. See here, he knew that in his position he was bound to be suspected, so he conceived the exceedingly clever idea of preparing a lot of manufactured evidence against himself. He wished to be suspected. He wished to be arrested. He would then produce his irreproachable alibi – and, hey presto, he was safe for life!'

'But I still don't see how he managed to prove his alibi, and yet go to the chemist's shop?'

Poirot stared at me in surprise.

'Is it possible? My poor friend! You have not yet realized that it was Miss Howard who went to the chemist's shop?'

'Miss Howard?'

'But, certainly. Who else? It was most easy for her. She is of a good height, her voice is deep and manly; moreover, remember, she and Inglethorp are cousins, and there is a distinct resemblance between them, especially in their gait and bearing. It was simplicity itself. They are a clever pair!'

'I am still a little fogged as to how exactly the bromide business was done,' I remarked.

'*Bon!* I will reconstruct for you as far as possible. I am inclined to think that Miss Howard was the master mind in that affair. You remember her once mentioning that her father was a doctor? Possibly she dispensed his medicines for him, or she may have taken the idea from one of the many books lying about when Mademoiselle Cynthia was studying for her exam. Anyway, she was familiar with the fact that the addition of a bromide to a mixture containing strychnine would cause the precipitation of the latter. Probably the idea came to her quite suddenly. Mrs Inglethorp had a box of bromide powders, which she occasionally took at night. What could be easier than quietly to dissolve one or more of those powders in Mrs Inglethorp's large-sized bottle of medicine when it came from Coot's? The risk is practically nil. The tragedy will not take place until nearly a fortnight later. If anyone has seen either of them touching the medicine, they will have forgotten it by that time. Miss Howard will have engineered her quarrel, and departed from the house. The lapse of time, and her absence, will defeat all suspicion. Yes, it was a clever idea! If they had left it alone, it is possible the crime might never have been brought home to them. But they were not satisfied. They tried to be too clever – and that was their undoing.'

Poirot puffed at his tiny cigarette, his eyes fixed on the ceiling.

'They arranged a plan to throw suspicion on John Cavendish, by buying strychnine at the village chemist's, and signing the register in his handwriting.

'On Monday Mrs Inglethorp will take the last dose of her medicine. On Monday, therefore, at six o'clock, Alfred Inglethorp arranges to be seen by a number of people at a spot far removed from the village. Miss Howard has previously made up a cock-and-bull story about him and Mrs Raikes to account for his holding his tongue afterwards. At six o'clock, Miss Howard, disguised as Alfred Inglethorp, enters the chemist's shop, with her story about a dog, obtains the strychnine, and writes the name of Alfred Inglethorp in John's handwriting, which she had previously studied carefully.

'But, as it will never do if John, too, can prove an alibi, she writes him an anonymous note – still copying his handwriting – which takes him to a remote spot where it is exceedingly unlikely that anyone will see him.

'So far, all goes well. Miss Howard goes back to Middlingham. Alfred Inglethorp returns to Styles. There is nothing that can compromise him in any way, since it is Miss Howard who has the strychnine, which, after all, is only wanted as a blind to throw suspicion on John Cavendish.

'But now a hitch occurs. Mrs Inglethorp does not take her medicine that night. The broken bell, Cynthia's absence – arranged by Inglethorp through his wife – all these are wasted. And then – he makes his slip.

'Mrs Inglethorp is out, and he sits down to write to his accomplice, who, he fears, may be in a panic at the non-success of their plan. It is probable that Mrs Inglethorp returned earlier than he expected. Caught in the act, and somewhat flurried, he hastily shuts and locks his desk. He fears that if he remains in the room he may have to open it again, and that Mrs Inglethorp might catch sight of the letter before he could snatch it up. So he goes out and walks in the woods, little dreaming that Mrs Inglethorp will open his desk, and discover the incriminating document.

'But this, as we know, is what happened. Mrs Inglethorp reads it, and becomes aware of the perfidy of her husband and Evelyn Howard, though, unfortunately, the sentence about the bromide conveys no warning to her mind. She knows that she is in danger – but is ignorant of where the danger lies. She decides to say nothing to her husband, but sits down and writes to her solicitor, asking him to come on the morrow, and she also determines to destroy immediately the will which she has just made. She keeps the fatal letter.'

'It was to discover that letter, then, that her husband forced the lock of the despatch-case?'

'Yes, and from the enormous risk he ran we can see how fully he realized its importance. That letter excepted, there was absolutely nothing to connect him with the crime.'

'There's only one thing I can't make out, why didn't he destroy it at once when he got hold of it?'

'Because he did not dare take the biggest risk of all – that of keeping it on his own person.'

'I don't understand.'

'Look at it from his point of view. I have discovered that

there were only five short minutes in which he could have taken it – the five minutes immediately before our own arrival on the scene, for before that time Annie was brushing the stairs, and would have seen anyone who passed going to the right wing. Figure to yourself the scene! He enters the room, unlocking the door by means of one of the other door-keys – they were all much alike. He hurries to the despatch-case – it is locked, and the keys are nowhere to be seen. That is a terrible blow to him, for it means that his presence in the room cannot be concealed as he had hoped. But he sees clearly that everything must be risked for the sake of that damning piece of evidence. Quickly, he forces the lock with a penknife, and turns over the papers until he finds what he is looking for.

'But now a fresh dilemma arises: he dare not keep that piece of paper on him. He may be seen leaving the room – he may be searched. If the paper is found on him, it is certain doom. Probably, at this minute, too, he hears the sounds below of Mr Wells and John leaving the boudoir. He must act quickly. Where can he hide this terrible slip of paper? The contents of the waste-paper basket are kept and, in any case, are sure to be examined. There are no means of destroying it; and he dare not keep it. He looks round, and he sees – what do you think, *mon ami?*'

I shook my head.

'In a moment, he has torn the letter into long thin strips, and rolling them up into spills he thrusts them hurriedly in amongst the other spills in the vase on the mantelpiece.'

I uttered an exclamation.

'No one would think of looking there,' Poirot continued. 'And he will be able, at his leisure, to come back and destroy this solitary piece of evidence against him.'

'Then, all the time, it was in the spill vase in Mrs Inglethorp's bedroom, under our very noses?' I cried.

Poirot nodded.

'Yes, my friend. That is where I discovered my "last link", and I owe that very fortunate discovery to you.'

'To me?'

'Yes. Do you remember telling me that my hand shook as I was straightening the ornaments on the mantelpiece?'

'Yes, but I don't see –'

'No, but I saw. Do you know, my friend, I remembered that earlier in the morning, when we had been there together, I had straightened all the objects on the mantelpiece. And, if they were already straightened, there would be no need to straighten them again, unless, in the meantime, someone else had touched them.'

'Dear me,' I murmured, 'so that is the explanation of your extraordinary behaviour. You rushed down to Styles, and found it still there?'

'Yes, and it was a race for time.'

'But I still can't understand why Inglethorp was such a fool as to leave it there when he had plenty of opportunity to destroy it.'

'Ah, but he had no opportunity. *I* saw to that.'

'You?'

'Yes. Do you remember reproving me for taking the household into my confidence on the subject?'

'Yes.'

'Well, my friend, I saw there was just one chance. I was not sure then if Inglethorp was the criminal or not, but if he was I reasoned that he would not have the paper on him, but would have hidden it somewhere, and by enlisting the sympathy of the household I could effectually prevent his destroying it. He was already under suspicion, and by making the matter public I secured the services of about ten amateur detectives, who would be watching him unceasingly, and being himself aware of their watchfulness he would not dare seek further to destroy the document. He was, therefore, forced to depart from the house, leaving it in the spill vase.'

'But surely Miss Howard had ample opportunities of aiding him.'

'Yes, but Miss Howard did not know of the paper's existence. In accordance with their pre-arranged plan, she never spoke to Alfred Inglethorp. They were supposed to be deadly enemies, and until John Cavendish was safely convicted they neither of them dared risk a meeting. Of course, I had a watch kept on Mr Inglethorp, hoping that sooner or later he would lead me to the hiding-place. But he was too clever to take any chances. The paper was safe where it was; since no one had thought of looking there in the first week, it was not likely they would do so afterwards. But for your lucky remark, we might never have been able to bring him to justice.'

'I understand that now; but when did you first begin to suspect Miss Howard?'

'When I discovered that she had told a lie at the inquest about the letter she had received from Mrs Inglethorp.'

'Why, what was there to lie about?'

'You saw that letter? Do you recall its general appearance?'

'Yes – more or less.'

'You will recollect, then, that Mrs Inglethorp wrote a very distinctive hand, and left large clear spaces between her words. But if you look at the date at the top of the letter you will notice that "July 17th" is quite different in this respect. Do you see what I mean?'

'No,' I confessed, 'I don't.'

'You do not see that that letter was not written on the 17th, but on the 7th – the day after Miss Howard's departure? The "1" was written in before the "7" to turn it into the "17th".'

'But why?'

'That is exactly what I asked myself. Why does Miss Howard suppress the letter written on the 17th, and produce this faked one instead? Because she did not wish to show the letter of the 17th. Why, again? Again at once a suspicion dawned in my mind. You will remember my saying that it was wise to beware of people who were not telling you the truth.'

'And yet,' I cried indignantly, 'after that, you gave me two reasons why Miss Howard could not have committed the crime!'

'And very good reasons too,' replied Poirot. 'For a long time they were a stumbling-block to me until I remembered a very significant fact: that she and Alfred Inglethorp were cousins. She could not have committed the crime single-handed, but the reasons against that did not debar her from being an accomplice. And, then, there was that rather over-vehement hatred of hers! It concealed a very opposite emotion. There was, undoubtedly, a tie of passion between them long before he came to Styles. They had already arranged their infamous plot – that he should marry this rich, but rather foolish old lady, induce her to make a will leaving her money to him, and then gain their ends by a very cleverly conceived crime. If all had gone as they planned, they would probably have left England, and lived together on their poor victim's money.

'They are a very astute and unscrupulous pair. While suspicion was to be directed against him, she would be making quiet preparations for a very different *dénouement*. She arrives from Middlingham with all the compromising items in her possession. No suspicion attaches to her. No notice is paid to her coming and going in the house. She hides the strychnine and glasses in John's room. She puts the beard in the attic. She will see to it that sooner or later they are duly discovered.'

'I don't quite see why they tried to fix the blame on John,' I remarked. 'It would have been much easier for them to bring the crime home to Lawrence.'

'Yes, but that was mere chance. All the evidence against him arose out of pure accident. It must, in fact, have been distinctly annoying to the pair of schemers.'

'His manner was unfortunate,' I observed thoughtfully.

'Yes. You realize, of course, what was at the back of that?'

'No.'

'You did not understand that he believed Mademoiselle Cynthia guilty of the crime?'

'No,' I exclaimed, astonished. 'Impossible!'

'Not at all. I myself nearly had the same idea. It was in my mind when I asked Mr Wells that first question about the will. Then there were the bromide powders which she had made up, and her clever male impersonations, as Dorcas recounted them to us. There was really more evidence against her than anyone else.'

'You are joking, Poirot!'

'No. Shall I tell you what made Monsieur Lawrence turn so pale when he first entered his mother's room on the fatal night? It was because, whilst his mother lay there, obviously poisoned, he saw, over your shoulder, that the door into Mademoiselle Cynthia's room was unbolted.'

'But he declared that he saw it bolted!' I cried.

'Exactly,' said Poirot dryly. 'And that was just what confirmed my suspicion that it was not. He was shielding Mademoiselle Cynthia.'

'But why should he shield her?'

'Because he is in love with her.'

I laughed.

'There, Poirot, you are quite wrong! I happen to know for a fact that, far from being in love with her, he positively dislikes her.'

'Who told you that, *mon ami*?'

'Cynthia herself.'

'*La pauvre petite!* And she was concerned?'

'She said that she did not mind at all.'

'Then she certainly did mind very much,' remarked Poirot. 'They are like that – *les femmes*!'

'What you say about Lawrence is a great surprise to me,' I said.

'But why? It was most obvious. Did not Monsieur Lawrence make the sour face every time Mademoiselle Cynthia spoke and laughed with his brother? He had taken it into his long head that Mademoiselle Cynthia was in love with Monsieur John. When he entered his mother's room, and saw her obviously poisoned, he jumped to the conclusion that Mademoiselle Cynthia knew something about the matter. He was nearly driven desperate. First he crushed the coffee-cup to powder under his feet, remembering that *she* had gone up with his mother the night before, and he determined that there should be no chance of testing its contents. Thenceforward, he strenuously, and quite uselessly, upheld the theory of "Death from natural causes".'

'And what about the "extra coffee-cup"?'

'I was fairly certain that it was Mrs Cavendish who had hidden it, but I had to make sure. Monsieur Lawrence did not know at all what I meant; but, on reflection, he came to the conclusion that if he could find an extra coffee-cup anywhere his lady love would be cleared of suspicion. And he was perfectly right.'

'One thing more. What did Mrs Inglethorp mean by her dying words?'

'They were, of course, an accusation against her husband.'

'Dear me, Poirot,' I said with a sigh, 'I think you have explained everything. I am glad it has all ended so happily. Even John and his wife are reconciled.'

'Thanks to me.'

'How do you mean – thanks to you?'

'My dear friend, do you realize that it was simply and solely the trial which has brought them together again? That John Cavendish still loved his wife, I was convinced. Also, that she was equally in love with him. But they had drifted very far apart. It all arose from a misunderstanding. She married him without love. He knew it. He is a sensitive man in his way, he would not force himself upon her if she did not want him. And, as he withdrew, her love awoke. But they are both unusually proud, and their pride held them inexorably apart. He drifted into an entanglement with Mrs Raikes, and she deliberately cultivated the friendship of Dr Bauerstein. Do you remember the day of John Cavendish's arrest, when you found me deliberating over a big decision?'

'Yes, I quite understood your distress.'

'Pardon me, *mon ami*, but you did not understand it in the least. I was trying to decide whether or not I would clear John Cavendish at once. I could have cleared him – though it might have meant a failure to convict the real criminals. They were entirely in the dark as to my real attitude up to the very last moment – which partly accounts for my success.'

'Do you mean that you could have saved John Cavendish from being brought to trial?'

'Yes, my friend. But I eventually decided in favour of "a woman's happiness". Nothing but the great danger through which they have passed could have brought these two proud souls together again.'

I looked at Poirot in silent amazement. The colossal cheek of the little man! Who on earth but Poirot would have thought of a trial for murder as a restorer of conjugal happiness!

'I perceive your thoughts, *mon ami*,' said Poirot, smiling at me. 'No one but Hercule Poirot would have attempted such a thing! And you are wrong in condemning it. The happiness of one man and woman is the greatest thing in all the world.'

His words took me back to earlier events. I remembered Mary as she lay white and exhausted on the sofa, listening, listening. There had come the sound of the bell below. She had started up. Poirot had opened the door, and meeting her agonized eyes had nodded gently. 'Yes, madame,' he said. 'I have brought him back to you.' He had stood aside, and as I went out I had seen the look in Mary's eyes, as John Cavendish had caught his wife in his arms.

'Perhaps you are right, Poirot,' I said gently. 'Yes, it is the greatest thing in the world.'

Suddenly, there was a tap at the door, and Cynthia peeped in.

'I – I – only –'

'Come in,' I said, springing up.

She came in, but did not sit down.

'I – only wanted to tell you something –'

'Yes?'

Cynthia fidgeted with a little tassel for some moments, then, suddenly exclaiming: 'You dears!' kissed first me and then Poirot, and rushed out of the room again.

'What on earth does this mean?' I asked, surprised.

It was very nice to be kissed by Cynthia, but the publicity of the salute rather impaired the pleasure.

'It means that she has discovered Monsieur Lawrence does

not dislike her as much as she thought,' replied Poirot philosophically.

'But –'

'Here he is.'

Lawrence at that moment passed the door.

'Eh! Monsieur Lawrence,' called Poirot. 'We must congratulate you, is it not so?'

Lawrence blushed, and then smiled awkwardly. A man in love is a sorry spectacle. Now Cynthia had looked charming.

I sighed.

'What is it, *mon ami*?'

'Nothing,' I said sadly. 'They are two delightful women!'

'And neither of them is for you?' finished Poirot. 'Never mind. Console yourself, my friend. We may hunt together again, who knows? And then –'

Postscript

'It was while working in the dispensary that I first conceived the idea of writing a detective story ... I began considering what kind of a detective story I could write. Since I was surrounded by poisons, perhaps it was natural that death by poisoning should be the method I selected.'

In her Autobiography *Agatha Christie writes extensively about the origins of* The Mysterious Affair at Styles, *her character research and her conception of the plot: 'The whole point of a good detective story was that it must be somebody obvious but at the same time, for some reason, you would find that it was not obvious, that he could not possibly have done it. Though really, of course, he had done it.'*

Well steeped in the Sherlock Holmes tradition, she envisaged a similar type of detective who, like Holmes, would team up with a butler. Then she remembered the Belgian refugees who lived in a nearby parish: 'There were all types of refugees. How about a refugee police officer? A retired police officer ... Anyway, I settled on a Belgian detective. He should have been an inspector, so that he would have a certain knowledge of crime. He would be meticulous, very tidy, I thought to myself, as I cleared away a good many untidy odds and ends in my own bedroom. A tidy little man. I could see him as a tidy little man, always arranging things, liking things in pairs, liking things square instead of round. And he should be very brainy – he should have little grey cells of mind – that was a good phrase: I must remember that – yes, he would have little grey cells. He would have rather a grand name – one of those names that Sherlock Holmes and his family had ... How about calling my little man Hercules? He would be a small man – Hercules: a good name. His last name was more difficult. I don't know why I settled on the name Poirot, whether it just came into my head or whether I saw it in some newspaper or written on something – anyway it came. It went well not with Hercules but Hercule – Hercule Poirot. That was all right – settled, thank goodness.'

Hercule Poirot was born, though Agatha Christie never did remember how the name Poirot came to her. Many critics pointed out the name's similarity to Hercule Popeau, a character created by Marie Belloc Lowndes (1868–1947), who wrote crime novels in the thirties, but the genesis of Poirot remains a mystery. After the maturation of her plot, Agatha Christie started typing chapter by chapter on her sister's typewriter. Halfway through, when she was enmeshed in the middle part of her book, Christie's mother advised her to take some time off and go to Dartmoor where, after a fortnight's holiday, the manuscript was nearly finished.

'Reasonably satisfied' with her work, Agatha Christie sent the manuscript to Hodder and Stoughton who returned it with a 'plain refusal, with no frills on it'. Immediately she bundled it off to another publisher.

Though written in 1916, The Mysterious Affair at Styles *was only published in 1920, by John Lane, who was then director of The Bodley Head publishers. Agatha Christie had sent him her manuscript eighteen months earlier, undeterred by six previous rejections. In the excitement of the war's ending, her husband Archie's return and the birth of her daughter Rosalind, Christie had forgotten all about her novel. One day she got a letter from John Lane asking her to call at his office. He told her that some of his readers had thought it showed promise; something might be made of it. But there would have to be considerable changes and, in particular, the last chapter would have to be completely rewritten. Excited at the thought of having her first book out in print, Agatha Christie did not think twice before signing a contract. Little did she realize that it would bind her to The Bodley Head for another five novels: 'Certainly at that moment I did not envisage writing any more books. I think if I had been asked I would have said that I would probably write stories from time to time. I was the complete amateur – nothing of the professional about me. For me, writing was fun.'*

Christie went home, told everything to her husband Archie and together they went to the Hammersmith Palais to celebrate: 'There was a third party with us, though I did not know it. Hercule Poirot, my Belgian invention, was hanging round my neck, firmly attached there like the old man of the sea.'

In spite of its 1920 copyright, The Mysterious Affair at Styles *was not published until 1921. It was serialized in the* Weekly Times, *for which the author received the meagre sum of £25.*

Of all the reviews at the time the one that pleased Christie most appeared in the Pharmaceutical Journal. *It praised 'this detective story for dealing with poisons in a knowledgeable way, without the nonsense about untraceable substances that so often happens. Miss Agatha Christie,' they said, 'knows her job.'*

THE SECRET
ADVERSARY

To all those who lead monotonous lives
in the hope that they may experience
at second-hand the delights and dangers of
adventure

Prologue

It was 2 p.m. on the afternoon of May 7th, 1915. The *Lusitania* and been struck by two torpedoes in succession and was sinking rapidly, while the boats were being launched with all possible speed. The women and children were being lined up awaiting their turn. Some still clung desperately to husbands and fathers; others clutched their children closely to their breasts. One girl stood alone, slightly apart from the rest. She was quite young, not more than eighteen. She did not seem afraid, and her grave steadfast eyes looked straight ahead.

'I beg your pardon.'

A man's voice beside her made her start and turn. She had noticed the speaker more than once amongst the first-class passengers. There had been a hint of mystery about him which had appealed to her imagination. He spoke to no one. If anyone spoke to him he was quick to rebuff the overture. Also he had a nervous way of looking over his shoulder with a swift, suspicious glance.

She noticed now that he was greatly agitated. There were beads of perspiration on his brow. He was evidently in a state of overmastering fear. And yet he did not strike her as the kind of man who would be afraid to meet death!

'Yes?' Her grave eyes met his inquiringly.

He stood looking at her with a kind of desperate irresolution.

'It must be!' he muttered to himself. 'Yes – it is the only way.' Then aloud he said abruptly: 'You are an American?'

'Yes.'

'A patriotic one?'

The girl flushed.

'I guess you've no right to ask such a thing! Of course I am!'

'Don't be offended. You wouldn't be if you knew how much there was at stake. But I've got to trust someone – and it must be a woman.'

'Why?'

'Because of "women and children first".' He looked round and lowered his voice. 'I'm carrying papers – vitally important papers. They may make all the difference to the Allies in the war. You understand? These papers have *got* to be saved! They've more chance with you than with me. Will you take them?'

The girl held out her hand.

'Wait – I must warn you. There may be a risk – if I've been followed. I don't think I have, but one never knows. If so, there will be danger. Have you the nerve to go through with it?'

The girl smiled.

'I'll go through with it all right. And I'm real proud to be chosen! What am I to do with them afterwards?'

'Watch the newspapers! I'll advertise in the personal column of *The Times*, beginning "Shipmate". At the end of three days if there's nothing – well, you'll know I'm down and out. Then take the packet to the American Embassy, and deliver it into the Ambassador's own hands. Is that clear?'

'Quite clear.'

'Then be ready – I'm going to say goodbye.' He took her hand in his. 'Goodbye. Good luck to you,' he said in a louder tone.

Her hand closed on the oilskin packet that had lain in his palm.

The *Lusitania* settled with a more decided list to starboard. In answer to a quick command, the girl went forward to take her place in the boat.

CHAPTER I

The Young Adventurers, Ltd

'Tommy, old thing!'

'Tuppence, old bean!'

The two young people greeted each other affectionately, and momentarily blocked the Dover Street Tube exit in doing so. The adjective 'old' was misleading. Their united ages would certainly not have totalled forty-five.

'Not seen you for simply centuries,' continued the young man. 'Where are you off to? Come and chew a bun with me. We're getting a bit unpopular here – blocking the gangway as it were. Let's get out of it.'

The girl assenting, they started walking down Dover Street towards Piccadilly.

'Now then,' said Tommy, 'where shall we go?'

The very faint anxiety which underlay his tone did not escape the astute ears of Miss Prudence Cowley, known to her intimate friends for some mysterious reason as 'Tuppence'. She pounced at once.

'Tommy, you're stony!'

'Not a bit of it,' declared Tommy unconvincingly. 'Rolling in cash.'

'You always were a shocking liar,' said Tuppence severely, 'though you did once persuade Sister Greenbank that the doctor had ordered you beer as a tonic, but forgotten to write it on the chart. Do you remember?'

Tommy chuckled.

'I should think I did! Wasn't the old cat in a rage when she found out? Not that she was a bad sort really, old Mother Greenbank! Good old hospital – demobbed like everything else, I suppose?'

Tuppence sighed.

'Yes. You too?'

Tommy nodded.

'Two months ago.'

'Gratuity?' hinted Tuppence.

'Spent.'

'Oh, Tommy!'

'No, old thing, not in riotous dissipation. No such luck! The cost of living – ordinary plain, or garden living nowadays is, I assure you, if you do not know –'

'My dear child,' interrupted Tuppence, 'there is nothing I do *not* know about the cost of living. Here we are at Lyons', and we will each of us pay for our own. That's that!' And Tuppence led the way upstairs.

The place was full, and they wandered about looking for a table, catching odds and ends of conversation as they did so.

'And – do you know, she sat down and *cried* when I told her she couldn't have the flat after all.' 'It was simply a *bargain*, my dear! Just like the one Mabel Lewis brought from Paris –'

'Funny scraps one does overhear,' murmured Tommy. 'I passed two Johnnies in the street today talking about someone called Jane Finn. Did you ever hear such a name?'

But at that moment two elderly ladies rose and collected parcels, and Tuppence deftly ensconced herself in one of the vacant seats.

Tommy ordered tea and buns. Tuppence ordered tea and buttered toast.

'And mind the tea comes in separate teapots,' she added severely.

Tommy sat down opposite her. His bared head revealed a shock of exquisitely slicked-back red hair. His face was pleasantly ugly – nondescript, yet unmistakably the face of a gentleman and a sportsman. His brown suit was well cut, but perilously near the end of its tether.

They were an essentially modern-looking couple as they sat there. Tuppence had no claim to beauty, but there was character and charm in the elfin lines of her little face, with its determined chin and large, wide-apart grey eyes that looked mistily out from under straight, black brows. She wore a small bright green toque over her black bobbed hair, and her extremely short and rather shabby skirt revealed a pair of uncommonly dainty ankles. Her appearance presented a valiant attempt at smartness.

The tea came at last, and Tuppence, rousing herself from a fit of meditation, poured it out.

'Now then,' said Tommy, taking a large bite of bun, 'let's get up-to-date. Remember, I haven't seen you since that time in hospital in 1916.'

'Very well.' Tuppence helped herself liberally to buttered toast. 'Abridged biography of Miss Prudence Cowley, fifth daughter of Archdeacon Cowley of Little Missendell, Suffolk. Miss Cowley left the delights (and drudgeries) of her home life early in the war and came up to London, where she entered an officers' hospital. First month: Washed up six hundred and forty-eight plates every day. Second month: Promoted to drying aforesaid plates. Third month: Promoted to peeling potatoes. Fourth month: Promoted to cutting bread and butter. Fifth month: Promoted one floor up to duties of wardmaid with mop and pail. Sixth month: Promoted to waiting at table. Seventh month: Pleasing appearance and nice manners so striking that am promoted to waiting on the Sisters! Eighth month: Slight check in career. Sister Bond ate Sister Westhaven's egg! Grand row! Wardmaid clearly to blame! Inattention in such important matters cannot be too highly censured. Mop and pail again! How are the mighty fallen! Ninth month: Promoted to sweeping out wards, where I found a friend of my childhood in Lieutenant Thomas Beresford (bow, Tommy!), whom I had not seen for five long years. The meeting was affecting! Tenth month: Reproved by matron for visiting the pictures in company with one of the patients, namely: the aforementioned Lieutenant Thomas Beresford. Eleventh and twelfth months: Parlourmaid duties resumed with entire success. At the end of the year left hospital in a blaze of glory. After that, the talented Miss Cowley drove successively a trade delivery van, a motor-lorry and a general. The last was the pleasantest. He was quite a young general!'

'What blighter was that?' inquired Tommy. 'Perfectly sickening the way those brass hats drove from the War Office to the Savoy, and from the Savoy to the War Office!'

'I've forgotten his name now,' confessed Tuppence. 'To resume, that was in a way the apex of my career. I next entered a Government office. We had several very enjoyable tea parties. I had intended to become a land girl, a postwoman, and a bus conductress by way of rounding off my career – but the Armistice intervened! I clung to the office with the true limpet touch for many long months, but, alas, I was combed out at last. Since then I've been looking for a job. Now then – your turn.'

'There's not so much promotion in mine,' said Tommy regretfully, 'and a great deal less variety. I went out to France again, as you know. Then they sent me to Mesopotamia, and I got wounded for the second time, and went into hospital out there. Then I got stuck in Egypt till the Armistice happened, kicked my heels there some time longer, and, as I told you, finally got demobbed. And, for ten long, weary months I've been job hunting! There aren't any jobs! And, if there were, they wouldn't give 'em to me. What good am I? What do I know about business? Nothing.'

Tuppence nodded gloomily.

'What about the colonies?' she suggested.

Tommy shook his head.

'I shouldn't like the colonies – and I'm perfectly certain they wouldn't like me!'

'Rich relations?'

Again Tommy shook his head.

'Oh, Tommy, not even a great-aunt?'

'I've got an old uncle who's more or less rolling, but he's no good.'

'Why not?'

'Wanted to adopt me once. I refused.'

'I think I remember hearing about it,' said Tuppence slowly. 'You refused because of your mother –'

Tommy flushed.

'Yes, it would have been a bit rough on the mater. As you know, I was all she had. Old boy hated her – wanted to get me away from her. Just a bit of spite.'

'Your mother's dead, isn't she?' said Tuppence gently.

Tommy nodded.

Tuppence's large grey eyes looked misty.

'You're a good sort, Tommy. I always knew it.'

'Rot!' said Tommy hastily. 'Well, that's my position. I'm just about desperate.'

'So am I! I've hung out as long as I could. I've touted round. I've answered advertisements. I've tried every mortal blessed thing. I've screwed and saved and pinched! But it's no good. I shall have to go home!'

'Don't you want to?'

'Of course I don't want to! What's the good of being sentimental? Father's a dear – I'm awfully fond of him – but you've no idea how I worry him! He has that delightful early Victorian view that short skirts and smoking are immoral. You can imagine what a thorn in the flesh I am to him! He just heaved a sigh of relief when the war took me off. You see, there are seven of us at home. It's awful! All housework and mothers' meetings! I have always been the changeling. I don't want to go back, but – oh, Tommy, what else is there to do?'

Tommy shook his head sadly. There was a silence, and then Tuppence burst out:

'Money, money, money! I think about money morning, noon and night! I dare say it's mercenary of me, but there it is!'

'Same here,' agreed Tommy with feeling.

'I've thought over every imaginable way of getting it too,' continued Tuppence. 'There are only three! To be left it, to marry it, or to make it. First is ruled out. I haven't got any rich elderly relatives. Any relatives I have are in homes for decayed gentlewomen! I always help old ladies over crossings, and pick up parcels for old gentlemen, in case they should turn out to be eccentric millionaires. But not one of them has ever asked me my name – and quite a lot never said "Thank you." '

There was a pause.

'Of course,' resumed Tuppence, 'marriage is my best chance. I made up my mind to marry money when I was quite young. Any thinking girl would! I'm not sentimental, you know.' She paused. 'Come now, you can't say I'm sentimental,' she added sharply.

'Certainly not,' agreed Tommy hastily. 'No one would ever think of sentiment in connection with you.'

'That's not very polite,' replied Tuppence. 'But I dare say you mean it all right. Well, there it is! I'm ready and willing – but I never meet any rich men! All the boys I know are about as hard up as I am.'

'What about the general?' inquired Tommy.

'I fancy he keeps a bicycle shop in time of peace,' explained Tuppence. 'No, there it is! Now *you* could marry a rich girl.'

'I'm like you. I don't know any.'

'That doesn't matter. You can always get to know one. Now, if I see a man in a fur coat come out of the Ritz I can't rush up to him and say: "Look here, you're rich. I'd like to know you." '

'Do you suggest that I should do that to a similarly garbed female?'

'Don't be silly. You tread on her foot, or pick up her handkerchief, or something like that. If she thinks you want to know her she's flattered, and will manage it for you somehow.'

'You overrate my manly charms,' murmured Tommy.

'On the other hand,' proceeded Tuppence, 'my millionaire would probably run for his life! No – marriage is fraught with difficulties. Remains – to *make* money!'

'We've tried that, and failed,' Tommy reminded her.

'We've tried all the orthodox ways, yes. But suppose we try the unorthodox. Tommy, let's be adventurers!'

'Certainly,' replied Tommy cheerfully. 'How do we begin?'

'That's the difficulty. If we could make ourselves known, people might hire us to commit crimes for them.'

'Delightful,' commented Tommy. 'Especially coming from a clergyman's daughter!'

'The moral guilt,' Tuppence pointed out, 'would be theirs – not mine. You must admit that there's a difference between stealing a diamond necklace for yourself and being hired to steal it?'

'There wouldn't be the least difference if you were caught!'

'Perhaps not. But I shouldn't be caught. I'm so clever.'

'Modesty always was your besetting sin,' remarked Tommy.

'Don't rag. Look here, Tommy, shall we really? Shall we form a business partnership?'

'Form a company for the stealing of diamond necklaces?'

'That was only an illustration. Let's have a – what do you call it in book-keeping?'

'Don't know. Never did any.'

'I have – but I always got mixed up, and used to put credit entries on the debit side, and vice versa – so they fired me out. Oh, I know – a joint venture! It struck me as such a romantic phrase to come across in the middle of musty old figures. It's got an Elizabethan flavour about it – makes one think of galleons and doubloons. A joint venture!'

'Trading under the name of the Young Adventurers, Ltd? Is that your idea, Tuppence?'

'It's all very well to laugh, but I feel there might be something in it.'

'How do you propose to get in touch with your would-be employers?'

'Advertisement,' replied Tuppence promptly. 'Have you got a bit of paper and a pencil? Men usually seem to have. Just like we have hairpins and powder-puffs.'

Tommy handed over a rather shabby green notebook, and Tuppence began writing busily.

'Shall we begin: "Young officer, twice wounded in the war –"'

'Certainly not.'

'Oh, very well, my dear boy. But I can assure you that that sort of thing might touch the heart of an elderly spinster, and she might adopt you, and then there would be no need for you to be a young adventurer at all.'

'I don't want to be adopted.'

'I forgot you had a prejudice against it. I was only ragging you! The papers are full up to the brim with that type of thing. Now listen – how's this? "Two young adventurers for hire. Willing to do anything, go anywhere. Pay must be good." (We might as well make that clear from the start.) Then we might add: "No reasonable offer refused" – like flats and furniture.'

'I should think any offer we get in answer to that would be a pretty *un*reasonable one!'

'Tommy! You're a genius! That's ever so much more chic. "No unreasonable offer refused – if pay is good." How's that?'

'I shouldn't mention pay again. It looks rather eager.'

'It couldn't look as eager as I feel! But perhaps you are right. Now I'll read it straight through. "Two young adventurers for hire. Willing to do anything, go anywhere. Pay must be good. No unreasonable offer refused." How would that strike you if you read it?'

'It would strike me as either being a hoax, or else written by a lunatic.'

'It's not half so insane as a thing I read this morning beginning "Petunia" and signed "Best Boy".' She tore out the leaf and handed it to Tommy. 'There you are. *The Times*, I think. Reply to Box so-and-so. I expect it will be about five shillings. Here's half a crown for my share.'

Tommy was holding the paper thoughtfully. His face burned a deeper red.

'Shall we really try it?' he said at last. 'Shall we, Tuppence? Just for the fun of the thing?'

'Tommy, you're a sport! I knew you would be! Let's drink to success.' She poured some cold dregs of tea into the two cups.

'Here's to our joint venture, and may it prosper!'

'The Young Adventurers, Ltd!' responded Tommy.

They put down the cups and laughed rather uncertainly. Tuppence rose.

'I must return to my palatial suite at the hostel.'

'Perhaps it is time I strolled round to the Ritz,' agreed Tommy with a grin. 'Where shall we meet? And when?'

'Twelve o'clock tomorrow. Piccadilly Tube station. Will that suit you?'

'My time is my own,' replied Mr Beresford magnificently.

'So long, then.'

'Goodbye, old thing.'

The two young people went off in opposite directions. Tuppence's hostel was situated in what was charitably called Southern Belgravia. For reasons of economy she did not take a bus.

She was half-way across St James's Park, when a man's voice behind her made her start.

'Excuse me,' it said. 'But may I speak to you for a moment?'

CHAPTER II

Mr Whittington's Offer

Tuppence turned sharply, but the words hovering on the tip of her tongue remained unspoken for the man's appearance and manner did not bear out her first and most natural assumption. She hesitated. As if he read her thoughts, the man said quickly:

'I can assure you I mean no disrespect.'

Tuppence believed him. Although she disliked and distrusted him instinctively, she was inclined to acquit him of the particular motive which she had at first attributed to him. She looked him up and down. He was a big man, clean shaven, with a heavy jowl. His eyes were small and cunning, and shifted their glance under her direct gaze.

'Well, what is it?' she asked.

The man smiled.

'I happened to overhear part of your conversation with the young gentleman in Lyons'.'

'Well – what of it?'

'Nothing – except that I think I may be of some use to you.'

Another inference forced itself into Tuppence's mind.

'You followed me here?'

'I took that liberty.'

'And in what way do you think you could be of use to me?'

The man took a card from his pocket and handed it to her with a bow.

Tuppence took it and scrutinized it carefully. It bore the inscription 'Mr Edward Whittington'. Below the name were the words 'Esthonia Glassware Co.,' and the address of a city office. Mr Whittington spoke again:

'If you will call upon me tomorrow morning at eleven

o'clock, I will lay the details of my proposition before you.'

'At eleven o'clock?' said Tuppence doubtfully.

'At eleven o'clock.'

Tuppence made up her mind.

'Very well. I'll be there.'

'Thank you. Good evening.'

He raised his hat with a flourish, and walked away. Tuppence remained for some minutes gazing after him. Then she gave a curious movement of her shoulders, rather as a terrier shakes himself.

'The adventures have begun,' she murmured to herself. 'What does he want me to do, I wonder? There's something about you, Mr Whittington, that I don't like at all. But, on the other hand, I'm not the least bit afraid of you. And as I've said before, and shall doubtless say again, little Tuppence can look after herself, thank you!'

And with a short, sharp nod of her head she walked briskly onward. As a result of further meditations, however, she turned aside from the direct route and entered a post office. There she pondered for some moments, a telegraph form in her hand. The thought of a possible five shillings spent unnecessarily spurred her to action, and she decided to risk the waste of ninepence.

Disdaining the spiky pen and thick, black treacle which a beneficent Government had provided, Tuppence drew out Tommy's pencil which she had retained and wrote rapidly: 'Don't put in advertisement. Will explain tomorrow.' She addressed it to Tommy at his club, from which in one short month he would have to resign, unless a kindly fortune permitted him to renew his subscription.

'It may catch him,' she murmured. 'Anyway it's worth trying.'

After handing it over the counter she set out briskly for home, stopping at a baker's to buy three-pennyworth of new buns.

Later, in her tiny cubicle at the top of the house she munched buns and reflected on the future. What was the

Esthonia Glassware Co., and what earthly need could it have for her services? A pleasurable thrill of excitement made Tuppence tingle. At any rate, the country vicarage had retreated into the background again. The morrow held possibilities.

It was a long time before Tuppence went to sleep that night, and, when at length she did, she dreamed that Mr Whittington had set her to washing up a pile of Esthonia Glassware, which bore an unaccountable resemblance to hospital plates!

It wanted some five minutes to eleven when Tuppence reached the block of buildings in which the offices of the Esthonia Glassware Co. were situated. To arrive before the time would look over-eager. So Tuppence decided to walk to the end of the street and back again. She did so. On the stroke of eleven she plunged into the recesses of the building. The Esthonia Glassware Co. was on the top floor. There was a lift, but Tuppence chose to walk up.

Slightly out of breath, she came to a halt outside the ground glass door with the legend painted across it: 'Esthonia Glassware Co.'

Tuppence knocked. In response to a voice from within, she turned the handle and walked into a small, rather dirty office.

A middle-aged clerk got down from a high stool at a desk near the window and came towards her inquiringly.

'I have an appointment with Mr Whittington,' said Tuppence.

'Will you come this way, please.' He crossed to a partition door with 'Private' on it, knocked, then opened the door and stood aside to let her pass in.

Mr Whittington was seated behind a large desk covered with papers. Tuppence felt her previous judgement confirmed. There was something wrong about Mr Whittington. The combination of his sleek prosperity and his shifty eye was not attractive.

He looked up and nodded.

'So you've turned up all right? That's good. Sit down, will you?'

Tuppence sat down on the chair facing him. She looked particularly small and demure this morning. She sat there meekly with downcast eyes whilst Mr Whittington sorted and rustled amongst his papers. Finally he pushed them away, and leaned over the desk.

'Now, my dear young lady, let us come to business.' His large face broadened into a smile. 'You want work? Well, I have work to offer you. What should you say now to £100 down, and all expenses paid?' Mr Whittington leaned back in his chair, and thrust his thumbs into the arm-holes of his waistcoat.

Tuppence eyed him warily.

'And the nature of the work?' she demanded.

'Nominal – purely nominal. A pleasant trip, that is all.'

'Where to?'

Mr Whittington smiled again.

'Paris.'

'Oh!' said Tuppence thoughtfully. To herself she said: 'Of course, if father heard that he would have a fit! But somehow I don't see Mr Whittington in the role of the gay deceiver.'

'Yes,' continued Whittington. 'What could be more delightful? To put the clock back a few years – a very few, I am sure – and re-enter one of those charming *pensionnats de jeunes filles* with which Paris abounds –'

Tuppence interrupted him.

'A *pensionnat?*'

'Exactly. Madame Colombier's in the Avenue de Neuilly.'

Tuppence knew the name well. Nothing could have been more select. She had had several American friends there. She was more than ever puzzled.

'You want me to go to Madame Colombier's? For how long?'

'That depends. Possibly three months.'

'And that is all? There are no other conditions?'

'None whatever. You would, of course, go in the character of my ward, and you would hold no communication with your friends. I should have to request absolute secrecy for the time being. By the way, you are English, are you not?'

'Yes.'

'Yet you speak with a slight American accent?'

'My great pal in hospital was a little American girl. I dare say I picked it up from her. I can soon get out of it again.'

'On the contrary, it might be simpler for you to pass as an American. Details about your past life in England might be more difficult to sustain. Yes, I think that would be decidedly better. Then –'

'One moment, Mr Whittington! You seem to be taking my consent for granted.'

Whittington looked surprised.

'Surely you are not thinking of refusing? I can assure you that Madame Colombier's is a most high-class and orthodox establishment. And the terms are most liberal.'

'Exactly,' said Tuppence. 'That's just it. The terms are almost too liberal, Mr Whittington. I cannot see any way in which I can be worth that amount of money to you.'

'No?' said Whittington softly. 'Well, I will tell you. I could doubtless obtain someone else for very much less. What I am willing to pay for is a young lady with sufficient intelligence and presence of mind to sustain her part well, and also one who will have sufficient discretion not to ask too many questions.'

Tuppence smiled a little. She felt that Whittington had scored.

'There's another thing. So far there has been no mention of Mr Beresford. Where does he come in?'

'Mr Beresford?'

'My partner,' said Tuppence with dignity. 'You saw us together yesterday.'

'Ah, yes. But I'm afraid we shan't require his services.'

'Then it's off!' Tuppence rose. 'It's both or neither. Sorry – but that's how it is. Good morning, Mr Whittington.'

'Wait a minute. Let us see if something can't be managed. Sit down again, Miss –' He paused interrogatively.

Tuppence's conscience gave her a passing twinge as she remembered the archdeacon. She seized hurriedly on the first name that came into her head.

'Jane Finn,' she said hastily; and then paused open-mouthed at the effect of those two simple words.

All the geniality had faded out of Whittington's face. It was purple with rage, and the veins stood out on the forehead. And behind it all there lurked a sort of incredulous dismay. He leaned forward and hissed savagely:

'So that's your little game, is it?'

Tuppence, though utterly taken aback, nevertheless kept her head. She had not the faintest comprehension of his meaning, but she was naturally quick-witted, and felt it imperative to 'keep her end up' as she phrased it.

Whittington went on:

'Been playing with me, have you, all the time, like a cat and mouse? Knew all the time what I wanted you for, but kept up the comedy. Is that it, eh?' He was cooling down. The red colour was ebbing out of his face. He eyed her keenly. 'Who's been blabbing? Rita?'

Tuppence shook her head. She was doubtful as to how long she could sustain this illusion, but she realized the importance of not dragging an unknown Rita into it.

'No,' she replied with perfect truth. 'Rita knows nothing about me.'

His eyes still bored into her like gimlets.

'How much do you know?' he shot out.

'Very little indeed,' answered Tuppence, and was pleased to note that Whittington's uneasiness was augmented instead of allayed. To have boasted that she knew a lot might have raised doubts in his mind.

'Anyway,' snarled Whittington, 'you knew enough to come in here and plump out that name.'

'It might be my own name,' Tuppence pointed out.

'It's likely, isn't it, that there would be two girls with a name like that?'

'Or I might just have hit upon it by chance,' continued Tuppence, intoxicated with the success of truthfulness.

Mr Whittington brought his fist down upon the desk with a bang.

'Quit fooling! How much do you know? And how much do you want?'

The last five words took Tuppence's fancy mightily, especially after a meagre breakfast and a supper of buns the night before. Her present part was of the adventuress rather than the adventurous order, but she did not deny its possibilities. She sat up and smiled with the air of one who has the situation thoroughly well in hand.

'My dear Mr Whittington,' she said, 'let us by all means lay our cards upon the table. And pray do not be so angry. You heard me say yesterday that I proposed to live by my wits. It seems to me that I have now proved I have some wits to live by! I admit I have knowledge of a certain name, but perhaps my knowledge ends there.'

'Yes – and perhaps it doesn't,' snarled Whittington.

'You insist on misjudging me,' said Tuppence, and sighed gently.

'As I said once before,' said Whittington angrily, 'quit fooling, and come to the point. You can't play the innocent with me. You know a great deal more than you're willing to admit.'

Tuppence paused a moment to admire her own ingenuity, and then said softly:

'I shouldn't like to contradict you, Mr Whittington.'

'So we come to the usual question – how much?'

Tuppence was in a dilemma. So far she had fooled Whittington with complete success, but to mention a palpably impossible sum might awaken his suspicions. An idea flashed across her brain.

'Suppose we say a little something down, and a fuller discussion of the matter later?'

Whittington gave her an ugly glance.

'Blackmail, eh?'

Tuppence smiled sweetly.

'Oh no! Shall we say payment of services in advance?'

Whittington grunted.

'You see,' explained Tuppence sweetly, 'I'm not so very fond of money!'

'You're about the limit, that's what you are,' growled Whittington, with a sort of unwilling admiration. 'You took me in all right. Thought you were quite a meek little kid with just enough brains for my purpose.'

'Life,' moralized Tuppence, 'is full of surprises.'

'All the same,' continued Whittington, 'someone's been talking. You say it isn't Rita. Was it –? Oh, come in?'

The clerk followed his discreet knock into the room, and laid a paper at his master's elbow.

'Telephone message just come for you, sir.'

Whittington snatched it up and read it. A frown gathered on his brow.

'That'll do, Brown. You can go.'

The clerk withdrew, closing the door behind him. Whittington turned to Tuppence.

'Come tomorrow at the same time. I'm busy now. Here's fifty to go on with.'

He rapidly sorted out some notes, and pushed them across the table to Tuppence, then stood up, obviously impatient for her to go.

The girl counted the notes in a business-like manner, secured them in her handbag, and rose.

'Good morning, Mr Whittington,' she said politely. 'At least *au revoir*, I should say.'

'Exactly. *Au revoir!*' Whittington looked almost genial again, a reversion that aroused in Tuppence a faint misgiving. '*Au revoir*, my clever and charming young lady.'

Tuppence sped lightly down the stairs. A wild elation possessed her. A neighbouring clock showed the time to be five minutes to twelve.

'Let's give Tommy a surprise!' murmured Tuppence, and hailed a taxi.

The cab drew up outside the Tube station. Tommy was just within the entrance. His eyes opened to their fullest extent as he hurried forward to assist Tuppence to alight. She smiled at him affectionately, and remarked in a slightly affected voice:

'Pay the thing, will you, old bean? I've got nothing smaller than a five-pound note!'

CHAPTER III

A Setback

The moment was not quite so triumphant as it ought to have been. To begin with, the resources of Tommy's pockets were somewhat limited. In the end the fare was managed, the lady recollecting a plebeian twopence, and the driver, still holding the varied assortment of coins in his hand, was prevailed upon to move on, which he did after one last hoarse demand as to what the gentleman thought he was giving him?

'I think you've given him too much, Tommy,' said Tuppence innocently. 'I fancy he wants to give some of it back.'

It was possibly this remark which induced the driver to move away.

'Well,' said Mr Beresford, at length able to relieve his feelings, 'what the – dickens, did you want to take a taxi for?'

'I was afraid I might be late and keep you waiting,' said Tuppence gently.

'Afraid – you – might – be – late! Oh, Lord, I give it up!' said Mr Beresford.

'And really and truly,' continued Tuppence, opening her eyes very wide, 'I haven't got anything smaller than a five-pound note.'

'You did that part of it very well, old bean, but all the same the fellow wasn't taken in – not for a moment!'

'No,' said Tuppence thoughtfully, 'he didn't believe it. That's the curious part about speaking the truth. No one does believe it. I found that out this morning. Now let's go to lunch. How about the Savoy?'

Tommy grinned.

'How about the Ritz?'

'On second thoughts, I prefer the Piccadilly. It's nearer. We shan't have to take another taxi. Come along.'

'Is this a new brand of humour? Or is your brain really unhinged?' inquired Tommy.

'Your last supposition is the correct one. I have come into money, and the shock has been too much for me! For that particular form of mental trouble an eminent physician recommends unlimited *hors d'oeuvre*, lobster *à l'américaine*, chicken Newberg, and *pêche Melba*! Let's go and get them!'

'Tuppence, old girl, what has really come over you?'

'Oh, unbelieving one!' Tuppence wrenched open her bag. 'Look here, and here, and here!'

'My dear girl, don't wave pound notes aloft like that!'

'They're not pound notes. They're five times better, and this one's ten times better!'

Tommy groaned.

'I must have been drinking unawares! Am I dreaming, Tuppence, or do I really behold a large quantity of five-pound notes being waved about in a dangerous fashion?'

'Even so, O King! *Now*, will you come and have lunch?'

'I'll come anywhere. But what have you been doing? Holding up a bank?'

'All in good time. What an awful place Piccadilly Circus is. There's a huge bus bearing down on us. It would be too terrible if they killed the five-pound notes!'

'Grill room?' inquired Tommy, as they reached the opposite pavement in safety.

'The other's more expensive,' demurred Tuppence.

'That's mere wicked wanton extravagance. Come on below.'

'Are you sure I can get all the things I want there?'

'That extremely unwholesome menu you were outlining just now? Of course you can – or as much as is good for you, anyway.'

'And now tell me,' said Tommy, unable to restrain his pent-up curiosity any longer, as they sat in state surrounded by the many *hors d'oeuvre* of Tuppence's dreams.

Miss Cowley told him.

'And the curious part of it is,' she ended, 'that I really did invent the name of Jane Finn! I didn't want to give my own because of poor father – in case I should get mixed up in anything shady.'

'Perhaps that's so,' said Tommy slowly. 'But you didn't invent it.'

'What?'

'No. *I* told it to you. Don't you remember, I said yesterday I'd overheard two people talking about a female called Jane Finn? That's what brought the name into your mind so pat.'

'So you did. I remember now. How extraordinary –' Tuppence tailed off into silence. Suddenly she roused herself. 'Tommy!'

'Yes?'

'What were they like, the two men you passed?'

Tommy frowned in an effort at remembrance.

'One was a big fat sort of chap. Clean shaven. I think – and dark.'

'That's him,' cried Tuppence, in an ungrammatical squeal. 'That's Whittington! What was the other man like?'

'I can't remember. I didn't notice him particularly. It was really the outlandish name that caught my attention.'

'And people say that coincidences don't happen!' Tuppence tackled her *pêche Melba* happily.

But Tommy had become serious.

'Look here, Tuppence, old girl, what is this going to lead to?'

'More money,' replied his companion.

'I know that. You've only got one idea in your head. What I mean is, what about the next step? How are you going to keep the game up?'

'Oh!' Tuppence laid down her spoon. 'You're right, Tommy, it is a bit of a poser.'

'After all, you know, you can't bluff him for ever. You're sure to slip up sooner or later. And, anyway, I'm not at all sure that it isn't actionable – blackmail, you know.'

'Nonsense. Blackmail is saying you'll tell unless you are

given money. Now, there's nothing I could tell, because I don't really know anything.'

'H'm,' said Tommy doubtfully. 'Well, anyway, what *are* we going to do? Whittington was in a hurry to get rid of you this morning, but next time he'll want to know something more before he parts with his money. He'll want to know how much you know, and where you got your information from, and a lot of other things that you can't cope with. What are you going to do about it?'

Tuppence frowned severely.

'We must think. Order some Turkish coffee, Tommy. Stimulating to the brain. Oh, dear, what a lot I have eaten!'

'You have made rather a hog of yourself! So have I for that matter, but I flatter myself that my choice of dishes was more judicious than yours. Two coffees.' (This was to the waiter.) 'One Turkish, one French.'

Tuppence sipped her coffee with a deeply reflective air, and snubbed Tommy when he spoke to her.

'Be quiet. I'm thinking.'

'Shades of Pelmanism!' said Tommy, and relapsed into silence.

'There!' said Tuppence at last. 'I've got a plan. Obviously what we've got to do is find out more about it all.'

Tommy applauded.

'Don't jeer. We can only find out through Whittington. We must discover where he lives, what he does – sleuth him, in fact! Now I can't do it, because he knows me, but he only saw you for a minute or two in Lyons'. He's not likely to recognize you. After all, one young man is much like another.'

'I repudiate that remark utterly. I'm sure my pleasing features and distinguished appearance would single me out from any crowd.'

'My plan is this,' Tuppence went on calmly. 'I'll go alone tomorrow. I'll put him off again like I did today. It doesn't matter if I don't get any more money at once. Fifty pounds ought to last us a few days.'

'Or even longer!'

'You'll hang about outside. When I come out I shan't speak to you in case he's watching. But I'll take up my stand somewhere near, and when he comes out of the building I'll drop a handkerchief or something, and off you go!'

'Off I go where?'

'Follow him, of course, silly! What do you think of the idea?'

'Sort of thing one reads about in books. I somehow feel that in real life one will feel a bit of an ass standing in the street for hours with nothing to do. People will wonder what I'm up to.'

'Not in the city. Everyone's in such a hurry. Probably no one will even notice you at all.'

'That's the second time you've made that sort of remark. Never mind, I forgive you. Anyway, it will be rather a lark. What are you doing this afternoon?'

'Well,' said Tuppence meditatively. 'I *had* thought of hats! Or perhaps silk stockings! Or perhaps –'

'Hold hard,' admonished Tommy. 'There's a limit to fifty pounds! But let's do dinner and a show tonight at all events.'

'Rather.'

The day passed pleasantly. The evening even more so. Two of the five-pound notes were now irretrievably dead.

They met by arrangement the following morning, and proceeded citywards. Tommy remained on the opposite side of the road while Tuppence plunged into the building.

Tommy strolled slowly down to the end of the street, then back again. Just as he came abreast of the buildings, Tuppence darted across the road.

'Tommy!'

'Yes. What's up?'

'The place is shut. I can't make anyone hear.'

'That's odd.'

'Isn't it? Come up with me, and let's try again.'

Tommy followed her. As they passed the third floor landing a young clerk came out of an office. He hesitated a moment, then addressed himself to Tuppence.

'Were you wanting the Esthonia Glassware?'

'Yes, please.'

'It's closed down. Since yesterday afternoon. Company being wound up, they say. Not that I've ever heard of it myself. But anyway the office is to let.'

'Th – thank you,' faltered Tuppence. 'I suppose you don't know Mr Whittington's address?'

'Afraid I don't. They left rather suddenly.'

'Thank you very much,' said Tommy. 'Come on, Tuppence.'

They descended to the street again where they gazed at one another blankly.

'That's torn it,' said Tommy at length.

'And I never suspected it,' wailed Tuppence.

'Cheer up, old thing, it can't be helped.'

'Can't it, though!' Tuppence's little chin shot out defiantly. 'Do you think this is the end? If so, you're wrong. It's just the beginning!'

'The beginning of what?'

'Of our adventure! Tommy, don't you see, if they are scared enough to run away like this, it shows that there must be a lot in this Jane Finn business! Well, we'll get to the bottom of it. We'll run them down! We'll be sleuths in earnest!'

'Yes, but there's no one left to sleuth.'

'No, that's why we'll have to start all over again. Lend me that bit of pencil. Thanks. Wait a minute – don't interrupt. There!' Tuppence handed back the pencil, and surveyed the piece of paper on which she had written with a satisfied eye.

'What's that?'

'Advertisement.'

'You're not going to put that thing in after all?'

'No, it's a different one.' She handed him the slip of paper. Tommy read the words on it aloud:

'WANTED, any information respecting Jane Finn. Apply Y. A.'

CHAPTER IV

Who Is Jane Finn?

The next day passed slowly. It was necessary to curtail expenditure. Carefully husbanded, forty pounds will last a long time. Luckily the weather was fine, and 'walking is cheap', dictated Tuppence. An outlying picture house provided them with recreation for the evening.

The day of disillusionment had been a Wednesday. On Thursday the advertisement had duly appeared. On Friday letters might be expected to arrive at Tommy's rooms.

He had been bound by an honourable promise not to open any such letters if they did arrive, but to repair to the National Gallery, where his colleague would meet him at ten o'clock.

Tuppence was first at the rendezvous. She ensconced herself on a red velvet seat, and gazed at the Turners with unseeing eyes until she saw the familiar figure enter the room.

'Well?'

'Well,' returned Mr Beresford provokingly. 'Which is your favourite picture?'

'Don't be a wretch. Aren't there *any* answers?'

Tommy shook his head with a deep and somewhat over-acted melancholy.

'I didn't want to disappoint you, old thing, by telling you right off. It's too bad. Good money wasted.' He sighed. 'Still, there it is. The advertisement has appeared, and – there are only two answers!'

'Tommy, you devil!' Tuppence almost screamed. 'Give them to me. How could you be so mean!'

'Your luggage, Tuppence, your luggage! They're very particular at the National Gallery. Government show, you know.

And do remember, as I have pointed out to you before, that as a clergyman's daughter –'

'I ought to be on the stage!' finished Tuppence with a snap.

'That is not what I intended to say. But if you are sure that you have enjoyed to the full the reaction of joy after despair with which I have kindly provided you free of charge, let us get down to our mail, as the saying goes.'

Tuppence snatched the two precious envelopes from him unceremoniously, and scrutinized them carefully.

'Thick paper, this one. It looks rich. We'll keep it to the last and open the other first.'

'Right you are. One, two, three, go!'

Tuppence's little thumb ripped open the envelope, and she extracted the contents.

> Dear Sir,
>   Referring to your advertisement in this morning's paper, I may be able to be of some use to you. Perhaps you could call and see me at the above address at eleven o'clock tomorrow morning.
>
>   Yours truly,
>   A. Carter

'27 Carshalton Terrace,' said Tuppence, referring to the address. 'That's Gloucester Road way. Plenty of time to get there if we Tube.'

'The following,' said Tommy, 'is the plan of campaign. It is my turn to assume the offensive. Ushered into the presence of Mr Carter, he and I wish each other good morning as is customary. He then says: "Please take a seat, Mr – er?" To which I reply promptly and significantly: "Edward Whittington!" whereupon Mr Carter turns purple in the face and gasps out: "How much?" Pocketing the usual fee of fifty pounds, I rejoin you in the road outside, and we proceed to the next address and repeat the performance.'

'Don't be absurd, Tommy. Now for the other letter. Oh, this is from the Ritz!'

'A hundred pounds instead of fifty!'
'I'll read it:

'Dear Sir,
   'Re your advertisement, I should be glad if you would
call round somewhere about lunch-time.
                              'Yours truly,
                              'Julius P. Hersheimmer.'

'Ha!' said Tommy. 'Do I smell a Boche? Or only an American millionaire of unfortunate ancestry? At all events we'll call
at lunch-time. It's a good time – frequently leads to free food
for two.'

Tuppence nodded assent.

'Now for Carter. We'll have to hurry.'

Carshalton Terrace proved to be an unimpeachable row of
what Tuppence called 'ladylike looking houses'. They rang
the bell at No. 27, and a neat maid answered the door. She
looked so respectable that Tuppence's heart sank. Upon
Tommy's request for Mr Carter, she showed them into a small
study on the ground floor, where she left them. Hardly a
minute elapsed, however, before the door opened, and a tall
man with a lean hawklike face and a tired manner entered the
room.

'Mr Y. A.?' he said, and smiled. His smile was distinctly
attractive. 'Do sit down, both of you.'

They obeyed. He himself took a chair opposite to Tuppence
and smiled at her encouragingly. There was something in the
quality of his smile that made the girl's usual readiness desert
her.

As he did not seem inclined to open the conversation, Tuppence was forced to begin.

'We wanted to know – that is, would you be so kind as to
tell us anything you know about Jane Finn?'

'Jane Finn? Ah!' Mr Carter appeared to reflect. 'Well, the
question is, what do you know about her?'

Tuppence drew herself up.

'I don't see that that's got anything to do with it.'

'No? But it has, you know, really it has.' He smiled again in his tired way, and continued reflectively. 'So that brings us down to it again. What do *you* know about Jane Finn?'

'Come now,' he continued, as Tuppence remained silent. 'You must know *something* to have advertised as you did?' He leaned forward a little, his weary voice held a hint of persuasiveness. 'Suppose you tell me . . .'

There was something very magnetic about Mr Carter's personality. Tuppence seemed to shake herself free of it with an effort, as she said:

'We couldn't do that, could we, Tommy?'

But to her surprise, her companion did not back her up. His eyes were fixed on Mr Carter, and his tone when he spoke held an unusual note of deference.

'I dare say the little we know won't be any good to you, sir. But such as it is, you're welcome to it.'

'Tommy!' cried out Tuppence in surprise.

Mr Carter slewed round in his chair. His eyes asked a question.

Tommy nodded.

'Yes, sir, I recognized you at once. Saw you in France when I was with the Intelligence. As soon as you came into the room, I knew –'

Mr Carter held up his hand.

'No names, please. I'm known as Mr Carter here. It's my cousin's house, by the way. She's willing to lend it to me sometimes when it's a case of working on strictly unofficial lines. Well, now,' – he looked from one to the other – 'who's going to tell me the story?'

'Fire ahead, Tuppence,' directed Tommy. 'It's your yarn.'

'Yes, little lady, out with it.'

And obediently Tuppence did out with it, telling the whole story from the forming of the Young Adventurers, Ltd, downwards.

Mr Carter listened in silence with a resumption of his tired manner. Now and then he passed his hand across his lips as though to hide a smile. When she had finished he nodded gravely.

'Not much. But suggestive. Quite suggestive. If you'll excuse me saying so, you're a curious young couple. I don't know – you might succeed where others have failed . . . I believe in luck, you know – always have . . .'

He paused a moment and then went on.

'Well, how about it? You're out for adventure. How would you like to work for me? All quite unofficial, you know. Expenses paid, and a moderate screw?'

Tuppence gazed at him, her lips parted, her eyes growing wider and wider. 'What should we have to do?' she breathed.

Mr Carter smiled.

'Just go on with what you're doing now. *Find Jane Finn.*'

'Yes, but – who is Jane Finn?'

Mr Carter nodded gravely.

'Yes, you're entitled to know that, I think.'

He leaned back in his chair, crossed his legs, brought the tips of his fingers together, and began in a low monotone:

'Secret diplomacy (which, by the way, is nearly always bad policy!) does not concern you. It will be sufficient to say that in the early days of 1915 a certain document came into being. It was the draft of a secret agreement – treaty – call it what you like. It was drawn up ready for signature by the various representatives, and drawn up in America – at that time a neutral country. It was dispatched to England by a special messenger selected for that purpose, a young fellow called Danvers. It was hoped that the whole affair had been kept so secret that nothing would have leaked out. That kind of hope is usually disappointed. Somebody always talks!

'Danvers sailed for England on the *Lusitania*. He carried the precious papers in an oilskin packet which he wore next his skin. It was on that particular voyage that the *Lusitania* was torpedoed and sunk. Danvers was among the list of those missing. Eventually his body was washed ashore, and identified beyond any possible doubt. But the oilskin packet was missing!

'The question was, had it been taken from him, or had he himself passed it on into another's keeping? There were a few incidents that strengthened the possibility of the latter theory. After the torpedo struck the ship, in the few moments during the launching of the boats, Danvers was seen speaking to a young American girl. No one actually saw him pass anything to her, but he might have done so. It seems to me quite likely that he entrusted the papers to this girl, believing that she, as a woman, had a greater chance of bringing them safely to shore.

'But if so, where was the girl, and what had she done with the papers? By later advice from America it seemed likely that Danvers had been closely shadowed on the way over. Was this girl in league with his enemies? Or had she, in her turn, been shadowed and either tricked or forced into handing over the precious packet?

'We set to work to trace her out. It proved unexpectedly difficult. Her name was Jane Finn, and it duly appeared among the list of the survivors, but the girl herself seemed to have vanished completely. Inquiries into her antecedents did little to help us. She was an orphan, and had been what we should call over here a pupil teacher in a small school out West. Her passport had been made out for Paris, where she was going to join the staff of a hospital. She had offered her services voluntarily, and after some correspondence they had been accepted. Having seen her name in the list of the saved from the *Lusitania*, the staff of the hospital were naturally very surprised at her not arriving to take up her billet, and at not hearing from her in any way.

'Well, every effort was made to trace the young lady – but all in vain. We tracked her across Ireland, but nothing could be heard of her after she set foot in England. No use was made of the draft treaty – as might very easily have been done – and we therefore came to the conclusion that Danvers had, after all, destroyed it. The war entered on another phase, the diplomatic aspect changed accordingly, and the treaty was never redrafted. Rumours as to its existence were emphatically

denied. The disappearance of Jane Finn was forgotten and the
whole affair was lost in oblivion.'

Mr Carter paused, and Tuppence broke in impatiently:

'But why has it all cropped up again? The war's over.'

A hint of alertness came into Mr Carter's manner.

'Because it seemed that the papers were not destroyed after
all, and that they might be resurrected today with a new and
deadly significance.'

Tuppence stared. Mr Carter nodded.

'Yes, five years ago, that draft treaty was a weapon in our
hands; today it is a weapon against us. It was a gigantic
blunder. If its terms were made public, it would mean disaster
. . . It might possibly bring about another war – not with
Germany this time! That is an extreme possibility, and I do
not believe in its likelihood myself, but that document
undoubtedly implicates a number of our statesmen whom we
cannot afford to have discredited in any way at the present
moment. As a party cry for Labour it would be irresistible,
and a Labour Government at this juncture would, in my
opinion, be a grave disability for British trade, but that is a
mere nothing to the *real* danger.'

He paused, and then said quietly:

'You may perhaps have heard or read that there is Bolshevist influence at work behind the present labour unrest?'

Tuppence nodded.

'That is the truth, Bolshevist gold is pouring into this
country for the specific purpose of procuring a Revolution.
And there is a certain man, a man whose real name is unknown
to us, who is working in the dark for his own ends. The Bolshevists are behind the labour unrest – but this man is *behind
the Bolshevists*. Who is he? We do not know. He is always spoken
of by the unassuming title of "Mr Brown". But one thing is
certain, he is the master criminal of this age. He controls a
marvellous organization. Most of the peace propaganda during the war was originated and financed by him. His spies are
everywhere.'

'A naturalized German?' asked Tommy.

'On the contrary, I have every reason to believe he is an Englishman. He was pro-German, as he would have been pro-Boer. What he seeks to attain we do not know – probably supreme power for himself, of a kind unique in history. We have no clue as to his real personality. It is reported that even his own followers are ignorant of it. Where we have come across his tracks, he has always played a secondary part. Somebody else assumes the chief role. But afterwards we always find that there had been some nonentity, a servant or a clerk, who had remained in the background unnoticed, and that the elusive Mr Brown has escaped us once more.'

'Oh!' Tuppence jumped. 'I wonder –'

'Yes?'

'I remember in Mr Whittington's office. The clerk – he called him Brown. You don't think –'

Carter nodded thoughtfully.

'Very likely. A curious point is that the name is usually mentioned. An idiosyncracy of genius. Can you describe him at all?'

'I really didn't notice. He was quite ordinary – just like anyone else.'

Mr Carter sighed in his tired manner.

'That is the invariable description of Mr Brown! Brought a telephone message to the man Whittington, did he? Notice a telephone in the outer office?'

Tuppence thought.

'No, I don't think I did.'

'Exactly. That "message" was Mr Brown's way of giving an order to his subordinate. He overheard the whole conversation of course. Was it after that that Whittington handed you over the money, and told you to come the following day?'

Tuppence nodded.

'Yes, undoubtedly the hand of Mr Brown!' Mr Carter paused. 'Well, there it is, you see what you are pitting yourself against? Possibly the finest criminal brain of the age. I don't quite like it, you know. You're such young things, both of you. I shouldn't like anything to happen to you.'

'It won't,' Tuppence assured him positively.

'I'll look after her, sir,' said Tommy.

'And *I'll* look after you,' retorted Tuppence, resenting the manly assertion.

'Well, then, look after each other,' said Mr Carter, smiling. 'Now let's get back to business. There's something mysterious about this draft treaty that we haven't fathomed yet. We've been threatened with it – in plain and unmistakable terms. The Revolutionary elements as good as declared that it's in their hands, and that they intend to produce it at a given moment. On the other hand, they are clearly at fault about many of its provisions. The Government consider it as mere bluff on their part, and, rightly or wrongly, have stuck to the policy of absolute denial. I'm not so sure. There have been hints, indiscreet allusions, that seem to indicate that the menace is a real one. The position is much as though they had got hold of an incriminating document, but couldn't read it because it was in cipher – but we know that the draft treaty wasn't in cipher – couldn't be in the nature of things – so that won't wash. But there's *something*. Of course, Jane Finn may be dead for all we know – but I don't think so. The curious thing is that *they're trying to get information about the girl from us.*'

'What?'

'Yes. One or two little things have cropped up. And your story, little lady, confirms my idea. They know we're looking for Jane Finn. Well, they'll produce a Jane Finn of their own – say at a *pensionnat* in Paris.' Tuppence gasped, and Mr Carter smiled. 'No one knows in the least what she looks like, so that's all right. She's primed with a trumped-up tale, and her real business is to get as much information as possible out of us. See the idea?'

'Then you think' – Tuppence paused to grasp the supposition fully – 'that it *was* as Jane Finn that they wanted me to go to Paris?'

Mr Carter smiled more wearily than ever.

'I believe in coincidences, you know,' he said.

CHAPTER V

Mr Julius P. Hersheimmer

'Well,' said Tuppence, recovering herself, 'it really seems as though it were meant to be.'

Carter nodded.

'I know what you mean. I'm superstitious myself. Luck, and all that sort of thing. Fate seems to have chosen you out to be mixed up in this.'

Tommy indulged in a chuckle.

'My word! I don't wonder Whittington got the wind up when Tuppence plumped out that name! I should have myself. But look here, sir, we're taking up an awful lot of your time. Have you any tips to give us before we clear out?'

'I think not. My experts, working in stereotyped ways, have failed. You will bring imagination and an open mind to the task. Don't be discouraged if that too does not succeed. For one thing there is a likelihood of the pace being forced.'

Tuppence frowned uncomprehendingly.

'When you had that interview with Whittington, they had time before them. I have information that the big *coup* was planned for early in the new year. But the Government is contemplating legislative action which will deal effectually with the strike menace. They'll get wind of it soon, if they haven't already, and it's possible that they may bring things to a head. I hope it will myself. The less time they have to mature their plans the better. I'm just warning you that you haven't much time before you, and that you needn't be cast down if you fail. It's not an easy proposition anyway. That's all.'

Tuppence rose.

'I think we ought to be business-like. What exactly can we count upon you for, Mr Carter?'

Mr Carter's lips twitched slightly, but he replied succinctly:

'Funds within reason, detailed information on any point, and no *official recognition*. I mean that if you get yourselves into trouble with the police, I can't officially help you out of it. You're on your own.'

Tuppence nodded sagely.

'I quite understand that. I'll write out a list of the things I want to know when I've had time to think. Now – about money –'

'Yes, Miss Tuppence. Do you want to say how much?'

'Not exactly. We've got plenty to go on with for the present, but when we want more –'

'It will be waiting for you.'

'Yes, but – I'm sure I don't want to be rude about the Government if you've got anything to do with it, but you know one really has the devil of a time getting anything out of it! And if we have to fill up a blue form and send it in, and then, after three months, they send us a green one, and so on – well, that won't be much use, will it?'

Mr Carter laughed outright.

'Don't worry, Miss Tuppence. You will send a personal demand to me here, and the money, in notes, shall be sent by return of post. As to salary, shall we say at the rate of three hundred a year? And an equal sum for Mr Beresford, of course.'

Tuppence beamed upon him.

'How lovely. You are kind. I do love money! I'll keep beautiful accounts of our expenses – all debit and credit, and the balance on the right side, and a red line drawn sideways with the totals the same at the bottom. I really know how to do it when I think.'

'I'm sure you do. Well, goodbye, and good luck to you both.'

He shook hands with them and in another minute they were

descending the steps of 27 Carshalton Terrace with their heads in a whirl.

'Tommy! Tell me at once, who is "Mr Carter"?'

Tommy murmured a name in her ear.

'Oh!' said Tuppence, impressed.

'And I can tell you, old bean, he's rr!'

'Oh!' said Tuppence again. Then she added reflectively: 'I like him, don't you? He looks so awfully tired and bored, and yet you feel that underneath he's just like steel, all keen and flashing. Oh!' She gave a skip. 'Pinch me, Tommy, do pinch me. I can't believe it's real!'

Mr Beresford obliged.

'Ow! That's enough! Yes, we're not dreaming. We've got a job!'

'And what a job! The joint venture has really begun.'

'It's more respectable than I thought it would be,' said Tuppence thoughtfully.

'Luckily I haven't got your craving for crime! What time is it? Let's have lunch – oh!'

The same thought sprang to the minds of each. Tommy voiced it first.

'Julius P. Hersheimmer!'

'We never told Mr Carter about hearing from him.'

'Well, there wasn't much to tell – not till we've seen him. Come on, we'd better take a taxi.'

'Now who's being extravagant?'

'All expenses paid, remember. Hop in.'

'At any rate, we shall make a better effect arriving this way,' said Tuppence, leaning back luxuriously. 'I'm sure black-mailers never arrive in buses!'

'We've ceased being blackmailers,' Tommy pointed out.

'I'm not sure I have,' said Tuppence darkly.

On inquiring for Mr Hersheimmer, they were at once taken up to his suite. An impatient voice cried 'Come in' in answer to the page-boy's knock, and the lad stood aside to let them pass in.

Mr Julius P. Hersheimmer was a great deal younger than

either Tommy or Tuppence had pictured him. The girl put him down as thirty-five. He was of middle height, and squarely built to match his jaw. His face was pugnacious but pleasant. No one could have mistaken him for anything but an American, though he spoke with very little accent.

'Get my note? Sit down and tell me right away all you know about my cousin.'

'Your cousin?'

'Sure thing. Jane Finn.'

'Is she your cousin?'

'My father and her mother were brother and sister,' explained Mr Hersheimmer meticulously.

'Oh!' cried Tuppence. 'Then you know where she is?'

'No!' Mr Hersheimmer brought down his fist with a bang on the table. 'I'm darned if I do! Don't you?'

'We advertised to receive information, not to give it,' said Tuppence severely.

'I guess I know that. I can read. But I thought maybe it was her back history you were after, and that you'd know where she was now?'

'Well, we wouldn't mind hearing her back history,' said Tuppence guardedly.

But Mr Hersheimmer seemed to grow suddenly suspicious.

'See here,' he declared. 'This isn't Sicily! No demanding ransom or threatening to crop her ears if I refuse. These are the British Isles, so quit the funny business, or I'll just sing out for that beautiful big British policeman I see out there in Piccadilly.'

Tommy hastened to explain.

'We haven't kidnapped your cousin. On the contrary, we're trying to find her. We're employed to do so.'

Mr Hersheimmer leant back in his chair.

'Put me wise,' he said succinctly.

Tommy fell in with this demand in so far as he gave him a guarded version of the disappearance of Jane Finn, and of the possibility of her having been mixed up unawares in 'some political show'. He alluded to Tuppence and himself as 'private inquiry agents' commissioned to find her, and added that they would therefore be glad of any details Mr Hersheimmer could give them.

That gentleman nodded approval.

'I guess that's my right. I was just a mite hasty. But London gets my goat! I only know little old New York. Just trot your questions and I'll answer.'

For the moment this paralysed the Young Adventurers, but Tuppence, recovering herself, plunged boldly into the breach with a reminiscence culled from detective fiction.

'When did you last see the dece – your cousin, I mean?'

'Never seen her,' responded Mr Hersheimmer.

'What?' demanded Tommy astonished.

Hersheimmer turned to him.

'No, sir. As I said before, my father and her mother were brother and sister, just as you might be' – Tommy did not correct this view of their relationship – 'but they didn't always get on together. And when my aunt made up her mind to marry Amos Finn, who was a poor school teacher out West, my father was just mad! Said if he made his pile, as he seemed in a fair way to do, she'd never see a cent of it. Well, the upshot was that Aunt Jane went out West and we never heard from her again.

'The old man *did* pile it up. He went into oil, and he went into steel, and he played a bit with railroads, and I can tell you he made Wall Street sit up!' He paused. 'Then he died – last fall – and I got the dollars. Well, would you believe it, my conscience got busy! Kept knocking me up and saying: What about your Aunt Jane, way out West? It worried me some. You see, I figured it out that Amos Finn would never make good. He wasn't the sort. End of it was, I hired a man to hunt her down. Result, she was dead, and Amos Finn was dead, but they'd left a daughter – Jane – who'd been torpedoed in the *Lusitania* on her way to Paris. She was saved all right, but they didn't seem able to hear of her over this side. I guessed they weren't hustling any, so I thought I'd come along over, and speed things up. I phoned Scotland Yard and the

Admiralty first thing. The Admiralty rather choked me off, but Scotland Yard were very civil – said they would make inquiries, even sent a man round this morning to get her photograph. I'm off to Paris tomorrow, just to see what the Prefecture is doing. I guess if I go to and fro hustling them, they ought to get busy!'

The energy of Mr Hersheimmer was tremendous. They bowed before it.

'But say now,' he ended, 'you're not after her for anything? Contempt of court, or something British? A proud-spirited young American girl might find your rules and regulations in war time rather irksome, and get up against it. If that's the case, and there's such a thing as graft in this country, I'll buy her off.'

Tuppence reassured him.

'That's good. Then we can work together. What about some lunch? Shall we have it up here, or go down to the restaurant?'

Tuppence expressed a preference for the latter, and Julius bowed to her decision.

Oysters had just given place to Sole Colbert when a card was brought to Hersheimmer.

'Inspector Japp, CID Scotland Yard again. Another man this time. What does he expect I can tell him that I didn't tell the first chap? I hope they haven't lost that photograph. That Western photographer's place was burned down and all his negatives destroyed – this is the only copy in existence. I got it from the principal of the college there.'

An unformulated dread swept over Tuppence.

'You – you don't know the name of the man who came this morning?'

'Yes, I do. No, I don't. Half a second. It was on his card. Oh, I know! Inspector Brown. Quiet unassuming sort of chap.'

CHAPTER VI

A Plan of Campaign

A veil might with profit be drawn over the events of the next half-hour. Suffice it to say that no such person as 'Inspector Brown' was known to Scotland Yard. The photograph of Jane Finn, which would have been of the utmost value to the police in tracing her, was lost beyond recovery. Once again 'Mr Brown' had triumphed.

The immediate result of this set-back was to effect a *rapprochement* between Julius Hersheimmer and the Young Adventurers. All barriers went down with a crash, and Tommy and Tuppence felt they had known the young American all their lives. They abandoned the discreet reticence of 'private inquiry agents', and revealed to him the whole history of the joint venture, whereat the young man declared himself 'tickled to death'.

He turned to Tuppence at the close of the narration.

'I've always had a kind of idea that English girls were just a mite moss-grown. Old-fashioned and sweet, you know, but scared to move round without a footman or a maiden aunt. I guess I'm a bit behind the times!'

The upshot of these confidential relations was that Tommy and Tuppence took up their abode forthwith at the Ritz, in order, as Tuppence put it, to keep in touch with Jane Finn's only living relation. 'And put like that,' she added confidentially to Tommy, 'nobody could boggle at the expense!'

Nobody did, which was the great thing.

'And now,' said the young lady on the morning after their installation, 'to work!'

Mr Beresford put down the *Daily Mail*, which he was reading, and applauded with somewhat unnecessary vigour. He was politely requested by his colleague not to be an ass.

'Dash it all, Tommy, we've got to *do* something for our money.'

Tommy sighed.

'Yes, I fear even the dear old Government will not support us at the Ritz in idleness for ever.'

'Therefore, as I said before, we must *do* something.'

'Well,' said Tommy, picking up the *Daily Mail* again, '*do* it. I shan't stop you.'

'You see,' continued Tuppence. 'I've been thinking –'

She was interrupted by a fresh bout of applause.

'It's all very well for you to sit there being funny, Tommy. It would do you no harm to do a little brain work too.'

'My union, Tuppence, my union! It does not permit me to work before 11 a.m.'

'Tommy, do you want something thrown at you? It is absolutely essential that we should without delay map out a plan of campaign.'

'Hear, hear!'

'Well, let's do it.'

Tommy laid his paper finally aside. 'There's something of the simplicity of the truly great mind about you, Tuppence. Fire ahead. I'm listening.'

'To begin with,' said Tuppence, 'what have we to go upon?'

'Absolutely nothing,' said Tommy cheerily.

'Wrong!' Tuppence wagged an energetic finger. 'We have two distinct clues.'

'What are they?'

'First clue, we know one of the gang.'

'Whittington?'

'Yes. I'd recognize him anywhere.'

'Hum,' said Tommy doubtfully. 'I don't call that much of a clue. You don't know where to look for him, and it's about a thousand to one against your running against him by accident.'

'I'm not so sure about that,' replied Tuppence thoughtfully. 'I've often noticed that once coincidences start happening they go on happening in the most extraordinary way. I dare say it's some natural law that we haven't found out. Still, as you say, we can't rely on that. But there *are* places in London where simply everyone is bound to turn up sooner or later. Piccadilly Circus, for instance. One of my ideas was to take up my stand there every day with a tray of flags.'

'What about meals?' inquired the practical Tommy.

'How like a man! What does mere food matter?'

'That's all very well. You've just had a thundering good breakfast. No one's got a better appetite than you have, Tuppence, and by tea-time you'd be eating the flags, pins and all. But, honestly, I don't think much of the idea. Whittington mayn't be in London at all.'

'That's true. Anyway, I think clue No. 2 is more promising.'

'Let's hear it.'

'It's nothing much. Only a Christian name – Rita. Whittington mentioned it that day.'

'Are you proposing a third advertisement: Wanted, female crook, answering to the name of Rita?'

'I am not. I propose to reason in a logical manner. That man, Danvers, was shadowed on the way over, wasn't he? And it's more likely to have been a woman than a man –'

'I don't see that at all.'

'I am absolutely certain that it would be a woman, and a good-looking one,' replied Tuppence calmly.

'On these technical points I bow to your decision,' murmured Mr Beresford.

'Now, obviously, this woman, whoever she was, was saved.'

'How do you make that out?'

'If she wasn't, how would they have known Jane Finn had got the papers?'

'Correct. Proceed, O Sherlock!'

'Now there's just a chance, I admit it's only a chance, that this woman may have been "Rita".'

'And if so?'

'If so, we've got to hunt through the survivors of the *Lusitania* till we find her.'

'Then the first thing is to get a list of the survivors.'

'I've got it. I wrote a long list of things I wanted to know, and sent it to Mr Carter. I got his reply this morning, and among other things it encloses the official statement of those saved from the *Lusitania*. How's that for clever little Tuppence?'

'Full marks for industry, zero for modesty. But the great point is, is there a "Rita" on the list?'

'That's just what I don't know,' confessed Tuppence.

'Don't know?'

'Yes, look here.' Together they bent over the list. 'You see, very few Christian names are given. They're nearly all Mrs or Miss.'

Tommy nodded.

'That complicates matters,' he murmured thoughtfully.

Tuppence gave her characteristic 'terrier' shake.

'Well, we've just got to get down to it, that's all. We'll start with the London area. Just note down the addresses of any of the females who live in London or roundabout, while I put on my hat.'

Five minutes later the young couple emerged into Piccadilly, and a few seconds later a taxi was bearing them to The Laurels, Glendower Road, N.7, the residence of Mrs Edgar Keith, whose name figured first in a list of seven reposing in Tommy's pocket-book.

The Laurels was a dilapidated house, standing back from the road with a few grimy bushes to support the fiction of a front garden. Tommy paid off the taxi, and accompanied Tuppence to the front door bell. As she was about to ring it, he arrested her hand.

'What are you going to say?'

'What am I going to say? Why, I shall say – Oh dear, I don't know. It's very awkward.'

'I thought as much,' said Tommy with satisfaction. 'How like a woman! No foresight! Now just stand aside, and see how easily the mere male deals with the situation.' He pressed the bell. Tuppence withdrew to a suitable spot.

A slatternly-looking servant, with an extremely dirty face and a pair of eyes that did not match, answered the door.

Tommy had produced a notebook and pencil.

'Good morning,' he said briskly and cheerfully. 'From the Hampstead Borough Council. The New Voting Register. Mrs Edgar Keith lives here, does she not?'

'Yaas,' said the servant.

'Christian name?' asked Tommy, his pencil poised.

'Missus's? Eleanor Jane.'

'Eleanor,' spelt Tommy. 'Any sons or daughters over twenty-one?'

'Naow.'

'Thank you.' Tommy closed the notebook with a brisk snap. 'Good morning.'

The servant volunteered her first remark:

'I thought perhaps as you'd come about the gas,' she observed cryptically, and shut the door.

Tommy rejoined his accomplice.

'You see, Tuppence,' he observed. 'Child's play to the masculine mind.'

'I don't mind admitting that for once you've scored handsomely. I should never have thought of that.'

'Good wheeze, wasn't it? And we can repeat it *ad lib*.'

Lunch-time found the young couple attacking steak and chips in an obscure hostelry with avidity. They had collected a Gladys Mary and a Marjorie, been baffled by one change of address, and had been forced to listen to a long lecture on universal suffrage from a vivacious American lady whose Christian name had proved to be Sadie.

'Ah!' said Tommy, imbibing a long draught of beer. 'I feel better. Where's the next draw?'

The notebook lay on the table between them. Tuppence picked it up.

'Mrs Vandemeyer,' she read, '20 South Audley Mansions. Miss Wheeler, 43 Clapington Road, Battersea. She's a lady's maid, as far as I remember, so probably won't be there, and, anyway, she's not likely.'

'Then the Mayfair lady is clearly indicated as the first port of call.'

'Tommy, I'm getting discouraged.'

'Buck up, old bean. We always knew it was an outside chance. And, anyway, we're only starting. If we draw a blank in London, there's a fine tour of England, Ireland and Scotland before us.'

'True,' said Tuppence, her flagging spirits reviving. 'And all expenses paid! But, oh, Tommy, I do like things to happen quickly. So far, adventure has succeeded adventure, but this morning has been dull as dull.'

'You must stifle this longing for vulgar sensation, Tuppence. Remember that if Mr Brown is all he is reported to be, it's a wonder that he has not ere now done us to death. That's a good sentence, quite a literary flavour about it.'

'You're really more conceited than I am – with less excuse! Ahem! But it certainly is queer that Mr Brown has not yet wreaked vengeance upon us. (You see, I can do it too.) We pass on our way unscathed.'

'Perhaps he doesn't think us worth bothering about,' suggested the young man simply.

Tuppence received the remark with great disfavour.

'How horrid you are, Tommy. Just as though we didn't count.'

'Sorry, Tuppence. What I meant was that we work like moles in the dark, and that he has no suspicion of our nefarious schemes. Ha ha!'

'Ha ha!' echoed Tuppence approvingly, as she rose.

South Audley Mansions was an imposing looking block of flats just off Park Lane. No. 20 was on the second floor.

Tommy had by this time the glibness born of practice. He rattled off the formula to the elderly woman, looking more like a housekeeper than a servant, who opened the door to him.

'Christian name?'

'Margaret.'

Tommy spelt it, but the other interrupted him.

'No, *g u e*.'

'Oh, Marguerite; French way, I see.' He paused then plunged boldly. 'We had her down as Rita Vandemeyer, but I suppose that's correct?'

'She's mostly called that, sir, but Marguerite's her name.'

'Thank you. That's all. Good morning.'

Hardly able to contain his excitement, Tommy hurried down the stairs. Tuppence was waiting at the angle of the turn.

'You heard?'

'Yes. Oh, *Tommy*!'

Tommy squeezed her arm sympathetically.

'I know, old thing. I feel the same.'

'It's – it's so lovely to think of things – and then for them really to happen!' cried Tuppence enthusiastically.

Her hand was still in Tommy's. They had reached the entrance hall. There were footsteps on the stairs above them, and voices.

Suddenly, to Tommy's complete surprise, Tuppence dragged him into the little space by the side of the lift where the shadow was deepest.

'What the –'

'Hush!'

Two men came down the stairs and passed out through the entrance. Tuppence's hand closed tighter on Tommy's arm.

'Quick – follow them. I daren't. He might recognize me. I don't know who the other man is, but the bigger of the two was Whittington.'

CHAPTER VII

The House in Soho

Whittington and his companion were walking at a good pace. Tommy started in pursuit at once, and was in time to see them turn the corner of the street. His vigorous strides soon enabled him to gain upon them, and by the time he, in his turn, reached the corner the distance between them was sensibly lessened. The small Mayfair streets were comparatively deserted, and he judged it wise to content himself with keeping them in sight.

The sport was a new one to him. Though familiar with the technicalities from a course of novel reading, he had never before attempted to 'follow' anyone, and it appeared to him at once that, in actual practice, the proceeding was fraught with difficulties. Supposing, for instance, that they should suddenly hail a taxi? In books, you simply leapt into another, promised the driver a sovereign – or its modern equivalent – and there you were. In actual fact, Tommy foresaw that it was extremely likely there would be no second taxi. Therefore he would have to run. What happened in actual fact to a young man who ran incessantly and persistently through the London streets? In a main road he might hope to create the illusion that he was merely running for a bus. But in these obscure aristocratic byways he could not but feel that an officious policeman might stop him to explain matters.

At this juncture in his thoughts a taxi with flag erect turned the corner of the street ahead. Tommy held his breath. Would they hail it?

He drew a sigh of relief as they allowed it to pass unchallenged. Their course was a zigzag one designed to bring them as quickly as possible to Oxford Street. When at length they turned into it, proceeding in an easterly direction, Tommy slightly increased his pace. Little by little he gained upon them. On the crowded pavement there was little chance of his attracting their notice, and he was anxious if possible to catch a word or two of their conversation. In this he was completely foiled: they spoke low and the din of the traffic drowned their voices effectually.

Just before the Bond Street Tube station they crossed the road, Tommy, unperceived, faithfully at their heels, and entered the big Lyons'. There they went up to the first floor, and sat at a small table in the window. It was late, and the place was thinning out. Tommy took a seat at the table next to them sitting directly behind Whittington in case of recognition. On the other hand, he had a full view of the second man and studied him attentively. He was fair, with a weak, unpleasant face, and Tommy put him down as being either a Russian or a Pole. He was probably about fifty years of age, his shoulders cringed a little as he talked, and his eyes, small and crafty, shifted unceasingly.

Having already lunched heartily, Tommy contented himself with ordering a Welsh rarebit and a cup of coffee. Whittington ordered a substantial lunch for himself and his companion; then, as the waitress withdrew, he moved his chair a little closer to the table and began to talk earnestly in a low voice. The other man joined in. Listen as he would, Tommy could only catch a word here and there; but the gist of it seemed to be some directions or orders which the big man was impressing on his companion, and with which the latter seemed from time to time to disagree. Whittington addressed the other as Boris.

Tommy caught the word 'Ireland' several times, also 'propaganda', but of Jane Finn there was no mention. Suddenly, in a lull in the clatter of the room, he got one phrase entire. Whittington was speaking. 'Ah, but you don't know Flossie. She's a marvel. An archbishop would swear she was his own mother. She gets the voice right every time, and that's really the principal thing.'

Tommy did not hear Boris's reply, but in response to it

Whittington said something that sounded like: 'of course – only in an emergency . . .'

Then he lost the thread again. But presently the phrases became distinct again, whether because the other two had insensibly raised their voices, or because Tommy's ears were getting more attuned, he could not tell. But two words certainly had a most stimulating effect upon the listener. They were uttered by Boris and they were: 'Mr Brown.'

Whittington seemed to remonstrate with him, but he merely laughed.

'Why not, my friend? It is a name most respectable – most common. Did he not choose it for that reason? Ah, I should like to meet him – Mr Brown.'

There was a steely ring in Whittington's voice as he replied: 'Who knows? You may have met him already.'

'Bah!' retorted the other. 'That is children's talk – a fable for the police. Do you know what I say to myself sometimes? That he is a fable invented by the Inner Ring, a bogy to frighten us with. It might be so.'

'And it might not.'

'I wonder . . . or is it indeed true that he is with us and amongst us, unknown to all but a chosen few? If so, he keeps his secret well. And the idea is a good one, yes. We never know. We look at each other – *one of us is Mr Brown* – which? He commands – but also he serves. Among us – in the midst of us. And no one knows which he is . . .'

With an effort the Russian shook off the vagary of his fancy. He looked at his watch.

'Yes,' said Whittington. 'We might as well go.'

He called the waitress and asked for his bill. Tommy did likewise, and a few moments later was following the two men down the stairs.

Outside, Whittington hailed a taxi, and directed the driver to Waterloo.

Taxis were plentiful here, and before Whittington's had driven off another was drawing up to the curb in obedience to Tommy's peremptory hand.

'Follow that other taxi,' directed the young man. 'Don't lose it.'

The elderly chauffeur showed no interest. He merely grunted and jerked down his flag. The drive was uneventful. Tommy's taxi came to rest at the departure platform just after Whittington's. Tommy was behind him at the booking-office. He took a first-class single to Bournemouth, Tommy did the same. As he emerged, Boris remarked, glancing up at the clock: 'You are early. You have nearly half an hour.'

Boris's words had aroused a new train of thought in Tommy's mind. Clearly Whittington was making the journey alone, while the other remained in London. Therefore he was left with a choice as to which he would follow. Obviously, he could not follow both of them unless – Like Boris, he glanced up at the clock, and then to the announcement board of the trains. The Bournemouth train left at 3.30. It was now ten past. Whittington and Boris were walking up and down by the bookstall. He gave one doubtful look at them, then hurried into an adjacent telephone box. He dared not waste time in trying to get hold of Tuppence. In all probability she was still in the neighbourhood of South Audley Mansions. But there remained another ally. He rang up the Ritz and asked for Julius Hersheimmer. There was a click and a buzz. Oh, if only the young American was in his room! There was another click, and then 'Hello' in unmistakable accents came over the wire.

'That you, Hersheimmer? Beresford speaking. I'm at Waterloo. I've followed Whittington and another man here. No time to explain. Whittington's off to Bournemouth by the 3.30. Can you get here by then?'

The reply was reassuring.

'Sure. I'll hustle.'

The telephone rang off. Tommy put back the receiver with a sigh of relief. His opinion of Julius's power of hustling was high. He felt instinctively that the American would arrive in time.

Whittington and Boris were still where he had left them. If

Boris remained to see his friend off, all was well. Then Tommy fingered his pocket thoughtfully. In spite of the carte blanche assured to him, he had not yet acquired the habit of going about with any considerable sum of money on him. The taking of the first-class ticket to Bournemouth had left him with only a few shillings in his pocket. It was to be hoped that Julius would arrive better provided.

In the meantime, the minutes were creeping by: 3.15, 3.20, 3.25, 3.27. Supposing Julius did not get there in time. 3.29 . . . Doors were banging. Tommy felt cold waves of despair pass over him. Then a hand fell on his shoulder.

'Here I am, son. Your British traffic beats description! Put me wise to the crooks right away.'

'That's Whittington – there, getting in now, that big dark man. The other is the foreign chap he's talking to.'

'I'm on to them. Which of the two is my bird?'

Tommy had thought out this question.

'Got any money with you?'

Julius shook his head, and Tommy's face fell.

'I guess I haven't more than three or four hundred dollars with me at the moment,' explained the American.

Tommy gave a faint whoop of relief.

'Oh, Lord, you millionaires! You don't talk the same language! Climb aboard the lugger. Here's your ticket. Whittington's your man.'

'Me for Whittington!' said Julius darkly. The train was just starting as he swung himself aboard. 'So long, Tommy.' The train slid out of the station.

Tommy drew a deep breath. The man Boris was coming along the platform towards him. Tommy allowed him to pass and then took up the chase once more.

From Waterloo Boris took the Tube as far as Piccadilly Circus. Then he walked up Shaftesbury Avenue, finally turning off into the maze of mean streets round Soho. Tommy followed him at a judicious distance.

They reached at length a small dilapidated square. The houses there had a sinister air in the midst of their dirt and decay. Boris looked round, and Tommy drew back into the shelter of a friendly porch. The place was almost deserted. It was a cul-de-sac, and consequently no traffic passed that way. The stealthy way the other had looked round stimulated Tommy's imagination. From the shelter of the doorway he watched him go up the steps of a particularly evil-looking house and rap sharply, with a peculiar rhythm, on the door. It was opened promptly, he said a word or two to the door-keeper, then passed inside. The door was shut to again.

It was at this juncture that Tommy lost his head. What he ought to have done, what any sane man would have done, was to remain patiently where he was and wait for his man to come out again. What he did do was entirely foreign to the sober common sense which was, as a rule, his leading characteristic. Something, as he expressed it, seemed to snap in his brain. Without a moment's pause for reflection he, too, went up the steps, and reproduced as far as he was able the peculiar knock.

The door swung open with the same promptness as before. A villainous-faced man with close-cropped hair stood in the doorway.

'Well?' he grunted.

It was at that moment that the full realization of his folly began to come home to Tommy. But he dared not hesitate. He seized at the first words that came into his mind.

'Mr Brown?' he said.

To his surprise the man stood aside.

'Upstairs,' he said, jerking his thumb over his shoulder, 'second door on your left.'

CHAPTER VIII

The Adventures of Tommy

Taken aback though he was by the man's words, Tommy did not hesitate. If audacity had successfully carried him so far, it was to be hoped it would carry him yet farther. He quietly passed into the house and mounted the ramshackle staircase. Everything in the house was filthy beyond words. The grimy paper, of a pattern now indistinguishable, hung in loose festoons from the wall. In every angle was a grey mass of cobweb.

Tommy proceeded leisurely. By the time he reached the bend of the staircase, he had heard the man below disappear into a back room. Clearly no suspicion attached to him as yet. To come to the house and ask for 'Mr Brown' appeared indeed to be a reasonable and natural proceeding.

At the top of the stairs Tommy halted to consider his next move. In front of him ran a narrow passage, with doors opening on either side of it. From the one nearest him on the left came a low murmur of voices. It was this room which he had been directed to enter. But what held his glance fascinated was a small recess immediately on his right, half concealed by a torn velvet curtain. It was directly opposite the left-hand door and, owing to its angle, it also commanded a good view of the upper part of the staircase. As a hiding-place for one or, at a pinch, two men, it was ideal, being about two feet deep and three feet wide. It attracted Tommy mightily. He thought things over in his usual slow and steady way, deciding that the mention of 'Mr Brown' was not a request for an individual, but in all probability a password used by the gang. His lucky use of it had gained him admission. So far he had aroused no suspicion. But he must decide quickly on his next step.

Suppose he were boldly to enter the room on the left of the passage. Would the mere fact of his having been admitted to the house be sufficient? Perhaps a further password would be required, or, at any rate, some proof of identity. The door-keeper clearly did not know all the members of the gang by sight, but it might be different upstairs. On the whole it seemed to him that luck had served him very well so far, but that there was such a thing as trusting it too far. To enter that room was a colossal risk. He could not hope to sustain his part indefinitely; sooner or later he was almost bound to betray himself, and then he would have thrown away a vital chance in mere foolhardiness.

A repetition of the signal sounded on the door below, and Tommy, his mind made up, slipped quickly into the recess, and cautiously drew the curtain farther across so that it shielded him completely from sight. There were several rents and slits in the ancient material which afforded him a good view. He would watch events, and any time he chose could, after all, join the assembly, modelling his behaviour on that of the new arrival.

The man who came up the staircase with a furtive, soft-footed tread was quite unknown to Tommy. He was obviously of the very dregs of society. The low beetling brows, and the criminal jaw, the bestiality of the whole countenance were new to the young man, though he was of a type that Scotland Yard would have recognized at a glance.

The man passed the recess, breathing heavily as he went. He stopped at the door opposite, and gave a repetition of the signal knock. A voice inside called out something, and the man opened the door and passed in, affording Tommy a momentary glimpse of the room inside. He thought there must be about four or five people seated round a long table that took up most of the space, but his attention was caught and held by a tall man with close-cropped hair and a short, pointed, naval-looking beard, who sat at the head of the table with papers in front of him. As the newcomer entered he glanced up, and with a correct, but curiously precise enunciation, which attracted Tommy's notice, he asked: 'Your number, comrade?'

'Fourteen, guv'nor,' replied the other hoarsely.

'Correct.'

The door shut again.

'If that isn't a Hun, I'm a Dutchman!' said Tommy to himself. 'And running the show darned systematically, too – as they always do. Lucky I didn't roll in. I'd have given the wrong number, and there would have been the deuce to pay. No, this is the place for me. Hullo, here's another knock.'

This visitor proved to be of an entirely different type to the last. Tommy recognized in him an Irish Sinn Feiner. Certainly Mr Brown's organization was a far-reaching concern. The common criminal, the well-bred Irish gentleman, the pale Russian, and the efficient German master of the ceremonies! Truly a strange and sinister gathering! Who was this man who held in his fingers these curiously variegated links of an unknown chain?

In this case, the procedure was exactly the same. The signal knock, the demand for a number, and the reply 'Correct.'

Two knocks followed in quick succession on the door below. The first man was quite unknown to Tommy, who put him down as a city clerk. A quiet, intelligent-looking man, rather shabbily dressed. The second was of the working classes, and his face was vaguely familiar to the young man.

Three minutes later came another, a man of commanding appearance, exquisitely dressed, and evidently well born. His face, again, was not unknown to the watcher, though he could not for the moment put a name to it.

After his arrival there was a long wait. In fact, Tommy concluded that the gathering was now complete, and was just cautiously creeping out from his hiding-place, when another knock sent him scuttling back to cover.

This last-comer came up the stairs so quietly that he was almost abreast of Tommy before the young man had realized his presence.

He was a small man, very pale, with a gentle almost

womanish air. The angle of the cheek-bones hinted at his Slavonic ancestry, otherwise there was nothing to indicate his nationality. As he passed the recess, he turned his head slowly. The strange light eyes seemed to burn through the curtain; Tommy could hardly believe that the man did not know he was there and in spite of himself he shivered. He was no more fanciful than the majority of young Englishmen, but he could not rid himself of the impression that some unusually potent force emanated from the man. The creature reminded him of a venomous snake.

A moment later his impression was proved correct. The newcomer knocked on the door as all had done, but his reception was very different. The bearded man rose to his feet, and all the others followed suit. The German came forward and shook hands. His heels clicked together.

'We are honoured,' he said. 'We are greatly honoured. I much feared that it would be impossible.'

The other answered in a low voice that had a kind of hiss in it:

'There were difficulties. It will not be possible again, I fear. But one meeting is essential – to define my policy. I can do nothing without – Mr Brown. He is here?'

The change in the German's air was audible as he replied with slight hesitation:

'We have received a message. It is impossible for him to be present in person.' He stopped, giving a curious impression of having left the sentence unfinished.

A very slow smile overspread the face of the other. He looked round at a circle of uneasy faces.

'Ah! I understand. I have read of his methods. He works in the dark and trusts no one. But, all the same, it is possible that he is among us now . . .' He looked round him again, and again that expression of fear swept over the group. Each man seemed to be eyeing his neighbour doubtfully.

The Russian tapped his cheek.

'So be it. Let us proceed.'

The German seemed to pull himself together. He indicated

the place he had been occupying at the head of the table. The Russian demurred, but the other insisted.

'It is the only possible place,' he said, 'for – Number One. Perhaps Number Fourteen will shut the door!'

In another moment Tommy was once more confronting bare wooden panels, and the voices within had sunk once more to a mere undistinguishable murmur. Tommy became restive. The conversation he had overheard had stimulated his curiosity. He felt that, by hook or by crook, he must hear more.

There was no sound from below, and it did not seem likely that the door-keeper would come upstairs. After listening intently for a minute or two, he put his head round the curtain. The passage was deserted. Tommy bent down and removed his shoes, then, leaving them behind the curtain, he walked gingerly out on his stockinged feet, and kneeling down by the closed door he laid his ear cautiously to the crack. To his intense annoyance he could distinguish little more; just a chance word here and there if a voice was raised, which merely served to whet his curiosity still further.

He eyed the handle of the door tentatively. Could he turn it by degrees so gently and imperceptibly that those in the room would notice nothing? He decided that with great care it could be done. Very slowly, a fraction of an inch at a time, he moved it round, holding his breath in his excessive care. A little more – a little more still – would it never be finished? Ah! at last it would turn no farther.

He stayed so for a minute or two, then drew a deep breath, and pressed it ever so slightly inward. The door did not budge. Tommy was annoyed. If he had to use too much force, it would almost certainly creak. He waited until the voices rose a little, then he tried again. Still nothing happened. He increased the pressure. Had the beastly thing stuck? Finally, in desperation, he pushed with all his might. But the door remained firm, and at last the truth dawned upon him. It was locked or bolted on the inside.

For a moment or two Tommy's indignation got the better of him.

'Well, I'm damned!' he said. 'What a dirty trick!'

As his indignation cooled, he prepared to face the situation. Clearly the first thing to be done was to restore the handle to its original position. If he let it go suddenly, the men inside would be almost certain to notice it, so with the same infinite pains he reversed his former tactics. All went well, and with a sigh of relief the young man rose to his feet. There was a certain bulldog tenacity about Tommy that made him slow to admit defeat. Checkmated for the moment, he was far from abandoning the conflict. He still intended to hear what was going on in the locked room. As one plan had failed, he must hunt about for another.

He looked round him. A little farther along the passage on the left was a second door. He slipped silently along to it. He listened for a moment or two, then tried the handle. It yielded, and he slipped inside.

The room, which was untenanted, was furnished as a bedroom. Like everything else in the house, the furniture was falling to pieces, and the dirt was, if anything, more abundant.

But what interested Tommy was the thing he had hoped to find, a communicating door between the two rooms, up on the left by the window. Carefully closing the door into the passage behind him, he stepped across to the other and examined it closely. The bolt was shot across it. It was very rusty, and had clearly not been used for some time. By gently wriggling it to and fro, Tommy managed to draw it back without making too much noise. Then he repeated his former manœuvres with the handle – this time with complete success. The door swung open – a crack, a mere fraction, but enough for Tommy to hear what went on. There was a velvet *portière* on the inside of this door which prevented him from seeing, but he was able to recognize the voices with a reasonable amount of accuracy.

The Sinn Feiner was speaking. His rich Irish voice was unmistakable:

'That's all very well. But more money is essential. No money – no results!'

Another voice which Tommy rather thought was that of Boris replied:

'Will you guarantee that there *are* results?'

'In a month from now – sooner or later as you wish – I will guarantee you such a reign of terror in Ireland as shall shake the British Empire to its foundations.'

There was a pause, and then came the soft, sibilant accents of Number One:

'Good! You shall have the money. Boris, you will see to that.'

Boris asked a question:

'Via the Irish Americans, and Mr Potter as usual?'

'I guess that'll be all right!' said a new voice, with a transatlantic intonation, 'though I'd like to point out, here and now, that things are getting a mite difficult. There's not the sympathy there was, and a growing disposition to let the Irish settle their own affairs without interference from America.'

Tommy felt that Boris had shrugged his shoulders as he answered:

'Does that matter, since the money only nominally comes from the States?'

'The chief difficulty is the landing of the ammunition,' said the Sinn Feiner. 'The money is conveyed in easily enough – thanks to our colleague here.'

Another voice, which Tommy fancied was that of the tall, commanding-looking man whose face had seemed familiar to him, said:

'Think of the feelings of Belfast if they could hear you!'

'That is settled, then,' said the sibilant tones. 'Now, in the matter of the loan to an English newspaper, you have arranged the details satisfactorily, Boris?'

'I think so.'

'That is good. An official denial from Moscow will be forthcoming if necessary.'

There was a pause, and then the clear voice of the German broke the silence:

'I am directed by – Mr Brown, to place the summaries of the reports from the different unions before you. That of the miners is most satisfactory. We must hold back the railways. There may be trouble with the ASE.'

For a long time there was a silence, broken only by the rustle of papers and an occasional word of explanation from the German. Then Tommy heard the light tap-tap of fingers drumming on the table.

'And – the date, my friend?' said Number One.

'The 29th.'

The Russian seemed to consider.

'That is rather soon.'

'I know. But it was settled by the principal Labour leaders, and we cannot seem to interfere too much. They must believe it to be entirely their own show.'

The Russian laughed softly, as though amused.

'Yes, yes,' he said. 'That is true. They must have no inkling that we are using them for our own ends. They are honest men – and that is their value to us. It is curious – but you cannot make a revolution without honest men. The instinct of the populace is infallible.' He paused, and then repeated, as though the phrase pleased him: 'Every revolution has had its honest men. They are soon disposed of afterwards.'

There was a sinister note in his voice.

The German resumed:

'Clymes must go. He is too far-seeing. Number Fourteen will see to that.'

There was a hoarse murmur.

'That's all right, guv'nor.' And then after a moment or two: 'Suppose I'm nabbed.'

'You will have the best legal talent to defend you,' replied the German quietly. 'But in any case you will wear gloves fitted with the finger-prints of a notorious housebreaker. You have little to fear.'

'Oh, I ain't afraid, guv'nor. All for the good of the cause. The streets is going to run with blood, so they say.' He spoke with a grim relish. 'Dreams of it, sometimes, I does. And diamonds and pearls rolling about in the gutter for anyone to pick up!'

Tommy heard a chair shifted. Then Number One spoke:

'Then all is arranged. We are assured of success?'

'I – I think so.' But the German spoke with less than his usual confidence.

Number One's voice held suddenly a dangerous quality:

'What has gone wrong?'

'Nothing; but –'

'But what?'

'The labour leaders. Without them, as you say, we can do nothing. If they do not declare a general strike on the 29th –'

'Why should they not?'

'As you've said, they're honest. And, in spite of everything we've done to discredit the Government in their eyes, I'm not sure that they haven't got a sneaking faith and belief in it.'

'But –'

'I know. They abuse it unceasingly. But, on the whole, public opinion swings to the side of the Government. They will not go against it.'

Again the Russian's fingers drummed on the table.

'To the point, my friend. I was given to understand that there was a certain document in existence which assured success.'

'That is so. If that document were placed before the leaders, the result would be immediate. They would publish it broadcast throughout England, and declare for the revolution without a moment's hesitation. The Government would be broken finally and completely.'

'Then what more do you want?'

'The document itself,' said the German bluntly.

'Ah! It is not in your possession? But you know where it is?'

'No.'

'Does anyone know where it is?'

'One person – perhaps. And we are not sure of that even.'

'Who is this person?'

'A girl.'

Tommy held his breath.

'A girl?' The Russian's voice rose contemptuously. 'And you have not made her speak? In Russia we have ways of making a girl talk.'

'This case is different,' said the German sullenly.

'How – different?' He paused a moment, then went on: 'Where is the girl now?'

'The girl?'

'Yes.'

'She is –'

But Tommy heard no more. A crashing blow descended on his head, and all was darkness.

CHAPTER IX

Tuppence Enters Domestic Service

When Tommy set forth on the trail of the two men, it took all Tuppence's self-command to refrain from accompanying him. However, she contained herself as best she might, consoled by the reflection that her reasoning had been justified by events. The two men had undoubtedly come from the second floor flat, and that one slender thread of the name 'Rita' had set the Young Adventurers once more upon the track of the abductors of Jane Finn.

The question was what to do next? Tuppence hated letting the grass grow under her feet. Tommy was amply employed, and debarred from joining him in the chase, the girl felt at a loose end. She retraced her steps to the entrance hall of the mansions. It was now tenanted by a small lift-boy, who was polishing brass fittings, and whistling the latest air with a good deal of vigour and a reasonable amount of accuracy.

He glanced round at Tuppence's entry. There was a certain amount of the gamin element in the girl, at all events she invariably got on well with small boys. A sympathetic bond seemed instantly to be formed. She reflected that an ally in the enemy's camp, so to speak, was not to be despised.

'Well, William,' she remarked cheerfully, in the best approved hospital-early-morning style, 'getting a good shine up?'

The boy grinned responsively.

'Albert, miss,' he corrected.

'Albert be it,' said Tuppence. She glanced mysteriously round the hall. The effect was purposely a broad one in case Albert should miss it. She leaned towards the boy and dropped her voice: 'I want a word with you, Albert.'

Albert ceased operations on the fittings and opened his mouth slightly.

'Look! Do you know what this is?' With dramatic gesture she flung back the left side of her coat and exposed a small enamelled badge. It was extremely unlikely that Albert would have any knowledge of it – indeed, it would have been fatal for Tuppence's plans, since the badge in question was the device of a local training corps originated by the archdeacon in the early days of the war. Its presence in Tuppence's coat was due to the fact that she had used it for pinning in some flowers a day or two before. But Tuppence had sharp eyes, and had noted the corner of a threepenny detective novel protruding from Albert's pocket, and the immediate enlargement of his eyes told her that her tactics were good, and that the fish would rise to the bait.

'American Detective Force!' she hissed.

Albert fell for it.

'Lord!' he murmured ecstatically.

Tuppence nodded at him with the air of one who has established a thorough understanding.

'Know who I'm after?' she inquired genially.

Albert, still round-eyed, demanded breathlessly:

'One of the flats?'

Tuppence nodded and jerked a thumb up the stairs.

'No. 20. Calls herself Vandemeyer. Vandemeyer! Ha! ha!'

Albert's hand stole to his pocket.

'A crook?' he queried eagerly.

'A crook? I should say so. Ready Rita they call her in the States.'

'Ready Rita,' repeated Albert deliriously. 'Oh, ain't it just like the pictures!'

It was. Tuppence was a great frequenter of the cinema.

'Annie always said as how she was a bad lot,' continued the boy.

'Who's Annie?' inquired Tuppence idly.

''Ouse-parlourmaid. She's leaving today. Many's the time Annie's said to me: "Mark my words, Albert, I wouldn't

wonder if the police was to come after her one of these days."
Just like that. But she's a stunner to look at, ain't she?'

'She's some peach,' allowed Tuppence carefully. 'Finds it
useful in her lay-out, you bet. Has she been wearing any of
the emeralds, by the way?'

'Emeralds? Them's the green stones, isn't they?'

Tuppence nodded.

'That's what we're after her for. You know old man
Rysdale?'

Albert shook his head.

'Peter B. Rysdale, the oil king?'

'It seems sort of familiar to me.'

'The sparklers belonged to him. Finest collection of emeralds in the world. Worth a million dollars!'

'Lumme!' came ecstatically from Albert. 'It sounds more
like the pictures every minute.'

Tuppence smiled, gratified at the success of her efforts.

'We haven't exactly proved it yet. But we're after her. And'
– she produced a long drawn-out wink – 'I guess she won't
get away with the goods this time.'

Albert uttered another ejaculation indicative of delight.

'Mind you, sonny, not a word of this,' said Tuppence suddenly. 'I guess I oughtn't to have put you wise, but in the
States we know a real smart lad when we see one.'

'I'll not breathe a word,' protested Albert eagerly. 'Ain't
there anything I could do? A bit of shadowing, maybe, or
suchlike?'

Tuppence affected to consider, then shook her head.

'Not at the moment, but I'll bear you in mind, son. What's
this about the girl you say is leaving?'

'Annie? Regular turn up, they 'ad. As Annie said, servants
is someone nowadays, and to be treated accordingly, and,
what with her passing the word round, she won't find it so
easy to get another.'

'Won't she?' said Tuppence thoughtfully. 'I wonder –'

An idea was dawning in her brain. She thought a minute
or two, then tapped Albert on the shoulder.

'See here, son, my brain's got busy. How would it be if you mentioned that you'd got a young cousin, or a friend of yours had, that might suit the place. You get me?'

'I'm there,' said Albert instantly. 'You leave it to me, miss, and I'll fix the whole thing up in two ticks.'

'Some lad!' commented Tuppence, with a nod of approval. 'You might say that the young woman could come right away. You let me know, and if it's OK I'll be round tomorrow at eleven o'clock.'

'Where am I to let you know to?'

'Ritz,' replied Tuppence laconically. 'Name of Cowley.'

Albert eyed her enviously.

'It must be a good job, this tec business.'

'It sure is,' drawled Tuppence, 'especially when old man Rysdale backs the bill. But don't fret, son. If this goes well, you shall come in on the ground floor.'

With which promise she took leave of her new ally, and walked briskly away from South Audley Mansions, well pleased with her morning's work.

But there was no time to be lost. She went straight back to the Ritz and wrote a few brief words to Mr Carter. Having dispatched this, and Tommy not having yet returned – which did not surprise her – she started off on a shopping expedition which, with an interval for tea and assorted creamy cakes, occupied her until well after six o'clock, and she returned to the hotel jaded, but satisfied with her purchases. Starting with a cheap clothing store, and passing through one or two second-hand establishments, she had finished the day at a well-known hair-dresser's. Now, in the seclusion of her bedroom, she unwrapped that final purchase. Five minutes later she smiled contentedly at her reflection in the glass. With an actress's pencil she had slightly altered the line of her eye-brows, and that, taken in conjunction with the new luxuriant growth of fair hair above, so changed her appearance that she felt confident that even if she came face to face with Whittington he would not recognize her. She would wear elevators in her shoes, and the cap and apron would be an even more valuable disguise. From hospital experience she knew only too well that a nurse out of uniform is frequently unrecognized by her patients.

'Yes,' said Tuppence aloud, nodding at the pert reflection in the glass, 'you'll do.' She then resumed her normal appearance.

Dinner was a solitary meal. Tuppence was rather surprised at Tommy's non-return. Julius, too, was absent – but that to the girl's mind was more easily explained. His 'hustling' activities were not confined to London, and his abrupt appearances and disappearances were fully accepted by the Young Adventurers as part of the day's work. It was quite on the cards that Julius P. Hersheimmer had left for Constantinople at a moment's notice if he fancied that a clue to his cousin's disappearance was to be found there. The energetic young man had succeeded in making the lives of several Scotland Yard men unbearable to them, and the telephone girls at the Admiralty had learned to know and dread the familiar 'Hullo!' He had spent three hours in Paris hustling the Prefecture, and had returned from there imbued with the idea, possibly inspired by a weary French official, that the true clue to the mystery was to be found in Ireland.

'I dare say he's dashed off there now,' thought Tuppence. 'All very well, but this is very dull for *me*! Here I am bursting with news, and absolutely no one to tell it to! Tommy might have wired, or something. I wonder where he is. Anyway, he can't have "lost the trail" as they say. That reminds me –' And Miss Cowley broke off in her meditations, and summoned a small boy.

Ten minutes later the lady was ensconced comfortably on her bed, smoking cigarettes and deep in the perusal of *Barnaby Williams, the Boy Detective*, which, with other threepenny works of lurid fiction, she had sent out to purchase. She felt, and rightly, that before the strain of attempting further intercourse with Albert, it would be as well to fortify herself with a good supply of local colour.

The morning brought a note from Mr Carter:

Dear Miss Tuppence,

You have made a splendid start, and I congratulate you. I feel, though, that I should like to point out to you once more the risks you are running, especially if you pursue the course you indicate. Those people are absolutely desperate and incapable of either mercy or pity. I feel that you probably underestimate the danger, and therefore warn you again that I can promise you no protection. You have given us valuable information, and if you choose to withdraw now no one could blame you. At any rate, think the matter over well before you decide.

If, in spite of my warnings, you make up your mind to go through with it, you will find everything arranged. You have lived for two years with Miss Dufferin, the Parsonage, Llanelly, and Mrs Vandemeyer can apply to her for a reference.

May I be permitted a word or two of advice? Stick as near to the truth as possible – it minimizes the danger of 'slips'. I suggest that you should represent yourself to be what you are, a former VAD, who has chosen domestic service as a profession. There are many such at the present time. That explains away any incongruities of voice or manner which otherwise might awaken suspicion.

Whichever way you decide, good luck to you.

Your sincere friend,
Mr Carter.

Tuppence's spirits rose mercurially. Mr Carter's warnings passed unheeded. The young lady had far too much confidence in herself to pay any heed to them.

With some reluctance she abandoned the interesting part she had sketched out for herself. Although she had no doubts of her own powers to sustain a role indefinitely, she had too much common sense not to recognize the force of Mr Carter's arguments.

There was still no word or message from Tommy, but the

morning post brought a somewhat dirty postcard with the words: 'It's OK' scrawled upon it.

At 10.30 Tuppence surveyed with pride a slightly battered tin trunk containing her new possessions. It was artistically corded. It was with a slight blush that she rang the bell and ordered it to be placed in a taxi. She drove to Paddington, and left the box in the cloak room. She then repaired with a handbag to the fastnesses of the ladies' waiting-room. Ten minutes later a metamorphosed Tuppence walked demurely out of the station and entered a bus.

It was a few minutes past eleven when Tuppence again entered the hall of South Audley Mansions. Albert was on the look-out, attending to his duties in a somewhat desultory fashion. He did not immediately recognize Tuppence. When he did, his admiration was unbounded.

'Blest if I'd have known you! That rig-out's top-hole.'

'Glad you like it, Albert,' replied Tuppence modestly. 'By the way, am I your cousin, or am I not?'

'Your voice too,' cried the delighted boy. 'It's as English as anything! No, I said as a friend of mine knew a young gal. Annie wasn't best pleased. She stopped on till today – to oblige, *she* said, but really it's so as to put you against the place.'

'Nice girl,' said Tuppence.

Albert suspected no irony.

'She's style about her, and keeps her silver a treat – but, my word, ain't she got a temper. Are you going up now, miss? Step inside the lift. No. 20 did you say?' And he winked.

Tuppence quelled him with a stern glance, and stepped inside.

As she rang the bell of No. 20 she was conscious of Albert's eyes descending beneath the level of the floor.

A smart young woman opened the door.

'I've come about the place,' said Tuppence.

'It's a rotten place,' said the young woman without hesitation. 'Regular old cat – always interfering. Accused me of tampering with her letters. Me! The flap was half undone anyway. There's never anything in the waste-paper basket – she burns everything. She's a wrong 'un, that's what she is. Swell clothes but no class. Cook knows something about her – but she won't tell – scared to death of her. And suspicious! She's on to you in a minute if you as much as speak to a fellow. I can tell you –'

But what more Annie could tell, Tuppence was never destined to learn, for at that moment a clear voice with a peculiarly steely ring to it called:

'Annie!'

The smart young woman jumped as if she had been shot.

'Yes, ma'am?'

'Who are you talking to?'

'It's a young woman about the situation, ma'am.'

'Show her in then. At once.'

'Yes, ma'am.'

Tuppence was ushered into a room on the right of the long passage. A woman was standing by the fire-place. She was no longer in her first youth, and the beauty she undeniably possessed was hardened and coarsened. In her youth she must have been dazzling. Her pale gold hair, owing a slight assistance to art, was coiled low on her neck, her eyes, of a piercing electric blue, seemed to possess a faculty of boring into the very soul of the person she was looking at. Her exquisite figure was enhanced by a wonderful gown of indigo charmeuse. And yet, despite her swaying grace, and the almost ethereal beauty of her face, you felt instinctively the presence of something hard and menacing, a kind of metallic strength that found expression in the tones of her voice and in that gimlet-like quality of her eyes.

For the first time Tuppence felt afraid. She had not feared Whittington, but this woman was different. As if fascinated, she watched the long cruel line of the red curving mouth, and again she felt that sensation of panic pass over her. Her usual self-confidence deserted her. Vaguely she felt that deceiving this woman would be very different to deceiving Whittington.

Mr Carter's warning recurred to her mind. Here, indeed, she might expect no mercy.

Fighting down that instinct of panic which urged her to turn tail and run without further delay, Tuppence returned the lady's gaze firmly and respectfully.

As though that first scrutiny had been satisfactory, Mrs Vandemeyer motioned to a chair.

'You can sit down. How did you hear I wanted a house-parlourmaid?'

'Through a friend who knows the lift-boy here. He thought the place might suit me.'

Again that basilisk glance seemed to pierce her through.

'You speak like an educated girl?'

Glibly enough, Tuppence ran through her imaginary career on the lines suggested by Mr Carter. It seemed to her, as she did so, that the tension of Mrs Vandemeyer's attitude relaxed.

'I see,' she remarked at length. 'Is there anyone I can write to for a reference?'

'I lived last with a Miss Dufferin, The Parsonage, Llanelly. I was with her two years.'

'And then you thought you would get more money by coming to London, I suppose? Well, it doesn't matter to me. I will give you £50–£60 – whatever you want. You can come at once?'

'Yes, ma'am. Today, if you like. My box is at Paddington.'

'Go and fetch it by taxi, then. It's an easy place. I am out a good deal. By the way, what's your name?'

'Prudence Cooper, ma'am.'

'Very well, Prudence. Go away and fetch your box. I shall be out to lunch. The cook will show you where everything is.'

'Thank you, ma'am.'

Tuppence withdrew. The smart Annie was not in evidence. In the hall below a magnificent hall porter had relegated Albert to the background. Tuppence did not even glance at him as she passed meekly out.

The adventure had begun, but she felt less elated than she had done earlier in the morning. It crossed her mind that if the unknown Jane Finn had fallen into the hands of Mrs Vandemeyer, it was likely to have gone hard with her.

CHAPTER X

Enter Sir James Peel Edgerton

Tuppence betrayed no awkwardness in her new duties. The daughters of the archdeacon were well grounded in household tasks. They were also experts in training a 'raw girl', the inevitable result being that the raw girl, once trained, departed somewhere where her newly-acquired knowledge commanded a more substantial remuneration than the archdeacon's meagre purse allowed.

Tuppence had therefore very little fear of proving inefficient. Mrs Vandemeyer's cook puzzled her. She evidently went in deadly terror of her mistress. The girl thought it probable that the other woman had some hold over her. For the rest, she cooked like a *chef*, as Tuppence had an opportunity of judging that evening. Mrs Vandemeyer was expecting a guest to dinner, and Tuppence accordingly laid the beautifully polished table for two. She was a little exercised in her own mind as to this visitor. It was highly possible that it might prove to be Whittington. Although she felt fairly confident that he would not recognize her, yet she would have been better pleased had the guest proved to be a total stranger. However, there was nothing for it but to hope for the best.

At a few minutes past eight the front door bell rang, and Tuppence went to answer it with some inward trepidation. She was relieved to see that the visitor was the second of the two men whom Tommy had taken upon himself to follow.

He gave his name as Count Stepanov. Tuppence announced him, and Mrs Vandemeyer rose from her seat on a low divan with a quick murmur of pleasure.

'It is delightful to see you, Boris Ivanovitch,' she said.

'And you, madame!' He bowed low over her hand.

Tuppence returned to the kitchen.

'Count Stepanov, or some such,' she remarked, and affecting a frank and unvarnished curiosity: 'Who's he?'

'A Russian gentleman, I believe.'

'Come here much?'

'Once in a while. What d'you want to know for?'

'Fancied he might be sweet on the missus, that's all,' explained the girl, adding with an appearance of sulkiness: 'How you do take one up!'

'I'm not quite easy in my mind about the *soufflé*,' explained the other.

'You know something,' thought Tuppence to herself, but aloud she only said: 'Going to dish up now? Right-o.'

Whilst waiting at table, Tuppence listened closely to all that was said. She remembered that this was one of the men Tommy was shadowing when she had last seen him. Already, although she would hardly admit it, she was becoming uneasy about her partner. Where was he? Why had no word of any kind come from him? She had arranged before leaving the Ritz to have all letters or messages sent on at once by special messenger to a small stationer's shop near at hand where Albert was to call in frequently. True, it was only yesterday morning that she had parted from Tommy, and she told herself that any anxiety on his behalf would be absurd. Still, it was strange he had sent no word of any kind.

But, listen as she might, the conversation presented no clue. Boris and Mrs Vandemeyer talked on purely indifferent subjects: plays they had seen, new dances, and the latest society gossip. After dinner they repaired to the small boudoir where Mrs Vandemeyer, stretched on the divan, looked more wickedly beautiful than ever. Tuppence brought in the coffee and liqueurs and unwillingly retired. As she did so, she heard Boris say:

'New, isn't she?'

'She came in today. The other was a fiend. This girl seems all right. She waits well.'

Tuppence lingered a moment longer by the door which she had carefully neglected to close, and heard him say:

'Quite safe, I suppose?'

'Really, Boris, you are absurdly suspicious. I believe she's the cousin of the hall porter, or something of the kind. And nobody even dreams that I have any connection with our – mutual friend, Mr Brown.'

'For heaven's sake, be careful, Rita. That door isn't shut.'

'Well, shut it then,' laughed the woman.

Tuppence removed herself speedily.

She dared not absent herself longer from the back premises, but she cleared away and washed up with a breathless speed acquired in hospital. Then she slipped quietly back to the boudoir door. The cook, more leisurely, was still busy in the kitchen and, if she missed the other, would only suppose her to be turning down the beds.

Alas! The conversation inside was being carried on in too low a tone to permit of her hearing anything of it. She dared not reopen the door, however gently. Mrs Vandemeyer was sitting almost facing it, and Tuppence respected her mistress's lynx-eyed powers of observation.

Nevertheless, she felt she would give a good deal to overhear what was going on. Possibly, if anything unforeseen had happened, she might get news of Tommy. For some moments she reflected desperately, then her face brightened. She went quickly along the passage to Mrs Vandemeyer's bedroom, which had long french windows leading on to a balcony that ran the length of the flat. Slipping quickly through the window, Tuppence crept noiselessly along till she reached the boudoir window. As she had thought it stood a little ajar, and the voices within were plainly audible.

Tuppence listened attentively, but there was no mention of anything that could be twisted to apply to Tommy. Mrs Vandemeyer and the Russian seemed to be at variance over some matter, and finally the latter exclaimed bitterly:

'With your persistent recklessness, you will end by ruining us!'

'Bah!' laughed the woman. 'Notoriety of the right kind is the best way of disarming suspicion. You will realize that one of these days – perhaps sooner than you think!'

'In the meantime, you are going about everywhere with Peel Edgerton. Not only is he, perhaps, the most celebrated KC in England, but his special hobby is criminology! It is madness!'

'I know that his eloquence has saved untold men from the gallows,' said Mrs Vandemeyer calmly. 'What of it? I may need his assistance in that line myself some day. If so, how fortunate to have such a friend at court – or perhaps it would be more to the point to say *in* court.'

Boris got up and began striding up and down. He was very excited.

'You are a clever woman, Rita; but you are also a fool! Be guided by me, and give up Peel Edgerton.'

Mrs Vandemeyer shook her head gently.

'I think not.'

'You refuse?' There was an ugly ring in the Russian's voice.

'I do.'

'Then, by heaven,' snarled the Russian, 'we will see –'

But Mrs Vandemeyer also rose to her feet, her eyes flashing.

'You forget, Boris,' she said. 'I am accountable to no one. I take my orders only from – Mr Brown.'

The other threw up his hands in despair.

'You are impossible,' he muttered. 'Impossible! Already it may be too late. They say Peel Edgerton can *smell* a criminal! How do we know what is at the bottom of his sudden interest in you? Perhaps even now his suspicions are aroused. He guesses –'

Mrs Vandemeyer eyed him scornfully.

'Reassure yourself, my dear Boris. He suspects nothing. With less than your usual chivalry, you seem to forget that I am commonly accounted a beautiful woman. I assure you that is all that interests Peel Edgerton.'

Boris shook his head doubtfully.

'He has studied crime as no other man in this kingdom has studied it. Do you fancy that you can deceive him?'

Mrs Vandemeyer's eyes narrowed.

'If he is all that you say – it would amuse me to try!'

'Good heavens, Rita –'

'Besides,' added Mrs Vandemeyer, 'he is extremely rich. I am not one who despises money. The "sinews of war" you know, Boris!'

'Money – money! That is always the danger with you, Rita. I believe you would sell your soul for money. I believe –' He paused, then in a low, sinister voice he said slowly: 'Sometimes I believe that you would sell – *us!*'

Mrs Vandemeyer smiled and shrugged her shoulders.

'The price, at any rate, would have to be enormous,' she said lightly. 'It would be beyond the power of anyone but a millionaire to pay.'

'Ah!' snarled the Russian. 'You see, I was right.'

'My dear Boris, can you not take a joke?'

'Was it a joke?'

'Of course.'

'Then all I can say is that your ideas of humour are peculiar, my dear Rita.'

Mrs Vandemeyer smiled.

'Let us not quarrel, Boris. Touch the bell. We will have some drinks.'

Tuppence beat a hasty retreat. She paused a moment to survey herself in Mrs Vandemeyer's long glass, and be sure that nothing was amiss with her appearance. Then she answered the bell demurely.

The conversation that she had overheard, although interesting in that it proved beyond doubt the complicity of both Rita and Boris, threw very little light on the present preoccupations. The name of Jane Finn had not even been mentioned.

The following morning a few brief words with Albert informed her that nothing was waiting for her at the stationer's. It seemed incredible that Tommy, if all was well with him, should not send any word to her. A cold hand seemed to close round her heart . . . Supposing . . . She choked her fears down bravely. It was no good worrying. But she leapt at a chance offered her by Mrs Vandemeyer.

'What day do you usually go out, Prudence?'

'Friday's my usual day, ma'am.'

Mrs Vandemeyer lifted her eyebrows.

'And today is Friday! But I suppose you hardly wish to go out today, as you only came yesterday.'

'I was thinking of asking you if I might, ma'am.'

Mrs Vandemeyer looked at her a minute longer, and then smiled.

'I wish Count Stepanov could hear you. He made a suggestion about you last night.' Her smile broadened, cat-like. 'Your request is very – typical. I am satisfied. You do not understand all this – but you can go out today. It makes no difference to me, as I shall not be dining at home.'

'Thank you, ma'am.'

Tuppence felt a sensation of relief once she was out of the other's presence. Once again she admitted to herself that she was afraid, horribly afraid, of the beautiful woman with the cruel eyes.

In the midst of a final desultory polishing of her silver, Tuppence was disturbed by the ringing of the front door bell, and went to answer it. This time the visitor was neither Whittington nor Boris, but a man of striking appearance.

Just a shade over average height, he nevertheless conveyed the impression of a big man. His face, clean-shaven and exquisitely mobile, was stamped with an expression of power and force far beyond the ordinary. Magnetism seemed to radiate from him.

Tuppence was undecided for the moment whether to put him down as an actor or a lawyer, but her doubts were soon solved as he gave her his name: Sir James Peel Edgerton.

She looked at him with renewed interest. This, then, was the famous K C whose name was familiar all over England. She had heard it said that he might one day be Prime Minister.

He was known to have refused office in the interests of his profession, preferring to remain a simple Member for a Scotch constituency.

Tuppence went back to her pantry thoughtfully. The great man had impressed her. She understood Boris's agitation. Peel Edgerton would not be an easy man to deceive.

In about a quarter of an hour the bell rang, and Tuppence repaired to the hall to show the visitor out. He had given her a piercing glance before. Now, as she handed him his hat and stick, she was conscious of his eyes raking her through. As she opened the door and stood aside to let him pass out, he stopped in the doorway.

'Not been doing this long, eh?'

Tuppence raised her eyes, astonished. She read in his glance kindliness, and something else more difficult to fathom.

He nodded as though she had answered.

'VAD and hard up, I suppose?'

'Did Mrs Vandemeyer tell you that?' asked Tuppence suspiciously.

'No, child. The look of you told me. Good place here?'

'Very good, thank you, sir.'

'Ah, but there are plenty of good places nowadays. And a change does no harm sometimes.'

'Do you mean –?' began Tuppence.

But Sir James was already on the topmost stair. He looked back with his kindly, shrewd glance.

'Just a hint,' he said. 'That's all.'

Tuppence went back to the pantry more thoughtful than ever.

CHAPTER XI

Julius Tells a Story

Dressed appropriately, Tuppence duly sallied forth for her 'afternoon out'. Albert was in temporary abeyance, but Tuppence went herself to the stationer's to make quite sure that nothing had come for her. Satisfied on this point, she made her way to the Ritz. On inquiry she learnt that Tommy had not yet returned. It was the answer she had expected, but it was another nail in the coffin of her hopes. She resolved to appeal to Mr Carter, telling him when and where Tommy had started on his quest, and asking him to do something to trace him. The prospect of his aid revived her mercurial spirits, and she next inquired for Julius Hersheimmer. The reply she got was to the effect that he had returned about half an hour ago, but had gone out immediately.

Tuppence's spirits revived still more. It would be something to see Julius. Perhaps he could devise some plan for finding out what had become of Tommy. She wrote her note to Mr Carter in Julius's sitting-room, and was just addressing the envelope when the door burst open.

'What the hell—' began Julius, but checked himself abruptly. 'I beg your pardon, Miss Tuppence. Those fools down at the office would have it that Beresford wasn't here any longer – hadn't been here since Wednesday. Is that so?'

Tuppence nodded.

'You don't know where he is?' she asked faintly.

'I? How should I know? I haven't had one darned word from him, though I wired him yesterday morning.'

'I expect your wire's at the office unopened.'

'But where is he?'

'I don't know. I hoped you might.'

'I tell you I haven't had one darned word from him since we parted at the depot on Wednesday.'

'What depot?'

'Waterloo. Your London and South Western road.'

'Waterloo?' frowned Tuppence.

'Why, yes. Didn't he tell you?'

'I haven't seen him either,' replied Tuppence impatiently. 'Go on about Waterloo. What were you doing there?'

'He gave me a call. Over the phone. Told me to get a move on, and hustle. Said he was trailing two crooks.'

'Oh!' said Tuppence, her eyes opening. 'I see. Go on.'

'I hurried along right away. Beresford was there. He pointed out the crooks. The big one was mine, the guy you bluffed. Tommy shoved a ticket into my hand and told me to get aboard the cars. He was going to sleuth the other crook.' Julius paused. 'I thought for sure you'd know all this.'

'Julius,' said Tuppence firmly, 'stop walking up and down. It makes me giddy. Sit down in that arm-chair, and tell me the whole story with as few fancy turns of speech as possible.'

Mr Hersheimmer obeyed.

'Sure,' he said. 'Where shall I begin?'

'Where you left off. At Waterloo.'

'Well,' began Julius, 'I got into one of your dear old-fashioned first-class British compartments. The train was just off. First thing I knew a guard came along and informed me mightily politely that I wasn't in a smoking-carriage. I handed him out half a dollar, and that settled that. I did a bit of prospecting along the corridor to the next coach. Whittington was there right enough. When I saw the skunk, with his big sleek fat face, and thought of poor little Jane in his clutches, I felt real mad that I hadn't got a gun with me. I'd have tickled him up some.

'We got to Bournemouth all right. Whittington took a cab and gave the name of an hotel. I did likewise, and we drove up within three minutes of each other. He hired a room, and I hired one too. So far it was all plain sailing. He hadn't the remotest notion that anyone was on to him. Well, he just sat around in the hotel lounge, reading the papers and so on, till it was time for dinner. He didn't hurry any over that either.

'I began to think that there was nothing doing, that he'd just come on the trip for his health, but I remembered that he hadn't changed for dinner, though it was by way of being a slap-up hotel, so it seemed likely enough that he'd be going out on his real business afterwards.

'Sure enough, about nine o'clock, so he did. Took a car across the town – mighty pretty place by the way, I guess I'll take Jane there for a spell when I find her – and then paid it off and struck out along those pine-woods on the top of the cliff. I was there too, you understand. We walked, maybe, for half an hour. There's a lot of villas all the way along, but by degrees they seemed to get more and more thinned out, and in the end we got to one that seemed the last of the bunch. Big house it was, with a lot of piny grounds around it.

'It was a pretty black night, and the carriage drive up to the house was dark as pitch. I could hear him ahead, though I couldn't see him. I had to walk carefully in case he might get on to it that he was being followed. I turned a curve and I was just in time to see him ring the bell and get admitted to the house. I just stopped where I was. It was beginning to rain, and I was soon pretty near soaked through. Also, it was almighty cold.

'Whittington didn't come out again, and by and by I got kind of restive, and began to mooch around. All the ground floor windows were shuttered tight, but upstairs, on the first floor (it was a two-storeyed house) I noticed a window with a light burning and the curtains not drawn.

'Now, just opposite to that window, there was a tree growing. It was about thirty foot away from the house, maybe, and I sort of got it into my head that, if I climbed up that tree, I'd very likely be able to see into that room. Of course, I knew there was no reason why Whittington should be in that room rather than in any other – less reason, in fact, for the betting would be on his being in one of the reception-rooms down-stairs. But I guess I'd got the hump from standing so long in the rain, and anything seemed better than going on doing nothing. So I started up.

'It wasn't so easy, by a long chalk! The rain had made the boughs mighty slippery, and it was all I could do to keep a foothold, but bit by bit I managed it, until at last there I was level with the window.

'But then I was disappointed. I was too far to the left. I could only see sideways into the room. A bit of curtain, and a yard of wall-paper was all I could command. Well, that wasn't any manner of good to me, but just as I was going to give it up, and climb down ignominiously, someone inside moved and threw his shadow on my little bit of wall – and, by gum, it was Whittington!

'After that, my blood was up. I'd just *got* to get a look into that room. It was up to me to figure out how. I noticed that there was a long branch running out from the tree in the right direction. If I could only swarm about half-way along it, the proposition would be solved. But it was mighty uncertain whether it would bear my weight. I decided I'd just got to risk that, and I started. Very cautiously, inch by inch, I crawled along. The bough creaked and swayed in a nasty fashion, and it didn't do to think of the drop below, but at last I got safely to where I wanted to be.

'The room was medium-sized, furnished in a kind of bare hygienic way. There was a table with a lamp on it in the middle of the room, and sitting at that table, facing towards me, was Whittington right enough. He was talking to a woman dressed as a hospital nurse. She was sitting with her back to me, so I couldn't see her face. Although the blinds were up, the window itself was shut, so I couldn't catch a word of what they said. Whittington seemed to be doing all the talking, and the nurse just listened. Now and then she nodded, and sometimes she'd shake her head, as though she were answering questions. He seemed very emphatic – once or twice he beat with his fist on the table. The rain had stopped now, and the sky was clearing in that sudden way it does.

'Presently, he seemed to get to the end of what he was

saying. He got up, and so did she. He looked towards the window and asked something – I guess it was whether it was raining. Anyway, she came right across and looked out. Just then the moon came out from behind the clouds. I was scared the woman would catch sight of me, for I was full in the moonlight. I tried to move back a bit. The jerk I gave was too much for that rotten old branch. With an almighty crash, down it came, and Julius P. Hersheimmer with it!'

'Oh, Julius,' breathed Tuppence, 'how exciting! Go on.'

'Well, luckily for me, I pitched down into a good soft bed of earth – but it put me out of action for the time, sure enough. The next thing I knew, I was lying in bed with a hospital nurse (not Whittington's one) on one side of me, and a little black-bearded man with gold glasses, and medical man written all over him, on the other. He rubbed his hands together, and raised his eyebrows as I stared at him. "Ah!" he said. "So our young friend is coming round again. Capital. Capital."

'I did the usual stunt. Said: "What's happened?" And "Where am I?" But I knew the answer to the last well enough. There's no moss growing on my brain. "I think that'll do for the present, sister," said the little man, and the nurse left the room in a sort of brisk well-trained way. But I caught her handing me out a look of deep curiosity as she passed through the door.

'That look of hers gave me an idea. "Now then, doc," I said, and tried to sit up in bed, but my right foot gave me a nasty twinge as I did so. "A slight sprain," explained the doctor. "Nothing serious. You'll be about again in a couple of days."

'I noticed you walked lame,' interpolated Tuppence.

Julius nodded, and continued:

'"How did it happen?" I asked again. He replied dryly. "You fell, with a considerable portion of one of my trees, into one of my newly-planted flower-beds."

'I liked the man. He seemed to have a sense of humour. I felt sure that he, at least, was plumb straight. "Sure, doc," I said, "I'm sorry about the tree, and I guess the new bulbs will be on me. But perhaps you'd like to know what I was doing in your garden?" "I think the facts do call for an explanation," he replied. "Well, to begin with, I wasn't after the spoons."

'He smiled. "My first theory. But I soon altered my mind. By the way, you are an American, are you not?" I told him my name. "And you?" "I am Dr Hall, and this, as you doubtless know, is my private nursing home."

'I didn't know, but wasn't going to put him wise. I was just thankful for the information. I liked the man, and I felt he was straight, but I wasn't going to give him the whole story. For one thing he probably wouldn't have believed it.

'I made up my mind in a flash. "Why, doctor," I said, "I guess I feel an almighty fool, but I owe it to you to let you know that it wasn't the Bill Sikes business I was up to." Then I went on and mumbled out something about a girl. I trotted out the stern guardian business, and a nervous breakdown, and finally explained that I had fancied I recognized her among the patients at the home, hence my nocturnal adventures.

'I guess it was just the kind of story he was expecting. "Quite a romance," he said genially, when I'd finished. "Now, doc," I went on, "will you be frank with me? Have you here now, or have you had here at any time, a young girl called Jane Finn?" He repeated the name thoughtfully. "Jane Finn?" he said. "No."

'I was chagrined, and I guess I showed it. "You are sure?" "Quite sure, Mr Hersheimmer. It is an uncommon name, and I should not have been likely to forget it."

'Well, that was flat. It laid me out for a space. I'd kind of hoped my search was at an end. "That's that," I said at last. "Now, there's another matter. When I was hugging that darned branch I thought I recognized an old friend of mine talking to one of your nurses." I purposely didn't mention any name because, of course, Whittington might be calling himself something quite different down here, but the doctor answered at once. "Mr Whittington, perhaps?" "That's the fellow," I replied. "What's he doing down here? Don't tell me *his* nerves are out of order?"

'Dr Hall laughed. "No. He came down to see one of my nurses, Nurse Edith, who is a niece of his." "Why, fancy that!" I exclaimed, "Is he still here?" "No, he went back to town almost immediately." "What a pity!" I ejaculated. "But perhaps I could speak to his niece – Nurse Edith, did you say her name was?"

'But the doctor shook his head. "I'm afraid that, too, is impossible. Nurse Edith left with a patient tonight also." "I seem to be real unlucky," I remarked. "Have you Mr Whittington's address in town? I guess I'd like to look him up when I get back." "I don't know his address. I can write to Nurse Edith for it if you like." I thanked him. "Don't say who it is wants it. I'd like to give him a little surprise."

'That was about all I could do for the moment. Of course, if the girl was really Whittington's niece, she might be too cute to fall into the trap, but it was worth trying. Next thing I did was to write out a wire to Beresford saying where I was, and that I was laid up with a sprained foot, and telling him to come down if he wasn't busy. I had to be guarded in what I said. However, I didn't hear from him, and my foot soon got all right. It was only ricked, not really sprained, so today I said goodbye to the little doctor chap, asked him to send me word if he heard from Nurse Edith, and came right away back to town. Say, Miss Tuppence, you're looking mighty pale?'

'It's Tommy,' said Tuppence. 'What can have happened to him?'

'Buck up, I guess he's all right really. Why shouldn't he be? See here, it was a foreign-looking guy he went off after. Maybe they've gone abroad – to Poland, or something like that?'

Tuppence shook her head.

'He couldn't without passports and things. Besides I've seen that man, Boris Something, since. He dined with Mrs Vandemeyer last night.'

'Mrs Who?'

'I forgot. Of course you don't know all that.'

'I'm listening,' said Julius, and gave vent to his favourite expression. 'Put me wise.'

Tuppence thereupon related the events of the last two days. Julius's astonishment and admiration were unbounded.

'Bully for you! Fancy you a menial. It just tickles me to death!' Then he added seriously: 'But say now, I don't like it, Miss Tuppence, I sure don't. You're just as plucky as they make 'em, but I wish you'd keep right out of this. These crooks we're up against would as soon croak a girl as a man any day.'

'Do you think I'm afraid?' said Tuppence indignantly, valiantly repressing memories of the steely glitter in Mrs Vandemeyer's eyes.

'I said before you were darned plucky. But that doesn't alter facts.'

'Oh, bother *me*!' said Tuppence impatiently. 'Let's think about what can have happened to Tommy. I've written to Mr Carter about it,' she added, and told him the gist of her letter.

Julius nodded gravely.

'I guess that's good as far as it goes. But it's for us to get busy and do something.'

'What can we do?' asked Tuppence, her spirits rising.

'I guess we'd better get on the track of Boris. You say he's been to your place. Is he likely to come again?'

'He might. I really don't know.'

'I see. Well, I guess I'd better buy a car, a slap-up one, dress as a chauffeur and hang about outside. Then if Boris comes, you could make some kind of signal, and I'd trail him. How's that?'

'Splendid, but he mightn't come for weeks.'

'We'll have to chance that. I'm glad you like the plan.' He rose.

'Where are you going?'

'To buy the car, of course,' replied Julius, surprised. 'What make do you like? I guess you'll do some riding in it before we've finished.'

'Oh,' said Tuppence faintly. 'I *like* Rolls-Royces, but –'

'Sure,' agreed Julius. 'What you say goes. I'll get one.'

'But you can't at once,' cried Tuppence. 'People wait ages sometimes.'

'Little Julius doesn't,' affirmed Mr Hersheimmer. 'Don't you worry any. I'll be round in the car in half an hour.'

Tuppence got up.

'You're awfully good, Julius. But I can't help feeling that it's rather a forlorn hope. I'm really pinning my faith to Mr Carter.'

'Then I shouldn't.'

'Why?'

'Just an idea of mine.'

'Oh, but he must do something. There's no one else. By the way, I forgot to tell you of a queer thing that happened this morning.'

And she narrated her encounter with Sir James Peel Edgerton. Julius was interested.

'What did the guy mean, do you think?' he asked.

'I don't quite know,' said Tuppence meditatively. 'But I think that, in an ambiguous, legal, without prejudishish lawyer's way, he was trying to warn me.'

'Why should he?'

'I don't know,' confessed Tuppence. 'But he looked kind, and simply awfully clever. I wouldn't mind going to him and telling him everything.'

Somewhat to her surprise, Julius negatived the idea sharply.

'See here,' he said, 'we don't want any lawyers mixed up in this. That guy couldn't help us any.'

'Well, I believe he could,' reiterated Tuppence obstinately.

'Don't you think it. So long. I'll be back in half an hour.'

Thirty-five minutes had elapsed when Julius returned. He took Tuppence by the arm, and walked her to the window.

'There she is.'

'Oh!' said Tuppence with a note of reverence in her voice, as she gazed down at the enormous car.

'She's some pace-maker, I can tell you,' said Julius complacently.

'How did you get it?' gasped Tuppence.

'She was just being sent home to some bigwig.'

'Well?'

'I went round to his house,' said Julius. 'I said that I reckoned a car like that was worth every penny of twenty thousand dollars. Then I told him that it was worth just about fifty thousand dollars to me if he'd get out.'

'Well?' said Tuppence, intoxicated.

'Well,' returned Julius, 'he got out, that's all.'

CHAPTER XII

A Friend in Need

Friday and Saturday passed uneventfully. Tuppence had received a brief answer to her appeal from Mr Carter. In it he pointed out that the Young Adventurers had undertaken the work at their own risk, and had been fully warned of the dangers. If anything had happened to Tommy he regretted it deeply, but he could do nothing.

This was cold comfort. Somehow, without Tommy, all the savour went out of the adventure, and, for the first time, Tuppence felt doubtful of success. While they had been together she had never questioned it for a minute. Although she was accustomed to take the lead, and to pride herself on her quick-wittedness, in reality she had relied upon Tommy more than she realized at the time. There was something so eminently sober and clear-headed about him, his common sense and soundness of vision were so unvarying, that without him Tuppence felt much like a rudderless ship. It was curious that Julius, who was undoubtedly much cleverer than Tommy, did not give her the same feeling of support. She had accused Tommy of being a pessimist, and it is certain that he always saw the disadvantages and difficulties which she herself was optimistically given to overlooking, but nevertheless she had really relied a good deal on his judgement. He might be slow, but he was very sure.

It seemed to the girl that, for the first time, she realized the sinister character of the mission they had undertaken so light-heartedly. It had begun like a page of romance. Now, shorn of its glamour, it seemed to be turning to grim reality. Tommy – that was all that mattered. Many times in the day Tuppence blinked the tears out of her eyes resolutely. 'Little fool,' she would apostrophize herself, 'don't snivel. Of course you're fond of him. You've known him all your life. But there's no need to be sentimental about it.'

In the meantime, nothing more was seen of Boris. He did not come to the flat, and Julius and the car waited in vain. Tuppence gave herself over to new meditations. Whilst admitting the truth of Julius's objections, she had nevertheless not entirely relinquished the idea of appealing to Sir James Peel Edgerton. Indeed, she had gone so far as to look up his address in the *Red Book*. Had he meant to warn her that day? If so, why? Surely she was at least entitled to demand an explanation. He had looked at her so kindly. Perhaps he might tell them something concerning Mrs Vandemeyer which might lead to a clue to Tommy's whereabouts.

Anyway, Tuppence decided, with her usual shake of the shoulders, it was worth trying, and try it she would. Sunday was her afternoon out. She would meet Julius, persuade him to her point of view, and they would beard the lion in his den.

When the day arrived Julius needed a considerable amount of persuading, but Tuppence held firm. 'It can do no harm,' was what she always came back to. In the end Julius gave in, and they proceeded in the car to Carlton House Terrace.

The door was opened by an irreproachable butler. Tuppence felt a little nervous. After all, perhaps it *was* colossal cheek on her part. She had decided not to ask if Sir James was 'at home', but to adopt a more personal attitude.

'Will you ask Sir James if I can see him for a few minutes? I have an important message for him.'

The butler retired, returning a moment or two later.

'Sir James will see you. Will you step this way?'

He ushered them into a room at the back of the house, furnished as a library. The collection of books was a magnificent one, and Tuppence noticed that all one wall was devoted to works on crime and criminology. There were several deep-padded leather armchairs, and an old-fashioned open hearth. In the window was a big roll-top desk strewn with papers at which the master of the house was sitting.

He rose as they entered.

'You have a message for me? Ah' – he recognized Tuppence with a smile – 'it's you, is it? Brought a message from Mrs Vandemeyer, I suppose?'

'Not exactly,' said Tuppence. 'In fact, I'm afraid I only said that to be quite sure of getting in. Oh, by the way, this is Mr Hersheimmer, Sir James Peel Edgerton.'

'Pleased to meet you,' said the American, shooting out a hand.

'Won't you both sit down?' asked Sir James. He drew forward two chairs.

'Sir James,' said Tuppence, plunging boldly, 'I dare say you will think it is most awful cheek of me coming here like this. Because, of course, it's nothing whatever to do with you, and then you're a very important person, and of course Tommy and I are very unimportant.' She paused for breath.

'Tommy?' queried Sir James, looking across at the American.

'No, that's Julius,' explained Tuppence. 'I'm rather nervous, and that makes me tell it badly. What I really want to know is what you meant by what you said to me the other day? Did you mean to warn me against Mrs Vandemeyer? You did, didn't you?'

'My dear young lady, as far as I recollect I only mentioned that there were equally good situations to be obtained elsewhere.'

'Yes, I know. But it was a hint, wasn't it?'

'Well, perhaps it was,' admitted Sir James gravely.

'Well, I want to know more. I want to know just *why* you gave me a hint.'

Sir James smiled at her earnestness.

'Suppose the lady brings a libel action against me for defamation of character?'

'Of course,' said Tuppence. 'I know lawyers are always dreadfully careful. But can't we say "without prejudice" first, and then say just what we want to.'

'Well,' said Sir James, still smiling, 'without prejudice, then, if I had a young sister forced to earn her living, I should not like to see her in Mrs Vandemeyer's service. I felt it incumbent on me just to give you a hint. It is no place for a young and inexperienced girl. That is all I can tell you.'

'I see,' said Tuppence thoughtfully. 'Thank you very much. But I'm not *really* inexperienced, you know. I knew perfectly that she was a bad lot when I went there – as a matter of fact that's *why* I went –' She broke off, seeing some bewilderment on the lawyer's face, and went on: 'I think perhaps I'd better tell you the whole story, Sir James. I've a sort of feeling that you'd know in a minute if I didn't tell the truth, and so you might as well know all about it from the beginning. What do you think, Julius?'

'As you're bent on it, I'd go right ahead with the facts,' replied the American, who had so far sat in silence.

'Yes, tell me all about it,' said Sir James. 'I want to know who Tommy is.'

Thus encouraged Tuppence plunged into her tale, and the lawyer listened with close attention.

'Very interesting,' he said, when she finished. 'A great deal of what you tell me, child, is already known to me. I've had certain theories of my own about this Jane Finn. You've done extraordinarily well so far, but it's rather too bad of – what do you know him as? – Mr Carter to pitchfork you two young things into an affair of this kind. By the way, where did Mr Hersheimmer come in originally? You didn't make that clear?'

Julius answered for himself.

'I'm Jane's first cousin,' he explained, returning the lawyer's keen gaze.

'Ah!'

'Oh, Sir James,' broke out Tuppence, 'what do you think has become of Tommy?'

'H'm.' The lawyer rose, and paced slowly up and down. 'When you arrived, young lady, I was just packing up my traps. Going to Scotland by the night train for a few days' fishing. But there are different kinds of fishing. I've a good mind to stay, and see if we can't get on the track of that young chap.'

'Oh!' Tuppence clasped her hands ecstatically.

'All the same, as I said before, it's too bad of – of Carter to set you two babies on a job like this. Now, don't get offended, Miss – er –'

'Cowley. Prudence Cowley. But my friends call me Tuppence.'

'Well, Miss Tuppence, then, as I'm certainly going to be a friend. Don't be offended because I think you're young. Youth is a failing only too easily outgrown. Now, about this young Tommy of yours –'

'Yes.' Tuppence clasped her hands.

'Frankly, things look bad for him. He's been butting in somewhere where he wasn't wanted. Not a doubt of it. But don't give up hope.'

'And you really will help us? There, Julius! He didn't want me to come,' she added by way of explanation.

'H'm,' said the lawyer, favouring Julius with another keen glance. 'And why was that?'

'I reckoned it would be no good worrying you with a petty little business like this.'

'I see.' He paused a moment. 'This petty little business, as you call it, bears directly on a very big business, bigger perhaps than either of you or Miss Tuppence know. If this boy is alive, he may have very valuable information to give us. Therefore, we must find him.'

'Yes, but how?' cried Tuppence. 'I've tried to think of everything.'

Sir James smiled.

'And yet there's one person quite near at hand who in all probability knows where he is, or at all events where he is likely to be.'

'Who is that?' asked Tuppence, puzzled.

'Mrs Vandemeyer.'

'Yes, but she'd never tell us.'

'Ah, that is where I come in. I think it quite likely that I shall be able to make Mrs Vandemeyer tell me what I want to know.'

'How?' demanded Tuppence, opening her eyes very wide.

'Oh, just by asking her questions,' replied Sir James easily. 'That's the way we do it, you know.'

He tapped with his fingers on the table, and Tuppence felt again the intense power that radiated from the man.

'And if she won't tell?' asked Julius suddenly.

'I think she will. I have one or two powerful levers. Still, in that unlikely event, there is always the possibility of bribery.'

'Sure. And that's where I come in!' cried Julius, bringing his fist down on the table with a bang. 'You can count on me, if necessary, for one million dollars. Yes, sir, one million dollars!'

Sir James sat down and subjected Julius to a long scrutiny.

'Mr Hersheimmer,' he said at last, 'that is a very large sum.'

'I guess it'll have to be. These aren't the kind of folk to offer sixpence to.'

'At the present rate of exchange it amounts to considerably over two hundred and fifty thousand pounds.'

'That's so. Maybe you think I'm talking through my hat, but I can deliver the goods all right, with enough over to spare for your fee.'

Sir James flushed slightly.

'There is no question of a fee, Mr Hersheimmer. I am not a private detective.'

'Sorry. I guess I was just a mite hasty, but I've been feeling bad about this money question. I wanted to offer a big reward for news of Jane some days ago, but your crusted institution of Scotland Yard advised me against it. Said it was undesirable.'

'They were probably right,' said Sir James dryly.

'But it's all OK about Julius,' put in Tuppence. 'He's not pulling your leg. He's got simply pots of money.'

'The old man piled it up in style,' explained Julius. 'Now, let's get down to it. What's your idea?'

Sir James considered for a moment or two.

'There is no time to be lost. The sooner we strike the better.'
He turned to Tuppence. 'Is Mrs Vandemeyer dining out
tonight, do you know?'

'Yes, I think so, but she will not be out late. Otherwise, she
would have taken the latch-key.'

'Good. I will call upon her about ten o'clock. What time
are you supposed to return.'

'About nine-thirty or ten, but I could go back earlier.'

'You must not do that on any account. It might arouse
suspicion if you did not stay out till the usual time. Be back
by nine-thirty. I will arrive at ten. Mr Hersheimmer will wait
below in a taxi perhaps.'

'He's got a new Rolls-Royce car,' said Tuppence with vicari-
ous pride.

'Even better. If I succeed in obtaining the address from her,
we can go there at once, taking Mrs Vandemeyer with us if
necessary. You understand?'

'Yes.' Tuppence rose to her feet with a skip of delight. 'Oh,
I feel so much better!'

'Don't build on it too much, Miss Tuppence. Go easy.'

Julius turned to the lawyer.

'Say, then, I'll call for you in the car round about nine-
thirty. Is that right?'

'Perhaps that will be the best plan. It would be unnecessary
to have two cars waiting about. Now, Miss Tuppence, my
advice to you is to go and have a good dinner, a *really* good
one, mind. And don't think ahead more than you can help.'

He shook hands with them both, and a moment later they
were outside.

'Isn't he a duck?' inquired Tuppence ecstatically, as she
skipped down the steps. 'Oh, Julius, isn't he just a duck?'

'Well, I allow he seems to be the goods all right. And I was
wrong about its being useless to go to him. Say, shall we go
right away back to the Ritz?'

'I must walk a bit, I think. I feel so excited. Drop me in
the Park, will you? Unless you'd like to come too?'

Julius shook his head.

'I want to get some petrol,' he explained. 'And send off a cable or two.'

'All right. I'll meet you at the Ritz at seven. We'll have to dine upstairs. I can't show myself in these glad rags.'

'Sure. I'll get Felix to help me choose the menu. He's some head waiter, that. So long.'

Tuppence walked briskly along towards the Serpentine, first glancing at her watch. It was nearly six o'clock. She remembered that she had had no tea, but felt too excited to be conscious of hunger. She walked as far as Kensington Gardens and then slowly retraced her steps, feeling infinitely better for the fresh air and exercise. It was not so easy to follow Sir James's advice and put the possible events of the evening out of her head. As she drew nearer and nearer to Hyde Park Corner, the temptation to return to South Audley Mansions was almost irresistible.

At any rate, she decided, it would do no harm just to go and *look* at the building. Perhaps, then, she could resign herself to waiting patiently for ten o'clock.

South Audley Mansions looked exactly the same as usual. What Tuppence had expected she hardly knew, but the sight of its red brick solidity slightly assuaged the growing and entirely unreasonable uneasiness that possessed her. She was just turning away when she heard a piercing whistle, and the faithful Albert came running from the building to join her.

Tuppence frowned. It was no part of the programme to have attention called to her presence in the neighbourhood, but Albert was purple with suppressed excitement.

'I say, miss, she's a-going!'

'Who's going?' demanded Tuppence sharply.

'The crook. Ready Rita. Mrs Vandemeyer. She's a-packing up, and she's just sent down word for me to get her a taxi.'

'What?' Tuppence clutched his arm.

'It's the truth, miss. I thought maybe as you didn't know about it.'

'Albert,' cried Tuppence, 'you're a brick. If it hadn't been for you we'd have lost her.'

Albert flushed with pleasure at this tribute.

'There's no time to lose,' said Tuppence, crossing the road. 'I've got to stop her. At all costs I must keep her here until –' She broke off. 'Albert, there's a telephone here, isn't there?'

The boy shook his head.

'The flats mostly have their own, miss. But there's a box just round the corner.'

'Go to it then, at once, and ring up the Ritz Hotel. Ask for Mr Hersheimmer, and when you get him tell him to get Sir James and come at once, as Mrs Vandemeyer is trying to hook it. If you can't get him, ring up Sir James Peel Edgerton, you'll find his number in the book, and tell him what's happening. You won't forget the names, will you?'

Albert repeated them glibly. 'You trust to me, miss, it'll be all right. But what about you? Aren't you afraid to trust yourself with her?'

'No, no, that's all right. *But go and telephone*. Be quick.'

Drawing a long breath, Tuppence entered the Mansions and ran up to the door of No. 20. How she was to detain Mrs Vandemeyer until the two men arrived, she did not know, but somehow or other it had to be done, and she must accomplish the task single-handed. What had occasioned this precipitate departure? Did Mrs Vandemeyer suspect her?

Speculations were idle. Tuppence pressed the bell firmly. She might learn something from the cook.

Nothing happened and, after waiting some minutes, Tuppence pressed the bell again, keeping her finger on the button for some little while. At last she heard footsteps inside, and a moment later Mrs Vandemeyer herself opened the door. She lifted her eyebrows at the sight of the girl.

'You?'

'I had a touch of toothache, ma'am,' said Tuppence glibly. 'So thought it better to come home and have a quiet evening.'

Mrs Vandemeyer said nothing, but she drew back and let Tuppence pass into the hall.

'How unfortunate for you,' she said coldly. 'You had better go to bed.'

'Oh, I shall be all right in the kitchen, ma'am. Cook will –'

'Cook is out,' said Mrs Vandemeyer, in a rather disagreeable tone. 'I sent her out. So you see you had better go to bed.'

Suddenly Tuppence felt afraid. There was a ring in Mrs Vandemeyer's voice that she did not like at all. Also, the other woman was slowly edging her up the passage. Tuppence turned at bay.

'I don't want –'

Then, in a flash, a rim of cold steel touched her temple, and Mrs Vandemeyer's voice rose cold and menacing:

'You damned little fool! Do you think I don't know? No, don't answer. If you struggle or cry out, I'll shoot you like a dog.'

The rim of steel pressed a little harder against the girl's temple.

'Now then, march,' went on Mrs Vandemeyer. 'This way – into my room. In a minute, when I've done with you, you'll go to bed as I told you to. And you'll sleep – oh yes, my little spy, you'll sleep all right!'

There was a sort of hideous geniality in the last words which Tuppence did not at all like. For the moment there was nothing to be done, and she walked obediently into Mrs Vandemeyer's bedroom. The pistol never left her forehead. The room was in a state of wild disorder, clothes were flung about right and left, a suitcase and a hat box, half-packed, stood in the middle of the floor.

Tuppence pulled herself together with an effort. Her voice shook a little, but she spoke out bravely.

'Come now,' she said, 'this is nonsense. You can't shoot me. Why, everyone in the building would hear the report.'

'I'd risk that,' said Mrs Vandemeyer cheerfully. 'But, as long as you don't sing out for help, you're all right – and I don't think you will. You're a clever girl. You deceived *me* all right. I hadn't a suspicion of you! So I've no doubt that you understand perfectly well that this is where I'm on top and you're underneath. Now then – sit on the bed. Put your hands above your head, and if you value your life don't move them.'

Tuppence obeyed passively. Her good sense told her that there was nothing else to do but accept the situation. If she shrieked for help there was very little chance of anyone hearing her, whereas there was probably quite a good chance of Mrs Vandemeyer's shooting her. In the meantime, every minute of delay gained was valuable.

Mrs Vandemeyer laid down the revolver on the edge of the wash-stand within reach of her hand, and, still eyeing Tuppence like a lynx in case the girl should attempt to move, she took a little stoppered bottle from its place on the marble and poured some of its contents into a glass which she filled up with water.

'What's that?' asked Tuppence sharply.

'Something to make you sleep soundly.'

Tuppence paled a little.

'Are you going to poison me?' she asked in a whisper.

'Perhaps,' said Mrs Vandemeyer, smiling agreeably.

'Then I shan't drink it,' said Tuppence firmly. 'I'd much rather be shot. At any rate that would make a row, and someone might hear it. But I won't be killed off quietly like a lamb.'

Mrs Vandemeyer stamped her foot.

'Don't be a little fool! Do you really think I want a hue and cry for murder out after me? If you've any sense at all, you'll realize that poisoning you wouldn't suit my book at all. It's a sleeping-draught, that's all. You'll wake up tomorrow morning none the worse. I simply don't want the bother of tying you up and gagging you. That's the alternative – and you won't like it, I can tell you! I can be very rough if I choose. So drink this down like a good girl, and you'll be none the worse for it.'

In her heart of hearts Tuppence believed her. The arguments she had adduced rang true. It was a simple and effective method of getting her out of the way for the time being. Nevertheless, the girl did not take kindly to the idea of being tamely put to sleep without as much as one bid for freedom. She felt that once Mrs Vandemeyer gave them the slip, the last hope of finding Tommy would be gone.

Tuppence was quick in her mental processes. All these reflections passed through her mind in a flash, and she saw where a chance, a very problematic chance, lay, and she determined to risk all in one supreme effort.

Accordingly, she lurched suddenly off the bed and fell on her knees before Mrs Vandemeyer, clutching her skirts frantically.

'I don't believe it,' she moaned. 'It's poison – I know it's poison. Oh, don't make me drink it' – her voice rose to a shriek – 'don't make me drink it!'

Mrs Vandemeyer, glass in hand, looked down with a curling lip at this sudden collapse.

'Get up, you little idiot! Don't go on drivelling there. How you ever had the nerve to play your part as you did I can't think.' She stamped her foot. 'Get up, I say.'

But Tuppence continued to cling and sob, interjecting her sobs with incoherent appeals for mercy. Every minute gained was to the good. Moreover, as she grovelled, she moved imperceptibly nearer to her objective.

Mrs Vandemeyer gave a sharp impatient exclamation, and jerked the girl to her knees.

'Drink it at once!' Imperiously she pressed the glass to the girl's lips.

Tuppence gave one last despairing moan.

'You swear it won't hurt me?' she temporized.

'Of course it won't hurt you. Don't be a fool.'

'Will you swear it?'

'Yes, yes,' said the other impatiently. 'I swear it.'

Tuppence raised a trembling left hand to the glass.

'Very well.' Her mouth opened meekly.

Mrs Vandemeyer gave a sigh of relief, off her guard for the moment. Then, quick as a flash, Tuppence jerked the glass upward as hard as she could. The fluid in it splashed into Mrs Vandemeyer's face, and during her momentary gasp, Tuppence's right hand shot out and grasped the revolver where it lay on the edge of the wash-stand. The next moment she had sprung back a pace, and the revolver pointed straight at Mrs Vandemeyer's heart, with no unsteadiness in the hand that held it.

In the moment of victory, Tuppence betrayed a somewhat unsportsman-like triumph.

'Now who's on top and who's underneath?' she crowed.

The other's face was convulsed with rage. For a minute Tuppence thought she was going to spring upon her, which would have placed the girl in an unpleasant dilemma, since she meant to draw the line at actually letting off the revolver. However, with an effort, Mrs Vandemeyer controlled herself, and at last a slow evil smile crept over her face.

'Not a fool then, after all! You did that well, girl. But you shall pay for it – oh, yes, you shall pay for it! I have a long memory!'

'I'm surprised you should have been gulled so easily,' said Tuppence scornfully. 'Did you really think I was the kind of girl to roll about on the floor and whine for mercy?'

'You may do – some day!' said the other significantly.

The cold malignity of her manner sent an unpleasant chill down Tuppence's spine, but she was not going to give in to it.

'Supposing we sit down,' she said pleasantly. 'Our present attitude is a little melodramatic. No – not on the bed. Draw a chair up to the table, that's right. Now I'll sit opposite you with the revolver in front of me – just in case of accidents. Splendid. Now, let's talk.'

'What about?' said Mrs Vandemeyer sullenly.

Tuppence eyed her thoughtfully for a minute. She was remembering several things. Boris's words, 'I believe you would sell – *us*!' and her answer, 'The price would have to be enormous,' given lightly, it was true, yet might not there be a substratum of truth in it? Long ago, had not Whittington asked: 'Who's been blabbing? Rita?' Would Rita Vandemeyer prove to be the weak spot in the armour of Mr Brown?

Keeping her eyes fixed steadily on the other's face, Tuppence replied quietly:

'Money –'

Mrs Vandemeyer started. Clearly, the reply was unexpected.

'What do you mean?'

'I'll tell you. You said just now that you had a long memory. A long memory isn't half as useful as a long purse! I dare say it relieves your feelings a good deal to plan out all sorts of dreadful things to do to me, but is that *practical*? Revenge is very unsatisfactory. Everyone always says so. But money' – Tuppence warmed to her pet creed – 'well, there's nothing unsatisfactory about money, is there?'

'Do you think,' said Mrs Vandemeyer scornfully, 'that I am the kind of woman to sell my friends?'

'Yes,' said Tuppence promptly, 'if the price was big enough.'

'A paltry hundred pounds or so!'

'No,' said Tuppence. 'I should suggest – a hundred thousand!'

Her economical spirit did not permit her to mention the whole million dollars suggested by Julius.

A flush crept over Mrs Vandemeyer's face.

'What did you say?' she asked, her fingers playing nervously with a brooch on her breast. In that moment Tuppence knew that the fish was hooked, and for the first time she felt a horror of her own money-loving spirit. It gave her a dreadful sense of kinship to the woman fronting her.

'A hundred thousand pounds,' repeated Tuppence.

The light died out of Mrs Vandemeyer's eyes. She leaned back in her chair.

'Bah!' she said. 'You haven't got it.'

'No,' admitted Tuppence, 'I haven't – but I know someone who has.'

'Who?'

'A friend of mine.'

'Must be a millionaire,' remarked Mrs Vandemeyer unbelievingly.

'As a matter of fact he is. He's an American. He'll pay you

that without a murmur. You can take it from me that it's a perfectly genuine proposition.'

Mrs Vandemeyer sat up again.

'I'm inclined to believe you,' she said slowly.

There was silence between them for some time, then Mrs Vandemeyer looked up.

'What does he want to know, this friend of yours?'

Tuppence went through a momentary struggle, but it was Julius's money, and his interests must come first.

'He wants to know where Jane Finn is,' she said boldly.

Mrs Vandemeyer showed no surprise.

'I'm not sure where she is at the present moment,' she replied.

'But you could find out?'

'Oh, yes,' returned Mrs Vandemeyer carelessly. 'There would be no difficulty about that.'

'Then' – Tuppence's voice shook a little – 'there's a boy, a friend of mine. I'm afraid something's happened to him, through your pal, Boris.'

'What's his name?'

'Tommy Beresford.'

'Never heard of him. But I'll ask Boris. He'll tell me anything he knows.'

'Thank you.' Tuppence felt a terrific rise in her spirits. It impelled her to more audacious efforts. 'There's one thing more.'

'Well?'

Tuppence leaned forward and lowered her voice.

'*Who is Mr Brown?*'

Her quick eyes saw the sudden paling of the beautiful face. With an effort Mrs Vandemeyer pulled herself together and tried to resume her former manner. But the attempt was a mere parody.

She shrugged her shoulders.

'You can't have learnt much about us if you don't know that *nobody knows who Mr Brown is* . . .'

'You do,' said Tuppence quietly.

Again the colour deserted the other's face.

'What makes you think that?'

'I don't know,' said the girl truthfully. 'But I'm sure.'

Mrs Vandemeyer stared in front of her for a long time.

'Yes,' she said hoarsely, at last, '*I* know. I was beautiful, you see – very beautiful –'

'You are still,' said Tuppence with admiration.

Mrs Vandemeyer shook her head. There was a strange gleam in her electric-blue eyes.

'Not beautiful enough,' she said in a soft dangerous voice. 'Not – beautiful – enough! And sometimes, lately, I've been afraid . . . It's dangerous to know too much!' She leaned forward across the table. 'Swear that my name shan't be brought into it – that no one shall ever know.'

'I swear it. And, once he's caught, you'll be out of danger.'

A terrified look swept across Mrs Vandemeyer's face.

'Shall I? Shall I ever be?' She clutched Tuppence's arm. 'You're sure about the money?'

'Quite sure.'

'When shall I have it? There must be no delay.'

'This friend of mine will be here presently. He may have to send cables, or something like that. But there won't be any delay – he's a terrific hustler.'

A resolute look settled on Mrs Vandemeyer's face.

'I'll do it. It's a great sum of money, and besides' – she gave a curious smile – 'it is not – wise to throw over a woman like me!'

For a moment or two, she remained smiling, and lightly tapping her fingers on the table. Suddenly she started, and her face blanched.

'What was that?'

'I heard nothing.'

Mrs Vandemeyer gazed round her fearfully.

'If there should be someone listening –'

'Nonsense. Who could there be?'

'Even the walls might have ears,' whispered the other. 'I tell you I'm frightened. You don't know him!'

'Think of the hundred thousand pounds,' said Tuppence soothingly.

Mrs Vandemeyer passed her tongue over her dried lips.

'You don't know him,' she reiterated hoarsely. 'He's – ah!'

With a shriek of terror she sprang to her feet. Her outstretched hand pointed over Tuppence's head. Then she swayed to the ground in a dead faint.

Tuppence looked round to see what had startled her.

In the doorway were Sir James Peel Edgerton and Julius Hersheimmer.

CHAPTER XIII

The Vigil

Sir James brushed past Julius and hurriedly bent over the fallen woman.

'Heart,' he said sharply. 'Seeing us so suddenly must have given her a shock. Brandy – and quickly, or she'll slip through our fingers.'

Julius hurried to the wash-stand.

'Not here,' said Tuppence over her shoulder. 'In the tantalus in the dining-room. Second door down the passage.'

Between them Sir James and Tuppence lifted Mrs Vandemeyer and carried her to the bed. There they dashed water on her face, but with no result. The lawyer fingered her pulse.

'Touch and go,' he muttered. 'I wish that young fellow would hurry up with the brandy.'

At that moment Julius re-entered the room, carrying a glass half full of the spirit which he handed to Sir James. While Tuppence lifted her head the lawyer tried to force a little of the spirit between her closed lips. Finally the woman opened her eyes feebly. Tuppence held the glass to her lips.

'Drink this.'

Mrs Vandemeyer complied. The brandy brought the colour back to her white cheeks, and revived her in a marvellous fashion. She tried to sit up – then fell back with a groan, her hand to her side.

'It's my heart,' she whispered. 'I mustn't talk.'

She lay back with closed eyes.

Sir James kept his finger on her wrist a minute longer, then withdrew it with a nod.

'She'll do now.'

All three moved away, and stood together talking in low voices. One and all were conscious of a certain feeling of anticlimax. Clearly any scheme for cross-questioning the lady was out of the question for the moment. For the time being they were baffled, and could do nothing.

Tuppence related how Mrs Vandemeyer had declared herself willing to disclose the identity of Mr Brown, and how she had consented to discover and reveal to them the whereabouts of Jane Finn. Julius was congratulatory.

'That's all right, Miss Tuppence. Splendid! I guess that hundred thousand pounds will look just as good in the morning to the lady as it did over night. There's nothing to worry over. She won't speak without the cash anyway, you bet!'

There was certainly a good deal of common sense in this, and Tuppence felt a little comforted.

'What you say is true,' said Sir James meditatively. 'I must confess, however, that I cannot help wishing we had not interrupted at the minute we did. Still, it cannot be helped, it is only a matter of waiting until the morning.'

He looked across at the inert figure on the bed. Mrs Vandemeyer lay perfectly passive with closed eyes. He shook his head.

'Well,' said Tuppence, with an attempt at cheerfulness, 'we must wait until the morning, that's all. But I don't think we ought to leave the flat.'

'What about leaving that bright boy of yours on guard?'

'Albert? And suppose she came round again and hooked it. Albert couldn't stop her.'

'I guess she won't want to make tracks away from the dollars.'

'She might. She seemed very frightened of "Mr Brown".'

'What? Real plumb scared of him?'

'Yes. She looked round and said even walls had ears.'

'Maybe she meant a dictaphone,' said Julius with interest.

'Miss Tuppence is right,' said Sir James quietly. 'We must not leave the flat – if only for Mrs Vandemeyer's sake.'

Julius stared at him.

'You think he'd get after her? Between now and tomorrow morning. How could he know, even?'

'You forget your own suggestion of a dictaphone,' said Sir James dryly. 'We have a very formidable adversary. I believe, if we exercise all due care, that there is a very good chance of his being delivered into our hands. But we must neglect no precaution. We have an important witness, but she must be safeguarded. I would suggest that Miss Tuppence should go to bed, and that you and I, Mr Hersheimmer, should share the vigil.'

Tuppence was about to protest, but happening to glance at the bed she saw Mrs Vandemeyer, her eyes half-open, with such an expression of mingled fear and malevolence on her face that it quite froze the words on her lips.

For a moment she wondered whether the faint and the heart attack had been a gigantic sham, but remembering the deadly pallor she could hardly credit the supposition. As she looked the expression disappeared as by magic, and Mrs Vandemeyer lay inert and motionless as before. For a moment the girl fancied she must have dreamt it. But she determined nevertheless to be on the alert.

'Well,' said Julius, 'I guess we'd better make a move out of here anyway.'

The others fell in with his suggestion. Sir James again felt Mrs Vandemeyer's pulse.

'Perfectly satisfactory,' he said in a low voice to Tuppence. 'She'll be absolutely all right after a night's rest.'

The girl hesitated a moment by the bed. The intensity of the expression she had surprised had impressed her powerfully. Mrs Vandemeyer lifted her eyelids. She seemed to be struggling to speak. Tuppence bent over her.

'Don't – leave –' she seemed unable to proceed, murmuring something that sounded like 'sleepy'. Then she tried again.

Tuppence bent lower still. It was only a breath.

'Mr – Brown –' The voice stopped.

But the half-closed eyes seemed still to send an agonized message.

Moved by a sudden impulse, the girl said quickly:

'I shan't leave the flat. I shall sit up all night.'

A flash of relief showed before the lids descended once more. Apparently Mrs Vandemeyer slept. But her words had awakened a new uneasiness in Tuppence. What had she meant by that low murmur, 'Mr Brown'? Tuppence caught herself nervously looking over her shoulder. The big wardrobe loomed up in a sinister fashion before her eyes. Plenty of room for a man to hide in that . . . Half-ashamed of herself Tuppence pulled it open and looked inside. No one – of course! She stooped down and looked under the bed. There was no other possible hiding-place.

Tuppence gave her familiar shake of the shoulders. It was absurd, this giving way to nerves! Slowly she went out of the room. Julius and Sir James were talking in a low voice. Sir James turned to her.

'Lock the door on the outside, please, Miss Tuppence, and take out the key. There must be no chance of anyone entering that room.'

The gravity of his manner impressed them, and Tuppence felt less ashamed of her attack of 'nerves'.

'Say,' remarked Julius suddenly, 'there's Tuppence's bright boy. I guess I'd better go down and ease his young mind. That's some lad, Tuppence.'

'How did you get in, by the way?' asked Tuppence suddenly. 'I forgot to ask.'

'Well, Albert got me on the phone all right. I ran round for Sir James here, and we came right on. The boy was on the look out for us, and was just a mite worried about what might have happened to you. He'd been listening outside the door of the flat, but couldn't hear anything. Anyhow he suggested sending us up in the coal lift instead of ringing the bell. And sure enough we landed in the scullery and came right along to find you. Albert's still below, and must be hopping mad by this time.' With which Julius departed abruptly.

'Now then, Miss Tuppence,' said Sir James, 'you know this

place better than I do. Where do you suggest we should take up our quarters?'

Tuppence considered for a moment or two.

'I think Mrs Vandemeyer's boudoir would be the most comfortable,' she said at last, and led the way there.

Sir James looked round approvingly.

'This will do very well, and now, my dear young lady, do go to bed and get some sleep.'

Tuppence shook her head resolutely.

'I couldn't, thank you, Sir James. I should dream of Mr Brown all night!'

'But you'll be so tired, child.'

'No, I shan't. I'd rather stay up – really.'

The lawyer gave in.

Julius reappeared some minutes later, having reassured Albert and rewarded him lavishly for his services. Having in his turn failed to persuade Tuppence to go to bed, he said decisively:

'At any rate, you've got to have something to eat right away. Where's the larder?'

Tuppence directed him, and he returned in a few minutes with a cold pie and three plates.

After a hearty meal, the girl felt inclined to pooh-pooh her fancies of half an hour before. The power of the money bribe could not fail.

'And now, Miss Tuppence,' said Sir James, 'we want to hear your adventures.'

'That's so,' agreed Julius.

Tuppence narrated her adventures with some complacence. Julius occasionally interjected an admiring 'Bully'. Sir James said nothing until she had finished, when his quiet 'Well done, Miss Tuppence,' made her flush with pleasure.

'There's one thing I don't get clearly,' said Julius. 'What put her up to clearing out?'

'I don't know,' confessed Tuppence.

Sir James stroked his chin thoughtfully.

'The room was in great disorder. That looks as though her

flight was unpremeditated. Almost as though she got a sudden warning to go from someone.'

'Mr Brown, I suppose,' said Julius scoffingly.

The lawyer looked at him deliberately for a minute or two.

'Why not?' he said. 'Remember, you yourself have once been worsted by him.'

Julius flushed with vexation.

'I feel just mad when I think of how I handed out Jane's photograph to him like a lamb. Gee, if I ever lay hands on it again, I'll freeze on to it – like hell!'

'That contingency is likely to be a remote one,' said the other dryly.

'I guess you're right,' said Julius frankly. 'And, in any case, it's the original I'm out after. Where do you think she can be, Sir James?'

The lawyer shook his head.

'Impossible to say. But I've a very good idea where she *has* been.'

'You have? Where?'

Sir James smiled.

'At the scene of your nocturnal adventures, the Bournemouth nursing home.'

'There? Impossible. I asked.'

'No, my dear sir, you asked if anyone of the name of Jane Finn had been there. Now, if the girl had been placed there it would almost certainly be under an assumed name.'

'Bully for you,' cried Julius. 'I never thought of that!'

'It was fairly obvious,' said the other.

'Perhaps the doctor's in it too,' suggested Tuppence.

Julius shook his head.

'I don't think so. I took to him at once. No, I'm pretty sure Dr Hall's all right.'

'Hall, did you say?' asked Sir James. 'That is curious – really very curious.'

'Why?' demanded Tuppence.

'Because I happened to meet him this morning. I've known

him slightly on and off for some years, and this morning I ran across him in the street. Staying at the Metropole, he told me.' He turned to Julius. 'Didn't he tell you he was coming up to town?'

Julius shook his head.

'Curious,' mused Sir James. 'You did not mention his name this afternoon, or I would have suggested your going to him for further information with my card as introduction.'

'I guess I'm a mutt,' said Julius with unusual humility. 'I ought to have thought of the false name stunt.'

'How could you think of anything after falling out of that tree?' cried Tuppence. 'I'm sure anyone else would have been killed right off.'

'Well, I guess it doesn't matter now, anyway,' said Julius. 'We've got Mrs Vandemeyer on a string, and that's all we need.'

'Yes,' said Tuppence, but there was a lack of assurance in her voice.

A silence settled down over the party. Little by little the magic of the night began to gain hold on them. There were sudden creaks in the furniture, imperceptible rustlings in the curtains. Suddenly Tuppence sprang up with a cry.

'I can't help it. I know Mr Brown's somewhere in the flat! I can *feel* him.'

'Sure, Tuppence, how could he be? This door's open into the hall. No one could have come in by the front door without our seeing and hearing him.'

'I can't help it. I *feel* he's here!'

She looked appealingly at Sir James, who replied gravely:

'With due deference to your feelings, Miss Tuppence (and mine as well for that matter), I do not see how it is humanly possible for anyone to be in the flat without our knowledge.'

The girl was a little comforted by his words.

'Sitting up at night is always rather jumpy,' she confessed.

'Yes,' said Sir James. 'We are in the condition of people holding a séance. Perhaps if a medium were present we might get some marvellous results.'

'Do you believe in spiritualism?' asked Tuppence, opening her eyes wide.

The lawyer shrugged his shoulders.

'There is some truth in it, without a doubt. But most of the testimony would not pass muster in the witness-box.'

The hours drew on. With the first faint glimmerings of dawn, Sir James drew aside the curtains. They beheld, what few Londoners see, the slow rising of the sun over the sleeping city. Somehow, with the coming of the light, the dreads and fancies of the past night seemed absurd. Tuppence's spirits revived to the normal.

'Hooray!' she said. 'It's going to be a gorgeous day. And we shall find Tommy. And Jane Finn. And everything will be lovely. I shall ask Mr Carter if I can't be made a Dame!'

At seven o'clock Tuppence volunteered to go and make some tea. She returned with a tray, containing the teapot and four cups.

'Who's the other cup for?' inquired Julius.

'The prisoner, of course. I suppose we might call her that?'

'Taking her tea seems a kind of anti-climax to last night,' said Julius thoughtfully.

'Yes, it does,' admitted Tuppence. 'But, anyway, here goes. Perhaps you'd both come, too, in case she springs on me, or anything. You see, we don't know what mood she'll wake up in.'

Sir James and Julius accompanied her to the door.

'Where's the key? Oh, of course, I've got it myself.'

She put it in the lock, and turned it, then paused.

'Supposing, after all, she's escaped?' she murmured in a whisper.

'Plumb impossible,' replied Julius reassuringly.

But Sir James said nothing.

Tuppence drew a long breath and entered. She heaved a sigh of relief as she saw that Mrs Vandemeyer was lying on the bed.

'Good morning,' she remarked cheerfully. 'I've brought you some tea.'

Mrs Vandemeyer did not reply. Tuppence put down the cup on the table by the bed and went across to draw up the blinds. When she turned, Mrs Vandemeyer still lay without a movement. With a sudden fear clutching at her heart, Tuppence ran to the bed. The hand she lifted was cold as ice . . . Mrs Vandemeyer would never speak now . . .

Her cry brought the others. A very few minutes sufficed. Mrs Vandemeyer was dead – must have been dead some hours. She had evidently died in her sleep.

'If that isn't the cruellest luck,' cried Julius in despair.

The lawyer was calmer, but there was a curious gleam in his eyes.

'If it is luck,' he replied.

'You don't think – but, say, that's plumb impossible – no one could have got in.'

'No,' admitted the lawyer. 'I don't see how they could. And yet – she is on the point of betraying Mr Brown, and – she dies. Is it only chance?'

'But how –'

'Yes, *how*! That is what we must find out.' He stood there silently, gently stroking his chin. 'We must find out,' he said quietly, and Tuppence felt that if she was Mr Brown she would not like the tone of those simple words.

Julius's glance went to the window.

'The window's open,' he remarked. 'Do you think –'

Tuppence shook her head.

'The balcony only goes along as far as the boudoir. We were there.'

'He might have slipped out –' suggested Julius.

But Sir James interrupted him.

'Mr Brown's methods are not so crude. In the meantime we must send for a doctor, but before we do so is there anything in this room that might be of value to us?'

Hastily, the three searched. A charred mass in the grate indicated that Mrs Vandemeyer had been burning papers on the eve of her flight. Nothing of importance remained, though they searched the other rooms as well.

'There's that,' said Tuppence suddenly, pointing to a small, old-fashioned safe let into the wall. 'It's for jewellery, I believe, but there might be something else in it.'

The key was in the lock, and Julius swung open the door, and searched inside. He was some time over the task.

'Well,' said Tuppence impatiently.

There was a pause before Julius answered, then he withdrew his head and shut the door.

'Nothing,' he said.

In five minutes a brisk young doctor arrived, hastily summoned. He was deferential to Sir James, whom he recognized.

'Heart failure, or possibly an overdose of some sleeping-draught.' He sniffed. 'Rather an odour of chloral in the air.'

Tuppence remembered the glass she had upset. A new thought drove her to the wash-stand. She found the little bottle from which Mrs Vandemeyer had poured a few drops.

It had been three parts full. Now – *it was empty.*

CHAPTER XIV

A Consultation

Nothing was more surprising and bewildering to Tuppence than the ease and simplicity with which everything was arranged, owing to Sir James's skilful handling. The doctor accepted quite readily the theory that Mrs Vandemeyer had accidentally taken an overdose of chloral. He doubted whether an inquest would be necessary. If so, he would let Sir James know. He understood that Mrs Vandemeyer was on the eve of departure for abroad, and that the servants had already left? Sir James and his young friends had been paying a call upon her, when she was suddenly stricken down and they had spent the night in the flat, not liking to leave her alone. Did they know of any relatives? They did not, but Sir James referred him to Mrs Vandemeyer's solicitor.

Shortly afterwards a nurse arrived to take charge, and the others left the ill-omened building.

'And what now?' asked Julius, with a gesture of despair. 'I guess we're down and out for good.'

Sir James stroked his chin thoughtfully.

'No,' he said quietly. 'There is still the chance that Dr Hall may be able to tell us something.'

'Gee! I'd forgotten him.'

'The chance is slight, but it must not be neglected. I think I told you that he is staying at the Metropole. I should suggest that we call upon him there as soon as possible. Shall we say after a bath and breakfast?'

It was arranged that Tuppence and Julius should return to the Ritz, and call for Sir James in the car. The programme was faithfully carried out, and a little after eleven they drew up before the Metropole. They asked for Dr Hall, and a page-boy went in search of him. In a few minutes the little doctor came hurrying towards them.

'Can you spare us a few minutes, Dr Hall?' said Sir James pleasantly. 'Let me introduce you to Miss Cowley. Mr Hersheimmer, I think, you already know.'

A quizzical gleam came into the doctor's eye as he shook hands with Julius.

'Ah, yes, my young friend of the tree episode! Ankle all right, eh?'

'I guess it's cured owing to your skilful treatment, doc.'

'And the heart trouble? Ha! ha!'

'Still searching,' said Julius briefly.

'To come to the point, can we have a word with you in private?' asked Sir James.

'Certainly. I think there is a room here where we shall be quite undisturbed.'

He led the way, and the others followed him. They sat down, and the doctor looked inquiringly at Sir James.

'Dr Hall, I am very anxious to find a certain young lady for the purpose of obtaining a statement from her. I have reason to believe that she has been at one time or another in your establishment at Bournemouth. I hope I am transgressing no professional etiquette in questioning you on the subject?'

'I suppose it is a matter of testimony?'

Sir James hesitated a moment, then he replied:

'Yes.'

'I shall be pleased to give you any information in my power. What is the young lady's name? Mr Hersheimmer asked me, I remember —' He half turned to Julius.

'The name,' said Sir James bluntly, 'is really immaterial. She would be almost certainly sent to you under an assumed one. But I should like to know if you are acquainted with a Mrs Vandemeyer?'

'Mrs Vandemeyer, of 20 South Audley Mansions? I know her slightly.'

'You are not aware of what has happened?'

'What do you mean?'

'You do not know that Mrs Vandemeyer is dead?'

'Dear, dear, I had no idea of it! When did it happen?'

'She took an overdose of chloral last night.'

'Purposely?'

'Accidentally, it is believed. I should not like to say myself. Anyway, she was found dead this morning.'

'Very sad. A singularly handsome woman. I presume she was a friend of yours, since you are acquainted with all these details.'

'I am acquainted with the details because – well, it was I who found her dead.'

'Indeed,' said the doctor, starting.

'Yes,' said Sir James, and stroked his chin reflectively.

'This is very sad news, but you will excuse me if I say that I do not see how it bears on the subject of your inquiry?'

'It bears on it in this way, is it not a fact that Mrs Vandemeyer committed a young relative of hers to your charge?'

Julius leaned forward eagerly.

'That is the case,' said the doctor quietly.

'Under the name of – ?'

'Janet Vandemeyer. I understood her to be a niece of Mrs Vandemeyer's.'

'And she came to you?'

'As far as I can remember in June or July of 1915.'

'Was she a mental case?'

'She is perfectly sane, if that is what you mean. I understood from Mrs Vandemeyer that the girl had been with her on the *Lusitania* when that ill-fated ship was sunk, and had suffered a severe shock in consequence.'

'We're on the right track, I think?' Sir James looked round.

'As I said before, I'm a mutt!' returned Julius.

The doctor looked at them all curiously.

'You spoke of wanting a statement from her,' he said. 'Supposing she is not able to give one?'

'What? You have just said that she is perfectly sane.'

'So she is. Nevertheless, if you want a statement from her

concerning any events prior to May 7, 1915, she will not be able to give it to you.'

They looked at the little man, stupefied. He nodded cheerfully.

'It's a pity,' he said. 'A great pity, especially as I gather, Sir James, that the matter is important. But there it is, she can tell you nothing.'

'But why, man? Darn it all, why?'

The little man shifted his benevolent glance to the excited young American.

'Because Janet Vandemeyer is suffering from a complete loss of memory!'

'*What?*'

'Quite so. An interesting case, a *very* interesting case. Not so uncommon, really, as you would think. There are several very well-known parallels. It's the first case of the kind that I've had under my own personal observation, and I must admit that I've found it of absorbing interest.' There was something rather ghoulish in the little man's satisfaction.

'And she remembers nothing,' said Sir James slowly.

'Nothing prior to May 7, 1915. After that date her memory is as good as yours or mine.'

'Then the first thing she remembers?'

'Is landing with the survivors. Everything before that is a blank. She did not know her own name, or where she had come from, or where she was. She couldn't even speak her own tongue.'

'But surely all this is most unusual?' put in Julius.

'No, my dear sir. Quite normal under the circumstances. Severe shock to the nervous system. Loss of memory proceeds nearly always on the same lines. I suggested a specialist, of course. There's a very good man in Paris – makes a study of these cases – but Mrs Vandemeyer opposed the idea of publicity that might result from such a course.'

'I can imagine she would,' said Sir James grimly.

'I fell in with her views. There *is* a certain notoriety given to these cases. And the girl was very young – nineteen, I believe. It seemed a pity that her infirmity should be talked about – might damage her prospects. Besides, there is no special treatment to pursue in such cases. It is really a matter of waiting.'

'Waiting?'

'Yes, sooner or later, the memory will return – as suddenly as it went. But in all probability the girl will have entirely forgotten the intervening period, and will take up life where she left off – at the sinking of the *Lusitania*.'

'And when do you expect this to happen?'

The doctor shrugged his shoulders.

'Ah, that I cannot say. Sometimes it is a matter of months, sometimes it has been known to be as long as twenty years! Sometimes another shock does the trick. One restores what the other took away.'

'Another shock, eh?' said Julius thoughtfully.

'Exactly. There was a case in Colorado –' The little man's voice trailed on, voluble, mildly enthusiastic.

Julius did not seem to be listening. He had relapsed into his own thoughts and was frowning. Suddenly he came out of his brown study, and hit the table such a resounding bang with his fist that everyone jumped, the doctor most of all.

'I've got it! I guess, doc, I'd like your medical opinion on the plan I'm about to outline. Say Jane was to cross the herring pond again, and the same thing was to happen. The sub-marine, the sinking ship, everyone to take to the boats – and so on. Wouldn't that do the trick? Wouldn't it give a mighty big bump to her subconscious self, or whatever the jargon is, and start it functioning again right away?'

'A very interesting speculation, Mr Hersheimmer. In my own opinion, it would be successful. It is unfortunate that there is no chance of the conditions repeating themselves as you suggest.'

'Not by nature, perhaps, doc. But I'm talking about art.'

'Art?'

'Why, yes. What's the difficulty? Hire the liner –'

'A liner!' murmured Dr Hall faintly.

'Hire some passengers, hire a submarine – that's the only difficulty, I guess. Governments are apt to be a bit hidebound over their engines of war. They won't sell to the first comer. Still, I guess that can be got over. Ever heard of the word "graft", sir? Well, graft gets there every time! I reckon that we shan't really need to fire a torpedo. If everyone hustles round and screams loud enough that the ship is sinking, it ought to be enough for an innocent young girl like Jane. By the time she's got a life-belt on her, and is being hustled into a boat, with a well-drilled lot of artistes doing the hysterical stunt on deck, why – she ought to be right back again where she was in May, 1915. How's that for the bare outline?'

Dr Hall looked at Julius. Everything that he was for the moment incapable of saying was eloquent in that look.

'No,' said Julius, in answer to it, 'I'm not crazy. The thing's perfectly possible. It's done every day in the States for the movies. Haven't you seen trains in collision on the screen? What's the difference between buying up a train and buying up a liner? Get the properties and you can go right ahead!'

Dr Hall found his voice.

'But the expense, my dear sir.' His voice rose. 'The expense! It will be *colossal*!'

'Money doesn't worry me any,' explained Julius simply.

Dr Hall turned an appealing face to Sir James, who smiled slightly.

'Mr Hersheimmer is very well off – very well off indeed.'

The doctor's glance came back to Julius with a new and subtle quality in it. This was no longer an eccentric young fellow with a habit of falling off trees. The doctor's eyes held the deference accorded to a really rich man.

'Very remarkable plan. Very remarkable,' he murmured. 'The movies – of course! Your American word for the cinema. Very interesting. I fear we are perhaps a little behind the times over here in our methods. And you really mean to carry out this remarkable plan of yours.'

'You bet your bottom dollar I do.'

The doctor believed him – which was a tribute to his

nationality. If an Englishman had suggested such a thing, he
would have had grave doubts as to his sanity.

'I cannot guarantee a cure,' he pointed out. 'Perhaps I ought
to make that quite clear.'

'Sure, that's all right,' said Julius. 'You just trot out Jane,
and leave the rest to me.'

'Jane?'

'Miss Janet Vandemeyer, then. Can we get on the long
distance to your place right away, and ask them to send her
up; or shall I run down and fetch her in my car?'

The doctor stared.

'I beg your pardon, Mr Hersheimmer. I thought you
understood.'

'Understood what?'

'That Miss Vandemeyer is no longer under my care.'

CHAPTER XV

Tuppence Receives a Proposal

Julius sprang up.

'What?'

'I thought you were aware of that.'

'When did she leave?'

'Let me see. Today is Monday, is it not? It must have been last Wednesday – why, surely – yes, it was the same evening that you – er – fell out of my tree.'

'That evening? Before, or after?'

'Let me see – oh yes, afterwards. A very urgent message arrived from Mrs Vandemeyer. The young lady and the nurse who was in charge of her left by the night train.'

Julius sank back again into his chair.

'Nurse Edith – left with a patient – I remember,' he muttered. 'My God, to have been so near!'

Dr Hall looked bewildered.

'I don't understand. Is the young lady not with her aunt, after all?'

Tuppence shook her head. She was about to speak when a warning glance from Sir James made her hold her tongue. The lawyer rose.

'I'm much obliged to you, Hall. We're very grateful for all you've told us. I'm afraid we're now in the position of having to track Miss Vandemeyer anew. What about the nurse who accompanied her; I suppose you don't know where she is?'

The doctor shook his head.

'We've not heard from her, as it happens. I understood she was to remain with Miss Vandemeyer for a while. But what can have happened? Surely the girl has not been kidnapped.'

'That remains to be seen,' said Sir James gravely.

The other hesitated.

'You do not think I ought to go to the police?'

'No, no. In all probability the young lady is with other relations.'

The doctor was not completely satisfied, but he saw that Sir James was determined to say no more, and realized that to try to extract more information from the famous KC would be mere waste of labour. Accordingly, he wished them goodbye, and they left the hotel. For a few minutes they stood by the car talking.

'How maddening,' cried Tuppence. 'To think that Julius must have been actually under the same roof with her for a few hours.'

'I was a darned idiot,' muttered Julius gloomily.

'You couldn't know,' Tuppence consoled him. 'Could he?' She appealed to Sir James.

'I should advise you not to worry,' said the latter kindly. 'No use crying over spilt milk, you know.'

'The great thing is what to do next,' added Tuppence the practical.

Sir James shrugged his shoulders.

'You might advertise for the nurse who accompanied the girl. That is the only course I can suggest, and I must confess I do not hope for much result. Otherwise there is nothing to be done.'

'Nothing?' said Tuppence blankly. 'And – Tommy?'

'We must hope for the best,' said Sir James. 'Oh yes, we must go on hoping.'

But over her downcast head his eyes met Julius's, and almost imperceptibly he shook his head. Julius understood. The lawyer considered the case hopeless. The young American's face grew grave. Sir James took Tuppence's hand.

'You must let me know if anything further comes to light. Letters will always be forwarded.'

Tuppence stared at him blankly.

'You are going away?'

'I told you. Don't you remember? To Scotland.'

'Yes, but I thought –' The girl hesitated.

Sir James shrugged his shoulders.

'My dear young lady, I can do nothing more, I fear. Our clues have all ended in thin air. You can take my word for it that there is nothing more to be done. If anything should arise, I shall be glad to advise you in any way I can.'

His words gave Tuppence an extraordinary desolate feeling.

'I suppose you're right,' she said. 'Anyway, thank you very much for trying to help us. Goodbye.'

Julius was bending over the car. A momentary pity came into Sir James's keen eyes, as he gazed into the girl's downcast face.

'Don't be too disconsolate, Miss Tuppence,' he said in a low voice. 'Remember, holiday-time isn't always all playtime. One sometimes manages to put in some work as well.'

Something in his tone made Tuppence glance up sharply. He shook his head with a smile.

'No, I shan't say any more. Great mistake to say too much. Remember that. Never tell all you know – not even to the person you know best. Understand? Goodbye.'

He strode away. Tuppence stared after him. She was beginning to understand Sir James's methods. Once before he had thrown her a hint in the same careless fashion. Was this a hint? What exactly lay behind those last brief words? Did he mean that, after all, he had not abandoned the case: that secretly, he would be working on it still while –

Her meditations were interrupted by Julius, who adjured her to 'get right in'.

'You're looking kind of thoughtful,' he remarked as they started off. 'Did the old guy say anything more?'

Tuppence opened her mouth impulsively, and then shut it again. Sir James's words sounded in her ears: 'Never tell all you know – not even to the person you know best.' And like a flash there came into her mind another memory. Julius before the safe in the flat, her own question and the pause before his reply, 'Nothing.' Was there really nothing? Or had he found something he wished to keep to himself? If he could make a reservation, so could she.

'Nothing particular,' she replied.

She felt rather than saw Julius throw a sideways glance at her.

'Say, shall we go for a spin in the park?'

'If you like.'

For a while they ran on under the trees in silence. It was a beautiful day. The keen rush through the air brought a new exhilaration to Tuppence.

'Say, Miss Tuppence, do you think I'm ever going to find Jane?'

Julius spoke in a discouraged voice. The mood was so alien to him that Tuppence turned and stared at him in surprise. He nodded.

'That's so. I'm getting down and out over the business. Sir James today hadn't got any hope at all, I could see that. I don't like him – we don't gee together somehow – but he's pretty cute, and I guess he wouldn't quit if there was any chance of success – now, would he?'

Tuppence felt rather uncomfortable, but clinging to her belief that Julius also had withheld something from her, she remained firm.

'He suggested advertising for the nurse,' she reminded him.

'Yes, with a "forlorn hope" flavour to his voice! No – I'm about fed up. I've half a mind to go back to the States right away.'

'Oh no!' cried Tuppence. 'We've got to find Tommy.'

'I sure forgot Beresford,' said Julius contritely. 'That's so. We must find him. But after – well, I've been day-dreaming ever since I started on this trip – and these dreams are rotten poor business. I'm quit of them. Say, Miss Tuppence, there's something I'd like to ask you.'

'Yes.'

'You and Beresford. What about it?'

'I don't understand you,' replied Tuppence with dignity, adding rather inconsequently: 'And, anyway, you're wrong!'

'Not got a sort of kindly feeling for one another?'

'Certainly not,' said Tuppence with warmth. 'Tommy and I are friends – nothing more.'

'I guess every pair of lovers has said that some time or another,' observed Julius.

'Nonsense!' snapped Tuppence. 'Do I look the sort of girl that's always falling in love with every man she meets?'

'You do not. You look the sort of girl that's mighty often getting fallen in love with!'

'Oh!' said Tuppence, rather taken aback. 'That's a compliment, I suppose?'

'Sure. Now let's get down to this. Supposing we never find Beresford and – and –'

'All right – say it! I can face facts. Supposing he's – dead! Well?'

'And all this business fiddles out. What are you going to do?'

'I don't know,' said Tuppence forlornly.

'You'll be darned lonesome, you poor kid.'

'I shall be all right,' snapped Tuppence with her usual resentment of any kind of pity.

'What about marriage?' inquired Julius. 'Got any views on the subject?'

'I intend to marry, of course,' replied Tuppence. 'That is, if' – she paused, knew a momentary longing to draw back, and then stuck to her guns bravely – 'I can find someone rich enough to make it worth my while. That's frank, isn't it? I dare say you despise me for it.'

'I never despise business instinct,' said Julius. 'What particular figure have you in mind?'

'Figure?' asked Tuppence, puzzled. 'Do you mean tall or short?'

'No. Sum – income.'

'Oh, I – haven't quite worked that out.'

'What about me?'

'*You?*'

'Sure thing.'

'Oh, I couldn't!'

'Why not?'

'I tell you I couldn't.'

'Again, why not?'

'It would seem so unfair.'

'I don't see anything unfair about it. I call your bluff, that's all. I admire you immensely, Miss Tuppence, more than any girl I've ever met. You're so darned plucky. I'd just love to give you a real, rattling good time. Say the word, and we'll run round right away to some high-class jeweller, and fix up the ring business.'

'I can't,' gasped Tuppence.

'Because of Beresford?'

'No, no, *no*!'

'Well then?'

Tuppence merely continued to shake her head violently.

'You can't reasonably expect more dollars than I've got.'

'Oh, it isn't that,' gasped Tuppence with an almost hysterical laugh. 'But thanking you very much, and all that, I think I'd better say no.'

'I'd be obliged if you'd do me the favour to think it over until tomorrow.'

'It's no use.'

'Still, I guess we'll leave it like that.'

'Very well,' said Tuppence meekly.

Neither of them spoke again until they reached the Ritz.

Tuppence went upstairs to her room. She felt morally battered to the ground after her conflict with Julius's vigorous personality. Sitting down in front of the glass, she stared at her own reflection for some minutes.

'Fool,' murmured Tuppence at length, making a grimace. 'Little fool. Everything you want – everything you've ever hoped for, and you go and bleat out "no" like an idiotic little sheep. It's your one chance. Why don't you take it? Grab it? Snatch at it? What more do you want?'

As if in answer to her own question, her eyes fell on a small snapshot of Tommy that stood on her dressing-table in a shabby frame. For a moment she struggled for self-control, and then abandoning all pretence, she held it to her lips and burst into a fit of sobbing.

'Oh, Tommy, Tommy,' she cried, 'I do love you so – and I may never see you again . . .'

At the end of five minutes Tuppence sat up, blew her nose, and pushed back her hair.

'That's that,' she observed sternly. 'Let's look facts in the face. I seem to have fallen in love – with an idiot of a boy who probably doesn't care two straws about me.' Here she paused. 'Anyway,' she resumed, as though arguing with an unseen opponent, 'I don't *know* that he does. He'd never have dared to say so. I've always jumped on sentiment – and here I am being more sentimental than anybody. What idiots girls are! I've always thought so. I suppose I shall sleep with his photograph under my pillow, and dream about him all night. It's dreadful to feel you've been false to your principles.'

Tuppence shook her head sadly, as she reviewed her backsliding.

'I don't know what to say to Julius, I'm sure. Oh, what a fool I feel! I'll have to say *something* – he's so American and thorough, he'll insist upon having a reason. I wonder if he did find anything in that safe –'

Tuppence's meditations went off on another track. She reviewed the events of last night carefully and persistently. Somehow, they seemed bound up with Sir James's enigmatical words . . .

Suddenly she gave a great start – the colour faded out of her face. Her eyes, fascinated, gazed in front of her, the pupils dilated.

'Impossible,' she murmured. 'Impossible! I must be going mad even to think of such a thing . . .'

Monstrous – yet it explained everything . . .

After a moment's reflection she sat down and wrote a note, weighing each word as she did so. Finally she nodded her head as though satisfied, and slipped it into an envelope which she addressed to Julius. She went down the passage to his sitting-room and knocked at the door. As she had expected, the room was empty. She left the note on the table.

A small page-boy was waiting outside her own door when she returned to it.

'Telegram for you, miss.'

Tuppence took it from the salver, and tore it open carelessly. Then she gave a cry. The telegram was from Tommy!

CHAPTER XVI

Further Adventures of Tommy

From a darkness punctuated with throbbing stabs of fire, Tommy dragged his senses slowly back to life. When he at last opened his eyes, he was conscious of nothing but an excruciating pain through his temples. He was vaguely aware of unfamiliar surroundings. Where was he? What had happened? He blinked feebly. This was not his bedroom at the Ritz. And what the devil was the matter with his head?

'Damn!' said Tommy, and tried to sit up. He had remembered. He was in that sinister house in Soho. He uttered a groan and fell back. Through his almost-closed eyelids he reconnoitred carefully.

'He is coming to,' remarked a voice very near Tommy's ear. He recognized it at once for that of the bearded and efficient German, and lay artistically inert. He felt that it would be a pity to come round too soon; and until the pain in his head became a little less acute, he felt quite incapable of collecting his wits. Painfully he tried to puzzle out what had happened. Obviously somebody must have crept up behind him as he listened and struck him down with a blow on the head. They knew him now for a spy, and would in all probability give him short shrift. Undoubtedly he was in a tight place. Nobody knew where he was, therefore he need expect no outside assistance, and must depend solely on his own wits.

'Well, here goes,' murmured Tommy to himself, and repeated his former remark.

'Damn!' he observed, and this time succeeded in sitting up.

In a minute the German stepped forward and placed a glass to his lips, with the brief command 'Drink.' Tommy obeyed.

The potency of the draught made him choke, but it cleared his brain in a marvellous manner.

He was lying on a couch in the room in which the meeting had been held. On one side of him was the German, on the other the villainous-faced door-keeper who had let him in. The others were grouped together at a little distance away. But Tommy missed one face. The man known as Number One was no longer of the company.

'Feel better?' asked the German, as he removed the empty glass.

'Yes, thanks,' returned Tommy cheerfully.

'Ah, my young friend, it is lucky for you your skull is so thick. The good Conrad struck hard.' He indicated the evil-faced door-keeper by a nod.

The man grinned.

Tommy twisted his head round with an effort.

'Oh,' he said, 'so you're Conrad, are you? It strikes me the thickness of my skull was lucky for you too. When I look at you I feel it's almost a pity I've enabled you to cheat the hangman.'

The man snarled, and the bearded man said quietly:

'He would have run no risk of that.'

'Just as you like,' replied Tommy. 'I know it's the fashion to run down the police. I rather believe in them myself.'

His manner was nonchalant to the last degree. Tommy Beresford was one of those young Englishmen not distinguished by any special intellectual ability, but who are emphatically at their best in what is known as a 'tight place'. Their natural diffidence and caution falls from them then like a glove. Tommy realized perfectly that in his own wits lay the only chance of escape, and behind his casual manner he was racking his brains furiously.

The cold accents of the German took up the conversation:

'Have you anything to say before you are put to death as a spy?'

'Simply lots of things,' replied Tommy with the same urbanity as before.

'Do you deny that you were listening at that door?'

'I do not. I must really apologize – but your conversation was so interesting that it overcame my scruples.'

'How did you get in?'

'Dear old Conrad here.' Tommy smiled deprecatingly at him. 'I hesitate to suggest pensioning off a faithful servant, but you really ought to have a better watchdog.'

Conrad snarled impotently, and said sullenly, as the man with the beard swung round upon him:

'He gave the word. How was I to know?'

'Yes,' Tommy chimed in. 'How was he to know? Don't blame the poor fellow. His hasty action has given me the pleasure of seeing you all face to face.'

He fancied that his words caused some discomposure among the group, but the watchful German stilled it with a wave of his hand.

'Dead men tell no tales,' he said evenly.

'Ah,' said Tommy, 'but I'm not dead yet!'

'You soon will be, my young friend,' said the German.

An assenting murmur came from the others.

Tommy's heart beat faster, but his casual pleasantness did not waver.

'I think not,' he said firmly. 'I should have a great objection to dying.'

He had got them puzzled, he saw that by the look on his captor's face.

'Can you give us any reason why we should not put you to death?' asked the German.

'Several,' replied Tommy. 'Look here, you've been asking me a lot of questions. Let me ask you one for a change. Why didn't you kill me off at once before I regained consciousness?'

The German hesitated, and Tommy seized his advantage.

'Because you didn't know how much I knew – and where I obtained that knowledge. If you kill me now, you never will know.'

But here the emotions of Boris became too much for him. He stepped forward waving his arms.

'You hell-hound of a spy,' he screamed. 'We will give you short shrift. Kill him! Kill him!'

There was a roar of applause.

'You hear?' said the German, his eyes on Tommy. 'What have you got to say to that?'

'Say?' Tommy shrugged his shoulders. 'Pack of fools. Let them ask themselves a few questions. How did I get into this place? Remember what dear old Conrad said – *with your own password*, wasn't it? How did I get hold of that? You don't suppose I came up those steps haphazard and said the first thing that came into my head?'

Tommy was pleased with the concluding words of this speech. His only regret was that Tuppence was not present to appreciate its full flavour.

'That is true,' said the working man suddenly. 'Comrades, we have been betrayed!'

An ugly murmur arose. Tommy smiled at them encouragingly.

'That's better. How can you hope to make a success of any job if you don't use your brains?'

'You will tell us who has betrayed us,' said the German. 'But that shall not save you – oh, no! You shall tell us all that you know. Boris, here, knows pretty ways of making people speak!'

'Bah!' said Tommy scornfully, fighting down a singularly unpleasant feeling in the pit of his stomach. 'You will neither torture me nor kill me.'

'And why not?' asked Boris.

'Because you'd kill the goose that lays the golden eggs,' replied Tommy quietly.

There was a momentary pause. It seemed as though Tommy's persistent assurance was at last conquering. They were no longer completely sure of themselves. The man in the shabby clothes stared at Tommy searchingly.

'He's bluffing you, Boris,' he said quietly.

Tommy hated him. Had the man seen through him?

The German, with an effort, turned roughly to Tommy.

'What do you mean?'

'What do you think I mean?' parried Tommy, searching desperately in his own mind.

Suddenly Boris stepped forward, and shook his fist in Tommy's face.

'Speak, you swine of an Englishman – speak!'

'Don't get so excited, my good fellow,' said Tommy calmly. 'That's the worst of you foreigners. You can't keep calm. Now, I ask you, do I look as though I thought there were the least chance of your killing me?'

He looked confidently round, and was glad they could not hear the persistent beating of his heart which gave the lie to his words.

'No,' admitted Boris at last sullenly, 'you do not.'

'Thank God, he's not a mind reader,' thought Tommy. Aloud he pursued his advantage:

'And why am I so confident? Because I know something that puts me in a position to propose a bargain.'

'A bargain?' The bearded man took him up sharply.

'Yes – a bargain. My life and liberty against –' He paused. 'Against what?'

The group pressed forward. You could have heard a pin drop.

Slowly Tommy spoke.

'The papers that Danvers brought over from America in the *Lusitania*.'

The effect of his words was electrical. Everyone was on his feet. The German waved them back. He leaned over Tommy, his face purple with excitement.

'*Himmel!* You have got them, then?'

With magnificent calm Tommy shook his head.

'You know where they are?' persisted the German.

Again Tommy shook his head. 'Not in the least.'

'Then – then –' angry and baffled, the words failed him.

Tommy looked round. He saw anger and bewilderment on every face, but his calm assurance had done its work – no one doubted but that something lay behind his words.

'I don't know where the papers are – but I believe that I can find them. I have a theory –'

'Pah!'

Tommy raised his hand, and silenced the clamours of disgust.

'I call it a theory – but I'm pretty sure of my facts – facts that are known to no one but myself. In any case what do you lose? If I can produce the papers – you give me my life and liberty in exchange. Is it a bargain?'

'And if we refuse?' said the German quietly.

Tommy lay back on the couch.

'The 29th,' he said thoughtfully, 'is less than a fortnight ahead –'

For a moment the German hesitated. Then he made a sign to Conrad.

'Take him into the other room.'

For five minutes Tommy sat on the bed in the dingy room next door. His heart was beating violently. He had risked all on this throw. How would they decide? And all the while that this agonized questioning went on within him, he talked flippantly to Conrad, enraging the cross-gained door-keeper to the point of homicidal mania.

At last the door opened, and the German called imperiously to Conrad to return.

'Let's hope the judge hasn't put his black cap on,' remarked Tommy frivolously. 'That's right, Conrad, march me in. The prisoner is at the bar, gentlemen.'

The German was seated once more behind the table. He motioned to Tommy to sit down opposite to him.

'We accept,' he said harshly, 'on terms. The papers must be delivered to us before you go free.'

'Idiot!' said Tommy amiably. 'How do you think I can look for them if you keep me tied by the leg here?'

'What do you expect, then?'

'I must have liberty to go about the business in my own way.'

The German laughed.

'Do you think we are little children to let you walk out of here leaving us a pretty story full of promises?'

'No,' said Tommy thoughtfully. 'Though infinitely simpler for me, I did not really think you would agree to that plan. Very well, we must arrange a compromise. How would it be if you attached little Conrad here to my person. He's a faithful fellow, and very ready with the fist.'

'We prefer,' said the German coldly, 'that you should remain here. One of our number will carry out your instructions minutely. If the operations are complicated, he will return to you with a report and you can instruct him further.'

'You're tying my hands,' complained Tommy. 'It's a very delicate affair, and the other fellow will muff it up as likely as not, and then where shall I be? I don't believe one of you has got an ounce of tact.'

The German rapped the table.

'Those are our terms. Otherwise, death!'

Tommy leaned back wearily.

'I like your style. Curt, but attractive. So be it, then. But one thing is essential, I must see the girl.'

'What girl?'

'Jane Finn, of course.'

The other looked at him curiously for some minutes, then he said slowly, and as though choosing his words with care:

'Do you not know that she can tell you nothing?'

Tommy's heart beat a little faster. Would he succeed in coming face to face with the girl he was seeking?

'I shall not ask her to tell me anything,' he said quietly. 'Not in so many words, that is.'

'Then why see her?'

Tommy paused.

'To watch her face when I ask her one question,' he replied at last.

Again there was a look in the German's eyes that Tommy did not quite understand.

'She will not be able to answer your question.'

'That does not matter. I shall have seen her face when I ask it.'

'And you think that will tell you anything?' He gave a short disagreeable laugh. More than ever, Tommy felt that there was a factor somewhere that he did not understand. The German looked at him searchingly. 'I wonder whether, after all, you know as much as we think?' he said softly.

Tommy felt his ascendancy less sure than a moment before. His hold had slipped a little. But he was puzzled. What had he said wrong? He spoke out on the impulse of the moment.

'There may be things that you know which I do not. I have not pretended to be aware of all the details of your show. But equally I've got something up my sleeve that *you* don't know about. And that's where I mean to score. Danvers was a damned clever fellow –' He broke off as if he had said too much.

But the German's face had lightened a little.

'Danvers,' he murmured. 'I see –' He paused a minute, then waved to Conrad. 'Take him away. Upstairs – you know.'

'Wait a minute,' said Tommy. 'What about the girl?'

'That may perhaps be arranged.'

'It must be.'

'We will see about it. Only one person can decide that.'

'Who?' asked Tommy. But he knew the answer.

'Mr Brown –'

'Shall I see him?'

'Perhaps.'

'Come,' said Conrad harshly.

Tommy rose obediently. Outside the door his gaoler motioned to him to mount the stairs. He himself followed close behind. On the floor above Conrad opened a door and Tommy passed into a small room. Conrad lit a hissing gas burner and went out. Tommy heard the sound of the key being turned in the lock.

He set to work to examine his prison. It was a smaller room than the one downstairs, and there was something peculiarly airless about the atmosphere of it. Then he realized that there was no window. He walked round it. The walls were filthily dirty, as everywhere else. Four pictures hung crookedly on the wall representing scenes from *Faust*, Marguerite with her box of jewels, the church scene, Siebel and his flowers, and Faust and Mephistopheles. The latter brought Tommy's mind back to Mr Brown again. In this sealed and closed chamber, with its close-fitting heavy door, he felt cut off from the world, and the sinister power of the arch-criminal seemed more real. Shout as he would, no one could ever hear him. The place was a living tomb. . .

With an effort Tommy pulled himself together. He sank on to the bed and gave himself up to reflection. His head ached badly; also, he was hungry. The silence of the place was dispiriting.

'Anyway,' said Tommy, trying to cheer himself, 'I shall see the chief – the mysterious Mr Brown, and with a bit of luck in bluffing I shall see the mysterious Jane Finn also. After that –'

After that Tommy was forced to admit the prospect looked dreary.

CHAPTER XVII

Annette

The troubles of the future, however, soon faded before the troubles of the present. And of these, the most immediate and pressing was that of hunger. Tommy had a healthy and vigorous appetite. The steak and chips partaken of for lunch seemed now to belong to another decade. He regretfully recognized the fact that he would not make a success of a hunger strike.

He prowled aimlessly about his prison. Once or twice he discarded dignity, and pounded on the door. But nobody answered the summons.

'Hang it all!' said Tommy indignantly. 'They can't mean to starve me to death.' A new-born fear passed through his mind that this might, perhaps, be one of those 'pretty ways' of making a prisoner speak, which had been attributed to Boris. But on reflection he dismissed the idea.

'It's that sour-faced brute Conrad,' he decided. 'That's a fellow I shall enjoy getting even with one of these days. This is just a bit of spite on his part. I'm certain of it.'

Further meditations induced in him the feeling that it would be extremely pleasant to bring something down with a whack on Conrad's egg-shaped head. Tommy stroked his own head tenderly, and gave himself up to the pleasures of imagination. Finally a bright idea flashed across his brain. Why not convert imagination into reality! Conrad was undoubtedly the tenant of the house. The others, with the possible exception of the bearded German, merely used it as a rendezvous. Therefore, why not wait in ambush for Conrad behind the door, and when he entered bring down a chair, or one of the decrepit pictures, smartly on to his head. One would, of course, be careful not to hit too hard. And then – and then, simply walk out! If he met anyone on the way down, well – Tommy brightened at the thought of an encounter with his fists. Such an affair was infinitely more in his line than the verbal encounter of this afternoon. Intoxicated by his plan, Tommy gently unhooked the picture of the Devil and Faust, and settled himself in position. His hopes were high. The plan seemed to him simple but excellent.

Time went on, but Conrad did not appear. Night and day were the same in this prison room, but Tommy's wrist-watch, which enjoyed a certain degree of accuracy, informed him that it was nine o'clock in the evening. Tommy reflected gloomily that if supper did not arrive soon it would be a question of waiting for breakfast. At ten o'clock hope deserted him, and he flung himself on the bed to seek consolation in sleep. In five minutes his woes were forgotten.

The sound of the key turning in the lock awoke him from his slumbers. Not belonging to the type of hero who is famous for awaking in full possession of his faculties, Tommy merely blinked at the ceiling and wondered vaguely where he was. Then he remembered, and looked at his watch. It was eight o'clock.

'It's either early morning tea or breakfast,' deduced the young man, 'and pray God it's the latter!'

The door swung open. Too late, Tommy remembered his scheme of obliterating the unprepossessing Conrad. A moment later he was glad that he had, for it was not Conrad who entered, but a girl. She carried a tray which she set down on the table.

In the feeble light of the gas burner Tommy blinked at her. He decided at once that she was one of the most beautiful girls he had ever seen. Her hair was a full rich brown, with sudden glints of gold in it as though there were imprisoned sunbeams struggling in its depths. There was a wild-rose quality about her face. Her eyes, set wide apart, were hazel, a golden hazel that again recalled a memory of sunbeams.

A delirious thought shot through Tommy's mind.

'Are you Jane Finn?' he asked breathlessly.

The girl shook her head wonderingly.

'My name is Annette, monsieur.'

She spoke in a soft, broken English.

'Oh!' said Tommy, rather taken aback. '*Française?*' he hazarded.

'*Oui, monsieur. Monsieur parle français?*'

'Not for any length of time,' said Tommy. 'What's that? Breakfast?'

The girl nodded. Tommy dropped off the bed and came and inspected the contents of the tray. It consisted of a loaf, some margarine, and a jug of coffee.

'The living is not equal to the Ritz,' he observed with a sigh. 'But for what we are at last about to receive the Lord has made me truly thankful. Amen.'

He drew up a chair, and the girl turned away to the door.

'Wait a sec,' cried Tommy. 'There are lots of things I want to ask you, Annette. What are you doing in this house? Don't tell me you're Conrad's niece, or daughter, or anything, because I can't believe it.'

'I do the *service*, monsieur. I am not related to anybody.'

'I see,' said Tommy. 'You know what I asked you just now. Have you ever heard that name?'

'I have heard people speak of Jane Finn, I think.'

'You don't know where she is?'

Annette shook her head.

'She's not in this house, for instance?'

'Oh no, monsieur. I must go now – they will be waiting for me.'

She hurried out. The key turned in the lock.

'I wonder who "they" are,' mused Tommy, as he continued to make inroads on the loaf. 'With a bit of luck, that girl might help me to get out of here. She doesn't look like one of the gang.'

At one o'clock Annette reappeared with another tray, but this time Conrad accompanied her.

'Good morning,' said Tommy amiably. 'You have *not* used Pear's soap, I see.'

Conrad growled threateningly.

'No light repartee, have you, old bean? There, there, we can't always have brains as well as beauty. What have we for lunch? Stew? How did I know? Elementary, my dear Watson – the smell of onions is unmistakable.'

'Talk away,' grunted the man. 'It's little enough time you'll have to talk in, maybe.'

The remark was unpleasant in its suggestion, but Tommy ignored it. He sat down at the table.

'Retire, varlet,' he said, with a wave of his hand. 'Prate not to thy betters.'

That evening Tommy sat on the bed, and cogitated deeply. Would Conrad again accompany the girl? If he did not, should he risk trying to make an ally of her? He decided that he must leave no stone unturned. His position was desperate.

At eight o'clock the familiar sound of the key turning made him spring to his feet. The girl was alone.

'Shut the door,' he commanded. 'I want to speak to you.'

She obeyed.

'Look here, Annette, I want you to help me get out of this.'

She shook her head.

'Impossible. There are three of them on the floor below.'

'Oh!' Tommy was secretly grateful for the information. 'But you would help me if you could?'

'No, monsieur.'

'Why not?'

The girl hesitated.

'I think – they are my own people. You have spied upon them. They are quite right to keep you here.'

'They're a bad lot, Annette. If you'll help me, I'll take you away from the lot of them. And you'd probably get a good whack of money.'

But the girl merely shook her head.

'I dare not, monsieur. I am afraid of them.'

She turned away.

'Wouldn't you do anything to help another girl?' cried Tommy. 'She's about your age too. Won't you save her from their clutches?'

'You mean Jane Finn?'

'Yes.'

'It is her you came here to look for? Yes?'

'That's it.'

The girl looked at him, then passed her hand across her forehead.

'Jane Finn. Always I hear that name. It is familiar.'

Tommy came forward eagerly.

'You must know *something* about her?'

But the girl turned away abruptly.

'I know nothing – only the name.' She walked towards the door. Suddenly she uttered a cry. Tommy stared. She had caught sight of the picture he had laid against the wall the night before. For a moment he caught a look of terror in her eyes. As inexplicably it changed to relief. Then abruptly, she went out of the room. Tommy could make nothing of it. Did she fancy that he had meant to attack her with it? Surely not. He rehung the picture on the wall thoughtfully.

Three more days went by in dreary inaction. Tommy felt the strain telling on his nerves. He saw no one but Conrad and Annette, and the girl had become dumb. She spoke only in monosyllables. A kind of dark suspicion smouldered in her eyes. Tommy felt that if this solitary confinement went on much longer he would go mad. He gathered from Conrad that they were waiting for orders from 'Mr Brown'. Perhaps, thought Tommy, he was abroad or away, and they were obliged to wait for his return.

But the evening of the third day brought a rude awakening.

It was barely seven o'clock when he heard the tramp of footsteps outside in the passage. In another minute the door was flung open. Conrad entered. With him was the evil-looking Number Fourteen. Tommy's heart sank at the sight of them.

'Evenin', gov'nor,' said the man with a leer. 'Got those ropes, mate?'

The silent Conrad produced a length of fine cord. The next minute Number Fourteen's hands, horribly dexterous, were winding the cord round his limbs, while Conrad held him down.

'What the devil –?' began Tommy.

But the slow, speechless grin of the silent Conrad froze the words on his lips.

Number Fourteen proceeded deftly with his task. In another minute Tommy was a mere helpless bundle. Then at last Conrad spoke:

'Thought you'd bluffed us, did you? With what you knew, and what you didn't know. Bargained with us! And all the time it was bluff! Bluff! You know less than a kitten. But your number's up all right, you b— swine.'

Tommy lay silent. There was nothing to say. He had failed. Somehow or other the omnipotent Mr Brown had seen through his pretensions. Suddenly a thought occurred to him.

'A very good speech, Conrad,' he said approvingly. 'But wherefore the bonds and fetters? Why not let this kind gentleman here cut my throat without delay?'

'Garn,' said Number Fourteen unexpectedly. 'Think we're as green as to do you in here, and have the police nosing round? Not 'alf! We've ordered the carriage for your lordship tomorrow mornin', but in the meantime we're not taking any chances, see!'

'Nothing,' said Tommy, 'could be plainer than your words – unless it was your face.'

'Stow it,' said Number Fourteen.

'With pleasure,' replied Tommy. 'You're making a sad mistake – but yours will be the loss.'

'You don't kid us that way again,' said Number Fourteen. 'Talking as though you were still at the blooming Ritz, aren't you?'

Tommy made no reply. He was engaged in wondering how Mr Brown had discovered his identity. He decided that

Tuppence, in the throes of anxiety, had gone to the police, and that his disappearance having been made public the gang had not been slow to put two and two together.

The two men departed and the door slammed. Tommy was left to his meditations. They were not pleasant ones. Already his limbs felt cramped and stiff. He was utterly helpless, and he could see no hope anywhere.

About an hour had passed when he heard the key softly turned, and the door opened. It was Annette. Tommy's heart beat a little faster. He had forgotten the girl. Was it possible that she had come to his help?

Suddenly he heard Conrad's voice:

'Come out of it, Annette. He doesn't want any supper tonight.'

'*Oui, oui, je sais bien.* But I must take the other tray. We need the things on it.'

'Well, hurry up,' growled Conrad.

Without looking at Tommy the girl went over to the table, and picked up the tray. She raised a hand and turned out the light.

'Curse you,' – Conrad had come to the door – 'why did you do that?'

'I always turn it out. You should have told me. Shall I relight it, Monsieur Conrad?'

'No, come on out of it.'

'*Le beau petit monsieur,*' cried Annette, pausing by the bed in the darkness. 'You have tied him up well, *hein*? He is like a trussed chicken!' The frank amusement in her tone jarred on the boy but at that moment to his amazement, he felt her hand running lightly over his bonds, and something small and cold was pressed into the palm of his hand.

'Come on, Annette.'

'*Mais me voilà.*'

The door shut. Tommy heard Conrad say:

'Lock it and give me the key.'

The footsteps died away. Tommy lay petrified with amazement. The object Annette had thrust into his hand was a small penknife, the blade open. From the way she had studiously avoided looking at him, and her action with the light, he came to the conclusion that the room was overlooked. There must be a peep-hole somewhere in the walls. Remembering how guarded she had always been in her manner, he saw that he had probably been under observation all the time. Had he said anything to give himself away? Hardly. He had revealed a wish to escape and a desire to find Jane Finn, but nothing that could have given a clue to his own identity. True, his question to Annette had proved that he was personally unacquainted with Jane Finn, but he had never pretended otherwise. The question now was, did Annette really know more? Were her denials intended primarily for the listeners? On that point he could come to no conclusion.

But there was a more vital question that drove out all others. Could he, bound as he was, manage to cut his bonds? He essayed cautiously to rub the open blade up and down on the cord that bound his two wrists together. It was an awkward business and drew a smothered 'Ow' of pain from him as the knife cut into his wrist. But slowly and doggedly he went on sawing to and fro. He cut the flesh badly, but at last he felt the cord slacken. With his hands free, the rest was easy. Five minutes later he stood upright with some difficulty owing to the cramp in his limbs. His first care was to bind up his bleeding wrist. Then he sat on the edge of the bed to think. Conrad had taken the key of the door, so he could expect little more assistance from Annette. The only outlet from the room was the door, consequently he would perforce have to wait until the two men returned to fetch him. But when they did . . . Tommy smiled! Moving with infinite caution in the dark room, he found and unhooked the famous picture. He felt an economical pleasure that his first plan would not be wasted. There was now nothing to do but to wait. He waited.

The night passed slowly. Tommy lived through an eternity of hours, but at last he heard footsteps. He stood upright, drew a deep breath, and clutched the picture firmly.

The door opened. A faint light streamed in from outside.

Conrad went straight towards the gas to light it. Tommy deeply regretted that it was he who had entered first. It would have been pleasant to get even with Conrad. Number Fourteen followed. As he stepped across the threshold, Tommy brought the picture down with terrific force on his head. Number Fourteen went down amidst a stupendous crash of broken glass. In a minute Tommy had slipped out and pulled to the door. The key was in the lock. He turned it and withdrew it just as Conrad hurled himself against the door from the inside with a volley of curses.

For a moment Tommy hesitated. There was the sound of someone stirring on the floor below. Then the German's voice came up the stairs.

'*Gott im Himmel!* Conrad, what is it?'

Tommy felt a small hand thrust into his. Beside him stood Annette. She pointed up a rickety ladder that apparently led to some attics.

'Quick – up here!' She dragged him after her up the ladder. In another moment they were standing in a dusty garret littered with lumber. Tommy looked round.

'This won't do. It's a regular trap. There's no way out.'

'Hush! Wait.' The girl put her finger to her lips. She crept to the top of the ladder and listened.

The banging and beating on the door was terrific. The German and another were trying to force the door in. Annette explained in a whisper:

'They will think you are still inside. They cannot hear what Conrad says. The door is too thick.'

'I thought you could hear what went on in the room?'

'There is a peep-hole into the next room. It was clever of you to guess. But they will not think of that – they are only anxious to get in.'

'Yes – but look here –'

'Leave it to me.' She bent down. To his amazement, Tommy saw that she was fastening the end of a long piece of string to the handle of a big cracked jug. She arranged it carefully, then turned to Tommy.

'Have you the key of the door?'

'Yes.'

'Give it to me.'

He handed it to her.

'I am going down. Do you think you can go half-way, and then swing yourself down *behind* the ladder, so that they will not see you?'

Tommy nodded.

'There's a big cupboard in the shadow of the landing. Stand behind it. Take the end of this string in your hand. When I've let the others out – *pull*!'

Before he had time to ask her anything more, she had flitted lightly down the ladder and was in the midst of the group with a loud cry:

'*Mon Dieu! Mon Dieu! Qu'est-ce qu'il y a?*'

The German turned on her with an oath.

'Get out of this. Go to your room!'

Very cautiously Tommy swung himself down the back of the ladder. So long as they did not turn round, all was well. He crouched behind the cupboard. They were still between him and the stairs.

'Ah!' Annette appeared to stumble over something. She stooped. '*Mon Dieu, voilà la clef!*'

The German snatched it from her. He unlocked the door. Conrad stumbled out, swearing.

'Where is he? Have you got him?'

'We have seen no one,' said the German sharply. His face paled. 'Who do you mean?'

Conrad gave vent to another oath.

'He's got away.'

'Impossible. He would have passed us.'

At that moment, with an ecstatic smile Tommy pulled the string. A crash of crockery came from the attic above. In a trice the men were pushing each other up the rickety ladder and had disappeared into the darkness above.

Quick as a flash Tommy leapt from his hiding-place and dashed down the stairs, pulling the girl with him. There was no one in the hall. He fumbled over the bolts and chain. At last they yielded, the door swung open. He turned. Annette had disappeared.

Tommy stood spell-bound. Had she run upstairs again? What madness possessed her! He fumed with impatience, but he stood his ground. He would not go without her.

And suddenly there was an outcry overhead, an exclamation from the German, and then Annette's voice, clear and high:

'*Ma foi*, he has escaped! And quickly! Who would have thought it?'

Tommy still stood rooted to the ground. Was that a command to him to go? He fancied it was.

And then, louder still, the words floated down to him:

'This is a terrible house. I want to go back to Marguerite. To Marguerite. *To Marguerite!*'

Tommy had run back to the stairs. She wanted him to go and leave her? But why? At all costs he must try to get her away with him. Then his heart sank. Conrad was leaping down the stairs uttering a savage cry at the sight of him. After him came the others.

Tommy stopped Conrad's rush with a straight blow with his fist. It caught the other on the point of the jaw and he fell like a log. The second man tripped over his body and fell. From higher up the staircase there was a flash, and a bullet grazed Tommy's ear. He realized that it would be good for his health to get out of this house as soon as possible. As regards Annette he could do nothing. He had got even with Conrad, which was one satisfaction. The blow had been a good one.

He leapt for the door, slamming it behind him. The square was deserted. In front of the house was a baker's van. Evidently he was to have been taken out of London in that, and his body found many miles from the house in Soho. The driver jumped to the pavement and tried to bar Tommy's way. Again Tommy's fist shot out, and the driver sprawled on the pavement.

Tommy took to his heels and ran – none too soon. The front

door opened and a hail of bullets followed him. Fortunately none of them hit him. He turned the corner of the square.

'There's one thing,' he thought to himself, 'they can't go on shooting. They'll have the police after them if they do. I wonder they dared to there.'

He heard the footsteps of his pursuers behind him, and redoubled his own pace. Once he got out of these byways he would be safe. There would be a policeman about somewhere – not that he really wanted to invoke the aid of the police if he could possibly do without it. It meant explanation, and general awkwardness. In another moment he had reason to bless his luck. He stumbled over a prostrate figure, which started up with a yell of alarm and dashed off down the street. Tommy drew back into a doorway. In a minute he had the pleasure of seeing his two pursuers, of whom the German was one, industriously tracking down the red herring!

Tommy sat down quietly on the doorstep and allowed a few moments to elapse while he recovered his breath. Then he strolled gently in the opposite direction. He glanced at his watch. It was a little after half-past five. It was rapidly growing light. At the next corner he passed a policeman. The policeman cast a suspicious eye on him. Tommy felt slightly offended. Then, passing his hand over his face, he laughed. He had not shaved or washed for three days! What a guy he must look.

He betook himself without more ado to a Turkish Bath establishment which he knew to be open all night. He emerged into the busy daylight feeling himself once more, and able to make plans.

First of all, he must have a square meal. He had eaten nothing since midday yesterday. He turned into an ABC shop and ordered eggs and bacon and coffee. Whilst he ate, he read a morning paper propped up in front of him. Suddenly he stiffened. There was a long article on Kramenin, who was described as the 'man behind Bolshevism' in Russia, and who had just arrived in London – some thought as an unofficial envoy. His career was sketched lightly, and it was firmly asserted that he, and not the figurehead leaders, had been the author of the Russian Revolution.

In the centre of the page was his portrait.

'So that's who Number One is,' said Tommy with his mouth full of eggs and bacon. 'Not a doubt about it. I must push on.'

He paid for his breakfast, and betook himself to Whitehall. There he sent up his name, and the message that it was urgent. A few minutes later he was in the presence of the man who did not here go by the name of 'Mr Carter'. There was a frown on his face.

'Look here, you've no business to come asking for me in this way. I thought that was distinctly understood?'

'It was, sir. But I judged it important to lose no time.'

And as briefly and succinctly as possible he detailed the experiences of the last few days.

Half-way through, Mr Carter interrupted him to give a few cryptic orders through the telephone. All traces of displeasure had now left his face. He nodded energetically when Tommy had finished.

'Quite right. Every moment's of value. Fear we shall be too late anyway. They wouldn't wait. Would clear out at once. Still, they may have left something behind them that will be a clue. You say you've recognized Number One to be Kramenin? That's important. We want something against him badly to prevent the Cabinet falling on his neck too freely. What about the others? You say two faces were familiar to you? One's a Labour man, you think? Just look through these photos, and see if you can spot him.'

A minute later, Tommy held one up. Mr Carter exhibited some surprise.

'Ah, Westway! Shouldn't have thought it. Poses as being moderate. As for the other fellow, I think I can give a good guess.' He handed another photograph to Tommy, and smiled at the other's exclamation. 'I'm right, then. Who is he? Irishman. Prominent Unionist MP. All a blind, of course. We've suspected it – but couldn't get any proof. Yes, you've done very well, young man. The 29th, you say, is the date. That gives us very little time – very little time indeed.'

'But –' Tommy hesitated.

Mr Carter read his thoughts.

'We can deal with the General Strike menace, I think. It's a toss-up – but we've got a sporting chance! But if that draft treaty turns up – we're done. England will be plunged in anarchy. Ah, what's that? The car? Come on, Beresford, we'll go and have a look at this house of yours.'

Two constables were on duty in front of the house in Soho. An inspector reported to Mr Carter in a low voice. The latter turned to Tommy.

'The birds have flown – as we thought. We might as well go over it.'

Going over the deserted house seemed to Tommy to partake of the character of a dream. Everything was just as it had been. The prison room with the crooked pictures, the broken jug in the attic, the meeting room with its long table. But nowhere was there a trace of papers. Everything of that kind had either been destroyed or taken away. And there was no sign of Annette.

'What you tell me about the girl puzzled me,' said Mr Carter. 'You believe that she deliberately went back?'

'It would seem so, sir. She ran upstairs while I was getting the door open.'

'H'm, she must belong to the gang, then; but, being a woman, didn't feel like standing by to see a personable young man killed. But evidently she's in with them, or she wouldn't have gone back.'

'I can't believe she's really one of them, sir. She – seemed so different –'

'Good-looking, I suppose?' said Mr Carter with a smile that made Tommy flush to the roots of his hair.

He admitted Annette's beauty rather shame-facedly.

'By the way,' observed Mr Carter, 'have you shown yourself to Miss Tuppence yet? She's been bombarding me with letters about you.'

'Tuppence? I was afraid she might get a bit rattled. Did she go to the police?'

Mr Carter shook his head.

'Then I wonder how they twigged me.'

Mr Carter looked inquiringly at him, and Tommy explained. The other nodded thoughtfully.

'True, that's rather a curious point. Unless the mention of the Ritz was an accidental remark?'

'It might have been, sir. But they must have found out about me suddenly in some way.'

'Well,' said Mr Carter, looking round him, 'there's nothing more to be done here. What about some lunch with me?'

'Thanks awfully, sir. But I think I'd better get back and rout out Tuppence.'

'Of course. Give her my kind regards and tell her not to believe you're killed too readily next time.'

Tommy grinned.

'I take a lot of killing, sir.'

'So I perceive,' said Mr Carter dryly. 'Well, goodbye. Remember you're a marked man now, and take reasonable care of yourself.'

'Thank you, sir.'

Hailing a taxi briskly Tommy stepped in, and was swiftly borne to the Ritz, dwelling the while on the pleasurable anticipation of startling Tuppence.

'Wonder what she's been up to. Dogging "Rita" most likely. By the way, I suppose that's who Annette meant by Marguerite. I didn't get it at the time.' The thought saddened him a little, for it seemed to prove that Mrs Vandemeyer and the girl were on intimate terms.

The taxi drew up at the Ritz. Tommy burst into its sacred portals eagerly, but his enthusiasm received a check. He was informed that Miss Cowley had gone out a quarter of an hour ago.

CHAPTER XVIII

The Telegram

Baffled for the moment, Tommy strolled into the restaurant, and ordered a meal of surpassing excellence. His four days' imprisonment had taught him anew to value good food.

He was in the middle of conveying a particularly choice morsel of *sole à la Jeannette* to his mouth, when he caught sight of Julius entering the room. Tommy waved a menu cheerfully, and succeeded in attracting the other's attention. At the sight of Tommy, Julius's eyes seemed as though they would pop out of his head. He strode across, and pump-handled Tommy's hand with what seemed to the latter quite unnecessary vigour.

'Holy snakes!' he ejaculated. 'Is it really you?'

'Of course it is. Why shouldn't it be?'

'Why shouldn't it be? Say, man, don't you know you've been given up for dead? I guess we'd have had a solemn requiem for you in another few days.'

'Who thought I was dead?' demanded Tommy.

'Tuppence.'

'She remembered the proverb about the good dying young, I suppose. There must be a certain amount of original sin in me to have survived. Where is Tuppence, by the way?'

'Isn't she here?'

'No, the fellows at the office said she'd just gone out.'

'Gone shopping, I guess. I dropped her here in the car about an hour ago. But, say, can't you shed that British calm of yours, and get down to it? What on God's earth have you been doing all this time?'

'If you're feeding here,' replied Tommy, 'order now. It's going to be a long story.'

Julius drew up a chair to the opposite side of the table,

summoned a hovering waiter, and dictated his wishes. Then he turned to Tommy.

'Fire ahead. I guess you've had some few adventures.'

'One or two,' replied Tommy modestly, and plunged into his recital.

Julius listened spell-bound. Half the dishes that were placed before him he forgot to eat. At the end he heaved a long sigh.

'Bully for you. Reads like a dime novel!'

'And now for the home front,' said Tommy, stretching out his hand for a peach.

'W–ell,' drawled Julius, 'I don't mind admitting we've had some adventures too.'

He, in his turn, assumed the role of narrator. Beginning with his unsuccessful reconnoitring at Bournemouth, he passed on to his return to London, the buying of the car, the growing anxieties of Tuppence, the call upon Sir James, and the sensational occurrences of the previous night.

'But who killed her?' asked Tommy. 'I don't quite understand.'

'The doctor kidded himself she took it herself,' replied Julius dryly.

'And Sir James? What did he think?'

'Being a legal luminary, he is likewise a human oyster,' replied Julius. 'I should say he "reserved judgement".' He went on to detail the events of the morning.

'Lost her memory, eh?' said Tommy with interest. 'By Jove, that explains why they looked at me so queerly when I spoke of questioning her. Bit of a slip on my part, that! But it wasn't the sort of thing a fellow would be likely to guess.'

'They didn't give you any sort of hint as to where Jane was?'

Tommy shook his head regretfully.

'Not a word. I'm a bit of an ass, as you know. I ought to have got more out of them somehow.'

'I guess you're lucky to be here at all. That bluff of yours was the goods all right. How you ever came to think of it all so pat beats me to a frazzle!'

'I was in such a funk I had to think of something,' said Tommy simply.

There was a moment's pause, and then Tommy reverted to Mrs Vandemeyer's death.

'There's no doubt it was chloral?'

'I believe not. At least they call it heart failure induced by an overdose, or some such claptrap. It's all right. We don't want to be worried with an inquest. But I guess Tuppence and I and even the highbrow Sir James have all got the same idea.'

'Mr Brown?' hazarded Tommy.

'Sure thing.'

Tommy nodded.

'All the same,' he said thoughtfully, 'Mr Brown hasn't got wings. I don't see how he got in and out.'

'How about some high-class thought transference stunt? Some magnetic influence that irresistibly impelled Mrs Vandemeyer to commit suicide?'

Tommy looked at him with respect.

'Good, Julius. Distinctly good. Especially the phraseology. But it leaves me cold. I yearn for a real Mr Brown of flesh and blood. I think the gifted young detectives must get to work, study the entrances and exits, and tap the bumps on their foreheads until the solution of the mystery dawns on them. Let's go round to the scene of the crime. I wish we could get hold of Tuppence. The Ritz would enjoy the spectacle of the glad reunion.'

Inquiry at the office revealed the fact that Tuppence had not yet returned.

'All the same, I guess I'll have a look round upstairs,' said Julius. 'She might be in my sitting-room.' He disappeared.

Suddenly a diminutive boy spoke at Tommy's elbow:

'The young lady – she's gone away by train, I think, sir,' he murmured shyly.

'What?' Tommy wheeled round upon him.

The small boy became pinker than before.

'The taxi, sir. I heard her tell the driver Charing Cross and to look sharp.'

Tommy stared at him, his eyes opening wide in surprise. Emboldened, the small boy proceeded. 'So I thought, having asked for an ABC and a Bradshaw.'

Tommy interrupted him:

'When did she ask for an ABC and a Bradshaw?'

'When I took her the telegram, sir.'

'A telegram?'

'Yes, sir.'

'When was that?'

'About half-past twelve, sir.'

'Tell me exactly what happened.'

The small boy drew a long breath.

'I took up a telegram to No. 891 – the lady was there. She opened it and gave a gasp, and then she said, very jolly like: "Bring me up a Bradshaw, and an ABC, and look sharp, Henry." My name isn't Henry, but –'

'Never mind your name,' said Tommy impatiently. 'Go on.'

'Yes, sir. I brought them, and she told me to wait, and looked up something. And then she looks up at the clock, and "Hurry up," she says. "Tell them to get me a taxi," and she begins a-shoving on of her hat in front of the glass, and she was down in two ticks, almost as quick as I was, and I seed her going down the steps and into the taxi, and I heard her call out what I told you.'

The small boy stopped and replenished his lungs. Tommy continued to stare at him. At that moment Julius rejoined him. He held an open letter in his hand.

'I say, Hersheimmer,' – Tommy turned to him – 'Tuppence has gone off sleuthing on her own.'

'Shucks!'

'Yes, she has. She went off in a taxi to Charing Cross in the deuce of a hurry after getting a telegram.' His eye fell on the letter in Julius's hand. 'Oh; she left a note for you. That's all right. Where's she off to?'

Almost unconsciously, he held out his hand for the letter, but Julius folded it up and placed it in his pocket. He seemed a trifle embarrassed.

'I guess this is nothing to do with it. It's about something else – something I asked her that she was to let me know about.'

'Oh!' Tommy looked puzzled, and seemed waiting for more.

'See here,' said Julius suddenly, 'I'd better put you wise. I asked Miss Tuppence to marry me this morning.'

'Oh!' said Tommy mechanically. He felt dazed. Julius's words were totally unexpected. For the moment they benumbed his brain.

'I'd like to tell you,' continued Julius, 'that before I suggested anything of the kind to Miss Tuppence, I made it clear that I didn't want to butt in in any way between her and you –'

Tommy roused himself.

'That's all right,' he said quickly. 'Tuppence and I have been pals for years. Nothing more.' He lit a cigarette with a hand that shook ever so little. 'That's quite all right. Tuppence always said that she was looking out for –'

He stopped abruptly, his face crimsoning, but Julius was in no way discomposed.

'Oh, I guess it'll be the dollars that'll do the trick. Miss Tuppence put me wise to that right away. There's no humbug about her. We ought to gee along together very well.'

Tommy looked at him curiously for a minute, as though he were about to speak, then changed his mind and said nothing. Tuppence and Julius! Well, why not? Had she not lamented the fact that she knew no rich men? Had she not openly avowed her intention of marrying for money if she ever had the chance? Her meeting with the young American millionaire had given her the chance – and it was unlikely she would be slow to avail herself of it. She was out for money. She had always said so. Why blame her because she had been true to her creed?

Nevertheless, Tommy did blame her. He was filled with a passionate and utterly illogical resentment. It was all very well to *say* things like that – but a *real* girl would never marry for money. Tuppence was utterly cold-blooded and selfish, and he would be delighted if he never saw her again! And it was a rotten world!

Julius's voice broke in on these meditations.

'Yes, we ought to gee along together very well. I've heard that a girl always refuses you once – a sort of convention.'

Tommy caught his arm.

'Refuses? Did you say *refuses*?'

'Sure thing. Didn't I tell you that? She just rapped out a "no" without any kind of reason to it. The eternal feminine, the Huns call it, I've heard. But she'll come round right enough. Likely enough, I hustled her some –'

But Tommy interrupted regardless of decorum.

'What did she say in that note?' he demanded fiercely.

The obliging Julius handed it to him.

'There's no earthly clue in it as to where she's gone,' he assured Tommy. 'But you might as well see for yourself if you don't believe me.'

The note, in Tuppence's well-known schoolboy writing, ran as follows:

Dear Julius,

It's always better to have things in black and white. I don't feel I can be bothered to think of marriage until Tommy is found. Let's leave it till then.

> Yours affectionately,
> Tuppence.

Tommy handed it back, his eyes shining. His feelings had undergone a sharp reaction. He now felt that Tuppence was all that was noble and disinterested. Had she not refused Julius without hesitation? True, the note betokened signs of weakening, but he could excuse that. It read almost like a bribe to Julius to spur him on in his efforts to find Tommy, but he supposed she had not really meant it that way. Darling Tuppence, there was not a girl in the world to touch her! When he saw her – His thoughts were brought up with a sudden jerk.

'As you say,' he remarked, pulling himself together, 'there's not a hint here as to what she's up to. Hi – Henry!'

The small boy came obediently. Tommy produced five shillings.

'One thing more. Do you remember what the young lady did with the telegram?'

Henry gasped and spoke.

'She crumpled it up into a ball and threw it into the grate, and made a sort of noise like "Whoop!" sir.'

'Very graphic, Henry,' said Tommy. 'Here's your five shillings. Come on, Julius. We must find that telegram.'

They hurried upstairs. Tuppence had left the key in her door. The room was as she had left it. In the fire-place was a crumpled ball of orange and white. Tommy disentangled it and smoothed out the telegram.

Come at once, Moat House, Ebury, Yorkshire, great developments – Tommy.

They looked at each other in stupefaction. Julius spoke first:

'*You* didn't send it?'

'Of course not. What does it mean?'

'I guess it means the worst,' said Julius quietly. 'They've got her.'

'*What?*'

'Sure thing! They signed your name, and she fell into the trap like a lamb.'

'My God! What shall we do?'

'Get busy, and go after her! Right now! There's no time to waste. It's almighty luck that she didn't take the wire with her. If she had we'd probably never have traced her. But we've got to hustle. Where's that Bradshaw?'

The energy of Julius was infectious. Left to himself, Tommy would probably have sat down to think things out for a good half-hour before he decided on a plan of action. But with Julius Hersheimmer about, hustling was inevitable.

After a few muttered imprecations he handed the Bradshaw to Tommy as being more conversant with its mysteries. Tommy abandoned it in favour of an ABC.

'Here we are. Ebury, Yorks. From King's Cross. Or St Pancras. (Boy must have made a mistake. It was King's Cross, not *Charing Cross*.) 12.50, that's the train she went by; 2.10, that's gone; 3.20 is the next – and a damned slow train, too.'

'What about the car?'

Tommy shook his head.

'Send it up if you like, but we'd better stick to the train. The great thing is to keep calm.'

Julius groaned.

'That's so. But it gets my goat to think of that innocent young girl in danger!'

Tommy nodded abstractedly. He was thinking. In a moment or two, he said:

'I say, Julius, what do they want her for, anyway?'

'Eh? I don't get you?'

'What I mean is that I don't think it's their game to do her any harm,' explained Tommy, puckering his brow with the strain of his mental processes. 'She's a hostage, that's what she is. She's in no immediate danger, because if we tumble on to anything, she'd be damned useful to them. As long as they've got her, they've got the whip hand of us. See?'

'Sure thing,' said Julius thoughtfully. 'That's so.'

'Besides,' added Tommy, as an afterthought, 'I've great faith in Tuppence.'

The journey was wearisome, with many stops, and crowded carriages. They had to change twice, once at Doncaster, once at a small junction. Ebury was a deserted station with a solitary porter, to whom Tommy addressed himself:

'Can you tell me the way to the Moat House?'

'The Moat House? It's a tidy step from here. The big house near the sea, you mean?'

Tommy assented brazenly. After listening to the porter's meticulous but perplexing directions, they prepared to leave the station. It was beginning to rain, and they turned up the collars of their coats as they trudged through the slush of the road. Suddenly Tommy halted.

'Wait a moment.' He ran back to the station and tackled the porter anew.

'Look here, do you remember a young lady who arrived by an earlier train, the 12.10 from London? She'd probably ask you the way to the Moat House.'

He described Tuppence as well as he could, but the porter shook his head. Several people had arrived by the train in question. He could not call to mind one young lady in particular. But he was quite certain that no one had asked him the way to the Moat House.

Tommy rejoined Julius, and explained. Depression was settling down on him like a leaden weight. He felt convinced that their quest was going to be unsuccessful. The enemy had over three hours' start. Three hours was more than enough for Mr Brown. He would not ignore the possibility of the telegram having been found.

The way seemed endless. Once they took the wrong turning and went nearly half a mile out of their direction. It was past seven o'clock when a small boy told them that 't' Moat House' was just past the next corner.

A rusty iron gate swinging dismally on its hinges! An overgrown drive thick with leaves. There was something about the place that struck a chill to both their hearts. They went up the deserted drive. The leaves deadened their footsteps. The daylight was almost gone. It was like walking in a world of ghosts. Overhead the branches flapped and creaked with a mournful note. Occasionally a sodden leaf drifted silently down, startling them with its cold touch on their cheeks.

A turn of the drive brought them in sight of the house. That, too, seemed empty and deserted. The shutters were closed, the steps up to the door overgrown with moss. Was it indeed to this desolate spot that Tuppence had been decoyed? It seemed hard to believe that a human footstep had passed this way for months.

Julius jerked the rusty bell handle. A jangling peal rang
discordantly, echoing through the emptiness within. No one
came. They rang again and again – but there was no sign of
life. Then they walked completely round the house. Everywhere silence, and shuttered windows. If they could believe
the evidence of their eyes the place was empty.

'Nothing doing,' said Julius.

They retraced their steps slowly to the gate.

'There must be a village handy,' continued the young
American. 'We'd better make inquiries there. They'll know
something about the place, and whether there's been anyone
there lately.'

'Yes, that's not a bad idea.'

Proceeding up the road they soon came to a little hamlet.
On the outskirts of it, they met a workman swinging his bag
of tools, and Tommy stopped him with a question.

'The Moat House? It's empty. Been empty for years. Mrs
Sweeney's got the key if you want to go over it – next to the
post office.'

Tommy thanked him. They soon found the post office,
which was also a sweet and general fancy shop, and knocked at
the door of the cottage next to it. A clean, wholesome-looking
woman opened it. She readily produced the key of the Moat
House.

'Though I doubt if it's the kind of place to suit you, sir. In
a terrible state of repair. Ceilings leaking and all. 'Twould
need a lot of money spent on it.'

'Thanks,' said Tommy cheerily. 'I dare say it'll be a wash-
out, but houses are scarce nowadays.'

'That they are,' declared the woman heartily. 'My daughter
and son-in-law have been looking for a decent cottage for I
don't know how long. It's all the war. Upset things terribly,
it has. But excuse me, sir, it'll be too dark for you to see much
of the house. Hadn't you better wait until tomorrow?'

'That's all right. We'll have a look round this evening, anyway. We'd have been here before only we lost our way. What's
the best place to stay at for the night round here?'

Mrs Sweeney looked doubtful.

'There's the Yorkshire Arms, but it's not much of a place for gentlemen like you.'

'Oh, it will do very well. Thanks. By the way, you've not had a young lady here asking for this key today?'

The woman shook her head.

'No one's been over the place for a long time.'

'Thanks very much.'

They retraced their steps to the Moat House. As the front door swung back on its hinges, protesting loudly, Julius struck a match and examined the floor carefully. Then he shook his head.

'I'd swear no one's passed this way. Look at the dust. Thick. Not a sign of a footmark.'

They wandered round the deserted house. Everywhere the same tale. Thick layers of dust apparently undisturbed.

'This gets me,' said Julius. 'I don't believe Tuppence was ever in this house.'

'She must have been.'

Julius shook his head without replying.

'We'll go over it again tomorrow,' said Tommy. 'Perhaps we'll see more in the daylight.'

On the morrow they took up the search once more, and were reluctantly forced to the conclusion that the house had not been invaded for some considerable time. They might have left the village altogether but for a fortunate discovery of Tommy's. As they were retracing their steps to the gate, he gave a sudden cry, and stooping, picked something up from among the leaves, and held it out to Julius. It was a small gold brooch.

'That's Tuppence's!'

'Are you sure?'

'Absolutely. I've often seen her wear it.'

Julius drew a deep breath.

'I guess that settles it. She came as far as here, anyway. We'll make that pub our headquarters, and raise hell round here until we find her. Somebody *must* have seen her.'

Forthwith the campaign began. Tommy and Julius worked separately and together, but the result was the same. Nobody answering to Tuppence's description had been seen in the vicinity. They were baffled – but not discouraged. Finally they altered their tactics. Tuppence had certainly not remained long in the neighbourhood of the Moat House. That pointed to her having been overcome and carried away in a car. They renewed inquiries. Had anyone seen a car standing somewhere near the Moat House that day? Again they met with no success.

Julius wired to town for his own car, and they scoured the neighbourhood daily with unflagging zeal. A grey limousine on which they had set high hopes was traced to Harrogate, and turned out to be the property of a highly respectable maiden lady!

Each day saw them set out on a new quest. Julius was like a hound on the leash. He followed up the slenderest clue. Every car that had passed through the village on the fateful day was tracked down. He forced his way into country properties and submitted the owners of the cars to searching cross-examination. His apologies were as thorough as his methods, and seldom failed in disarming the indignation of his victims; but, as day succeeded day, they were no nearer to discovering Tuppence's whereabouts. So well had the abduction been planned that the girl seemed literally to have vanished into thin air.

And another preoccupation was weighing on Tommy's mind.

'Do you know how long we've been here?' he asked one morning as they sat facing each other at breakfast. 'A week! We're no nearer to finding Tuppence, *and next Sunday is the 29th!*'

'Shucks!' said Julius thoughtfully. 'I'd almost forgotten about the 29th. I've been thinking of nothing but Tuppence.'

'So have I. At least, I hadn't forgotten about the 29th, but it didn't seem to matter a damn in comparison to finding Tuppence. But today's the 23rd, and time's getting short. If we're ever going to get hold of her at all, we must do it before the 29th – her life won't be worth an hour's purchase afterwards. The hostage game will be played out by then. I'm beginning to feel that we've made a big mistake in the way we've set about this. We've wasted time and we're no forrader.'

'I'm with you there. We've been a couple of mutts, who've bitten off a bigger bit than they can chew. I'm going to quit fooling right away!'

'What do you mean?'

'I'll tell you. I'm going to do what we ought to have done a week ago. I'm going right back to London to put the case in the hands of your British police. We fancied ourselves as sleuths. Sleuths! It was a piece of damn-fool foolishness! I'm through! I've had enough of it. Scotland Yard for me!'

'You're right,' said Tommy slowly. 'I wish to God we'd gone there right away.'

'Better late than never. We've been like a couple of babes playing "Here we go round the Mulberry Bush". Now I'm going right along to Scotland Yard to ask them to take me by the hand and show me the way I should go. I guess the professional always scores over the amateur in the end. Are you coming along with me?'

Tommy shook his head.

'What's the good? One of us is enough. I might as well stay here and nose round a bit longer. Something *might* turn up. One never knows.'

'Sure thing. Well, so long. I'll be back in a couple of shakes with a few inspectors along. I shall tell them to pick out their brightest and best.'

But the course of events was not to follow the plan Julius had laid down. Later in the day Tommy received a wire:

Join me Manchester Midland Hotel. Important news – Julius.

At 7.30 that night Tommy alighted from a slow cross-country train. Julius was on the platform.

'Thought you'd come by this train if you weren't out when my wire arrived.'

Tommy grasped him by the arm.

'What is it? Is Tuppence found?'

Julius shook his head.

'No. But I found this waiting in London. Just arrived.'

He handed the telegraph form to the other. Tommy's eyes opened as he read:

Jane Finn found. Come Manchester Midland Hotel immediately – Peel Edgerton.

Julius took the form back and folded it up.

'Queer,' he said thoughtfully. 'I thought that lawyer chap had quit!'

CHAPTER XIX

Jane Finn

'My train got in half an hour ago,' explained Julius, as he led the way out of the station. 'I reckoned you'd come by this before I left London, and wired accordingly to Sir James. He's booked rooms for us, and will be round to dine at eight.'

'What made you think he'd ceased to take any interest in the case?' asked Tommy curiously.

'What he said,' replied Julius dryly. 'The old bird's as close as an oyster! Like all the darned lot of them, he wasn't going to commit himself till he was sure he could deliver the goods.'

'I wonder,' said Tommy thoughtfully.

Julius turned on him.

'You wonder what?'

'Whether that was his real reason.'

'Sure. You bet your life it was.'

Tommy shook his head unconvinced.

Sir James arrived punctually at eight o'clock, and Julius introduced Tommy. Sir James shook hands with him warmly.

'I am delighted to make your acquaintance, Mr Beresford. I have heard so much about you from Miss Tuppence' – he smiled involuntarily – 'that it really seems as though I already know you quite well.'

'Thank you, sir,' said Tommy with his cheerful grin. He scanned the great lawyer eagerly. Like Tuppence, he felt the magnetism of the other's personality. He was reminded of Mr Carter. The two men, totally unlike so far as physical resemblance went, produced a similar effect. Beneath the weary manner of the one and the professional reserve of the other, lay the same quality of mind, keen-edged like a rapier.

In the meantime he was conscious of Sir James's close

scrutiny. When the lawyer dropped his eyes the young man had the feeling that the other had read him through and through like an open book. He could not but wonder what the final judgement was, but there was little chance of learning that. Sir James took in everything, but gave out only what he chose. A proof of that occurred almost at once.

Immediately the first greetings were over Julius broke out into a flood of eager questions. How had Sir James managed to track the girl? Why had he not let them know that he was still working on the case? And so on.

Sir James stroked his chin and smiled. At last he said:

'Just so, just so. Well, she's found. And that's the great thing, isn't it? Eh! Come now, that's the great thing?'

'Sure it is. But just how did you strike her trail? Miss Tuppence and I thought you'd quit for good and all.'

'Ah!' The lawyer shot a lightning glance at him, then resumed operations on his chin. 'You thought that, did you? Did you really? H'm, dear me.'

'But I guess I can take it we were wrong,' pursued Julius.

'Well, I don't know that I should go so far as to say that. But it's certainly fortunate for all parties that we've managed to find the young lady.'

'But where is she?' demanded Julius, his thoughts flying off on another tack. 'I thought you'd be sure to bring her along?'

'That would hardly be possible,' said Sir James gravely.

'Why?'

'Because the young lady was knocked down in a street accident, and has sustained slight injuries to the head. She was taken to the infirmary, and on recovering consciousness gave her name as Jane Finn. When – ah! – I heard that, I arranged for her to be removed to the house of a doctor – a friend of mine, and wired at once for you. She relapsed into unconsciousness and has not spoken since.'

'She's not seriously hurt?'

'Oh, a bruise and a cut or two; really, from a medical point of view, absurdly slight injuries to have produced such a condition. Her state is probably to be attributed to the mental shock consequent on recovering her memory.'

'It's come back?' cried Julius excitedly.

Sir James tapped the table rather impatiently.

'Undoubtedly, Mr Hersheimmer, since she was able to give her real name. I thought you had appreciated that point.'

'And you just happened to be on the spot,' said Tommy. 'Seems quite like a fairy tale?'

But Sir James was far too wary to be drawn.

'Coincidences are curious things,' he said dryly.

Nevertheless, Tommy was now certain of what he had before only suspected. Sir James's presence in Manchester was not accidental. Far from abandoning the case, as Julius supposed, he had by some means of his own successfully run the missing girl to earth. The only thing that puzzled Tommy was the reason for all this secrecy? He concluded that it was a foible of the legal mind.

Julius was speaking.

'After dinner,' he announced, 'I shall go right away and see Jane.'

'That will be impossible, I fear,' said Sir James. 'It is very unlikely they would allow her to see visitors at this time of night. I should suggest tomorrow morning about ten o'clock.'

Julius flushed. There was something in Sir James which always stirred him to antagonism. It was a conflict of two masterful personalities.

'All the same, I reckon I'll go round there tonight and see if I can't ginger them up to break through their silly rules.'

'It will be quite useless, Mr Hersheimmer.'

The words came out like the crack of a pistol, and Tommy looked up with a start. Julius was nervous and excited. The hand with which he raised his glass to his lips shook slightly, but his eyes held Sir James's defiantly. For a moment the hostility between the two seemed likely to burst into flame, but in the end Julius lowered his eyes, defeated.

'For the moment, I reckon you're the boss.'

'Thank you,' said the other. 'We will say ten o'clock then?'

With consummate ease of manner he turned to Tommy. 'I must confess, Mr Beresford, that it was something of a surprise to me to see you here this evening. The last I heard of you was that your friends were in grave anxiety on your behalf. Nothing had been heard of you for some days, and Miss Tuppence was inclined to think you had got into difficulties.'

'I had, sir!' Tommy grinned reminiscently. 'I was never in a tighter place in my life.'

Helped out by questions from Sir James, he gave an abbreviated account of his adventures. The lawyer looked at him with renewed interest as he brought the tale to a close.

'You got yourself out of a tight place very well,' he said gravely. 'I congratulate you. You displayed a great deal of ingenuity and carried your part through well.'

Tommy blushed, his face assuming a prawn-like hue at the praise.

'I couldn't have got away but for the girl, sir.'

'No.' Sir James smiled a little. 'It was lucky for you she happened to – er – take a fancy to you.' Tommy appeared about to protest, but Sir James went on. 'There's no doubt about her being one of the gang, I suppose?'

'I'm afraid not, sir. I thought perhaps they were keeping her there by force, but the way she acted didn't fit in with that. You see, she went back to them when she could have got away.'

Sir James nodded thoughtfully.

'What did she say? Something about wanting to be taken to Marguerite?'

'Yes, sir. I suppose she meant Mrs Vandemeyer.'

'She always signed herself Rita Vandemeyer. All her friends spoke of her as Rita. Still, I suppose the girl must have been in the habit of calling her by her full name. And, at the moment she was crying out to her, Mrs Vandemeyer was either dead or dying! Curious! There are one or two points that strike me as being obscure – their sudden change of attitude towards yourself, for instance. By the way, the house was raided, of course?'

'Yes, sir, but they'd cleared out.'

'Naturally,' said Sir James dryly.

'And not a clue left behind.'

'I wonder –' The lawyer tapped the table thoughtfully.

Something in his voice made Tommy look up. Would this man's eyes have seen something where theirs had been blind? He spoke impulsively:

'I wish you'd been there, sir, to go over the house!'

'I wish I had,' said Sir James quietly. He sat for a moment in silence. Then he looked up. 'And since then? What have you been doing?'

For a moment, Tommy stared at him. Then it dawned on him that of course the lawyer did not know.

'I forgot that you didn't know about Tuppence,' he said slowly. The sickening anxiety, forgotten for a while in the excitement of knowing Jane Finn found at last, swept over him again.

The lawyer laid down his knife and fork sharply.

'Has anything happened to Miss Tuppence?' His voice was keen-edged.

'She's disappeared,' said Julius.

'When?'

'A week ago.'

'How?'

Sir James's questions fairly shot out. Between them Tommy and Julius gave the history of the last week and their futile search.

Sir James went at once to the root of the matter.

'A wire signed with your name? They knew enough of you both for that. They weren't sure of how much you had learnt in that house. Their kidnapping of Miss Tuppence is the counter-move to your escape. If necessary they could seal your lips with what might happen to her.'

Tommy nodded.

'That's just what I thought, sir.'

Sir James looked at him keenly. '*You* had worked that out, had you? Not bad – not at all bad. The curious thing is that they certainly did not know anything about you when they first held you prisoner. You are sure that you did not in any way disclose your identity?'

Tommy shook his head.

'That's so,' said Julius with a nod. 'Therefore I reckon someone put them wise – and not earlier than Sunday afternoon.'

'Yes, but who?'

'That almighty omniscient Mr Brown, of course!'

There was a faint note of derision in the American's voice which made Sir James look up sharply.

'You don't believe in Mr Brown, Mr Hersheimmer?'

'No, sir, I do not,' returned the young American with emphasis. 'Not as such, that is to say. I reckon it out that he's a figurehead – just a bogy name to frighten the children with. The real head of this business is that Russian chap Kramenin. I guess he's quite capable of running revolutions in three countries at once if he chose! The man Whittington is probably the head of the English branch.'

'I disagree with you,' said Sir James shortly. 'Mr Brown exists.' He turned to Tommy. 'Did you happen to notice where that wire was handed in?'

'No, sir, I'm afraid I didn't.'

'H'm. Got it with you?'

'It's upstairs, sir, in my kit.'

'I'd like to have a look at it sometime. No hurry. You've wasted a week,' – Tommy hung his head – 'a day or so more is immaterial. We'll deal with Miss Jane Finn first. Afterwards, we'll set to work to rescue Miss Tuppence from bondage. I don't think she's in any immediate danger. That is, so long as they don't know that we've got Jane Finn, and that her memory has returned. We must keep that dark at all costs. You understand?'

The other two assented, and, after making arrangements for meeting on the morrow, the great lawyer took his leave.

At ten o'clock, the two young men were at the appointed spot. Sir James had joined them on the doorstep. He alone appeared unexcited. He introduced them to the doctor.

'Mr Hersheimmer – Mr Beresford – Dr Roylance. How's the patient?'

'Going on well. Evidently no idea of the flight of time. Asked this morning how many had been saved from the *Lusitania*. Was it in the papers yet? That, of course, was only what was to be expected. She seems to have something on her mind, though.'

'I think we can relieve her anxiety. May we go up?'

'Certainly.'

Tommy's heart beat sensibly faster as they followed the doctor upstairs. Jane Finn at last! The long-sought, the mysterious, the elusive Jane Finn! How wildly improbable success had seemed! And here in this house, her memory almost miraculously restored, lay the girl who held the future of England in her hands. A half groan broke from Tommy's lips. If only Tuppence could have been at his side to share in the triumphant conclusion of their joint venture! Then he put the thought of Tuppence resolutely aside. His confidence in Sir James was growing. There was a man who would unerringly ferret out Tuppence's whereabouts. In the meantime, Jane Finn! And suddenly a dread clutched at his heart. It seemed too easy . . . Suppose they should find her dead . . . stricken down by the hand of Mr Brown?

In another minute he was laughing at these melodramatic fancies. The doctor held open the door of a room and they passed in. On the white bed, bandages round her head, lay the girl. Somehow the whole scene seemed unreal. It was so exactly what one expected that it gave the effect of being beautifully staged.

The girl looked from one to the other of them with large wondering eyes. Sir James spoke first.

'Miss Finn,' he said, 'this is your cousin, Mr Julius P. Hersheimmer.'

A faint flush flitted over the girl's face, as Julius stepped forward and took her hand.

'How do, Cousin Jane?' he said lightly.

But Tommy caught the tremor in his voice.

'Are you really Uncle Hiram's son?' she asked wonderingly.

Her voice, with the slight warmth of the Western accent, had an almost thrilling quality. It seemed vaguely familiar to Tommy, but he thrust the impression aside as impossible.

'Sure thing.'

'We used to read about Uncle Hiram in the newspapers,' continued the girl, in her soft tones. 'But I never thought I'd meet you one day. Mother figured it out that Uncle Hiram would never get over being mad with her.'

'The old man was like that,' admitted Julius. 'But I guess the new generation's sort of different. Got no use for the family feud business. First thing I thought about, soon as the war was over, was to come along and hunt you up.'

A shadow passed over the girl's face.

'They've been telling me things – dreadful things – that my memory went, and that there are years I shall never know about – years lost out of my life.'

'You didn't realize that yourself?'

The girl's eyes opened wide.

'Why, no. It seems to me as though it were no time since we were being hustled into those boats. I can see it all now!' She closed her eyes with a shudder.

Julius looked across at Sir James, who nodded.

'Don't worry any. It isn't worth it. Now, see here, Jane, there's something we want to know about. There was a man aboard that boat with some mighty important papers on him, and the big guns in this country have got a notion that he passed on the goods to you. Is that so?'

The girl hesitated, her glance shifting to the other two. Julius understood.

'Mr Beresford is commissioned by the British Government to get those papers back. Sir James Peel Edgerton is an English Member of Parliament, and might be a big gun in the Cabinet if he liked. It's owing to him that we've ferreted you out at last. So you can go right ahead and tell us the whole story. Did Danvers give you the papers?'

'Yes. He said they'd have a better chance with me, because they would have the women and children first.'

'Just as we thought,' said Sir James.

'He said they were very important – that they might make all the difference to the Allies. But, if it's all so long ago, and the war's over, what does it matter now?'

'I guess history repeats itself, Jane. First there was a great hue and cry over those papers, then it all died down, and now the whole caboodle's started all over again – for rather different reasons. Then you can hand them over to us right away?'

'But I can't.'

'What?'

'I haven't got them.'

'You – haven't – got them?' Julius punctuated the words with little pauses.

'No – I hid them.'

'You *hid* them?'

'Yes. I got uneasy. People seemed to be watching me. It scared me – badly.' She put her hand to her head. 'It's almost the last thing I remember before waking up in the hospital . . .'

'Go on,' said Sir James, in his quiet penetrating tones. 'What do you remember?'

She turned to him obediently.

'It was at Holyhead. I came that way – I don't remember why . . .'

'That doesn't matter. Go on.'

'In the confusion on the quay I slipped away. Nobody saw me. I took a car. Told the man to drive me out of the town. I watched when we got on the open road. No other car was following us. I saw a path at the side of the road. I told the man to wait.'

She paused, then went on. 'The path led to the cliff, and down to the sea between big yellow gorse bushes – they were like golden flames. I looked round. There wasn't a soul in sight. But just level with my head there was a hole in the rock. It was quite small – I could only just get my hand in, but it went a long way back. I took the oilskin packet from round my neck and shoved it right in as far as I could. Then I tore off a bit of gorse – My! but it did prick – and plugged the hole with it so that you'd never guess there was a crevice of any kind there. Then I marked the place carefully in my own mind, so that I'd find it again. There was a queer boulder in the path just there – for all the world like a dog sitting up begging. Then I went back to the road. The car was waiting, and I drove back. I just caught the train. I was a bit ashamed of myself for fancying things maybe, but, by and by, I saw the man opposite me wink at a woman who was sitting next to me, and I felt scared again, and was glad the papers were safe. I went out in the corridor to get a little air. I thought I'd slip into another carriage. But the woman called me back, said I'd dropped something, and when I stooped to look, something seemed to hit me – here.' She placed her hand to the back of her head. 'I don't remember anything more until I woke up in the hospital.'

There was a pause.

'Thank you, Miss Finn.' It was Sir James who spoke. 'I hope we have not tired you?'

'Oh, that's all right. My head aches a little, but otherwise I feel fine.'

Julius stepped forward and took her hand again.

'So long, Cousin Jane. I'm going to get busy after those papers, but I'll be back in two shakes of a dog's tail, and I'll tote you up to London and give you the time of your young life before we go back to the States! I mean it – so hurry up and get well.'

CHAPTER XX

Too Late

In the street they held an informal council of war. Sir James had drawn a watch from his pocket.

'The boat train to Holyhead stops at Chester at 12.14. If you start at once I think you can catch the connection.'

Tommy looked up, puzzled.

'Is there any need to hurry, sir? Today is only the 24th.'

'I guess it's always well to get up early in the morning,' said Julius, before the lawyer had time to reply. 'We'll make tracks for the depot right away.'

A little frown had settled on Sir James's brow.

'I wish I could come with you. I am due to speak at a meeting at two o'clock. It is unfortunate.'

The reluctance in his tone was very evident. It was clear, on the other hand, that Julius was easily disposed to put up with the loss of the other's company.

'I guess there's nothing complicated about this deal,' he remarked. 'Just a game of hide-and-seek, that's all.'

'I hope so,' said Sir James.

'Sure thing. What else could it be?'

'You are still young, Mr Hersheimmer. At my age you will probably have learnt one lesson: "Never underestimate your adversary."'

The gravity of his tone impressed Tommy, but had little effect upon Julius.

'You think Mr Brown might come along and take a hand! If he does, I'm ready for him.' He slapped his pocket. 'I carry a gun. Little Willie here travels round with me everywhere.' He produced a murderous-looking automatic, and tapped it affectionately before returning it to its home. 'But he won't be needed on this trip. There's nobody to put Mr Brown wise.'

The lawyer shrugged his shoulders.

'There was nobody to put Mr Brown wise to the fact that Mrs Vandemeyer meant to betray him. Nevertheless, *Mrs Vandemeyer died without speaking.*'

Julius was silenced for once, and Sir James added on a lighter note:

'I only want to put you on your guard. Goodbye, and good luck. Take no unnecessary risks once the papers are in your hands. If there is any reason to believe that you have been shadowed, destroy them at once. Good luck to you. The game is in your hands now.' He shook hands with them both.

Ten minutes later the two men were seated in a first-class carriage *en route* for Chester.

For a long time neither of them spoke. When at length Julius broke the silence, it was with a totally unexpected remark.

'Say,' he observed thoughtfully, 'did you ever make a darn fool of yourself over a girl's face?'

Tommy, after a moment's astonishment, searched his mind.

'Can't say I have,' he replied at last. 'Not that I can recollect, anyhow. Why?'

'Because for the last two months I've been making a sentimental idiot of myself over Jane! First moment I clapped eyes on her photograph my heart did all the usual stunts you read about in novels. I guess I'm ashamed to admit it, but I came over here determined to find her and fix it all up, and take her back as Mrs Julius P. Hersheimmer!'

'Oh!' said Tommy, amazed.

Julius uncrossed his legs brusquely and continued:

'Just shows what an almighty fool a man can make of himself! One look at the girl in the flesh, and I was cured!'

Feeling more tongue-tied than ever, Tommy ejaculated 'Oh!' again.

'No disparagement to Jane, mind you,' continued the other. 'She's a real nice girl, and some fellow will fall in love with her right away.'

'I thought her a very good-looking girl,' said Tommy, finding his tongue.

'Sure she is. But she's not like her photo one bit. At least I suppose she is in a way – must be – because I recognized her right off. If I'd seen her in a crowd I'd have said "There's a girl whose face I know" right away without hesitation. But there was something about that photo' – Julius shook his head, and heaved a sigh – 'I guess romance is a mighty queer thing!'

'It must be,' said Tommy coldly, 'if you can come over here in love with one girl, and propose to another within a fortnight.'

Julius had the grace to look discomposed.

'Well, you see, I'd got sort of tired feeling that I'd never find Jane – and that it was all plumb foolishness anyway. And then – oh well, the French, for instance, are much more sensible in the way they look at things. They keep romance and marriage apart –'

Tommy flushed.

'Well, I'm damned! If that's –'

Julius hastened to interrupt.

'Say now, don't be hasty. I don't mean what you mean. I take it Americans have a higher opinion of morality than you have even. What I meant was that the French set about marriage in a business-like way – find two people who are suited to one another, look after the money affairs, and see the whole thing practically, and in a business-like spirit.'

'If you ask me,' said Tommy, 'we're all too damned business-like nowadays. We're always saying, "Will it pay?" The men are bad enough, and the girls are worse!'

'Cool down, son. Don't get so heated.'

'I feel heated,' said Tommy.

Julius looked at him and judged it wise to say no more.

However, Tommy had plenty of time to cool down before they reached Holyhead, and the cheerful grin had returned to his countenance as they alighted at their destination.

After consultation and with the aid of a road map, they were fairly well agreed as to direction, so were able to hire a taxi without more ado and drive out on the road leading to Treaddur Bay. They instructed the man to go slowly, and watched narrowly so as not to miss the path. They came to it not long after leaving the town, and Tommy stopped the car promptly, asked in a casual tone whether the path led down to the sea, and hearing it did paid off the man in handsome style.

A moment later the taxi was slowly chugging back to Holyhead. Tommy and Julius watched it out of sight, and then turned to the narrow path.

'It's the right one, I suppose?' asked Tommy doubtfully. 'There must be simply heaps along here.'

'Sure it is. Look at the gorse. Remember what Jane said?'

Tommy looked at the swelling hedges of golden blossom which bordered the path on either side, and was convinced.

They went down in single file, Julius leading. Twice Tommy turned his head uneasily. Julius looked back.

'What is it?'

'I don't know. I've got the wind up somehow. Keep fancying there's someone following us.'

'Can't be,' said Julius positively. 'We'd see him.'

Tommy had to admit that this was true. Nevertheless, his sense of uneasiness deepened. In spite of himself he believed in the omniscience of the enemy.

'I rather wish that fellow would come along,' said Julius. He patted his pocket. 'Little William here is just aching for exercise!'

'Do you always carry it – him – with you?' inquired Tommy with burning curiosity.

'Most always. I guess you never know what might turn up.'

Tommy kept a respectful silence. He was impressed by Little William. It seemed to remove the menace of Mr Brown farther away.

The path was now running along the side of the cliff, parallel to the sea. Suddenly Julius came to such an abrupt halt that Tommy cannoned into him.

'What's up?' he inquired.

'Look there. If that doesn't beat the band!'

Tommy looked. Standing out and half obstructing the path was a huge boulder which certainly bore a fanciful resemblance to a 'begging' terrier.

'Well,' said Tommy, refusing to share Julius's emotion, 'it's what we expected to see, isn't it?'

Julius looked at him sadly and shook his head.

'British phlegm! Sure we expected it – but it kind of rattles me, all the same, to see it sitting there just where we expected to find it!'

Tommy, whose calm was, perhaps, more assumed than natural, moved his feet impatiently.

'Push on. What about the hole?'

They scanned the cliff-side narrowly. Tommy heard himself saying idiotically:

'The gorse won't be there after all these years.'

And Julius replied solemnly:

'I guess you're right.'

Tommy suddenly pointed with a shaking hand.

'What about that crevice there?'

Julius replied in an awestricken voice:

'That's it – for sure.'

They looked at each other.

'When I was in France,' said Tommy reminiscently, 'whenever my batman failed to call me, he always said that he had come over queer. I never believed it. But whether he felt it or not, there *is* such a sensation. I've got it now! Badly!'

He looked at the rock with a kind of agonized passion.

'Damn it!' he cried. 'It's impossible! Five years! Think of it! Birds'-nesting boys, picnic parties, thousands of people passing! It can't be there! It's a hundred to one against its being there! It's against all reason!'

Indeed, he felt it to be impossible – more, perhaps, because he could not believe in his own success where so many others had failed. The thing was too easy, therefore it could not be. The hole would be empty.

Julius looked at him with a widening smile.

'I guess you're rattled now all right,' he drawled with some enjoyment. 'Well, here goes!' He thrust his hand into the crevice, and made a slight grimace. 'It's a tight fit. Jane's hand must be a few sizes smaller than mine. I don't feel anything – no – say, what's this? Gee whiz!' And with a flourish he waved aloft a small discoloured packet. 'It's the goods all right. Sewn up in oilskin. Hold it while I get my penknife.'

The unbelievable had happened. Tommy held the precious packet tenderly between his hands. They had succeeded!

'It's queer,' he murmured idly, 'you'd think the stitches would have rotted. They look just as good as new.'

They cut them carefully and ripped away the oilskin. Inside was a small folded sheet of paper. With trembling fingers they unfolded it. The sheet was blank! They stared at each other, puzzled.

'A dummy!' hazarded Julius. 'Was Danvers just a decoy?'

Tommy shook his head. That solution did not satisfy him. Suddenly his face cleared.

'I've got it! *Sympathetic ink!*'

'You think so?'

'Worth trying anyhow. Heat usually does the trick. Get some sticks. We'll make a fire.'

In a few minutes the little fire of twigs and leaves was blazing merrily. Tommy held the sheet of paper near the glow. The paper curled a little with the heat. Nothing more.

Suddenly Julius grasped his arm, and pointed to where characters were appearing in a faint brown colour.

'Gee whiz! You've got it! Say, that idea of yours was great. It never occurred to me.'

Tommy held the paper in position some minutes longer until he judged the heat had done its work. Then he withdrew it. A moment later he uttered a cry.

Across the sheet in neat brown printing ran the words:

WITH THE COMPLIMENTS OF MR BROWN.

CHAPTER XXI

Tommy Makes a Discovery

For a moment or two they stood staring at each other stupidly, dazed with the shock. Somehow, inexplicably, Mr Brown had forestalled them. Tommy accepted defeat quietly. Not so Julius.

'How in tarnation did he get ahead of us? That's what beats me!' he ended up.

Tommy shook his head, and said dully:

'It accounts for the stitches being new. We might have guessed . . .'

'Never mind the darned stitches. How did he get ahead of us? We hustled all we knew. It's downright impossible for anyone to get here quicker than we did. And, anyway, how did he know? Do you reckon there was a dictaphone in Jane's room? I guess there must have been.'

But Tommy's common sense pointed out objections.

'No one could have known beforehand that she was going to be in that house – much less that particular room.'

'That's so,' admitted Julius. 'Then one of the nurses was a crook and listened at the door. How's that?'

'I don't see that it matters anyway,' said Tommy wearily. 'He may have found out some months ago, and removed the papers, then – No, by Jove, that won't wash! They'd have been published at once.'

'Sure thing they would! No, someone's got ahead of us today by an hour or so. But how they did it gets my goat.'

'I wish that chap Peel Edgerton had been with us,' said Tommy thoughtfully.

'Why?' Julius stared. 'The mischief was done when we came.'

'Yes –' Tommy hesitated. He could not explain his own feeling – the illogical idea that the K C's presence would somehow have averted the catastrophe. He reverted to his former point of view. 'It's no good arguing about how it was done. The game's up. We've failed. There's only one thing for me to do.'

'What's that?'

'Get back to London as soon as possible. Mr Carter must be warned. It's only a matter of hours now before the blow falls. But, at any rate, he ought to know the worst.'

The duty was an unpleasant one, but Tommy had no intention of shirking it. He must report his failure to Mr Carter. After that his work was done. He took the midnight mail to London. Julius elected to stay the night at Holyhead.

Half an hour after arrival, haggard and pale, Tommy stood before his chief.

'I've come to report, sir. I've failed – failed badly.'

Mr Carter eyed him sharply.

'You mean that the treaty –'

'Is in the hands of Mr Brown, sir.'

'Ah!' said Mr Carter quietly. The expression on his face did not change, but Tommy caught the flicker of despair in his eyes. It convinced him as nothing else had done that the outlook was hopeless.

'Well,' said Mr Carter after a minute or two, 'we mustn't sag at the knees, I suppose. I'm glad to know definitely. We must do what we can.'

Through Tommy's mind flashed the assurance: 'It's hopeless, and he knows it's hopeless!'

The other looked up at him.

'Don't take it to heart, lad,' he said kindly. 'You did your best. You were up against one of the biggest brains of the century. And you came very near success. Remember that.'

'Thank you, sir. It's awfully decent of you.'

'I blame myself. I have been blaming myself ever since I heard this other news.'

Something in his tone attracted Tommy's attention. A new fear gripped at his heart.

'Is there – something more, sir?'

'I'm afraid so,' said Mr Carter gravely. He stretched out his hand to a sheet on the table.

'Tuppence –?' faltered Tommy.

'Read for yourself.'

The typewritten words danced before his eyes. The description of a green toque, a coat with a handkerchief in the pocket marked PLC. He looked an agonized question at Mr Carter. The latter replied to it:

'Washed up on the Yorkshire coast – near Ebury. I'm afraid – it looks very much like foul play.'

'My God!' gasped Tommy. '*Tuppence!* Those devils – I'll never rest till I've got even with them! I'll hunt them down! I'll –'

The pity on Mr Carter's face stopped him.

'I know what you feel like, my poor boy. But it's no good. You'll waste your strength uselessly. It may sound harsh, but my advice to you is: Cut your losses. Time's merciful. You'll forget.'

'Forget Tuppence? Never!'

Mr Carter shook his head.

'So you think now. Well, it won't bear thinking of – that brave little girl! I'm sorry about the whole business – confoundedly sorry.'

Tommy came to himself with a start.

'I'm taking up your time, sir,' he said with an effort. 'There's no need for you to blame yourself. I dare say we were a couple of young fools to take on such a job. You warned us all right. But I wish to God *I*'d been the one to get it in the neck. Goodbye, sir.'

Back at the Ritz, Tommy packed up his few belongings mechanically, his thoughts far away. He was still bewildered by the introduction of tragedy into his cheerful commonplace existence. What fun they had had together, he and Tuppence! And now – oh, he couldn't believe it – it couldn't be true!

Tuppence – dead! Little Tuppence, brimming over with life! It was a dream, a horrible dream. Nothing more.

They brought him a note, a few kind words of sympathy from Peel Edgerton, who had read the news in the paper. (There had been a large headline: EX-VAD FEARED DROWNED.) The letter ended with the offer of a post on a ranch in Argentine, where Sir James had considerable interests.

'Kind old beggar,' muttered Tommy, as he flung it aside.

The door opened, and Julius burst in with his usual violence. He held an open newspaper in his hand.

'Say, what's all this? They seem to have got some fool idea about Tuppence.'

'It's true,' said Tommy quietly.

'You mean they've done her in?'

Tommy nodded.

'I suppose when they got the treaty she – wasn't any good to them any longer, and they were afraid to let her go.'

'Well, I'm darned!' said Julius. 'Little Tuppence. She sure was the pluckiest little girl –'

But suddenly something seemed to crack in Tommy's brain. He rose to his feet.

'Oh, get out! You don't really care, damn you! You asked her to marry you in your rotten cold-blooded way, but I *loved* her. I'd have given the soul out of my body to save her from harm. I'd have stood by without a word and let her marry you, because you could have given her the sort of time she ought to have had, and I was only a poor devil without a penny to bless himself with. But it wouldn't have been because I didn't care!'

'See here,' began Julius temperately.

'Oh, go to the devil! I can't stand your coming here and talking about "little Tuppence". Go and look after your cousin. Tuppence is my girl! I've always loved her, from the time we played together as kids. We grew up and it was just the same. I shall never forget when I was in hospital, and she came in in that ridiculous cap and apron! It was like a miracle to see the girl I loved turn up in a nurse's kit –'

But Julius interrupted him.

'A nurse's kit! Gee whiz! I must be going to Coney Hatch! I could swear I've seen Jane in a nurse's cap too. And that's plumb impossible! No, by gum, I've got it! It was her I saw talking to Whittington at that nursing home in Bournemouth. She wasn't a patient there! She was a nurse!'

'I dare say,' said Tommy angrily, 'she's probably been in with them from the start. I shouldn't wonder if she stole those papers from Danvers to begin with.'

'I'm darned if she did!' shouted Julius. 'She's my cousin, and as patriotic a girl as ever stepped.'

'I don't care a damn who she is, but get out of here!' retorted Tommy also at the top of his voice.

The young men were on the point of coming to blows. But suddenly, with an almost magical abruptness, Julius's anger abated.

'All right, son,' he said quietly, 'I'm going. I don't blame you any for what you've been saying. It's mighty lucky you did say it. I've been the most almighty blithering darned idiot that it's possible to imagine. Calm down,' – Tommy had made an impatient gesture – 'I'm going right away now – going to the London and North Western Railway depot, if you want to know.'

'I don't care a damn where you're going,' growled Tommy.

As the door closed behind Julius, he returned to his suitcase.

'That's the lot,' he murmured, and rang the bell.

'Take my luggage down.'

'Yes, sir. Going away, sir?'

'I'm going to the devil,' said Tommy, regardless of the menial's feelings.

That functionary, however, merely replied respectfully:

'Yes, sir. Shall I call a taxi?'

Tommy nodded.

Where was he going? He hadn't the faintest idea. Beyond a fixed determination to get even with Mr Brown he had no plans. He had re-read Sir James's letter, and shook his head. Tuppence must be avenged. Still, it was kind of the old fellow.

'Better answer it, I suppose.' He went across to the writing-table. With the usual perversity of bedroom stationery, there were innumerable envelopes and no paper. He rang. No one came. Tommy fumed at the delay. Then he remembered that there was a good supply in Julius's sitting-room. The American had announced his immediate departure. There would be no fear of running up against him. Besides, he wouldn't mind if he did. He was beginning to be rather ashamed of the things he had said. Old Julius had taken them jolly well. He'd apologize if he found him there.

But the room was deserted. Tommy walked across to the writing-table, and opened the middle drawer. A photograph, carelessly thrust in face upwards, caught his eye. For a moment he stood rooted to the ground. Then he took it out, shut the drawer, walked slowly over to an arm-chair, and sat down still staring at the photograph in his hand.

What on earth was a photograph of the French girl Annette doing in Julius Hersheimmer's writing-table?

CHAPTER XXII

In Downing Street

The Prime Minister tapped the desk in front of him with nervous fingers. His face was worn and harassed. He took up his conversation with Mr Carter at the point it had broken off.

'I don't understand,' he said. 'Do you really mean that things are not so desperate after all?'

'So this lad seems to think.'

'Let's have a look at his letter again.'

Mr Carter handed it over. It was written in a sprawling boyish hand.

Dear Mr Carter,

Something's turned up that has given me a jar. Of course I may be simply making an awful ass of myself, but I don't think so. If my conclusions are right, that girl at Manchester was just a plant. The whole thing was prearranged, sham packet and all, with the object of making us think the game was up – therefore I fancy that we must have been pretty hot on the scent.

I think I know who the real Jane Finn is, and I've even got an idea where the papers are. That last's only a guess, of course, but I've a sort of feeling it'll turn out right. Anyhow, I enclose it in a sealed envelope for what it's worth. I'm going to ask you not to open it until the very last moment, midnight on the 28th, in fact. You'll understand why in a minute. You see, I've figured it out that those things of Tuppence's are a plant too, and she's no more drowned than I am. The way I reason is this: as a last chance they'll let Jane Finn escape in the hope that she's been shamming this memory stunt, and that once she thinks she's free she'll go right away to the cache. Of course it's an awful risk for them to take, because she knows all about them – but they're pretty desperate to get hold of that treaty. *But if they know that the papers have been recovered by us*, neither of those two girls' lives will be worth an hour's purchase. I must try and get hold of Tuppence before Jane escapes.

I want a repeat of that telegram that was sent to Tuppence at the Ritz. Sir James Peel Edgerton said you would be able to manage that for me. He's frightfully clever.

One last thing – please have that house in Soho watched day and night.

> Yours, etc.,
> Thomas Beresford

The Prime Minister looked up.

'The enclosure?'

Mr Carter smiled dryly.

'In the vaults of the Bank. I am taking no chances.'

'You don't think' – the Prime Minister hesitated a minute – 'that it would be better to open it now? Surely we ought to secure the document, that is, provided the young man's guess turns out to be correct, at once. We can keep the fact of having done so quite secret.'

'Can we? I'm not so sure. There are spies all round us. Once it's known I wouldn't give that' – he snapped his fingers – 'for the life of those two girls. No, the boy trusted me, and I shan't let him down.'

'Well, well, we must leave it at that, then. What's he like, this lad?'

'Outwardly, he's an ordinary clean-limbed, rather block-headed young Englishman. Slow in his mental processes. On the other hand, it's quite impossible to lead him astray through his imagination. He hasn't got any – so he's difficult to deceive. He worries things out slowly, and once he's got hold of anything he doesn't let go. The little lady's quite different. More intuition and less common sense. They make a pretty pair working together. Pace and stamina.'

'He seems confident,' mused the Prime Minister.

'Yes, and that's what gives me hope. He's the kind of diffident youth who would have to be *very* sure before he ventured an opinion at all.'

A half smile came to the other's lips.

'And it is this – boy who will defeat the master criminal of our time?'

'This – boy, as you say! But I sometimes fancy I see a shadow behind.'

'You mean?'

'Peel Edgerton.'

'Peel Edgerton?' said the Prime Minister in astonishment.

'Yes. I see his hand in *this*.' He struck the open letter. 'He's there – working in the dark, silently, unobtrusively. I've always felt that if anyone was to run Mr Brown to earth, Peel Edgerton would be the man. I tell you he's on the case now, but doesn't want it known. By the way, I got rather an odd request from him the other day.'

'Yes?'

'He sent me a cutting from some American paper. It referred to a man's body found near the docks in New York about three weeks ago. He asked me to collect any information on the subject I could.'

'Well?'

Carter shrugged his shoulders.

'I couldn't get much. Young fellow about thirty-five – poorly dressed – face very badly disfigured. He was never identified.'

'And you fancy that the two matters are connected in some way?'

'Somehow I do. I may be wrong, of course.'

There was a pause, then Mr Carter continued:

'I asked him to come round here. Not that we'll get anything out of him he doesn't want to tell. His legal instincts are too strong. But there's no doubt he can throw light on one or two obscure points in young Beresford's letter. Ah, here he is!'

The two men rose to greet the newcomer. A half whimsical thought flashed across the Premier's mind. 'My successor, perhaps!'

'We've had a letter from young Beresford,' said Mr Carter, coming to the point at once. 'You've seen him, I suppose?'

'You suppose wrong,' said the lawyer.

'Oh!' Mr Carter was a little nonplussed.

Sir James smiled, and stroked his chin.

'He rang me up,' he volunteered.

'Would you have any objection to telling us exactly what passed between you?'

'Not at all. He thanked me for a certain letter which I had written to him – as a matter of fact, I had offered him a job. Then he reminded me of something I had said to him at Manchester respecting that bogus telegram which lured Miss Cowley away. I asked him if anything untoward had occurred. He said it had – that in a drawer in Mr Hersheimmer's room he had discovered a photograph.' The lawyer paused, then continued: 'I asked him if the photograph bore the name and address of a Californian photographer. He replied: "You're on to it, sir. It had." Then he went on to tell me something I *didn't* know. The original of that photograph was the French girl, Annette, who saved his life.'

'What?'

'Exactly. I asked the young man with some curiosity what he had done with the photograph. He replied that he had put it back where he found it.' The lawyer paused again. 'That was good, you know – distinctly good. He can use his brains, that young fellow. I congratulated him. The discovery was a providential one. Of course, from the moment that the girl in Manchester was proved to be a plant everything was altered. Young Beresford saw that for himself without my having to tell it him. But he felt he couldn't trust his judgement on the subject of Miss Cowley. Did I think she was alive? I told him, duly weighing the evidence, that there was a very decided chance in favour of it. That brought us back to the telegram.'

'Yes?'

'I advised him to apply to you for a copy of the original wire. It had occurred to me as probable that, after Miss Cowley flung it on the floor, certain words might have been erased and altered with the express intention of setting searchers on a false trail.'

Carter nodded. He took a sheet from his pocket, and read aloud:

'Come at once, Astley Priors, Gatehouse, Kent. Great developments – Tommy.'

'Very simple,' said Sir James, 'and very ingenious. Just a few words to alter, and the thing was done. And the one important clue they overlooked.'

'What was that?'

'The page-boy's statement that Miss Cowley drove to Charing Cross. They were so sure of themselves that they took it for granted he had made a mistake.'

'Then young Beresford is now?'

'At Gatehouse, Kent, unless I am much mistaken.'

Mr Carter looked at him curiously.

'I rather wonder you're not there too, Peel Edgerton?'

'Ah, I'm busy on a case.'

'I thought you were on your holiday?'

'Oh, I've not been briefed. Perhaps it would be more correct to say I'm preparing a case. Any more facts about that American chap for me?'

'I'm afraid not. Is it important to find out who he was?'

'Oh, I know who he was,' said Sir James easily. 'I can't prove it yet – but I know.'

The other two asked no questions. They had an instinct that it would be mere waste of breath.

'But what I don't understand,' said the Prime Minister suddenly, 'is how that photograph came to be in Mr Hersheimmer's drawer?'

'Perhaps it never left it,' suggested the lawyer gently.

'But the bogus inspector? Inspector Brown?'

'Ah!' said Sir James thoughtfully. He rose to his feet. 'I mustn't keep you. Go on with the affairs of the nation. I must get back to – my case.'

Two days later Julius Hersheimmer returned from Manchester. A note from Tommy lay on his table:

Dear Hersheimmer,

Sorry I lost my temper. In case I don't see you again, goodbye. I've been offered a job in the Argentine, and might as well take it.

Yours,
Tommy Beresford

A peculiar smile lingered for a moment on Julius's face. He threw the letter into the waste-paper basket.

'The darned fool!' he murmured.

CHAPTER XXIII

A Race Against Time

After ringing up Sir James, Tommy's next procedure was to make a call at South Audley Mansions. He found Albert discharging his professional duties, and introduced himself without more ado as a friend of Tuppence's. Albert unbent immediately.

'Things has been very quiet here lately,' he said wistfully. 'Hope the young lady's keeping well, sir?'

'That's just the point, Albert. She's disappeared.'

'You don't mean as the crooks have got her?'

'They have.'

'In the Underworld?'

'No, dash it all, in this world!'

'It's a h'expression, sir,' explained Albert. 'At the pictures the crooks always have a restoorant in the Underworld. But do you think as they've done her in, sir?'

'I hope not. By the way, have you by any chance an aunt, a cousin, grandmother, or any other suitable female relation who might be represented as being likely to kick the bucket?'

A delighted grin spread slowly over Albert's countenance.

'I'm on, sir. My poor aunt what lives in the country has been mortal bad for a long time, and she's asking for me with her dying breath.'

Tommy nodded approval.

'Can you report this in the proper quarter and meet me at Charing Cross in an hour's time?'

'I'll be there, sir. You can count on me.'

As Tommy had judged, the faithful Albert proved an invaluable ally. The two took up their quarters at the inn in

Gatehouse. To Albert fell the task of collecting information. There was no difficulty about it.

Astley Priors was the property of a Dr Adams. The doctor no longer practised, had retired, the landlord believed, but he took a few private patients – here the good fellow tapped his forehead knowingly – 'Balmy ones! You understand!' The doctor was a popular figure in the village, subscribed freely to all the local sports – 'a very pleasant affable gentleman'. Been there long? Oh, a matter of ten years or so – might be longer. Scientific gentleman, he was. Professors and people often came down from town to see him. Anyway, it was a gay house, always visitors.

In the face of all this volubility, Tommy felt doubts. Was it possible that this genial, well-known figure could be in reality a dangerous criminal? His life seemed so open and above-board. No hint of sinister doings. Suppose it was all a gigantic mistake? Tommy felt a cold chill at the thought.

Then he remembered the private patients – 'balmy ones'. He inquired carefully if there was a young lady amongst them, describing Tuppence. But nothing much seemed to be known about the patients – they were seldom seen outside the grounds. A guarded description of Annette also failed to provoke recognition.

Astley Priors was a pleasant red-brick edifice, surrounded by well-wooded grounds which effectually shielded the house from observation from the road.

On the first evening Tommy, accompanied by Albert, explored the grounds. Owing to Albert's insistence they dragged themselves along painfully on their stomachs, thereby producing a great deal more noise than if they had stood upright. In any case, these precautions were totally unnecessary. The grounds, like those of any other private house after nightfall, seemed untenanted. Tommy had imagined a possible fierce watchdog. Albert's fancy ran to a puma, or a tame cobra. But they reached a shrubbery near the house quite unmolested.

The blinds of the dining-room window were up. There was a large company assembled round the table. The port was passing from hand to hand. It seemed a normal, pleasant company. Through the open window scraps of conversation floated out disjointedly on the night air. It was a heated discussion on county cricket!

Again Tommy felt that cold chill of uncertainty. It seemed impossible to believe that these people were other than they seemed. Had he been fooled once more? The fair-bearded, spectacled gentleman who sat at the head of the table looked singularly honest and normal.

Tommy slept badly that night. The following morning the indefatigable Albert, having cemented an alliance with the greengrocer's boy, took the latter's place and ingratiated himself with the cook at Malthouse. He returned with the information that she was undoubtedly 'one of the crooks', but Tommy mistrusted the vividness of his imagination. Questioned, he could adduce nothing in support of his statement except his own opinion that she wasn't the usual kind. You could see that at a glance.

The substitution being repeated (much to the pecuniary advantage of the real greengrocer's boy) on the following day, Albert brought back the first piece of hopeful news. There *was* a French young lady staying in the house. Tommy put his doubts aside. Here was confirmation of his theory. But time pressed. Today was the 27th. The 29th was the much-talked-of 'Labour Day', about which all sorts of rumours were running riot. Newspapers were getting agitated. Sensational hints of a Labour *coup d'état* were freely reported. The Government said nothing. It knew and was prepared. There were rumours of dissension among the Labour leaders. They were not of one mind. The more far-seeing among them realized that what they proposed might well be a death-blow to the England that at heart they loved. They shrank from the starvation and misery a general strike would entail, and were willing to meet the Government half-way. But behind them were subtle, insistent forces at work, urging the memories of old wrongs, deprecating the weakness of half-and-half measures, fomenting misunderstandings.

Tommy felt that, thanks to Mr Carter, he understood the

position fairly accurately. With the fatal document in the hands of Mr Brown, public opinion would swing to the side of the Labour extremists and revolutionists. Failing that, the battle was an even chance. The Government with a loyal army and police force behind them might win – but at a cost of great suffering. But Tommy nourished another and a preposterous dream. With Mr Brown unmasked and captured he believed, rightly or wrongly, that the whole organization would crumble ignominiously and instantaneously. The strange permeating influence of the unseen chief held it together. Without him, Tommy believed an instant panic would set in; and, the honest men left to themselves, an eleventh-hour reconciliation would be possible.

'This is a one-man show,' said Tommy to himself. 'The thing to do is to get hold of the man.'

It was partly in furtherance of this ambitious design that he had requested Mr Carter not to open the sealed envelope. The draft treaty was Tommy's bait. Every now and then he was aghast at his own presumption. How dared he think that he had discovered what so many wiser and cleverer men had overlooked? Nevertheless, he stuck tenaciously to his idea.

That evening he and Albert once more penetrated the grounds of Astley Priors. Tommy's ambition was somehow or other to gain admission to the house itself. As they approached cautiously, Tommy gave a sudden gasp.

On the second-floor window someone standing between the window and the light in the room threw a silhouette on the blind. It was one Tommy would have recognized anywhere! Tuppence was in that house!

He clutched Albert by the shoulder.

'Stay here! When I begin to sing, watch that window.'

He retreated hastily to a position on the main drive, and began in a deep roar, coupled with an unsteady gait, the following ditty:

> 'I am a soldier
> A jolly British soldier;
> You can see that I'm a soldier by my feet . . . ?'

It had been a favourite on the gramophone in Tuppence's hospital days. He did not doubt but that she would recognize it and draw her own conclusions. Tommy had not a note of music in his voice, but his lungs were excellent. The noise he produced was terrific.

Presently an unimpeachable butler, accompanied by an equally unimpeachable footman, issued from the front door. The butler remonstrated with him. Tommy continued to sing, addressing the butler affectionately as 'dear old whiskers'. The footman took him by one arm, the butler by the other. They ran him down the drive, and neatly out of the gate. The butler threatened him with the police if he intruded again. It was beautifully done – soberly and with perfect decorum. Anyone would have sworn that the butler was a real butler, the footman a real footman – only, as it happened, the butler was Whittington!

Tommy retired to the inn and waited for Albert's return. At last that worthy made his appearance.

'Well?' cried Tommy eagerly.

'It's all right. While they was a-running of you out the window opened, and something was chucked out.' He handed a scrap of paper to Tommy. 'It was wrapped round a letter-weight.'

On the paper were scrawled three words: 'Tomorrow – same time.'

'Good egg!' cried Tommy. 'We're getting going.'

'I wrote a message on a piece of paper, wrapped it round a stone, and chucked it through the window,' continued Albert breathlessly.

Tommy groaned.

'Your zeal will be the undoing of us, Albert. What did you say?'

'Said we was a-staying at the inn. If she could get away, to come there and croak like a frog.'

'She'll know that's you,' said Tommy with a sigh of relief. 'Your imagination runs away with you, you know, Albert.

Why, you wouldn't recognize a frog croaking if you heard it.'

Albert looked rather crestfallen.

'Cheer up,' said Tommy. 'No harm done. That butler's an old friend of mine – I bet he knew who I was, though he didn't let on. It's not their game to show suspicion. That's why we've found it fairly plain sailing. They don't want to discourage me altogether. On the other hand, they don't want to make it too easy. I'm a pawn in their game, Albert, that's what I am. You see, if the spider lets the fly walk out too easily, the fly might suspect it was a put-up job. Hence the usefulness of that promising youth, Mr T. Beresford, who's blundered in just at the right moment for them. But later, Mr T. Beresford had better look out!'

Tommy retired for the night in a state of some elation. He had elaborated a careful plan for the following evening. He felt sure that the inhabitants of Astley Priors would not interfere with him up to a certain point. It was after that that Tommy proposed to give them a surprise.

About twelve o'clock, however, his calm was rudely shaken. He was told that someone was demanding him in the bar. The applicant proved to be a rude-looking carter well coated with mud.

'Well, my good fellow, what is it?' asked Tommy.

'Might this be for you, sir?' The carter held out a very dirty folded note, on the outside of which was written: 'Take this to the gentleman at the inn near Astley Priors. He will give you ten shillings.'

The handwriting was Tuppence's. Tommy appreciated her quick-wittedness in realizing that he might be staying at the inn under an assumed name. He snatched at it.

'That's all right.'

The man withheld it.

'What about my ten shillings?'

Tommy hastily produced a ten-shilling note, and the man relinquished his find. Tommy unfastened it.

Dear Tommy,

I knew it was you last night. Don't go this evening. They'll be lying in wait for you. They're taking us away this morning. I heard something about Wales – Holyhead, I think. I'll drop this on the road if I get a chance. Annette told me how you'd escaped. Buck up.

> Yours,
> Twopence

Tommy raised a shout for Albert before he had even finished perusing this characteristic epistle.

'Pack my bag! We're off!'

'Yes, sir.' The boots of Albert could be heard racing upstairs.

Holyhead? Did that mean that, after all – Tommy was puzzled. He read on slowly.

The boots of Albert continued to be active on the floor above.

Suddenly a second shout came from below.

'Albert! I'm a damned fool! Unpack that bag!'

'Yes, sir.'

Tommy smoothed out the note thoughtfully.

'Yes, a damned fool,' he said softly. 'But so's someone else! And at last I know who it is!'

CHAPTER XXIV

Julius Takes a Hand

In his suite at Claridge's, Kramenin reclined on a couch and dictated to his secretary in sibilant Russian.

Presently the telephone at the secretary's elbow purred, and he took up the receiver, spoke for a minute or two, then turned to his employer.

'Someone below is asking for you.'

'Who is it?'

'He gives the name of Mr Julius P. Hersheimmer.'

'Hersheimmer,' repeated Kramenin thoughtfully. 'I have heard that name before.'

'His father was one of the steel kings of America,' explained the secretary, whose business it was to know everything. 'This young man must be a millionaire several times over.'

The other's eyes narrowed appreciatively.

'You had better go down and see him, Ivan. Find out what he wants.'

The secretary obeyed, closing the door noiselessly behind him. In a few minutes he returned.

'He declines to state his business – says it is entirely private and personal, and that he must see you.'

'A millionaire several times over,' murmured Kramenin. 'Bring him up, my dear Ivan.'

The secretary left the room once more, and returned escorting Julius.

'Monsieur Kramenin?' said the latter abruptly.

The Russian, studying him attentively with his pale venomous eyes, bowed.

'Pleased to meet you,' said the American. 'I've got some

very important business I'd like to talk over with you, if I can see you alone.' He looked pointedly at the other.

'My secretary, Monsieur Grieber, from whom I have no secrets.'

'That may be so – but I have,' said Julius dryly. 'So I'd be obliged if you'd tell him to scoot.'

'Ivan,' said the Russian softly, 'perhaps you would not mind retiring into the next room –'

'The next room won't do,' interrupted Julius. 'I know these ducal suites – and I want this one plumb empty except for you and me. Send him round to a store to buy a penn'orth of peanuts.'

Though not particularly enjoying the American's free and easy manner of speech, Kramenin was devoured by curiosity.

'Will your business take long to state?'

'Might be an all night job if you caught on.'

'Very good. Ivan, I shall not require you again this evening. Go to the theatre – take a night off.'

'Thank you, your excellency.'

The secretary bowed and departed.

Julius stood at the door watching his retreat. Finally, with a satisfied sigh, he closed it, and came back to his position in the centre of the room.

'Now, Mr Hersheimmer, perhaps you will be so kind as to come to the point?'

'I guess that won't take a minute,' drawled Julius. Then, with an abrupt change of manner: 'Hands up – or I shoot!'

For a moment Kramenin stared blindly into the big automatic, then, with almost comical haste, he flung up his hands above his head. In that instant Julius had taken his measure. The man he had to deal with was an abject physical coward – the rest would be easy.

'This is an outrage,' cried the Russian in a high hysterical voice. 'An outrage! Do you mean to kill me?'

'Not if you keep your voice down. Don't go edging sideways towards that bell. That's better.'

'What do you want? Do nothing rashly. Remember my life

is of the utmost value to my country. I may have been
maligned –'

'I reckon,' said Julius, 'that the man who let daylight into
you would be doing humanity a good turn. But you needn't
worry any. I'm not proposing to kill you this trip – that is, if
you're reasonable.'

The Russian quailed before the stern menace in the other's
eyes. He passed his tongue over his dry lips.

'What do you want? Money?'

'No. I want Jane Finn.'

'Jane Finn? I – never heard of her!'

'You're a darned liar! You know perfectly who I mean.'

'I tell you I've never heard of the girl.'

'And I tell you,' retorted Julius, 'that Little Willie here is
just hopping mad to go off!'

The Russian wilted visibly.

'You wouldn't dare –'

'Oh, yes I would, son!'

Kramenin must have recognized something in the voice that
carried conviction, for he said sullenly:

'Well? Granted I do know who you mean – what of it?'

'You will tell me now – right here – where she is to be
found.'

Kramenin shook his head.

'I daren't.'

'Why not?'

'I daren't. You ask an impossibility.'

'Afraid, eh? Of whom? Mr Brown? Ah, that tickles you up!
There is such a person, then? I doubted it. And the mere
mention of him scares you stiff!'

'I have seen him,' said the Russian slowly. 'Spoken to him
face to face. I did not know it until afterwards. He was one
of the crowd. I should not know him again. Who is he really?
I do not know. But I know this – he is a man to fear.'

'He'll never know,' said Julius.

'He knows everything – and his vengeance is swift. Even I
– Kramenin! – would not be exempt!'

'Then you won't do as I ask you?'

'You ask an impossibility.'

'Sure that's a pity for you,' said Julius cheerfully. 'But the world in general will benefit.' He raised the revolver.

'Stop,' shrieked the Russian. 'You cannot mean to shoot me?'

'Of course I do. I've always heard you Revolutionists held life cheap, but it seems there's a difference when it's your own life in question. I gave you just one chance of saving your dirty skin, and that you wouldn't take!'

'They would kill me!'

'Well,' said Julius pleasantly, 'it's up to you. But I'll just say this. Little Willie here is a dead cert, and if I was you I'd take a sporting chance with Mr Brown!'

'You will hang if you shoot me,' muttered the Russian irresolutely.

'No, stranger, that's where you're wrong. You forget the dollars. A big crowd of solicitors will get busy, and they'll get some high-brow doctors on the job, and the end of it all will be that they'll say my brain was unhinged. I shall spend a few months in a quiet sanatorium, my mental health will improve, the doctors will declare me sane again, and all will end happily for little Julius. I guess I can bear a few months' retirement in order to rid the world of you, but don't you kid yourself I'll hang for it!'

The Russian believed him. Corrupt himself, he believed implicitly in the power of money. He had read of American murder trials running much on the lines indicated by Julius. He had bought and sold justice himself. This virile young American with the significant drawling voice, had the whip hand of him.

'I'm going to count five,' continued Julius, 'and I guess, if you let me get past four, you needn't worry any about Mr Brown. Maybe he'll send some flowers to the funeral, but *you* won't smell them! Are you ready? I'll begin. One – two – three – four –'

The Russian interrupted with a shriek:

'Do not shoot. I will do all you wish.'

Julius lowered the revolver.

'I thought you'd hear sense. Where is the girl?'

'At Gatehouse, in Kent. Astley Priors, the place is called.'

'Is she a prisoner there?'

'She's not allowed to leave the house – though it's safe enough really. The little fool has lost her memory, curse her!'

'That's been annoying for you and your friends, I reckon. What about the other girl, the one you decoyed away over a week ago?'

'She's there too,' said the Russian sullenly.

'That's good,' said Julius. 'Isn't it all panning out beautifully? And a lovely night for the run!'

'What run?' demanded Kramenin, with a stare.

'Down to Gatehouse, sure. I hope you're fond of motoring?'

'What do you mean? I refuse to go.'

'Now don't get mad. You must see I'm not such a kid as to leave you here. You'd ring up your friends on that telephone first thing! Ah!' He observed the fall on the other's face. 'You see, you'd got it all fixed. No, sir, you're coming along with me. This your bedroom next door here? Walk right in. Little Willie and I will come behind. Put on a thick coat, that's right. Fur lined? And you a Socialist! Now we're ready. We walk downstairs and out through the hall to where my car's waiting. And don't you forget I've got you covered every inch of the way. I can shoot just as well through my coat pocket. One word or a glance even, at one of those liveried menials, and there'll sure be a strange face in the Sulphur and Brimstone Works!'

Together they descended the stairs, and passed out to the waiting car. The Russian was shaking with rage. The hotel servants surrounded them. A cry hovered on his lips, but at the last minute his nerve failed him. The American was a man of his word.

When they reached the car, Julius breathed a sigh of relief, the danger-zone was passed. Fear had successfully hypnotized the man by his side.

'Get in,' he ordered. Then as he caught the other's side-long glance, 'No, the chauffeur won't help you any. Naval man. Was on a submarine in Russia when the Revolution broke out. A brother of his was murdered by your people. George!'

'Yes, sir?' The chauffeur turned his head.

'This gentleman is a Russian Bolshevik. We don't want to shoot him, but it may be necessary. You understand?'

'Perfectly, sir.'

'I want to go to Gatehouse in Kent. Know the road at all?'

'Yes, sir, it will be about an hour and a half's run.'

'Make it an hour. I'm in a hurry.'

'I'll do my best, sir.' The car shot forward through the traffic.

Julius ensconced himself comfortably by the side of his victim. He kept his hand in the pocket of his coat, but his manner was urbane to the last degree.

'There was a man I shot once in Arizona –' he began cheerfully.

At the end of the hour's run the unfortunate Kramenin was more dead than alive. In succession to the anecdote of the Arizona man, there had been a tough from 'Frisco, and an episode in the Rockies. Julius's narrative style, if not strictly accurate, was picturesque!

Slowing down, the chauffeur called over his shoulder that they were just coming into Gatehouse. Julius bade the Russian direct them. His plan was to drive straight up to the house. There Kramenin was to ask for the two girls. Julius explained to him that Little Willie would not be tolerant of failure. Kramenin, by this time, was as putty in the other's hand. The terrific pace they had come had still further unmanned him. He had given himself up for dead at every corner.

The car swept up the drive, and stopped before the porch. The chauffeur looked round for orders.

'Turn the car first, George. Then ring the bell, and get back to your place. Keep the engine going, and be ready to scoot like hell when I give the word.'

'Very good, sir.'

The front door was opened by the butler. Kramenin felt the muzzle of the revolver pressed against his ribs.

'Now,' hissed Julius. 'And be careful.'

The Russian beckoned. His lips were white, and his voice was not very steady:

'It is I – Kramenin! Bring down the girl at once! There is no time to lose!'

Whittington had come down the steps. He uttered an exclamation of astonishment at seeing the other.

'You! What's up? Surely you know the plan –'

Kramenin interrupted him, using the words that have created many unnecessary panics:

'We have been betrayed! Plans must be abandoned. We must save our own skins. The girl! And at once! It's our only chance.'

Whittington hesitated, but for hardly a moment.

'You have orders – from *him*?'

'Naturally! Should I be here otherwise? Hurry! There is no time to be lost. The other little fool had better come too.'

Whittington turned and ran back into the house. The agonizing minutes went by. Then – two figures hastily huddled in cloaks appeared on the steps and were hustled into the car. The smaller of the two was inclined to resist and Whittington shoved her in unceremoniously. Julius leaned forward, and in doing so the light from the open door lit up his face. Another man on the steps behind Whittington gave a startled exclamation. Concealment was at an end.

'Get a move on, George,' shouted Julius.

The chauffeur slipped in his clutch, and with a bound the car started.

The man on the steps uttered an oath. His hand went to his pocket. There was a flash and a report. The bullet just missed the taller girl by an inch.

'Get down, Jane,' cried Julius. 'Flat on the bottom of the car.' He thrust her sharply forward, then standing up, he took careful aim and fired.

'Have you hit him?' cried Tuppence eagerly.

'Sure,' replied Julius. 'He isn't killed, though. Skunks like that take a lot of killing. Are you all right, Tuppence?'

'Of course I am. Where's Tommy? And who's this?' She indicated the shivering Kramenin.

'Tommy's making tracks for the Argentine. I guess he thought you'd turned up your toes. Steady through the gate, George! That's right. It'll take 'em at least five minutes to get busy after us. They'll use the telephone, I guess, so look out for snares ahead – and don't take the direct route. Who's this, did you say, Tuppence? Let me present Monsieur Kramenin. I persuaded him to come on the trip for his health.'

The Russian remained mute, still livid with terror.

'But what made them let us go?' demanded Tuppence suspiciously.

'I reckon Monsieur Kramenin here asked them so prettily they just couldn't refuse!'

This was too much for the Russian. He burst out vehemently:

'Curse you – curse you! They know now that I betrayed them. My life won't be safe for an hour in this country.'

'That's so,' assented Julius. 'I'd advise you to make tracks for Russia right away.'

'Let me go, then,' cried the other. 'I have done what you asked. Why do you still keep me with you?'

'Not for the pleasure of your company. I guess you can get right off now if you want to. I thought you'd rather I tooled you back to London.'

'You may never reach London,' snarled the other. 'Let me go here and now.'

'Sure thing. Pull up, George. The gentleman's not making the return trip. If I ever come to Russia, Monsieur Kramenin, I shall expect a rousing welcome and –'

But before Julius had finished his speech, and before the car had finally halted, the Russian had swung himself out and disappeared into the night.

'Just a mite impatient to leave us,' commented Julius, as the car gathered way again. 'And no idea of saying goodbye politely to the ladies. Say, Jane, you can get up on the seat now.'

For the first time the girl spoke.

'How did you "persuade" him?' she asked.

Julius tapped his revolver.

'Little Willie here takes the credit!'

'Splendid!' cried the girl. The colour surged into her face, her eyes looked admiringly at Julius.

'Annette and I didn't know what was going to happen to us,' said Tuppence. 'Old Whittington hurried us off. We thought it was lambs to the slaughter.'

'Annette,' said Julius. 'Is that what you call her?'

His mind seemed to be trying to adjust itself to a new idea.

'It's her name,' said Tuppence, opening her eyes very wide.

'Shucks!' retorted Julius. 'She may think it's her name, because her memory's gone, poor kid. But it's the one real and original Jane Finn we've got here.'

'What –?' cried Tuppence.

But she was interrupted. With an angry spurt, a bullet embedded itself in the upholstery of the car just behind her head.

'Down with you,' cried Julius. 'It's an ambush. These guys have got busy pretty quickly. Push her a bit, George.'

The car fairly leapt forward. Three more shots rang out, but went happily wide. Julius, upright, leant over the back of the car.

'Nothing to shoot at,' he announced gloomily. 'But I guess there'll be another little picnic soon. Ah!'

He raised his hand to his cheek.

'You are hurt?' said Annette quickly.

'Only a scratch.'

The girl sprang to her feet.

'Let me out! Let me out, I say! Stop the car. It is me they're after. I'm the one they want. You shall not lose your lives because of me. Let me go.' She was fumbling with the fastenings of the door.

Julius took her by both arms, and looked at her. She had spoken with no trace of foreign accent.

'Sit down, kid,' he said gently. 'I guess there's nothing wrong with your memory. Been fooling them all the time, eh?'

The girl looked at him, nodded, and then suddenly burst into tears. Julius patted her on the shoulder.

'There, there – just you sit tight. We're not going to let you quit.'

Through her sobs the girl said indistinctly:

'You're from home. I can tell by your voice. It makes me home-sick.'

'Sure I'm from home. I'm your cousin – Julius Hersheimmer. I came over to Europe on purpose to find you – and a pretty dance you've led me.'

The car slackened speed. George spoke over his shoulder:

'Cross-roads here, sir. I'm not sure of the way.'

The car slowed down till it hardly moved. As it did so a figure climbed suddenly over the back, and plunged head first into the midst of them.

'Sorry,' said Tommy, extricating himself.

A mass of confused exclamations greeted him. He replied to them severally:

'Was in the bushes by the drive. Hung on behind. Couldn't let you know before at the pace you were going. It was all I could do to hang on. Now then, you girls, get out!'

'Get out?'

'Yes. There's a station just up that road. Train due in three minutes. You'll catch it if you hurry.'

'What the devil are you driving at?' demanded Julius. 'Do you think you can fool them by leaving the car?'

'You and I aren't going to leave the car. Only the girls.'

'You're crazed, Beresford. Stark staring mad! You can't let those girls go off alone. It'll be the end of it if you do.'

Tommy turned to Tuppence.

'Get out at once, Tuppence. Take her with you, and do just as I say. No one will do you any harm. You're safe. Take the

train to London. Go straight to Sir James Peel Edgerton. Mr
Carter lives out of town, but you'll be safe with him.'

'Darn you!' cried Julius. 'You're mad. Jane, you stay where
you are.'

With a sudden swift movement, Tommy snatched the
revolver from Julius's hand, and levelled it at him.

'Now will you believe I'm in earnest? Get out, both of you,
and do as I say – or I'll shoot!'

Tuppence sprang out, dragging the unwilling Jane after her.

'Come on, it's all right. If Tommy's sure – he's sure. Be
quick. We'll miss the train.'

They started running.

Julius's pent-up rage burst forth.

'What the hell –'

Tommy interrupted him.

'Dry up! I want a few words with you, Mr Julius
Hersheimmer.'

CHAPTER XXV

Jane's Story

Her arm through Jane's, dragging her along, Tuppence reached the station. Her quick ears caught the sound of the approaching train.

'Hurry up,' she panted, 'or we'll miss it.'

They arrived on the platform just as the train came to a standstill. Tuppence opened the door of an empty first-class compartment, and the two girls sank down breathless on the padded seats.

A man looked in, then passed on to the next carriage. Jane started nervously. Her eyes dilated with terror. She looked questioningly at Tuppence.

'Is he one of them, do you think?' she breathed.

Tuppence shook her head.

'No, no. It's all right.' She took Jane's hand in hers. 'Tommy wouldn't have told us to do this unless he was sure we'd be all right.'

'But he doesn't know them as I do!' The girl shivered. 'You can't understand. Five years! Five long years! Sometimes I thought I should go mad.'

'Never mind. It's all over.'

'Is it?'

The train was moving now, speeding through the night at a gradually increasing rate. Suddenly Jane Finn started up.

'What was that? I thought I saw a face – looking in through the window.'

'No, there's nothing. See.' Tuppence went to the window, and lifting the strap let the pane down.

'You're sure?'

'Quite sure.'

The other seemed to feel some excuse was necessary:

'I guess I'm acting like a frightened rabbit, but I can't help it. If they caught me now they'd –' Her eyes opened wide and staring.

'*Don't!*' implored Tuppence. 'Lie back, and *don't think*. You can be quite sure that Tommy wouldn't have said it was safe if it wasn't.'

'My cousin didn't think so. He didn't want us to do this.'

'No,' said Tuppence, rather embarrassed.

'What are you thinking of?' said Jane sharply.

'Why?'

'Your voice was so – queer!'

'I *was* thinking of something,' confessed Tuppence. 'But I don't want to tell you – not now. I may be wrong, but I don't think so. It's just an idea that came into my head a long time ago. Tommy's got it too – I'm almost sure he has. But don't *you* worry – there'll be time enough for that later. And it mayn't be so at all! Do what I tell you – lie back and don't think of anything.'

'I'll try.' The long lashes drooped over the hazel eyes.

Tuppence, for her part, sat bolt upright – much in the attitude of a watchful terrier on guard. In spite of herself she was nervous. Her eyes flashed continually from one window to the other. She noted the exact position of the communication cord. What it was that she feared, she would have been hard put to it to say. But in her own mind she was far from feeling the confidence displayed in her words. Not that she disbelieved in Tommy, but occasionally she was shaken with doubts as to whether anyone so simple and honest as he was could ever be a match for the fiendish subtlety of the arch-criminal.

If they once reached Sir James Peel Edgerton in safety, all would be well. But would they reach him? Would not the silent forces of Mr Brown already be assembling against them? Even that last picture of Tommy, revolver in hand, failed to comfort her. By now he might be overpowered, borne down by sheer force of numbers . . . Tuppence mapped out her plan of campaign.

As the train at length drew slowly into Charing Cross, Jane Finn sat up with a start.

'Have we arrived? I never thought we should!'

'Oh, I thought we'd get to London all right. If there's going to be any fun, now is when it will begin. Quick, get out. We'll nip into a taxi.'

In another minute they were passing the barrier, had paid the necessary fares, and were stepping into a taxi.

'King's Cross,' directed Tuppence. Then she gave a jump. A man looked in at the window, just as they started. She was almost certain it was the same man who had got into the carriage next to them. She had a horrible feeling of being slowly hemmed in on every side.

'You see,' she explained to Jane, 'if they think we're going to Sir James, this will put them off the scent. Now they'll imagine we're going to Mr Carter. His country place is north of London somewhere.'

Crossing Holborn there was a block, and the taxi was held up. This was what Tuppence had been waiting for.

'Quick,' she whispered. 'Open the right-hand door!'

The two girls stepped out into the traffic. Two minutes later they were seated in another taxi and were retracing their steps, this time direct to Carlton House Terrace.

'There,' said Tuppence, with great satisfaction, 'this ought to do them. I can't help thinking that I'm really rather clever! How that other taxi man will swear! But I took his number, and I'll send him a postal order tomorrow, so that he won't lose by it if he happens to be genuine. What's this thing swerving – Oh!'

There was a grinding noise and a bump. Another taxi had collided with them.

In a flash Tuppence was out on the pavement. A policeman was approaching. Before he arrived Tuppence had handed the driver five shillings, and she and Jane had merged themselves in the crowd.

'It's only a step or two now,' said Tuppence breathlessly. The accident had taken place in Trafalgar Square.

'Do you think the collision was an accident, or done deliberately?'

'I don't know. It might have been either.'

Hand-in-hand, the two girls hurried along.

'It may be my fancy,' said Tuppence suddenly, 'but I feel as though there was someone behind us.'

'Hurry!' murmured the other. 'Oh, hurry!'

They were now at the corner of Carlton House Terrace, and their spirits lightened. Suddenly a large and apparently intoxicated man barred their way.

'Good evening, ladies,' he hiccupped. 'Whither away so fast?'

'Let us pass, please,' said Tuppence imperiously.

'Just a word with your pretty friend here.' He stretched out an unsteady hand, and clutched Jane by the shoulder. Tuppence heard other footsteps behind. She did not pause to ascertain whether they were friends or foes. Lowering her head, she repeated a manoeuvre of childish days, and butted their aggressor full in the capacious middle. The success of these unsportsman-like tactics was immediate. The man sat down abruptly on the pavement. Tuppence and Jane took to their heels. The house they sought was some way down. Other footsteps echoed behind them. Their breath was coming in choking gasps as they reached Sir James's door. Tuppence seized the bell and Jane the knocker.

The man who had stopped them reached the foot of the steps. For a moment he hesitated, and as he did so the door opened. They fell into the hall together. Sir James came forward from the library door.

'Hullo! What's this?'

He stepped forward and put his arm round Jane as she swayed uncertainly. He half carried her into the library, and laid her on the leather couch. From a tantalus on the table he poured out a few drops of brandy, and forced her to drink them. With a sigh she sat up, her eyes still wild and frightened.

'It's all right. Don't be afraid, my child. You're quite safe.'

Her breath came more normally, and the colour was

returning to her cheeks. Sir James looked at Tuppence quizzically.

'So you're not dead, Miss Tuppence, any more than that Tommy boy of yours was!'

'The Young Adventurers take a lot of killing,' boasted Tuppence.

'So it seems,' said Sir James dryly. 'Am I right in thinking that the joint venture has ended in success, and that this' – he turned to the girl on the couch – 'is Miss Jane Finn?'

Jane sat up.

'Yes,' she said quietly, 'I am Jane Finn. I have a lot to tell you.'

'When you are stronger –'

'No – now!' Her voice rose a little. 'I shall feel safer when I have told everything.'

'As you please,' said the lawyer.

He sat down in one of the big arm-chairs facing the couch. In a low voice Jane began her story.

'I came over on the *Lusitania* to take up a post in Paris. I was fearfully keen about the war, and just dying to help somehow or other. I had been studying French, and my teacher said they were wanting help in a hospital in Paris, so I wrote and offered my services, and they were accepted. I hadn't got any folk of my own, so it made it easy to arrange things.

'When the *Lusitania* was torpedoed, a man came up to me. I'd noticed him more than once – and I'd figured it out in my own mind that he was afraid of somebody or something. He asked me if I was a patriotic American, and told me he was carrying papers which were just life or death to the Allies. He asked me to take charge of them. I was to watch for an advertisement in *The Times*. If it didn't appear, I was to take them to the American Ambassador.

'Most of what followed seems like a nightmare still. I see it in my dreams sometimes . . . I'll hurry over that part. Mr Danvers had told me to watch out. He might have been shadowed from New York, but he didn't think so. At first I had no suspicions, but on the boat to Holyhead I began to

get uneasy. There was one woman who had been very keen
to look after me, and chum up with me generally – a Mrs
Vandemeyer. At first I'd been only grateful to her for being
so kind to me; but all the time I felt there was something
about her I didn't like, and on the Irish boat I saw her talking
to some queer-looking men, and from the way they looked I
saw that they were talking about me. I remembered that she'd
been quite near me on the *Lusitania* when Mr Danvers gave
me the packet, and before that she'd tried to talk to him once
or twice. I began to get scared, but I didn't quite see what
to do.

'I had a wild idea of stopping at Holyhead, and not going
on to London that day, but I soon saw that would be plumb
foolishness. The only thing was to act as though I'd noticed
nothing, and hope for the best. I couldn't see how they could
get me if I was on my guard. One thing I'd done already as
a precaution – ripped open the oilskin packet and substituted
blank paper, and then sewn it up again. So, if anyone did
manage to rob me of it, it wouldn't matter.

'What to do with the real thing worried me no end. Finally
I opened it out flat – there were only two sheets – and laid it
between two of the advertisement pages of a magazine. I stuck
the two pages together round the edge with some gum off an
envelope. I carried the magazine carelessly stuffed into the
pocket of my ulster.

'At Holyhead I tried to get into a carriage with people that
looked all right, but in a queer way there seemed always to
be a crowd round me shoving and pushing me just the way I
didn't want to go. There was something uncanny and frighten-
ing about it. In the end I found myself in a carriage with Mrs
Vandemeyer after all. I went out into the corridor, but all the
other carriages were full, so I had to go back and sit down. I
consoled myself with the thought that there were other people
in the carriage – there was quite a nice-looking man and his
wife sitting just opposite. So I felt almost happy about it until
just outside London. I had leaned back and closed my eyes.
I guess they thought I was asleep, but my eyes weren't quite

shut, and suddenly I saw the nice-looking man get something out of his bag and hand it to Mrs Vandemeyer, and as he did so he *winked* . . .

'I can't tell you how that wink sort of froze me through and through. My only thought was to get out in the corridor as quick as ever I could. I got up, trying to look natural and easy. Perhaps they saw something – I don't know – but suddenly Mrs Vandemeyer said "Now," and flung something over my nose and mouth as I tried to scream. At the same moment I felt a terrific blow on the back of my head . . .'

She shuddered. Sir James murmured something sympathetically. In a minute she resumed:

'I don't know how long it was before I came back to consciousness. I felt very ill and sick. I was lying on a dirty bed. There was a screen round it, but I could hear two people talking in the room. Mrs Vandemeyer was one of them. I tried to listen, but at first I couldn't take much in. When at last I did begin to grasp what was going on – I was just terrified! I wonder I didn't scream right out there and then.

'They hadn't found the papers. They'd got the oilskin packet with the blanks, and they were just mad! They didn't know whether I'd changed the papers, or whether Danvers had been carrying a dummy message, while the real one was sent another way. They spoke of' – she closed her eyes – 'torturing me to find out!'

'I'd never known what fear – really sickening fear – was before! Once they came to look at me. I shut my eyes and pretended to be still unconscious, but I was afraid they'd hear the beating of my heart. However, they went away again. I began thinking madly. What could I do? I knew I wouldn't be able to stand up against torture very long.

'Suddenly something put the thought of loss of memory into my head. The subject had always interested me, and I'd read an awful lot about it. I had the whole thing at my finger-tips. If only I could succeed in carrying the bluff through, it might save me. I said a prayer, and drew a long breath. Then I opened my eyes and started babbling in *French*!

'Mrs Vandemeyer came round the screen at once. Her face was so wicked I nearly died, but I smiled up at her doubtfully, and asked her in French where I was.

'It puzzled her, I could see. She called the man she had been talking to. He stood by the screen with his face in shadow. He spoke to me in French. His voice was very ordinary and quiet but somehow, I don't know why, he scared me, but I went on playing my part. I asked again where I was, and then went on that there was something I *must* remember – *must* remember – *only* for the moment it was all gone. I worked myself up to be more and more distressed. He asked me my name. I said I didn't know – that I couldn't remember anything at all.

'Suddenly he caught my wrist, and began twisting it. The pain was awful. I screamed. He went on. I screamed and screamed, but I managed to shriek out things in French. I don't know how long I could have gone on, but luckily I fainted. The last thing I heard was his voice saying: "That's not bluff! Anyway, a kid of her age wouldn't know enough.' I guess he forgot American girls are older for their age than English ones, and take more interest in scientific subjects.

'When I came to, Mrs Vandemeyer was sweet as honey to me. She'd had her orders, I guess. She spoke to me in French – told me I'd had a shock and been very ill. I should be better soon. I pretended to be rather dazed – murmured something about the "doctor" having hurt my wrist. She looked relieved when I said that.

'By and by she went out of the room altogether. I was suspicious still, and lay quite for some time. In the end, however, I got up and walked round the room, examining it. I thought that even if anyone *was* watching me from somewhere, it would seem natural enough under the circumstances. It was a squalid, dirty place. There were no windows, which seemed queer. I guessed the door would be locked, but I didn't try it. There were some battered old pictures on the walls, representing scenes from *Faust*.'

Jane's two listeners gave a simultaneous 'Ah!' The girl nodded.

'Yes – it was the place in Soho where Mr Beresford was imprisoned. Of course at the time I didn't even know if I was in London. One thing was worrying me dreadfully, but my heart gave a great throb of relief when I saw my ulster lying carelessly over the back of a chair. *And the magazine was still rolled up in the pocket!*

'If only I could be certain that I was not being overlooked! I looked carefully round the walls. There didn't seem to be a peep-hole of any kind – nevertheless I felt kind of sure there must be. All of a sudden I sat down on the edge of the table, and put my face in my hands, sobbing out a "Mon Dieu! Mon Dieu!" I've got very sharp ears. I distinctly heard the rustle of a dress, and slight creak. That was enough for me. I was being watched!

'I lay down on the bed again, and by and by Mrs Vandemeyer brought me some supper. She was still sweet as they make them. I guess she'd been told to win my confidence. Presently she produced the oilskin packet, and asked me if I recognized it, watching me like a lynx all the time.

'I took it and turned it over in a puzzled sort of way. Then I shook my head. I said that I felt I *ought* to remember something about it, that it was just as though it was all coming back, and then, before I could get hold of it, it went again. Then she told me that I was her niece, and that I was to call her "Aunt Rita". I did obediently, and she told me not to worry – my memory would soon come back.

'That was an awful night. I'd made my plan whilst I was waiting for her. The papers were safe so far, but I couldn't take the risk of leaving them there any longer. They might throw that magazine away any minute. I lay awake waiting until I judged it must be about two o'clock in the morning. Then I got up as softly as I could, and felt in the dark along the left-hand wall. Very gently, I unhooked one of the pictures from its nail – Marguerite with her casket of jewels. I crept over to my coat and took out the magazine, and an odd envelope or two that I had shoved in. Then I went to the wash-stand, and damped the brown paper at the back of the picture all round. Presently I was able to pull it away. I had already torn out the two stuck-together pages from the magazine, and now I slipped them with their precious enclosure between the picture and its brown paper backing. A little gum from the envelopes helped me to stick the latter up again. No one would dream the picture had ever been tampered with. I rehung it on the wall, put the magazine back in my coat pocket, and crept back to bed. I was pleased with my hiding-place. They'd never think of pulling to pieces one of their own pictures. I hoped that they'd come to the conclusion that Danvers had been carrying a dummy all along, and that, in the end, they'd let me go.

'As a matter of fact, I guess that's what they did think at first and, in a way, it was dangerous for me. I learnt afterwards that they nearly did away with me then and there – there was never much chance of their "letting me go" – but the first man, who was the boss, preferred to keep me alive on the chance of my having hidden them, and being able to tell where if I recovered my memory. They watched me constantly for weeks. Sometimes they'd ask me questions by the hour – I guess there was nothing they didn't know about the third degree! – but somehow I managed to hold my own. The strain of it was awful, though . . .

'They took me back to Ireland, and over every step of the journey again, in case I'd hidden it somewhere *en route*. Mrs Vandemeyer and another woman never left me for a moment. They spoke of me as a young relative of Mrs Vandemeyer's whose mind was affected by the shock of the *Lusitania*. There was no one I could appeal to for help without giving myself away to *them*, and if I risked it and failed – and Mrs Vandemeyer looked so rich, and so beautifully dressed, that I felt convinced they'd take her word against mine, and think it was part of my mental trouble to think myself "persecuted" – I felt that the horrors in store for me would be too awful once they knew I'd been only shamming.'

Sir James nodded comprehendingly.

'Mrs Vandemeyer was a woman of great personality. With that and her social position she would have had little difficulty in imposing her point of view in preference to yours. Your sensational accusations against her would not easily have found credence.'

'That's what I thought. It ended in my being sent to a sanatorium at Bournemouth. I couldn't make up my mind at first whether it was a sham affair or genuine. A hospital nurse had charge of me. I was a special patient. She seemed so nice and normal that at last I determined to confide in her. A merciful providence just saved me in time from falling into the trap. My door happened to be ajar, and I heard her talking to someone in the passage. *She was one of them!* They still fancied it might be a bluff on my part, and she was put in charge of me to make sure! After that, my nerve went completely. I dared trust nobody.

'I think I almost hypnotized myself. After a while, I almost forgot that I was really Jane Finn. I was so bent on playing the part of Janet Vandemeyer that my nerves began to play tricks. I became really ill – for months I sank into a sort of stupor. I felt sure I should die soon, and that nothing really mattered. A sane person shut up in a lunatic asylum often ends by becoming insane, they say. I guess I was like that. Playing my part had become second nature to me. I wasn't even unhappy in the end – just apathetic. Nothing seemed to matter. And the years went on.

'And then suddenly things seemed to change. Mrs Vandemeyer came down from London. She and the doctor asked me questions, experimented with various treatments. There was some talk of sending me to a specialist in Paris. In the end, they did not dare risk it. I overheard something that seemed to show that other people – friends – were looking for me. I learnt later that the nurse who had looked after me went to Paris, and consulted a specialist, representing herself to be me. He put her through some searching tests, and exposed her loss of memory to be fraudulent; but she had taken a note of his methods and reproduced them on me. I dare say I couldn't have deceived the specialist for a minute – a man who has made a lifelong study of a thing is unique – but I managed once again to hold my own with them. The fact that I'd not thought of myself as Jane Finn for so long made it easier.

'One night I was whisked off to London at a moment's notice. They took me back to the house in Soho. Once I got away from the sanatorium I felt different – as though something in me that had been buried for a long time was waking up again.

'They sent me in to wait on Mr Beresford. (Of course I didn't know his name then.) I was suspicious – I thought it was another trap. But he looked so honest, I could hardly believe it. However I was careful in all I said, for I knew we could be overheard. There's a small hole, high up in the wall.

'But on the Sunday afternoon a message was brought to the house. They were all very disturbed. Without their knowing, I listened. Word had come that he was to be killed. I needn't tell the next part, because you know it. I thought I'd have time to rush up and get the papers from their hiding-place, but I was caught. So I screamed out that he was escaping, and I said I wanted to go back to Marguerite. I shouted the name three times very loud. I knew the others would think I meant Mrs Vandemeyer, but I hoped it might make Mr Beresford think of the picture. He'd unhooked one the first day – that's what made me hesitate to trust him.'

She paused.

'Then the papers,' said Sir James slowly, 'are still at the back of the picture in that room.'

'Yes.' The girl had sunk back on the sofa exhausted with the strain of the long story.

Sir James rose to his feet. He looked at his watch.

'Come,' he said, 'we must go at once.'

'Tonight? queried Tuppence, surprised.

'Tomorrow may be too late,' said Sir James gravely. 'Besides, by going tonight we have the chance of capturing that great man and super-criminal – Mr Brown!'

There was dead silence, and Sir James continued:

'You have been followed here – not a doubt of it. When we leave the house we shall be followed again, but not molested *for it is Mr Brown's plan that we are to lead him*. But the Soho house is under police supervision night and day. There are several men watching it. When we enter that house, Mr Brown will not draw back – he will risk all, on the chance of obtaining the spark to fire his mine. And he fancies the risk not great – since he will enter in the guise of a friend!'

Tuppence flushed, then opened her mouth impulsively.

'But there's something you don't know – that we haven't told you.' Her eyes dwelt on Jane in perplexity.

'What is that?' asked the other sharply. 'No hesitations, Miss Tuppence. We need to be sure of our going.'

But Tuppence, for once, seemed tongue-tied.

'It's so difficult – you see, if I'm wrong – oh, it would be dreadful.' She made a grimace at the unconscious Jane. 'Never forgive me,' she observed cryptically.

'You want me to help you out, eh?'

'Yes, please. *You* know who Mr Brown is, don't you?'

'Yes,' said Sir James gravely. 'At last I do.'

'At last?' queried Tuppence doubtfully. 'Oh, but I thought –' She paused.

'You thought correctly, Miss Tuppence. I have been morally certain of his identity for some time – ever since the night of Mrs Vandemeyer's mysterious death.'

'Ah!' breathed Tuppence.

'For there we are up against the logic of facts. There are only two solutions. Either the chloral was administered by her own hand, which theory I reject utterly, or else –'

'Yes?'

'Or else it was administered in the brandy you gave her. Only three people touched that brandy – you, Miss Tuppence, I myself, and one other – Mr Julius Hersheimmer!'

Jane Finn stirred and sat up, regarding the speaker with wide astonished eyes.

'At first, the thing seemed utterly impossible. Mr

Hersheimmer, as the son of a prominent millionaire, was a well-known figure in America. It seemed utterly impossible that he and Mr Brown could be one and the same. But you cannot escape from the logic of facts. Since the thing was so – it must be accepted. Remember Mrs Vandemeyer's sudden and inexplicable agitation. Another proof, if proof was needed.

'I took an early opportunity of giving you a hint. From some words of Mr Hersheimmer's at Manchester, I gathered that you had understood and acted on that hint. Then I set to work to prove the impossible possible. Mr Beresford rang me up and told me, what I had already suspected, that the photograph of Miss Jane Finn had never really been out of Mr Hersheimmer's possession –'

But the girl interrupted. Springing to her feet, she cried out angrily:

'What do you mean? What are you trying to suggest? That Mr Brown is *Julius*? Julius – my own cousin!'

'No, Miss Finn,' said Sir James unexpectedly. 'Not your cousin. The man who calls himself Julius Hersheimmer is no relation to you whatsoever.'

CHAPTER XXVI

Mr Brown

Sir James's words came like a bombshell. Both girls looked equally puzzled. The lawyer went across to his desk, and returned with a small newspaper cutting, which he handed to Jane. Tuppence read it over her shoulder. Mr Carter would have recognized it. It referred to the mysterious man found dead in New York.

'As I was saying to Miss Tuppence,' resumed the lawyer, 'I set to work to prove the impossible possible. The great stumbling-block was the undeniable fact that Julius Hersheimmer was not an assumed name. When I came across this paragraph my problem was solved. Julius Hersheimmer set out to discover what had become of his cousin. He went out West, where he obtained news of her and her photograph to aid him in his search. On the eve of his departure from New York he was set upon and murdered. His body was dressed in shabby clothes, and the face disfigured to prevent identification. Mr Brown took his place. He sailed immediately for England. None of the real Hersheimmer's friends or intimates saw him before he sailed – though indeed it would hardly have mattered if they had, the impersonation was so perfect. Since then he had been hand in glove with those sworn to hunt him down. Every secret of theirs had been known to him. Only once did he come near disaster. Mrs Vandemeyer knew his secret. It was no part of his plan that that huge bribe should ever be offered to her. But for Miss Tuppence's fortunate change of plan, she would have been far away from the flat when we arrived there. Exposure stared him in the face. He took a desperate step, trusting in his assumed character to avert suspicion. He nearly succeeded – but not quite.'

'I can't believe it,' murmured Jane. 'He seemed so splendid.'

'The real Julius Hersheimmer *was* a splendid fellow! And Mr Brown is a consummate actor. But ask Miss Tuppence if she also has not had her suspicions.'

Jane turned mutely to Tuppence. The latter nodded.

'I didn't want to say it, Jane – I knew it would hurt you. And, after all, I couldn't be sure. I still don't understand why, if he's Mr Brown, he rescued us.'

'Was it Julius Hersheimmer who helped you to escape?'

Tuppence recounted to Sir James the exciting events of the evening, ending up: 'But I can't see *why*!'

'Can't you? I can. So can young Beresford, by his actions. As a last hope Jane Finn was to be allowed to escape – and the escape must be managed so that she harbours no suspicions of its being a put-up job. They're not averse to young Beresford's being in the neighbourhood, and, if necessary, communicating with you. They'll take care to get him out of the way at the right minute. Then Julius Hersheimmer dashes up and rescues you in true melodramatic style. Bullets fly – but don't hit anybody. What would have happened next? You would have driven straight to the house in Soho and secured the document which Miss Finn would probably have entrusted to her cousin's keeping. Or, if he conducted the search, he would have pretended to find the hiding-place already rifled. He would have had a dozen ways of dealing with the situation, but the result would have been the same. And I rather fancy some accident would have happened to both of you. You see, you know rather an inconvenient amount. That's a rough outline. I admit I was caught napping; but somebody else wasn't.'

'Tommy,' said Tuppence softly.

'Yes. Evidently when the right moment came to get rid of him – he was too sharp for them. All the same, I'm not too easy in my mind about him.'

'Why?'

'Because Julius Hersheimmer is Mr Brown,' said Sir James dryly. 'And it takes more than one man and a revolver to hold up Mr Brown . . .'

Tuppence paled a little.

'What can we do?'

'Nothing until we've been to the house in Soho. If Beresford has still got the upper hand, there's nothing to fear. If otherwise, our enemy will come to find us, and he will not find us unprepared!' From a drawer in the desk, he took a Service revolver, and placed it in his coat pocket.

'Now we're ready. I know better than even to suggest going without you, Miss Tuppence –'

'I should think so indeed!'

'But I do suggest that Miss Finn should remain here. She will be perfectly safe, and I am afraid she is absolutely worn out with all she has been through.'

But to Tuppence's surprise Jane shook her head.

'No. I guess I'm going too. Those papers were my trust. I must go through with this business to the end. I'm heaps better now anyway.'

Sir James's car was ordered round. During the short drive Tuppence's heart beat tumultuously. In spite of momentary qualms of uneasiness respecting Tommy, she could not but feel exultation. They were going to win!

The car drew up at the corner of the square and they got out. Sir James went up to a plain-clothes man who was on duty with several others, and spoke to him. Then he rejoined the girls.

'No one has gone into the house so far. It is being watched at the back as well, so they are quite sure of that. Anyone who attempts to enter after we have done so will be arrested immediately. Shall we go in?'

A policeman produced a key. They all knew Sir James well. They had also had orders respecting Tuppence. Only the third member of the party was unknown to them. The three entered the house, pulling the door to behind them. Slowly they mounted the rickety stairs. At the top was the ragged curtain hiding the recess where Tommy had hidden that day. Tuppence had heard the story from Jane in her character of 'Annette'. She looked at the tattered velvet with interest. Even now she could almost swear it moved – as though *someone* was behind it. So strong was the illusion that she almost fancied she could make out the outline of a form . . . Supposing Mr Brown – Julius – was there waiting . . .

Impossible of course! Yet she almost went back to put the curtain aside and make sure . . .

Now they were entering the prison room. No place for any-one to hide here, thought Tuppence, with a sigh of relief, then chided herself indignantly. She must not give way to this foolish fancying – this curious insistent feeling that *Mr Brown was in the house* . . . Hark! what was that? A stealthy footstep on the stairs? There *was* someone in the house! Absurd! She was becoming hysterical.

Jane had gone straight to the picture of Marguerite. She unhooked it with a steady hand. The dust lay thick upon it, and festoons of cobwebs lay between it and the wall. Sir James handed her a pocket-knife, and she stripped away the brown paper from the back . . . The advertisement page of a maga-zine fell out. Jane picked it up. Holding apart the frayed inner edges she extracted two thin sheets covered with writing!

No dummy this time! The real thing!

'We've got it,' said Tuppence. 'At last . . .'

The moment was almost breathless in its emotion. Forgotten the faint creakings, the imagined noises of a minute ago. None of them had eyes for anything but what Jane held in her hand.

Sir James took it, and scrutinized it attentively.

'Yes,' he said quietly, 'this is the ill-fated draft treaty!'

'We've succeeded,' said Tuppence. There was awe and an almost wondering unbelief in her voice.

Sir James echoed her words as he folded the paper carefully and put it away in his pocket-book, then he looked curiously round the dingy room.

'It was here that your young friend was confined for so long, was it not?' he said. 'A truly sinister room. You notice the absence of windows, and the thickness of the close-fitting door. Whatever took place here would never be heard by the outside world.'

Tuppence shivered. His words woke a vague alarm in her. What if there *was* someone concealed in the house? Someone who might bar that door on them, and leave them to die like rats in a trap? Then she realized the absurdity of her thought. The house was surrounded by police who, if they failed to reappear, would not hesitate to break in and make a thorough search. She smiled at her own foolishness – then looked up with a start to find Sir James watching her. He gave her an emphatic little nod.

'Quite right, Miss Tuppence. You scent danger. So do I. So does Miss Finn.'

'Yes,' admitted Jane. 'It's absurd – but I can't help it.'

Sir James nodded again.

'You feel – as we all feel – *the presence of Mr Brown.* Yes' – as Tuppence made a movement – 'not a doubt of it – Mr Brown is here . . .'

'In this house?'

'In this room . . . You don't understand? *I am Mr Brown . . .*'

Stupefied, unbelieving, they stared at him. The very lines of his face had changed. It was a different man who stood before them. He smiled a slow cruel smile.

'Neither of you will leave this room alive! You said just now we had succeeded. *I* have succeeded! The draft treaty is mine.' His smile grew wider as he looked at Tuppence. 'Shall I tell you how it will be? Sooner or later the police will break in, and they will find three victims of Mr Brown – three, not two, you understand, but fortunately the third will not be dead, only wounded, and will be able to describe the attack with a wealth of detail! The treaty? It is in the hands of Mr Brown. So no one will think of searching the pockets of Sir James Peel Edgerton!'

He turned to Jane.

'You outwitted me. I make my acknowledgements. But you will not do it again.'

There was a faint sound behind him, but intoxicated with success he did not turn his head.

He slipped his hand into his pocket.

'Checkmate to the Young Adventurers,' he said, and slowly raised the big automatic.

But, even as he did so, he felt himself seized from behind in a grip of iron. The revolver was wrenched from his hand, and the voice of Julius Hersheimmer said drawlingly:

'I guess you're caught red-handed with the goods upon you.'

The blood rushed to the KC's face, but his self-control was marvellous, as he looked from one to the other of his two captors. He looked longest at Tommy.

'You,' he said beneath his breath. '*You!* I might have known.'

Seeing that he was disposed to offer no resistance, their grip slackened. Quick as a flash his left hand, the hand which bore the big signet ring, was raised to his lips . . .

'"*Ave Caesar! te morituri salutant,*"' he said, still looking at Tommy.

Then his face changed, and with a long convulsive shudder he fell forward in a crumpled heap, whilst an odour of bitter almonds filled the air.

CHAPTER XXVII

A Supper Party at the Savoy

The supper party given by Mr Julius Hersheimmer to a few friends on the evening of the 30th will long be remembered in catering circles. It took place in a private room, and Mr Hersheimmer's orders were brief and forcible. He gave carte blanche – and when a millionaire gives carte blanche he usually gets it!

Every delicacy out of season was duly provided. Waiters carried bottles of ancient and royal vintage with loving care. The floral decorations defied the seasons, and fruits of the earth as far apart as May and November found themselves miraculously side by side. The list of guests was small and select. The American Ambassador, Mr Carter, who had taken the liberty, he said, of bringing an old friend, Sir William Beresford, with him, Archdeacon Cowley, Dr Hall, those two youthful adventurers, Miss Prudence Cowley and Mr Thomas Beresford, and last, but not least, as guest of honour, Miss Jane Finn.

Julius had spared no pains to make Jane's appearance a success. A mysterious knock had brought Tuppence to the door of the apartment she was sharing with the American girl. It was Julius. In his hand he held a cheque.

'Say, Tuppence,' he began, 'will you do me a good turn? Take this, and get Jane regularly togged up for this evening. You're all coming to supper with me at the Savoy. See? Spare no expense. You get me?'

'Sure thing,' mimicked Tuppence. 'We shall enjoy ourselves! It will be a pleasure dressing Jane. She's the loveliest thing I've ever seen.'

'That's so,' agreed Mr Hersheimmer fervently.

His fervour brought a momentary twinkle to Tuppence's eye.

'By the way, Julius,' she remarked demurely, 'I – haven't given you my answer yet.'

'Answer?' said Julius. His face paled.

'You know – when you asked me to – marry you,' faltered Tuppence, her eyes downcast in the true manner of the early Victorian heroine, 'and wouldn't take no for an answer. I've thought it well over –'

'Yes?' said Julius. The perspiration stood on his forehead. Tuppence relented suddenly.

'You great idiot!' she said. 'What on earth induced you to do it? I could see at the time you didn't care a twopenny dip for me!'

'Not at all. I had – and still have – the highest sentiments of esteem and respect – and admiration for you –'

'H'm!' said Tuppence. 'Those are the kind of sentiments that very soon go to the wall when the other sentiment comes along! Don't they, old thing?'

'I don't know what you mean,' said Julius stiffly, but a large and burning blush overspread his countenance.

'Shucks!' retorted Tuppence. She laughed and closed the door, reopening it to add with dignity: 'Morally, I shall always consider I have been jilted!'

'What was it?' asked Jane as Tuppence rejoined her.

'Julius.'

'What did he want?'

'Really, I think, he wanted to see you, but I wasn't going to let him. Not until tonight, when you're going to burst upon everyone like King Solomon in his glory! Come on! *We're going to shop!*'

To most people the 29th, the much-heralded 'Labour Day', had passed much as any other day. Speeches were made in the Park and Trafalgar Square. Straggling processions, singing *The Red Flag*, wandered through the streets in a more or less aimless manner. Newspapers which had hinted at a general strike, and the inauguration of a reign of terror, were forced to hide their diminished heads. The bolder and more astute among them sought to prove that peace had been effected by following their counsels. In the Sunday papers a brief notice of the sudden death of Sir James Peel Edgerton, the famous K C, had appeared. Monday's paper dealt appreciatively with the dead man's career. The exact manner of his sudden death was never made public.

Tommy had been right in his forecast of the situation. It had been a one-man show. Deprived of their chief, the organization fell to pieces. Kramenin had made a precipitate return to Russia, leaving England early on Sunday morning. The gang had fled from Astley Priors in a panic, leaving behind, in their haste, various damaging documents which compromised them hopelessly. With these proofs of conspiracy in their hands, aided further by a small brown diary, taken from the pocket of the dead man which had contained a full and damning résumé of the whole plot, the Government had called an eleventh-hour conference. The Labour leaders were forced to recognize that they had been used as a cat's paw. Certain concessions were made by the Government, and were eagerly accepted. It was to be Peace, not War!

But the Cabinet knew by how narrow a margin they had escaped utter disaster. And burnt in on Mr Carter's brain was the strange scene which had taken place in the house in Soho the night before.

He had entered the squalid room to find that great man, the friend of a lifetime, dead – betrayed out of his own mouth. From the dead man's pocket-book he had retrieved the ill-omened draft treaty, and then and there, in the presence of the other three, it had been reduced to ashes . . . England was saved!

And now, on the evening of the 30th, in a private room at the Savoy, Mr Julius P. Hersheimmer was receiving his guests.

Mr Carter was the first to arrive. With him was a choleric-looking old gentleman, at sight of whom Tommy flushed up to the roots of his hair. He came forward.

'Ha!' said the old gentleman surveying him apoplectically.

'So you're my nephew, are you? Not much to look at – but you've done good work, it seems. Your mother must have brought you up well after all. Shall we let bygones be bygones, eh? You're my heir, you know; and in future I propose to make you an allowance – and you can look upon Chalmers Park as your home.'

'Thank you, sir, it's awfully decent of you.'

'Where's this young lady I've been hearing such a lot about?'

Tommy introduced Tuppence.

'Ha!' said Sir William, eyeing her. 'Girls aren't what they used to be in my young days.'

'Yes, they are,' said Tuppence. 'Their clothes are different, perhaps, but they themselves are just the same.'

'Well, perhaps you're right. Minxes then – minxes now!'

'That's it,' said Tuppence. 'I'm a frightful minx myself.'

'I believe you,' said the old gentleman, chuckling, and pinched her ear in high good-humour. Most young women were terrified of the 'old bear', as they termed him. Tuppence's pertness delighted the old misogynist.

Then came the timid archdeacon, a little bewildered by the company in which he found himself, glad that his daughter was considered to have distinguished herself, but unable to help glancing at her from time to time with nervous apprehension. But Tuppence behaved admirably. She forbore to cross her legs, set a guard upon her tongue, and steadfastly refused to smoke.

Dr Hall came next, and he was followed by the American Ambassador.

'We might as well sit down,' said Julius, when he had introduced all his guests to each other. 'Tuppence, will you –'

He indicated the place of honour with a wave of his hand.

But Tuppence shook her head.

'No – that's Jane's place! When one thinks of how she's held out all these years, she ought to be made the queen of the feast tonight.'

Julius flung her a grateful glance, and Jane came forward

shyly to the allotted seat. Beautiful as she had seemed before, it was as nothing to the loveliness that now went fully adorned. Tuppence had performed her part faithfully. The model gown supplied by a famous dressmaker had been entitled 'A tiger lily'. It was all golds and reds and browns, and out of it rose the pure column of the girl's white throat, and the bronze masses of hair that crowned her lovely head. There was admiration in every eye, as she took her seat.

Soon the supper party was in full swing, and with one accord Tommy was called upon for a full and complete explanation.

'You've been too darned close about the whole business,' Julius accused him. 'You let on to me that you were off to the Argentine – though I guess you had your reasons for that. The idea of both you and Tuppence casting me for the part of Mr Brown just tickles me to death!'

'The idea was not original to them,' said Mr Carter gravely. 'It was suggested, and the poison very carefully instilled, by a past-master in the art. The paragraph in the New York paper suggested the plan to him, and by means of it he wove a web that nearly enmeshed you fatally.'

'I never liked him,' said Julius. 'I felt from the first that there was something wrong about him, and I always suspected that it was he who silenced Mrs Vandemeyer so appositely. But it wasn't till I heard that the order for Tommy's execution came right on the heels of our interview with him that Sunday that I began to tumble to the fact that he was the big bug himself.'

'I never suspected it at all,' lamented Tuppence. 'I've always thought I was so much cleverer than Tommy – but he's undoubtedly scored over me handsomely.'

Julius agreed.

'Tommy's been the goods this trip! And, instead of sitting there as dumb as a fish, let him banish his blushes, and tell us all about it.'

'Hear! hear!'

'There's nothing to tell,' said Tommy, acutely uncomfortable. 'I was an awful mug – right up to the time I found that photograph of Annette, and realized that she was Jane Finn. Then I remembered how persistently she had shouted out that word "Marguerite" – and I thought of the pictures, and – well, that's that. Then of course I went over the whole thing to see where I'd made an ass of myself.'

'Go on,' said Mr Carter, as Tommy showed signs of taking refuge in silence once more.

'That business about Mrs Vandemeyer had worried me when Julius told me about it. On the face of it, it seemed that he or Sir James must have done the trick. But I didn't know which. Finding that photograph in the drawer, after that story of how it had been got from him by Inspector Brown, made me suspect Julius. Then I remembered that it was Sir James who had discovered the false Jane Finn. In the end, I couldn't make up my mind – and just decided to take no chances either way. I left a note for Julius, in case he was Mr Brown, saying I was off to the Argentine, and I dropped Sir James's letter with the offer of the job by the desk so that he would see it was a genuine stunt. Then I wrote my letter to Mr Carter and rang up Sir James. Taking him into my confidence would be the best thing either way, so I told him everything except where I believed the papers to be hidden. The way he helped me to get on the track of Tuppence and Annette almost disarmed me, but not quite. I kept my mind open between the two of them. And then I got a bogus note from Tuppence – and then I knew!'

'But how?'

Tommy took the note in question from his pocket and passed it round the table.

'It's her handwriting all right, but I knew it wasn't from her because of the signature. She'd never spell her name "Twopence", but anyone who'd never seen it written might quite easily do so. Julius *had* seen it – he showed me a note of hers to him once – but *Sir James hadn't*! After that everything was plain sailing. I sent off Albert post-haste to Mr Carter. I pretended to go away, but doubled back again. When Julius came bursting up in his car, I felt it wasn't part of Mr Brown's plan – and that there would probably be trouble. Unless Sir James was actually caught in the act, so to speak, I knew Mr Carter would never believe it of him on my bare word –'

'I didn't,' interposed Mr Carter ruefully.

'That's why I sent the girls off to Sir James. I was sure they'd fetch up at the house in Soho sooner or later. I threatened Julius with the revolver, because I wanted Tuppence to repeat that to Sir James, so that he wouldn't worry about us. The moment the girls were out of sight I told Julius to drive like hell for London, and as we went along I told him the whole story. We got to the Soho house in plenty of time and met Mr Carter outside. After arranging things with him we went in and hid behind the curtain in the recess. The policemen had orders to say, if they were asked, that no one had gone into the house. That's all.'

And Tommy came to an abrupt halt.

There was silence for a moment.

'By the way,' said Julius suddenly, 'you're all wrong about that photograph of Jane. It *was* taken from me, but I found it again.'

'Where?' cried Tuppence.

'In that little safe on the wall in Mrs Vandermeyer's bedroom.'

'I knew you found something,' said Tuppence reproachfully. 'To tell you the truth, that's what started me off suspecting you. Why didn't you say?'

'I guess I was a mite suspicious too. It had been got away from me once, and I determined I wouldn't let on I'd got it until a photographer had made a dozen copies of it!'

'We all kept back something or other,' said Tuppence thoughtfully. 'I suppose secret service work makes you like that!'

In the pause that ensued, Mr Carter took from his pocket a small shabby brown book.

'Beresford has just said that I would not have believed Sir James Peel Edgerton to be guilty unless, so to speak, he was caught in the act. That is so. Indeed, not until I read the entries in this little book could I bring myself fully to credit the amazing truth. This book will pass into the possession of Scotland Yard, but it will never be publicly exhibited. Sir James's long association with the law would make it undesir-able. But to you, who know the truth, I propose to read certain passages which will throw some light on the extraordinary mentality of this great man.'

He opened the book, and turned the thin pages.

'. . . It is madness to keep this book. I know that. It is documentary evidence against me. But I have never shrunk from taking risks. And I feel an urgent need for self-expression . . . The book will only be taken from my dead body . . .

'. . . From an early age I realized that I had exceptional abilities. Only a fool underestimates his capabilities. My brain power was greatly above the average. I know that I was born to succeed. My appearance was the only thing against me. I was quiet and insignificant – utterly nondescript . . .

'. . . When I was a boy I heard a famous murder trial. I was deeply impressed by the power and eloquence of the coun-sel for the defence. For the first time I entertained the idea of taking my talents to that particular market . . . Then I studied the criminal in the dock . . . The man was a fool – he had been incredibly, unbelievably stupid. Even the eloquence of his counsel was hardly likely to save him . . . I felt an immeasurable contempt for him . . . Then it occurred to me that the criminal standard was a low one. It was the wastrels, the failures, the general riffraff of civilization who drifted into crime . . . Strange that men of brains had never realized its extraordinary opportunities . . . I played with the idea . . . What a magnificent field – what unlimited possibilities! It made my brain reel . . .

'. . . I read standard works on crime and criminals. They all confirmed my opinion. Degeneracy, disease – never the deliberate embracing of a career by a far-seeing man. Then I considered. Supposing my utmost ambitions were realized – that I was called to the bar, and rose to the height of my profession? That I entered politics – say, even, that I became

Prime Minister of England? What then? Was that power? Hampered at every turn by my colleagues, fettered by the democratic system of which I should be the mere figurehead! No – the power I dreamed of was absolute! An autocrat! A dictator! And such power could only be obtained by working outside the law. To play on the weaknesses of human nature, then on the weaknesses of nations – to get together and control a vast organization, and finally to overthrow the existing order, and rule! The thought intoxicated me . . .

'. . . I saw that I must lead two lives. A man like myself is bound to attract notice. I must have a successful career which would mask my true activities . . . Also I must cultivate a personality. I modelled myself upon famous KCs. I reproduced their mannerisms, their magnetism. If I had chosen to be an actor, I should have been the greatest actor living! No disguises – no grease paint – no false beards! Personality! I put it on like a glove! When I shed it, I was myself, quiet, unobtrusive, a man like every other man. I called myself Mr Brown. There are hundreds of men called Brown – there are hundreds of men looking just like me . . .

'. . . I succeeded in my false career. I was bound to succeed. I shall succeed in the other. A man like me cannot fail . . .

'. . . I have been reading a life of Napoleon. He and I have much in common . . .

'. . . I make a practice of defending criminals. A man should look after his own people . . .

'. . . Once or twice I have felt afraid. The first time was in Italy. There was a dinner given. Professor D—, the great alienist, was present. The talk fell on insanity. He said, "A great many men are mad, and no one knows it. They do not know it themselves." I do not understand why he looked at me when he said that. His glance was strange . . . I did not like it . . .

'. . . The war has disturbed me . . . I thought it would further my plans. The Germans are so efficient. Their spy system, too, was excellent. The streets are full of these boys in khaki. All empty-headed young fools . . . Yet I do not know . . . They won the war . . . It disturbs me . . .

'. . . My plans are going well . . . A girl butted in – I do not think she really knew anything . . . But we must give up the Esthonia . . . No risks now . . .

'. . . All goes well. The loss of memory is vexing. It cannot be a fake. No girl could deceive ME! . . .

'. . . The 29th . . . That is very soon . . .' Mr Carter paused.

'I will not read the details of the *coup* that was planned. But there are just two small entries that refer to the three of you. In the light of what happened they are interesting.

'. . . By inducing the girl to come to me of her own accord, I have succeeded in disarming her. But she has intuitive flashes that might be dangerous . . . She must be got out of the way . . . I can do nothing with the American. He suspects and dislikes me. But he cannot know. I fancy my armour is impregnable . . . Sometimes I fear I have underestimated the other boy. He is not clever, but it is hard to blind his eyes to facts . . .'

Mr Carter shut the book.

'A great man,' he said. 'Genius, or insanity, who can say?'

There was silence.

Then Mr Carter rose to his feet.

'I will give you a toast. The Joint Venture which has so amply justified itself by success!'

It was drunk with acclamation.

'There's something more we want to hear,' continued Mr Carter. He looked at the American Ambassador. 'I speak for you also, I know. We'll ask Miss Jane Finn to tell us the story that only Miss Tuppence has heard so far – but before we do so we'll drink her health. The health of one of the bravest of America's daughters, to whom is due the thanks and gratitude of two great countries!'

CHAPTER XXVIII

And After

'That was a mighty good toast, Jane,' said Mr Hersheimmer, as he and his cousin were being driven back in the Rolls-Royce to the Ritz.

'The one to the joint venture?'

'No – the one to you. There isn't another girl in the world who could have carried it though as you did. You were just wonderful!'

Jane shook her head.

'I don't feel wonderful. At heart I'm just tired and lonesome – and longing for my own country.'

'That brings me to something I wanted to say. I heard the Ambassador telling you his wife hoped you would come to them at the Embassy right away. That's good enough, but I've got another plan. Jane – I want you to marry me! Don't get scared and say no at once. You can't love me right away, of course, that's impossible. But I've loved you from the very moment I set eyes on your photo – and now I've seen you I'm simply crazy about you! If you'll only marry me, I won't worry you any – you shall take your own time. Maybe you'll never come to love me, and if that's the case I'll manage to set you free. But I want the right to look after you, and take care of you.'

'That's what I want,' said the girl wistfully. 'Someone who'll be good to me. Oh, you don't know how lonesome I feel!'

'Sure thing I do. Then I guess that's all fixed up, and I'll see the archbishop about a special licence tomorrow morning.'

'Oh, Julius!'

'Well, I don't want to hustle you any, Jane, but there's no

sense in waiting about. Don't be scared – I shan't expect you to love me all at once.'

But a small hand was slipped into his.

'I love you now, Julius,' said Jane Finn. 'I loved you that first moment in the car when the bullet grazed your cheek . . .'

Five minutes later Jane murmured softly:

'I don't know London very well, Julius, but is it such a very long way from the Savoy to the Ritz?'

'It depends how you go,' explained Julius unblushingly. 'We're going by way of Regent's Park!'

'Oh, Julius – what will the chauffeur think?'

'At the wages I pay him, he knows better than to do any independent thinking. Why, Jane, the only reason I had the supper at the Savoy was so that I could drive you home. I didn't see how I was ever going to get hold of you alone. You and Tuppence have been sticking together like Siamese twins. I guess another day of it would have driven me and Beresford stark staring mad!'

'Oh. Is he –?'

'Of course he is. Head over ears.'

'I thought so,' said Jane thoughtfully.

'Why?'

'From all the things Tuppence didn't say!'

'There you have me beat,' said Mr Hersheimmer.

But Jane only laughed.

In the meantime, the Young Adventurers were sitting bolt upright, very stiff and ill at ease, in a taxi which, with a singular lack of originality, was also returning to the Ritz via Regent's Park.

A terrible constraint seemed to have settled down between them. Without quite knowing what had happened, everything seemed changed. They were tongue-tied – paralysed. All the old *camaraderie* was gone.

Tuppence could think of nothing to say.

Tommy was equally afflicted.

They sat very straight and forbore to look at each other.

At last Tuppence made a desperate effort.

'Rather fun, wasn't it?'

'Rather.'

Another silence.

'I like Julius,' essayed Tuppence again.

Tommy was suddenly galvanized into life.

'You're not going to marry him, do you hear?' he said dictatorially. 'I forbid it.'

'Oh!' said Tuppence meekly.

'Absolutely, you understand.'

'He doesn't want to marry me – he really only asked me out of kindness.'

'That's not very likely,' scoffed Tommy.

'It's quite true. He's head over ears in love with Jane. I expect he's proposing to her now.'

'She'll do for him very nicely,' said Tommy condescendingly.

'Don't you think she's the most lovely creature you've ever seen?'

'Oh, I dare say.'

'But I suppose you prefer sterling worth,' said Tuppence demurely.

'I – oh, dash it all, Tuppence, you know!'

'I like your uncle, Tommy,' said Tuppence, hastily creating a diversion. 'By the way, what are you going to do, accept Mr Carter's offer of a Government job, or accept Julius's invitation and take a richly remunerated post in America on his ranch?'

'I shall stick to the old ship, I think, though it's awfully good of Hersheimmer. But I feel you'd be more at home in London.'

'I don't see where I come in.'

'I do,' said Tommy positively.

Tuppence stole a glance at him sideways.

'There's the money, too,' she observed thoughtfully.

'What money?'

'We're going to get a cheque each. Mr Carter told me so.'

'Did you ask how much?' inquired Tommy sarcastically.

'Yes,' said Tuppence triumphantly. 'But I shan't tell you.'

'Tuppence, you are the limit!'

'It has been fun, hasn't it, Tommy? I do hope we shall have lots more adventures.'

'You're insatiable, Tuppence. I've had quite enough adventures for the present.'

'Well, shopping is almost as good,' said Tuppence dreamily. 'Thinking of buying old furniture, and bright carpets, and futurist silk curtains, and a polished dining-table, and a divan with lots of cushions –'

'Hold hard,' said Tommy. 'What's all this for?'

'Possibly a house – but I think a flat.'

'Whose flat?'

'You think I mind saying it, but I don't in the least! *Ours*, so there!'

'You darling!' cried Tommy, his arms tightly round her. 'I was determined to make you say it. I owe you something for the relentless way you've squashed me whenever I've tried to be sentimental.'

Tuppence raised her face to his. The taxi proceeded on its course round the north side of Regent's Park.

'You haven't really proposed now,' pointed out Tuppence. 'Not what our grandmothers would call a proposal. But after listening to a rotten one like Julius's, I'm inclined to let you off.'

'You won't be able to get out of marrying me, so don't you think it.'

'What fun it will be,' responded Tuppence. 'Marriage is called all sorts of things, a haven, a refuge, and a crowning glory, and a state of bondage, and lots more. But do you know what I think it is?'

'What?'

'A sport!'

'And a damned good sport too,' said Tommy.

Postscript

It was Ashfield, the house in Torquay where she was born and spent her childhood, that made Agatha Christie decide to resume her writing and complete her second detective novel. After the crash of H.B. Chaflin & Co. in New York, the legal firm of which Agatha's grandfather had been a partner, Agatha's mother was struggling financially to keep on Ashfield. Agatha regretted that she was unable to contribute her small income towards the upkeep of Ashfield, as her sister Madge did. When she confessed as much to Archie he advised her to write another book. Agatha complained that The Mysterious Affair at Styles, *though it had sold 2,000 copies, had earned her a mere £25, which was not bad at that time for a detective story by an unknown author. Archie explained that a second book would surely be more successful. This time Agatha began to consider it . . .*

But what should her second book be about? That question was solved one day when she was having tea in an ABC tea room and overheard a conversation in which two people were talking at a table nearby, discussing somebody called Jane Fish. Christie was interested in the name which struck her as 'most entertaining': Jane Fish, or perhaps even better, Jane Finn. Christie settled for Jane Finn – and started writing straight away. She only needed to find the rest of the characters.

The struggle of the young people who served in the War and who, coming out of the Services, were unemployed, touched Christie and provided inspiration for two characters: a young girl who had been in the VAD (Volunteer Aid Detachment) – a group that provided help for the wounded and of which Christie herself had been a member – and a young man who, like Archie, had served in the Flying Corps. Tommy and Tuppence Beresford* were born. In their desperate search for a job,

---

* *More precisely, Tommy Beresford and Prudence Cowley, named Tuppence.*

they would become entangled in an espionage story linked to the enigmatic Jane Finn.

'This would be a spy book, a thriller, not a detective story. I liked the idea – it was a change after the detective work involved in The Mysterious Affair at Styles. So I started writing, in a sketchy kind of way. It was fun, on the whole, and much easier to write than a detective story, as thrillers always are.'

First entitled The Joyful Venture, *then* The Young Adventurers, *it finally became* The Secret Adversary. *Christie's editor John Lane, who did not like it very much since it was so different from her first book, nevertheless decided to publish it.*

The Secret Adversary, *like* The Mysterious Affair at Styles, *was again serialized in the* Weekly Times, *but sold much better. It earned Agatha Christie £50, which was encouraging – though 'not encouraging enough to make me think that I had as yet adopted anything so grand as a profession'.*

Agatha Christie remained particularly attached to the adventurous pair and it is easy to see in Tommy and Tuppence an idealized version of Agatha and Archie. Tommy and Tuppence continued to feature in Christie's novels throughout her career, appearing as late as 1973 in Postern of Fate.

MURDER ON
THE LINKS

CHAPTER I

A Fellow-Traveller

I believe that a well-known anecdote exists to the effect that a young writer, determined to make the commencement of his story forcible and original enough to catch and rivet the attention of the most blasé of editors, penned the following sentence:

'"Hell!" said the Duchess.'

Strangely enough, this tale of mine opens in much the same fashion. Only the lady who gave utterance to the exclamation was not a duchess.

It was a day in early June. I had been transacting some business in Paris and was returning by the morning service to London, where I was still sharing rooms with my old friend, the Belgian ex-detective, Hercule Poirot.

The Calais express was singularly empty – in fact, my own compartment held only one other traveller. I had made a somewhat hurried departure from the hotel and was busy assuring myself that I had duly collected all my traps, when the train started. Up till then I had hardly noticed my companion, but I was now violently recalled to the fact of her existence. Jumping up from her seat, she let down the window and stuck her head out, withdrawing it a moment later with the brief and forcible ejaculation 'Hell!'

Now I am old-fashioned. A woman, I consider, should be womanly. I have no patience with the modern neurotic girl who jazzes from morning to night, smokes like a chimney, and uses language which would make a Billingsgate fishwoman blush!

I looked up, frowning slightly, into a pretty, impudent face, surmounted by a rakish little red hat. A thick cluster of black curls hid each ear. I judged that she was little more than seventeen, but her face was covered with powder, and her lips were quite impossibly scarlet.

Nothing abashed, she returned my glance, and executed an expressive grimace.

'Dear me, we've shocked the kind gentleman!' she observed to an imaginary audience. 'I apologize for my language! Most unladylike, and all that, but, oh, Lord, there's reason enough for it! Do you know I've lost my only sister?'

'Really?' I said politely. 'How unfortunate.'

'He disapproves!' remarked the lady. 'He disapproves utterly – of me, and my sister – which last is unfair, because he hasn't seen her!'

I opened my mouth, but she forestalled me.

'Say no more! Nobody loves me! I shall go into the garden and eat worms! Boohoo. I am crushed!' ·

She buried herself behind a large comic French paper. In a minute or two I saw her eyes stealthily peeping at me over the top. In spite of myself I could not help smiling, and in a minute she had tossed the paper aside, and had burst into a merry peal of laughter.

'I knew you weren't such a mutt as you looked,' she cried.

Her laughter was so infectious that I could not help joining in, though I hardly cared for the word 'mutt'.

'There! Now we're friends!' declared the minx. 'Say you're sorry about my sister –'

'I am desolated!'

'That's a good boy!'

'Let me finish. I was going to add that, although I am desolated, I can manage to put up with her absence very well.' I made a little bow.

But this most unaccountable of damsels frowned and shook her head.

'Cut it out. I prefer the "dignified disapproval" stunt. Oh, your face! "Not one of us", it said. And you were right there – though, mind you, it's pretty hard to tell nowadays. It's not everyone who can distinguish between a demi and a duchess.

There now, I believe I've shocked you again! You've been dug out of the backwoods, you have. Not that I mind that. We could do with a few more of your sort. I just hate a fellow who gets fresh. It makes me mad.'

She shook her head vigorously.

'What are you like when you're mad?' I inquired with a smile.

'A regular little devil! Don't care what I say, or what I do, either! I nearly did a chap in once. Yes, really. He'd have deserved it too.'

'Well,' I begged, 'don't get mad with me.'

'I shan't. I like you – did the first moment I set eyes on you. But you looked so disapproving that I never thought we should make friends.'

'Well, we have. Tell me something about yourself.'

'I'm an actress. No – not the kind you're thinking of. I've been on the boards since I was a kid of six – tumbling.'

'I beg your pardon,' I said, puzzled.

'Haven't you ever seen child acrobats?'

'Oh, I understand!'

'I'm American born, but I've spent most of my life in England. We've got a new show now –'

'We?'

'My sister and I. Sort of song and dance, and a bit of patter, and a dash of the old business thrown in. It's quite a new idea, and it hits them every time. There's going to be money in it –'

My new acquaintance leaned forward, and discoursed volubly, a great many of her terms being quite unintelligible to me. Yet I found myself evincing an increasing interest in her. She seemed such a curious mixture of child and woman. Though perfectly worldly-wise, and able, as she expressed it, to take care of herself, there was yet something curiously ingenuous in her single-minded attitude towards life, and her wholehearted determination to 'make good'.

We passed through Amiens. The name awakened many memories. My companion seemed to have an intuitive knowledge of what was in my mind.

'Thinking of the War?'

I nodded.

'You were through it, I suppose?'

'Pretty well. I was wounded once, and after the Somme they invalided me out altogether. I'm a sort of private secretary now to an MP.'

'My! That's brainy!'

'No, it isn't. There's really awfully little to do. Usually a couple of hours every day sees me through. It's dull work too. In fact, I don't know what I should do if I hadn't got something to fall back upon.'

'Don't say you collect bugs!'

'No. I share rooms with a very interesting man. He's a Belgian – an ex-detective. He's set up as a private detective in London, and he's doing extraordinarily well. He's really a very marvellous little man. Time and again he has proved to be right where the official police have failed.'

My companion listened with widening eyes.

'Isn't that interesting now? I just adore crime. I go to all the mysteries on the movies. And when there's a murder on I just devour the papers.'

'Do you remember the Styles Case?' I asked.

'Let me see, was that the old lady who was poisoned? Somewhere down in Essex?'

I nodded.

'That was Poirot's first big case. Undoubtedly, but for him the murderer would have escaped scot-free. It was a most wonderful bit of detective work.'

Warming to my subject, I ran over the heads of the affair, working up to the triumphant and unexpected dénouement.

The girl listened spellbound. In fact, we were so absorbed that the train drew into Calais station before we realized it.

I secured a couple of porters, and we alighted on the platform. My companion held out her hand.

'Goodbye, and I'll mind my language better in future.'

'Oh, but surely you'll let me look after you on the boat?'

'Mayn't be on the boat. I've got to see whether that sister

of mine got aboard after all anywhere. But thanks, all the same.'

'Oh, but we're going to meet again, surely? Aren't you even going to tell me your name?' I cried, as she turned away.

She looked over her shoulder.

'Cinderella,' she said, and laughed.

But little did I think when and how I should see Cinderella again.

CHAPTER II

An Appeal for Help

It was five minutes past nine when I entered our joint sitting-room for breakfast on the following morning. My friend Poirot, exact to the minute as usual, was just tapping the shell of his second egg.

He beamed upon me as I entered.

'You have slept well, yes? You have recovered from the crossing so terrible? It is a marvel, almost you are exact this morning. *Pardon*, but your tie is not symmetrical. Permit that I rearrange him.'

Elsewhere, I have described Hercule Poirot. An extraordinary little man! Height, five feet four inches, egg-shaped head carried a little to one side, eyes that shone green when he was excited, stiff military moustache, air of dignity immense! He was neat and dandified in appearance. For neatness of any kind he had an absolute passion. To see an ornament set crookedly, or a speck of dust, or a slight disarray in one's attire, was torture to the little man until he could ease his feelings by remedying the matter. 'Order' and 'Method' were his gods. He had a certain disdain for tangible evidence, such as footprints and cigarette ash, and would maintain that, taken by themselves, they would never enable a detective to solve a problem. Then he would tap his egg-shaped head with absurd complacency, and remark with great satisfaction: 'The true work, it is done from *within. The little grey cells* – remember always the little grey cells, *mon ami.*'

I slipped into my seat, and remarked idly, in answer to Poirot's greeting, that an hour's sea passage from Calais to Dover could hardly be dignified by the epithet 'terrible'.

'Anything interesting come by the post?' I asked.

Poirot shook his head with a dissatisfied air.

'I have not yet examined my letters, but nothing of interest arrives nowadays. The great criminals, the criminals of method, they do not exist.'

He shook his head despondently, and I roared with laughter.

'Cheer up, Poirot, the luck will change. Open your letters. For all you know, there may be a great case looming on the horizon.'

Poirot smiled, and taking up the neat little letter opener with which he opened his correspondence he slit the tops of the several envelopes that lay by his plate.

'A bill. Another bill. It is that I grow extravagant in my old age. Aha! a note from Japp.'

'Yes?' I pricked up my ears. The Scotland Yard Inspector had more than once introduced us to an interesting case.

'He merely thanks me (in his fashion) for a little point in the Aberystwyth Case on which I was able to set him right. I am delighted to have been of service to him.'

Poirot continued to read his correspondence placidly.

'A suggestion that I should give a lecture to our local Boy Scouts. The Countess of Forfanock will be obliged if I will call and see her. Another lap-dog without doubt! And now for the last. Ah –'

I looked up, quick to notice the change of tone. Poirot was reading attentively. In a minute he tossed the sheet over to me.

'This is out of the ordinary, *mon ami*. Read for yourself.'

The letter was written on a foreign type of paper, in a bold characteristic hand:

> VILLA GENEVIÈVE,
> MERLINVILLE-SUR-MER,
> FRANCE

> Dear Sir, – I am in need of the services of a detective and, for reasons which I will give you later, do not wish to call in the official police. I have heard of you from several

quarters, and all reports go to show that you are not only a man of decided ability, but one who also knows how to be discreet. I do not wish to trust details to the post, but, on account of a secret I possess, I go in daily fear of my life. I am convinced that the danger is imminent, and therefore I beg that you will lose no time in crossing to France. I will send a car to meet you at Calais, if you will wire me when you are arriving. I shall be obliged if you will drop all cases you have on hand, and devote yourself solely to my interests. I am prepared to pay any compensation necessary. I shall probably need your services for a considerable period of time, as it may be necessary for you to go out to Santiago, where I spent several years of my life. I shall be content for you to name your own fee.

Assuring you once more that the matter is *urgent*.

Yours faithfully,
P. T. Renauld

Below the signature was a hastily scrawled line, almost illegible:

'For God's sake, come!'

I handed the letter back with quickened pulses.

'At last!' I said. 'Here is something distinctly out of the ordinary.'

'Yes, indeed,' said Poirot meditatively.

'You will go of course,' I continued.

Poirot nodded. He was thinking deeply. Finally he seemed to make up his mind, and glanced up at the clock. His face was very grave.

'See you, my friend, there is no time to lose. The Continental express leaves Victoria at 11 o'clock. Do not agitate yourself. There is plenty of time. We can allow ten minutes for discussion. You accompany me, *n'est-ce pas?*'

'Well –'

'You told me yourself that your employer needed you not for the next few weeks.'

'Oh, that's all right. But this Mr Renauld hints strongly that his business is private.'

'Ta-ta-ta! I will manage M. Renauld. By the way, I seem to know the name?'

'There's a well-known South American millionaire fellow. His name's Renauld. I don't know whether it could be the same.'

'But without doubt. That explains the mention of Santiago. Santiago is in Chile, and Chile it is in South America! Ah; but we progress finely! You remarked the postscript? How did it strike you?'

I considered.

'Clearly he wrote the letter keeping himself well in hand, but at the end his self-control snapped and, on the impulse of the moment, he scrawled those four desperate words.'

But my friend shook his head energetically.

'You are in error. See you not that while the ink of the signature is nearly black, that of the postscript is quite pale?'

'Well?' I said, puzzled.

'*Mon Dieu, mon ami*, but use your little grey cells. Is it not obvious? Mr Renault wrote his letter. Without blotting it, he re-read it carefully. Then, not on impulse, but deliberately, he added those last words, and blotted the sheet.'

'But why?'

'*Parbleu!* so that it should produce the effect upon me that it has upon you.'

'What?'

'*Mais oui* – to make sure of my coming! He re-read the letter and was dissatisfied. It was not strong enough!'

He paused, and then added softly, his eyes shining with that green light that always betokened inward excitement:

'And so, *mon ami*, since that postscript was added, not on impulse, but soberly, in cold blood, the urgency is very great, and we must reach him as soon as possible.'

'Merlinville,' I murmured thoughtfully. 'I've heard of it, I think.'

Poirot nodded.

'It is a quiet little place – but chic! It lies about midway between Boulogne and Calais. Mr Renauld has a house in England, I suppose?'

'Yes, in Rutland Gate, as far as I remember. Also a big place in the country, somewhere in Hertfordshire. But I really know very little about him, he doesn't do much in a social way. I believe he has large South American interests in the City, and has spent most of his life out in Chile and the Argentine.'

'Well, we shall hear all details from the man himself. Come, let us pack. A small suitcase each, and then a taxi to Victoria.'

Eleven o'clock saw our departure from Victoria on our way to Dover. Before starting Poirot had dispatched a telegram to Mr Renauld giving the time of our arrival at Calais.

On the boat, I knew better than to disturb my friend's solitude. The weather was gorgeous, and the sea as smooth as the proverbial mill-pond, so I was hardly surprised when a smiling Poirot joined me on disembarking at Calais. A disappointment was in store for us, as no car had been sent to meet us, but Poirot put this down to his telegram having been delayed in transit.

'We will hire a car,' he said cheerfully. And a few minutes later saw us creaking and jolting along, in the most ramshackle of automobiles that ever plied for hire, in the direction of Merlinville.

My spirits were at their highest, but my little friend was observing me gravely.

'You are what the Scotch people call "fey", Hastings. It presages disaster.'

'Nonsense. At any rate, you do not share my feelings.'

'No, but I am afraid.'

'Afraid of what?'

'I do not know. But I have a premonition – a *je ne sais quoi!*'

He spoke so gravely that I was impressed in spite of myself.

'I have a feeling,' he said slowly, 'that this is going to be a big affair – a long, troublesome problem that will not be easy to work out.'

I would have questioned him further, but we were just coming into the little town of Merlinville, and we slowed up to inquire the way to the Villa Geneviève.

'Straight on, monsieur, through the town. The Villa Geneviève is about half a mile the other side. You cannot miss it. A big villa, overlooking the sea.'

We thanked our informant, and drove on, leaving the town behind. A fork in the road brought us to a second halt. A peasant was trudging towards us, and we waited for him to come up to us in order to ask the way again. There was a tiny villa standing right by the road, but it was too small and dilapidated to be the one we wanted. As we waited, the gate of it swung open and a girl came out.

The peasant was passing us now, and the driver leaned forward from his seat and asked for direction.

'The Villa Geneviève? Just a few steps up this road to the right, monsieur. You could see it if it were not for the curve.'

The chauffeur thanked him, and started the car again. My eyes were fascinated by the girl who still stood, with one hand on the gate, watching us. I am an admirer of beauty, and here was one whom nobody could have passed without remark. Very tall, with the proportions of a young goddess, her uncovered golden head gleaming in the sunlight, I swore to myself that she was one of the most beautiful girls I had ever seen. As we swung up the rough road, I turned my head to look after her.

'By Jove, Poirot,' I exclaimed, 'did you see that young goddess?'

Poirot raised his eyebrows.

'*Ça commence!*' he murmured. 'Already you have seen a goddess!'

'But, hang it all, wasn't she?'

'Possibly, I did not remark the fact.'

'Surely you noticed her?'

'*Mon ami*, two people rarely see the same thing. You, for instance, saw a goddess. I –' He hesitated.

'Yes?'

'I saw only a girl with anxious eyes,' said Poirot gravely.

But at that moment we drew up at a big green gate, and, simultaneously, we both uttered an exclamation. Before it stood an imposing *sergent de ville*. He held up his hand to bar our way.

'You cannot pass, messieurs.'

'But we wish to see Mr Renauld,' I cried. 'We have an appointment. This is his villa, isn't it?'

'Yes, monsieur, but –'

Poirot leaned forward.

'But what?'

'Monsieur Renauld was murdered this morning.'

CHAPTER III

At the Villa Geneviève

In a moment Poirot had leapt from the car, his eyes blazing with excitement.

'What is that you say? Murdered? When? How?'

The *sergent de ville* drew himself up.

'I cannot answer any questions, monsieur.'

'True. I comprehend.' Poirot reflected for a minute. 'The Commissary of Police, he is without doubt within?'

'Yes, monsieur.'

Poirot took out a card, and scribbled a few words on it.

'*Voilà!* Will you have the goodness to see that this card is sent in to the commissary at once?'

The man took it and, turning his head over his shoulder, whistled. In a few seconds a comrade joined him, and was handed Poirot's message. There was a wait of some minutes, and then a short, stout man with a huge moustache came bustling down to the gate. The *sergent de ville* saluted and stood aside.

'My dear Monsieur Poirot,' cried the newcomer, 'I am delighted to see you. Your arrival is most opportune.'

Poirot's face had lighted up.

'Monsieur Bex! This is indeed a pleasure.' He turned to me. 'This is an English friend of mine, Captain Hastings – Monsieur Lucien Bex.'

The commissary and I bowed to each other ceremoniously, and M. Bex turned once more to Poirot.

'*Mon vieux*, I have not seen you since 1909, that time in Ostend. You have information to give which may assist us?'

'Possibly you know it already. You were aware that I had been sent for?'

'No. By whom?'

'The dead man. It seems that he knew an attempt was going to be made on his life. Unfortunately he sent for me too late.'

'*Sacré tonnerre!*' ejaculated the Frenchman. 'So he foresaw his own murder. That upsets our theories considerably! But come inside.'

He held the gate open, and we commenced walking towards the house. M. Bex continued to talk:

'The examining magistrate, Monsieur Hautet, must hear of this at once. He has just finished examining the scene of the crime and is about to begin his interrogations.'

'When was the crime committed?' asked Poirot.

'The body was discovered this morning about nine o'clock. Madame Renauld's evidence and that of the doctors goes to show that death must have occurred about 2 a.m. But enter, I pray of you.'

We had arrived at the steps which led up to the front door of the villa. In the hall another *sergent de ville* was sitting. He rose at sight of the commissary.

'Where is Monsieur Hautet now?' inquired the latter.

'In the *salon*, monsieur.'

M. Bex opened a door to the left of the hall, and we passed in. M. Hautet and his clerk were sitting at a big round table. They looked up as we entered. The commissary introduced us, and explained our presence.

M. Hautet, the Juge d'Instruction, was a tall gaunt man, with piercing dark eyes, and a neatly cut grey beard, which he had a habit of caressing as he talked. Standing by the mantelpiece was an elderly man, with slightly stooping shoulders, who was introduced to us as Dr Durand.

'Most extraordinary,' remarked M. Hautet as the commissary finished speaking. 'You have the letter here, monsieur?'

Poirot handed it to him, and the magistrate read it.

'H'm! He speaks of a secret. What a pity he was not more explicit. We are much indebted to you, Monsieur Poirot. I hope you will do us the honour of assisting us in our investigations. Or are you obliged to return to London?'

'Monsieur le juge, I propose to remain. I did not arrive in time to prevent my client's death, but I feel myself bound in honour to discover the assassin.'

The magistrate bowed.

'These sentiments do you honour. Also, without doubt, Madame Renauld will wish to retain your services. We are expecting M. Giraud from the Sûreté in Paris any moment, and I am sure that you and he will be able to give each other mutual assistance in your investigations. In the meantime, I hope that you will do me the honour to be present at my interrogations, and I need hardly say that if there is any assistance you require it is at your disposal.'

'I thank you, monsieur. You will comprehend that at present I am completely in the dark. I know nothing whatever.'

M. Hautet nodded to the commissary, and the latter took up the tale:

'This morning, the old servant Françoise, on descending to start her work, found the front door ajar. Feeling a momentary alarm as to burglars, she looked into the dining-room, but seeing the silver was safe she thought no more about it, concluding that her master had, without doubt, risen early, and gone for a stroll.'

'Pardon, monsieur, for interrupting, but was that a common practice of his?'

'No, it was not, but old Françoise has the common idea as regards the English – that they are mad, and liable to do the most unaccountable things at any moment! Going to call her mistress as usual, a young maid, Léonie, was horrified to discover her gagged and bound, and almost at the same moment news was brought that Monsieur Renauld's body had been discovered, stone dead, stabbed in the back.'

'Where?'

'That is one of the most extraordinary features of the case. Monsieur Poirot, the body was lying face downwards, *in an open grave.*'

'What?'

'Yes. The pit was freshly dug – just a few yards outside the boundary of the villa grounds.'

'And it had been dead – how long?'

Dr Durand answered this.

'I examined the body this morning at ten o'clock. Death must have taken place at least seven, and possibly ten hours previously.'

'H'm! that fixes it at between midnight and 3 a.m.'

'Exactly, and Mrs Renauld's evidence places it at after 2 a.m, which narrows the field still farther. Death must have been instantaneous, and naturally could not have been self-inflicted.'

Poirot nodded, and the commissary resumed:

'Madame Renauld was hastily freed from the cords that bound her by the horrified servants. She was in a terrible condition of weakness, almost unconscious from the pain of her bonds. It appears that two masked men entered the bedroom, gagged and bound her, while forcibly abducting her husband. This we know at second hand from the servants. On hearing the tragic news, she fell at once into an alarming state of agitation. On arrival, Dr Durand immediately prescribed a sedative, and we have not yet been able to question her. But without doubt she will awake more calm, and be equal to bearing the strain of the interrogation.'

The commissary paused.

'And the inmates of the house, monsieur?'

'There is old Françoise, the housekeeper, she lived for many years with the former owners of the Villa Geneviève. Then there are two young girls, sisters, Denise and Léonie Oulard. Their home is in Merlinville, and they come of most respectable parents. Then there is the chauffeur whom Monsieur Renauld brought over from England with him, but he is away on a holiday. Finally there are Madame Renauld and her son, Monsieur Jack Renauld. He, too, is away from home at present.'

Poirot bowed his head. M. Hautet spoke:

'Marchaud!'

The *sergent de ville* appeared.

'Bring in the woman Françoise.'

The man saluted, and disappeared. In a moment or two he returned, escorting the frightened Françoise.

'Your name is Françoise Arrichet?'

'Yes, monsieur.'

'You have been a long time in service at the Villa Geneviève?'

'Eleven years with Madame la Vicomtesse. Then when she sold the villa this spring, I consented to remain on with the English milor'. Never did I imagine –'

The magistrate cut her short.

'Without doubt, without doubt. Now, Françoise, in this matter of the front door, whose business was it to fasten it at night?'

'Mine, monsieur. Always I saw to it myself.'

'And last night?'

'I fastened it as usual.'

'You are sure of that?'

'I swear it by the blessed saints, monsieur.'

'What time would that be?'

'The same time as usual, half past ten, monsieur.'

'What about the rest of the household, had they gone up to bed?'

'Madame had retired some time before. Denise and Léonie went up with me. Monsieur was still in his study.'

'Then, if anyone unfastened the door afterwards, it must have been Monsieur Renauld himself?'

Françoise shrugged her broad shoulders.

'What should he do that for? With robbers and assassins passing every minute! A nice idea! Monsieur was not an imbecile. It is not as though he had had to let the lady out –'

The magistrate interrupted sharply:

'The lady? What lady do you mean?'

'Why, the lady who came to see him.'

'Had a lady been to see him that evening?'

'But yes, monsieur – and many other evenings as well.'

'Who was she? Did you know her?'

A rather cunning look spread over the woman's face.

'How should I know who it was?' she grumbled. 'I did not let her in last night.'

'Aha!' roared the examining magistrate, bringing his hand down with a bang on the table. 'You would trifle with the police, would you? I demand that you tell me at once the name of this woman who came to visit Monsieur Renauld in the evenings.'

'The police – the police,' grumbled Françoise. 'Never did I think that I should be mixed up with the police. But I know well enough who she was. It was Madame Daubreuil.'

The commissary uttered an exclamation, and leaned forward as though in utter astonishment.

'Madame Daubreuil – from the Villa Marguerite just down the road?'

'That is what I said, monsieur. Oh, she is a pretty one.'

The old woman tossed her head scornfully.

'Madame Daubreuil,' murmured the commissary. 'Impossible.'

'*Voilà*,' grumbled Françoise. 'That is all you get for telling the truth.'

'Not at all,' said the examining magistrate soothingly. 'We were surprised, that is all. Madame Daubreuil then, and Monsieur Renauld, they were –?' He paused delicately. 'Eh? It was that without doubt?'

'How should I know? But what will you? Monsieur, he was *milord anglais* – *très riche* – and Madame Daubreuil, she was poor, that one – and *très chic*, for all that she lives so quietly with her daughter. Not a doubt of it, she has had her history! She is no longer young, but *ma foi*! I who speak to you have seen the men's heads turn after her as she goes down the street. Besides lately, she had had more money to spend – all the town knows it. The little economies, they are at an end.' And Françoise shook her head with an air of unalterable certainty.

M. Hautet stroked his beard reflectively.

'And Madame Renauld?' he asked at length. 'How did she take this – friendship?'

Françoise shrugged her shoulders.

'She was always most amiable – most polite. One would say that she suspected nothing. But all the same, is it not so, the heart suffers, monsieur? Day by day, I have watched Madame grow paler and thinner. She was not the same woman who arrived here a month ago. Monsieur, too, has changed. He also has had his worries. One could see that he was on the brink of a crisis of the nerves. And who could wonder, with an affair conducted in such a fashion? No reticence, no discretion. *Style anglais*, without doubt!'

I bounded indignantly in my seat, but the examining magistrate was continuing his questions, undistracted by side issues.

'You say that Monsieur Renauld had not to let Madame Daubreuil out? Had she left, then?'

'Yes, monsieur. I heard them come out of the study and go to the door. Monsieur said goodnight, and shut the door after her.'

'What time was that?'

'About twenty-five minutes after ten, monsieur.'

'Do you know when Monsieur Renauld went to bed?'

'I heard him come up about ten minutes after we did. The stair creaks so that one hears everyone who goes up and down.'

'And that is all? You heard no sound of disturbance during the night?'

'Nothing whatever, monsieur.'

'Which of the servants came down the first in the morning?'

'I did, monsieur. At once I saw the door swinging open.'

'What about the other downstairs windows, were they all fastened?'

'Every one of them. There was nothing suspicious or out of place anywhere.'

'Good. Françoise, you can go.'

The old woman shuffled towards the door. On the theshold she looked back.

'I will tell you one thing, monsieur. That Madame Daubreuil she is a bad one! Oh, yes, one woman knows about another. She is a bad one, remember that.' And, shaking her head sagely, Françoise left the room.

'Léonie Oulard,' called the magistrate.

Léonie appeared dissolved in tears, and inclined to be hysterical. M. Hautet dealt with her adroitly. Her evidence was mainly concerned with the discovery of her mistress gagged and bound, of which she gave rather an exaggerated account. She, like Françoise, had heard nothing during the night.

Her sister, Denise, succeeded her. She agreed that her master had changed greatly of late.

'Every day he became more and more morose. He ate less. He was always depressed.' But Denise had her own theory. 'Without doubt it was the Mafia he had on his track! Two masked men – who else could it be? A terrible society that!'

'It is, of course, possible,' said the magistrate smoothly. 'Now, my girl, was it you who admitted Madame Daubreuil to the house last night?'

'Not *last* night, monsieur, the night before.'

'But Françoise has just told us that Madame Daubreuil was here last night?'

'No, monsieur. A lady *did* come to see Monsieur Renauld last night, but it was not Madame Daubreuil.'

Surprised, the magistrate insisted, but the girl held firm. She knew Madame Daubreuil perfectly by sight. This lady was dark also, but shorter, and much younger. Nothing could shake her statement.

'Had you ever seen this lady before?'

'Never, monsieur.' And then the girl added diffidently: 'But I think she was English.'

'English?'

'Yes, Monsieur. She asked for Monsieur Renauld in quite good French, but the accent – however slight one can always tell it. Besides, when they came out of the study they were speaking in English.'

'Did you hear what they said? Could you understand it, I mean?'

'Me, I speak the English very well,' said Denise with pride. 'The lady was speaking too fast for me to catch what she said, but I heard Monsieur's last words as he opened the door for her.' She paused, and then repeated carefully and laboriously: '"Yeas – yeas – but for Gaud's saike go nauw!"'

'Yes, yes, but for God's sake go now!' repeated the magistrate.

He dismissed Denise and, after a moment or two for consideration, recalled Françoise. To her he propounded the question as to whether she had not made a mistake in fixing the night of Madame Daubreuil's visit. Françoise, however, proved unexpectedly obstinate. It was last night that Madame Daubreuil had come. Without doubt it was she. Denise wished to make herself interesting, *voilà tout*! So she had cooked up this fine tale about a strange lady. Airing her knowledge of English, too! Probably Monsieur had never spoken that sentence in English at all, and, even if he had, it proved nothing, for Madame Daubreuil spoke English perfectly, and generally used that language when talking to Monsieur and Madame Renauld. 'You see, Monsieur Jack, the son of Monsieur, was usually here, and he spoke the French very badly.'

The magistrate did not insist. Instead, he inquired about the chauffeur, and learned that only yesterday Monsieur Renauld had declared that he was not likely to use the car, and that Masters might just as well take a holiday.

A perplexed frown was beginning to gather between Poirot's eyes.

'What is it?' I whispered.

He shook his head impatiently, and asked a question:

'Pardon, Monsieur Bex, but without doubt Monsieur Renauld could drive the car himself?'

The commissary looked over at Françoise, and the old woman replied promptly:

'No, Monsieur did not drive himself.'

Poirot's frown deepened.

'I wish you would tell me what is worrying you,' I said impatiently.

'See you not? In his letter Monsieur Renauld speaks of sending the car for me to Calais.'

'Perhaps he meant a hired car,' I suggested.

'Doubtless, that is so. But why hire a car when you have one of your own? Why choose yesterday to send away the chauffeur on a holiday – suddenly, at a moment's notice? Was it that for some reason he wanted him out of the way before we arrived?'

CHAPTER IV

The Letter Signed 'Bella'

Françoise had left the room. The magistrate was drumming thoughtfully on the table.

'Monsieur Bex,' he said at length, 'here we have directly conflicting testimony. Which are we to believe, Françoise or Denise?'

'Denise,' said the commissary decidedly. 'It was she who let the visitor in. Françoise is old and obstinate, and has evidently taken a dislike to Madame Daubreuil. Besides, our own knowledge tends to show that Renauld was entangled with another woman.'

'*Tiens!*' cried M. Hautet. 'We have forgotten to inform Monsieur Poirot of that.' He searched among the papers on the table, and finally handed the one he was in search of to my friend. 'This letter, Monsieur Poirot, we found in the pocket of the dead man's overcoat.'

Poirot took it and unfolded it. It was somewhat worn and crumpled, and was written in English in a rather unformed hand:

My Dearest One, – Why have you not written for so long? You do love me still, don't you? Your letters lately have been so different, cold, and strange, and now this long silence. It makes me afraid. If you were to stop loving me! But that's impossible – what a silly kid I am – always imagining things! But if you *did* stop loving me, I don't know what I should do – kill myself perhaps! I couldn't live without you. Sometimes I fancy another woman is coming between us. Let her look out, that's all

– and you too! I'd as soon kill you as let her have you! I mean it.

But there, I'm writing high-flown nonsense. You love me, and I love you – yes, love you, love you, love you!

> Your own adoring
> Bella

There was no address or date. Poirot handed it back with a grave face.

'And the assumption is – ?'

The examining magistrate shrugged his shoulders.

'Obviously Monsieur Renauld was entangled with this Englishwoman – Bella! He comes over here, meets Madame Daubreuil, and starts an intrigue with her. He cools off to the other, and she instantly suspects something. This letter contains a distinct threat. Monsieur Poirot, at first sight the case seemed simplicity itself. Jealousy! The fact that Monsieur Renauld was stabbed in the back seemed to point distinctly to its being a woman's crime.'

Poirot nodded.

'The stab in the back, yes – but not the grave! That was laborious work, hard work – no woman dug that grave, Monsieur. That was a man's doing.'

The commissary exclaimed excitedly:

'Yes, yes, you are right. We did not think of that.'

'As I said,' continued M. Hautet, 'at first sight the case seemed simple, but the masked men, and the letter you received from Monsieur Renauld, complicate matters. Here we seem to have an entirely different set of circumstances, with no relationship between the two. As regards the letter written to yourself, do you think it is possible that it referred in any way to this "Bella" and her threats?'

Poirot shook his head.

'Hardly. A man like Monsieur Renauld, who had led an adventurous life in out-of-the-way places, would not be likely to ask for protection against a woman.'

The examining magistrate nodded his head emphatically.

'My view exactly. Then we must look for the explanation of the letter –'

'In Santiago,' finished the commissary. 'I shall cable without delay to the police in that city, requesting full details of the murdered man's life out there, his love affairs, his business transactions, his friendships, and any enmities he may have incurred. It will be strange if, after that, we do not hold a clue to his mysterious murder.'

The commissary looked around for approval.

'Excellent!' said Poirot appreciatively.

'You have found no other letters from this Bella among Monsieur Renauld's effects?' asked Poirot.

'No. Of course one of our first proceedings was to search through his private papers in the study. We found nothing of interest, however. All seemed square and above-board. The only thing at all out of the ordinary was his will. Here it is.'

Poirot ran through the document.

'So. A legacy of a thousand pounds to Mr Stonor – who is he, by the way?'

'Monsieur Renauld's secretary. He remained in England, but was over here once or twice for a weekend.'

'And everything else left unconditionally to his beloved wife, Eloise. Simply drawn up, but perfectly legal. Witnessed by the two servants, Denise and Françoise. Nothing so very unusual about that.' He handed it back.

'Perhaps,' began Bex, 'you did not notice –'

'The date?' twinkled Poirot. 'But, yes, I noticed it. A fortnight ago. Possibly it marks his first intimation of danger. Many rich men die intestate through never considering the likelihood of their demise. But it is dangerous to draw conclusions prematurely. It points, however, to his having a real liking and fondness for his wife, in spite of his amorous intrigues.'

'Yes,' said M. Hautet doubtfully. 'But it is possibly a little unfair on his son, since it leaves him entirely dependent on his mother. If she were to marry again, and her second husband obtained an ascendancy over her, this boy might never touch a penny of his father's money.'

Poirot shrugged his shoulders.

'Man is a vain animal. Monsieur Renauld figured to himself, without doubt, that his widow would never marry again. As to the son, it may have been a wise precaution to leave the money in his mother's hands. The sons of rich men are proverbially wild.'

'It may be as you say. Now, Monsieur Poirot, you would without doubt like to visit the scene of the crime. I am sorry that the body has been removed, but of course photographs have been taken from every conceivable angle, and will be at your disposal as soon as they are available.'

'I thank you, monsieur, for all your courtesy.'

The commissary rose.

'Come with me, messieurs.'

He opened the door, and bowed ceremoniously to Poirot to precede him. Poirot, with equal politeness, drew back and bowed to the commissary.

'Monsieur.'

'Monsieur.'

At last they got out into the hall.

'That room there, it is the study, *hein*?' asked Poirot suddenly, nodding towards the door opposite.

'Yes. You would like to see it?' He threw open the door as he spoke, and we entered.

The room which M. Renauld had chosen for his own particular use was small, but furnished with great taste and comfort. A business-like writing-desk, with many pigeon-holes, stood in the window. Two large leather-covered armchairs faced the fireplace, and between them was a round table covered with the latest books and magazines.

Poirot stood a moment taking in the room, then he stepped forward, passed his hand lightly over the backs of the leather chairs, picked up a magazine from the table, and drew a finger gingerly over the surface of the oak sideboard. His face expressed complete approval.

'No dust?' I asked, with a smile.

He beamed on me, appreciative of my knowledge of his peculiarities.

'Not a particle, *mon ami*! And for once, perhaps, it is a pity.' His sharp, bird-like eyes darted here and there.

'Ah!' he remarked suddenly, with an intonation of relief. 'The hearth-rug is crooked,' and he bent down to straighten it.

Suddenly he uttered an exclamation and rose. In his hand he held a small fragment of pink paper.

'In France, as in England,' he remarked, 'the domestics omit to sweep under the mats?'

Bex took the fragment from him, and I came close to examine it.

'You recognize it – eh, Hastings?'

I shook my head, puzzled – and yet that particular shade of pink paper was very familiar.

The commissary's mental processes were quicker than mine.

'A fragment of a cheque,' he exclaimed.

The piece of paper was roughly about two inches square. On it was written in ink the word 'Duveen'.

'*Bien!*' said Bex. 'This cheque was payable to, or drawn by, someone named Duveen.'

'The former, I fancy,' said Poirot. 'For, if I am not mistaken, the handwriting is that of Monsieur Renauld.'

That was soon established, by comparing it with a memorandum from the desk.

'Dear me,' murmured the commissary, with a crestfallen air, 'I really cannot imagine how I came to overlook this.'

Poirot laughed.

'The moral of that is, always look under the mats! My friend Hastings here will tell you that anything in the least crooked is a torment to me. As soon as I saw that the hearth-rug was out of the straight, I said to myself: "*Tiens!* The legs of the chair caught it in being pushed back. Possibly there may be something beneath it which the good Françoise overlooked."'

'Françoise?'

'Or Denise, or Léonie. Whoever did this room. Since there is no dust, the room *must* have been done this morning. I reconstruct the incident like this. Yesterday, possibly last night, Monsieur Renauld drew a cheque to the order of someone named Duveen. Afterwards it was torn up, and scattered on the floor. This morning –'

But M. Bex was already pulling impatiently at the bell.

Françoise answered it. Yes, there had been a lot of pieces of paper on the floor. What had she done with them? Put them in the kitchen stove of course! What else?

With a gesture of despair, Bex dismissed her. Then, his face lightening, he ran to the desk. In a minute he was hunting through the dead man's cheque book. Then he repeated his former gesture. The last counterfoil was blank.

'Courage!' cried Poirot, clapping him on the back. 'Without doubt, Madame Renauld will be able to tell us all about this mysterious person named Duveen.'

The commissary's face cleared. 'That is true. Let us proceed.'

As we turned to leave the room, Poirot remarked casually: 'It was here that Monsieur Renauld received his guest last night, eh?'

'It was – but how did you know?'

'By *this*. I found it on the back of the leather chair.' And he held up between his finger and thumb a long black hair – a woman's hair!

M. Bex took us out by the back of the house to where there was a small shed leaning against the house. He produced a key from his pocket and unlocked it.

'The body is here. We moved it from the scene of the crime just before you arrived, as the photographers had done with it.'

He opened the door and we passed in. The murdered man lay on the ground, with a sheet over him. M. Bex dexterously whipped off the covering. Renauld was a man of medium height, slender, and lithe in figure. He looked about fifty years of age, and his dark hair was plentifully streaked with grey. He was clean-shaven with a long, thin nose, and eyes set rather close together, and his skin was deeply bronzed, as that of a man who had spent most of his life beneath tropical skies. His lips were drawn back from his teeth and an expression of absolute amazement and terror was stamped on the livid features.

'One can see by his face that he was stabbed in the back,' remarked Poirot.

Very gently, he turned the dead man over. There, between the shoulder-blades, staining the light fawn overcoat, was a round dark patch. In the middle of it there was a slit in the cloth. Poirot examined it narrowly.

'Have you any idea with what weapon the crime was committed?'

'It was left in the wound.' The commissary reached down a large glass jar. In it was a small object that looked to me more like a paper-knife than anything else. It had a black handle and a narrow shining blade. The whole thing was not more than ten inches long. Poirot tested the discoloured point gingerly with his finger-tip.

'*Ma foi!* but it is sharp! A nice easy little tool for murder!'

'Unfortunately, we could find no trace of fingerprints on it,' remarked Bex regretfully. 'The murderer must have worn gloves.'

'Of course he did,' said Poirot contemptuously. 'Even in Santiago they know enough for that. The veriest amateur of an English Mees knows it – thanks to the publicity the Bertillon system has been given in the Press. All the same, it interests me very much that there were no fingerprints. It is so amazingly simple to leave the fingerprints of someone else! And then the police are happy.' He shook his head. 'I very much fear our criminal is not a man of method – either that or he was pressed for time. But we shall see.'

He let the body fall back into its original position.

'He wore only underclothes under his overcoat, I see,' he remarked.

'Yes, the examining magistrate thinks that is rather a curious point.'

At this minute there was a tap on the door which Bex had

closed after him. He strode forward and opened it. Françoise was there. She endeavoured to peep in with ghoulish curiosity.

'Well, what is it?' demanded Bex impatiently.

'Madame. She sends a message that she is much recovered and is quite ready to receive the examining magistrate.'

'Good,' said M. Bex briskly. 'Tell Monsieur Hautet and say that we will come at once.'

Poirot lingered a moment, looking back towards the body. I thought for a moment that he was going to apostrophize it, to declare aloud his determination never to rest till he had discovered the murderer. But when he spoke, it was tamely and awkwardly, and his comment was ludicrously inappropriate to the solemnity of the moment.

'He wore his overcoat very long,' he said constrainedly.

CHAPTER V

Mrs Renauld's Story

We found M. Hautet awaiting us in the hall, and we all proceeded upstairs together, Françoise marching ahead to show
us the way. Poirot went up in a zigzag fashion which puzzled
me, until he whispered with a grimace:

'No wonder the servants heard M. Renauld mounting the
stairs, not a board of them but creaks fit to awake the dead!'

At the head of the staircase, a small passage branched off.

'The servants' quarters,' explained Bex.

We continued along a corridor, and Françoise tapped on
the last door to the right of it.

A faint voice bade us enter, and we passed into a large,
sunny apartment looking out towards the sea, which showed
blue and sparkling about a quarter of a mile distant.

On a couch, propped up with cushions, and attended by
Dr Durand, lay a tall, striking-looking woman. She was
middle-aged, and her once dark hair was now almost entirely
silvered, but the intense vitality, and strength of her personality would have made itself felt anywhere. You knew at once
that you were in the presence of what the French call *une
maîtresse femme*.

She greeted us with a dignified inclination of the head.

'Pray be seated, messieurs.'

We took chairs, and the magistrate's clerk established himself at a round table.

'I hope, madame,' began M. Hautet, 'that it will not distress
you unduly to relate to us what occurred last night?'

'Not at all, monsieur. I know the value of time, if these
scoundrelly assassins are to be caught and punished.'

'Very well, madame. It will fatigue you less, I think, if I

ask you questions and you confine yourself to answering them. At what time did you go to bed last night?'

'At half past nine, monsieur. I was tired.'

'And your husband?'

'About an hour later, I fancy.'

'Did he seem disturbed – upset in any way?'

'No, not more than usual.'

'What happened then?'

'We slept. I was awakened by a hand pressed over my mouth. I tried to scream out, but the hand prevented me. There were two men in the room. They were both masked.'

'Can you describe them at all, madame?'

'One was very tall, and had a long black beard, the other was short and stout. His beard was reddish. They both wore hats pulled down over their eyes.'

'H'm!' said the magistrate thoughtfully. 'Too much beard, I fear.'

'You mean they were false?'

'Yes, madame. But continue your story.'

'It was the short man who was holding me. He forced a gag into my mouth, and then bound me with rope hand and foot. The other man was standing over my husband. He had caught up my little dagger paper-knife from the dressing-table and was holding it with the point just over his heart. When the short man had finished with me, he joined the other, and they forced my husband to get up and accompany them into the dressing-room next door. I was nearly fainting with terror, nevertheless I listened desperately.

'They were speaking in too low a tone for me to hear what they said. But I recognized the language, a bastard Spanish such as is spoken in some parts of South America. They seemed to be demanding something from my husband, and presently they grew angry, and their voices rose a little. I think the tall man was speaking. "You know what we want?" he said. "*The secret!* Where is it?" I do not know what my husband answered, but the other replied fiercely: "You lie! We know you have it. Where are your keys?"'

'Then I heard sounds of drawers being pulled out. There is a safe on the wall of my husband's dressing-room in which he always keeps a fairly large amount of ready money. Léonie tells me this has been rifled and the money taken, but evidently what they were looking for was not there, for presently I heard the tall man, with an oath, command my husband to dress himself. Soon after that, I think some noise in the house must have disturbed them, for they hustled my husband out into my room only half dressed.'

'*Pardon*,' interrupted Poirot, 'but is there then no other egress from the dressing-room?'

'No, monsieur, there is only the communicating door into my room. They hurried my husband through, the short man in front, and the tall man behind him with the dagger still in his hand. Paul tried to break away to come to me. I saw his agonized eyes. He turned to his captors. "I must speak to her," he said. Then, coming to the side of the bed, "It is all right, Eloise," he said. "Do not be afraid. I shall return before morning." But, although he tried to make his voice confident, I could see the terror in his eyes. Then they hustled him out of the door, the tall man saying: "One sound – and you are a dead man, remember."

'After that,' continued Mrs Renauld, 'I must have fainted. The next thing I recollect is Léonie rubbing my wrists and giving me brandy.'

'Madame Renauld,' said the magistrate, 'had you any idea what it was for which the assassins were searching?'

'None whatever, monsieur.'

'Had you any knowledge that your husband feared something?'

'Yes. I had seen the change in him.'

'How long ago was that?'

Mrs Renauld reflected.

'Ten days, perhaps.'

'Not longer?'

'Possibly. I only noticed it then.'

'Did you question your husband at all as to the cause?'

'Once. He put me off evasively. Nevertheless, I was convinced that he was suffering some terrible anxiety. However, since he evidently wished to conceal the fact from me, I tried to pretend that I had noticed nothing.'

'Were you aware that he had called in the services of a detective?'

'A detective?' exclaimed Mrs Renauld, very much surprised.

'Yes, this gentleman – Monsieur Hercule Poirot.' Poirot bowed. 'He arrived today in response to a summons from your husband.' And taking the letter written by M. Renauld from his pocket he handed it to the lady.

She read it with apparently genuine astonishment.

'I had no idea of this. Evidently he was fully cognizant of the danger.'

'Now, madame, I will beg of you to be frank with me. Is there any incident in your husband's past life in South America which might throw light on his murder?'

Mrs Renauld reflected deeply, but at last shook her head.

'I can think of none. Certainly my husband had many enemies, people he had got the better of in some way or another, but I can think of no one distinctive case. I do not say there is no such incident – only that I am not aware of it.'

The examining magistrate stroked his beard disconsolately.

'And you can fix the time of this outrage?'

'Yes, I distinctly remember hearing the clock on the mantelpiece strike two.' She nodded towards an eight-day travelling clock in a leather case which stood in the centre of the chimney-piece.

Poirot rose from his seat, scrutinized the clock carefully, and nodded, satisfied.

'And here too,' exclaimed M. Bex, 'is a wristwatch, knocked off the dressing-table by the assassins, without doubt, and smashed to atoms. Little did they know it would testify against them.'

Gently he picked away the fragments of broken glass. Suddenly his face changed to one of utter stupefaction.

'*Mon Dieu!*' he ejaculated.

'What is it?'

'The hands of the watch point to seven o'clock!'

'What?' cried the examining magistrate, astonished.

But Poirot, deft as ever, took the broken trinket from the startled commissary, and held it to his ear. Then he smiled.

'The glass is broken, yes, but the watch itself is still going.'

The explanation of the mystery was greeted with a relieved smile. But the magistrate bethought him of another point.

'But surely it is not seven o'clock now?'

'No,' said Poirot gently, 'it is a few minutes after five. Possibly the watch gains, is that so, madame?'

Mrs Renauld was frowning perplexedly.

'It does gain,' she admitted. 'But I've never known it gain quite so much as that.'

With a gesture of impatience the magistrate left the matter of the watch and proceeded with his interrogatory.

'Madame, the front door was found ajar. It seems almost certain that the murderers entered that way, yet it has not been forced at all. Can you suggest any explanation?'

'Possibly my husband went out for a stroll the last thing, and forgot to latch it when he came in.'

'Is that a likely thing to happen?'

'Very. My husband was the most absent-minded of men.'

There was a slight frown on her brow as she spoke, as though this trait in the dead man's character had at times vexed her.

'There is one inference I think we might draw,' remarked the commissary suddenly. 'Since the men insisted on Monsieur Renauld dressing himself, it looks as though the place they were taking him to, the place where "the secret" was concealed, lay some distance away.'

The magistrate nodded.

'Yes, far, and yet not too far, since he spoke of being back by morning.'

'What time does the last train leave the station of Merlinville?' asked Poirot.

'11.50 one way, and 12.17 the other, but it is more probable that they had a motor waiting.'

'Of course,' agreed Poirot, looking somewhat crestfallen.

'Indeed, that might be one way of tracing them,' continued the magistrate, brightening. 'A motor containing two foreigners is quite likely to have been noticed. That is an excellent point, Monsieur Bex.'

He smiled to himself, and then, becoming grave once more, he said to Mrs Renauld:

'There is another question. Do you know anyone of the name of "Duveen"?'

'Duveen?' Mrs Renauld repeated thoughtfully. 'No, for the moment, I cannot say I do.'

'You have never heard your husband mention anyone of that name.'

'Never.'

'Do you know anyone whose Christian name is Bella?'

He watched Mrs Renauld narrowly as he spoke, seeking to surprise any signs of anger or consciousness, but she merely shook her head in quite a natural manner. He continued his questions.

'Are you aware that your husband had a visitor last night?'

Now he saw the red mount slightly in her cheeks, but she replied composedly:

'No, who was that?'

'A lady.'

'Indeed?'

But for the moment the magistrate was content to say no more. It seemed unlikely that Madame Daubreuil had any connection with the crime, and he was anxious not to upset Mrs Renauld more than necessary.

He made a sign to the commissary, and the latter replied with a nod. Then rising, he went across the room, and returned with the glass jar we had seen in the outhouse in his hand. From this he took the dagger.

'Madame,' he said gently, 'do you recognize this?'

She gave a little cry.

'Yes, that is my little dagger.' Then she saw the stained point, and she drew back, her eyes widening with horror. 'Is that – blood?'

'Yes, madame. Your husband was killed with this weapon.' He removed it hastily from sight. 'You are quite sure about its being the one that was on your dressing-table last night?'

'Oh, yes. It was a present from my son. He was in the Air Force during the war. He gave his age as older than it was.' There was a touch of the proud mother in her voice. 'This was made from a streamline aeroplane wire, and was given to me by my son as a souvenir of the war.'

'I see, madame. That brings us to another matter. Your son, where is he now? It is necessary that he should be telegraphed to without delay.'

'Jack? He is on his way to Buenos Aires.'

'What?'

'Yes. My husband telegraphed to him yesterday. He had sent him on business to Paris, but yesterday he discovered that it would be necessary for him to proceed without delay to South America. There was a boat leaving Cherbourg for Buenos Aires last night, and he wired him to catch it.'

'Have you any knowledge of what the business in Buenos Aires was?'

'No, monsieur, I know nothing of its nature, but Buenos Aires is not my son's final destination. He was going overland from there to Santiago.'

And, in unison, the magistrate and the commissary exclaimed:

'Santiago! Again Santiago!'

It was at this moment, when we were all stunned by the mention of that word, that Poirot approached Mrs Renauld. He had been standing by the window like a man lost in a dream, and I doubt if he had fully taken in what had passed. He paused by the lady's side with a bow.

'*Pardon*, madame, but may I examine your wrists?'

Though slightly surprised at the request, Mrs Renauld held them out to him. Round each of them was a cruel red mark where the cords had bitten into the flesh. As he examined them, I fancied that a momentary flicker of excitement I had seen in his eyes disappeared.

'They must cause you great pain,' he said, and once more he looked puzzled.

But the magistrate was speaking excitedly.

'Young Monsieur Renauld must be communicated with at once by wireless. It is vital that we should know anything he can tell us about this trip to Santiago.' He hesitated. 'I hoped he might have been near at hand, so that we could have saved you pain, madame.' He paused.

'You mean,' she said in a low voice, 'the identification of my husband's body?'

The magistrate bowed his head.

'I am a strong woman, monsieur. I can bear all that is required of me. I am ready – now.'

'Oh, tomorrow will be quite soon enough, I assure you –'

'I prefer to get it over,' she said in a low tone, a spasm of pain crossing her face. 'If you will be so good as to give me your arm, doctor?'

The doctor hastened forward, a cloak was thrown over Mrs Renauld's shoulders, and a slow procession went down the stairs. M. Bex hurried on ahead to open the door of the shed. In a minute or two Mrs Renauld appeared in the doorway. She was very pale, but resolute. She raised her hand to her face.

'A moment, messieurs, while I steel myself.'

She took her hand away and looked down at the dead man. Then the marvellous self-control which had upheld her so far deserted her.

'Paul!' she cried. 'Husband! Oh, God!' And pitching forward she fell unconscious to the ground.

Instantly Poirot was beside her, he raised the lid of her eye, felt her pulse. When he had satisfied himself that she had really fainted, he drew aside. He caught me by the arm.

'I am an imbecile, my friend! If ever there was love and grief in a woman's voice, I heard it then. My little idea was all wrong. *Eh bien!* I must start again!'

CHAPTER VI

The Scene of the Crime

Between them, the doctor and M. Hautet carried the unconscious woman into the house. The commissary looked after
them, shaking his head.

'*Pauvre femme*,' he murmured to himself. 'The shock was too
much for her. Well, well, we can do nothing. Now, Monsieur
Poirot, shall we visit the place where the crime was committed?'

'If you please, Monsieur Bex.'

We passed through the house, and out by the front door.
Poirot had looked up at the staircase in passing, and shook
his head in a dissatisfied manner.

'It is to me incredible that the servants heard nothing. The
creaking of that staircase, with *three* people descending it,
would awaken the dead!'

'It was the middle of the night, remember. They were sound
asleep by then.'

But Poirot continued to shake his head as though not fully
accepting the explanation. On the sweep of the drive he
paused, looking up at the house.

'What moved them in the first place to try if the front door
were open? It was a most unlikely thing that it should be. It
was far more probable that they should at once try to force a
window.'

'But all the windows on the ground floor are barred with
iron shutters,' objected the commissary.

Poirot pointed to a window on the first floor.

'That is the window of the bedroom we have just come
from, is it not? And see – there is a tree by which it would be
the easiest thing in the world to mount.'

'Possibly,' admitted the other. 'But they could not have done so without leaving footprints in the flower-bed.'

I saw the justice of his words. There were two large oval flower-beds planted with scarlet geraniums, one each side of the steps leading up to the front door. The tree in question had its roots actually at the back of the bed itself, and it would have been impossible to reach it without stepping on the bed.

'You see,' continued the commissary, 'owing to the dry weather no prints would show on the drive or paths; but, on the soft mould of the flower-bed, it would have been a very different affair.'

Poirot went close to the bed and studied it attentively. As Bex had said, the mould was perfectly smooth. There was not an indentation on it anywhere.

Poirot nodded, as though convinced, and we turned away, but he suddenly darted off and began examining the other flower-bed.

'Monsieur Bex!' he called. 'See here. Here are plenty of traces for you.'

The commissary joined him – and smiled.

'My dear Monsieur Poirot, those are without doubt the footprints of the gardener's large hobnailed boots. In any case, it would have no importance, since this side we have no tree, and consequently no means of gaining access to the upper storey.'

'True,' said Poirot, evidently crestfallen. 'So you think these footprints are of no importance?'

'Not the least in the world.'

Then, to my utter astonishment, Poirot pronounced these words:

'I do not agree with you. I have a little idea that these footprints are the most important things we have seen yet.'

M. Bex said nothing, merely shrugged his shoulders. He was far too courteous to utter his real opinion.

'Shall we proceed?' he asked, instead.

'Certainly. I can investigate this matter of the footprints later,' said Poirot cheerfully.

Instead of following the drive down to the gate, M. Bex turned up a path that branched off at right angles. It led, up a slight incline, round to the right of the house, and was bordered on either side by a kind of shrubbery. Suddenly it emerged into a little clearing from which one obtained a view of the sea. A seat had been placed here, and not far from it was a rather ramshackle shed. A few steps farther on, a neat line of small bushes marked the boundary of the Villa grounds. M. Bex pushed his way through these, and we found ourselves on a wide stretch of open downs. I looked round, and saw something that filled me with astonishment.

'Why, this is a golf course,' I cried.

Bex nodded.

'The links are not completed yet,' he explained. 'It is hoped to be able to open them some time next month. It was some of the men working on them who discovered the body early this morning.'

I gave a gasp. A little to my left, where for the moment I had overlooked it, was a long narrow pit and by it, face downwards, was the body of a man! For a moment my heart gave a terrible leap, and I had a wild fancy that the tragedy had been duplicated. But the commissary dispelled my illusion by moving forward with a sharp exclamation of annoyance:

'What have my police been about? They had strict orders to allow no one near the place without proper credentials!'

The man on the ground turned his head over his shoulder.

'But I have proper credentials,' he remarked, and rose slowly to his feet.

'My dear Monsieur Giraud,' cried the commissary. 'I had no idea that you had arrived, even. The examining magistrate has been awaiting you with the utmost impatience.'

As he spoke, I was scanning the newcomer with the keenest curiosity. The famous detective from the Paris Sûreté was familiar to me by name, and I was extremely interested to see him in the flesh. He was very tall, perhaps about thirty years of age, with auburn hair and moustache, and a military carriage. There was a trace of arrogance in his manner which showed that he was fully alive to his own importance. Bex introduced us, presenting Poirot as a colleague. A flicker of interest came into the detective's eye.

'I know you by name, Monsieur Poirot,' he said. 'You cut quite a figure in the old days, didn't you? But methods are very different now.'

'Crimes, though, are very much the same,' remarked Poirot gently.

I saw at once that Giraud was prepared to be hostile. He resented the other being associated with him, and I felt that if he came across any clue of importance he would be more than likely to keep it to himself.

'The examining magistrate –' began Bex again.

But Giraud interrupted rudely:

'A fig for the examining magistrate! The light is the important thing. For all practical purposes it will be gone in another half hour or so. I know all about the case, and the people at the house will do very well until tomorrow; but, if we're going to find a clue to the murderers, here is the spot we shall find it. Is it your police who have been trampling all over the place? I thought they knew better nowadays.'

'Assuredly they do. The marks you complain of were made by the workmen who discovered the body.'

The other grunted disgustedly.

'I can see the tracks where the three of them came through the hedge – but they were cunning. You can just recognize the centre footmarks as those of Monsieur Renauld, but those on either side have been carefully obliterated. Not that there would really be much to see anyway on this hard ground, but they weren't taking any chances.'

'The external sign,' said Poirot. 'That is what you seek, eh?'

The other detective stared.

'Of course.'

A very faint smile came to Poirot's lips. He seemed about to speak, but checked himself. He bent down to where a spade was lying.

'That's what the grave was dug with, right enough,' said

Giraud. 'But you'll get nothing from it. It was Renauld's own spade, and the man who used it wore gloves. Here they are.' He gesticulated with his foot to where two soil-stained gloves were lying. 'And they're Renauld's too – or at least his gardener's. I tell you, the men who carried out this crime were taking no chances. The man was stabbed with his own dagger, and would have been buried with his own spade. They counted on leaving no traces! But I'll beat them. There's always *something*! And I mean to find it.'

But Poirot was now apparently interested in something else, a short, discoloured piece of lead-piping which lay beside the spade. He touched it delicately with his finger.

'And does this, too, belong to the murdered man?' he asked, and I thought I detected a subtle flavour of irony in the question.

Giraud shrugged his shoulders to indicate that he neither knew nor cared.

'May have been lying around here for weeks. Anyway, it doesn't interest me.'

'I, on the contrary, find it very interesting,' said Poirot sweetly.

I guessed that he was merely bent on annoying the Paris detective and, if so, he succeeded. The other turned away rudely, remarking that he had no time to waste, and bending down he resumed his minute search of the ground.

Meanwhile, Poirot, as though struck by a sudden idea, stepped back over the boundary, and tried the door of the little shed.

'That's locked,' said Giraud over his shoulder. 'But it's only a place where the gardener keeps his rubbish. The spade didn't come from there, but from the tool-shed up by the house.'

'Marvellous,' murmured M. Bex ecstatically to me. 'He has been here but half an hour, and he already knows everything! What a man! Undoubtedly Giraud is the greatest detective alive today.'

Although I disliked the detective heartily, I nevertheless was secretly impressed. Efficiency seemed to radiate from the man. I could not help feeling that, so far, Poirot had not greatly distinguished himself, and it vexed me. He seemed to be directing his attention to all sorts of silly puerile points that had nothing to do with the case. Indeed, at this juncture, he suddenly asked:

'Monsieur Bex, tell me, I pray you, the meaning of this white-washed line that extends all round the grave. Is it a device of the police?'

'No, Monsieur Poirot, it is an affair of the golf course. It shows that there is here to be a "bunkair", as you call it.'

'A bunkair?' Poirot turned to me. 'That is the irregular hole filled with sand and a bank at one side, is it not?'

I concurred.

'Monsieur Renauld, without doubt he played the golf?'

'Yes, he was a keen golfer. It's mainly owing to him, and to his large subscriptions, that this work is being carried forward. He even had a say in the designing of it.'

Poirot nodded thoughtfully. Then he remarked:

'It was not a very good choice they made – of a spot to bury the body? When the men began to dig up the ground, all would have been discovered.'

'Exactly,' cried Giraud triumphantly. 'And that *proves* that they were strangers to the place. It's an excellent piece of indirect evidence.'

'Yes,' said Poirot doubtfully. 'No one who knew would bury a body there – unless they *wanted* it to be discovered. And that is clearly absurd, is it not?'

Giraud did not even trouble to reply.

'Yes,' said Poirot, in a somewhat dissatisfied voice. 'Yes – undoubtedly – absurd!'

CHAPTER VII

The Mysterious Madame Daubreuil

As we retraced our steps to the house, M. Bex excused himself for leaving us, explaining that he must immediately acquaint the examining magistrate with the fact of Giraud's arrival. Giraud himself had been obviously delighted when Poirot declared that he had seen all he wanted. The last thing we observed, as we left the spot, was Giraud, crawling about on all fours, with a thoroughness in his search that I could not but admire. Poirot guessed my thoughts, for as soon as we were alone he remarked ironically:

'At last you have seen the detective you admire – the human foxhound! Is it not so, my friend?'

'At any rate, he's *doing* something,' I said, with asperity. 'If there's anything to find he'll find it. Now you –'

'*Eh bien!* I also have found something! A piece of lead-piping.'

'Nonsense, Poirot. You know very well that's got nothing to do with it. I meant *little* things – traces that may lead us infallibly to the murderers.'

'*Mon ami*, a clue of two feet long is every bit as valuable as one measuring two millimetres! But it is the romantic idea that all important clues must be infinitesimal. As to the piece of lead-piping having nothing to do with the crime, you say that because Giraud told you so. No' – as I was about to interpose a question – 'we will say no more. Leave Giraud to his search, and me to my ideas. The case seems straightforward enough – and yet – and yet, *mon ami*, I am not satisfied! And do you know why? Because of the wristwatch that is two hours fast. And then there are several curious little points that do not seem to fit in. For instance, if the object of the murderers was revenge, why did they not stab Renauld in his sleep and have done with it?'

'They wanted the "secret",' I reminded him.

Poirot brushed a speck of dust from his sleeve with a dissatisfied air.

'Well, where is this "secret"? Presumably some distance away, since they wish him to dress himself. Yet he is found murdered close at hand, almost within ear-shot of the house. Then again, it is pure chance that a weapon such as the dagger should be lying about casually, ready to hand.'

He paused, frowning, and then went on:

'Why did the servants hear nothing? Were they drugged? Was there an accomplice, and did that accomplice see to it that the front door should remain open? I wonder if –'

He stopped abruptly. We had reached the drive in front of the house. Suddenly he turned to me.

'My friend, I am about to surprise you – to please you! I have taken your reproaches to heart! We will examine some footprints!'

'Where?'

'In that right-hand bed yonder. Monsieur Bex says that they are the footmarks of the gardener. Let us see if this is so. See, he approaches with his wheelbarrow.'

Indeed an elderly man was just crossing the drive with a barrowful of seedlings. Poirot called to him, and he set down the barrow and came hobbling towards us.

'You are going to ask him for one of his boots to compare with the footmarks?' I asked breathlessly. My faith in Poirot revived a little. Since he said the footprints in this right-hand bed were important, presumably they *were*.

'Exactly,' said Poirot.

'But won't he think it very odd?'

'He will not think about it at all.'

We could say no more, for the old man had joined us.

'You want me for something, monsieur?'

'Yes. You have been gardener here a long time, haven't you?'

'Twenty-four years, monsieur.'

'And your name is –?'

'Auguste, monsieur.'

'I was admiring these magnificent geraniums. They are truly superb. They have been planted long?'

'Some time, monsieur. But of course, to keep the beds looking smart, one must keep bedding out a few new plants, and remove those that are over, besides keeping the old blooms well picked off.'

'You put in some new plants yesterday, didn't you? Those in the middle there, and in the other bed also.'

'Monsieur has a sharp eye. It takes always a day or so for them to "pick up". Yes, I put ten new plants in each bed last night. As monsieur doubtless knows, one should not put in plants when the sun is hot.' Auguste was charmed with Poirot's interest, and was quite inclined to be garrulous.

'That is a splendid specimen there,' said Poirot, pointing. 'Might I perhaps have a cutting of it?'

'But certainly, monsieur.' The old fellow stepped into the bed, and carefully took a slip from the plant Poirot had admired.

Poirot was profuse in his thanks, and Auguste departed to his barrow.

'You see?' said Poirot with a smile, as he bent over the bed to examine the indentation of the gardener's hobnailed boot. 'It is quite simple.'

'I did not realize –'

'That the foot would be inside the boot? You do not use your excellent mental capacities sufficiently. Well, what of the footmark?'

I examined the bed carefully.

'All the footmarks in the bed were made by the same boot,' I said at length after a careful study.

'You think so? *Eh bien!* I agree with you,' said Poirot.

He seemed quite uninterested, and as though he were thinking of something else.

'At any rate,' I remarked, 'you will have one bee less in your bonnet now.'

'*Mon Dieu!* But what an idiom! What does it mean?'

'What I meant was that now you will give up your interest in these footmarks.'

But to my surprise Poirot shook his head.

'No, no, *mon ami*. At last I am on the right track. I am still in the dark, but, as I hinted just now to Monsieur Bex, these footmarks are the most important and interesting things in the case! That poor Giraud – I should not be surprised if he took no notice of them whatever.'

At that moment the front door opened, and M. Hautet and the commissary came down the steps.

'Ah, Monsieur Poirot, we were coming to look for you,' said the magistrate. 'It is getting late, but I wish to pay a visit to Madame Daubreuil. Without doubt she will be very much upset by Monsieur Renauld's death, and we may be fortunate enough to get a clue from her. The secret that he did not confide to his wife, it is possible that he may have told it to the woman whose love held him enslaved. We know where our Samsons are weak, don't we?'

We said no more, but fell into line. Poirot walked with the examining magistrate, and the commissary and I followed a few paces behind.

'There is no doubt that Françoise's story is substantially correct,' he remarked to me in a confidential tone. 'I have been telephoning headquarters. It seems that three times in the last six weeks – that is to say since the arrival of Monsieur Renauld at Merlinville – Madame Daubreuil has paid a large sum in notes into her banking account. Altogether the sum totals two hundred thousand francs!'

'Dear me,' I said, considering, 'that must be something like four thousand pounds!'

'Precisely. Yes, there can be no doubt that he was absolutely infatuated. But it remains to be seen whether he confided his secret to her. The examining magistrate is hopeful, but I hardly share his views.'

During this conversation we were walking down the lane towards the fork in the road where our car had halted earlier in the afternoon, and in another moment I realized that the Villa Marguerite, the home of the mysterious Madame Daubreuil, was the small house from which the beautiful girl had emerged.

'She has lived here for many years,' said the commissary nodding his head towards the house. 'Very quietly, very unobtrusively. She seems to have no friends or relations other than the acquaintances she has made in Merlinville. She never refers to the past, nor to her husband. One does not even know if he is alive or dead. There is a mystery about her, you comprehend.'

I nodded, my interest growing.

'And – the daughter?' I ventured.

'A truly beautiful young girl – modest, devout, all that she should be. One pities her, for, though she may know nothing of the past, a man who wants to ask her hand in marriage must necessarily inform himself, and then –' The commissary shrugged his shoulders cynically.

'But it would not be her fault!' I cried, with rising indignation.

'No. But what will you? A man is particular about his wife's antecedents.'

I was prevented from further argument by our arrival at the door. M. Hautet rang the bell. A few minutes elapsed, and then we heard a footfall within, and the door was opened. On the threshold stood my young goddess of that afternoon. When she saw us, the colour left her cheeks, leaving her deathly white, and her eyes widened with apprehension. There was no doubt about it, she was afraid!

'Mademoiselle Daubreuil,' said M. Hautet, sweeping off his hat, 'we regret infinitely to disturb you, but the exigencies of the Law, you comprehend? My compliments to madame your mother, and will she have the goodness to grant me a few moments' interview?'

For a moment the girl stood motionless. Her left hand was pressed to her side, as though to still the sudden unconquerable agitation of her heart. But she mastered herself, and said in a low voice:

'I will go and see. Please come inside.'

She entered a room on the left of the hall, and we heard the low murmur of her voice. And then another voice, much the same in timbre, but with a slightly harder inflection behind its mellow roundness, said:

'But certainly. Ask them to enter.'

In another minute we were face to face with the mysterious Madame Daubreuil.

She was not nearly so tall as her daughter, and the rounded curves of her figure had all the grace of full maturity. Her hair, again unlike her daughter's, was dark, and parted in the middle in the Madonna style. Her eyes, half hidden by the drooping lids, were blue. Though very well preserved, she was certainly no longer young, but her charm was of the quality which is independent of age.

'You wished to see me, monsieur?' she asked.

'Yes, madame.' M. Hautet cleared his throat. 'I am investigating the death of Monsieur Renauld. You have heard of it, no doubt?'

She bowed her head without speaking. Her expression did not change.

'We came to ask you whether you can – er – throw any light upon the circumstances surrounding it?'

'I?' The surprise of her tone was excellent.

'Yes, madame. We have reason to believe that you were in the habit of visiting the dead man at his villa in the evenings. Is that so?'

The colour rose in the lady's pale cheeks, but she replied quietly:

'I deny your right to ask me such a question!'

'Madame, we are investigating a murder.'

'Well, what of it? I had nothing to do with the murder.'

'Madame, we do not say that for a moment. But you knew the dead man well. Did he ever confide in you as to any danger that threatened him?'

'Never.'

'Did he ever mention his life in Santiago, and any enemies he may have made there?'

'No.'

'Then you can give us no help at all?'

'I fear not. I really do not see why you should come to me. Cannot his wife tell you what you want to know?' Her voice held a slender inflection of irony.

'Mrs Renauld has told us all she can.'

'Ah!' said Madame Daubreuil. 'I wonder –'

'You wonder what, madame?'

'Nothing.'

The examining magistrate looked at her. He was aware that he was fighting a duel, and that he had no mean antagonist.

'You persist in your statement that Monsieur Renauld confided nothing to you?'

'Why should you think it likely that he should confide in me?'

'Because, madame,' said M. Hautet, with calculated brutality, 'a man tells to his mistress what he does not always tell to his wife.'

'Ah!' She sprang forward. Her eyes flashed fire. 'Monsieur, you insult me! And before my daughter! I can tell you nothing. Have the goodness to leave my house!'

The honours undoubtedly rested with the lady. We left the Villa Marguerite like a shamefaced pack of schoolboys. The magistrate muttered angry ejaculations to himself. Poirot seemed lost in thought. Suddenly he came out of his reverie with a start, and inquired of M. Hautet if there was a good hotel near at hand.

'There is a small place, the Hôtel des Bains, on this side of the town. A few hundred yards down the road. It will be handy for your investigations. We shall see you in the morning, then, I presume?'

'Yes, I thank you, Monsieur Hautet.'

With mutual civilities we parted company, Poirot and I going towards Merlinville, and the others returning to the Villa Geneviève.

'The French police system is very marvellous,' said Poirot, looking after them. 'The information they possess about everyone's life, down to the most commonplace detail, is extraordinary. Though he has only been here a little over six weeks, they are perfectly well acquainted with Monsieur Renauld's tastes and pursuits, and at a moment's notice they can produce information as to Madame Daubreuil's banking account, and the sums that have lately been paid in! Undoubtedly the dossier is a great institution. But what is that?' He turned sharply.

A figure was running hatless down the road after us. It was Marthe Daubreuil.

'I beg your pardon,' she cried breathlessly, as she reached us. 'I – I should not do this, I know. You must not tell my mother. But is it true, what the people say, that Monsieur Renauld called in a detective before he died, and – and that you are he?'

'Yes, mademoiselle,' said Poirot gently. 'It is quite true. But how did you learn it?'

'Françoise told our Amélie,' explained Marthe with a blush.

Poirot made a grimace.

'The secrecy, it is impossible in an affair of this kind! Not that it matters. Well, mademoiselle, what is it you want to know?'

The girl hesitated. She seemed longing, yet fearing, to speak. At last, almost in a whisper, she asked:

'Is – anyone suspected?'

Poirot eyed her keenly.

Then he replied evasively:

'Suspicion is in the air at present, mademoiselle.'

'Yes, I know – but – anyone in particular?'

'Why do you want to know?'

The girl seemed frightened by the question. All at once Poirot's words about her earlier in the day occurred to me. The 'girl with the anxious eyes'.

'Monsieur Renauld was always very kind to me,' she replied at last. 'It is natural that I should be interested.'

'I see,' said Poirot. 'Well, mademoiselle, suspicion at present is hovering round two persons.'

'Two?'

I could have sworn there was a note of surprise and relief in her voice.

'Their names are unknown, but they are presumed to be Chileans from Santiago. And now, mademoiselle, you see what comes of being young and beautiful! I have betrayed professional secrets for you!'

The girl laughed merrily, and then, rather shyly, she thanked him.

'I must run back now. *Maman* will miss me.'

And she turned and ran back up the road, looking like a modern Atalanta. I stared after her.

'*Mon ami*,' said Poirot, in his gentle ironical voice, 'is it that we are to remain planted here all night – just because you have seen a beautiful young woman, and your head is in a whirl.'

I laughed and apologized.

'But she is beautiful, Poirot. Anyone might be excused for being bowled over by her.'

But to my surprise Poirot shook his head very earnestly.

'Ah, *mon ami*, do not set your heart on Marthe Daubreuil. She is not for you, that one! Take it from Papa Poirot!'

'Why,' I cried, 'the commissary assured me that she was as good as she is beautiful! A perfect angel!'

'Some of the greatest criminals I have known had the faces of angels,' remarked Poirot cheerfully. 'A malformation of the grey cells may coincide quite easily with the face of a Madonna.'

'Poirot,' I cried, horrified, 'you cannot mean that you suspect an innocent child like this!'

'Ta-ta-ta! Do not excite yourself! I have not said that I suspected her. But you must admit that her anxiety to know about the case is somewhat unusual.'

'For once I see farther than you do,' I said. 'Her anxiety is not for herself – but for her mother.'

'My friend,' said Poirot, 'as usual, you see nothing at all. Madame Daubreuil is very well able to look after herself without her daughter worrying about her. I admit I was teasing you just now, but all the same I repeat what I said before. Do not set your heart on that girl. She is not for you! I, Hercule Poirot, know it. *Sacré!* if only I could remember where I had seen that face?'

'What face?' I asked, surprised. 'The daughter's?'

'No. The mother's.'

Noting my surprise, he nodded emphatically.

'But yes – it is as I tell you. It was a long time ago, when I was still with the police in Belgium. I have never actually seen the woman before, but I have seen her picture – and in connection with some case. I rather fancy –'

'Yes?'

'I may be mistaken, but I rather fancy that it was a murder case!'

CHAPTER VIII

An Unexpected Meeting

We were up at the villa betimes next morning. The man on
guard at the gate did not bar our way this time. Instead, he
respectfully saluted us, and we passed on to the house. The
maid Léonie was just coming down the stairs, and seemed not
averse to the prospect of a little conversation.

Poirot inquired after the health of Mrs Renauld.

Léonie shook her head.

'She is terribly upset, the poor lady! She will eat nothing –
but nothing! And she is as pale as a ghost. It is heartrending
to see her. Ah, it is not I who would grieve like that for a man
who had deceived me with another woman!'

Poirot nodded sympathetically.

'What you say is very just, but what will you? The heart of
a woman who loves will forgive many blows. Still undoubtedly
there must have been many scenes of recrimination between
them in the last few months?'

Again Léonie shook her head.

'Never, monsieur. Never have I heard madame utter a word
of protest – of reproach, even! She had the temper and disposition of an angel – quite different to monsieur.'

'Monsieur Renauld had not the temper of an angel?'

'Far from it. When he enraged himself, the whole house
knew of it. The day that he quarrelled with Monsieur Jack –
ma foi! they might have been heard in the market-place, they
shouted so loud!'

'Indeed,' said Poirot. 'And when did this quarrel take
place?'

'Oh, it was just before Monsieur Jack went to Paris. Almost
he missed his train. He came out of the library, and caught

up his bag which he had left in the hall. The automobile, it was being repaired, and he had to run for the station. I was dusting the *salon*, and I saw him pass, and his face was white – white – with two burning spots of red. Ah, but he was angry!'

Léonie was enjoying her narrative thoroughly.

'And the dispute, what was it about?'

'Ah, that I do not know,' confessed Léonie. 'It is true that they shouted, but their voices were so loud and high, and they spoke so fast, that only one well acquainted with English could have comprehended. But monsieur, he was like a thundercloud all day! Impossible to please him!'

The sound of a door shutting upstairs cut short Léonie's loquacity.

'And Françoise who awaits me!' she exclaimed, awakening to a tardy remembrance of her duties. 'That old one, she always scolds.'

'One moment, mademoiselle. The examining magistrate, where is he?'

'They have gone out to look at the automobile in the garage. Monsieur the commissary had some idea that it might have been used on the night of the murder.'

'*Quelle idée*,' murmured Poirot, as the girl disappeared.

'You will go out and join them?'

'No, I shall await their return in the *salon*. It is cool there on this hot morning.'

This placid way of taking things did not quite commend itself to me.

'If you don't mind –' I said, and hesitated.

'Not in the least. You wish to investigate on your own account, eh?'

'Well, I'd rather like to have a look at Giraud, if he's anywhere about, and see what he's up to.'

'The human foxhound,' murmured Poirot, as he leaned back in a comfortable chair, and closed his eyes. 'By all means, my friend. Au revoir.'

I strolled out of the front door. It was certainly hot. I turned up the path we had taken the day before. I had a mind to study the scene of the crime myself. I did not go directly to the spot, however, but turned aside into the bushes, so as to come out on the links some hundred yards or so farther to the right. The shrubbery here was much denser, and I had quite a struggle to force my way through. When I emerged at last on the course, it was quite unexpectedly and with such vigour that I cannoned heavily into a young lady who had been standing with her back to the plantation.

She not unnaturally gave a suppressed shriek, but I, too, uttered an exclamation of surprise. For it was my friend of the train, Cinderella!

The surprise was mutual.

'You!' we both exclaimed simultaneously.

The young lady recovered herself first.

'My only aunt!' she exclaimed. 'What are you doing here?'

'For the matter of that, what are you?' I retorted.

'When last I saw you, the day before yesterday, you were trotting home to England like a good little boy.'

'When last I saw *you*,' I said, 'you were trotting home with your sister, like a good little girl. By the way, how is your sister?'

A flash of white teeth rewarded me.

'How kind of you to ask! My sister is well, I thank you.'

'She is here with you?'

'She remained in town,' said the minx with dignity.

'I don't believe you've got a sister,' I laughed. 'If you have, her name is Harris!'

'Do you remember mine?' she asked with a smile.

'Cinderella. But you're going to tell me the real one now, aren't you?'

She shook her head with a wicked look.

'Not even why you're here?'

'Oh, *that*! I suppose you've heard of members of my profession "resting".'

'At expensive French watering-places?'

'Dirt cheap if you know where to go.'

I eyed her keenly.

'Still, you'd no intention of coming here when I met you two days ago?'

'We all have our disappointments,' said Miss Cinderella sententiously. 'There now, I've told you quite as much as is good for you. Little boys should not be inquisitive. You've not yet told me what *you're* doing here?'

'You remember my telling you that my great friend was a detective?'

'Yes?'

'And perhaps you've heard about this crime – at the Villa Geneviève –?'

She stared at me. Her breast heaved, and her eyes grew wide and round.

'You don't mean – that you're in on *that*?'

I nodded. There was no doubt that I had scored heavily. Her emotion, as she regarded me, was only too evident. For some few seconds she remained silent, staring at me. Then she nodded her head emphatically.

'Well, if that doesn't beat the band! Tote me round. I want to see all the horrors.'

'What do you mean?'

'What I say. Bless the boy, didn't I tell you I doted on crimes? I've been nosing round for hours. It's a real piece of luck happening on you this way. Come on, show me all the sights.'

'But look here – wait a minute – I can't. Nobody's allowed in. They're awfully strict.'

'Aren't you and your friends the big bugs?'

I was loath to relinquish my position of importance.

'Why are you so keen?' I asked weakly. 'And what is it you want to see?'

'Oh, everything! The place where it happened, and the weapon, and the body, and any fingerprints or interesting things like that. I've never had a chance before of being right in on a murder like this. It'll last me all my life.'

I turned away, sickened. What were women coming to

nowadays? The girl's ghoulish excitement nauseated me.

'Come off your high horse,' said the lady suddenly. 'And don't give yourself airs. When you got called to this job, did you put your nose in the air and say it was a nasty business, and you wouldn't be mixed up in it?'

'No, but –'

'If you'd been here on a holiday, wouldn't you be nosing round just the same as I am? Of course you would.'

'I'm a man. You're a woman.'

'Your idea of a woman is someone who gets on a chair and shrieks if she sees a mouse. That's all prehistoric. But you *will* show me round, won't you? You see, it might make a big difference to me.'

'In what way?'

'They're keeping all the reporters out. I might make a big scoop with one of the papers. You don't know how much they pay for a bit of inside stuff.'

I hesitated. She slipped a small soft hand into mine.

'*Please* – there's a dear.'

I capitulated. Secretly, I knew that I should rather enjoy the part of showman.

We repaired first to the spot where the body had been discovered. A man was on guard there, who saluted respectfully, knowing me by sight, and raised no questions as to my companion. Presumably he regarded her as vouched for by me. I explained to Cinderella just how the discovery had been made, and she listened attentively, sometimes putting an intelligent question. Then we turned our steps in the direction of the villa. I proceeded rather cautiously, for, truth to tell, I was not at all anxious to meet anyone. I took the girl through the shrubbery round to the back of the house where the small shed was. I recollected that yesterday evening, after relocking the door, M. Bex had left the key with the *sergent de ville*, Marchaud, 'In case Monsieur Giraud should require it while we are upstairs.' I thought it quite likely that the Sûreté detective, after using it, had returned it to Marchaud again. Leaving the girl out of sight in the shrubbery, I entered the house.

Marchaud was on duty outside the door of the *salon*. From within came the murmur of voices.

'Monsieur desires Monsieur Hautet? He is within. He is again interrogating Françoise.'

'No,' I said hastily, 'I don't want him. But I should very much like the key of the shed outside if it is not against regulations.'

'But certainly, monsieur.' He produced it. 'Here it is. Monsieur Hautet gave orders that all facilities were to be placed at your disposal. You will return it to me when you have finished out there, that is all.'

'Of course.'

I felt a thrill of satisfaction as I realized that in Marchaud's eyes, at least, I ranked equally in importance with Poirot. The girl was waiting for me. She gave an exclamation of delight as she saw the key in my hand.

'You've got it then?'

'Of course,' I said coolly. 'All the same, you know, what I'm doing is highly irregular.'

'You've been a perfect duck, and I shan't forget it. Come along. They can't see us from the house, can they?'

'Wait a minute.' I arrested her eager advance. 'I won't stop you if you really wish to go in. But do you? You've seen the grave, and the grounds, and you've heard all the details of the affair. Isn't that enough for you? This is going to be gruesome, you know, and – unpleasant.'

She looked at me for a moment with an expression that I could not quite fathom. Then she laughed.

'Me for the horrors,' she said. 'Come along.'

In silence we arrived at the door of the shed. I opened it and we passed in. I walked over to the body, and gently pulled down the sheet as Bex had done the preceding afternoon. A little gasping sound escaped from the girl's lips, and I turned and looked at her. There was horror on her face now, and those debonair high spirits of hers were quenched utterly. She had not chosen to listen to my advice, and she was punished now for her disregard of it. I felt singularly merciless towards her. She should go through with it now. I turned the corpse over gently.

'You see,' I said. 'He was stabbed in the back.'

Her voice was almost soundless.

'With what?'

I nodded towards the glass jar.

'That dagger.'

Suddenly the girl reeled, and then sank down in a heap. I sprang to her assistance.

'You are faint. Come out of here. It has been too much for you.'

'Water,' she murmured. 'Quick. Water.'

I left her, and rushed into the house. Fortunately none of the servants were about, and I was able to secure a glass of water unobserved and add a few drops of brandy from a pocket flask. In a few minutes I was back again. The girl was lying as I had left her, but a few sips of the brandy and water revived her in a marvellous manner.

'Take me out of here – oh, quickly, quickly!' she cried, shuddering.

Supporting her with my arm, I led her out into the air, and she pulled the door to behind her. Then she drew a deep breath.

'That's better. Oh, it was horrible! Why did you ever let me go in?'

I felt this to be so feminine that I could not forbear a smile. Secretly, I was not dissatisfied with her collapse. It proved that she was not quite so callous as I had thought her. After all she was little more than a child, and her curiosity had probably been of the unthinking order.

'I did my best to stop you, you know,' I said gently.

'I suppose you did. Well, goodbye.'

'Look here, you can't start off like that – all alone. You're not fit for it. I insist on accompanying you back to Merlinville.'

'Nonsense. I'm quite all right now.'

'Supposing you felt faint again? No, I shall come with you.'

But this she combated with a good deal of energy. In the

end, however, I prevailed so far as to be allowed to accompany her to the outskirts of the town. We retraced our steps over our former route, passing the grave again, and making a detour on to the road. Where the first straggling line of shops began, she stopped and held out her hand.

'Goodbye, and thank you ever so much for coming with me.'

'Are you sure you're all right now?'

'Quite, thanks. I hope you don't get into any trouble over showing me things.'

I disclaimed the idea lightly.

'Well, goodbye.'

'Au revoir,' I corrected. 'If you're staying here, we shall meet again.'

She flashed a smile at me.

'That's so. Au revoir, then.'

'Wait a second, you haven't told me your address.'

'Oh, I'm staying at the Hôtel du Phare. It's a little place, but quite good. Come and look me up tomorrow.'

'I will,' I said, with perhaps rather unnecessary *empressement*.

I watched her out of sight, then turned and retraced my steps to the villa. I remembered that I had not relocked the door of the shed. Fortunately no one had noticed the oversight, and turning the key I removed it and returned it to the *sergent de ville*. And, as I did so, it came upon me suddenly that though Cinderella had given me her address I still did not know her name.

CHAPTER IX

M. Giraud Finds Some Clues

In the *salon* I found the examining magistrate busily interrogating the old gardener, Auguste. Poirot and the commissary,
who were both present, greeted me respectively with a smile
and a polite bow. I slipped quietly into a seat. M. Hautet was
painstaking and meticulous in the extreme, but did not succeed in eliciting anything of importance.

The gardening gloves Auguste admitted to be his. He wore
them when handling a certain species of primula plant which
was poisonous to some people. He could not say when he had
worn them last. Certainly he had not missed them. Where
were they kept? Sometimes in one place, sometimes in another.
The spade was usually to be found in the small tool-shed. Was
it locked? Of course it was locked. Where was the key kept?
Parbleu, it was in the door of course. There was nothing of
value to steal. Who would have expected a party of bandits,
or assassins? Such things did not happen in Madame la
Vicomtesse's time.

M. Hautet signifying that he had finished with him, the old
man withdrew, grumbling to the last. Remembering Poirot's
unaccountable insistence on the footprints in the flower-beds,
I scrutinized him narrowly as he gave his evidence. Either he
had nothing to do with the crime or he was a consummate
actor. Suddenly, just as he was going out of the door, an idea
struck me.

'*Pardon*, Monsieur Hautet,' I cried, 'but will you permit me
to ask him one question?'

'But certainly, monsieur.'

Thus encouraged, I turned to Auguste.

'Where do you keep your boots?'

'On my feet,' growled the old man. 'Where else?'

'But when you go to bed at night?'

'Under my bed.'

'But who cleans them?'

'Nobody. Why should they be cleaned? Is it that I promenade myself on the front like a young man? On Sunday I wear the Sunday boots, but otherwise –' He shrugged his shoulders.

I shook my head, discouraged.

'Well, well,' said the magistrate, 'we do not advance very much. Undoubtedly we are held up until we get the return cable from Santiago. Has anyone seen Giraud? In verity that one lacks politeness! I have a very good mind to send for him and –'

'You will not have to send far.'

The quiet voice startled us. Giraud was standing outside looking in through the open window.

He leapt lightly into the room and advanced to the table.

'Here I am, at your service. Accept my excuses for not presenting myself sooner.'

'Not at all – not at all!' said the magistrate, rather confused.

'Of course I am only a detective,' continued the other. 'I know nothing of interrogatories. Were I conducting one, I should be inclined to do so without an open window. Anyone standing outside can so easily hear all that passes. But no matter.'

M. Hautet flushed angrily. There was evidently going to be no love lost between the examining magistrate and the detective in charge of the case. They had fallen foul of each other at the start. Perhaps in any event it would have been much the same. To Giraud, all examining magistrates were fools, and to M. Hautet, who took himself seriously, the casual manner of the Paris detective could not fail to give offence.

'*Eh bien*, Monsieur Giraud,' said the magistrate rather sharply. 'Without doubt you have been employing your time to a marvel! You have the names of the assassins for us, have you not? And also the precise spot where they find themselves now?'

Unmoved by this irony, M. Giraud replied:

'I know at least where they have come from.'

Giraud took two small objects from his pocket and laid them down on the table. We crowded round. The objects were very simple ones: the stub of a cigarette and an unlighted match. The detective wheeled round on Poirot.

'What do you see there?' he asked.

There was something almost brutal in his tone. It made my cheeks flush. But Poirot remained unmoved. He shrugged his shoulders.

'A cigarette end and a match.'

'And what does that tell you?'

Poirot spread out his hands.

'It tells me – nothing.'

'Ah!' said Giraud, in a satisfied voice. 'You haven't made a study of these things. That's not an ordinary match – not in this country at least. It's common enough in South America. Luckily it's unlighted. I mightn't have recognized it otherwise. Evidently one of the men threw away his cigarette and lit another, spilling one match out of the box as he did so.'

'And the other match?' asked Poirot.

'Which match?'

'The one he *did* light his cigarette with. You have found that also?'

'No.'

'Perhaps you didn't search very thoroughly.'

'Not search thoroughly –' For a moment it seemed as though the detective was going to break out angrily, but with an effort he controlled himself. 'I see you love a joke, Monsieur Poirot. But in any case, match or no match, the cigarette end would be sufficient. It is a South American cigarette with liquorice pectoral paper.'

Poirot bowed. The commissary spoke:

'The cigarette end and match might have belonged to Monsieur Renauld. Remember, it is only two years since he returned from South America.'

'No,' replied the other confidently. 'I have already searched among the effects of Monsieur Renauld. The cigarettes he smoked and the matches he used are quite different.'

'You do not think it odd,' asked Poirot, 'that these strangers should come unprovided with a weapon, with gloves, with a spade, and that they should so conveniently find all these things?'

Giraud smiled in a rather superior manner.

'Undoubtedly it is strange. Indeed, without the theory that I hold, it would be inexplicable.'

'Aha!' said M. Hautet. 'An accomplice within the house!'

'Or outside it,' said Giraud, with a peculiar smile.

'But someone must have admitted them. We cannot allow that, by an unparalleled piece of good fortune, they found the door ajar for them to walk in?'

'The door was opened for them; but it could just as easily be opened from outside – by someone who possessed a key.'

'But who *did* possess a key?'

Giraud shrugged his shoulders.

'As for that, no one who possesses one is going to admit the fact if he can help it. But several people *might* have had one. Monsieur Jack Renauld, the son, for instance. It is true that he is on his way to South America, but he might have lost the key or had it stolen from him. Then there is the gardener – he has been here many years. One of the younger servants may have a lover. It is easy to take an impression of a key and have one cut. There are many possibilities. Then there is another person who, I should judge, is exceedingly likely to have such a thing.'

'Who is that?'

'Madame Daubreuil,' said the detective.

'Eh, eh!' said the magistrate. 'So you have heard about that, have you?'

'I hear everything,' said Giraud imperturbably.

'There is one thing I could swear you have not heard,' said M. Hautet, delighted to be able to show superior knowledge, and without more ado he retailed the story of the mysterious visitor the night before. He also touched on the cheque made out to 'Duveen', and finally handed Giraud the letter signed 'Bella'.

'All very interesting. But my theory remains unaffected.'

'And your theory is?'

'For the moment I prefer not to say. Remember, I am only just beginning my investigations.'

'Tell me one thing, Monsieur Giraud,' said Poirot suddenly. 'Your theory allows for the door being opened. It does not explain why it was *left* open. When they departed, would it not have been natural for them to close it behind them? If a *sergent de ville* had chanced to come up to the house, as is sometimes done to see that all is well, they might have been discovered and overtaken almost at once.'

'Bah! They forgot it. A mistake, I grant you.'

Then, to my surprise, Poirot uttered almost the same words as he had uttered to Bex the previous evening:

'*I do not agree with you*. The door being left open was the result of either design or necessity, and any theory that does not admit that fact is bound to prove vain.'

We all regarded the little man with a good deal of astonishment. The confession of ignorance drawn from him over the match end had, I thought, been bound to humiliate him, but here he was self-satisfied as ever, laying down the law to Giraud without a tremor.

The detective twisted his moustache, eyeing my friend in a somewhat bantering fashion.

'You don't agree with me, eh? Well, what strikes you particularly about the case? Let's hear your views.'

'One thing presents itself to me as being significant. Tell me, Monsieur Giraud, does nothing strike you as familiar about this case? Is there nothing it reminds you of?'

'Familiar? Reminds me of? I can't say off-hand. I don't think so, though.'

'You are wrong,' said Poirot quietly. 'A crime almost precisely similar has been committed before.'

'When? And where?'

'Ah, that, unfortunately, I cannot for the moment remember, but I shall do so. I had hoped *you* might be able to assist me.'

Giraud snorted incredulously.

'There have been many affairs of masked men. I cannot remember the details of them all. The crimes all resemble each other more or less.'

'There is such a thing as the individual touch.' Poirot suddenly assumed his lecturing manner, and addressed us collectively. 'I am speaking to you now of the psychology of crime. Monsieur Giraud knows quite well that each criminal has his particular method, and that the police, when called in to investigate, say, a case of burglary, can often make a shrewd guess at the offender, simply by the peculiar methods he has employed. (Japp would tell you the same, Hastings.) Man is an unoriginal animal. Unoriginal within the law in his daily respectable life, equally unoriginal outside the law. If a man commits a crime, any other crime he commits will resemble it closely. The English murderer who disposed of his wives in succession by drowning them in their baths was a case in point. Had he varied his methods, he might have escaped detection to this day. But he obeyed the common dictates of human nature, arguing that what had once succeeded would succeed again, and he paid the penalty of his lack of originality.'

'And the point of all this?' sneered Giraud.

'That, when you have two crimes precisely similar in design and execution, you find the same brain behind them both. I am looking for that brain, Monsieur Giraud, and I shall find it. Here we have a true clue – a psychological clue. You may know all about cigarettes and match ends, Monsieur Giraud, but I, Hercule Poirot, know the mind of man.'

Giraud remained singularly unimpressed.

'For your guidance,' continued Poirot, 'I will also advise you of one fact which might fail to be brought to your notice. The wristwatch of Madame Renauld, on the day following the tragedy, had gained two hours.'

Giraud stared.

'Perhaps it was in the habit of gaining?'

'As a matter of fact, I am told it did.'

'Very well, then.'

'All the same, two hours is a good deal,' said Poirot softly. 'Then there is the matter of the footprints in the flower-bed.'

He nodded his head towards the open window. Giraud took two eager strides, and looked out.

'But I see no footprints?'

'No,' said Poirot, straightening a little pile of books on a table. 'There are none.'

For a moment an almost murderous rage obscured Giraud's face. He took two strides towards his tormentor, but at that moment the salon door was opened, and Marchaud announced:

'Monsieur Stonor, the secretary, has just arrived from England. May he enter?'

CHAPTER X

Gabriel Stonor

The man who now entered the room was a striking figure. Very tall, with a well-knit, athletic frame, and a deeply bronzed face and neck, he dominated the assembly. Even Giraud seemed anaemic beside him. When I knew him better I realized that Gabriel Stonor was quite an unusual personality. English by birth, he had knocked about all over the world. He had shot big game in Africa, travelled in Korea, ranched in California, and traded in the South Sea islands.

His unerring eye picked out M. Hautet.

'The examining magistrate in charge of the case? Pleased to meet you, sir. This is a terrible business. How's Mrs Renauld? Is she bearing up fairly well? It must have been an awful shock to her.'

'Terrible, terrible,' said M. Hautet. 'Permit me to introduce Monsieur Bex, our commissary of police, Monsieur Giraud of the Sûreté. This gentleman is Monsieur Hercule Poirot. Mr Renauld sent for him, but he arrived too late to do anything to avert the tragedy. A friend of Monsieur Poirot's, Captain Hastings.'

Stonor looked at Poirot with some interest.

'Sent for you, did he?'

'You did not know, then, that Monsieur Renauld contemplated calling a detective?' interposed M. Bex.

'No, I didn't. But it doesn't surprise me a bit.'

'Why?'

'Because the old man was rattled. I don't know what it was all about. He didn't confide in me. We weren't on those terms. But rattled he was – and badly.'

'H'm!' said M. Hautet. 'But you have no notion of the cause?'

'That's what I said, sir.'

'You will pardon me, Monsieur Stonor, but we must begin with a few formalities. Your name?'

'Gabriel Stonor.'

'How long ago was it that you became secretary to Monsieur Renauld?'

'About two years ago, when he first arrived from South America. I met him through a mutual friend, and he offered me the post. A thundering good boss he was too.'

'Did he talk to you much about his life in South America?'

'Yes, a good bit.'

'Do you know if he was ever in Santiago?'

'Several times, I believe.'

'He never mentioned any special incident that occurred there – anything that might have provoked some vendetta against him?'

'Never.'

'Did he speak of any secret that he had acquired while sojourning there?'

'Not that I can remember. But, for all that, there *was* a mystery about him. I've never heard him speak of his boyhood, for instance, or of any incident prior to his arrival in South America. He was a French-Canadian by birth, I believe, but I've never heard him speak of his life in Canada. He could shut up like a clam if he liked.'

'So, as far as you know, he had no enemies, and you can give us no clue as to any secret to obtain possession of which he might have been murdered?'

'That's so.'

'Monsieur Stonor, have you ever heard the name of Duveen in connection with Monsieur Renauld?'

'Duveen. Duveen.' He tried the name over thoughtfully. 'I don't think I have. And yet it seems familiar.'

'Do you know a lady, a friend of Monsieur Renauld's, whose Christian name is Bella?'

Again Mr Stonor shook his head.

'Bella Duveen? Is that the full name? It's curious. I'm sure I know it. But for the moment I can't remember in what connection.'

The magistrate coughed.

'You understand, Monsieur Stonor – the case is like this. *There must be no reservations.* You might, perhaps, through a feeling of consideration for Madame Renauld – for whom, I gather, you have a great esteem and affection – you might – in fact!' said M. Hautet, getting rather tied up in his sentence, 'there must absolutely be no reservations.'

Stonor stared at him, a dawning light of comprehension in his eyes.

'I don't quite get you,' he said gently. 'Where does Mrs Renauld come in? I've an immense respect and affection for that lady; she's a very wonderful and unusual type, but I don't quite see how my reservations, or otherwise, could affect her.'

'Not if this Bella Duveen should prove to have been something more than a friend to her husband?'

'Ah!' said Stonor. 'I get you now. But I'll bet my bottom dollar that you're wrong. The old man never so much as looked at a petticoat. He just adored his own wife. They were the most devoted couple I know.'

M. Hautet shook his head gently.

'Monsieur Stonor, we hold absolute proof – a love-letter written by this Bella to Monsieur Renauld, accusing him of having tired of her. Moreover, we have further proof that, at the time of his death, he was carrying on an intrigue with a Frenchwoman, a Madame Daubreuil, who rents the adjoining villa.'

The secretary's eyes narrowed.

'Hold on, sir. You're barking up the wrong tree. I knew Paul Renauld. What you've just been saying is plumb impossible. There's some other explanation.'

The magistrate shrugged his shoulders.

'What other explanation could there be?'

'What leads you to think it was a love affair?'

'Madame Daubreuil was in the habit of visiting him here in the evenings. Also, since Monsieur Renauld came to the Villa Geneviève, Madame Daubreuil has paid large sums of money into the bank in notes. In all, the amount totals four thousand pounds of your English money.'

'I guess that's right,' said Stonor quietly. 'I transmitted him those sums in notes at his request. But it wasn't an intrigue.'

'What else could it be?'

'*Blackmail,*' said Stonor sharply, bringing down his hand with a slam on the table. 'That's what it was.'

'Ah!' cried the magistrate, shaken in spite of himself.

'Blackmail,' repeated Stonor. 'The old man was being bled – and at a good rate too. Four thousand in a couple of months. Whew! I told you just now there was a mystery about Renauld. Evidently this Madame Daubreuil knew enough of it to put the screw on.'

'It is possible,' the commissary cried excitedly. 'Decidedly it is possible.'

'Possible?' roared Stonor. 'It's certain. Tell me, have you asked Mrs Renauld about this love-affair stunt of yours?'

'No, monsieur. We did not wish to occasion her any distress if it could reasonably be avoided.'

'Distress? Why, she'd laugh in your face. I tell you, she and Renauld were a couple in a hundred.'

'Ah, that reminds me of another point,' said M. Hautet. 'Did Monsieur Renauld take you into his confidence at all as to the dispositions of his will?'

'I know all about it – took it to the lawyers for him after he'd drawn it out. I can give you the name of his solicitors if you want to see it. They've got it there. Quite simple. Half in trust to his wife for her lifetime, the other half to his son. A few legacies. I rather think he left me a thousand.'

'When was this will drawn up?'

'Oh, about a year and a half ago.'

'Would it surprise you very much, Monsieur Stonor, to hear that Monsieur Renauld had made another will, less than a fortnight ago?'

Stonor was obviously very much surprised.

'I'd no idea of it. What's it like?'

'The whole of his vast fortune is left unreservedly to his wife. There is no mention of his son.'

Mr Stonor gave vent to a prolonged whistle.

'I call that rather rough on the lad. His mother adores him of course, but to the world at large it looks rather like a want of confidence on his father's part. It will be rather galling to his pride. Still, it all goes to prove what I told you, that Renauld and his wife were on first-rate terms.'

'Quite so, quite so,' said M. Hautet. 'It is possible we shall have to revise our ideas on several points. We have, of course, cabled to Santiago, and are expecting a reply from there any minute. In all probability, everything will then be perfectly clear and straightforward. On the other hand, if your suggestion of blackmail is true, Madame Daubreuil ought to be able to give us valuable information.'

Poirot interjected a remark:

'Monsieur Stonor, the English chauffeur, Masters, had he been long with Monsieur Renauld?'

'Over a year.'

'Have you any idea whether he has ever been in South America?'

'I'm quite sure he hasn't. Before coming to M. Renauld he had been for many years with some people in Gloucestershire whom I know well.'

'In fact, you can answer for him as being above suspicion?'

'Absolutely.'

Poirot seemed somewhat crestfallen.

Meanwhile the magistrate had summoned Marchaud.

'My compliments to Madame Renauld, and I should be glad to speak to her for a few minutes. Beg her not to disturb herself. I will wait upon her upstairs.'

Marchaud saluted and disappeared.

We waited some minutes, and then, to our surprise, the door opened, and Mrs Renauld, deathly pale in her heavy mourning, entered the room.

M. Hautet brought forward a chair, uttering vigorous protestations, and she thanked him with a smile. Stonor was holding one hand of hers in his with an eloquent sympathy. Words evidently failed him. Mrs Renauld turned to M. Hautet.

'You wish to ask me something?'

'With your permission, madame. I understand your husband was a French-Canadian by birth. Can you tell me anything of his youth or upbringing?'

She shook her head.

'My husband was always very reticent about himself, monsieur. He came from the North-West, I know, but I fancy that he had an unhappy childhood, for he never cared to speak of that time. Our life was lived entirely in the present and the future.'

'Was there any mystery in his past life?'

Mrs Renauld smiled a little and shook her head.

'Nothing so romantic, I am sure, monsieur.'

M. Hautet also smiled.

'True, we must not permit ourselves to get melodramatic. There is one thing more –' He hesitated.

Stonor broke in impetuously:

'They've got an extraordinary idea into their heads, Mrs Renauld. They actually fancy that Mr Renauld was carrying on an intrigue with a Madame Daubreuil who, it seems, lives next door.'

The scarlet colour flamed into Mrs Renauld's cheeks. She flung her head up, then bit her lip, her face quivering. Stonor stood looking at her in astonishment, but M. Bex leaned forward and said gently:

'We regret to cause you pain, madame, but have you any reason to believe that Madame Daubreuil was your husband's mistress?'

With a sob of anguish, Mrs Renauld buried her face in her hands. Her shoulders heaved convulsively. At last she lifted her head and said brokenly:

'She may have been.'

Never, in all my life, have I seen anything to equal the blank amazement on Stonor's face. He was thoroughly taken aback.

CHAPTER XI

Jack Renauld

What the next development of the conversation would have been I cannot say, for at that moment the door was thrown open violently and a tall young man strode into the room.

Just for a moment I had the uncanny sensation that the dead man had come to life again. Then I realized that this dark head was untouched with grey, and that, in point of fact, it was a mere boy who now burst in among us with so little ceremony. He went straight to Mrs Renauld with an impetuosity that took no heed of the presence of others.

'Mother!'

'Jack!' With a cry she folded him in her arms. 'My dearest! But what brings you here? You were to sail on the *Anzora* from Cherbourg two days ago?' Then, suddenly recalling to herself the presence of others, she turned with a certain dignity: 'My son, messieurs.'

'Aha!' said M. Hautet, acknowledging the young man's bow. 'So you did not sail on the *Anzora*?'

'No, monsieur. As I was about to explain, the *Anzora* was detained twenty-four hours through engine trouble. I should have sailed last night instead of the night before, but, happening to buy an evening paper, I saw in it an account of the – the awful tragedy that had befallen us –' His voice broke and the tears came into his eyes. 'My poor father – my poor, poor father.'

Staring at him like one in a dream, Mrs Renauld repeated:

'So you did not sail?' And then, with a gesture of infinite weariness, she murmured as though to herself: 'After all, it does not matter – now.'

'Sit down, Monsieur Renauld, I beg of you,' said M. Hautet,

indicating a chair. 'My sympathy for you is profound. It must have been a terrible shock to you to learn the news as you did. However, it is most fortunate that you were prevented from sailing. I am in hopes that you may be able to give us just the information we need to clear up this mystery.'

'I am at your disposal, monsieur. Ask me any questions you please.'

'To begin with, I understand that this journey was being undertaken at your father's request?'

'Quite so, monsieur. I received a telegram bidding me to proceed without delay to Buenos Aires, and from thence *via* the Andes to Valparaiso, and on to Santiago.'

'Ah! And the object of this journey?'

'I have no idea.'

'What?'

'No. See, here in the telegram.'

The magistrate took it and read it aloud:

' "Proceed immediately Cherbourg embark *Anzora* sailing tonight Buenos Aires. Ultimate destination Santiago. Further instructions will await you Buenos Aires. Do not fail. Matter is of utmost importance. Renauld." And there had been no previous correspondence on the matter?'

Jack Renauld shook his head.

'That is the only intimation of any kind. I knew, of course, that my father, having lived so long out there, had necessarily many interests in South America. But he had never mooted any suggestion of sending me out.'

'You have, of course, been a good deal in South America, M. Renauld?'

'I was there as a child. But I was educated in England, and spent most of my holidays in that country, so I really know far less of South America than might be supposed. You see, the War broke out when I was seventeen.'

'You served in the English Flying Corps, did you not?'

'Yes, monsieur.'

M. Hautet nodded his head and proceeded with his inquiries along the, by now, well-known lines. In response,

Jack Renauld declared definitely that he knew nothing of any enmity his father might have incurred in the city of Santiago or elsewhere in the South American continent, that he had noticed no change in his father's manner of late, and that he had never heard him refer to a secret. He had regarded the mission to South America as connected with business interests.

As M. Hautet paused for a minute, the quiet voice of Giraud broke in:

'I should like to put a few questions of my own, Monsieur le juge.'

'By all means, Monsieur Giraud, if you wish,' said the magistrate coldly.

Giraud edged his chair a little nearer to the table.

'Were you on good terms with your father, Monsieur Renauld?'

'Certainly I was,' returned the lad haughtily.

'You assert that positively?'

'Yes.'

'No little disputes, eh?'

Jack shrugged his shoulders. 'Everyone may have a difference of opinion now and then.'

'Quite so, quite so. But, if anyone were to assert that you had a violent quarrel with your father on the eve of your departure for Paris, that person, without doubt, would be lying?'

I could not but admire the ingenuity of Giraud. His boast, 'I know everything,' had been no idle one. Jack Renauld was clearly disconcerted by the question.

'We – we did have an argument,' he admitted.

'Ah, an argument! In the course of that argument, did you use this phrase: "When you are dead I can do as I please"?'

'I may have done,' muttered the other. 'I don't know.'

'In response to that, did your father say: "But I am not dead yet!"? To which you responded: "I wish you were!"'

The boy made no answer. His hands fiddled nervously with the things on the table in front of him.

'I must request an answer, please, Monsieur Renauld,' said Giraud sharply.

With an angry exclamation, the boy swept a heavy paper-knife to the floor.

'What does it matter? You might as well know. Yes, I did quarrel with my father. I dare say I said all those things – I was so angry I cannot even remember what I said! I was furious – I could almost have killed him at that moment – there, make the most of that!' He leant back in his chair, flushed and defiant.

Giraud smiled, then, moving his chair back a little, said:

'That is all. You would, without doubt, prefer to continue the interrogatory, Monsieur Hautet.'

'Ah, yes, exactly,' said M. Hautet. 'And what was the subject of your quarrel?'

'That I decline to state.'

M. Hautet sat up in his chair.

'Monsieur Renauld, it is not permitted to trifle with the law!' he thundered. 'What was the subject of the quarrel?'

Young Renauld remained silent, his boyish face sullen and overcast. But another voice spoke, imperturbable and calm, the voice of Hercule Poirot:

'I will inform you, if you like, monsieur.'

'You know?'

'Certainly I know. The subject of the quarrel was Mademoiselle Marthe Daubreuil.'

Renauld sprang round, startled. The magistrate leaned forward.

'Is that so, monsieur?'

Jack Renauld bowed his head.

'Yes,' he admitted. 'I love Mademoiselle Daubreuil, and I wish to marry her. When I informed my father of the fact he flew at once into a violent rage. Naturally, I could not stand hearing the girl I loved insulted, and I, too, lost my temper.'

M. Hautet looked across at Mrs Renauld.

'You were aware of this – attachment, madame?'

'I feared it,' she replied simply.

'Mother,' cried the boy. 'You too! Marthe is as good as she is beautiful. What can you have against her?'

'I have nothing against Mademoiselle Daubreuil in any way. But I should prefer you to marry an Englishwoman, or if a Frenchwoman, not one who has a mother of doubtful antecedents!'

Her rancour against the older woman showed plainly in her voice, and I could well understand that it must have been a bitter blow to her when her only son showed signs of falling in love with the daughter of her rival.

Mrs Renauld continued, addressing the magistrate:

'I ought, perhaps, to have spoken to my husband on the subject, but I hoped that it was only a boy and girl flirtation which would blow over all the quicker if no notice was taken of it. I blame myself now for my silence, but my husband, as I told you, had seemed so anxious and careworn, different altogether from his normal self, that I was chiefly concerned not to give him any additional worry.'

M. Hautet nodded.

'When you informed your father of your intentions towards Mademoiselle Daubreuil,' he resumed, 'he was surprised?'

'He seemed completely taken aback. Then he ordered me peremptorily to dismiss any such idea from my mind. He would never give his consent to such a marriage. Nettled, I demanded what he had against Mademoiselle Daubreuil. To that he could give no satisfactory reply, but spoke in slighting terms of the mystery surrounding the lives of the mother and daughter. I answered that I was marrying Marthe and not her antecedents, but he shouted me down with a peremptory refusal to discuss the matter in any way. The whole thing must be given up. The injustice and high-handedness of it all maddened me – especially since he himself always seemed to go out of his way to be attentive to the Daubreuils and was always suggesting that they should be asked to the house. I lost my head, and we quarrelled in earnest. My father reminded me that I was entirely dependent on him, and it

must have been in answer to that that I made the remark
about doing as I pleased after his death –'

Poirot interrupted with a quick question:

'You were aware, then, of the terms of your father's will?'

'I knew that he had left half his fortune to me, the other
half in trust for my mother, to come to me at her death,'
replied the lad.

'Proceed with your story,' said the magistrate.

'After that we shouted at each other in sheer rage, until I
suddenly realized that I was in danger of missing my train to
Paris. I had to run for the station, still in a white heat of fury.
However, once well away, I calmed down. I wrote to Marthe,
telling her what had happened, and her reply soothed me still
further. She pointed out to me that we had only to be steadfast,
and any opposition was bound to give way at last. Our affection for each other must be tried and proved, and when my
parents realized that it was no light infatuation on my part
they would doubtless relent towards us. Of course, to her, I
had not dwelt on my father's principal objection to the match.
I soon saw that I should do my cause no good by violence.'

'To pass to another matter, are you acquainted with the
name of Duveen, Monsieur Renauld?'

'Duveen?' said Jack. 'Duveen?' He leant forward and slowly
picked up the paper-knife he had swept from the table. As he
lifted his head his eyes met the watching ones of Giraud.
'Duveen? No, I can't say I do.'

'Will you read this letter, Monsieur Renauld? And tell me
if you have any idea as to who the person was who addressed
it to your father.'

Jack Renauld took the letter and read it through, the colour
mounting in his face as he did so.

'Addressed to my father?' The emotion and indignation in
his tones were evident.

'Yes. We found it in the pocket of his coat.'

'Does –' He hesitated, throwing the merest fraction of a
glance towards his mother.

The magistrate understood.

'As yet – no. Can you give us any clue as to the writer?'

'I have no idea whatsoever.'

M. Hautet sighed.

'A most mysterious case. Ah, well, I suppose we can now rule out the letter altogether. Let me see, where were we? Oh, the weapon. I fear this may give you pain, Monsieur Renauld. I understand it was a present from you to your mother. Very sad – very distressing –'

Jack Renauld leaned forward. His face, which had flushed during the perusal of the letter, was now deadly white.

'Do you mean – that it was with an aeroplane wire paper-cutter that my father was – was killed? But it's impossible! A little thing like that!'

'Alas, Monsieur Renauld, it is only too true! An ideal little tool, I fear. Sharp and easy to handle.'

'Where is it? Can I see it? Is it still in the – the body?'

'Oh no, it has been removed. You would like to see it? To make sure? It would be as well, perhaps, though madame has already identified it. Still – Monsieur Bex, might I trouble you?'

'Certainly. I will fetch it immediately.'

'Would it not be better to take Monsieur Renauld to the shed?' suggested Giraud smoothly. 'Without doubt he would wish to see his father's body.'

The boy made a shivering gesture of negation, and the magistrate, always disposed to cross Giraud whenever possible, replied:

'But no – not at present. Monsieur Bex will be so kind as to bring it to us here.'

The commissary left the room. Stonor crossed to Jack and wrung him by the hand. Poirot had risen, and was adjusting a pair of candlesticks that struck his trained eye as being a shade askew. The magistrate was reading the mysterious love-letter through a last time, clinging desperately to his first theory of jealousy and a stab in the back.

Suddenly the door burst open and the commissary rushed in.

'Monsieur le juge! Monsieur le juge!'

'But yes. What is it?'

'The dagger! It is gone!'

'What – gone?'

'Vanished. Disappeared. The glass jar that contained it is empty!'

'What?' I cried. 'Impossible. Why, only this morning I saw –' The words died on my tongue.

But the attention of the entire room was diverted to me.

'What is that you say?' cried the commissary. 'This morning?'

'I saw it there this morning,' I said slowly. 'About an hour and a half ago, to be accurate.'

'You went to the shed, then? How did you get the key?'

'I asked the *sergent de ville* for it.'

'And you went there? Why?'

I hesitated, but in the end I decided that the only thing to do was to make a clean breast of it.

'Monsieur Hautet,' I said, 'I have committed a grave fault, for which I must crave your indulgence.'

'Proceed, monsieur.'

'The fact of the matter is,' I said, wishing myself anywhere else but where I was, 'that I met a young lady, an acquaintance of mine. She displayed a great desire to see everything that was to be seen, and I – well, in short, I took the key to show her the body.'

'Ah!' cried the magistrate indignantly. 'But it is a grave fault you have committed there, Captain Hastings. It is altogether most irregular. You should not have permitted yourself this folly.'

'I know,' I said meekly. 'Nothing that you can say could be too severe, monsieur.'

'You did not invite this lady to come here?'

'Certainly not. I met her quite by accident. She is an English lady who happens to be staying in Merlinville, though I was not aware of that until my unexpected meeting with her.'

'Well, well,' said the magistrate, softening. 'It was most

irregular, but the lady is without doubt young and beautiful. What it is to be young!' And he sighed sentimentally.

But the commissary, less romantic and more practical, took up the tale:

'But did you not reclose and lock the door when you departed?'

'That's just it,' I said slowly. 'That's what I blame myself for so terribly. My friend was upset at the sight. She nearly fainted. I got her some brandy and water, and afterwards insisted on accompanying her back to the town. In the excitement I forgot to relock the door. I only did so when I got back to the villa.'

'Then for twenty minutes at least –' said the commissary slowly. He stopped.

'Exactly,' I said.

'Twenty minutes,' mused the commissary.

'It is deplorable,' said M. Hautet, his sternness of manner returning. 'Without precedent.'

Suddenly another voice spoke.

'You find it deplorable?' asked Giraud.

'Certainly I do.'

'I find it admirable!' said the other imperturbably.

This unexpected ally quite bewildered me.

'Admirable, Monsieur Giraud?' asked the magistrate, studying him cautiously out of the corner of his eye.

'Precisely.'

'And why?'

'Because we know now that the assassin, or an accomplice of the assassin, has been near the villa only an hour ago. It will be strange if, with that knowledge, we do not shortly lay hands upon him.' There was a note of menace in his voice. He continued: 'He risked a good deal to gain possession of that dagger. Perhaps he feared that fingerprints might be discovered on it.'

Poirot turned to Bex.

'You said there were none?'

Giraud shrugged his shoulders.

'Perhaps he could not be sure.'

Poirot looked at him.

'You are wrong, Monsieur Giraud. The assassin wore gloves. So he must have been sure.'

'I do not say it was the assassin himself. It may have been an accomplice who was not aware of that fact.'

The magistrate's clerk was gathering up the papers on the table. M. Hautet addressed us:

'Our work here is finished. Perhaps, Monsieur Renauld, you will listen while your evidence is read over to you. I have purposely kept all the proceedings as informal as possible. I have been called original in my methods, but I maintain that there is much to be said for originality. The case is now in the clever hands of the renowned Monsieur Giraud. He will without doubt distinguish himself. Indeed, I wonder that he has not already laid his hands upon the murderers! Madame, again let me assure you of my heartfelt sympathy. Messieurs, I wish you all good day.' And, accompanied by his clerk and the commissary, he took his departure.

Poirot tugged out that large turnip of a watch of his and observed the time.

'Let us return to the hotel for lunch, my friend,' he said. 'And you shall recount to me in full the indiscretions of this morning. No one is observing us. We need make no adieux.'

We went quietly out of the room. The examining magistrate had just driven off in his car. I was going down the steps when Poirot's voice arrested me:

'One little moment, my friend.' Dexterously he whipped out his yard measure and proceeded, quite solemnly, to measure an overcoat hanging in the hall, from the collar to the hem. I had not seen it hanging there before, and guessed that it belonged to either Mr Stonor or Jack Renauld.

Then, with a little satisfied grunt, Poirot returned the measure to his pocket and followed me out into the open air.

CHAPTER XII

Poirot Elucidates Certain Points

'Why did you measure that overcoat?' I asked, with some curiosity, as we walked down the hot white road at a leisurely pace.

'*Parbleu!* to see how long it was,' replied my friend imperturbably.

I was vexed. Poirot's incurable habit of making a mystery out of nothing never failed to irritate me. I relapsed into silence, and followed a train of thought of my own. Although I had not noticed them specially at the time, certain words Mrs Renauld had addressed to her son now recurred to me, fraught with a new significance. 'So you did not sail?' she had said, and then had added: '*After all, it does not matter – now.*'

What had she meant by that? The words were enigmatical – significant. Was it possible that she knew more than we supposed? She had denied all knowledge of the mysterious mission with which her husband was to have entrusted his son. But was she really less ignorant than she pretended? Could she enlighten us if she chose, and was her silence part of a carefully thought out and preconceived plan?

The more I thought about it, the more I was convinced that I was right. Mrs Renauld knew more than she chose to tell. In her surprise at seeing her son, she had momentarily betrayed herself. I felt convinced that she knew, if not the assassins, at least the motive for the assassination. But some very powerful considerations must keep her silent.

'You think profoundly, my friend,' remarked Poirot, breaking in upon my reflections. 'What is it that intrigues you so?'

I told him, sure of my ground, though feeling expectant that he would ridicule my suspicions. But to my surprise he nodded thoughtfully.

'You are quite right, Hastings. From the beginning I have been sure that she was keeping something back. At first I suspected her, if not of inspiring, at least of conniving at the crime.'

'You suspected *her*?' I cried.

'But certainly. She benefits enormously – in fact, by this new will, she is the only person to benefit. So, from the start, she was singled out for attention. You may have noticed that I took an early opportunity of examining her wrists. I wished to see whether there was any possibility that she had gagged and bound herself. *Eh bien*, I saw at once that there was no fake, the cords had actually been drawn so tight as to cut into the flesh. That ruled out the possibility of her having committed the crime single-handed. But it was still possible for her to have connived at it, or to have been the instigator with an accomplice. Moreover, the story, as she told it, was singularly familiar to me – the masked men that she could not recognize, the mention of "the secret" – I had heard, or read, all these things before. Another little detail confirmed my belief that she was not speaking the truth. *The wristwatch, Hastings, the wristwatch!*'

Again that wristwatch! Poirot was eyeing me curiously.

'You see, *mon ami*? You comprehend?'

'No,' I replied with some ill humour. 'I neither see nor comprehend. You make all these confounded mysteries, and it's useless asking you to explain. You always like keeping something up your sleeve to the last minute.'

'Do not enrage yourself, my friend,' said Poirot, with a smile. 'I will explain if you wish. But not a word to Giraud, *c'est entendu*? He treats me as an old one of no importance! *We shall see!* In common fairness I gave him a hint. If he does not choose to act upon it, that is his own lookout.'

I assured Poirot that he could rely upon my discretion.

'*C'est bien!* Let us then employ our little grey cells. Tell me, my friend, at what time, according to you, did the tragedy take place?'

'Why, at two o'clock or thereabouts,' I said, astonished. 'You remember, Mrs Renauld told us that she heard the clock strike while the men were in the room.'

'Exactly, and on the strength of that, you, the examining magistrate, Bex, and everyone else, accept the time without further question. But I, Hercule Poirot, say that Madame Renauld lied. *The crime took place at least two hours earlier.*'

'But the doctors –'

'They declared, after examination of the body, that death had taken place between ten and seven hours previously. *Mon ami*, for some reason it was imperative that the crime should seem to have taken place later than it actually did. You have read of a smashed watch or clock recording the exact hour of a crime? So that the time should not rest on Madame Renauld's testimony alone, someone moved on the hands of that wristwatch to two o'clock, and then dashed it violently to the ground. But, as is often the case, they defeated their own object. The glass was smashed, but the mechanism of the watch was uninjured. It was a most disastrous manoeuvre on their part, for it at once drew my attention to two points – first, that Madame Renauld was lying; secondly, that there must be some vital reason for the postponement of the time.'

'But what reason could there be?'

'Ah, that is the question! There we have the whole mystery. As yet, I cannot explain it. There is only one idea that presents itself to me as having a possible connection.'

'And that is?'

'The last train left Merlinville at seventeen minutes past twelve.'

I followed it out slowly.

'So that, the crime apparently taking place some two hours later, anyone leaving by that train would have an unimpeachable alibi!'

'Perfect, Hastings! You have it!'

I sprang up.

'But we must inquire at the station! Surely they cannot have failed to notice two foreigners who left by that train! We must go there at once!'

'You think so, Hastings?'

'Of course. Let us go there now.'

Poirot restrained my ardour with a light touch upon the arm.

'Go by all means if you wish, *mon ami* – but if you go, I should not ask for particulars of two foreigners.'

I stared and he said rather impatiently:

'*Là, là*, you do not believe all that rigmarole, do you? The masked men and all the rest of *cette histoire-là*!'

His words took me so much aback, that I hardly knew how to respond. He went on serenely:

'You heard me say to Giraud, did you not, that all the details of this crime were familiar to me? *Eh bien*, that presupposes one of two things, either the brain that planned the first crime also planned this one, or else an account read of a *cause célèbre* unconsciously remained in our assassin's memory and prompted the details. I shall be able to pronounce definitely on that after –' He broke off.

I was revolving sundry matters in my mind.

'But Mr Renauld's letter? It distinctly mentions a secret and Santiago!'

'Undoubtedly there was a secret in Monsieur Renauld's life – there can be no doubt of that. On the other hand, the word Santiago, to my mind, is a red herring, dragged continually across the track to put us off the scent. It is possible that it was used in the same way on Monsieur Renauld, to keep him from directing his suspicions to a quarter nearer at hand. Oh, be assured, Hastings, the danger that threatened him was not in Santiago, it was near at hand, in France.'

He spoke so gravely, and with such assurance, that I could not fail to be convinced. But I essayed one final objection:

'And the match and cigarette end found near the body? What of them?'

A light of pure enjoyment lit up Poirot's face.

'Planted! Deliberately planted there for Giraud or one of his tribe to find! Ah, he is smart, Giraud, he can do his tricks! So can a good retriever dog. He comes in so pleased with himself. For hours he has crawled on his stomach. "See what I have found," he says. And then again to me: "What do you see here?" Me, I answer, with profound and deep truth, "Nothing." And Giraud, the great Giraud, he laughs, he thinks to himself, "Oh, he is imbecile, this old one!" *But we shall see . . .*'

But my mind had reverted to the main facts.

'Then all this story of the masked men –?'

'Is false.'

'What really happened?'

Poirot shrugged his shoulders.

'One person could tell us – Madame Renauld. But she will not speak. Threats and entreaties would not move her. A remarkable woman that, Hastings. I recognized as soon as I saw her that I had to deal with a woman of unusual character. At first, as I told you, I was inclined to suspect her of being concerned in the crime. Afterwards I altered my opinion.'

'What made you do that?'

'Her spontaneous and genuine grief at the sight of her husband's body. I could swear that the agony in that cry of hers was genuine.'

'Yes,' I said thoughtfully, 'one cannot mistake these things.'

'I beg your pardon, my friend – one can always be mistaken. Regard a great actress, does not her acting of grief carry you away and impress you with its reality? No, however strong my own impression and belief, I needed other evidence before I allowed myself to be satisfied. The great criminal can be a great actor. I base my certainty in this case not upon my own impression, but upon the undeniable fact that Madame Renauld actually fainted. I turned up her eyelids and felt her pulse. There was no deception – the swoon was genuine. Therefore I was satisfied that her anguish was real and not assumed. Besides, a small additional point without interest, it was unnecessary for Madame Renauld to exhibit unrestrained grief. She had had one paroxysm on learning of her husband's death, and there would be no need for her to simulate another such a violent one on beholding his body. No, Madame Renauld was not her husband's murderess. But why has she lied? She lied about the wristwatch, she lied about the masked men – she lied about a third thing. Tell me, Hastings, what is your explanation of the open door?'

'Well,' I said, rather embarrassed, 'I suppose it was an oversight. They forgot to shut it.'

Poirot shook his head, and sighed.

'That is the explanation of Giraud. It does not satisfy me. There is a meaning behind that open door which for the moment I cannot fathom. One thing I am fairly sure of – they did not leave through the door. They left by the window.'

'What?'

'Precisely.'

'But there were no footmarks in the flower-bed underneath.'

'No – and there ought to have been. Listen, Hastings. The gardener, Auguste, as you heard him say, planted both those beds the preceding afternoon. In the one there are plentiful impressions of his big hobnailed boots – in the other, *none!* You see? Someone had passed that way, someone who, to obliterate their footprints, smoothed over the surface of the bed with a rake.'

'Where did they get a rake?'

'Where they got the spade and the gardening gloves,' said Poirot impatiently. 'There is no difficulty about that.'

'What makes you think that they left that way, though? Surely it is more probable that they entered by the window, and left by the door?'

'That is possible, of course. Yet I have a strong idea that they left by the window.'

'I think you are wrong.'

'Perhaps, *mon ami.*'

I mused, thinking over the new field of conjecture that Poirot's deductions had opened up to me. I recalled my wonder at his cryptic allusion to the flower-bed and the wristwatch. His remarks had seemed so meaningless at the moment, and now, for the first time, I realized how remarkably, from a few slight incidents, he had unravelled much of the mystery that surrounded the case. I paid a belated homage to my friend.

'In the meantime,' I said, considering, 'although we know a great deal more than we did, we are no nearer to solving the mystery of who killed Mr Renauld.'

'No,' said Poirot cheerfully. 'In fact we are a great deal farther off.'

The fact seemed to afford him such peculiar satisfaction that I gazed at him in wonder. He met my eye and smiled.

Suddenly a light burst upon me.

'Poirot! Mrs Renauld! I see it now. She must be shielding somebody.'

From the quietness with which Poirot received my remark, I could see that the idea had already occurred to him.

'Yes,' he said thoughtfully. 'Shielding someone – or screening someone. One of the two.'

Then, as we entered our hotel, he enjoined silence on me with a gesture.

CHAPTER XIII

The Girl with the Anxious Eyes

We lunched with an excellent appetite. For a while we ate in silence, and then Poirot observed maliciously: '*Eh bien!* And your indiscretions! You recount them not?'

I felt myself blushing.

'Oh, you mean this morning?' I endeavoured to adopt a tone of absolute nonchalance.

But I was no match for Poirot. In a very few minutes he had extracted the whole story from me, his eyes twinkling as he did so.

'*Tiens!* A story of the most romantic. What is her name, this charming young lady?'

I had to confess that I did not know.

'Still more romantic! The first *rencontre* in the train from Paris, the second here. Journeys end in lovers' meetings, is not that the saying?'

'Don't be an ass, Poirot.'

'Yesterday it was Mademoiselle Daubreuil, today it is Mademoiselle – Cinderella! Decidedly you have the heart of a Turk, Hastings! You should establish a harem!'

'It's all very well to rag me. Mademoiselle Daubreuil is a very beautiful girl, and I do admire her immensely – I don't mind admitting it. The other's nothing – I don't suppose I shall ever see her again.'

'You do not propose to see the lady again?'

His last words were almost a question, and I was aware of the sharpness with which he darted a glance at me. And before my eyes, writ large in letters of fire, I saw the words 'Hôtel du Phare', and I heard again her voice saying, 'Come and look me up', and my own answering with *empressement* 'I will.'

I answered Poirot lightly enough:

'She asked me to look her up, but, of course, I shan't.'

'Why "of course"?'

'Well, I don't want to.'

'Mademoiselle Cinderella is staying at the Hôtel d'Angleterre you told me, did you not?'

'No. Hôtel du Phare.'

'True, I forgot.'

A moment's misgiving shot across my mind. Surely I had never mentioned any hotel to Poirot. I looked across at him and felt reassured. He was cutting his bread into neat little squares, completely absorbed in his task. He must have fancied I had told him where the girl was staying.

We had coffee outside facing the sea. Poirot smoked one of his tiny cigarettes, and then drew his watch from his pocket.

'The train to Paris leaves at 2.25,' he observed. 'I should be starting.'

'Paris?' I cried.

'That is what I said, *mon ami.*'

'You are going to Paris? But why?'

He replied very seriously:

'To look for the murderer of Monsieur Renauld.'

'You think he is in Paris?'

'I am quite certain that he is not. Nevertheless, it is there that I must look for him. You do not understand, but I will explain it all to you in good time. Believe me, this journey to Paris is necessary. I shall not be away long. In all probability I shall return tomorrow. I do not propose that you should accompany me. Remain here and keep an eye on Giraud. Also cultivate the society of Monsieur Renauld *fils.*'

'That reminds me,' I said. 'I meant to ask you how you knew about those two?'

'*Mon ami* – I know human nature. Throw together a boy like young Renauld and a beautiful girl like Mademoiselle Marthe and the result is almost inevitable. Then, the quarrel! It was money, or a woman, and, remembering Léonie's description of the lad's anger, I decided on the latter. So I made my guess – and I was right.'

'You already suspected that she loved young Renauld?' Poirot smiled.

'At any rate, *I saw that she had anxious eyes.* That is how I always think of Mademoiselle Daubreuil – *as the girl with the anxious eyes.*'

His voice was so grave that it impressed me uncomfortably.

'What do you mean by that, Poirot?'

'I fancy, my friend, that we shall see before very long. But I must start.'

'I will come and see you off,' I said, rising.

'You will do nothing of the sort. I forbid it.'

He was so peremptory that I stared at him in surprise. He nodded emphatically.

'I mean it, *mon ami.* Au revoir.'

I felt rather at a loose end after Poirot had left me. I strolled down to the beach and watched the bathers, without feeling energetic enough to join them. I rather fancied that Cinderella might be disporting herself among them in some wonderful costume, but I saw no signs of her. I strolled aimlessly along the sands towards the farther end of the town. It occurred to me that, after all, it would only be decent feeling on my part to inquire after the girl. And it would save trouble in the end. The matter would then be finished with. There would be no need for me to trouble about her any further. But if I did not go at all, she might quite possibly come and look me up at the villa.

Accordingly, I left the beach, and walked inland. I soon found the Hôtel du Phare, a very unpretentious building. It was annoying in the extreme not to know the lady's name and, to save my dignity, I decided to stroll inside and look around. Probably I should find her in the lounge. I went in, but there was no sign of her. I waited for some time, till my impatience got the better of me. I took the concierge aside and slipped five francs into his hand.

'I wish to see a lady who is staying here. A young English lady, small and dark. I am not sure of her name.'

The man shook his head and seemed to be suppressing a grin.

'There is no such lady as you describe staying here.'

'But the lady told me she was staying here.'

'Monsieur must have made a mistake – or it is more likely the lady did, since there has been another gentleman here inquiring for her.'

'What is that you say?' I cried, surprised.

'But yes, monsieur. A gentleman who described her just as you have done.'

'What was he like?'

'He was a small gentleman, well dressed, very neat, very spotless, the moustache very stiff, the head of a peculiar shape, and the eyes green.'

Poirot! So that was why he refused to let me accompany him to the station. The impertinence of it! I would thank him not to meddle in my concerns. Did he fancy I needed a nurse to look after me?

Thanking the man, I departed, somewhat at a loss, and still much incensed with my meddlesome friend.

But where was the lady? I set aside my wrath and tried to puzzle it out. Evidently, through inadvertence, she had named the wrong hotel. Then another thought struck me. Was it inadvertence? Or had she deliberately withheld her name and given me the wrong address?

The more I thought about it, the more I felt convinced that this last surmise of mine was right. For some reason or other she did not wish to let the acquaintance ripen into friendship. And, though half an hour earlier this had been precisely my own view, I did not enjoy having the tables turned upon me. The whole affair was profoundly unsatisfactory, and I went up to the Villa Geneviève in a condition of distinct ill humour. I did not go to the house, but went up the path to the little bench by the shed, and sat there moodily enough.

I was distracted from my thoughts by the sound of voices

close at hand. In a second or two I realized that they came, not from the garden I was in, but from the adjoining garden of the Villa Marguerite, and that they were approaching rapidly. A girl's voice was speaking, a voice that I recognized as that of the beautiful Marthe.

'*Chéri*,' she was saying, 'is it really true? Are all our troubles over?'

'You know it, Marthe,' Jack Renauld replied. 'Nothing can part us now, beloved. The last obstacle to our union is removed. Nothing can take you from me.'

'Nothing?' the girl murmured. 'Oh Jack, Jack – I am afraid.'

I had moved to depart, realizing that I was quite unintentionally eavesdropping. As I rose to my feet, I caught sight of them through a gap in the hedge. They stood together facing me, the man's arm round the girl, his eyes looking into hers. They were a splendid-looking couple, the dark, well-knit boy, and the fair young goddess. They seemed made for each other as they stood there, happy in spite of the terrible tragedy that overshadowed their young lives.

But the girl's face was troubled, and Jack Renauld seemed to recognize it, as he held her closer to him and asked:

'But what are you afraid of, darling? What is there to fear – now?'

And then I saw the look in her eyes, the look Poirot had spoken of, as she murmured, so that I almost guessed at the words:

'I am afraid – for *you*.'

I did not hear young Renauld's answer, for my attention was distracted by an unusual appearance a little farther down the hedge. There appeared to be a brown bush there, which seemed odd, to say the least of it, so early in the summer. I stepped along to investigate, but, at my advance, the brown bush withdrew itself precipitately, and faced me with a finger to its lips. It was Giraud.

Enjoining caution, he led the way round the shed until we were out of ear-shot.

'What were you doing there?' I asked.

'Exactly what you were doing – listening.'

'But I was not there on purpose!'

'Ah!' said Giraud. 'I was.'

As always, I admired the man while disliking him. He looked me up and down with a sort of contemptuous disfavour.

'You didn't help matters by butting in. I might have heard something useful in a minute. What have you done with your old fossil?'

'Monsieur Poirot has gone to Paris,' I replied coldly.

Giraud snapped his fingers disdainfully. 'So he has gone to Paris, has he? Well, a good thing. The longer he stays there the better. But what does he think he will find there?'

I thought I read in the question a tinge of uneasiness. I drew myself up.

'That I am not at liberty to say,' I said quietly.

Giraud subjected me to a piercing stare.

'He has probably enough sense not to tell *you*,' he remarked rudely. 'Good afternoon. I'm busy.' And with that he turned on his heel, and left me without ceremony.

Matters seemed at a standstill at the Villa Geneviève. Giraud evidently did not desire my company and, from what I had seen, it seemed fairly certain that Jack Renauld did not either.

I went back to the town, had an enjoyable bathe, and returned to the hotel. I turned in early, wondering whether the following day would bring forth anything of interest.

I was wholly unprepared for what it did bring forth. I was eating my *petit déjeuner* in the dining-room, when the waiter, who had been talking to someone outside, came back in obvious excitement. He hesitated for a minute, fidgeting with his napkin, and then burst out:

'Monsieur will pardon me, but he is connected, is he not, with the affair at the Villa Geneviève?'

'Yes,' I said eagerly. 'Why?'

'Monsieur has not heard the news, though?'

'What news?'

'That there has been another murder there last night!'

'*What?*'

Leaving my breakfast, I caught up my hat and ran as fast as I could. Another murder – and Poirot away! What fatality. But who had been murdered?

I dashed in at the gate. A group of servants were in the drive, talking and gesticulating. I caught hold of Françoise.

'What has happened?'

'Oh, monsieur! monsieur! Another death! It is terrible. There is a curse upon the house. But yes, I say it, a curse! They should send for Monsieur le Curé to bring some holy water. Never will I sleep another night under that roof. It might be my turn, who knows?'

She crossed herself.

'Yes,' I cried, 'but who has been killed?'

'Do I know – me? A man – a stranger. They found him up there – in the shed – not a hundred yards from where they found poor Monsieur. And that is not all. He is stabbed – stabbed to the heart *with the same dagger!*'

CHAPTER XIV

The Second Body

Waiting for no more, I turned and ran up the path to the shed. The two men on guard there stood aside to let me pass and, filled with excitement, I entered.

The light was dim, the place was a mere rough wooden erection to keep old pots and tools in. I had entered impetuously, but on the threshold I checked myself, fascinated by the spectacle before me.

Giraud was on his hands and knees, a pocket torch in his hand with which he was examining every inch of the ground. He looked up with a frown at my entrance, then his face relaxed a little in a sort of good-humoured contempt.

'There he is,' said Giraud, flashing his torch to the far corner.

I stepped across.

The dead man lay straight upon his back. He was of medium height, swarthy of complexion, and possibly about fifty years of age. He was neatly dressed in a dark blue suit, well cut, and probably made by an expensive tailor, but not new. His face was terribly convulsed, and on his left side, just over the heart, the hilt of a dagger stood up, black and shining. I recognized it. It was the same dagger I had seen reposing in the glass jar the preceding morning!

'I'm expecting the doctor any minute,' explained Giraud. 'Although we hardly need him. There's no doubt what the man died of. He was stabbed to the heart, and death must have been pretty well instantaneous.'

'When was it done? Last night?'

Giraud shook his head.

'Hardly. I don't lay down the law on medical evidence, but

the man's been dead well over twelve hours. When do you say you last saw that dagger?'

'About ten o'clock yesterday morning.'

'Then I should be inclined to fix the crime as being done not long after that.'

'But people were passing and repassing this shed continually.'

Giraud laughed disagreeably.

'You progress to a marvel! Who told you he was killed in this shed?'

'Well –' I felt flustered. 'I – I assumed it.'

'Oh, what a fine detective! Look at him. Does a man stabbed to the heart fall like that – neatly with his feet together, and his arms to his sides? No. Again, does a man lie down on his back and permit himself to be stabbed without raising a hand to defend himself? It is absurd, is it not? But see here – and here –' He flashed the torch along the ground. I saw curious irregular marks in the soft dirt. 'He was dragged here after he was dead. Half dragged, half carried by two people. Their tracks do not show on the hard ground outside, and here they have been careful to obliterate them; but one of the two was a woman, my young friend.'

'A woman?'

'Yes.'

'But if the tracks are obliterated, how do you know?'

'Because, blurred as they are, the prints of the woman's shoe are unmistakable. Also, by *this*.' And, leaning forward, he drew something from the handle of the dagger and held it up for me to see. It was a woman's long black hair, similar to the one Poirot had taken from the armchair in the library.

With a slightly ironic smile he wound it round the dagger again.

'We will leave things as they are as much as possible,' he explained. 'It pleases the examining magistrate. Well, do you notice anything else?'

I was forced to shake my head.

'Look at his hands.'

I did. The nails were broken and discoloured and the skin was hard. It hardly enlightened me as much as I should have liked it to have done. I looked up at Giraud.

'They are not the hands of a gentleman,' he said, answering my look. 'On the contrary, his clothes are those of a well-to-do man. That is curious, is it not?'

'Very curious,' I agreed.

'And none of his clothing is marked. What do we learn from that? This man was trying to pass himself off as other than he was. He was masquerading. Why? Did he fear something? Was he trying to escape by disguising himself? As yet we do not know, but one thing we do know – he was as anxious to conceal his identity as we are to discover it.'

He looked down at the body again.

'As before, there are no fingerprints on the handle of the dagger. The murderer again wore gloves.'

'You think, then, that the murderer was the same in both cases?' I asked eagerly.

Giraud became inscrutable.

'Never mind what I think. We shall see. Marchaud!'

The *sergent de ville* appeared at the door.

'Monsieur?'

'Why is Madame Renauld not here? I sent for her a quarter of an hour ago.'

'She is coming up the path now, monsieur, and her son with her.'

'Good. I only want one at a time, though.'

Marchaud saluted and disappeared again. A moment later he reappeared with Mrs Renauld.

'Here is Madame.'

Giraud came forward with a curt bow.

'This way, madame.' He led her across, and then, standing suddenly aside, 'Here is the man. Do you know him?'

And as he spoke, his eyes, gimlet-like, bored into her face, seeking to read her mind, noting every indication of her manner.

But Mrs Renauld remained perfectly calm – too calm, I

felt. She looked down at the corpse almost without interest, certainly without any sign of agitation or recognition.

'No,' she said. 'I have never seen him in my life. He is quite a stranger to me.'

'You are sure?'

'Quite sure.'

'You do not recognize in him one of your assailants, for instance?'

'No.' She seemed to hesitate, as though struck by the idea. 'No, I do not think so. Of course they wore beards – false ones the examining magistrate thought – but still, no.' Now she seemed to make her mind up definitely. 'I am sure neither of the two was this man.'

'Very well, madame. That is all, then.'

She stepped out with head erect, the sun flashing on the silver threads in her hair. Jack Renauld succeeded her. He, too, failed to identify the man in a completely natural manner.

Giraud merely grunted. Whether he was pleased or chagrined I could not tell. He called to Marchaud.

'You have got the other there?'

'Yes, monsieur.'

'Bring her in, then.'

'The other' was Madame Daubreuil. She came indignantly, protesting with vehemence.

'I object, monsieur! This is an outrage! What have I to do with all this?'

'Madame,' said Giraud brutally, 'I am investigating not one murder, but two murders! For all I know you may have committed them both.'

'How dare you?' she cried. 'How dare you insult me by such a wild accusation! It is infamous!'

'Infamous, is it? What about this?' Stooping, he again detached the hair, and held it up. 'Do you see this, madame?' He advanced towards her. 'You permit that I see whether it matches?'

With a cry she started backwards, white to the lips.

'It is false, I swear it. I know nothing of the crime – of either

crime. Anyone who says I do lies! Ah, *mon Dieu*, what shall I
do?'

'Calm yourself, madame,' said Giraud coldly. 'No one has
accused you as yet. But you will do well to answer my questions without more ado.'

'Anything you wish, monsieur.'

'Look at the dead man. Have you ever seen him before?'

Drawing nearer, a little of the colour creeping back to her
face, Madame Daubreuil looked down at the victim with a
certain amount of interest and curiosity. Then she shook her
head.

'I do not know him.'

It seemed impossible to doubt her, the words came so naturally. Giraud dismissed her with a nod of the head.

'You are letting her go?' I asked in a low voice. 'Is that
wise? Surely that black hair is from her head.'

'I do not need teaching my business,' said Giraud dryly.
'She is under surveillance. I have no wish to arrest her as yet.'

Then, frowning, he gazed down at the body.

'Should you say that was a Spanish type at all?' he asked
suddenly.

I considered the face carefully.

'No,' I said at last. 'I should put him down as a Frenchman
most decidedly.'

Giraud gave a grunt of dissatisfaction.

'Same here.'

He stood there for a moment, then with an imperative gesture he waved me aside, and once more, on hands and knees,
he continued his search of the floor of the shed. He was marvellous. Nothing escaped him. Inch by inch he went over the
floor, turning over pots, examining old sacks. He pounced on
a bundle by the door, but it proved to be only a ragged coat
and trousers, and he flung it down again with a snarl. Two
pairs of old gloves interested him, but in the end he shook his
head and laid them aside. Then he went back to the pots,
methodically turning them over one by one. In the end he
rose to his feet, and shook his head thoughtfully. He seemed

baffled and perplexed. I think he had forgotten my presence.

But at that moment a stir and bustle was heard outside, and our old friend, the examining magistrate, accompanied by his clerk and M. Bex, with the doctor behind them, came bustling in.

'But this is extraordinary, Monsieur Giraud,' cried M. Hautet. 'Another crime! Ah, we have not got to the bottom of this case. There is some deep mystery here. But who is the victim this time?'

'That is just what nobody can tell us, monsieur. He has not been identified.'

'Where is the body?' asked the doctor.

Giraud moved aside a little.

'There in the corner. He has been stabbed to the heart, as you see. And with the dagger that was stolen yesterday morning. I fancy that the murder followed hard upon the theft – but that is for you to say. You can handle the dagger freely – there are no fingerprints on it.'

The doctor knelt down by the dead man, and Giraud turned to the examining magistrate.

'A pretty little problem, is it not? But I shall solve it.'

'And so no one can identify him,' mused the magistrate. 'Could it possibly be one of the assassins? They may have fallen out among themselves.'

Giraud shook his head.

'The man is a Frenchman – I would take my oath on that –'

But at that moment they were interrupted by the doctor, who was sitting back on his heels with a perplexed expression.

'You say he was killed yesterday morning?'

'I fix it by the theft of the dagger,' explained Giraud. 'He may, of course, have been killed later in the day.'

'Later in the day? Fiddlesticks! This man has been dead at least forty-eight hours, and probably longer.'

We stared at each other in blank amazement.

CHAPTER XV

A Photograph

The doctor's words were so surprising that we were all momentarily taken aback. Here was a man stabbed with a dagger which we knew to have been stolen only twenty-four hours previously, and yet Dr Durand asserted positively that he had been dead at least forty-eight hours! The whole thing was fantastic to the last extreme.

We were still recovering from the surprise of the doctor's announcement, when a telegram was brought to me. It had been sent up from the hotel to the villa. I tore it open. It was from Poirot, and announced his return by the train arriving at Merlinville at 12.28.

I looked at my watch and saw that I had just time to get comfortably to the station and meet him there. I felt that it was of the utmost importance that he should know at once of the new and startling developments in the case.

Evidently, I reflected, Poirot had had no difficulty in finding what he wanted in Paris. The quickness of his return proved that. Very few hours had sufficed. I wondered how he would take the exciting news I had to impart.

The train was some minutes late, and I strolled aimlessly up and down the platform, until it occurred to me that I might pass the time by asking a few questions as to who had left Merlinville by the last train on the evening of the tragedy.

I approached the chief porter, an intelligent-looking man, and had little difficulty in persuading him to enter upon the subject. It was a disgrace to the police, he hotly affirmed, that such brigands or assassins should be allowed to go about unpunished. I hinted that there was some possibility they might have left by the midnight train, but he negatived the idea decidedly. He would have noticed two foreigners – he was sure of it. Only about twenty people had left by the train, and he could not have failed to observe them.

I do not know what put the idea into my head – possibly it was the deep anxiety underlying Marthe Daubreuil's tones – but I asked suddenly:

'Young Monsieur Renauld – he did not leave by that train, did he?'

'Ah, no, monsieur. To arrive and start off again within half an hour, it would not be amusing, that!'

I stared at the man, the significance of his words almost escaping me. Then I saw.

'You mean,' I said, my heart beating a little, 'that Monsieur Jack Renauld arrived at Merlinville that evening?'

'But yes, monsieur. By the last train arriving the other way, the 11.40.'

My brain whirled. That, then, was the reason of Marthe's poignant anxiety. Jack Renauld had been in Merlinville on the night of the crime. But why had he not said so? Why, on the contrary, had he led us to believe that he had remained in Cherbourg? Remembering his frank boyish countenance, I could hardly bring myself to believe that he had any connection with the crime. Yet why this silence on his part about so vital a matter? One thing was certain, Marthe had known all along. Hence her anxiety, and her eager questioning of Poirot as to whether anyone was suspected.

My cogitations were interrupted by the arrival of the train, and in another moment I was greeting Poirot. The little man was radiant. He beamed and vociferated and, forgetting my English reluctance, embraced me warmly on the platform.

'*Mon cher ami*, I have succeeded – but succeeded to a marvel!'

'Indeed? I'm delighted to hear it. Have you heard the latest here?'

'How would you that I should hear anything? There have been some developments, eh? The brave Giraud, he has made an arrest? Or even arrests, perhaps? Ah, but I will make him look foolish, that one! But where are you taking me, my friend?

Do we not go to the hotel? It is necessary that I attend to my moustaches – they are deplorably limp from the heat of travelling. Also, without doubt, there is dust on my coat. And my tie, that I must rearrange.'

I cut short his remonstrances.

'My dear Poirot – never mind all that. We must go to the villa at once. *There has been another murder!*'

Never have I seen a man so flabbergasted. His jaw dropped. All the jauntiness went out of his bearing. He stared at me open-mouthed.

'What is that you say? Another murder? Ah, then, but I am all wrong. I have failed. Giraud may mock himself at me – he will have reason!'

'You did not expect it, then?'

'I? Not the least in the world. It demolishes my theory – it ruins everything – it – Ah, no!' He stopped dead, thumping himself on the chest. 'It is impossible. I *cannot* be wrong! The facts, taken methodically, and in their proper order, admit of only one explanation. I must be right! I *am* right!'

'But then –'

He interrupted me.

'Wait, my friend. I must be right, therefore this new murder is impossible unless – unless – Oh, wait, I implore you. Say no word.'

He was silent for a moment or two, then resuming his normal manner, he said in a quiet assured voice:

'The victim is a man of middle age. His body was found in the locked shed near the scene of the crime and had been dead at least forty-eight hours. And it is most probable that he was stabbed in a similar manner to Mr Renauld, though not necessarily in the back.'

It was my turn to gape – and gape I did. In all my knowledge of Poirot he had never done anything so amazing as this. And, almost inevitably, a doubt crossed my mind.

'Poirot,' I cried, 'you're pulling my leg. You've heard all about it already.'

He turned his earnest gaze upon me reproachfully.

'Would I do such a thing? I assure you that I have heard nothing whatsoever. Did you not observe the shock your news was to me?'

'But how on earth could you know all that?'

'I was right, then? But I knew it. The little grey cells, my friend, the little grey cells! They told me. Thus, and in no other way, could there have been a second death. Now tell me all. If we go round to the left here, we can take a short cut across the golf links which will bring us to the back of the Villa Geneviève much more quickly.'

As we walked, taking the way he had indicated, I recounted all I knew. Poirot listened attentively.

'The dagger was in the wound, you say? That is curious. You are sure it was the same one?'

'Absolutely certain. That's what makes it so impossible.'

'Nothing is impossible. There may have been two daggers.'

I raised my eyebrows.

'Surely that is in the highest degree unlikely? It would be a most extraordinary coincidence.'

'You speak as usual, without reflection, Hastings. In some cases two identical weapons *would* be highly improbable. But not here. This particular weapon was a war souvenir which was made to Jack Renauld's orders. It is really highly unlikely, when you come to think of it, that he should have had only one made. Very probably he would have another for his own use.'

'But nobody has mentioned such a thing,' I objected.

A hint of the lecturer crept into Poirot's tone.

'My friend, in working upon a case, one does not take into account only the things that are "mentioned". There is no reason to mention many things which may be important. Equally, there is often an excellent reason for *not* mentioning them. You can take your choice of the two motives.'

I was silent, impressed in spite of myself. Another few minutes brought us to the famous shed. We found all our friends there, and after an interchange of polite amenities, Poirot began his task.

Having watched Giraud at work, I was keenly interested. Poirot bestowed but a cursory glance on the surroundings. The only thing he examined was the ragged coat and trousers by the door. A disdainful smile rose to Giraud's lips, and, as though noting it, Poirot flung the bundle down again.

'Old clothes of the gardener's?' he queried.

'Exactly,' said Giraud.

Poirot knelt down by the body. His fingers were rapid but methodical. He examined the texture of the clothes, and satisfied himself that there were no marks on them. The boots he subjected to special care, also the dirty and broken fingernails. While examining the latter he threw a quick question at Giraud.

'You saw them?'

'Yes, I saw them,' replied the other. His face remained inscrutable.

Suddenly Poirot stiffened.

'Dr Durand!'

'Yes?' The doctor came forward.

'There is foam on the lips. You observed it?'

'I didn't notice it, I must admit.'

'But you observe it now?'

'Oh, certainly.'

Poirot again shot a question at Giraud.

'You noticed it without doubt?'

The other did not reply. Poirot proceeded. The dagger had been withdrawn from the wound. It reposed in a glass jar by the side of the body. Poirot examined it, then he studied the wound closely. When he looked up, his eyes were excited and shone with the green light I knew so well.

'It is a strange wound, this! It has not bled. There is no stain on the clothes. The blade of the dagger is slightly discoloured, that is all. What do you think, *monsieur le docteur*?'

'I can only say that it is most abnormal.'

'It is not abnormal at all. It is most simple. The man was stabbed *after he was dead*.' And, stilling the clamour of voices that arose with a wave of his hand, Poirot turned to Giraud and added: 'M. Giraud agrees with me, do you not, monsieur?'

Whatever Giraud's real belief, he accepted the position without moving a muscle. Calmly and almost scornfully he replied:

'Certainly I agree.'

The murmur of surprise and interest broke out again.

'But what an idea!' cried M. Hautet. 'To stab a man after he is dead! Barbaric! Unheard of! Some unappeasable hate perhaps.'

'No,' said Poirot. 'I should fancy it was done quite cold-bloodedly – to create an impression.'

'What impression?'

'The impression it nearly did create,' returned Poirot oracularly.

M. Bex had been thinking.

'How, then, was the man killed?'

'He was not killed. He died. He died, if I am not much mistaken, of an epileptic fit!'

This statement of Poirot's again aroused considerable excitement. Dr Durand knelt down again, and made a searching examination. At last he rose to his feet.

'Monsieur Poirot, I am inclined to believe that you are correct in your assertion. I was misled to begin with. The incontrovertible fact that the man had been stabbed distracted my attention from any other indications.'

Poirot was the hero of the hour. The examining magistrate was profuse in compliments. Poirot responded gracefully, and then excused himself on the pretext that neither he nor I had yet lunched, and that he wished to repair the ravages of the journey. As we were about to leave the shed, Giraud approached us.

'One other thing, Monsieur Poirot,' he said, in his suave mocking voice. 'We found this coiled round the handle of the dagger – a woman's hair.'

'Ah!' said Poirot. 'A woman's hair? What woman's, I wonder?'

'I wonder also,' said Giraud. Then, with a bow, he left us.

'He was insistent, the good Giraud,' said Poirot thought-fully, as we walked towards the hotel. 'I wonder in what direction he hopes to mislead me? A woman's hair – h'm!'

We lunched heartily, but I found Poirot somewhat distrait and inattentive. Afterwards, we went up to our sitting-room, and there I begged him to tell me something of his mysterious journey to Paris.

'Willingly, my friend. I went to Paris to find *this*.'

He took from his pocket a small faded newspaper cutting. It was the reproduction of a woman's photograph. He handed it to me. I uttered an exclamation.

'You recognize it, my friend?'

I nodded. Although the photo obviously dated from very many years back, and the hair was dressed in a different style, the likeness was unmistakable.

'Madame Daubreuil!' I exclaimed.

Poirot shook his head with a smile.

'Not quite correct, my friend. She did not call herself by that name in those days. That is a picture of the notorious Madame Beroldy!'

Madame Beroldy! In a flash the whole thing came back to me. The murder trial that had evoked such world-wide interest.

The Beroldy Case.

CHAPTER XVI

The Beroldy Case

Some twenty years or so before the opening of the present story, Monsieur Arnold Beroldy, a native of Lyons, arrived in Paris accompanied by his pretty wife and their little daughter, a mere babe. Monsieur Beroldy was a junior partner in a firm of wine merchants, a stout middle-aged man, fond of the good things of life, devoted to his charming wife, and altogether unremarkable in every way. The firm in which Monsieur Beroldy was a partner was a small one and, although doing well, it did not yield a large income to the junior partner. The Beroldys had a small apartment and lived in a very modest fashion to begin with.

But, unremarkable though Monsieur Beroldy might be, his wife was plentifully gilded with the brush of Romance. Young and good-looking, and gifted withal with a singular charm of manner, Madame Beroldy at once created a stir in the quarter, especially when it began to be whispered that some interesting mystery surrounded her birth. It was rumoured that she was the illegitimate daughter of a Russian Grand Duke. Others asserted that it was an Austrian Arch-duke, and that the union was legal, though morganatic. But all stories agreed upon one point, that Jeanne Beroldy was the centre of an interesting mystery.

Among the friends and acquaintances of the Beroldys was a young lawyer, Georges Conneau. It was soon evident that the fascinating Jeanne had completely enslaved his heart. Madame Beroldy encouraged the young man in a discreet fashion, but always being careful to affirm her complete devotion to her middle-aged husband. Nevertheless, many spiteful persons did not hesitate to declare that young Conneau was her lover – and not the only one!

When the Beroldys had been in Paris about three months, another personage came upon the scene. This was Mr Hiram P. Trapp, a native of the United States, and extremely wealthy. Introduced to the charming and mysterious Madame Beroldy, he fell a prompt victim to her fascinations. His admiration was obvious, though strictly respectful.

About this time, Madame Beroldy became more outspoken in her confidences. To several friends, she declared herself greatly worried on her husband's behalf. She explained that he had been drawn into several schemes of a political nature, and also referred to some important papers that had been entrusted to him for safe-keeping and which concerned a 'secret' of far-reaching European importance. They had been entrusted to his custody to throw pursuers off the track, but Madame Beroldy was nervous, having recognized several important members of the Revolutionary Circle in Paris.

On the 28th day of November the blow fell. The woman who came daily to clean and cook for the Beroldys was surprised to find the door of the apartment standing wide open. Hearing faint moans issuing from the bedroom, she went in. A terrible sight met her eyes. Madame Beroldy lay on the floor bound hand and foot, uttering feeble moans, having managed to free her mouth from a gag. On the bed was Monsieur Beroldy, lying in a pool of blood, with a knife driven through his heart.

Madame Beroldy's story was clear enough. Suddenly awakened from sleep, she had discerned two masked men bending over her. Stifling her cries, they had bound and gagged her. They had then demanded of Monsieur Beroldy the famous 'secret'.

But the intrepid wine merchant refused point-blank to accede to their request. Angered by his refusal, one of the men incontinently stabbed him through the heart. With the dead man's keys, they had opened the safe in the corner, and had carried away with them a mass of papers. Both men were heavily bearded, and had worn masks, but Madame Beroldy declared positively that they were Russians.

The affair created an immense sensation. Time went on,

and the mysterious bearded men were never traced. And then, just as public interest was beginning to die down, a startling development occurred: Madame Beroldy was arrested and charged with the murder of her husband.

The trial, when it came on, aroused widespread interest. The youth and beauty of the accused, and her mysterious history, were sufficient to make of it a *cause célèbre*.

It was proved beyond doubt that Jeanne Beroldy's parents were a highly respectable and prosaic couple, fruit merchants, who lived on the outskirts of Lyons. The Russian Grand Duke, the court intrigues, and the political schemes – all the stories current were traced back to the lady herself! Remorselessly, the whole story of her life was laid bare. The motive for the murder was found in Mr Hiram P. Trapp. Mr Trapp did his best, but, relentlessly and agilely cross-questioned, he was forced to admit that he loved the lady, and that, had she been free, he would have asked her to be his wife. The fact that the relations between them were admittedly platonic strengthened the case against the accused. Debarred from becoming his mistress by the simple honourable nature of the man, Jeanne Beroldy had conceived the monstrous project of ridding herself of her elderly, undistinguished husband and becoming the wife of the rich American.

Throughout, Madame Beroldy confronted her accusers with complete sang-froid and self-possession. Her story never varied. She continued to declare strenuously that she was of royal birth and that she had been substituted for the daughter of the fruit-seller at an early age. Absurd and completely unsubstantiated as these statements were, a great number of people believed implicitly in their truth.

But the prosecution was implacable. It denounced the masked 'Russians' as a myth, and asserted that the crime had been committed by Madame Beroldy and her lover, Georges Conneau. A warrant was issued for the arrest of the latter, but he had wisely disappeared. Evidence showed that the bonds which secured Madame Beroldy were so loose that she could easily have freed herself.

And then, towards the close of the trial, a letter, posted in Paris, was sent to the Public Prosecutor. It was from Georges Conneau and, without revealing his whereabouts it contained a full confession of the crime. He declared that he had indeed struck the fatal blow at Madame Beroldy's instigation. The crime had been planned between them. Believing that her husband ill-treated her, and maddened by his own passion for her, a passion which he believed her to return, he had planned the crime and struck the fatal blow that should free the woman he loved from a hateful bondage. Now, for the first time, he learnt of Mr Hiram P. Trapp, and realized that the woman he loved had betrayed him! Not for his sake did she wish to be free, but in order to marry the wealthy American. She had used him as a cat's paw, and now, in his jealous rage, he turned and denounced her, declaring that throughout he had acted at her instigation.

And then Madame Beroldy proved herself the remarkable woman she undoubtedly was. Without hesitation, she dropped her previous defence, and admitted that the 'Russians' were a pure invention on her part. The real murderer was Georges Conneau. Maddened by passion, he had committed the crime, vowing that if she did not keep silence he would exact a terrible vengeance from her. Terrified by his threats, she had consented – also fearing it likely that if she told the truth she might be accused of conniving at the crime. But she had steadfastly refused to have anything more to do with her husband's murderer, and it was in revenge for this attitude on her part that he had written this letter accusing her. She swore solemnly that she had had nothing to do with the planning of the crime, that she had awoke on that memorable night to find Georges Conneau standing over her, the blood-stained knife in his hand.

It was a touch-and-go affair. Madame Beroldy's story was hardly credible. But her address to the jury was a masterpiece. The tears streaming down her face, she spoke of her child, of her woman's honour – of her desire to keep her reputation untarnished for the child's sake. She admitted that, Georges

Conneau having been her lover, she might perhaps be held morally responsible for the crime – but, before God, nothing more! She knew that she had committed a grave fault in not denouncing Conneau to the law, but she declared in a broken voice that that was a thing no woman could have done. She had loved him! Could she let her hand be the one to send him to the guillotine? She had been guilty of much, but she was innocent of the terrible crime imputed to her.

However that may have been, her eloquence and personality won the day. Madame Beroldy, amidst a scene of unparalleled excitement, was acquitted.

Despite the utmost endeavours of the police, Georges Conneau was never traced. As for Madame Beroldy, nothing more was heard of her. Taking the child with her, she left Paris to begin a new life.

CHAPTER XVII

We Make Further Investigations

I have set down the Beroldy case in full. Of course all the details did not present themselves to my memory as I have recounted them here. Nevertheless, I recalled the case fairly accurately. It had attracted a great deal of interest at the time, and had been fully reported by the English papers, so that it did not need much effort of memory on my part to recollect the salient details.

Just for the moment, in my excitement, it seemed to clear up the whole matter. I admit that I am impulsive, and Poirot deplores my custom of jumping to conclusions, but I think I had some excuse in this instance. The remarkable way in which this discovery justified Poirot's point of view struck me at once.

'Poirot,' I said, 'I congratulate you. I see everything now.'

Poirot lit one of his little cigarettes with his usual precision. Then he looked up.

'And since you see everything now, *mon ami*, what exactly is it that you see?'

'Why, that it was Madame Daubreuil – Beroldy – who murdered Mr Renauld. The similarity of the two cases proves that beyond a doubt.'

'Then you consider that Madame Beroldy was wrongly acquitted? That in actual fact she was guilty of connivance in her husband's murder?'

I opened my eyes wide.

'Of course! Don't you?'

Poirot walked to the end of the room, absent-mindedly straightened a chair, and then said thoughtfully:

'Yes, that is my opinion. But there is no "of course" about

it, my friend. Technically speaking, Madame Beroldy is innocent.'

'Of that crime, perhaps. But not of this.'

Poirot sat down again, and regarded me, his thoughtful air more marked than ever.

'So it is definitely your opinion, Hastings, that Madame Daubreuil murdered Monsieur Renauld?'

'Yes.'

'Why?'

He shot the question at me with such suddenness that I was taken aback.

'Why?' I stammered. 'Why? Oh, because –' I came to a stop.

Poirot nodded his head at me.

'You see, you come to a stumbling-block at once. Why should Madame Daubreuil (I shall call her that for clearness' sake) murder Monsieur Renauld? We can find no shadow of a motive. She does not benefit by his death; considered as either mistress or blackmailer she stands to lose. You cannot have a murder without motive. The first crime was different – there we had a rich lover waiting to step into her husband's shoes.'

'Money is not the only motive for murder,' I objected.

'True,' agreed Poirot placidly. 'There are two others, the *crime passionnel* is one. And there is the third rare motive, murder for an idea, which implies some form of mental derangement on the part of the murderer. Homicidal mania and religious fanaticism belong to that class. We can rule it out here.'

'But what about the *crime passionnel*? Can you rule that out? If Madame Daubreuil was Renauld's mistress, if she found that his affection was cooling, or if her jealousy was aroused in any way, might she not have struck him down in a moment of anger?'

Poirot shook his head.

'If – I say *if*, you note – Madame Daubreuil was Renauld's mistress, he had not had time to tire of her. And in any case you mistake her character. She is a woman who can simulate great emotional stress. She is a magnificent actress. But, looked at dispassionately, her life disproves her appearance. Throughout, if we examine it, she has been cold-blooded and calculating in her motives and actions. It was not to link her life with that of her young lover that she connived at her husband's murder. The rich American, for whom she probably did not care a button, was her objective. If she committed a crime, she would always do so for gain. Here there was no gain. Besides, how do you account for the digging of the grave? That was a man's work.'

'She might have had an accomplice,' I suggested, unwilling to relinquish my belief.

'I pass to another objection. You have spoken of the similarity between the two crimes. Wherein does that lie, my friend?'

I stared at him in astonishment.

'Why, Poirot, it was you who remarked on that! The story of the masked men, the "secret", the papers!'

Poirot smiled a little.

'Do not be so indignant, I beg of you. I repudiate nothing. The similarity of the two stories links the two cases together inevitably. But reflect now on something very curious. It is not Madame Daubreuil who tells us this tale – if it were, all would indeed be plain sailing – it is Madame Renauld. Is she then in league with the other?'

'I can't believe that,' I said slowly. 'If she is, she must be the most consummate actress the world has ever known.'

'Ta-ta-ta!' said Poirot impatiently. 'Again you have the sentiment and not the logic! If it is necessary for a criminal to be a consummate actress, then by all means assume her to be one. But is it necessary? I do not believe Mrs Renauld to be in league with Madame Daubreuil for several reasons, some of which I have already enumerated to you. The others are self-evident. Therefore, that possibility eliminated, we draw very near to the truth, which is, as always, very curious and interesting.'

'Poirot,' I cried, 'what more do you know?'

'*Mon ami*, you must make your own deductions. You have "access to the facts". Concentrate your grey cells. Reason – not like Giraud – but like Hercule Poirot!'

'But are you *sure*?'

'My friend, in many ways I have been an imbecile. But at last I see clearly.'

'You know everything?'

'I have discovered what Monsieur Renauld sent for me to discover.'

'And you know the murderer?'

'I know one murderer.'

'What do you mean?'

'We talk a little at cross-purposes. There are here not one crime, but two. The first I have solved, the second – *eh bien*, I will confess, I am not sure!'

'But, Poirot, I thought you said the man in the shed had died a natural death?'

'Ta-ta-ta!' Poirot made his favourite ejaculation of impatience. 'Still you do not understand. One may have a crime without a murderer, but for two crimes it is essential to have two bodies.'

His remark struck me as so peculiarly lacking in lucidity that I looked at him in some anxiety. But he appeared perfectly normal. Suddenly he rose and strolled to the window.

'Here he is,' he observed.

'Who?'

'Monsieur Jack Renauld. I sent a note up to the villa to ask him to come here.'

That changed the course of my ideas, and I asked Poirot if he knew that Jack Renauld had been in Merlinville on the night of the crime. I had hoped to catch my astute little friend napping, but as usual he was omniscient. He, too, had inquired at the station.

'And without doubt we are not original in the idea, Hastings. The excellent Giraud, he also has probably made his inquiries.'

'You don't think –' I said, and then stopped. 'Ah, no, it would be too horrible!'

Poirot looked inquiringly at me, but I said no more. It had just occurred to me that though there were seven women, directly and indirectly connected with the case – Mrs Renauld, Madame Daubreuil and her daughter, the mysterious visitor, and the three servants – there was, with the exception of old Auguste, who could hardly count, only one man – Jack Renauld. *And a man must have dug the grave.*

I had no time to develop farther the appalling idea that had occurred to me, for Jack Renauld was ushered into the room.

Poirot greeted him in business-like manner.

'Take a seat, monsieur. I regret infinitely to derange you, but you will perhaps understand that the atmosphere of the villa is not too congenial to me. Monsieur Giraud and I do not see eye to eye about everything. His politeness to me has not been striking, and you will comprehend that I do not intend any little discoveries I may make to benefit him in any way.'

'Exactly, Monsieur Poirot,' said the lad. 'That fellow Giraud is an ill-conditioned brute, and I'd be delighted to see someone score at his expense.'

'Then I may ask a little favour of you?'

'Certainly.'

'I will ask you to go to the railway station and take a train to the next station along the line, Abbalac. Ask at the cloak-room whether two foreigners deposited a valise there on the night of the murder. It is a small station, and they are almost certain to remember. Will you do this?'

'Of course I will,' said the boy, mystified, though ready for the task.

'I and my friend, you comprehend, have business else-where,' explained Poirot. 'There is a train in a quarter of an hour, and I will ask you not to return to the villa, as I have no wish for Giraud to get an inkling of your errand.'

'Very well, I will go straight to the station.'

He rose to his feet. Poirot's voice stopped him:

'One moment, Monsieur Renauld, there is one little matter that puzzles me. Why did you not mention to Monsieur Hautet this morning that you were in Merlinville on the night of the crime?'

Jack Renauld's face went crimson. With an effort he controlled himself.

'You have made a mistake. I was in Cherbourg as I told the examining magistrate this morning.'

Poirot looked at him, his eyes narrowed, cat-like, until they only showed a gleam of green.

'Then it is a singular mistake that I have made there – for it is shared by the station staff. They say you arrived by the 11.40 train.'

For a moment Jack Renauld hesitated, then he made up his mind.

'And if I did? I suppose you do not mean to accuse me of participating in my father's murder?' He asked the question haughtily, his head thrown back.

'I should like an explanation of the reason that brought you here.'

'That is simple enough. I came to see my fiancée, Mademoiselle Daubreuil. I was on the eve of a long voyage, uncertain as to when I should return. I wished to see her before I went, to assure her of my unchanging devotion.'

'And did you see her?' Poirot's eyes never left the other's face.

There was an appreciable pause before Renauld replied. Then he said:

'Yes.'

'And afterwards?'

'I found I had missed the last train. I walked to St Beauvais, where I knocked up a garage and got a car to take me back to Cherbourg.'

'St Beauvais? That is fifteen kilometres. A long walk, M. Renauld.'

'I – I felt like walking.'

Poirot bowed his head as a sign that he accepted the

explanation. Jack Renauld took up his hat and cane and departed. In a trice Poirot jumped to his feet.

'Quick, Hastings. We will go after him.'

Keeping a discreet distance behind our quarry, we followed him through the streets of Merlinville. But when Poirot saw that he took the turning to the station he checked himself.

'All is well. He has taken the bait. He will go to Abbalac, and will inquire for the mythical valise left by the mythical foreigners. Yes, *mon ami*, all that was a little invention of my own.'

'You wanted him out of the way!' I exclaimed.

'Your penetration is amazing, Hastings! Now, if you please, we will go up to the Villa Geneviève.'

CHAPTER XVIII

Giraud Acts

Arrived at the villa, Poirot led the way up to the shed where the second body had been discovered. He did not, however, go in, but paused by the bench which I have mentioned before as being set some few yards away from it. After contemplating it for a moment or two, he paced carefully from it to the hedge which marked the boundary between the Villa Geneviève and the Villa Marguerite. Then he paced back again, nodding his head as he did so. Returning again to the hedge, he parted the bushes with his hands.

'With good fortune,' he remarked to me over his shoulder, 'Mademoiselle Marthe may find herself in the garden. I desire to speak to her and would prefer not to call formally at the Villa Marguerite. Ah, all is well, there she is. Pst, Mademoiselle! Pst! *Un moment, s'il vous plaît.*'

I joined him at the moment that Marthe Daubreuil, looking slightly startled, came running up to the hedge at his call.

'A little word with you, mademoiselle, if it is permitted?'

'Certainly, Monsieur Poirot.'

Despite her acquiescence, her eyes looked troubled and afraid.

'Mademoiselle, do you remember running after me on the road the day that I came to your house with the examining magistrate? You asked me if anyone were suspected of the crime.'

'And you told me two Chileans.' Her voice sounded rather breathless, and her left hand stole to her breast.

'Will you ask me the same question again, mademoiselle?'

'What do you mean?'

'This. If you were to ask me that question again, I should

give you a different answer. Someone is suspected – but not a Chilean.'

'Who?' The word came faintly between her parted lips.

'Monsieur Jack Renauld.'

'What?' It was a cry. 'Jack? Impossible. Who dares to suspect him?'

'Giraud.'

'Giraud!' The girl's face was ashy. 'I am afraid of that man. He is cruel. He will – he will –' She broke off. There was courage gathering in her face, and determination. I realized in that moment that she was a fighter. Poirot, too, watched her intently.

'You know, of course, that he was here on the night of the murder?' he asked.

'Yes,' she replied mechanically. 'He told me.'

'It was unwise to have tried to conceal the fact,' ventured Poirot.

'Yes, yes,' she replied impatiently. 'But we cannot waste time on regrets. We must find something to save him. He is innocent, of course; but that will not help him with a man like Giraud, who has his reputation to think of. He must arrest someone, and that someone will be Jack.'

'The facts will tell against him,' said Poirot. 'You realize that?'

She faced him squarely.

'I am not a child, monsieur. I can be brave and look facts in the face. He is innocent, and we must save him.'

She spoke with a kind of desperate energy, then was silent, frowning as she thought.

'Mademoiselle,' said Poirot, observing her keenly, 'is there not something that you are keeping back that you could tell us?'

She nodded perplexedly.

'Yes, there is something, but I hardly know whether you will believe it – it seems so absurd.'

'At any rate, tell us, mademoiselle.'

'It is this. M. Giraud sent for me, as an afterthought, to see if I could identify the man in there.' She signed with her head towards the shed. 'I could not. At least I could not at the moment. But since I have been thinking –'

'Well?'

'It seems so queer, and yet I am almost sure. I will tell you. On the morning of the day Monsieur Renauld was murdered, I was walking in the garden here, when I heard a sound of men's voices quarrelling. I pushed aside the bushes and looked through. One of the men was Monsieur Renauld and the other was a tramp, a dreadful-looking creature in filthy rags. He was alternately whining and threatening. I gathered he was asking for money, but at that moment *maman* called me from the house, and I had to go. That is all, only – I am almost sure that the tramp and the dead man in the shed are one and the same.'

Poirot uttered an exclamation.

'But why did you not say at the time, mademoiselle?'

'Because at first it only struck me that the face was vaguely familiar in some way. The man was differently dressed, and apparently belonged to a superior station in life.'

A voice called from the house.

'*Maman*,' whispered Marthe: 'I must go.' And she slipped away through the trees.

'Come,' said Poirot and, taking my arm, turned in the direction of the villa.

'What do you really think?' I asked in some curiosity. 'Was that story true, or did the girl make it up in order to divert suspicion from her lover?'

'It is a curious tale,' said Poirot, 'but I believe it to be the absolute truth. Unwittingly, Mademoiselle Marthe told us the truth on another point – and incidentally gave Jack Renauld the lie. Did you notice his hesitation when I asked him if he saw Marthe Daubreuil on the night of the crime? He paused and then said "Yes". I suspected that he was lying. It was necessary for me to see Mademoiselle Marthe before he could put her on her guard. Three little words gave me the information I wanted. When I asked her if she knew that Jack

Renauld was here that night, she answered, "He *told* me."
Now, Hastings, what was Jack Renauld doing here on that
eventful evening, and if he did not see Mademoiselle Marthe
whom did he see?'

'Surely, Poirot,' I cried, aghast, 'you cannot believe that a
boy like that would murder his own father!'

'*Mon ami*,' said Poirot. 'You continue to be of a sentimentality unbelievable! I have seen mothers who murdered their
little children for the sake of the insurance money! After that,
one can believe anything.'

'And the motive?'

'Money of course. Remember that Jack Renauld thought
that he would come into half his father's fortune at the latter's
death.'

'But the tramp. Where does he come in?'

Poirot shrugged his shoulders.

'Giraud would say that he was an accomplice – an apache
who helped young Renauld to commit the crime, and who
was conveniently put out of the way afterwards.'

'But the hair round the dagger? The woman's hair?'

'Ah!' said Poirot, smiling broadly. 'That is the cream of
Giraud's little jest. According to him, it is not a woman's hair
at all. Remember that the youths of today wear their hair
brushed straight back from the forehead with pomade or hair
wash to make it lie flat. Consequently some of the hairs are
of considerable length.'

'And you believe that too?'

'No,' said Poirot, with a curious smile. 'For I know it to be
the hair of a woman – and more, which woman!'

'Madame Daubreuil,' I announced positively.

'Perhaps,' said Poirot, regarding me quizzically. But I
refused to allow myself to get annoyed.

'What are we going to do now?' I asked, as we entered the
hall of the Villa Geneviève.

'I wish to make a search among the effects of M. Jack
Renauld. That is why I had to get him out of the way for a
few hours.'

Neatly and methodically, Poirot opened each drawer in turn, examined the contents, and returned them exactly to their places. It was a singularly dull and uninteresting proceeding. Poirot waded on through collars, pyjamas, and socks. A purring noise outside drew me to the window. Instantly I became galvanized into life.

'Poirot!' I cried. 'A car has just driven up. Giraud is in it, and Jack Renauld, and two gendarmes.'

'*Sacré tonnerre!*' growled Poirot. 'That animal of a Giraud, could he not wait? I shall not be able to replace the things in this last drawer with the proper method. Let us be quick.'

Unceremoniously he tumbled out the things on the floor, mostly ties and handkerchiefs. Suddenly with a cry of triumph Poirot pounced on something, a small square of cardboard, evidently a photograph. Thrusting it into his pocket, he returned the things pell-mell to the drawer, and seizing me by the arm dragged me out of the room and down the stairs. In the hall stood Giraud, contemplating his prisoner.

'Good afternoon, Monsieur Giraud,' said Poirot. 'What have we here?'

Giraud nodded his head towards Jack.

'He was trying to make a getaway, but I was too sharp for him. He's under arrest for the murder of his father, Monsieur Paul Renauld.'

Poirot wheeled round to confront the boy, who was leaning limply against the door, his face ashy pale.

'What do you say to that, *jeune homme*?'

Jack Renauld stared at him stonily.

'Nothing,' he said.

CHAPTER XIX

I Use My Grey Cells

I was dumbfounded. Up to the last, I had not been able to bring myself to believe Jack Renauld guilty. I had expected a ringing proclamation of his innocence when Poirot challenged him. But now, watching him as he stood, white and limp against the wall, and hearing the damning admission fall from his lips, I doubted no longer.

But Poirot had turned to Giraud.

'What are your grounds for arresting him?'

'Do you expect me to give them to you?'

'As a matter of courtesy, yes.'

Giraud looked at him doubtfully. He was torn between a desire to refuse rudely and the pleasure of triumphing over his adversary.

'You think I have made a mistake, I suppose?' he sneered.

'It would not surprise me,' replied Poirot, with a soupçon of malice.

Giraud's face took on a deeper tinge of red.

'*Eh bien*, come in here. You shall judge for yourself.'

He flung open the door of the salon, and we passed in, leaving Jack Renauld in the care of the two other men.

'Now, Monsieur Poirot,' said Giraud, laying his hat on the table, and speaking with the utmost sarcasm, 'I will treat you to a little lecture on detective work. I will show how we moderns work.'

'*Bien!*' said Poirot, composing himself to listen. 'I will show you how admirably the Old Guard can listen.' And he leaned back and closed his eyes, opening them for a moment to remark: 'Do not fear that I shall sleep. I will attend most carefully.'

'Of course,' began Giraud, 'I soon saw through all that

Chilean tomfoolery. Two men were in it – but they were not mysterious foreigners! All that was a blind.'

'Very creditable so far, my dear Giraud,' murmured Poirot. 'Especially after that clever trick of theirs with the match and cigarette end.'

Giraud glared, but continued.

'A man must have been connected with the case, in order to dig the grave. There is no man who actually benefits by the crime, but there was a man who *thought* he would benefit. I heard of Jack Renauld's quarrel with his father, and of the threats that he had used. The motive was established. Now as to means. Jack Renauld was in Merlinville that night. He concealed the fact – which turned suspicion into certainty. Then we found a second victim – *stabbed with the same dagger.* We know when that dagger was stolen. Captain Hastings here can fix the time. Jack Renauld, arriving from Cherbourg, was the only person who could have taken it. I have accounted for all the other members of the household.'

Poirot interrupted.

'You are wrong. There is one other person who could have taken the dagger.'

'You refer to Monsieur Stonor? He arrived at the front door, in an automobile which had brought him straight from Calais. Ah! believe me, I have looked into everything. Monsieur Jack Renauld arrived by train. An hour elapsed between his arrival and the moment when he presented himself at the house. Without doubt, he saw Captain Hastings and his companion leave the shed, slipped in himself and took the dagger, stabbed his accomplice in the shed –'

'Who was already dead!'

Giraud shrugged his shoulders.

'Possibly he did not observe that. He may have judged him to be sleeping. Without doubt they had a rendezvous. In any case he knew this apparent second murder would greatly complicate the case. It did.'

'But it could not deceive Monsieur Giraud,' murmured Poirot.

'You mock at me! But I will give you one last irrefutable proof. Madame Renauld's story was false – a fabrication from beginning to end. We believe Madame Renauld to have loved her husband – *yet she lied to shield his murderer*. For whom will a woman lie? Sometimes for herself, usually for the man she loves, *always* for her children. That is the last – the irrefutable proof. You cannot get round it.'

Giraud paused, flushed and triumphant. Poirot regarded him steadily.

'That is my case,' said Giraud. 'What have you to say to it?'

'Only that there is one thing you have failed to take into account.'

'What is that?'

'Jack Renauld was presumably acquainted with the planning out of the golf course. He knew that the body would be discovered almost at once, when they started to dig the bunker.'

Giraud laughed out loud.

'But it is idiotic what you say there! He wanted the body to be found! Until it was found, he could not presume death, and would have been unable to enter into his inheritance.'

I saw a quick flash of green in Poirot's eyes as he rose to his feet.

'Then why bury it?' he asked very softly. 'Reflect, Giraud. Since it was to Jack Renauld's advantage that the body should be found without delay, *why dig a grave at all*?'

Giraud did not reply. The question found him unprepared. He shrugged his shoulders as though to intimate that it was of no importance.

Poirot moved towards the door. I followed him.

'There is one more thing that you have failed to take into account,' he said over his shoulder.

'What is that?'

'The piece of lead-piping,' said Poirot, and left the room.

Jack Renauld still stood in the hall, with a white dumb face, but as we came out of the salon he looked up sharply. At the same moment there was the sound of a footfall on the staircase. Mrs Renauld was descending it. At the sight of her son, standing between the two myrmidons of the law, she stopped as though petrified.

'Jack,' she faltered. 'Jack, what is this?'

He looked up at her, his face set.

'They have arrested me, mother.'

'What?'

She uttered a piercing cry, and before anyone could get to her, swayed, and fell heavily. We both ran to her and lifted her up. In a minute Poirot stood up again.

'She has cut her head badly, on the corner of the stairs. I fancy there is slight concussion also. If Giraud wants a statement from her, he will have to wait. She will probably be unconscious for at least a week.'

Denise and Françoise had run to their mistress, and leaving her in their charge Poirot left the house. He walked with his head down, frowning thoughtfully. For some time I did not speak, but at last I ventured to put a question to him:

'Do you believe then, in spite of all appearances to the contrary, that Jack Renauld may not be guilty?'

Poirot did not answer at once, but after a long wait he said gravely:

'I do not know, Hastings. There is just a chance of it. Of course Giraud is all wrong – wrong from beginning to end. If Jack Renauld is guilty, it is in spite of Giraud's arguments, not *because* of them. And the gravest indictment against him is known only to me.'

'What is that?' I asked, impressed.

'If you would use your grey cells, and see the whole case clearly as I do, you too would perceive it, my friend.'

This was what I called one of Poirot's irritating answers. He went on, without waiting for me to speak:

'Let us walk this way to the sea. We will sit on that little mound there, overlooking the beach, and review the case. You shall know all that I know, but I would prefer that you should come at the truth by your own efforts – not by my leading you by the hand.'

We established ourselves on the grassy knoll as Poirot had suggested, looking out to sea.

'Think, my friend,' said Poirot's voice encouragingly. 'Arrange your ideas. Be methodical. Be orderly. There is the secret of success.'

I endeavoured to obey him, casting my mind back over all the details of the case. And suddenly I started as an idea of bewildering luminosity shot into my brain. Tremblingly I built up my hypothesis.

'You have a little idea, I see, *mon ami*! Capital. We progress.'

I sat up, and lit a pipe.

'Poirot,' I said, 'it seems to me we have been strangely remiss. I say *we* – although I dare say *I* would be nearer the mark. But you must pay the penalty of your determined secrecy. So I say again we have been strangely remiss. There is someone we have forgotten.'

'And who is that?' inquired Poirot, with twinkling eyes.

'Georges Conneau!'

CHAPTER XX

An Amazing Statement

The next moment Poirot embraced me warmly on the cheek.

'*Enfin!* You have arrived! And all by yourself. It is superb! Continue your reasoning. You are right. Decidedly we have done wrong to forget Georges Conneau.'

I was so flattered by the little man's approval that I could hardly continue. But at last I collected my thoughts and went on.

'Georges Conneau disappeared twenty years ago, but we have no reason to believe that he is dead.'

'*Aucunement*,' agreed Poirot. 'Proceed.'

'Therefore we will assume that he is alive.'

'Exactly.'

'Or that he was alive until recently.'

'*De mieux en mieux!*'

'We will presume,' I continued, my enthusiasm rising, 'that he has fallen on evil days. He has become a criminal, an apache, a tramp – a what you will. He chances to come to Merlinville. There he finds the woman he has never ceased to love.'

'Eh eh! The sentimentality,' warned Poirot.

'Where one hates one also loves,' I quoted or misquoted. 'At any rate he finds her there, living under an assumed name. But she has a new lover, the Englishman, Renauld. Georges Conneau, the memory of old wrongs rising in him, quarrels with this Renauld. He lies in wait for him as he comes to visit his mistress, and stabs him in the back. Then, terrified at what he has done, he starts to dig a grave. I imagine it likely that Madame Daubreuil comes out to look for her lover. She and Conneau have a terrible scene. He drags her into the shed,

and there suddenly falls down in an epileptic fit. Now supposing Jack Renauld to appear. Madame Daubreuil tells him all,
points out to him the dreadful consequences to her daughter
if this scandal of the past is revived. His father's murderer is
dead – let them do their best to hush it up. Jack Renauld
consents – goes to the house and has an interview with his
mother, winning her over to his point of view. Primed with
the story that Madame Daubreuil has suggested to him, she
permits herself to be gagged and bound. There, Poirot, what
do you think of that?' I leaned back, flushed with the pride of
successful reconstruction.

Poirot looked at me thoughtfully.

'I think that you should write for the Kinema, *mon ami*,' he
remarked at last.

'You mean –'

'It would mean a good film, the story that you have
recounted to me there – but it bears no sort of resemblance
to everyday life.'

'I admit that I haven't gone into all the details, but –'

'You have gone farther – you have ignored them magnificently. What about the way the two men were dressed? Do
you suggest that after stabbing his victim, Conneau removed
his suit of clothes, donned it himself, and replaced the dagger?'

'I don't see that that matters,' I objected rather huffily.
'He may have obtained clothes and money from Madame
Daubreuil by threats earlier in the day.'

'By threats – eh? You seriously advance that supposition?'

'Certainly. He could have threatened to reveal her identity
to the Renaulds, which would probably have put an end to
all hopes of her daughter's marriage.'

'You are wrong, Hastings. He could not blackmail her, for
she had the whip-hand. Georges Conneau, remember, is still
wanted for murder. A word from her and he is in danger of
the guillotine.'

I was forced, rather reluctantly, to admit the truth of this.

'*Your* theory,' I remarked acidly, 'is doubtless correct as to
all the details?'

'My theory is the truth,' said Poirot quietly. 'And the truth is necessarily correct. In your theory you made a fundamental error. You permitted your imagination to lead you astray with midnight assignations and passionate love scenes. But in investigating crime we must take our stand upon the commonplace. Shall I demonstrate my methods to you?'

'Oh, by all means let us have a demonstration!'

Poirot sat very upright and began, wagging his forefinger emphatically to emphasize his points:

'I will start as you started from the basic fact of Georges Conneau. Now the story told by Madame Beroldy in court as to the "Russians" was admittedly a fabrication. If she was innocent of connivance in the crime, it was concocted by her, and by her only as she stated. If, on the other hand, she was *not* innocent, it might have been invented by either her or Georges Conneau.

'Now, in this case we are investigating, we meet the same tale. As I pointed out to you, the facts render it very unlikely that Madame Daubreuil inspired it. So we turn to the hypothesis that the story had its origin in the brain of Georges Conneau. Very good. Georges Conneau, therefore, planned the crime, with Mrs Renauld as his accomplice. She is in the limelight, and behind her is a shadowy figure whose present *alias* is unknown to us.

'Now let us go carefully over the Renauld Case from the beginning, setting down each significant point in its chronological order. You have a notebook and pencil? Good. Now what is the earliest point to note down?'

'The letter to you?'

'That was the first we knew of it, but it is not the proper beginning of the case. The first point of any significance, I should say, is the change that came over Monsieur Renauld shortly after arriving in Merlinville, and which is attested to by several witnesses. We have also to consider his friendship with Madame Daubreuil, and the large sums of money paid over to her. From thence we can come directly to the 23rd May.'

Poirot paused, cleared his throat, and signed to me to write:

'*23rd May*. M. Renauld quarrels with his son over latter's wish to marry Marthe Daubreuil. Son leaves for Paris.

'*24th May*. M. Renauld alters his will, leaving entire control of his fortune in his wife's hands.

'*7th June*. Quarrel with tramp in garden, witnessed by Marthe Daubreuil.

'Letter written to M. Hercule Poirot, imploring assistance.

'Telegram sent to M. Jack Renauld, bidding him proceed by the *Anzora* to Buenos Aires.

'Chauffeur, Masters, sent off on a holiday.

'Visit of a lady that evening. As he is seeing her out, his words are "Yes, yes – but for God's sake go now . . ."'

Poirot paused.

'There, Hastings, take each of those facts one by one, consider them carefully by themselves and in relation to the whole, and see if you do not get new light on the matter.'

I endeavoured conscientiously to do as he had said. After a moment or two, I said rather doubtfully:

'As to the first points, the question seems to be whether we adopt the theory of blackmail, or of an infatuation for this woman.'

'Blackmail, decidedly. You heard what Stonor said as to his character and habits.'

'Mrs Renauld did not confirm his view,' I argued.

'We have already seen that Madame Renauld's testimony cannot be relied upon in any way. We must trust to Stonor on that point.'

'Still, if Renauld had an affair with a woman called Bella, there seems no inherent improbability in his having another with Madame Daubreuil.'

'None whatever, I grant you, Hastings. But did he?'

'The letter, Poirot. You forget the letter.'

'No, I do not forget. But what makes you think that letter was written to Monsieur Renauld?'

'Why, it was found in his pocket, and – and –'

'And that is all!' cut in Poirot. 'There was no mention of any name to show to whom the letter was addressed. We assumed it was to the dead man because it was in the pocket of his overcoat. Now, *mon ami*, something about that overcoat struck me as unusual. I measured it, and made the remark that he wore his overcoat very long. That remark should have given you to think.'

'I thought you were just saying it for the sake of saying something,' I confessed.

'Ah, *quelle idée*! Later you observed me measuring the overcoat of Monsieur Jack Renauld. *Eh bien*, Monsieur Jack Renauld wears his overcoat very short. Put those two facts together with a third, namely, that Monsieur Jack Renauld flung out of the house in a hurry on his departure for Paris, and tell me what you make of it!'

'I see,' I said slowly, as the meaning of Poirot's remarks bore in upon me. 'That letter was written to Jack Renauld – not to his father. He caught up the wrong overcoat in his haste and agitation.'

Poirot nodded.

'*Précisément!* We can return to this point later. For the moment let us content ourselves with accepting the letter as having nothing to do with Monsieur Renauld *père*, and pass to the next chronological event.'

'"*23rd May*."' I read: '"M. Renauld quarrels with his son over latter's wish to marry Marthe Daubreuil. Son leaves for Paris." I don't see anything much to remark upon there, and the altering of the will the following day seems straightforward enough. It was the direct result of the quarrel.'

'We agree, *mon ami* – at least as to the cause. But what exact motive underlay this procedure of Monsieur Renauld's?'

I opened my eyes in surprise.

'Anger against his son of course.'

'Yet he wrote him affectionate letters to Paris?'

'So Jack Renauld says, but he cannot produce them.'

'Well, let us pass from that.'

'Now we come to the day of the tragedy. You have placed

the events of the morning in a certain order. Have you any justification for that?'

'I have ascertained that the letter to me was posted at the same time as the telegram was dispatched. Masters was informed he could take a holiday shortly afterwards. In my opinion the quarrel with the tramp took place anterior to these happenings.'

'I do not see that you can fix that definitely unless you question Mademoiselle Daubreuil again.'

'There is no need. I am sure of it. And if you do not see that, you see nothing, Hastings!'

I looked at him for a moment.

'Of course! I am an idiot. If the tramp was Georges Conneau, it was after the stormy interview with him that Mr Renauld apprehended danger. He sent away the chauffeur, Masters, whom he suspected of being in the other's pay, he wired to his son, and sent for you.'

A faint smile crossed Poirot's lips.

'You do not think it strange that he should use exactly the same expressions in his letter as Madame Renauld used, later in her story? If the mention of Santiago was a blind, why should Renauld speak of it, and – what is more – send his son there?'

'It is puzzling, I admit, but perhaps we shall find some explanation later. We come now to the evening, and the visit of the mysterious lady. I confess that that fairly baffles me, unless it was indeed Madame Daubreuil, as Françoise all along maintained.'

Poirot shook his head.

'My friend, my friend, where are your wits wandering? Remember the fragment of cheque, and the fact that the name Bella Duveen was faintly familiar to Stonor, and I think we may take it for granted that Bella Duveen is the full name of Jack's unknown correspondent, and that it was she who came to the Villa Geneviève that night. Whether she intended to see Jack, or whether she meant all along to appeal to his father, we cannot be certain, but I think we may assume that this is what occurred. She produced her claim upon Jack, probably showed letters that he had written her, and the older man tried to buy her off by writing a cheque. This she indignantly tore up. The terms of her letter are those of a woman genuinely in love, and she would probably deeply resent being offered money. In the end he got rid of her, and here the words that he used are significant.'

' "Yes, yes, but for God's sake go now",' I repeated. 'They seem to me a little vehement, perhaps, that is all.'

'That is enough. He was desperately anxious for the girl to go. Why? Not because the interview was unpleasant. No, it was the time that was slipping by, and for some reason time was precious.'

'Why should it be?' I asked bewildered.

'That is what we ask ourselves. Why should it be? But later we have the incident of the wristwatch – which again shows us that time plays a very important part in the crime. We are now fast approaching the actual drama. It is half past ten when Bella Duveen leaves, and by the evidence of the wristwatch we know that the crime was committed, or at any rate that it was staged, before twelve o'clock. We have reviewed all the events anterior to the murder, there remains only one unplaced. By the doctor's evidence, the tramp, when found, had been dead at least forty-eight hours – with a possible margin of twenty-four hours more. Now, with no other facts to help me than those we have discussed, I place the death as having occurred on the morning of 7th June.'

I stared at him, stupefied.

'But how? Why? How can you possibly know?'

'Because only in that way can the sequence of events be logically explained. *Mon ami*, I have taken you step by step along the way. Do you not now see what is so glaringly plain?'

'My dear Poirot, I can't see anything glaring about it. I did think I was beginning to see my way before, but I'm now hopelessly fogged. For goodness' sake, get on, and tell me who killed Mr Renauld.'

'That is just what I am not sure of as yet.'

'But you said it was glaringly clear!'

'We talk at cross-purposes, my friend. Remember, it is *two* crimes we are investigating – for which, as I pointed out to you, we have the necessary two bodies. There, there, *ne vous impatientez pas*! I explain all. To begin with, we apply our psychology. We find three points at which Monsieur Renauld displays a distinct change of view and action – three psychological points therefore. The first occurs immediately after arriving in Merlinville, the second after quarrelling with his son on a certain subject, the third on the morning of 7th June. Now for the three causes. We can attibute No. 1 to meeting Madame Daubreuil. No. 2 is indirectly connected with her, since it concerns a marriage between Monsieur Renauld's son and her daughter. But the cause of No. 3 is hidden from us. We had to deduce it. Now, *mon ami*, let me ask you a question: whom do we believe to have planned this crime?'

'Georges Conneau,' I said doubtfully, eyeing Poirot warily.

'Exactly. Now Giraud laid it down as an axiom that a woman lies to save herself, the man she loves, and her child. Since we are satisfied that it was Georges Conneau who dictated the lie to her, and as Georges Conneau is not Jack Renauld, it follows that the third case is put out of court. And, still attributing the crime to Georges Conneau, the first is equally so. So we are forced to the second – that Madame Renauld lied for the sake of the man she loved – or in other words, for the sake of Georges Conneau. You agree to that?'

'Yes,' I admitted. 'It seems logical enough.'

'*Bien!* Madame Renauld loves Georges Conneau. Who, then, is Georges Conneau?'

'The tramp.'

'Have we any evidence to show that Madame Renauld loved the tramp?'

'No, but –'

'Very well then. Do not cling to theories where facts no longer support them. Ask yourself instead whom Madame Renauld *did* love.'

I shook my head perplexed.

'*Mais oui*, you know perfectly. Whom did Madame Renauld love so dearly that when she saw his dead body she fell down in a swoon?'

I stared dumbfounded.

'Her husband?' I gasped.

Poirot nodded.

'Her husband – or Georges Conneau, whichever you like to call him.'

I rallied myself.

'But it's impossible.'

'How "impossible"? Did we not agree just now that Madame Daubreuil was in a position to blackmail Georges Conneau?'

'Yes, but –'

'And did she not very effectively blackmail Monsieur Renauld?'

'That may be true enough, but –'

'And is it not a fact that we know nothing of Monsieur Renauld's youth and upbringing? That he springs suddenly into existence as a French-Canadian exactly twenty-two years ago?'

'All that is so,' I said more firmly, 'but you seem to me to be overlooking one salient point.'

'What is that, my friend?'

'Why, we have admitted that Georges planned the crime. That brings us to the ridiculous statement *that he planned his own murder!*'

'*Eh bien, mon ami*,' said Poirot placidly, 'that is just what he did do!'

CHAPTER XXI

Hercule Poirot on the Case

In a measured voice Poirot began his exposition.

'It seems strange to you, *mon ami*, that a man should plan his own death? So strange, that you prefer to reject the truth as fantastic, and to revert to a story that is in reality ten times more impossible. Yes, Monsieur Renauld planned his own death, but there is one detail that perhaps escapes you – he did not intend to die.'

I shook my head, bewildered.

'But no, it is all most simple really,' said Poirot kindly. 'For the crime that Monsieur Renauld proposed a murderer was not necessary, as I told you, but a body was. Let us reconstruct, seeing events this time from a different angle.

'Georges Conneau flies from justice – to Canada. There, under an assumed name, he marries, and finally acquires a vast fortune in South America. But there is a nostalgia upon him for his own country. Twenty years have elapsed, he is considerably changed in appearance, besides being a man of such eminence that no one is likely to connect him with a fugitive from justice many years ago. He deems it quite safe to return. He takes up his headquarters in England, but intends to spend the summers in France. And ill fortune, or that obscure justice which shapes men's ends and will not allow them to evade the consequences of their acts, takes him to Merlinville. There, in the whole of France, is the one person who is capable of recognizing him. It is, of course, a gold mine to Madame Daubreuil, and a gold mine of which she is not slow to take advantage. He is helpless, absolutely in her power. And she bleeds him heavily.

'And then the inevitable happens. Jack Renauld falls in love with the beautiful girl he sees almost daily, and wishes to marry her. That rouses his father. At all costs, he will prevent his son marrying the daughter of this evil woman. Jack Renauld knows nothing of his father's past, but Madame Renauld knows everything. She is a woman of great force of character and passionately devoted to her husband. They take counsel together. Renauld sees only one way of escape – death. He must appear to die, in reality escaping to another country where he will start again under an assumed name and where Madame Renauld, having played the widow's part for a while, can join him. It is essential that she should have control of the money, so he alters his will. How they meant to manage the body business originally, I do not know – possibly an art student's skeleton and a fire – or something of the kind, but long before their plans have matured an event occurs which plays into their hands. A rough tramp, violent and abusive, finds his way into the garden. There is a struggle, Renauld seeks to eject him, and suddenly the tramp, an epileptic, falls down in a fit. He is dead. Renauld calls his wife. Together they drag him into the shed – as we know the event had occurred just outside – and they realize the marvellous opportunity that has been vouchsafed them. The man bears no resemblance to Renauld but he is middle-aged, of a usual French type. That is sufficient.

'I rather fancy that they sat on the bench up there, out of earshot from the house, discussing matters. Their plan was quickly made. The identification must rest solely on Madame Renauld's evidence. Jack Renauld and the chauffeur (who had been with his master two years) must be got out of the way. It was unlikely that the French women servants would go near the body, and in any case Renauld intended to take measures to deceive anyone not likely to appreciate details. Masters was sent off, a telegram dispatched to Jack, Buenos Aires being selected to give credence to the story that Renauld had decided upon. Having heard of me as a rather obscure elderly detective, he wrote his appeal for help, knowing that when I arrived, the production of the letter would have a profound effect upon the examining magistrate – which, of course, it did.

'They dressed the body of the tramp in a suit of Renauld's and left his ragged coat and trousers by the door of the shed, not daring to take them into the house. And then, to give credence to the tale Madame Renauld was to tell, they drove the aeroplane dagger through his heart. That night Renauld will first bind and gag his wife, and then, taking a spade, will dig a grave in that particular plot of ground where he knows a – how do you call it? – bunkair? is to be made. It is essential that the body should be found – Madame Daubreuil must have no suspicions. On the other hand, if a little time elapses, any dangers as to identity will be greatly lessened. Then, Renauld will don the tramp's rags, and shuffle off to the station, where he will leave, unnoticed, by the 12.10 train. Since the crime will be supposed to have taken place two hours later, no suspicion can possibly attach to him.

'You see now his annoyance at the inopportune visit of the girl, Bella. Every moment of delay is fatal to his plans. He gets rid of her as soon as he can, however. Then, to work! He leaves the front door slightly ajar to create the impression that assassins left that way. He binds and gags Madame Renauld, correcting his mistake of twenty-two years ago, when the looseness of the bonds caused suspicion to fall upon his accomplice, but leaving her primed with essentially the same story as he had invented before, proving the unconscious recoil of the mind against originality. The night is chilly, and he slips on an overcoat over his under-clothing, intending to cast it into the grave with the dead man. He goes out by the window, smoothing over the flower-bed carefully, and thereby furnishing the most positive evidence against himself. He goes out on to the lonely golf links, and he digs – And then –'

'Yes?'

'And then,' said Poirot gravely, 'the justice that he has so long eluded overtakes him. An unknown hand stabs him in the back . . . Now, Hastings, you understand what I mean when I talk of *two* crimes. The first crime, the crime that

Monsieur Renauld, in his arrogance, asked us to investigate, is solved. But behind it lies a deeper riddle. And to solve that will be difficult – since the criminal, in his wisdom, has been content to avail himself of the devices prepared by Renauld. It has been a particularly perplexing and baffling mystery to solve.'

'You're marvellous, Poirot,' I said, with admiration. 'Absolutely marvellous. No one on earth but you would have done it!'

I think my praise pleased him. For once in his life he looked almost embarrassed.

'That poor Giraud,' said Poirot, trying unsuccessfully to look modest. 'Without doubt it is not all stupidity. He has had *la mauvaise chance* once or twice. That dark hair coiled round the dagger, for instance. To say the least, it was misleading.'

'To tell you the truth, Poirot,' I said slowly, 'even now I don't quite see – whose hair was it?'

'Madame Renauld's, of course. That is where *la mauvaise chance* came in. Her hair, dark originally, is almost completely silvered. It might just as easily have been a grey hair – and then, by no conceivable effort could Giraud have persuaded himself it came from the head of Jack Renauld! But it is all of a piece. Always the facts must be twisted to fit the theory!

'Without doubt, when Madame Renauld recovers, she will speak. The possibility of her son being accused of the murder never occurred to her. How should it, when she believed him safely at sea on board the *Anzora*? Ah! *voilà une femme*, Hastings! What force, what self-command! She only made one slip. On his unexpected return: "It does not matter – *now*." And no one noticed – no one realized the significance of those words. What a terrible part she has had to play, poor woman. Imagine the shock when she goes to identify the body and, instead of what she expects, sees the actual lifeless form of the husband she has believed miles away by now. No wonder she fainted! But since then, despite her grief and her despair, how resolutely she has played her part and how the anguish of it must wring her. She cannot say a word to set us on the track of the real murderers. For her son's sake, no one must know that Paul Renauld was Georges Conneau, the criminal. Final and most bitter blow, she has admitted publicly that Madame Daubreuil was her husband's mistress – for a hint of blackmail might be fatal to her secret. How cleverly she dealt with the examining magistrate when he asked her if there was any mystery in her husband's past life. "Nothing so romantic, I am sure, monsieur." It was perfect, the indulgent tone, the soupçon of sad mockery. At once Monsieur Hautet felt himself foolish and melodramatic. Yes, she is a great woman! If she loved a criminal, she loved him royally!'

Poirot lost himself in contemplation.

'One thing more, Poirot, what about the piece of lead-piping?'

'You do not see? To disfigure the victim's face so that it would be unrecognizable. It was that which first set me on the right track. And that imbecile of a Giraud, swarming all over it to look for match ends! Did I not tell you that a clue of two foot long was quite as good as a clue of two inches? You see, Hastings, we must now start again. Who killed Monsieur Renauld? Someone who was near the villa just before twelve o'clock that night, someone who would benefit by his death – the description fits Jack Renauld only too well. The crime need not have been premeditated. And then the dagger!'

I started, I had not realized that point.

'Of course,' I said, 'Mrs Renauld's dagger was the second one we found in the tramp. There *were* two, then?'

'Certainly, and since they were duplicates, it stands to reason that Jack Renauld was the owner. But that would not trouble me so much. In fact, I had a little idea as to that. No, the worst indictment against him is again psychological – heredity, *mon ami*, heredity! Like father, like son – Jack Renauld, when all is said or done, is the son of Georges Conneau.'

His tone was grave and earnest, and I was impressed in spite of myself.

'What is your little idea that you mentioned just now?' I asked.

For answer, Poirot consulted his turnip-faced watch, and then asked:

'What time is the afternoon boat from Calais?'

'About five, I believe.'

'That will do very well. We shall just have time.'

'You are going to England?'

'Yes, my friend.'

'Why?'

'To find a possible – witness.'

'Who?'

With a rather peculiar smile upon his face, Poirot replied: 'Miss Bella Duveen.'

'But how will you find her – what do you know about her?'

'I know nothing about her – but I can guess a good deal. We may take it for granted that her name *is* Bella Duveen, and since that name was faintly familiar to Monsieur Stonor, though evidently not in connection with the Renauld family, it is probable that she is on the stage. Jack Renauld was a young man with plenty of money, and twenty years of age. The stage is sure to have been the home of his first love. It tallies, too, with Monsieur Renauld's attempt to placate her with a cheque. I think I shall find her all right – especially with the help of *this*.'

And he brought out the photograph I had seen him take from Jack Renauld's drawer. 'With love from Bella' was scrawled across the corner, but it was not that which held my eyes fascinated. The likeness was not first rate – but for all that it was unmistakable to me. I felt a cold sinking, as though some unutterable calamity had befallen me.

It was the face of Cinderella.

CHAPTER XXII

I Find Love

For a moment or two I sat as though frozen, the photograph still in my hand. Then summoning all my courage to appear unmoved, I handed it back. At the same time I stole a quick glance at Poirot. Had he noticed anything? But to my relief he did not seem to be observing me. Anything unusual in my manner had certainly escaped him.

He rose briskly to his feet.

'We have no time to lose. We must make our departure with all dispatch. All is well – the sea it will be calm!'

In the bustle of departure, I had no time for thinking, but once on board the boat, secure from Poirot's observation, I pulled myself together, and attacked the facts dispassionately. How much did Poirot know, and why was he bent on finding this girl? Did he suspect her of having seen Jack Renauld commit the crime? Or did he suspect – But that was impossible! The girl had no grudge against the elder Renauld, no possible motive for wishing his death. What had brought her back to the scene of the murder? I went over the facts carefully. She must have left the train at Calais where I parted from her that day. No wonder I had been unable to find her on the boat. If she had dined in Calais, and then taken a train out to Merlinville, she would have arrived at the Villa Geneviève just about the time that Françoise said. What had she done when she left the house just after ten? Presumably either gone to an hotel, or returned to Calais. And then? The crime had been committed on Tuesday night. On Thursday morning she was once more in Merlinville. Had she ever left France at all? I doubted it very much. What kept her there – the hope of seeing Jack Renauld? I had told her (as at the time we believed) that he was on the high seas *en route* to Buenos Aires. Possibly she was aware that the *Anzora* had not sailed. But to know that she must have seen Jack. Was that what Poirot was after? Had Jack Renauld, returning to see Marthe Daubreuil, come face to face instead with Bella Duveen, the girl he had heartlessly thrown over?

I began to see daylight. If that were indeed the case, it might furnish Jack with the alibi he needed. Yet under those circumstances his silence seemed difficult to explain. Why could he not have spoken out boldly? Did he fear for this former entanglement of his to come to the ears of Marthe Daubreuil? I shook my head, dissatisfied. The thing had been harmless enough, a foolish boy-and-girl affair, and I reflected cynically that the son of a millionaire was not likely to be thrown over by a penniless French girl, who moreover loved him devotedly, without a much graver cause.

Poirot reappeared brisk and smiling at Dover, and our journey to London was uneventful. It was past nine o'clock when we arrived, and I suppose that we should return straight away to our rooms and do nothing till the morning.

But Poirot had other plans.

'We must lose no time, *mon ami*. The news of the arrest will not be in the English papers until the day after tomorrow, but still we must lose no time.'

I did not quite follow his reasoning, but I merely asked how he proposed to find the girl.

'You remember Joseph Aarons, the theatrical agent? No? I assisted him in a little matter of a Japanese wrestler. A pretty little problem, I must recount it to you one day. He, without doubt, will be able to put us in the way of finding out what we want to know.'

It took us some time to run Mr Aarons to earth, and it was after midnight when we finally managed it. He greeted Poirot with every evidence of warmth, and professed himself ready to be of service to us in any way.

'There's not much about the profession I don't know,' he said, beaming genially.

'*Eh bien*, Monsieur Aarons, I desire to find a young girl called Bella Duveen.'

'Bella Duveen. I know the name, but for a moment I can't place it. What's her line?'

'That I do not know – but here is her photograph.'

Mr Aarons studied it for a moment, then his face lighted.

'Got it!' He slapped his thigh. 'The Dulcibella Kids, by the Lord!'

'The Dulcibella Kids?'

'That's it. They're sisters. Acrobats, dancers, and singers. Give quite a good little turn. They're in the provinces, somewhere, I believe – if they're not resting. They've been on in Paris for the last two or three weeks.'

'Can you find out for me exactly where they are?'

'Easy as a bird. You go home, and I'll send you round the dope in the morning.'

With this promise we took leave of him. He was as good as his word. About eleven o'clock the following day, a scribbled note reached us.

'The Dulcibella Sisters are on at the Palace in Coventry. Good luck to you.'

Without more ado, we started for Coventry. Poirot made no inquiries at the theatre, but contented himself with booking stalls for the variety performance that evening.

The show was wearisome beyond words – or perhaps it was only my mood that made it seem so. Japanese families balanced themselves precariously, would-be fashionable men, in greenish evening dress and exquisitely slicked hair, reeled off society patter and danced marvellously. Stout prima donnas sang at the top of the human register, a comic comedian endeavoured to be Mr George Robey and failed signally.

At last the number went up which announced the Dulcibella Kids. My heart beat sickeningly. There she was – there they both were, the pair of them, one flaxen-haired, one dark, matching as to size, with short fluffy skirts and immense 'Buster Brown' bows. They looked a pair of extremely piquant

children. They began to sing. Their voices were fresh and true,
rather thin and music-hally, but attractive.

It was quite a pretty little turn. They danced neatly, and did
some clever little acrobatic feats. The words of their songs were
crisp and catchy. When the curtain fell, there was a full meed
of applause. Evidently the Dulcibella Kids were a success.

Suddenly I felt that I could remain no longer. I must get
out into the air. I suggested leaving to Poirot.

'Go by all means, *mon ami*. I amuse myself, and will stay to
the end. I will rejoin you later.'

It was only a few steps from the theatre to the hotel. I went
up to the sitting-room, ordered a whisky and soda, and sat
drinking it, staring meditatively into the empty grate. I heard
the door open, and turned my head, thinking it was Poirot.
Then I jumped to my feet. It was Cinderella who stood in
the doorway. She spoke haltingly, her breath coming in little
gasps.

'I saw you in front. You and your friend. When you got up
to go, I was waiting outside and followed you. Why are you
here – in Coventry? What were you doing there tonight? Is
the man who was with you the – the detective?'

She stood there, the cloak she had wrapped round her stage
dress slipping from her shoulders. I saw the whiteness of her
cheeks under the rouge, and heard the terror in her voice. And
in that moment I understood everything – understood why
Poirot was seeking her, and what she feared, and understood
at last my own heart . . .

'Yes,' I said gently.

'Is he looking for – me?' she half whispered.

Then, as I did not answer for a moment, she slipped down
by the big chair, and burst into violent bitter weeping.

I knelt down by her, holding her in my arms, and smoothing
the hair back from her face.

'Don't cry, child, don't cry, for God's sake. You're safe here.
I'll take care of you. Don't cry, darling. Don't cry. I know –
I know everything.'

'Oh, but you don't!'

'I think I do.' And after a moment, as her sobs grew quieter, I asked: 'It was you who took the dagger, wasn't it?'

'Yes.'

'That was why you wanted me to show you round? And why you pretended to faint?'

Again she nodded.

'Why did you take the dagger?' I asked presently.

She replied as simply as a child:

'I was afraid there might be fingermarks on it.'

'But didn't you remember that you had worn gloves?'

She shook her head as though bewildered, and then said slowly:

'Are you going to give me up to – to the police?'

'Good God! no.'

Her eyes sought mine long and earnestly, and then she asked in a little quiet voice that sounded afraid of itself:

'Why not?'

It seemed a strange place and a strange time for a declaration of love – and God knows, in all my imagining, I had never pictured love coming to me in such a guise. But I answered simply and naturally enough:

'Because I love you, Cinderella.'

She bent her head down, as though ashamed, and muttered in a broken voice:

'You can't – you can't – not if you knew –' And then, as though rallying herself, she faced me squarely, and asked, 'What do you know, then?'

'I know that you came to see Mr Renauld that night. He offered you a cheque and you tore it up indignantly. Then you left the house –' I paused.

'Go on – what next?'

'I don't know whether you knew Jack Renauld would be coming that night, or whether you just waited about on the chance of seeing him, but you did wait about. Perhaps you were just miserable and walked aimlessly – but at any rate just before twelve you were still near there, and you saw a man on the golf links –'

Again I paused. I had leapt to the truth in a flash as she entered the room, but now the picture rose before me even more convincingly. I saw vividly the peculiar pattern of the overcoat on the dead body of Mr Renauld, and I remembered the amazing likeness that had startled me into believing for one instant that the dead man had risen from the dead when his son burst into our conclave in the salon.

'Go on,' repeated the girl steadily.

'I fancy his back was to you – but you recognized him, or thought you recognized him. The gait and the carriage were familiar to you, and the pattern of his overcoat.' I paused. 'You used a threat in one of your letters to Jack Renauld. When you saw him there, your anger and jealousy drove you mad – and you struck! I don't believe for a minute that you meant to kill him. But you did kill him, Cinderella.'

She had flung up her hands to cover her face, and in a choked voice she said:

'You're right . . . you're right . . . I can see it all as you tell it.' Then she turned on me almost savagely. 'And you love me? Knowing what you do, how can you love me?'

'I don't know,' I said a little wearily. 'I think love is like that – a thing one cannot help. I have tried, I know – ever since the first day I met you. And love has been too strong for me.'

And then suddenly, when I least expected it, she broke down again, casting herself down on the floor and sobbing wildly.

'Oh, I can't!' she cried. 'I don't know what to do. I don't know which way to turn. Oh, pity me, pity me, someone, and tell me what to do!'

Again I knelt by her, soothing her as best I could.

'Don't be afraid of me, Bella. For God's sake don't be afraid of me. I love you, that's true – but I don't want anything in return. Only let me help you. Love him still if you have to, but let me help you, as he can't.'

It was as though she had been turned to stone by my words. She raised her head from her hands and stared at me.

'You think that?' she whispered. 'You think that I love Jack Renauld?'

Then, half laughing, half crying, she flung her arms passionately round my neck, and pressed her sweet wet face to mine.

'Not as I love you,' she whispered. 'Never as I love you!'

Her lips brushed my cheek, and then, seeking my mouth, kissed me again and again with a sweetness and fire beyond belief. The wildness of it – and the wonder, I shall not forget – no, not as long as I live!

It was a sound in the doorway that made us look up. Poirot was standing there looking at us.

I did not hesitate. With a bound I reached him and pinioned his arms to his sides.

'Quick,' I said to the girl. 'Get out of here. As fast as you can. I'll hold him.'

With one look at me, she fled out of the room past us. I held Poirot in a grip of iron.

'*Mon ami*,' observed the latter mildly, 'you do this sort of thing very well. The strong man holds me in his grasp and I am helpless as a child. But all this is uncomfortable and slightly ridiculous. Let us sit down and be calm.'

'You won't pursue her?'

'*Mon Dieu!* no. Am I Giraud? Release me, my friend.'

Keeping a suspicious eye upon him, for I paid Poirot the compliment of knowing that I was no match for him in astuteness, I relaxed my grip, and he sank into an armchair, feeling his arms tenderly.

'It is that you have the strength of a bull when you are roused, Hastings! *Eh bien*, and do you think you have behaved well to your old friend? I show you the girl's photograph and you recognize it, but you never say a word.'

'There was no need if you knew that I recognized it,' I said rather bitterly. So Poirot had known all along! I had not deceived him for an instant.

'Ta-ta! You did not know that I knew that. And tonight you help the girl to escape when we have found her with so much trouble. *Eh bien!* it comes to this – are you going to work with me or against me, Hastings?'

For a moment or two I did not answer. To break with my old friend gave me great pain. Yet I must definitely range myself against him. Would he ever forgive me, I wondered? He had been strangely calm so far, but I knew him to possess marvellous self-command.

'Poirot,' I said, 'I'm sorry. I admit I've behaved badly to you over this. But sometimes one has no choice. And in future I must take my own line.'

Poirot nodded his head several times.

'I understand,' he said. The mocking light had quite died out of his eyes, and he spoke with a sincerity and kindness that surprised me. 'It is that, my friend, is it not? It is love that has come – not as you imagined it, all cock-a-hoop with fine feathers, but sadly, with bleeding feet. Well, well – I warned you. When I realized that this girl must have taken the dagger, I warned you. Perhaps you remember. But already it was too late. But, tell me, how much do you know?'

I met his eyes squarely.

'Nothing that you could tell me would be any surprise to me, Poirot. Understand that. But in case you think of resuming your search for Miss Duveen, I should like you to know one thing clearly. If you have any idea that she was concerned in the crime, or was the mysterious lady who called upon Mr Renauld that night, you are wrong. I travelled home from France with her that day, and parted from her at Victoria that evening, so that it is clearly impossible for her to have been in Merlinville.'

'Ah!' Poirot looked at me thoughtfully. 'And you would swear to that in a court of law?'

'Most certainly I would.'

Poirot rose and bowed.

'*Mon ami! Vive l'amour!* It can perform miracles. It is decidedly ingenious what you have thought of there. It defeats even Hercule Poirot!'

CHAPTER XXIII

Difficulties Ahead

After a moment of stress, such as I have just described, reaction is bound to set in. I retired to rest that night on a note of triumph, but I awoke to realize that I was by no means out of the wood. True, I could see no flaw in the alibi I had so suddenly conceived. I had but to stick to my story, and I failed to see how Bella could be convicted in face of it.

But I felt the need of treading warily. Poirot would not take defeat lying down. Somehow or other, he would endeavour to turn the tables on me, and that in the way, and at the moment, when I least expected it.

We met at breakfast the following morning as though nothing had happened. Poirot's good temper was imperturbable, yet I thought I detected a film of reserve in his manner which was new. After breakfast, I announced my intention of going out for a stroll. A malicious gleam shot through Poirot's eyes.

'If it is information you seek, you need not be at the pains of deranging yourself. I can tell you all you wish to know. The Dulcibella Sisters have cancelled their contract, and have left Coventry for an unknown destination.'

'Is that really so, Poirot?'

'You can take it from me, Hastings. I made inquiries the first thing this morning. After all, what else did you expect?'

True enough, nothing else could be expected under the circumstances. Cinderella had profited by the slight start I had been able to secure her, and would certainly not lose a moment in removing herself from the reach of the pursuer. It was what I had intended and planned. Nevertheless, I was aware of being plunged into a network of fresh difficulties.

I had absolutely no means of communicating with the girl,

and it was vital that she should know the line of defence that had occurred to me, and which I was prepared to carry out. Of course it was possible that she might try to send word to me in some way or another, but I hardly thought it likely. She would know the risk she ran of a message being intercepted by Poirot, thus setting him on her track once more. Clearly her only course was to disappear utterly for the time being.

But, in the meantime, what was Poirot doing? I studied him attentively. He was wearing his most innocent air, and staring meditatively into the far distance. He looked altogether too placid and supine to give me reassurance. I had learned, with Poirot, that the less dangerous he looked, the more dangerous he was. His quiescence alarmed me. Observing a troubled quality in my glance, he smiled benignantly.

'You are puzzled, Hastings? You ask yourself why I do not launch myself in pursuit?'

'Well – something of the kind.'

'It is what you would do, were you in my place. I understand that. But I am not of those who enjoy rushing up and down a country seeking a needle in a haystack, as you English say. No – let Mademoiselle Bella Duveen go. Without doubt, I shall be able to find her when the time comes. Until then, I am content to wait.'

I stared at him doubtfully. Was he seeking to mislead me? I had an irritating feeling that, even now, he was master of the situation. My sense of superiority was gradually waning. I had contrived the girl's escape, and evolved a brilliant scheme for saving her from the consequences of her rash act – but I could not rest easy in my mind. Poirot's perfect calm awakened a thousand apprehensions.

'I suppose, Poirot,' I said rather diffidently, 'I mustn't ask what your plans are? I've forfeited the right.'

'But not at all. There is no secret about them. We return to France without delay.'

'*We?*'

'Precisely – "*we*"! You know very well that you cannot afford to let Papa Poirot out of your sight. Eh? is it not so, my friend? But remain in England by all means if you wish –'

I shook my head. He had hit the nail on the head. I could not afford to let him out of my sight. Although I could not expect his confidence after what had happened, I could still check his actions. The only danger to Bella lay with him. Giraud and the French police were indifferent to her existence. At all costs I must keep near Poirot.

Poirot observed me attentively as these reflections passed through my mind, and gave me a nod of satisfaction.

'I am right, am I not? And as you are quite capable of trying to follow me, disguised with some absurdity such as a false beard – which everyone would perceive, *bien entendu* – I much prefer that we should voyage together. It would annoy me greatly that anyone should mock themselves at you.'

'Very well, then. But it's only fair to warn you –'

'I know – I know all. You are my enemy! Be my enemy, then. It does not worry me at all.'

'So long as it's all fair and above-board, I don't mind.'

'You have to the full the English passion for "fair play"! Now your scruples are satisfied, let us depart immediately. There is no time to be lost. Our stay in England has been short but sufficient. I know – what I wanted to know.'

The tone was light, but I read a veiled menace into the words.

'Still –' I began, and stopped.

'Still – as you say! Without doubt you are satisfied with the part you are playing. Me, I preoccupy myself with Jack Renauld.'

Jack Renauld! The words gave me a start. I had completely forgotten that aspect of the case. Jack Renauld, in prison, with the shadow of the guillotine looming over him. I saw the part I was playing in a more sinister light. I could save Bella – yes, but in doing so I ran the risk of sending an innocent man to his death.

I pushed the thought from me with horror. It could not be. He would be acquitted. Certainly he would be acquitted. But the cold fear came back. Suppose he were not? What then?

Could I have it on my conscience – horrible thought! Would it come to that in the end? A decision. Bella or Jack Renauld? The promptings of my heart were to save the girl I loved at any cost to myself. But, if the cost were to another, the problem was altered.

What would the girl herself say? I remembered that no word of Jack Renauld's arrest had passed my lips. As yet she was in total ignorance of the fact that her former lover was in prison charged with a hideous crime which he had not committed. When she knew, how would she act? Would she permit her life to be saved at the expense of his? Certainly she must do nothing rash. Jack Renauld might, and probably would, be acquitted without any intervention on her part. If so, good. But if he was not! That was the terrible, the unanswerable problem. I fancied that she ran no risk of the extreme penalty. The circumstances of the crime were quite different in her case. She could plead jealousy and extreme provocation, and her youth and beauty would go for much. The fact that by a tragic mistake it was Mr Renauld, and not his son, who paid the penalty would not alter the motive of the crime. But in any case, however lenient the sentence of the Court, it must mean a long term of imprisonment.

No, Bella must be protected. And, at the same time, Jack Renauld must be saved. How this was to be accomplished I did not see clearly. But I pinned my faith to Poirot. He *knew*. Come what might, he would manage to save an innocent man. He must find some pretext other than the real one. It might be difficult, but he would manage it somehow. And with Bella unsuspected, and Jack Renauld acquitted, all would end satisfactorily.

So I told myself repeatedly, but at the bottom of my heart there still remained a cold fear.

CHAPTER XXIV

'Save Him!'

We crossed from England by the evening boat, and the following morning saw us in St Omer, whither Jack Renauld had been taken. Poirot lost no time in visiting M. Hautet. As he did not seem disposed to make any objections to my accompanying him, I bore him company.

After various formalities and preliminaries, we were conducted to the examining magistrate's room. He greeted us cordially.

'I was told that you had returned to England, Monsieur Poirot. I am glad to find that such is not the case.'

'It is true I went there, monsieur, but it was only for a flying visit. A side issue, but one that I fancied might repay investigation.'

'And it did – eh?'

Poirot shrugged his shoulders. M. Hautet nodded, sighing.

'We must resign ourselves, I fear. That animal Giraud, his manners are abominable, but he is undoubtedly clever! Not much chance of that one making a mistake.'

'You think not?'

It was the examining magistrate's turn to shrug his shoulders.

'Oh, well, speaking frankly – in confidence, of course – can you come to any other conclusion?'

'Frankly, there seem to me to be many points that are obscure.'

'Such as –?'

But Poirot was not to be drawn.

'I have not yet tabulated them,' he remarked. 'It was a general reflection that I was making. I liked the young man, and should be sorry to believe him guilty of such a hideous crime. By the way, what has he to say for himself on the matter?'

The magistrate frowned.

'I cannot understand him. He seems incapable of putting up any sort of defence. It has been most difficult to get him to answer questions. He contents himself with a general denial, and beyond that takes refuge in a most obstinate silence. I am interrogating him again tomorrow, perhaps you would like to be present?'

We accepted the invitation with *empressement*.

'A distressing case,' said the magistrate with a sigh. 'My sympathy for Madame Renauld is profound.'

'How is Madame Renauld?'

'She has not yet recovered consciousness. It is merciful in a way, poor woman, she is being spared much. The doctors say that there is no danger, but that when she comes to herself she must be kept as quiet as possible. It was, I understand, quite as much the shock as the fall which caused her present state. It would be terrible if her brain became unhinged; but I should not wonder at all – no, really, not at all.'

M. Hautet leaned back, shaking his head, with a sort of mournful enjoyment, as he envisaged the gloomy prospect.

He roused himself at length, and observed with a start:

'That reminds me. I have here a letter for you, Monsieur Poirot. Let me see, where did I put it?'

He proceeded to rummage among his papers. At last he found the missive, and handed it to Poirot.

'It was sent under cover to me in order that I might forward it to you,' he explained. 'But as you left no address I could not do so.'

Poirot studied the letter curiously. It was addressed in a long, sloping, foreign hand, and the writing was decidedly a woman's. Poirot did not open it. Instead he put it in his pocket and rose to his feet.

'Till tomorrow then. Many thanks for your courtesy and amiability.'

'But not at all. I am always at your service.'

We were just leaving the building when we came face to face with Giraud, looking more dandified than ever, and thoroughly pleased with himself.

'Aha! Monsieur Poirot,' he cried airily. 'You have returned from England then?'

'As you see,' said Poirot.

'The end of the case is not far off now, I fancy.'

'I agree with you, Monsieur Giraud.'

Poirot spoke in a subdued tone. His crestfallen manner seemed to delight the other.

'Of all the milk-and-water criminals! Not an idea of defending himself. It is extraordinary!'

'So extraordinary that it gives one to think, does it not?' suggested Poirot mildly.

But Giraud was not even listening. He twirled his cane amicably.

'Well, good day, Monsieur Poirot. I am glad you're satisfied of young Renauld's guilt at last.'

'*Pardon!* But I am not in the least satisfied. Jack Renauld is innocent.'

Giraud stared for a moment – then burst out laughing, tapping his head significantly with the brief remark: '*Toqué!*'

Poirot drew himself up. A dangerous light showed in his eyes.

'Monsieur Giraud, throughout the case your manner to me has been deliberately insulting. You need teaching a lesson. I am prepared to wager you five hundred francs that I find the murderer of Monsieur Renauld before you do. Is it agreed?'

Giraud stared helplessly at him, and murmured again: '*Toqué!*'

'Come now,' urged Poirot, 'is it agreed?'

'I have no wish to take your money from you.'

'Make your mind easy – you will not!'

'Oh, well then, I agree! You speak of my manner to you being insulting. Well, once or twice, *your* manner has annoyed *me*.'

'I am enchanted to hear it,' said Poirot. 'Good morning, Monsieur Giraud. Come, Hastings.'

I said no word as we walked along the street. My heart was heavy. Poirot had displayed his intentions only too plainly. I doubted more than ever my powers of saving Bella from the consequences of her act. This unlucky encounter with Giraud had roused Poirot and put him on his mettle.

Suddenly I felt a hand laid on my shoulder, and turned to face Gabriel Stonor. We stopped and greeted him, and he proposed strolling with us back to our hotel.

'And what are you doing here, Monsieur Stonor?' inquired Poirot.

'One must stand by one's friends,' replied the other dryly. 'Especially when they are unjustly accused.'

'Then you do not believe that Jack Renauld committed the crime?' I asked eagerly.

'Certainly I don't. I know the lad. I admit that there have been one or two things in this business that have staggered me completely, but none the less, in spite of his fool way of taking it, I'll never believe that Jack Renauld is a murderer.'

My heart warmed to the secretary. His words seemed to lift a secret weight from my heart.

'I have no doubt that many people feel as you do,' I exclaimed. 'There is really absurdly little evidence against him. I should say that there was no doubt of his acquittal – no doubt whatever.'

But Stonor hardly responded as I could have wished.

'I'd give a lot to think as you do,' he said gravely. He turned to Poirot. 'What's your opinion, monsieur?'

'I think that things look very black against him,' said Poirot quietly.

'You believe him guilty?' said Stonor sharply.

'No. But I think he will find it hard to prove his innocence.'

'He's behaving so damned queerly,' muttered Stonor. 'Of course, I realize that there's a lot more in this affair than meets the eye. Giraud's not wise to that because he's an outsider, but the whole thing has been damned odd. As to that, least said soonest mended. If Mrs Renauld wants to hush anything up, I'll take my cue from her. It's her show, and I've too much respect for her judgement to shove my oar in, but I can't get behind this attitude of Jack's. Anyone would think he *wanted* to be thought guilty.'

'But it's absurd,' I cried, bursting in. 'For one thing, the dagger –' I paused, uncertain as to how much Poirot would wish me to reveal. I continued, choosing my words carefully, 'We know that the dagger could not have been in Jack Renauld's possession that evening. Mrs Renauld knows that.'

'True,' said Stonor. 'When she recovers, she will doubtless say all this and more. Well, I must be leaving you.'

'One moment.' Poirot's hand arrested his departure. 'Can you arrange for word to be sent to me at once should Mrs Renauld recover consciousness?'

'Certainly. That's easily done.'

'That point about the dagger is good, Poirot,' I urged as we went upstairs. 'I couldn't speak very plainly before Stonor.'

'That was quite right of you. We might as well keep the knowledge to ourselves as long as we can. As to the dagger, your point hardly helps Jack Renauld. You remember that I was absent for an hour this morning, before we started from London?'

'Yes?'

'Well, I was employed in trying to find the firm Jack Renauld employed to convert his souvenirs. It was not very difficult. *Eh bien*, Hastings, they made to his order not *two* paper knives, but *three*.'

'So that –'

'So that, after giving one to his mother and one to Bella Duveen, there was a third which he doubtless retained for his own use. No, Hastings, I fear the dagger question will not help us to save him from the guillotine.'

'It won't come to that,' I cried, stung.

Poirot shook his head uncertainly.

'You will save him,' I cried positively.

Poirot glanced at me dryly.

'Have you not rendered it impossible, *mon ami*?'

'Some other way,' I muttered.

'Ah! *Sapristi!* But it is miracles you ask from me. No – say no more. Let us instead see what is in this letter.'

And he drew out the envelope from his breast pocket.

His face contracted as he read, then he handed the one flimsy sheet to me.

'There are other women in the world who suffer, Hastings.'

The writing was blurred and the note had evidently been written in great agitation.

Dear M. Poirot – If you get this, I beg of you to come to my aid. I have no one to turn to, and at all costs Jack must be saved. I implore of you on my knees to help us.

Marthe Daubreuil

I handed it back, moved.

'You will go?'

'At once. We will command an auto.'

Half an hour later saw us at the Villa Marguerite. Marthe was at the door to meet us, and let Poirot in, clinging with both hands to one of his.

'Ah, you have come – it is good of you. I have been in despair, not knowing what to do. They will not let me go to see him in prison even. I suffer horribly. I am nearly mad.

'Is it true what they say, that he does not deny the crime? But that is madness. It is impossible that he should have done it! Never for one minute will I believe it.'

'Neither do I believe it, mademoiselle,' said Poirot gently.

'But then why does he not speak? I do not understand.'

'Perhaps because he is screening someone,' suggested Poirot, watching her.

Marthe frowned.

'Screening someone? Do you mean his mother? Ah, from the beginning I have suspected her. Who inherits all that vast fortune? She does. It is easy to wear widow's weeds and play the hypocrite. And they say that when he was arrested she fell down like *that*!' She made a dramatic gesture. 'And without doubt, Monsieur Stonor, the secretary, he helped her. They are thick as thieves, those two. It is true she is older than he – but what do men care – if a woman is rich!'

There was a hint of bitterness in her tone.

'Stonor was in England,' I put in.

'He says so – but who knows?'

'Mademoiselle,' said Poirot quietly, 'if we are to work together, you and I, we must have things clear. First, I will ask you a question.'

'Yes, monsieur?'

'Are you aware of your mother's real name?'

Marthe looked at him for a minute, then, letting her head fall forward on her arms, she burst into tears.

'There, there,' said Poirot, patting her on the shoulder. 'Calm yourself, *petite*, I see that you know. Now a second question – did you know who Monsieur Renauld was?'

'Monsieur Renauld,' she raised her head from her hands and gazed at him wonderingly.

'Ah, I see you do not know that. Now listen to me carefully.'

Step by step, he went over the case, much as he had done to me on the day of our departure for England. Marthe listened spellbound. When he had finished, she drew a long breath.

'But you are wonderful – magnificent! You are the greatest detective in the world.'

With a swift gesture she slipped off her chair and knelt before him with an abandonment that was wholly French.

'Save him, monsieur,' she cried. 'I love him so. Oh, save him, save him – save him!'

CHAPTER XXV

An Unexpected Dénouement

We were present the following morning at the examination of Jack Renauld. Short as the time had been, I was shocked at the change that had taken place in the young prisoner. His cheeks had fallen in, there were deep black circles round his eyes, and he looked haggard and distraught, as one who had wooed sleep in vain for several nights. He betrayed no emotion at seeing us.

'Renauld,' began the magistrate, 'do you deny that you were in Merlinville on the night of the crime?'

Jack did not reply at once, then he said with a hesitancy of manner which was piteous:

'I – I – told you that I was in Cherbourg.'

The magistrate turned sharply.

'Send in the station witnesses.'

In a moment or two the door opened to admit a man whom I recognized as being a porter at Merlinville station.

'You were on duty on the night of 7th June?'

'Yes, monsieur.'

'You witnessed the arrival of the 11.40 train?'

'Yes, monsieur.'

'Look at the prisoner. Do you recognize him as having been one of the passengers to alight?'

'Yes, monsieur.'

'There is no possibility of your being mistaken?'

'No, monsieur. I know Monsieur Jack Renauld well.'

'Nor of your being mistaken as to the date?'

'No, monsieur. Because it was the following morning, 8th June, that we heard of the murder.'

Another railway official was brought in, and confirmed the

first one's evidence. The magistrate looked at Jack Renauld.

'These men have identified you positively. What have you to say?'

Jack shrugged his shoulders.

'Nothing.'

'Renauld,' continued the magistrate, 'do you recognize this?'

He took something from the table by his side and held it out to the prisoner. I shuddered as I recognized the aeroplane dagger.

'Pardon,' cried Jack's counsel, Maître Grosier. 'I demand to speak to my client before he answers that question.'

But Jack Renauld had no consideration for the feelings of the wretched Grosier. He waved him aside, and replied quietly:

'Certainly I recognize it. It was a present given by me to my mother, as a souvenir of the war.'

'Is there, as far as you know, any duplicate of that dagger in existence?'

Again Maître Grosier burst out, and again Jack overrode him.

'Not that I know of. The setting was my own design.'

Even the magistrate almost gasped at the boldness of the reply. It did, in very truth, seem as though Jack was rushing on his fate. I realized, of course, the vital necessity he was under of concealing, for Bella's sake, the fact that there was a duplicate dagger in the case. So long as there was supposed to be only one weapon, no suspicion was likely to attach to the girl who had had the second paper-knife in her possession. He was valiantly shielding the woman he had once loved – but at what cost to himself! I began to realize the magnitude of the task I had so lightly set Poirot. It would not be easy to secure the acquittal of Jack Renauld by anything short of the truth.

M. Hautet spoke again, with a peculiarly biting inflection:

'Madame Renauld told us that this dagger was on her dressing-table on the night of the crime. But Madame Renauld is a mother! It will doubtless astonish you, Renauld, but I consider it highly likely that Madame Renauld was mistaken, and that, by inadvertence perhaps, you had taken it with you to Paris. Doubtless you will contradict me –'

I saw the lad's handcuffed hands clench themselves. The perspiration stood out in beads upon his brow, as with a supreme effort he interrupted M. Hautet in a hoarse voice:

'I shall not contradict you. It is possible.'

It was a stupefying moment. Maître Grosier rose to his feet, protesting:

'My client has undergone a considerable nervous strain. I should wish it put on record that I do not consider him answerable for what he says.'

The magistrate quelled him angrily. For a moment a doubt seemed to arise in his own mind. Jack Renauld had almost overdone his part. He leaned forward, and gazed at the prisoner searchingly.

'Do you fully understand, Renauld, that on the answers you have given me I shall have no alternative but to commit you for trial?'

Jack's pale face flushed. He looked steadily back.

'Monsieur Hautet, I swear that I did not kill my father.'

But the magistrate's brief moment of doubt was over. He laughed a short unpleasant laugh.

'Without doubt, without doubt – they are always innocent, our prisoners! By your own mouth you are condemned. You can offer no defence, no alibi – only a mere assertion which would not deceive a babe! – that you are not guilty. You killed your father, Renauld – a cruel and cowardly murder – for the sake of the money which you believed would come to you at his death. Your mother was an accessory after the fact. Doubtless, in view of the fact that she acted as a mother, the courts will extend an indulgence to her that they will not accord to you. And rightly so! Your crime was a horrible one – to be held in abhorrence by gods and men!'

M. Hautet was interrupted – to his intense annoyance. The door was pushed open.

'Monsieur le juge, Monsieur le juge,' stammered the attendant, 'there is a lady who says – who says –'

'Who says what?' cried the justly incensed magistrate. 'This is highly irregular. I forbid it – I absolutely forbid it.'

But a slender figure pushed the stammering gendarme aside. Dressed all in black, with a long veil that hid her face, she advanced into the room.

My heart gave a sickening throb. She had come then! All my efforts were in vain. Yet I could not but admire the courage that had led her to take this step so unfalteringly.

She raised her veil – and I gasped. For, though as like her as two peas, this girl was not Cinderella! On the other hand, now that I saw her without the fair wig she had worn on the stage, I recognized her as the girl of the photograph in Jack Renauld's room.

'You are the Juge d'Instruction, Monsieur Hautet?' she queried.

'Yes, but I forbid –'

'My name is Bella Duveen. I wish to give myself up for the murder of Mr Renauld.'

CHAPTER XXVI

I Receive a Letter

'My friend, – You will know all when you get this. Nothing that I can say will move Bella. She has gone out to give herself up. I am tired out with struggling.

'You will know now that I deceived you, that where you gave me trust I repaid you with lies. It will seem, perhaps, indefensible to you, but I should like, before I go out of your life for ever, to show you just how it all came about. If I knew that you forgave me, it would make life easier for me. It wasn't for myself I did it – that's the only thing I can put forward to say for myself.

'I'll begin from the day I met you in the boat train from Paris. I was uneasy then about Bella. She was just desperate about Jack Renauld, she'd have lain down on the ground for him to walk on, and when he began to change, and to stop writing so often, she began getting in a state. She got it into her head that he was keen on another girl – and of course, as it turned out afterwards, she was quite right there. She'd made up her mind to go to their villa at Merlinville, and try and see Jack. She knew I was against it, and tried to give me the slip. I found she was not on the train at Calais, and determined I would not go on to England without her. I'd an uneasy feeling that something awful was going to happen if I couldn't prevent it.

'I met the next train from Paris. She was on it, and set upon going out then and there to Merlinville. I argued with her for all I was worth, but it wasn't any good. She was all strung up and set upon having her own way. Well, I washed my hands of it. I'd done all I could. It was getting late. I went to an hotel, and Bella started for Merlinville. I still couldn't shake off my feeling of what the books call "impending disaster".

'The next day came – but no Bella. She'd made a date with me to meet at the hotel, but she didn't keep it. No sign of her all day. I got more and more anxious. Then came an evening paper with the news.

'It was awful! I couldn't be sure, of course – but I was terribly afraid. I figured it out that Bella had met Papa Renauld and told him about her and Jack, and that he'd insulted her or something like that. We've both got terribly quick tempers.

'Then all the masked foreigner business came out, and I began to feel more at ease. But it still worried me that Bella hadn't kept her date with me.

'By the next morning I was so rattled that I'd just got to go and see what I could. First thing, I ran up against you. You know all that . . . When I saw the dead man, looking so like Jack, and wearing Jack's fancy overcoat, I knew! And there was the identical paper-knife – wicked little thing! – that Jack had given Bella! Ten to one it had her fingermarks on it. I can't hope to explain to you the sort of helpless horror of that moment. I only saw one thing clearly – I must get hold of that dagger, and get right away with it before they found out it was gone. I pretended to faint, and while you were away getting water I took the thing and hid it away in my dress.

'I told you that I was staying at the Hôtel du Phare, but of course really I made a bee-line back to Calais, and then on to England by the first boat. When we were in mid-Channel I dropped that little devil of a dagger into the sea. Then I felt I could breathe again.

'Bella was in our digs in London. She looked like nothing on God's earth. I told her what I'd done, and that she was pretty safe for the time being. She stared at me, and then began laughing . . . laughing . . . laughing . . . it was horrible to hear her! I felt that the best thing to do was to keep busy. She'd go mad if she had time to brood on what she'd done. Luckily we got an engagement at once.

'And then, I saw you and your friend watching us that night . . . I was frantic. You must suspect, or you wouldn't have tracked us down. I had to know the worst, so I followed you. I was desperate. And then, before I'd had time to say anything, I tumbled to it that it was me you suspected, not Bella! Or at least that you thought I *was* Bella, since I'd stolen the dagger.

'I wish, honey, that you could see back into my mind at that moment . . . you'd forgive me, perhaps . . . I was so frightened, and muddled, and desperate . . . All I could get clearly was that you would try and save me – I didn't know whether you'd be willing to save her . . . I thought very likely not – It wasn't the same thing! And I couldn't risk it! Bella's my twin – I'd got to do the best for her. So I went on lying. I felt mean – I feel mean still . . . That's all – enough too, you'll say, I expect. I ought to have trusted you . . . If I had –

'As soon as the news was in the paper that Jack Renauld had been arrested, it was all up. Bella wouldn't even wait to see how things went . . .

'I'm very tired. I can't write any more.'

She had begun to sign herself Cinderella, but had crossed that out and written instead 'Dulcie Duveen'.

It was an ill-written, blurred epistle – but I have kept it to this day.

Poirot was with me when I read it. The sheets fell from my hand, and I looked across at him.

'Did you know all the time that it was – the other?'

'Yes, my friend.'

'Why did you not tell me?'

'To begin with, I could hardly believe it conceivable that you could make such a mistake. You had seen the photograph. The sisters are very alike, but by no means incapable of distinguishment.'

'But the fair hair?'

'A wig, worn for the sake of a piquant contrast on the stage.

Is it conceivable that with twins one should be fair and one dark?'

'Why didn't you tell me that night at the hotel in Coventry?'

'You were rather high-handed in your methods, *mon ami*,' said Poirot dryly. 'You did not give me a chance.'

'But afterwards?'

'Ah, afterwards! Well, to begin with, I was hurt at your want of faith in me. And then, I wanted to see whether your – feelings would stand the test of time. In fact, whether it was love, or a flash in the pan, with you. I should not have left you long in your error.'

I nodded. His tone was too affectionate for me to bear resentment. I looked down on the sheets of the letter. Suddenly I picked them up from the floor, and pushed them across to him.

'Read that,' I said. 'I'd like you to.'

He read it through in silence, then he looked up at me.

'What is it that worries you, Hastings?'

This was quite a new mood in Poirot. His mocking manner seemed laid quite aside. I was able to say what I wanted without too much difficulty.

'She doesn't say – she doesn't say – well, not whether she cares for me or not?'

Poirot turned back the pages.

'I think you are mistaken, Hastings.'

'Where?' I cried, leaning forward eagerly.

Poirot smiled.

'She tells you that in every line of the letter, *mon ami*.'

'But where am I to find her? There's no address on the letter. There's a French stamp, that's all.'

'Excite yourself not! Leave it to Papa Poirot. I can find her for you as soon as I have five little minutes!'

CHAPTER XXVII

Jack Renauld's Story

'Congratulations, Monsieur Jack,' said Poirot, wringing the lad warmly by the hand.

Young Renauld had come to us as soon as he was liberated – before starting for Merlinville to rejoin Marthe and his mother. Stonor accompanied him. His heartiness was in strong contrast to the lad's wan looks. It was plain that the boy was on the verge of a nervous breakdown. He smiled mournfully at Poirot, and said in a low voice:

'I went through it to protect her, and now it's all no use.'

'You could hardly expect the girl to accept the price of your life,' remarked Stonor dryly. 'She was bound to come forward when she saw you heading straight for the guillotine.'

'*Eh ma foi!* and you were heading for it too!' added Poirot, with a slight twinkle. 'You would have had Maître Grosier's death from rage on your conscience if you had gone on.'

'He was a well meaning ass, I suppose,' said Jack. 'But he worried me horribly. You see, I couldn't very well take him into my confidence. But, my God! what's going to happen about Bella?'

'If I were you,' said Poirot frankly, 'I should not distress myself unduly. The French Courts are very lenient to youth and beauty, and the *crime passionnel*! A clever lawyer will make out a great case of extenuating circumstances. It will not be pleasant for you –'

'I don't care about that. You see, Monsieur Poirot, in a way I *do* feel guilty of my father's murder. But for me, and my entanglement with this girl, he would be alive and well today.

And then my cursed carelessness in taking away the wrong overcoat. I can't help feeling responsible for his death. It will haunt me for ever!'

'No, no,' I said soothingly.

'Of course it's horrible to me to think that Bella killed my father,' resumed Jack. 'But I'd treated her shamefully. After I met Marthe, and realized I'd made a mistake, I ought to have written and told her so honestly. But I was so terrified of a row, and of its coming to Marthe's ears, and her thinking there was more in it than there ever had been, that – well, I was a coward, and went on hoping the thing would die down of itself. I just drifted, in fact – not realizing that I was driving the poor kid desperate. If she'd really knifed me, as she meant to, I should have got no more than my deserts. And the way she's come forward now is downright plucky. I'd have stood the racket, you know – up to the end.'

He was silent for a moment or two, and then burst out on another tack:

'What gets me is why the Governor should be wandering about in underclothes and my overcoat at that time of night. I suppose he'd just given the foreign johnnies the slip, and my mother must have made a mistake about its being two o'clock when they came. Or – or, it wasn't all a frame-up, was it? I mean, my mother didn't think – couldn't think – that – that it was *me*?'

Poirot reassured him quickly.

'No, no, Monsieur Jack. Have no fears on that score. As for the rest, I will explain it to you one of these days. It is rather curious. But will you recount to us exactly what did occur on that terrible evening?'

'There's very little to tell. I came from Cherbourg, as I told you, in order to see Marthe before going to the other end of the world. The train was late, and I decided to take the short cut across the golf links. I could easily get into the grounds of the Villa Marguerite from there. I had nearly reached the place when –'

He paused and swallowed.

'Yes?'

'I heard a terrible cry. It wasn't loud – a sort of choke and gasp – but it frightened me. For a moment I stood rooted to the spot. Then I came round the corner of a bush. There was moonlight. I saw the grave, and a figure lying face downwards with a dagger sticking in the back. And then – and then – I looked up and saw *her*. She was looking at me as though she saw a ghost – it's what she must have thought me at first – all expression seemed frozen out of her face by horror. And then she gave a cry, and turned and ran.'

He stopped, trying to master his emotion.

'And afterwards?' asked Poirot gently.

'I really don't know. I stayed there for a time, dazed. And then I realized I'd better get away as fast as I could. It didn't occur to me that they would suspect me, but I was afraid of being called upon to give evidence against her. I walked to St Beauvais as I told you, and got a car from there back to Cherbourg.'

A knock came at the door, and a page entered with a telegram which he delivered to Stonor. He tore it open. Then he got up from his seat.

'Mrs Renauld has regained consciousness,' he said.

'Ah!' Poirot sprang to his feet. 'Let us all go to Merlinville at once!'

A hurried departure was made forthwith. Stonor, at Jack's instance, agreed to stay behind and do all that could be done for Bella Duveen. Poirot, Jack Renauld, and I set off in the Renauld car.

The run took just over forty minutes. As we approached the doorway of the Villa Marguerite Jack Renauld shot a questioning glance at Poirot.

'How would it be if you went on first – to break the news to my mother that I am free –'

'While you break it in person to Mademoiselle Marthe, eh?' finished Poirot, with a twinkle. 'But yes, by all means, I was about to propose such an arrangement myself.'

Jack Renauld did not wait for more. Stopping the car, he

swung himself out, and ran up the path to the front door. We went on in the car to the Villa Geneviève.

'Poirot,' I said, 'do you remember how we arrived here that first day? And were met by the news of Mr Renauld's murder?'

'Ah, yes, truly. Not so long ago either. But what a lot of things have happened since then – especially for *you, mon ami!*'

'Yes, indeed,' I sighed.

'You are regarding it from the sentimental standpoint, Hastings. That was not my meaning. We will hope that Mademoiselle Bella will be dealt with leniently, and after all Jack Renauld cannot marry both the girls! I spoke from a professional standpoint. This is not a crime well ordered and regular, such as a detective delights in. The *mise en scène* designed by Georges Conneau, that indeed is perfect, but the *dénouement* – ah, no! A man killed by accident in a girl's fit of anger – ah, indeed, what order or method is there in that?'

And in the midst of a fit of laughter on my part at Poirot's peculiarities, the door was opened by Françoise.

Poirot explained that he must see Mrs Renauld at once, and the old woman conducted him upstairs. I remained in the salon. It was some time before Poirot reappeared. He was looking unusually grave.

'*Vous voilà*, Hastings! *Sacré tonnerre!* but there are squalls ahead!'

'What do you mean?' I cried.

'I would hardly have credited it,' said Poirot thoughtfully, 'but women are very unexpected.'

'Here are Jack and Marthe Daubreuil,' I exclaimed, looking out of the window.

Poirot bounded out of the room, and met the young couple on the steps outside.

'Do not enter. It is better not. Your mother is very upset.'

'I know, I know,' said Jack Renauld. 'I must go up to her at once.'

'But no, I tell you. It is better not.'

'But Marthe and I –'

'In any case, do not take Mademoiselle with you. Mount,

if you must, but you would be wise to be guided by me.'

A voice on the stairs behind made us all start.

'I thank you for your good offices, Monsieur Poirot, but I will make my own wishes clear.'

We stared in astonishment. Descending the stairs, leaning on Léonie's arm, was Mrs Renauld, her head still bandaged. The French girl was weeping, and imploring her mistress to return to bed.

'Madame will kill herself. It is contrary to all the doctor's orders!'

But Mrs Renauld came on.

'Mother,' cried Jack, starting forward.

But with a gesture she drove him back.

'I am no mother of yours! You are no son of mine! From this day and hour I renounce you.'

'Mother!' cried the lad, stupefied.

For a moment she seemed to waver, to falter before the anguish in his voice. Poirot made a mediating gesture. But instantly she regained command of herself.

'Your father's blood is on your head. You are morally guilty of his death. You thwarted and defied him over this girl, and by your heartless treatment of another girl, you brought about his death. Go out from my house. Tomorrow I intend to take such steps as shall make it certain that you shall never touch a penny of his money. Make your way in the world as best you can with the help of the girl who is the daughter of your father's bitterest enemy!'

And slowly, painfully, she retraced her way upstairs.

We were all dumbfounded – totally unprepared for such a demonstration. Jack Renauld, worn out with all he had already gone through, swayed and nearly fell. Poirot and I went quickly to his assistance.

'He is overdone,' murmured Poirot to Marthe. 'Where can we take him?'

'But home! To the Villa Marguerite. We will nurse him, my mother and I. My poor Jack!'

We got the lad to the villa, where he dropped limply on to

a chair in a semi-dazed condition. Poirot felt his head and hands.

'He has fever. The long strain begins to tell. And now this shock on top of it. Get him to bed, and Hastings and I will summon a doctor.'

A doctor was soon procured. After examining the patient, he gave it as his opinion that it was simply a case of nerve strain. With perfect rest and quiet, the lad might be almost restored by the next day, but, if excited, there was a chance of brain fever. It would be advisable for someone to sit up all night with him.

Finally, having done all we could, we left him in the charge of Marthe and her mother, and set out for the town. It was past our usual hour of dining, and we were both famished. The first restaurant we came to assuaged the pangs of hunger with an excellent omelette, and an equally excellent entrecôte to follow.

'And now for quarters for the night,' said Poirot, when at length *café noir* had completed the meal. 'Shall we try our old friend, the Hôtel de Bains?'

We traced our steps there without more ado. Yes, Messieurs could be accommodated with two good rooms overlooking the sea. Then Poirot asked a question which surprised me:

'Has an English lady, Miss Robinson, arrived?'

'Yes, Monsieur. She is in the little salon.'

'Ah!'

'Poirot,' I cried, keeping pace with him, as he walked along the corridor, 'who on earth is Miss Robinson?'

Poirot beamed kindly on me.

'It is that I have arranged you a marriage, Hastings.'

'But I say –'

'Bah!' said Poirot, giving me a friendly push over the threshold of the door. 'Do you think I wish to trumpet aloud in Merlinville the name of Duveen?'

It was indeed Cinderella who rose to greet us. I took her hand in both of mine. My eyes said the rest.

Poirot cleared his throat.

'*Mes enfants*,' he said, 'for the moment we have no time for sentiment. There is work ahead of us. Mademoiselle, were you able to do what I asked you?'

In response, Cinderella took from her bag an object wrapped up in paper, and handed it silently to Poirot. The latter unwrapped it. I gave a start – for it was the aeroplane dagger which I understood she had cast into the sea. Strange, how reluctant women always are to destroy the most compromising of objects and documents!

'*Très bien, mon enfant*,' said Poirot. 'I am pleased with you. Go now and rest yourself. Hastings here and I have work to do. You shall see him tomorrow.'

'Where are you going?' asked the girl, her eyes widening.

'You shall hear all about it tomorrow.'

'Because wherever you're going, I'm coming too.'

'But, mademoiselle –'

'I'm coming too, I tell you.'

Poirot realized that it was futile to argue. He gave in.

'Come then, mademoiselle. But it will not be amusing. In all probability nothing will happen.'

The girl made no reply.

Twenty minutes later we set forth. It was quite dark now, a close oppressive evening. Poirot led the way out of the town in the direction of the Villa Geneviève. But when he reached the Villa Marguerite he paused.

'I should like to assure myself that all goes well with Jack Renauld. Come with me, Hastings. Mademoiselle will perhaps remain outside. Madame Daubreuil might say something which would wound her.'

We unlatched the gate, and walked up the path. As we went round to the side of the house, I drew Poirot's attention to a window on the first floor. Thrown sharply on the blind was the profile of Marthe Daubreuil.

'Ah!' said Poirot. 'I figure to myself that that is the room where we shall find Jack Renauld.'

Madame Daubreuil opened the door to us. She explained that Jack was much the same, but perhaps we would like to see for ourselves. She led us upstairs and into the bedroom. Marthe Daubreuil was sitting by a table with a lamp on it, working. She put her finger to her lips as we entered.

Jack Renauld was sleeping an uneasy, fitful sleep, his head turning from side to side, and his face still unduly flushed.

'Is the doctor coming again?' asked Poirot in a whisper.

'Not unless we send. He is sleeping – that is the great thing. *Maman* made him a tisane.'

She sat down again with her embroidery as we left the room. Madame Daubreuil accompanied us down the stairs. Since I had learned of her past history, I viewed this woman with increased interest. She stood there with her eyes cast down, the same very faint enigmatical smile that I remembered on her lips. And suddenly I felt afraid of her, as one might feel afraid of a beautiful poisonous snake.

'I hope we have not deranged you, madame,' said Poirot politely, as she opened the door for us to pass out.

'Not at all, monsieur.'

'By the way,' said Poirot, as though struck by an after-thought, 'Monsieur Stonor has not been in Merlinville today, has he?'

I could not at all fathom the point of this question, which I well knew to be meaningless as far as Poirot was concerned.

Madame Daubreuil replied quite composedly:

'Not that I know of.'

'He has not had an interview with Madame Renauld?'

'How should I know that, monsieur?'

'True,' said Poirot. 'I thought you might have seen him coming or going, that is all. Goodnight, madame.'

'Why –' I began.

'No whys, Hastings. There will be time for that later.'

We rejoined Cinderella and made our way rapidly in the direction of the Villa Geneviève. Poirot looked over his shoulder once at the lighted window and the profile of Marthe as she bent over her work.

'He is being guarded at all events,' he muttered.

Arrived at the Villa Geneviève, Poirot took up his stand

behind some bushes to the left of the drive, where, while enjoying a good view ourselves, we were completely hidden from sight. The villa itself was in total darkness, everybody was without doubt in bed and asleep. We were almost immediately under the window of Mrs Renauld's bedroom, which window, I noticed, was open. It seemed to me that it was upon this spot that Poirot's eyes were fixed.

'What are we going to do?' I whispered.

'Watch.'

'But –'

'I do not expect anything to happen for at least an hour, probably two hours, but the –'

His words were interrupted by a long, thin drawn cry:

'Help!'

A light flashed up in the first-floor room on the right-hand side of the front door. The cry came from there. And even as we watched there came a shadow on the blind as of two people struggling.

'*Mille tonnerres!*' cried Poirot. 'She must have changed her room.'

Dashing forward, he battered wildly on the front door. Then rushing to the tree in the flower-bed, he swarmed up it with the agility of a cat. I followed him, as with a bound he sprang in through the open window. Looking over my shoulder, I saw Dulcie reaching the branch behind me.

'Take care,' I exclaimed.

'Take care of your grandmother!' retorted the girl. 'This is child's play to me.'

Poirot had rushed through the empty room and was pounding on the door.

'Locked and bolted on the outside,' he growled. 'And it will take time to burst it open.'

The cries for help were getting noticeably fainter. I saw despair in Poirot's eyes. He and I together put our shoulders to the door.

Cinderella's voice, calm and dispassionate, came from the window:

'You'll be too late. I guess I'm the only one who can do anything.'

Before I could move a hand to stop her, she appeared to leap from the window into space. I rushed and looked out. To my horror, I saw her hanging by her hands from the roof, propelling herself along by jerks in the direction of the lighted window.

'Good heavens! She'll be killed,' I cried.

'You forget. She's a professional acrobat, Hastings. It was the providence of the good God that made her insist on coming with us tonight. I only pray that she may be in time. Ah!'

A cry of absolute terror floated out on to the night, as the girl disappeared through the window, and then in Cinderella's clear tones came the words:

'No, you don't! I've got you – and my wrists are just like steel.'

At the same moment the door of our prison was opened cautiously by Françoise. Poirot brushed her aside unceremoniously and rushed down the passage to where the other maids were grouped round the farther door.

'It's locked on the inside, monsieur.'

There was the sound of a heavy fall within. After a moment or two the key turned and the door swung slowly open. Cinderella, very pale, beckoned us in.

'She is safe?' demanded Poirot.

'Yes, I was just in time. She was exhausted.'

Mrs Renauld was half sitting, half lying on the bed. She was gasping for breath.

'Nearly strangled me,' she murmured painfully.

The girl picked up something from the floor and handed it to Poirot. It was a rolled-up ladder of silk rope, very fine but quite strong.

'A getaway,' said Poirot. 'By the window, while we were battering at the door. Where is – the other?'

The girl stood aside a little and pointed. On the ground lay a figure wrapped in some dark material, a fold of which hid the face.

'Dead?'

She nodded.

'I think so. Head must have struck the marble fender.'

'But who is it?' I cried.

'The murderer of Renauld, Hastings. And the would-be murderer of Madame Renauld.'

Puzzled and uncomprehending, I knelt down, and lifting the fold of cloth, looked into the dead beautiful face of Marthe Daubreuil!

CHAPTER XXVIII

Journey's End

I have confused memories of the further events of that night. Poirot seemed deaf to my repeated questions. He was engaged in overwhelming Françoise with reproaches for not having told him of Mrs Renauld's change of sleeping quarters.

I caught him by the shoulder, determined to attract his attention, and make myself heard.

'But you *must* have known,' I expostulated. 'You were taken up to see her this afternoon.'

Poirot deigned to attend to me for a brief moment.

'She had been wheeled on a sofa into the middle room – her boudoir,' he explained.

'But, monsieur,' cried Françoise, 'Madame changed her room almost immediately after the crimes. The associations – they were too distressing!'

'Then why was I not told?' vociferated Poirot, striking the table, and working himself into a first-class passion. 'I demand of you – why – was – I – not – told? You are an old woman completely imbecile! And Léonie and Denise are no better. All of you are triple idiots! Your stupidity has nearly caused the death of your mistress. But for this courageous child –'

He broke off, and, darting across the room to where the girl was bending over ministering to Mrs Renauld, he embraced her with Gallic fervour – slightly to my annoyance.

I was aroused from my condition of mental fog by a sharp command from Poirot to fetch the doctor immediately on Mrs Renauld's behalf. After that, I might summon the police. And he added, to complete my dudgeon:

'It will hardly be worth your while to return here. I shall

be too busy to attend to you, and of Mademoiselle here I make a *garde-malade*.'

I retired with what dignity I could command. Having done my errands, I returned to the hotel. I understood next to nothing of what had occurred. The events of the night seemed fantastic and impossible. Nobody would answer my questions. Nobody had seemed to hear them. Angrily, I flung myself into bed, and slept the sleep of the bewildered and utterly exhausted.

I awoke to find the sun pouring in through the open windows and Poirot, neat and smiling, sitting beside the bed.

'*Enfin*, you wake! But it is that you are a famous sleeper, Hastings! Do you know that it is nearly eleven o'clock?'

I groaned and put a hand to my head.

'I must have been dreaming,' I said. 'Do you know, I actually dreamt that we found Marthe Daubreuil's body in Mrs Renauld's room, and that you declared her to have murdered Mr Renauld?'

'You were not dreaming. All that is quite true.'

'But Bella Duveen killed Mr Renauld?'

'Oh no, Hastings, she did not! She said she did – yes – but that was to save the man she loved from the guillotine.'

'What?'

'Remember Jack Renauld's story. They both arrived on the scene on the same instant, and each took the other to be the perpetrator of the crime. The girl stares at him in horror, and then with a cry rushes away. But, when she hears that the crime has been brought home to him, she cannot bear it, and comes forward to accuse herself and save him from certain death.'

Poirot leaned back in his chair, and brought the tips of his fingers together in familiar style.

'The case was not quite satisfactory to me,' he observed judicially. 'All along I was strongly under the impression that we were dealing with a cold-blooded and premeditated crime committed by someone who had contented themselves (very cleverly) with using Monsieur Renauld's own plans for

throwing the police off the track. The great criminal (as you
may remember my remarking to you once) is always
supremely simple.'

I nodded.

'Now, to support this theory, the criminal must have been
fully cognizant of Monsieur Renauld's plans. That leads us to
Mrs Renauld. But facts fail to support any theory of her guilt.
Is there anyone else who might have known of them? Yes.
From Marthe Daubreuil's own lips we have the admission
that she overheard Mr Renauld's quarrel with the tramp. If
she could overhear that, there is no reason why she should
not have heard everything else, especially if Mr and Madame
Renauld were imprudent enough to discuss their plans sitting
on the bench. Remember how easily you overheard Marthe's
conversation with Jack Renauld from that spot.'

'But what possible motive could Marthe have for murdering
Mr Renauld?' I argued.

'What motive! Money! Renauld was a millionaire several
times over, and at his death (or so she and Jack believed) half
that vast fortune would pass to his son. Let us reconstruct the
scene from the standpoint of Marthe Daubreuil.

'Marthe Daubreuil overhears what passes between Renauld
and his wife. So far he has been a nice little source of income
to the Daubreuil mother and daughter, but now he proposes
to escape from their toils. At first, possibly, her idea is to
prevent that escape. But a bolder idea takes its place, and one
that fails to horrify the daughter of Jeanne Beroldy! At present
Renauld stands inexorably in the way of her marriage with
Jack. If the latter defies his father, he will be a pauper – which
is not at all to the mind of Mademoiselle Marthe. In fact, I
doubt if she has ever cared a straw for Jack Renauld. She
can simulate emotion but in reality she is of the same cold,
calculating type as her mother. I doubt, too, whether she was
really very sure of her hold over the boy's affections. She had
dazzled and captivated him, but separated from her, as his
father could so easily manage to separate him, she might lose
him. But with Renauld dead, and Jack the heir to half his

millions, the marriage can take place at once, and at a stroke she will attain wealth – not the beggarly thousands that have been extracted from him so far. And her clever brain takes in the simplicity of the thing. It is all so easy. Renauld is planning all the circumstances of his death – she has only to step in at the right moment and turn the farce into a grim reality. And here comes in the second point which led me infallibly to Marthe Daubreuil – the dagger! Jack Renauld had *three* souvenirs made. One he gave to his mother, one to Bella Duveen – was it not highly probable that he had given the third one to Marthe Daubreuil?

'So, then, to sum up, there were four points of note against Marthe Daubreuil:

(1) Marthe Daubreuil could have overheard Renauld's plans.
(2) Marthe Daubreuil had a direct interest in causing Renauld's death.
(3) Marthe Daubreuil was the daughter of the notorious Madame Beroldy who in my opinion was morally and virtually the murderess of her husband, although it may have been Georges Conneau's hand which struck the actual blow.
(4) Marthe Daubreuil was the only person, besides Jack Renauld, likely to have the third dagger in her possession.'

Poirot paused and cleared his throat.

'Of course, when I learned of the existence of the other girl, Bella Duveen, I realized that it was quite possible that *she* might have killed Renauld. The solution did not commend itself to me, because, as I pointed out to you, Hastings, an expert, such as I am, likes to meet a foeman worthy of his steel. Still, one must take crimes as one finds them, not as one would like them to be. It did not seem very likely that Bella Duveen would be wandering about carrying a souvenir paper-knife in her hand, but of course she might have had some idea all the time of revenging herself on Jack Renauld. When she actually came forward and confessed to the murder, it seemed that all was over. And yet – I was not satisfied, *mon ami. I was not satisfied* . . .

'I went over the case again minutely, and I came to the same conclusion as before. If it was *not* Bella Duveen, the only other person who could have committed the crime was Marthe Daubreuil. But I had not one single proof against her!

'And then you showed me that letter from Mademoiselle Dulcie, and I saw a chance of settling the matter once for all. The original dagger was stolen by Dulcie Duveen and thrown into the sea – since, as she thought, it belonged to her sister. But if, by any chance, it was *not* her sister's, but the one given by Jack to Marthe Daubreuil – why then, Bella Duveen's dagger would be still intact! I said no word to you, Hastings (it was no time for romance), but I sought out Mademoiselle Dulcie, told her as much as I deemed needful, and set her to search among the effects of her sister. Imagine my elation, when she sought me out (according to my instructions) as Miss Robinson, with the precious souvenir in her possession!

'In the meantime I had taken steps to force Mademoiselle Marthe into the open. By my orders, Madame Renauld repulsed her son, and declared her intention of making a will on the morrow which should cut him off from ever enjoying even a portion of his father's fortune. It was a desperate step, but a necessary one, and Madame Renauld was fully prepared to take the risk – though unfortunately she also never thought of mentioning her change of room. I suppose she took it for granted that I knew. All happened as I thought. Marthe Daubreuil made a last bold bid for the Renauld millions – and failed!'

'What absolutely bewilders me,' I said, 'is how she ever got into the house without our seeing her. It seems an absolute miracle. We left her behind at the Villa Marguerite, we go straight to the Villa Geneviève – and yet she is there before us!'

'Ah, but we did not leave her behind. She was out of the

Villa Marguerite by the back way while we were talking to her mother in the hall. That is where, as the Americans say, she "put it over" on Hercule Poirot!'

'But the shadow on the blind? We saw it from the road.'

'*Eh bien*, when we looked up, Madame Daubreuil had just had time to run upstairs and take her place.'

'Madame Daubreuil?'

'Yes. One is old, and one is young, one dark, and one fair, but, for the purpose of a silhouette on a blind, their profiles are singularly alike. Even I did not suspect – triple imbecile that I was! I thought I had plenty of time before me – that she would not try to gain admission to the villa until much later. She had brains, that beautiful Mademoiselle Marthe.'

'And her object was to murder Mrs Renauld?'

'Yes. The whole fortune would then pass to her son. But it would have been suicide, *mon ami*! On the floor by Marthe Daubreuil's body, I found a pad and a little bottle of chloroform and a hypodermic syringe containing a fatal dose of morphine. You understand? The chloroform first – then when the victim is unconscious the prick of the needle. By the morning the smell of the chloroform has quite disappeared, and the syringe lies where it has fallen from Madame Renauld's hand. What would he say, the excellent Monsieur Hautet? "Poor woman! What did I tell you? The shock of joy, it was too much on top of the rest! Did I not say that I should not be surprised if her brain became unhinged. Altogether a most tragic case, the Renauld Case!"

'However, Hastings, things did not go quite as Mademoiselle Marthe had planned. To begin with, Madame Renauld was awake and waiting for her. There is a struggle. But Madame Renauld is terribly weak still. There is a last chance for Marthe Daubreuil. The idea of suicide is at an end, but if she can silence Madame Renauld with her strong hands, make a getaway with her little silk ladder while we are still battering on the inside of the farther door, and be back at the Villa Marguerite before we return there, it will be hard to prove anything against her. But she was check-mated, not by

Hercule Poirot, but by *la petite acrobate* with her wrists of steel.'

I mused over the whole story.

'When did you first begin to suspect Marthe Daubreuil, Poirot? When she told us she had overheard the quarrel in the garden?'

Poirot smiled.

'My friend, do you remember when we drove into Merlinville that first day? And the beautiful girl we saw standing at the gate? You asked me if I had noticed a young goddess, and I replied to you that I had seen only a girl with anxious eyes. That is how I have thought of Marthe Daubreuil from the beginning. *The girl with the anxious eyes!* Why was she anxious? Not on Jack Renauld's behalf, for she did not know then that he had been in Merlinville the previous evening.'

'By the way,' I exclaimed, 'how is Jack Renauld?'

'Much better. He is still at the Villa Marguerite. But Madame Daubreuil has disappeared. The police are looking for her.'

'Was she in with her daughter, do you think?'

'We shall never know. Madame is a lady who can keep her secrets. And I doubt very much if the police will ever find her.'

'Has Jack Renauld been – told?'

'Not yet.'

'It will be a terrible shock to him.'

'Naturally. And yet, do you know, Hastings, I doubt if his heart was ever seriously engaged? So far we have looked upon Bella Duveen as a siren, and Marthe Daubreuil as the girl he really loved. But I think that if we reversed the terms we should come nearer to the truth. Marthe Daubreuil was very beautiful. She set herself to fascinate Jack, and she succeeded, but remember his curious reluctance to break with the other girl. And see how he was willing to go to the guillotine rather than implicate her. I have a little idea that when he learns the truth, he will be horrified – revolted, and his false love will wither away.'

'What about Giraud?'

'He has a *crise* of the nerves, that one! He has been obliged to return to Paris.'

We both smiled.

Poirot proved a fairly true prophet. When at length the doctor pronounced Jack Renauld strong enough to hear the truth, it was Poirot who broke it to him. The shock was indeed terrific. Yet Jack rallied better than I could have supposed possible. His mother's devotion helped him to live through those difficult days. The mother and son were inseparable now.

There was a further revelation to come. Poirot had acquainted Mrs Renauld with the fact that he knew her secret, and had represented to her that Jack should not be left in ignorance of his father's past.

'To hide the truth, never does it avail, madame! Be brave and tell him everything.'

With a heavy heart Mrs Renauld consented, and her son learned that the father he had loved had been in actual fact a fugitive from justice. A halting question was promptly answered by Poirot.

'Reassure yourself, Monsieur Jack. The world knows nothing. As far as I can see, there is no obligation for me to take the police into my confidence. Throughout the case I have acted, not for them, but for your father. Justice overtook him at last, but no one need ever know that he and Georges Conneau were one and the same.'

There were, of course, various points in the case that remained puzzling to the police, but Poirot explained things in so plausible a fashion that all query about them was gradually stilled.

Shortly after we got back to London, I noticed a magnificent model of a foxhound adorning Poirot's mantelpiece. In answer to my inquiring glance, Poirot nodded.

'*Mais oui*! I got my five hundred francs! Is he not a splendid fellow? I call him Giraud!'

A few days later Jack Renauld came to see us with a resolute expression on his face.

'Monsieur Poirot, I've come to say goodbye. I'm sailing for South America almost immediately. My father had large interests over the continent, and I mean to start a new life out there.'

'You go alone, Monsieur Jack?'

'My mother comes with me – and I shall keep Stonor on as my secretary. He likes out-of-the-way parts of the world.'

'No one else goes with you?'

Jack flushed.

'You mean –?'

'A girl who loves you very dearly – who has been willing to lay down her life for you.'

'How could I ask her?' muttered the boy. 'After all that has happened, could I go to her and – Oh, what sort of a lame story could I tell?'

'*Les femmes* – they have a wonderful genius for manufacturing crutches for stories like that.'

'Yes, but – I've been such a damned fool.'

'So have all of us, one time and another,' observed Poirot philosophically.

But Jack's face had hardened.

'There's something else. I'm my father's son. Would anyone marry me, knowing that?'

'You are your father's son, you say. Hastings here will tell you that I believe in heredity –'

'Well, then –'

'Wait. I know a woman, a woman of courage and endurance, capable of great love, of supreme self-sacrifice –'

The boy looked up. His eyes softened.

'My mother!'

'Yes. You are your mother's son as well as your father's. Then go to Mademoiselle Bella. Tell her everything. Keep nothing back – and see what she will say!'

Jack looked irresolute.

'Go to her as a boy no longer, but a man – a man bowed by the fate of the Past, and the fate of Today, but looking forward to a new and wonderful life. Ask her to share it with